The Gothengau Colony

The Gothengau Colony

W. F. LOGAN

Published by Heart of the Bruce, London, England.

A CIP catalogue for this book is available from the British Library.

Typeset in Garamond Classic 10.25/12.5 by Hewer Text UK Ltd, Edinburgh

Paperback ISBN: 978-1-7396659-1-3

eBook ISBN: 978-1-7396659-0-6

Prologue

Western Siberia, May 1st, 1965.

Fir, larch, pine, and spruce stretched into the horizon. Their tallest reaches scraped the helicopter's fuselage. In the near distance, the missile smouldered over the trees.

Konrad turned from the cockpit door to face his convicts. "This is the real one!"

"The 500th." The troops raised their fists.

Metal dug into his shoulder when the chopper braked hard. Nose down, the gunship swung up and around the clearing, a swastika-bearing projectile in front of them. Ragged soldiers pelted away.

Cannon fodder. All fell before the rotating barrels. Body parts, the dead, and the dying surrounded the launch vehicle.

These few deaths might save thousands of lives. This rocket must not fire.

He grabbed a rope hanging from the ceiling, brushed the door aside and jumped out. Palms burned as he dropped. Earth banged against his feet, his knees. Soil. Forearms protected his face. Grass. Scorched hands pushed him up. Firearm switched from shouldered to brandished.

Peeled skin smarted from the wooden stock.

In the driver's cab two men gurgled and twitched their way to eternal rest. Only one more, suicidal, launching option to check. He sprinted across the front. Movement near the smoking engine cone. In three bounds he exposed the final threat.

Danger screamed from a lever's sign. A bloodied hand rested there by the time he aimed the gun. The broken Soviet soldier grinned and pulled, but Konrad pressed the trigger. No chance to hit Berlin now.

Only an impotent click. At least he warned Petra so there may be fewer killed.

Incineration stopped the Russian's laughter. Airborne from the blast, Konrad witnessed failure accelerate away.

Chapter 1

New York, August 1946.

Metal screeched on metal as the train braked. Konrad almost filled the boxcar when he stooped through the sliding door. Seeing the track's pebbles passing slowly enough to follow individual stones, he leapt down and strolled out of the yard.

Konrad - no country bumpkin now - had seen cities before, but not one as bustling and crowded as this. Despite hopes of anonymity, necks craned to see him better. Not surprising as he towered above everyone else. He roamed along the pavement, flinching with each brush of a passing coat. Would the local cops have received a wire yet? "Suspect nearly seven-feet tall" should do it.

A gaudy building caught his eye. Its glittering sign proclaimed that the 'Bow Tie' offered a double bill of moving pictures all day, every day. Konrad had never been to a cinema before, but he knew they were dark, comfortable, and safe. An ideal spot to think of a solution.

The peroxide-blonde clerk looked up from her magazine. Eyes down, startled by a glimpse of blue-veined cleavage, he paid and walked into the foyer. The theatre showed 'Nazi Titanic'. A scarlet-uniformed, gum-chewing boy in a pillbox hat eagerly checked his ticket, and Konrad walked in, the only one occupying the massive room, besides stale cigarette smoke and the stench of yesterday's hotdogs.

After Konrad sat at the back, the drapes parted, and light streamed out from just above him, its twinkling shafts painting moving pictures on the screen. Bold text and stirring music introduced something called 'Answer the Call'. A soothing voice narrated over a scene of tall, blonde people laughing and playing volleyball.

'Do you have a German grandparent? Are you an Aryan?'

Konrad wasn't entirely sure what that was and had little idea why they asked.

'Then you are a Volksdeutsche. You could Answer the Call! Come to live in the Reich. Look what the Fatherland has to offer to American Volksdeutsche like you.'

A man overseeing a production line in a small factory appeared. He gave orders in fluent German. The taciturn fellow looked to the camera.

'This is Otto. Where are you from, Otto?'

'I'm from Iowa, originally, but I answered the call in '36, and now I own my own business.'

'That's great, Otto. Did you come to Germany with money to start your company?'

'No, sir. I didn't even speak good German. The government helped with that at the absorption centre. Then they gave me a grant to start this place.'

'Thanks, Otto! If you like the joy of raising children, come to the Reich.'

A scene of tranquil home life - an ornately tiled stove, a mother nursing a baby in a rocking chair, and father playing with two toddlers on the rug - comforted Konrad.

'This lovely couple are Edwin and Margaret. Where are you two from, Edwin?'

Edwin's collarless shirt revealed the sinewy form of his skinny frame. He looked up from the game. *'We're from Minnesota, been living here since '38.'*

'How many kids do you have?'

Edwin grinned. *'We have ten.'*

'My, that must keep you busy, Margaret. How do you manage?'

Margaret's smile showed her straight teeth. *'There's extra cash comes in from the government, and there are so many nannying services that I never worry about time or money.'*

'That's great. The Fatherland thanks you for helping us reach our population goal. By 2010, we aim for the Reich to have 2 billion people.'

A map appeared. Red covered almost all of Europe, and three points marked out the colonies.

'Our settlements in the East need people, people of good German stock, to relocate. Imagine the space you and your family could enjoy in the Baltic. Ingermannland and Memel-Narev welcome returning Germans.'

Drab shopping streets appeared. At least they filmed when the weather was good, thought Konrad. It looked dead.

Surprisingly, the next scene showed cowboys lassoing a steer.

'But this is Gothengau, on the shores of the Black Sea, where SS soldiers grow our food and make their own, unique entertainment.'

It looked fantastic. Before he could get more interested, the scene changed to King Edward visiting Berlin, greeting crowds by Hitler's side.

'None of this would be possible without the Anglo-German Entente. Here, on its tenth anniversary, the King of England, Edward the Eighth with his Queen Barbara visit the Führer in Berlin.

All this was news to Konrad. He hadn't followed the war, and by the time he joined the circus the fighting was over. Germany dominated Europe from the Pyrenees to the Urals, while Britain ruled the waves and expanded her global empire. A flicker of hope awakened in him. Heck, Konrad had four German grandparents, and he didn't need help speaking German either. Maybe he could have a family, and a farm.

'Sailings every Wednesday at noon from the Hamburg America Line docks in Hoboken.'

That meant there would be one the next day. Maybe he'd think about it and even go next week, with emigrating being so drastic he might need to consider it a little more thoroughly. Then Alabama's electric chair crackled to life in his mind.

Konrad, sufficiently heartened at the potential end of his dilemma, relaxed and enjoyed the entertainment. The crazy Captain kept driving the doomed ship forward to meet its fate, just so the greedy ship owners could break the Atlantic crossing record and make even more money. Only the solitary German officer saw they were sailing into icefloes, but he put principles and people before profit. He saved the German passengers even though the grasping, clueless English ignored him, and let the ship sink.

Germans, these films told Konrad, were good sorts. It might be a good idea to go there and seek out the life that fate had denied him in America.

Intense pangs of hunger woke him from dreams where tall, blonde Nazis dressed like cowboys threw limbless Ed around. Konrad didn't know how long he had been asleep or, momentarily, where he was, and it slowed his thinking. On the screen the settlement film played again.

Konrad had to eat and find a bed, so he stood. Next to the cinema, the diner's pulsating sign beckoned him. Konrad obeyed. Several heads along the bar turned before the sudden silence encouraged everybody in the cubicles to stare at him as well. Some even stepped out to get a better look. No way, thought Konrad, could he make it to Canada without being caught. Even getting across the river to Manhattan appeared impossible.

"Hey there, big guy." The rotund, grey-haired man behind the counter wore a name badge saying Klaus. "What you having?"

Above Klaus colour photographs illustrated the menu.

"Hamburger and fries, please. And a coffee, too."

"What brings you around here?" asked the red-haired man beside him.

What business was it of his? Since killing the sheriff, nothing anybody said or did meant what it had before. There was always a subtext, an ulterior motive.

"I'm sailing to Germany tomorrow."

"Don't you worry about going there? I heard they sent the Jews to death-mills."

Klaus looked up from wiping the counter. "Oh, the kikes are asking for it."

Red-hair shook his head and smacked his lips. "Nobody asks to be treated like that."

"Pah, those death camps are just stories. Nobody at the Bund believes a word of it." Klaus waved a hand. "They used to say stuff like that about Germans throwing babies on pitch forks in the Great War and it was a bare-faced lie then."

"Well, the Jews ain't there now, so what do you think happened to them?"

Klaus shrugged. "Someone told me they sent them to Siberia."

"My grandfather was Jewish - would you have me sent to a death mill or Siberia too, Klaus?"

The waiter lowered his eyes and wiped the far end of the counter

"I've never heard anything like that." Konrad hadn't, as far as he knew, met any Jews. Their treatment through history had always perplexed him. "Weren't Jesus and the apostles Jewish?"

"I guess they were." He looked surprised at this information. "How are you getting to Germany? The Hamburg-America line?"

"You ask a lot of questions." Konrad pushed back the scowl creeping across his face.

"That's what my wife always says. I guess it comes from my job."

A chance for Konrad to overcome his new suspicious nature arrived. "What do you do?"

"Cop."

Looking down, Konrad couldn't see his heart pumping under his shirt, though its beats resounded through his eardrums. He sipped on coffee and the invigorating heat squeezed a sigh out of him.

"Sounds like you needed that. I'm Jack, by the way. I didn't catch your name."

Civility compelled Konrad to return Jack's favour. "Hercules."

"Suits you, but that's your nickname, right?"

Klaus served Konrad's food, and Jack at last fell silent. Konrad wanted to keep it that way – Jack's interrogation returned Alabama's sparking chair to the front of his mind.

"Is there a hotel around here?" Konrad asked Klaus.

"Why sure, there's the Palace on Newark Avenue. It's only a couple of blocks away. You sure can eat fast!" He laughed as Konrad consumed his meal.

"It's good, and I'm starving." The complete version went unmentioned. A few mouthfuls later and Konrad settled the bill.

"Bon voyage, Hercules." Jack waved as Konrad sped out.

Konrad ignored him.

Like Klaus had said, the Palace stood close by. Its no-vacancy sign illuminated the alley opposite where there was room for Konrad to lie down. He got little rest on the kerb. All night he chased sleep in an eternal battle to put recent events from his mind.

Vehicles woke him. Three police trucks stood outside the hotel, Jack's voice shouted orders to his colleagues in blue. Keeping to the back ways, Konrad hurried away from the main streets for the six blocks between him and Pier C where a ship would take him to his destiny.

Before breaking cover to board the liner, he poked his head around the corner. Police uniforms appeared regularly amongst the passengers and their well-wishers. Sweat stung Konrad's brow when he searched for an answer. Boarding would end soon, the crew already finished putting friends and loved ones ashore.

Now the cops' task neared completion without any sign of their prey, they looked uninterested. Some congregated in small groups to chat conspiratorially. A dark blue vehicle arrived, and they all trotted to it, ready to get in when the back door opened.

If Konrad didn't run now, he would never make it.

He sprinted to the waving crowds at the stern of the black-hulled ocean liner *St. Louis*. Its foghorn blew, and smoke billowed from its two striped funnels. The side boarding hatch banged closed. His heart and lungs burned. You can do this, Konrad told himself.

"It's him." A policeman raised his baton. "Stop!"

Those waving farewell looked towards the shouting and scattered out of Konrad's way. When the walkway slammed on to the dock, a wave of tight muscle raced down Konrad's thigh, through the calf, and into his left foot. Propellers churned the river. Every fibre of strength in Konrad's massive body flowed into a single purpose. Bounding up from his right leg's thick coiled spring he pushed his left foot down on the iron mooring and flew high into the air.

"Stop or we'll shoot."

Konrad's hands clawed at the stern railings, smashing his fingers. He grabbed a metal strut. A foot found a porthole. Another hand wrapped around a chain.

Shots whizzed by. In two reaches his nose touched the bottom of the guardrail. One more and the top of the barrier became his tipping point. He flipped over the fence and onto the rear deck.

After his breathing calmed, Konrad noticed applause. Jackboots filled his vision until a bottle appeared. He took the drink.

The Nazi officer helped Konrad to his feet. "*Sie haben das verdient.*" Why Konrad had earned that in a Texan accent confounded him.

They raised their glasses. "To one of us!"

Konrad swigged the scorching alcohol down when they drank to him. Scrunching his eyes from the fiery liquid he doubted the officers' words, having heard 'one of us' before. Now Konrad had a chance to look at the young men, the more toothy-smiled and all-American they appeared. A barrier separated them from the passengers waving farewell on the narrow deck.

"What are you guys doing in those outfits?" Konrad asked.

"You boarding like that, and us in these uniforms?" The Texan laughed, highlighting his lined brow. "We should be asking you." His bottom lip pouted youthfully, but receding, thinning hair mocked his boyish facial expression.

Immediately Konrad entered he ran to the white porcelain bathroom and started a shower. After the refreshing cleansing, Konrad didn't relish donning the same filthy old clothes he'd worn for the last week. Somebody, however, had let themselves in and left fresh clothing on the bed. A pair of pants that almost reached his ankles and a tuxedo whose sleeves nearly touched his wrists exceeded Konrad's hopes. He stepped out into the hallway and followed the signs to the ballroom.

Pushing the double doors, Konrad stood at the top of a twin staircase looking down into the sea of well-dressed emigrants returning to their roots. Their attire varied between dinner jackets, dresses, suits, leather-shorts and *dirndls*. Examining his ill-fitting clothing, the shame made it difficult to look back up at the guests swirling on the dancefloor.

The three SS men stood at the foot of the stairs with their drinks held high. Tex stood at the front. "Here's Konrad, our vaulting star!"

When his gaze returned to the party below, all eyes were on him. Shoulders back, he descended the grand steps, and rivulets of clapping merged into a flood of applause. Pride battled shame within Konrad, before the smile on his lips showed pride's victory. He held up his arms to the crowd's whoops.

Minnesota tapped Konrad's arm. "We have a VIP here tonight who would love to meet you," Minnesota turned to a man all in morning dress, besides the top hat. "Allow us to introduce the Reich Minister of Transport, Julius Dorpmüller."

A sour-faced, stocky, bald man stuck out his hand to shake Konrad's. His grey pencil moustache stayed straight along his upper lip when he stared.

"It's an honour to meet you." Konrad meant it only as a pleasantry.

"The feeling is mutual." Julius' stony expression lent his words as much faith.

A teenager with eager blue eyes stepped forward and grabbed the VIP's hand before he could return it. "I'm Karl Dietrich."

Julius' pupils dilated. Konrad thought he saw the minister's thin lips pursing before showing his teeth in an unexpectedly vigorous display of pleasure. His hand rested on Karl's shoulder.

"Good day young man, welcome to the Reich. May I be of any assistance to you in your exciting new life in Germany?"

Konrad found their dialogue a little strange, and when he looked around in bemusement, Minnesota's jaw hung open in disbelief.

Brooklyn let a wrist go limp, then inched away from Julius. Tex rolled his eyes at his colleagues.

"Why, of course Minister Dorpmüller. I'll do anything to ensure a good future for myself in the glorious new world of the Reich."

"Well, I'm here all evening." The minister laughed to himself. "Perhaps we could talk about your talents and abilities, and I'll see if and how the Reich transport ministry can put them to use." He turned to Konrad. "You American volksdeutsches really go and grab the things you want."

Brooklyn hurried away, hand over mouth and shoulders heaving.

Tex sighed. "Seasickness."

Dorpmüller frowned. "But it's flat calm. What's he doing on this duty?"

"Good question, minister. It might well be his last."

"Everybody." At the top of the staircases, a woman waved. "Look over here everybody."

Her blonde perm rested above garish make-up and her bosom struggled to remain inside her frilly red dress. She and a small, sallow-skinned pubescent girl stood on the balcony connecting the staircases.

"This is my daughter, Petra. She's gonna be the Fatherland's singing sensation, you mark my words."

Konrad pitied the poor young girl. Frills and epaulettes decorated the sailor dress she wore, emphasising its suitability for one five years younger. Despite her mother's arm on her shoulder, she cast her eyes down. The woman tucked Petra under the chin and whispered to her.

The delicate bones of Minnesota's face turned to Konrad. "Here's another American volksdeutsche grabbing what they want with both hands. The only question is what she tells Petra to sing."

While her stage-mother continued her encouragement, Petra launched into a strong-voiced rendition of 'You'll Never Walk Alone'. Cheers went up. Konrad willingly participated. "She's got a lovely voice."

Tex nodded. "She might go far. Who knows? The Reich is the real New World. Anything could happen. When my folks took me to the Fatherland, I didn't think I'd be living the high life on ocean liners, that's for sure."

Petra's mother bustled into the VIP group. She squeezed past Konrad, rubbing her breasts along his stomach as she pushed up against him.

The mother dragged Petra behind her, who gawked up at him, then down at the tent in his pants. Konrad deflated instantly. The sin of lust simmered on his cheeks. After he waved at her she ran behind her mother's skirt.

"Don't you worry about her. That's how she shows she likes someone. I'm too big to hide behind skirts myself. I'm Barbara." She stuck out her hand and they shook. "Like the Queen of England. Don't worry, I know your name. Everybody does. That was quite a stunt you pulled to get on the boat. You're a real action man. The Fatherland is lucky to get you." It startled Konrad when she reached up and caressed his upper arm. "Is it like that between your legs as well?"

A meek man in a crumpled dark suit sidled up beside Barbara and harrumphed with a hand to his lips. She looked away and stopped fondling Konrad.

"This is my husband, Markus."

When Konrad stepped away from the woman, he bumped into someone. "Excuse me."

"Watch where you're going, you big show-off," said a voice soft enough that only Konrad heard it.

Konrad turned and scowled at Karl, who stepped back, spun around, and pushed through the people glowering behind him. Julius exclaimed when Karl stepped on his foot.

"I'm so sorry, Minister Dorpmüller. Please, may I get you something for the pain? A Scotch, perhaps?"

"No thanks, but I will have a brandy." Dorpmüller grabbed Karl's arm before he could turn. "And join me on the deck afterwards while I smoke a cigar – we can talk about your future in Germany with some . . . privacy."

"I bet that man has a lot of nephews over to visit," said Barbara.

Her husband nodded. "Yes, dear."

"Why don't you get me a drink, instead of hanging around like a bad smell?" Barbara punched Markus in the shoulder. "Would you like one, too, Konrad?"

"No." He didn't want to be in her debt, avoiding eye contact when she gazed up at him.

"Can we go out on deck as well, mummy?" Petra asked.

"Maybe. Konrad, would you like to walk on deck with us?"

Petra grabbed on to Konrad's pants. "Please, please, Konrad. Please come with us."

Barbara slipped her hand through Konrad's elbow and linked her arm to his. He had to lean over to accommodate her, close enough for her to whisper. "Come on, I know you want to."

Surprised, Konrad reached up to scratch his ear and wrenched his arm from hers. There needed to be some distance between him and this woman. He grabbed Petra's clasping hand from his trouser. "Race you there, Petra."

Once through the door the salty air invigorated him. Out at sea, the setting sun glinted on the mill-pond stillness of the Atlantic. Birds followed the boat, filling the evening with their calls.

"Put me on your shoulders," Petra begged. "I want to see even further than you."

Smiling, he lifted her behind his head.

"Wow, Konrad. I think I can still see America. It must be great to be as big as you."

"Petra! Konrad!" cried Barbara.

"Let's hide." Petra's eyes gleamed with mischief. "She'll make me sing again and I don't want to."

Konrad obliged. In front of them, the deck widened. They hurried to it, slipping behind the bulkhead. He heard pacing. "Shhh."

Petra kissed the top of his head. Footfalls increased, but it still startled Konrad when Barbara and Markus walked by.

"Petra!" cried her mother when she disappeared from view.

Konrad turned and trotted in the opposite direction. "That was close."

They reached a point where a higher deck jutted out. Smoke wafted over them.

"Pooh." Petra faked a cough. "Cigars stink. It's the minister and that horrible Karl."

Not the tallest, for once, Konrad only saw two pairs of feet on the deck above them. One, by the railings, sported leather and spats. Facing them stood feet shod with canvas tied with mismatched laces. He heard grunts. The pair of knees with the cheap footwear banged on the deck, drawing a wince of sympathetic pain from Konrad. It appeared that the minister had forced Karl to do something, despite the Bible's ban on man laying with men. Maybe the minister wanted that of Karl.

One of Karl's knees raised, freeing a foot that pushed hard on the deck. "Get off me you fairy."

One of the minister's feet stepped back, trying to regain balance. "Help!" Dorpmüller's other foot lifted from the deck. Shoes waggled desperately for support. Then they flew up.

"Hee-." The call increased. "-eelp!" then instantly diminished as it fell away to the rhythm of limbs against hull. A splash ended his descent. Konrad gasped. Two unnatural deaths in a week, at least this one had no connection with him. A prayer came to mind, but before it started, a sharp poke in the small of his back snatched him from his devotion.

"What are you two doing out here on your own?" Barbara screamed.

After he set Petra back on the floor, Konrad turned.

"You dirty man, walking off with my little girl. She's thirteen! You ought to be ashamed of yourself."

Barbara turned to her husband, hiding in the shadows.

"Well, aren't you going to defend her honour? What are you? A man or a mouse?"

Twisting around, she jumped up and tried slapping Konrad's face, but he stepped back.

"And what about you, little madam, dragging on his pants! You're too old for that kind of shenanigans now, young lady."

"Then stop dressing me like a little girl and quit forcing yourself on men. I've seen you. Everybody's seen you. What about Dad? Don't you ever think about him?"

Her father wagged his finger. "Don't talk to your mother like that, have some respect."

Petra stamped a foot. "Have some for yourself." She span on a heel and grunted before sprinting away.

"Well, don't just stand there, do something." Barbara shoved the little man. "Go after her!"

Markus fled. When he disappeared, Barbara stepped forward and touched Konrad's crotch. Horrified, he dashed after her husband and daughter.

With the sun almost beneath the horizon and an exhausting day nearly behind him, Konrad felt the pull of his sumptuous accommodation. He knew that he should report the crime to the Captain. Minister Dorpmüller's disappearance needed investigation, but Konrad and an under-age girl raised suspicion. Karl might be well-connected and protected. They could blame Konrad. Had the minister observed Konrad misbehaving with her? Did he throw Dorpmüller overboard to avoid detection?

He would say nothing of this and would deny seeing the politician after the ballroom. He couldn't afford to be dragged into another killing, to waste this chance of a new life before it had even begun.

Konrad sailed on into the night, leaving Hercules and his troubles behind. Or so he wished.

Chapter 2

Gothengau, The Reich. Saturday, May 1st, 1965.

Konrad brushed a fly away from his eyes. Though the action got rid of the buzzing nuisance, it deepened his scowl. A carved Nazi eagle crowning the totem pole irked him. For everyone else present, Konrad's facial expression meant protection from the glaring sun, but not for his wife.

Diana peered up at him, her teasing smile twinkling her emerald eyes. Bobbed brown hair fell back and framed her strong jaw and aquiline nose. Safely standing outside the other guests' earshot, he stooped to listen without fear of being overheard when she tugged his arm.

"I see that look on your face. When are you going to get used to this?"

"I don't know. Maybe never."

Platinum-haired Himmler Youth sextuplets grasped the ribbons streaming down. They began hopping one way, then skipping the other.

"The Wild West didn't look this way." Konrad covered his face against the blazing sky and shook his head at the spurious imitation of the short-lived era. "They didn't have totem poles, and even if they did, they never danced around them on May Day. It's nonsense. Yet another empty gesture for the German people. There's nothing like this in America, where do they get these ideas?"

"Do I have to tell you again?" Diana raised her thin eyebrow and curled her lips. "From touring cowboy shows and Karl May books. They were very popular when Baer was a kid, and this is his frontier."

"It's ridiculous."

"Yes, but you get something out of it."

The blond boys reached the song's crescendo, then stopped moving and clapped in unison. With beetled brows and straightened mouths, the children turned to a nearby flag and gave the straight-arm salute.

"*Heil* Gothengau."

Despite his feelings, Konrad emulated the gesture. He towered above the tallest men in the colony and rarely escaped attention. Baer, Gothengau's leader, hosted this deceptively peaceful family event at his ranch every year. All the province's elite stood around the totem-cum-maypole.

Although Konrad and Diana's children took after their father in stature, clothing further distinguished them. Others wore uniforms or ersatz Wild West costumes, but not the Lapp family. His three girls wore plain blue dresses, white aprons, and hats. That indulgence of Konrad's Amish heritage from the Gothengau community made his presence there almost tolerable. Mousey-haired, pug-nosed Mary, Susan, and Alice ran to their parents, revealing their teeth through open-mouthed grins. Mary hadn't become accustomed to her arms and legs, which had rapidly lengthened since reaching adolescence. Identical Susan and Alice didn't yet show any signs of adulthood. Konrad had hoped the gangly phase would pass by the time Mary turned sixteen, but that wish faded as her birthday loomed only months away. After the calm of the dance had ended the sun still shone, but storm clouds gathered in Konrad's mind. The next course of entertainment would be less wholesome.

The twins spoke the words at the same moment, each movement reflecting the other. "Can we go to the rodeo now?"

"Of course, you can." Konrad didn't want to stop their fun, even though their excitement always ended when the games got going.

Diana stepped over to the twins. "Make sure you drink enough water. We don't want you getting dehydrated."

"Will it be a rodeo like in America, dad?" Susan asked.

"I only ever went to one back in America. It was nothing like the one here."

"Did you win the rodeo, daddy?" Mary got anxious when the twins hogged Konrad's attention.

Alice's small eyes squinted shut, and she hopped up and down waving her hands. "Can you lasso a cow, daddy?"

"You all know I never did any of those things! I'm from a small village, and the Amish don't have rodeos or cowboys. They live simple lives farming the land."

"Did you have a totem pole, dad?" Mary asked.

"No, they don't have any in Lancaster County. I did see one once, though, but that was miles away, in Seattle. America's not like Karl May stories, you know. Outside the Reich, nobody's even heard of him."

The children's misguided beliefs in Konrad's American background swaddled him in their naïve love. On rare occasions, life in the Reich's breadbasket brought the simple pleasures of family and belonging to the fore, pushing the everyday aside.

Susan tapped her twin's elbow and ran down the hundred-metre avenue, its yellowed grass enclosed by long, thin swastika banners fluttering in the warm, gentle breeze. She stopped to look back over her shoulder until Alice scampered towards the bleachers with her. Mary shook her head and carried on at her own pace.

Below Konrad, Diana's hair bounced as they ambled to the show. Many near-identical blonde children darted around them, laughing and whooping, firing their toy guns and rubber-tipped arrows in mock battle.

They reached the arena and walked to the front of the stand, where the pen faced them. Rows of seats on either side formed the playing field, a thirty-by-thirty metre square of yellowing grass sprouting from gnarled, hoof-print rutted soil. A shoulder-high barrier of strong wooden staves protected the seating. A massive bull rattled its bucking chute, his long, sharp horns only visible when he cast his head back. Above the animal a cowboy paced, assessing the safest way to mount. The white number seven on his back contrasted against his black shirt.

Diana nudged Konrad and sighed. "Oh no, Baer and Mengele are coming over. I'm going to make sure the girls are okay."

Diana stood, looming over the new arrivals. Her gingham dress blended with their American-style clothing, but Diana's bearing set her apart. She only held her back so straight when she protected their children. Baer's relaxed swagger spoke of carefree leadership. She waved to acknowledge their greetings, her posture belying sincerity. Konrad felt no calm, either. His adrenaline surged when talking to the Colony leader, or *Gauleiter*, and the doctor, his awareness as high as on patrol in Siberia.

Even though his belly strained the buttons of his embroidered black shirt, fifty-something Baer still sauntered around like a movie-star cowboy. His black Stetson covered his thinning locks and dark glasses masked his wrinkled eyes, but his exposed cheeks sagged prematurely.

Despite their similar ages, denim-clad Dr Mengele's full head of combed back, greying hair atop a lean frame painted a picture of modest, healthy diets and regular spa visits. With a hand tucked between his shirt's buttons, he lingered over Baer's shoulder, leering at Konrad with a precise stare. Mengele cocked his head to one side and parted his thin lips mawkishly. Konrad's nerves produced a bigger grin than usual. That smirk bared Konrad's teeth right to the gums. It frightened his own children and might explain the doctor's hesitation before speaking.

"It's wonderful to see you, Konrad. Are your twins here as well?"

"Mengele," Baer said. "Remember what we agreed about twins, or you won't be welcome at my house again."

"But I'm only about science." Mengele shook his head. "Natural twins are perfect for my experiments. Look at the results." His arm swept across the sea of blonde children. "Without my IVF work, there wouldn't be any multiple births. Then how would the Reich get the population it needs?"

"Yeah, yeah, yeah. That's not what I think when you ogle my wives, and I bet Konrad feels the same about you asking after his kids. Shut up about it now, the show's going to start."

An alarm bell sounded. Konrad faced the action just before the native Crimean cowboy jumped on the caged beast. Another buzzer blared. The pen's gate shot open. Instantly, the huge black animal hurled itself into the arena. Its powerful, broad, tall shoulders rippled as they beat the steer's long hind legs on the turf like a piston. Snot and condensation snorted from its nostrils. On its back, the cowboy grasped the rope tying him to the beast. Konrad barely had time to sympathise with rider or bull. Its head down, divots of soil flicked from the tips of the animal's horns. Number Seven's hat came off. Onlookers hooted cheers, both of encouragement and derision. Konrad's cheeks pumped hot with blood. Seven flapped around loosely, limbs flailing independently. Airborne, he gripped the cord until the bull's hooves hit him in the abdomen and he flew back.

Konrad had broken several ribs during his paratrooper career. In sympathy with Seven's possible condition, he rubbed his old injuries. Seven struck the ground. Bouncing back like a small, hard rubber ball, seven sprang to his feet. Only earth got gored. The cowboy scampered for shelter behind the stakes of the wooden blockade. Seven got there with millimetres separating him from the ruminant's flat head when it rammed the wall.

"Excellent!" Baer applauded. "That was a great opening performance. My money's on number seven next round. It's a lot harder to stay on a Heck bull for eight seconds than to keep hold of an American bull for an hour, eh Konrad?"

"I wouldn't know."

Mengele turned. "But ethnic Germans are famed for their Wild-West skills!"

"Of course." Konrad knew otherwise but didn't disagree with the Doctor. "But not in my community. We maintained our old German ways."

Baer grabbed Mengele. "Haven't you heard his story before, Mengele? He's our only genuine part of the Wild West, but his people are a religious cult." Baer's eyes burrowed into Konrad. "The Amish must be a dull lot if May never bothered writing about them. Konrad's best off away from that nonsense. Now keep it down. The next ride is on!"

Konrad wanted to tell Baer that they did no harm, but sense held him back. Cowboy number eight climbed on the supports around the bucking chute, eyeing the best way to bestride his steer. On the field, the tied bull hit the ground. They attached it to a tractor to drag the snorting, writhing animal back to the pens.

"Oh no, what's Aurelian coming over for?" asked Baer.

Baer's four-storey ranch stood a hundred metres left of the rodeo. Middle-aged, balding Aurelian stopped running and bent over panting, little more than halfway to Konrad.

"He needs more exercise," laughed Baer.

"Maybe he doesn't have time if he works on May Day," Konrad said.

"He's been assigned a special task. No way can he have a day off today. I shouldn't be here myself. Himmler ordered me to the Berlin parade. He's making some big announcement about Max Hellfeier's next achievement."

"Bigger than breaking the sound barrier?"

Baer nodded. "Yes, a lot bigger. Von Braun will be there too, so I think it's about the space program. His dreams of going to the moon are nonsense, pure fairy tales, and a complete waste of time. And money! All the money in the Fatherland isn't enough for that man's desires." Baer patted Konrad's knee. "We need to put the world to rights before we go to space. There's plenty for us to get on with down here, and if I were in charge, that's all that we'd do. Still, at least Petra's going to be there."

"I know Petra. We left America on the same boat."

"You're a quiet one. I love Petra." Baer winked at him and grinned. "Do you think you could get me an introduction?"

Konrad shrugged. "It's been a while since we saw each other."

Aurelian straightened up. He struggled to smile through his exhaustion, and as he sauntered over, the flabby signs of his condition bulged from his hips and waist. His white shirt, damp under the armpits, had a tide mark of salt at the edges of the sweat stains. Even the buttocks of his jodhpurs didn't hide his body fat.

"Good news," Aurelian gasped for air as his leaden feet climbed the stairs. "They destroyed the rocket."

Baer grinned and clapped. "Excellent! Have a break. Sit down and watch the show for a while."

"Okay, but just until I get my breath back. They are about to go and clean up the area."

To Konrad, these events sounded too important to be excluded from. "What happened?"

"The Reds stole a missile on patrol in Siberia." Baer's manner was offhand enough as though explaining the loss of an umbrella on a train journey.

Konrad's inner voice screamed. He didn't lose his cool demeanour while he attempted to make some sense of the rocket's disappearance.

"Siberia's a terrible place. What are we doing driving rockets around there?"

"We're only obeying orders. High Priest Drachenblut thinks there's a Japanese threat, and he has Himmler in his pocket with all his mumbo-jumbo."

"So, because Drachenblut suspects a threat from Japan, you take rockets outside of the Reich, the two-day drive past the Ural Barrier?" Konrad had to consciously shut his mouth after the sentence ended.

"That's right."

"Why didn't you send my men and me to get the missile back? That's a perfect job for paratroopers."

"Relax, it's fixed now." Baer waved a hand like he refused another serving of dessert. "Aurelian sent the Barrier Boys to make it right."

"Those drunks? When they're sent to me, it takes a lot to bring them up to scratch."

Baer's gritted teeth reminded Konrad that he'd been too emotional. Losing one of the Reich's unique weapons in the anarchic maelstrom of Siberia stoked Konrad's anger. He held back, a little.

"You only get the worst ones in the 500th - the thieves, cowards, drinkers, and brawlers." Baer put a thumb down. "You haven't seen the best of them. Not by a long way."

"I've seen the best of the Ural Boys, and they're the ones that stay in the 500th after their sentence ends. If something big is happening in Berlin today, the Reds couldn't pick a better time to launch the rocket,"

"Are you kidding? Even if it hadn't been taken out, they'd never be able to do that. They've only had it a day. Our guys need a two-week course before they can even switch it on, let alone aim it."

Mengele leaned into the conversation. "German technology leads the world, but something so advanced is not easy to operate. Those Reds don't have the brains to work it out."

Konrad would be pushing his luck too far to remind them of the Hare and the Tortoise. Aurelian stood and wiped the droplets of sweat from his brow.

"I'm going back to my office to see how the clean-up is going." He trotted down the steps.

Something about the relationship between the gauleiter and his deputy mystified Konrad. "You put Aurelian under a lot of pressure."

"He gets the rewards, don't worry."

"Commitment doesn't just come from money, though, does it?"

"He's a good Nazi. Always has been."

Maybe Konrad could scratch a little more of the surface from the situation. "Isn't there a deeper reason?"

With a wave of the hand, Baer ignored the question. On the field, the tractor dragged the writhing, screaming bull back to the pens. It repulsed Konrad, and the crowd's enjoyment worsened his loathing. He needed to invest in a pair of shades. The mirrored sort, so nobody could see his eyes, then he could look away much more discreetly. Number Thirteen stood ready for the next round before he leapt down out of view. A few seconds later he reappeared, pacing around the pen carefully.

A mocking laugh seeped from Baer. "Who picked that number for him? The fool's asking for trouble."

Again, Thirteen vanished. Konrad thought that very smart of him. Better to be careful than dead.

"Not only a fool but a coward too!"

Konrad looked away and clenched his fist. Heck riding had a high death rate and even herding them could be fatal. No tales of Baer's valour had ever reached Konrad's ears.

Thirteen got back up and walked around the steer again. This time, Thirteen nodded his assent to a darkened figure below. The bell rang, and he jumped to mount, but the bull rose on its hind legs before the gate shot open. It pelted outside, Thirteen trailing behind in the dirt. After several paces, Thirteen still gripped the rope.

"Hah! What an idiot!" Baer shouted. "Why the hell is he holding on when he's already been knocked out?"

When the bull's hoof made contact with Thirteen's head, he grasped the cord no more. Konrad groaned in sympathy, but the crowd laughed at the epileptic twitching of the local cowpoke. Baer glanced at Konrad and sneered. The spectators roared, and Konrad squirmed inside; the bull scooped Thirteen from the floor on his horns. It pranced around the playing field, head held high with Thirteen, impaled and limp, gracing the beast's rippling shoulders. Blood oozed on the animal's back, adding deep red lustre to its black hide.

Baer gestured to the casualty. "What did I tell you about that number? He was asking for that."

As before, the herding crew tried to rope the bull, but Thirteen's corpse blocked landing places for the lassos. Head low, the bull scraped the earth with a front foot, snorting clouds of vapour and mucus. The roping team split up to surround the animal, but it made a run for one of them. Its target had no room to escape and crumpled under the beast's momentum.

The floored cattleman's brains spilt from his shattered skull when the Heck bull cleared the ropers. Blood from the head wound rinsed the grey matter within a couple of heartbeats. Konrad hoped Diana had removed their children from the sight of this disgusting spectacle.

The crowd cheered. Konrad seethed, wondering how the audience had so little humanity. Feeling a grimace forming, telling the world his internal disgust, he put on the deadpan expression that had helped him survive here. Breathing slowly and picturing his gentle, pastoral childhood calmed him down enough to jeer at the fatalities along with everyone else. Baer's eyes met his again, this time with an approving smile.

Looking away from the horror on the pitch relieved Konrad of some tension until he noticed Aurelian running towards them, red-faced and puffing. Konrad nudged Baer.

"Aurelian's coming back."

"For God's sake, it's all done with the rocket. What the hell does he want now?"

Aurelian didn't slow from a sprint. When he reached Baer, he collapsed.

Baer leaned in closer to his prostrate sidekick. "What is it, man?"

Aurelian's blue eyes looked wildly from Baer to Konrad, to Mengele. His mouth opened and closed, but hardly a sound came out.

"Well, spit it out!" Baer screamed. "You're ruining the whole day!"

"They . . . didn't . . . get the rocket." Aurelian panted, the half sentence draining him of any energy remaining from the dash. "They got . . . they got . . . a decoy."

Konrad gripped Baer's arm. "I'll try. It still might not happen."

Baer nodded vigorously. "There's a helicopter standing behind the ranch. That will get you to your base quicker. Now go!"

Now Konrad had something to do that took his mind from the butchery on the playing field. An essential duty of service to the German people beckoned him. Lives could still be saved. The whole bleacher shook as the Gentle Giant leapt down the stairs. If Konrad got to the phone, and Petra was still home, he may have the power to rescue her again. A long way stood between him and the missile. There had to be a telephone somewhere. He would use the first he saw. Konrad galloped through the Baer homestead, stopping when he saw a receiver. He picked it up, dialling the number from memory with hope. It rang. The ringing tone again. Once more the telephone at the line's other end clamoured for attention. Maybe he had the wrong number. Or maybe she already left.

As Konrad took the phone from his ear, a famous voice answered.

"Hello?" asked Petra.

"It's Konrad. There might be trouble when you get to Berlin."

Petra laughed. "Are you saving my life again?"

Chapter 3

Berlin, Saturday, May 1st, 1965.

Petra ignored Max's stare burning into her as she struggled to end the conversation. The Hero of the Fatherland squinted at his watch, drummed his fingers on the steering wheel then glanced at the time again. Hitler's violently trembling hands gave Max the Porsche's keys shortly before the Great Führer's death. Max basked in the early afternoon glow, its light reflected by his silver-grey uniform. It gilded his blonde hair and highlighted his cheekbones in shadow. Voted the sexiest man in the Reich by Popular Observer viewers, he looked every bit the heroic guest at Berlin's May Day parade. She knew people envied her. Why wouldn't they? Her husband put both hands on the centre of the steering wheel and held them there. A finger in her ear drowned out some of the klaxon.

"Yes, it's Max honking at me. Bye Konrad, and thanks."

At last, Petra replaced the receiver. From their villa's doorway, she teetered across the drive to the car, looking to the eastern skies. Diminutive Petra liked wearing heels. She bumped into the passenger door, cushioned by the tulle beneath her taffeta dress. After seating herself, she straightened out the black ruffles and smoothed the headscarf protecting her dark beehived hair, all the while still looking east. Entering the forest at the end of the drive, spring's scents filled the air. Max touched her stockinged knee as he changed gear.

"What are you looking at?"

After Petra checked the back seat, she passed their child a toy.

"Lothar. Here, play with Daddy's spaceship."

That ensured that Lothar paid their conversation no mind. Petra cast her eyes east again.

"It was Konrad on the phone. He said the Reds ambushed a Siberian missile patrol, stole one of Gothengau's rockets, and now he's taking his men to find it before it's launched."

"That's not going to stop us attending, but you won't see it coming." He checked the left lane. "Well, not so you'll be able to get away from it." Max looked in the wing mirror and indicated. "We'll be alright, so long as we're underground or a block away from the blast." Acceleration forced Petra's head back when Max overtook the car in front. "Konrad's your guardian angel, isn't he? It's like Hamburg all over again."

"No, Hamburg was different. If Konrad hadn't stopped me getting on that train, then I wouldn't be here today. There's no guarantee this rocket will be fired, though, and even if it does, who's to say it will hit Berlin?"

"I'm glad one of us knows someone in Gothengau. Otherwise, there'd be no warning at all. Why do they drive rocket launchers in Siberia?"

"He mentioned something about Drachenblut, but I didn't get the connection."

"You know an Odinist priest, don't you?"

"Yes, a pretty boy called Karl." Petra indeed knew Karl. "We came over from America in the same boat. I believe he's quite senior now." She caught Max staring east far longer than he needed to. "You said there's no point in looking out for a rocket."

He smiled, his teeth sparkling white in the sunshine. "It's hard to ignore fifteen years of training."

Petra showed her appreciation by weaving her slender digits with his sturdy fingers.

"Everybody knows Konrad's battalion are the best paratroopers around. Why didn't they send him in the first place?"

"He didn't say. I was too pushed for time to ask."

"Losing one of those rockets is pretty useless, though!" Max cackled with laughter. "The SS isn't getting any better with age. When I was in the Luftwaffe, we were always bailing them out of trouble. Hitlerstadt would still be called Stalingrad if it wasn't for us."

"Daddy helps useless SS!" cried Lothar.

"Daddy helps brave SS." Petra poked his thigh. "Careful, the Gestapo have agents in kindergartens."

"Daddy helps brave SS."

Petra drew a long, calming breath. Keeping that boy's ears out of their conversations grew more critical by the day. They joined the autobahn and the clear line of sight to the capital revealed Berlin's gigantic dome shimmering in the distance. For the next twenty minutes it occupied a little more of their field of vision every meter they moved forward.

Berlin's new, monumental centre dwarfed Rome, Paris, and London. Cool shade and the smell of concrete greeted their entry to the underground car park. Max jumped from the Porsche, tapping his feet while Petra took Lothar in her arms. Before she had settled him in place, Max ran to the stairs. He lingered just in front of her until they reached the door. The family emerged from the parking garage behind the massive dais constructed across the entrance to the domed Volkshalle's main square.

The Hellfeiers walked past a radio installation manned by jumpy SS officers. One of the crew - tan uniform, a sour, balding smoker with a cigarette between his lips - recognised her. Pleasure swept across his face.

"Hi Petra! Will you be singing for us today?" His half-smoked cigarette stayed at the corner of his mouth.

Petra shook her head and smiled at the soldier.

Max squeezed her hand. "I can't believe you still get recognised all these years later. I should have more fans by now!"

"Don't play modest, you know you have. I've seen all the women staring at you."

A smug grin curled up his lip and died. "Women always stared at me."

"Men always stared at me, too, but I was never tempted. Just don't act on it again, please."

Two tiers of guest seating had a catwalk jutting from the first row. It pointed down the Boulevard of Splendours at the massive Arch of Total Victory and the South Railway Station. Giant screens relayed images from the stage to the tens of thousands of people filling the enormous avenue. Many of the men and women wore an SS uniform of some description. They stood at attention around the tanks, cannons, and rockets lined along the thoroughfare. Arms stretched in salute they repeatedly, in unison, cried "Heil Himmler!"

Max sat in the front, Petra and Lothar in the back row. The Luftwaffe Air Marshal, all rugged good looks and fair hair, turned to wink at her.

She repressed disapproval, familiar with his persistent flirtations but also glad of them. In a little over two weeks, Petra would be two years past thirty and didn't know how long her looks would last.

"Give it a rest, Fritz."

Max met her eye when turning to his colleague, the beautiful Eva Reitsch. Petra felt a tinge of jealousy, and anger tensed her mouth. Max completely ignored her requests to stay faithful. She may as well have talked to herself.

The head of the army passed by and greeted Petra with a nod and an intense stare. The chief admiral remained motionless, his rough, pitted skin lending him a stone-hewn appearance. From behind the dais, Petra heard the radio set broadcasting a gun battle before a sheepish officer muted it.

Silence began to fall when the Führer stood. Stubble jutted from the back of his sweaty neck. Himmler remained quiet, staring around the crowd until the audience muted their praise. "Aryan people of the Reich, I stand before you today with High Priest Drachenblut, the leaders of our glorious colonies of Ingermanland and Memel-Narev."

Petra noted Gothengau Leader Richard Baer's absence. Only serious discord between the Führer and the Gauleiter could account for Baer's empty seat. Himmler nodded toward the group on his left. "Our spiritual leader and the Vestal Virgins are here to perform the blessings of Spring in the manner of our ancient Germanic forefathers." The Führer looked to his right. "The Wehrmacht Chiefs, Western Defenders of the Fatherland, Air Marshall von Hohenzollern, Field Marshal Mannteufel, and Admiral Geissler, offer us their support through their defence against Britain and America."

Himmler continued addressing the assembly. He didn't even mention Gothengau.

"But first I will tell you something. I'll tell you how the Reich Space Agency will take a leap in technology further than America, Britain, or Japan have even dreamed. Today, I let it be known that the Fatherland will be the first nation to put a man in space. Yes, through the brilliance of our scientists we can truly be above all, as rulers of the skies. This is the first step for the Aryan people to continue their natural domination from planet Earth into other worlds."

The crowd initially shouted as individuals, then announced their pride collectively with a rhythmic chant of *Deutschland Über Alles.*

Himmler let them continue for a minute before slashing the air with his arm to stop their tribute.

"We shall colonise and populate the moon, Mars, the cold outer reaches of the Solar System, then the stars. First, we shall send the finest specimens of the Aryan race to take that vital, initial leap. They must be strong in mind and body, skilled aviators, and at the pinnacle of their generation.

"Who will be the first? Who has that mental fortitude and the high levels of physical ability demanded? Could there be anyone except the Hero of the Battle for Russian Skies, the first to break the speed of sound, and Pride of the Fatherland? Max Hellfeier!" Max bristled with pride, looked around him, then stood and bowed.

In the moments of relative silence between the speeches and their matching rounds of applause, Petra monitored the panicked radio officers. Himmler further detailed his plans for the Third Reich's domination of space.

"The rubble in the asteroid belt is our new source of mineral wealth."

Wernher von Braun, rocket pioneer and visionary, had his accomplishments usurped, but his expression betrayed no feelings. When not looking at the radio set, Petra watched out for the rocket. Max did too. The glances seemed more than instinctive despite his protestations driving over.

Himmler neared the end of his speech. "I give you my word that we will, by the end of this decade, put a man in space. We do this not because it is easy, but because it is hard; because that challenge is one that we are willing to accept, one we are unwilling to postpone, and one which we intend to win."

Little Lothar trembled on Petra's knee when the audience responded with seismic applause. She sympathised, drawing him closer to her. Lothar's behind felt damp with urine. She didn't swear, nor raise her voice, but a long breath always accompanied her admonitions. Petra knew Lothar's familiarity with her behaviour. He wept gently.

Raising his hands high, Himmler basked in the adulation before ceding the podium to the High Priest. Drachenblut rose. His six-and-a-half-foot frame loomed over Petra. Her skin tingled, feeling his messianic presence. She felt like this once before: when Konrad stopped the SS rounding her up for the Auschwitz train. The memory almost made her wet herself as well. The High Priest breezed past the dais' sentries with a few long strides. He turned, and when the cloak arced through the air, the silver threads in its embroidery glinted in the sunshine. His loose tunic and boots laced over the trousers mimicked the ancient Teutonic style but remodelled with the fearsome iconography and stylish lines of the SS.

Rising at Drachenblut's beckoning the Vestal Virgins snaked toward him in line. Their powder-blue, billowing silk robes appeared to conjoin them; the colour of their coiled, braided hair the only distinguishing feature. They bent down and picked up the blue and white pole lying on the runway, seductively raising it and placing it in its socket on the podium. Red-headed Helga, the Chief Vestal and daughter of propaganda minister Josef Goebbels, stepped forward. Grimhilt, the blonde Vestal remained still. Edda, mouth perpetually agape, stepped back to reflect her place in the hierarchy.

The May Day fertility blessing started with Drachenblut raising Helga's leg and running his hand along her bare thigh. She coiled and uncoiled her leg around him, then flung herself over to the maypole. Grimhilt replaced Helga as the High Priest's dancing partner, while Helga wrapped herself around the strut, spinning and dancing up and down it.

Petra's smoking admirer from the radio installation ran up the stairs towards the Führer. She jumped so hard Lothar's toy spaceship flew from his hand. It smashed to pieces on the floor. Ignoring his screams, she leant forward to Max.

"I think the rocket is coming." Petra motioned at her breathless fan spraying Himmler's ear with saliva. "Look at the Führer."

The messenger finally got his information across to Himmler. Wiping his face, the Führer shot up and bounded to the steps. Jealousy stung Petra when Max grasped Eva's thigh and whispered to her. Eva jumped and ran to the stairs. Max followed her. Petra picked up Lothar, but by now almost half the guests had moved to the exit, keeping her apart from Max. On stage, Drachenblut disentangled himself from the Vestals to watch the impromptu evacuation.

If the crowd received no warning of the attack, the rocket strike could kill many thousands. That might sit fine with Himmler, but Petra couldn't just allow it. She let those behind her push past, jumped over to Himmler's empty chair and grabbed the microphone. But she couldn't hang around.

"Run! Run!" The crowd remained motionless.

A cameraman focused on her, the camera's light glowing red. The screens down the avenue showed her face. Little time remained to get to safety. This must be her last attempt to save them before she saved herself. Using the expression reserved for the saddest songs in her repertoire, she begged the crowd.

"Run! A rocket's coming! Run now!"

All this got recorded. Petra still knew this business. A tear ran from the eye during a camera close up. Old tricks came back so easily.

On the grand boulevard, the ordered ranks of demonstrators became a crazed mob. Radiating from the screens like toppling dominoes, individuals pelted from their regimented places. People at the edges ran under the rocket launchers and climbed over the tanks. Artillery hindered the exit for those in the centre. Petra's eyes glued to the desperation. Had her weeping really been the catalyst for this? Behind them, thousands of Nazi men, women, and teenagers escaped the middle. They ran until they pushed the reticent over and ground their boots on the dawdlers. A missile could hit any second. Back in the present moment, Petra gulped air. She had forgotten to breathe.

Petra stood between the mob and the stairs. She grabbed Lothar and jumped into the fray of pampered outfits. The crush swept them along. Petra thought she would tear the boy in two when the crowd pulled his feet away so forcefully. His terrified glare and piercing scream cut into her, almost tearing her away from her survival instinct. Energised, she tugged again, and his shoes came off. He shot back into her arms. Sticking a foot back, she recovered her balance.

The tsunami of people flowed down the stairs. The horde pushed Lothar's face to her chest. Petra worried about him suffocating, but the mob spewed them to the ground. He gasped, compensating for his missed breaths, eyes bulging and lips blue. Petra stood close to the stage looking down the boulevard at the melee. The crowd kicked one of the Himmler Youth out from under it. Whoever it was, the body's battered, bloody condition erased any clues about gender.

When Petra looked around for cover, she glimpsed Max and Eva running to a massive Hitler statue that disguised a car park entrance. She dashed into Hitler's shadow as an orange glow illuminated their world. On the cusp of taking a breath, the blast hit. The explosion's power ripped the air from her mouth and wrenched Lothar's hand from hers, spinning her around. His body shot towards a wall, but Petra had no air to scream with. The concrete stopped his little body dead. Clutching at her face, she watched Lothar's crumpled, snapped form slide to the ground leaving a trail of blood and gore behind it.

Petra fought through stinging dust to reach him. She knelt to check his neck for a pulse, bent closer to feel his breath. No signs of life remained. Not recoiling from the internal fluids (this was no time for prissiness), she cradled the still body in her arms.

The memory of Wieland's harrowing death fleetingly brushed aside the anguish Petra felt for Lothar. Ears ringing, she carried Lothar to the parking garage, stepping around the Hitler head and arm thrown to the ground by the explosion. Petra kicked the door open and rushed downstairs. When she reached the basement, shock caught up with her. She collapsed over the dead child, wracked with sobs.

Disoriented, Petra picked up Lothar's body and staggered towards her car. Desperate to avoid the carnage outside, as well as Max, Petra staggered to the vehicle, raising herself with every step. When she regained her erect posture, their Porsche became visible. As did Max. He consoled Eva, steadfastly supporting her buttocks in this hour of Petra's need. Petra's vision blurred. There was just no stopping that guy. At least she had stopped him at first base.

Eva's eyes lifted from Max's comforting shoulder, the fire in them turning vibrantly startled. Petra glared at her, and Eva recoiled when she saw the red and white bouquet of compound fractures dangling from Petra's arms. Eva straightened her posture, casually pushed Max away and strode to the exit.

Max's haunted expression showed his guilt, but remorse wasn't enough to pay for Petra's hurt. She handed the body to him, showing no emotion. Her self-control kept her calm. "He needs the burial ceremony." Petra held back her emotions. "Take him to the Children's Valhalla Temple."

Petra got in the car. She pressed a button and as the roof drew back, she drove back up to the street. Acrid fumes and choking soot filled her lungs. When her coughing became too much, she stopped the car until regaining her composure. The roof went back up and she drove again. Ghost-like, the dust-covered survivors roamed, dazed and aimless across her path. She sounded the horn briefly. Nobody reacted, and she leant on the klaxon again for several seconds. People noticed, their eyes wandering to the driver of the noisy car.

"Petra!" one of them cried.

More heads rose when they heard her name.

"You saved us!" said another.

Clutch balanced, she edged the Porsche forward at a rheumatic walking pace. Her right foot fluttered between gas and brake pedals. The crowd, unwillingly and under duress, parted around the vehicle with the viscosity of molasses. As she meandered past them, they began to murmur her name. By the time she reached the end of their number, it became a rhythmic chant and her vision blurred through the tears and mascara that streamed down her face. This was a comeback she hadn't planned on.

Chapter 4

Gothengau, Monday, March 1st,1948

Ploughing the field with a tractor back in Amish country would have got Konrad chased out of town and maybe even banished for life. Mechanisation made everything easier, though. He turned his head to admire the straight clay markings where the harrow split the baked, ashy surface and exposed the unbleached, dark brown fertile ground to sunlight. Time to plant Konrad's first summer wheat crop had arrived. His dreams of raising grain and children had come true. He had been in the Reich almost two years and the convicts, farm and family took Konrad's mind away from his unexpected new reality. Before he had time to dwell further, the end of the field arrived. Turning the vehicle required concentration, making it easy to push thoughts about the Nazis to the back of his mind. When he faced the other direction, Yuri ran toward Konrad, waving his arms. Squat Yuri sported an old, brown pair of patches held together by trousers and an equally brown, hole-strewn sweater. Konrad sped over to his local help.

"Is important telephone for you, mister Konrad."

The engine rasped when Konrad raced back to the white, clapboard farmhouse at the bottom of the field. Braking hard splattered soil over the back porch of the recently finished two-storey house. He ran in to the phone that lay off its hook on the table. The place still smelled of fresh paint

"You spattered mud all over the window and back wall again." Diana rocked in the comfort of her nursing chair. Young Mary burped when she'd reached her fill of milk.

"Sorry, Yuri told me there's an important call."

Diana beamed and nodded toward the receiver lying beside the telephone cradle. Konrad picked it up.

"Konrad Lapp speaking." He sat on the cushioned seat built into the bureau.

"Heil Hitler. This is Otto Günsche, the Führer's personal adjutant."

Yuri hadn't exaggerated the significance of the call. Konrad had only met the Führer once, when Konrad bowed deep so that Hitler could hang the Giant's Cross medal around his neck. Adolf was a strange little man, staring deep in Konrad's eyes. Most of the time he held himself like he had wind. The gentle murmur and smell of farts followed him everywhere. Otto had arranged it all then, too.

"Heil Hitler."

"For the Führer's 59th birthday next month there is to be a special event. As one of the prime examples of Aryan development, you are to be an important guest.

"On March the 15th, a flight will take you from Gothengau to Hamburg for you to be instructed and rehearsed in your part of the celebration."

Yet another outing to display Konrad, just like back in the freakshow. Would they have him lifting tractors, dragging ploughs, throwing anvils again here? Sometimes, he felt like a microscope focussed on him, magnifying every mundane part of his life, his physique, to be spied on by the general public, monitored by amoral scientists and studied by anthropologists in the futile search to prove racial superiority.

"You will return to Gothengau two days later, until April 19th, when you will again be in Hamburg to take part in the official celebrations for two days."

Would spending time in Germany proper improve his feelings about the Reich? It sounded as if he would be too busy to think about it.

"Then you will go back to Gothengau. That is all. Do you have any questions?"

He certainly did. "What will I do during these activities?"

"You will be on stage with a group of other exceptional Aryans."

"Just standing?"

"I believe so, although that is not a guarantee. You should be prepared to do some lifting."

"Okay, Mr Günsche. I shall see you in two weeks." Konrad replaced the receiver.

Diana held their baby over her shoulder, gently patting its back, her bobbed brown hair bouncing in time. "Where are you going?"

"I've to be displayed again. In Hamburg, this time, for the benefit of the Führer."

Diana's downturned mouth didn't hide the sympathy in her eyes. "It's the right kind of attention."

"Yes, I'm lucky." His suspicions pulled his mood further down. "I'm going back to the fields."

"What about the dirt on the window and the back of the house?"

"Ask Yuri to clean it."

Konrad returned to the tractor. While ploughing the straightest furrows in Gothengau, he daydreamed of redemption. Saving just one life might be enough.

Gothengau, Monday, March 15th

Diana stood in the doorway cradling and cooing to Mary, dawn's early light enhancing her sandy golden glow. She waved to Konrad while he started the army car. He waved back, smiling in contentment. On the way to the airport the road took him through the ploughed fields of the Reich's breadbasket. Unripe grain swayed in the breeze. Combine harvesters chewed up the ripened seed, leaving a trail of stubble behind. Within half an hour, Konrad arrived at the solitary hut near which an aircraft with propellers on its nose and each wing idled its engines.

Airfield would be a more appropriate name for the terminus, but not for long. Beside the pasture, troopers forced men in striped costumes to labour on the concrete runway. Konrad parked and lifted up the hood to retrieve his bag. While his face was hidden, Konrad grimaced at the use of slaves captured in Siberia. A bald man in uniform with a forehead reminiscent of sperm whales, trotted from the corrugated airplane, arms waving.

"Konrad. We're ready for lift-off. Please board and take a seat."

Konrad strode to the silver flying machine and followed the attendant up the steps into the empty cabin. Good, he thought, I'll get a seat with enough legroom near the door. As soon as the dome-headed man closed the door, the airliner moved. Usually, Konrad thought as the plane hurtled forward, these Nazi displays were very well lit, graceful shows of German pride. By the time he came back, everything would be clearer. The plane left the ground and Konrad fell soundly asleep.

An abrupt change in the engine note woke Konrad. By the way they angled up, the aircraft was about to land. He couldn't help but stretch after the slumber, and by the time the vehicle touched the tarmac he had satisfied the urgent desire. The plane taxied to its stand by a terminal building and the flight attendant opened the door after the stairs were in place. Downy fluff on the steward's scalp locked drops of perspiration in place. Konrad's greeter, a young man with dark hair, scowling eyes and a smile, hopped from foot to foot. He needed no sign to recognize his giant charge, and the SS-officer marched over to the foot of the steps when Konrad squeezed through the door.

"Konrad Lapp, I presume?" The smiling greeter stretched out an arm. "Heil Hitler."

"Heil Hitler." Konrad raised his palm.

"I am Section Leader Magnus Heiligmann." His broken nose made Magnus sound more adenoidal. "I'm your escort to the rehearsal. Please follow me, and I will drive you there."

Heiligmann walked back to his Mercedes, a beautiful silver confection of flowing arcs free of a roof flying a swastika flag from the bonnet. When the car moved, Konrad's fine hair flew around as much as its short length allowed. Morning traffic advanced slowly, and the reduction of speed let Konrad's mop fall back in place. Fields dominated the journey into Hamburg's centre. When they neared the river, concrete replaced crops and the city's conurbation rose up. Low-rise blocks of flats lined Airport Street, seeming to stretch on indefinitely, though within thirty minutes they neared the German Playhouse.

Trains gained superiority over cars the closer they came to the Playhouse. On a bridge across a lake the rail neared the road. Traffic halted, and the stench of the farmyard blended with the fragrance of open toilets smacked Konrad's senses. With his nose scrunched, Konrad peeked around for the source of the foul odour. There was no origin apart from the train standing next to the road. Several cattle trucks waited to enter the main station. Human hands reached out of the breathing slats along the doors and panels. The inhabitants caterwauled in a piercing high note that undulated in volume as choristers joined and departed from the discordant acapella.

Heat ran through Konrad and his scalp tightened. This was the veracity behind the stories told abroad. Without losing his own life, even his family's lives, he could do nothing to help the wretched souls destined for resettlement in the East. Konrad suspected that they got no further than Poland. How Konrad, let alone the German people, could atone for this baffled him. His driver looked away from the horror. Konrad wished for such wilful blindness.

Congestion eased once they crossed the bridge, and they left the train still standing. Hamburg began to look familiar from the brief time Konrad spent here when the *St. Louis* docked and released him into this terrifying new world. After passing the main station, their destination appeared. A squat, white building with a colonnaded front and a dome topped with slate, the German Playhouse was much grander than almost everything Konrad had seen in rough-and-ready Gothengau. Heiligmann stopped the car between the building's Swastika banners, stepped out and opened Konrad's door.

"I shall return tomorrow to take you to your flight back."

Konrad climbed the few steps to the entrance and walked into the grand rotunda, its floor ornately patterned with tiles and its walls and ceilings with swirls of plaster relief. A fleur-de-lis motif ran through all the adornments, but for Konrad all Teutonic beauty had been debased. Konrad couldn't see it without picturing the hands grasping the air from inside cattle trucks.

A wall of doors faced Konrad. One of them opened, releasing the hubbub of voices and activities from the theatre and a handsome woman strode out. Her beaming smile exposed the laugh-lines under her defined cheekbones.

"Heil Hitler." She raised her palm. "I'm Leni. How are you, Konrad?"

"I'm fine. And you?"

"It's how you are that counts!" Leni's smile spanned her face. "You certainly look wonderful, a figure of Aryan beauty if ever I saw one. You are going to be the perfect centrepiece for the show. Now that I've seen you in person, I have a much better idea of how you'll fit in to the scheme of the performance. I might even have a rethink and make you more the focal point."

Leni stepped back and scrutinised Konrad. Her hand rubbed her chin, but occasionally flicked a stray black curl from her right eye. The shoulder length hair allowed her femininity to overcome the shapeless grey crew-neck and flannel pants adorning her. A puppy-eyed, leotard clad man opened the theatre door. His stare did not stray from Leni.

"We're all ready for you, Leni, darling."

"Look who it is, Johan." Leni turned to the interloper. "It's Konrad Lapp, the Führer's giant."

"Yeah. I'm not blind." Johan crossed his arms. "Come on, we're all waiting for you."

"Stop bullying me with this 'all ready for you', 'all waiting for you'. I'm speaking to Konrad. They can wait a moment."

Johan exhaled deeply then let the door bang shut behind him.

"We're using this for rehearsals. The real show will be on an artificial island of some kind in the Aussenalster lake. Most likely you crossed it when you arrived here."

That's where the cattle-trucks had sat next to his open-top car. He swore that the train's faecal emanations still almost lingered in his nose. Keeping his face, his voice, and even his tiniest movements free from emotion still took the utmost concentration.

"I will be making a film of it, about the Thousand-Year Reich that our Führer led us to. The working title is 'the Dream Realised'. Have you ever seen a film called 'Triumph of the Will'?"

Konrad nodded. At the absorption camp, Hitler's 1935 visit to the Nazi Party conference had been compulsory viewing.

"This will be something like a sequel. Its centrepiece will be on this island. I'll be filming from the ground, the air, and you will represent the pinnacle of Aryan evolution which helped the Führer achieve his goal. You will be making some simple movements, synchronising them with the other performers." Leni pawed his arm. "We have an outfit for you to wear. It's backstage, in the changing room." She tugged his sleeve. "Follow me, I'll take you."

They walked through the door into the three-tiered room. On stage various young, leotard-clad people stood by plinths and on tables. Spotlights focussed their glare on several of the youths. Konrad followed Leni along the gangway between the red seats, and up to the footlights. The players all greeted Konrad, then he followed Leni backstage. She opened a door to a large, messy chamber filled with racks of clothing and decked with mirrors.

"The changing room." Leni strode to an enlarged version of the leotard everyone else wore. "Here you are." She handed him the clothing. "Don't worry, I won't watch. See you back onstage in a few minutes, okay?"

Alone, Konrad donned the elegant, contour-hugging clothing. His thoughts returned to the people in the train's cattle trucks. Scripture says to save a single life is to save the world entire. After changing, Konrad headed back to the stage.

Leni halted rehearsal when Konrad appeared. The cast groaned.

"Don't worry, the main event is here now. Come Konrad, climb on to the highest pedestal."

Resentment radiated from some colleagues. Their facial expressions and sounds of exasperation betrayed jealousy. He ignored their childishness. As Leni had said, her requirements were simple, and she directed them through the graceful, if monotonous, changes in position.

"Imagine the camera on you. Show your pride in the Aryan race for the audience out there. This is the birth of the Thousand Year Reich, and it's because of you, and the people like you that this could happen."

Konrad didn't need to stretch his powers of imagination too hard to think of the camera on him. By behaving as if the spotlights were cameras, he got the same effect.

"Good, Konrad. You're a natural." Grumbles emerged from the performers. "Oh, stop with your jealousy, Johan. How can you compete with Konrad? He's a giant, and a perfect specimen. Look, Konrad's blushing!"

Although on the highest perch in the hall, Konrad wanted to crawl under a rock. He breathed deeply a few times until the sizzling in his face reduced. The Nazis painted him as the tip of the evolutionary spear, but even someone so advanced could do nothing about the heinous crime back on the railway though the station stood only moments away from the theatre. Leni clapped her hands.

"Okay, everyone." The cast turned to her. "That's it for today."

Leni sashayed over to Konrad as he climbed down from his eyrie.

"Why don't you come with me after you get changed? We could see the city together. The Führer has told me so much about you, but only as a fine specimen of Aryan manhood. I'd like to get the know the real you."

Although Konrad preferred not to spend time alone with women other than his wife, there seemed to be no way to refuse. That would damage his own good standing in those far-off pinnacles of the Reich leadership. "Of course, it would be my pleasure."

While Konrad changed back into his black suit, he wondered how to use this encounter to do something about the ghastly situation in the cattle-trucks without drawing attention to himself. According to Leni, Hitler followed Konrad's activities closely. Anything untoward on Konrad's behalf held dangers for his family. Perhaps an amble past the cattle trucks, just to see what opportunities arose for Konrad's assistance, was not too much to hope for.

Konrad walked back to the stage, where Leni tapped her feet and glanced at her watch. She waved.

"Come Konrad, let's go out. I feel so cramped in here. This room isn't big enough for spirits like ours."

Leni reached up and linked arms with Konrad and they returned to the marble-tiled entrance hall before setting feet on the pavement. Dragging Konrad to a halt, Leni drew in a great breath.

"Ah, the smell of the German Ocean is so briny, don't you think?"

Konrad didn't have that sort of olfactory sensitivity, and his imagination still held the stench of the train. They were several kilometres away from the sea along the Elbe and Konrad wasn't sure how Leni could detect the salty air, other than in her mind.

"I can't tell." Konrad took a step toward the road. "Shall we walk through the train station?"

Without waiting for Leni's answer, Konrad moved off towards the rail terminus.

"Seems like you've already decided we're going there!" Leni smiled, her feet planted firmly on the ground. "But it's a good route through to the city centre from here."

Across the street, the station's tower loomed above the dirty, metal and glass arches that covered the platforms. Traffic stopped, horns honked, and drivers stepped out of cars to gawp at the giant dragging the movie director along by the hand. Konrad felt his hand being pulled back. Couldn't Leni walk and talk at the same time?

"You're in quite a rush." Leni looked exasperated. "Where's the fire?"

Burning in me, thought Konrad. He marched across the plaza to the entrance of the main station, Leni struggling to maintain pace, keep her feet on the floor, and not be swept off her feet. Surely now that faecal stench was in his nostrils, not just his mind. He looked down at Leni, but her face could have been contorted by the journey. "Are you okay?"

Leni stopped moving. "Yes, but this isn't what I expected time alone with you to be like. Can you slow down, please?"

Better had, thought Konrad. Didn't want Hitler getting any reports of disconcerting behaviour about his giant.

"Of course. So sorry for rushing, it's just I felt really constrained from being in the theatre, especially after the flight from Gothengau. Please, you lead the way - I'm never sure of anybody else's walking speed."

Opening the door for Leni, Konrad allowed her to get a few steps ahead of him. While he dawdled behind her, Konrad looked around. After the acrid aroma of smoke from the remaining steam locomotives, another biological scent probed Konrad's mind through his most primal sense. That stink was from the cattle trucks, he could see them at a far platform. Konrad could do nothing.

"Come, Konrad." Leni tugged his sleeve. "I can't drag you like you can me. What are you looking at?" Leni turned to see. "Yes, they are clearing the town of any remaining sub-humans today. There are still some Jews, Gypsies and deviants around, the Führer believes."

"And what do you believe?" Konrad surprised himself at taking the risk to which this line of questioning led.

"There are always going to be those sorts. It's a continual battle to relocate them. They insist on coming back, or more appear from nowhere like mushrooms."

"Lead on." Konrad held out a hand and Leni started walking.

SS uniforms sandwiched a procession of a dozen such undesirables near the cattle trucks. Konrad sucked on his teeth and trudged forward, despondency digging a hole in his gut. He would never be able to save a single soul. As he reached the doors a familiar voice sang out.

"Konrad!" cried the girl. "Konrad help me!"

Chapter 5

Hamburg, Monday, March 15th, 1948.

Preparations for the Führer's impending birthday - signs, banners, spotlights, giant tents, and firework installations - blocked Petra's way from Central Station through the narrow alleys and gabled houses of the old town, past the waterfront, and right to the steps of the city-hall tower. At a billboard in the square, a chill ran through Petra when she saw her own picture - a poster for a recently given concert to honour the German soldiers in the East - being daubed with plaster and emblazoned with those of the official celebration. At least it was for something important, though: the international recognition of the birth of the Thousand Year Reich to honour Hitler. Petra had booked quite a few paid singing engagements for the festivities. She would meet her most prestigious client after the formalities with the stern, bald, paper-skinned clerks in half-moon rimless spectacles, eyes down over their desks, under the vaulted stone arches of the city-hall's interior.

Petra took a deep breath and held it, trying to calm her fluttering stomach. This was the most adult thing that she had ever done on her own, and she had worn her most mature outfit - a dark blue dress and a navy jacket. Stale odours of unopened folders hung heavier the closer Petra came to the desks. The clerk's pen stopped scratching away at the pad. An opportunity for Petra to interrupt. "Excuse me?"

"Heil Hitler." He raised his right palm a little

"Heil Hitler."

"How can I help you?" He looked up.

"I'm here to see Albrecht Schmitt, the city clerk."

"Yes, I know who he is." His eyes rolled. "Do you have an appointment?"

"Of course! It's at two-thirty."

The clerk cocked his head. "And your name, young lady?"

"Petra Vierjahn."

"Oh yes." He leafed through a few sheets of a large, cloth bound book and then closed it. Moments afterward he nodded to her and sighed.

"Are you still here? It's on the second floor, fourth door on the left."

Petra's high heels clomped up the stairs, the sound reverberating through the arched corridors of sandstone and plaster. Beyond the ground floor, the interior looked utilitarian. Corridors of glass and wood with doors into the offices spaced at irregular intervals. Meticulously painted names adorned the doors, but the *fraktur* demanded more attention of Petra to comprehend it than she cared to give. Fortunately, she didn't need to, only to reach the fourth door on the left where she paused before knocking, long enough to figure that the ornate font introduced Albrecht Schmitt, City Clerk.

Petra worked up the nerve to tap her knuckles on the glass door panel. "Enter."

She walked in the small office. Filing cabinets lined the walls, leaving only enough room for a petite desk. A large, bald, beady eyed man squeezed behind it. Presumably this was Albrecht Schmitt.

"Petra?" His smile obscured his eyes and shifted his wire spectacles. "It is, isn't it? I've seen your posters. You may go through and see Mr Schmitt straight away."

Only when the secretary told her that did she notice that she stood in an anteroom.

"Thank you." She stepped through the door the secretary guarded.

Albrecht, a bald man with a toothbrush moustache and little higher that Petra in stature, stood with his arm outstretched.

"Heil Hitler."

Petra raised her hand to return the greeting.

"Heil Hitler."

"It is wonderful to meet you, Petra." He dived in to land a slobbering kiss on each cheek.

Petra stepped back. Don't wipe it, she thought. You want this job, don't you? She smiled, the effort almost making her lips tremble.

Albrecht's hand caressed her upper arm. "Come, sit."

He guided her to the guest chair by her elbow, another hand landing on her hip soon after. Petra's eyebrows raised, but she stayed silent. She had to see this opportunity fulfilled. It could be the start of a life of fame, internationally even, with the recognition from America, the British Empire, and maybe far-off Japan. So much glamour and a host of opportunities to escape her overbearing mother.

Albrecht rolled his chair over to hers and they sat face-to-face, their knees touching.

"So, Petra. You are comfortable singing in English?"

"Oh yes, Mr. Schmitt." Petra tapped a foot. He already knows I'm American. "It's the first language I ever sang in."

"Perhaps you could also sing something in Japanese?"

Petra thought about that. "With somebody coaching me." Confidence fed her enough to power an emphasis. "Yes. Yes, I could."

"I'm sure, I've no doubt about it at all. I heard that you're a very clever young woman who won the mathematics prize for the schoolchildren in the whole of the Reich."

"Well, yes." Petra always found talking about maths uncomfortable. "I just spot patterns. Numbers don't really interest me." Her eyebrows neared each other. Many of the other contestants were undergraduates. "But it wasn't just kids that entered."

"Then it seems we have the perfect candidate to lead the children's chorus for the celebration of the Reich's birth." Albrecht's thin-lipped smile sharpened his high cheekbones. "Of course, you will sing the American and English anthems solo." He patted her knee, his eyes not meeting hers. "It's lucky for you they haven't finished rebuilding Berlin yet, otherwise the role would have gone to one of their local heroines." Now his hand rubbed her thigh. "You will receive a thousand Reichsmarks for this, as well as the international exposure. No longer." He touched her crotch while she bit her lip. "Will you only be known in the Hamburg area, Petra." Heavy breathing. "This could be your big break."

Albrecht's knee worked its way between hers. Petra clenched her jaw and kept her legs shut tight. She knew what this was about, she'd witnessed her mother's lewd conduct and even walked in on the act itself.

"No." The highest volume she could raise was only a mumble.

He touched between her legs again. How could she stop this, a tiny young woman like her? No ideas came to her and fear's paralysis blanketed her. Tears brimmed in her eyelids, blurring her vision. One rolled down her cheek.

"Of course, you are still not sixteen. How foolish of me, and there's no fool like an old fool as they say."

Petra's chest felt tight from the tension, and she could barely speak, her mouth was so dry. Her tongue rubbed the roof of her mouth.

"I know you are famed for your exotic looks." Albrecht looked away and tugged at his collar. "Which means you should know that undesirables are being cleared from the city ahead of the celebrations - I fear that you may be caught in the dragnet. Be careful walking around. We wouldn't want anything to happen to you."

"Thank you for the warning." Petra's voice now managed a rasp. "I shall go straight home." She wouldn't, she had another appointment.

"Very good. You know the way out. Thanks for your visit, it was a pleasure."

Petra's relief at the end of the ordeal sent a chill down her and she shivered. Spinning around, she took dainty but rapid paces towards the corridor. Her next meeting shared something with the one at the town hall - unrequited love, although Petra was the unsated half of the relationship. Merely imagining the rough-hewn jaw and dimpled chin of Hans Bader calmed her from the anxiety from the meeting with Albrecht. Hans held a masterful, near paternal, authority over her, and he was old enough, just, to be her father.

Ignoring Albrecht's warning, she walked to the station and took the tram to Reeperbahn. Her mind wandered to the romantic possibilities she felt sure Hans ignored, Petra believed, purely for professional reasons. They were meeting in a theatre to discuss business, and such a professional strived to separate it from pleasure. When the streetcar passed the SS stormtroopers and the undesirables they herded she barely noticed. By the time she reached her stop, they were out of both her sight and mind. Her destination, the Trichter Theatre, stood close by. She skipped towards the box office. Its occupant smiled broadly in recognition.

"Hi Petra." Animation livened the grey-bearded concierge's face. "Hans and his friend are waiting for you upstairs."

Petra trotted up the wooden staircase, and along the white corridor. She tried the handle of his door, but it was locked. She heard some fluttering and banging, then the door opened.

"Hi Hans." Petra stepped into the room, looking at the floor. "I did the deal with City Hall. That Albrecht's so creepy, though. I almost burst into tears when I was on my own with him."

Silence greeted her, and she looked up at Hans' well-built young friend rearranging the tuck of the shirt in his pants. He had the face of a hectored and harried angel. Beautiful lines and milky skin blotched with red and covered in a patina of sweat.

"So, I'll see you about that next time and we'll finish where we left off." The friend rushed past Petra to the exit.

"That's great news about Albrecht, though." Hans smiled when he turned to her. "He does seem a little peculiar, I must say. You're going to be a very busy girl with all these international bookings. What will you do with all the money?"

"I'm going to get my own flat the minute I'm sixteen." Petra couldn't say that without grinning.

"Oh yes?" Hans pursed his lips.

"Yes. It's too much pressure, being an only child in that house."

Hans laughed, his eyes sparkling. For her?

"Well, I've seen your mother in action. I'm not surprised you're going to flee the nest as soon as you can. But you should watch out. Not all the men you'll meet in this business are as respectful as I am."

"I think I just found that out for myself. He must have felt guilty afterwards, because he warned me about SS patrols cleaning up the city for the celebrations."

"Really?" Hans raised an eyebrow. "I wish you'd said before Jürgen left." He paused, biting his lip. "Anyway, yes. Well as you're not really a little girl any more, you'll have to be more careful when and where you meet men. Perhaps I'll be your agent, then you'll always be chaperoned."

"I would like that." Then, Petra thought, I would have more time on my own with him. We'd definitely end up married, her a singer him an impresario. Two lovely children - one boy, one girl - and a dog in a cottage in the countryside somewhere. And there would be roses around the door.

"So, we were thinking of having you here on a short residency after the Führer's birthday. Just while we see how it works out. You never know, it could become permanent."

"That's wonderful, Hans." Petra made some calculations, "I'll get my own place with the money. You will come and see me, won't you?"

Hans' square, dimpled chin framed his beguiling smile. His nostrils flared.

"Of course, Petra. Of course! So, you should be on the lookout for the SS, you exotic little beauty. If I were an SS officer, I'd round you up on sight! You'd better go now we've let each other know the good news. My friend Jürgen is sure to come back any minute." Hans checked his watch and tutted. "I hope so, anyway."

"I'll get going back home, then. See you on Wednesday."

Petra smelt Hans' aftershave, breathing it deeply to enjoy its aroma, as he held the door for her.

A fine mist of rain met her when she stepped back on the pavement, and Petra pulled her jacket up over her head to prevent her auburn hair frizzing up. After she scooted under the awning of a cinema she looked around. Handsome Jürgen caught her eye. He shouted and threw aside an SS guard's hands. He bounded from the SS and their group of undesirables, his mouth showing the effort.

"Stop!" Shouted the strikingly tall officer.

Petra couldn't take her eyes from the SS leader, who drew his pistol. Something about him made her tingle all over. She wanted to step back, turn and run, but the gunman's magnetism compelled her to stop and watch.

"Stop, or I'll shoot!"

Petra brought her hand to her face but peeked through her fingers. She could not unsee the flash from the muzzle, the smoke from the gun. Blood appeared on Jürgen's shirt. Colour drained from his sweet face. His eyes swam with confusion. He tumbled over, hitting the pavement arms akimbo. A sob burst from her, loudly enough to bring her to the shooter's attention. He nodded to a subordinate, then looked straight at Petra. She couldn't move, or her bladder would empty right here, in daylight, in the theatre district's epicentre. There was no air to scream with when the stormtrooper trotted to her, double-time. His arm reached out and his hand seized her shoulder. The warmth of urine flowed down her legs and filled her shoes. She couldn't stop it now. Everybody pointed at her, laughing. She wanted to curl up inside herself and die, instead she was roughly shoved in the back. Struggling to stay on her feet, he marched her, squelching in her own waste, to the crowd of deplorables trailing his compelling SS officer.

"Show's over for you lot." The officer strutted along his prisoners. "We're taking you to the station for the train east. Sergeant, get them in marching order."

"Yes, Unterscharführer Drachenblut."

The sergeant and his four underlings set to work poking the itinerants with bayonetted rifles. Petra, the last in line moved fast when she saw the flash of the blade. Not fast enough. The sound of her dress tearing preceded a sharp pain. Looking down, she already saw blood around her skirt. Standing as straight as possible, her torn and bloody frock blended her right in to the motley procession of rough-sleepers, miscreants, effeminate men, and masculine women.

Pedestrians stopped and stared at them marching double time past St. Michael's Church. Petra found it hard to keep up, but whenever the distance between her and the next victim became too large a bayonet ripped at her dress. She worried it would fall apart and she would need to walk through the streets naked.

By the time they crossed the canals and entered Rödings Market, one of the camp men fell, panting for breath. He scrabbled for the wig that now lay an arms-reach away from his mottled, pink scalp. Its nudity enhanced the make-up on his face.

Drachenblut bounded over to him. "Get up."

The portly man scrabbled on the ground but couldn't push himself up. The soldiers pulled him upright by the armpits.

"No more delays." Drachenblut smacked the hostage's pate. "You're keeping the train waiting."

Petra didn't know how she would carry on at double time, but fortunately the sergeant put them to a manageable pace. People seemed to stop what they were doing to turn and watch their procession. At least she wasn't being harried by the soldier's blade anymore. Central Station appeared. How, Petra wondered could she tell Hans? What would become of her nascent career? Her parents came to mind last. Petra's mother would miss her progeny more now the bud of Petra's success had been nipped.

None of the eyes staring at them at Central Station showed indicators of help, or even signs of interest. A steam train towing cattle trucks sat at one of the platforms. Petra looked around wildly. In the distance, in the throng she made somebody out. Someone exceptionally tall. My word, what an amazing coincidence! Her friend from the boat, it had to be Konrad. Not believing her luck, joy overcame her. She drew several deep, excited breaths, puffed her chest out and stood on tiptoes.

"Konrad," she near sang.

No response, but for the guard marching towards her. Elation left her. A panicked note infused her voice.

"Konrad help me!"

He turned and came towards them just as Drachenblut struck her around the face and sent her flying. Nothing and nobody had ever hit her like that before. Surprised and stunned, Petra raised a hand to her jaw. Her teeth felt loose. Head throbbing, she reached up to soothe it, but a hand grabbed her throat. Drachenblut lifted her to his eye-level and she gurgled and gagged, her legs jerking. From under Drachenblut's caldera brow ridge, his hooded lava lake eyes seared into her. Everything else dimmed. Energy poured out of her. On the point of passing out, she hit the ground, staying alert.

Petra looked up, dazed. Konrad had Drachenblut by the throat, raising the snatch-squad leader to Konrad's eye-level. Drachenblut's limbs reached out to strike Konrad, but none matched the Amish giant's reach. Before the guards realised what Konrad did to their boss, Drachenblut's eyes closed. Suddenly aware of the danger, they bolted towards Konrad. Konrad grabbed Drachenblut's ankles and bowled their leader at them. They toppled. While they wriggled on the ground, struggling to stand, Konrad leapt, arms and legs spread. His body landed on the goons and squeezed grunts and groans from them.

"I'm the Führer's giant." Konrad stood. "This girl arrived with me from America on the same ship. Why are you trying to put her on that train?" Konrad wrenched the gun from Drachenblut and brandished it at him. "If Hitler hears about this, you will pay. But now you've released her, he won't hear about it from me."

Petra stood and wrapped her arms around one of Konrad's legs, safe at last.

Chapter 6

Wewelsburg, Saturday, May 1st, 1965.

In the castle's most recently and lavishly decorated room, the headrests of its plush leather armchairs prevented the draught from biting too hard on a winter's day. Oak panelling lent the chamber a warm appearance. All the chairs were arranged before a tall, walnut box in imitation of a fireplace, and bearded, long-haired men occupied all fifteen seats. Recent technological developments made this castle chamber exempt from the normal power structure. When High Priest Drachenblut was absent, Second Priest Karl held sway in the rest of the spiritual centre. But not here. The one who held The Wand had total control of the room. The pro-Drachenblut contingent held great store in its possession. As the earliest risers, it usually fell into their hands. Today, Karl brandished The Wand with pride. Drachenblut's acolytes had been too busy squabbling to pay it attention. Now Karl determined the agenda in the whole of the castle without exception, and the colour television showed what he dictated: the May Day celebration, live from Berlin. Their bickering only increased.

"Oh, be quiet for Loki's sake." Karl had reached his limit. "It's not like this May Day thing of Drachenblut's is anything like what Odinism was in its heyday."

Hegel snorted. "You're jealous because it's popular and he thought of it."

"You're jealous of the ones that were invited - the Vestal Virgins. Getting green eyed over a man paying attention to women. Borderline homosexuality."

Hegel lunged at Karl, getting so close Karl smelled his acid breath. His proximity gave Karl the chance to examine Hegel's cheek scar through his black facial hair. Burly Rolf tumbled in, all red hair and beard. He held Hegel back by the shoulders.

"Don't give him the satisfaction." Rolf held Karl's gaze. "Pretty boy isn't worth it."

Everybody returned to their original places. In Berlin, Drachenblut and the Vestals began their dance and the broadcast switched off. A black screen, then a patriotic tune with a Nazi pennant fluttering. In front of the flag, text reassured viewers the current technical problem would shortly be corrected.

"The program's gone off." Karl felt a wave of satisfaction warm him. "That's not Odinism, not real Odinism. It's a sexy stage show playing on people's lowest instincts."

"Change the record." Hegel shook his head, lips taut and angry. "Everyone loves them dancing around the Maypole." Hegel slashed the air with his hand then caressed his holstered firearm.

"Do you think you're still in Siberia? What does that gun protect you from around here? Mobs of angry squirrels?"

"I'm the only one of us that's seen Siberia."

With so much hair, reading facial expressions became near impossible for Karl. Hegel continued fondling the gun, his eyes peering right into Karl's. The cocky priest was armed and backed up, the pressure in Karl's skull so explosive it almost released a scream. Karl stormed out. When the door slammed, they laughed and humiliation prickled his skin from face to feet. Karl seethed and pounded the corridor until meeting a thick-browed sentry bearing a rifle.

"Give me your gun."

The guard didn't flinch.

"Did you hear me? Give me your gun."

When the sentry still stood mute, Karl pulled at the rifle. He didn't get it.

"Give me your gun." Karl lost it, raging at the implacable trooper. "I'm your senior officer."

With that, the soldier relinquished his weapon. Karl ran back to the television lounge and kicked the door open. He stood in the doorway and cocked the rifle, then brandished it at Hegel.

"You're not the only one with a gun now."

"I'm the only one with the balls to use it." Hegel drew his pistol.

A wave washed over Karl, front to back, sparkling and tingling the minute fine hairs on his bald skin. Hegel was right. Squeezing the trigger felt like squeezing granite. Karl wouldn't shoot, but resolving this impasse daunted him. Then the television broadcast returned. He exhaled, shock spreading across his chest.

"Run! A rocket's coming! Run now!"

All turned to the television. Karl and Hegel lowered their weapons. On screen, tears flowed down Petra Hellfeier's face as she begged the massed crowd to flee the boulevard. Glad as Karl was of her breaking the stalemate, why did this woman have to keep popping into his life? At least she wasn't blackmailing him this time.

The camera panned to the Vestals and Drachenblut untangling themselves while behind them a crowd boiled over into side streets. Then they showed the rocket coming in from a distance, the dot growing until its shape became clear, then closer, and then the signal went dead. Cries and wails entered the room when a half-mast Nazi flag was shown for a moment, then Petra's weeping restarted the cycle. Hegel holstered his gun. As the video played through another time, Karl shouldered his rifle. Then Olaf spoke.

"Hail the new High Priest." Olaf's eyebrows, a pair of elevated circumflexes, didn't necessarily mean surprise.

"Don't jump the gun." Sceptical Hegel shook his head. "Nothing's been said yet."

"The flag's at half-mast. I just thought it must mean Drachenblut didn't make it. That makes Karl the new High Priest of the German Religion."

Pride scoured Karl, exfoliating the grime of his prior indefinite subordination. He had resisted drawing the conclusion that Drachenblut had died. Now Olaf had spoken Karl's truth it became more malleable. He could touch it, grab it, embrace a new reality.

Hegel sprang from his chair and ran in front of Olaf, fist raised. "Why don't you let Karl speak for himself?"

Olaf shrank back. "I was only saying what we're all thinking." A murmur of agreement ran through the room.

Hegel let it go, relaxing his threatening stance. "If that's the case, we should hold a moment's silence."

Fabric and leather rustled together when the score of Odinist priests in the room stood, their faces tilted to the floor. Somebody wept, and Karl felt sure the sobbing came from Hadwin. Karl reflected on the situation. He needed to share his thoughts.

"Drachenblut will long be remembered as the greatest Odinist High

Priest. Now, surely, he is seated in Valhalla feasting beside Odin, Thor, Freya, and the others. Holy be his name forevermore."

"Excellent thoughts, High Priest."

Karl opened his eyes. Olaf and tear-stained Hadwin still had theirs closed. Hegel, however, stared at Karl and a fraction of a second after their gaze met, he bowed his head with slow deliberation. What a creep. But certainly an improvement on his own acolytes Olaf and blubbering Hadwin.

"No word for the Vestals, High Priest?"

Tears almost burst from his dry eyes when he realised he would never smell Virgin Grimhilt's blonde, streaked hair again, nor repeat running his hands down her silken belly to caress her pudenda. He held back his sobs. As High Priest, he would take another lover. Maybe it could even be one of the next batch of Virgins. Or more than one.

"Vestals Helga, Grimhilt, and Edda will forever be remembered as true servants of the German Religion. Their virtuous lives, leading to today's ultimate sacrifice shall not be forgotten."

"Probably cavorting in Valhalla with the Gods." After a chilling pause, Olaf yammered a vowel repeatedly, the remainder of the sobs held fast inside.

Hegel levelled a dead-eye stare at him, mouthing the word 'fairy'. "How could this happen? I saw where that missile came from. Gothengau are the Eastern Defenders, but they let something fly into the net."

"Drachenblut made Gothengau patrol those rockets around Siberia," said Olaf.

"You think I don't know that?" Hegel lunged in Olaf's direction. "I was one of his inner circle, soft lad."

Karl envied Drachenblut. His followers were more forthright, stronger, and, in Hegel's case, substantially more aggressive. Hegel's conversion may be transparent, but it pleased High Priest Karl to be followed by a real man, and not by the pansies that had trailed him before Drachenblut's death.

Hegel raised his hand, the preferred pupil confidently requesting a favour that the rest of the class abhorred. "What will you do first as the High Priest?"

"Good question." Satisfaction bubbled up through Karl to become a smirk.

Karl's shoulders swung back while he considered his answer. He had longed for this moment for several years but now wondered why he never conceived a plan for what to do on day one. Don't look wavering, he told himself. Keep your jaw straight and look towards the heavens. Inspiration will come to you.

"We shall have a celebration of the lives of the High Priest and Vestals."

Muted applause rippled around the room.

"That's a great idea, High Priest." Hegel had made every one of Karl's notions a brilliant, shining beacon of glory in the last few minutes. It didn't take much getting used to.

"I want everybody here to get down to the organisation of the grieving process," Karl flaunted his management skills. "Divide into four groups." Delineating the people in the rom by where they sat, Karl waved a hand to mark them. "The two on my left, I want proposals for the ceremony and service for Drachenblut. The two on my right, do the same for the Vestals. I want the teams to work against each other so we get the best results."

"Consider that this is also a terrible time for the Reich, that they are not the only deaths, not by any means. One can only imagine how many are dead and dying right now, at this moment. The people of the Reich need Odinism now, more than ever, to console them in the great loss that we all share.

"Hadwin and Olaf, come with me."

Before Karl could leave, Hegel's arm blocked his way.

"Can't I help?" Hegel whispered. "I've got experience and skills you know these two don't have."

Rolf stared at Karl with puppy eyes. No, thought Karl, Rolf was not needed. Then he looked at Hadwin. Karl's mind changed.

"Please join us."

Karl pushed through the crowd, returned to the corridor and padded to the steps. His pace increased on the spiral staircase. No paint had ever been applied to those, making it one of the few places in the castle to have the solid, protective aroma of stone. When passing Drachenblut's room, the Second Priest looked forward to taking possession of the High Priest's adjacent real-estate. Its increased space and a stunning view over the Wewelsburg Centre's steel and glass arcs on the plain below the castle lent its occupant a God-like quality. Given privacy, Karl and his followers would soon put Odinism right, especially with the new members of the team. He unlocked the heavy, nailed wooden door, pushing it open.

"Come in." That invitation should remind his followers of their place.

Olaf, the last to enter, closed it behind him. Now, Karl needed to come up with the changes he had long dreamed of and for which he had yearned since joining the order. Thoughts arrived in his mind, but the image of the rocket attack displaced them before he could explore. He couldn't plan his succession. Maybe Rolf, Hadwin, Olaf, and Hegel could help by giving him a figurative push.

"I can't believe he's gone." Dark facial hair left Hadwin's elegant nose and sensitive eyes unhidden, and tears streaked down his exposed skin.

When Olaf shook his head, his blonde mane trembled in response but his eyebrows stayed v-shaped. The new High Priest saw under Rolf's moustache, and his lips were pursed. Hegel glared at Hadwin. It seemed like only Karl needed to hide his pleasure in the day's events. He pictured his favourite pet dog, long gone. Grief dripped down his face. Safe grief, one against which time had long since inoculated his tears.

"What are we going to do now?" Hadwin wailed.

"Stop your weeping, woman," Hegel shouted. "It won't bring them back. We need action, not tears."

"Quite right, Hegel." Karl admired his new enforcer already. "Your sobbing never fixed anything, Hadwin. Dry your eyes."

Hadwin blew his nose and, with mouth downturned, stared at the floor. Well handled, thought Karl. Hegel is the man to keep the troops in order.

"This is a harrowing day for the Reich and even more than that for us." Karl let that hang aloft, looking from man to man. "We lost our leader and our Vestals. It would be so easy to let this grief overwhelm us, but we must take Odinism forward for the German People. Nor must we forget the contribution that Drachenblut made to Odinism."

"You never used to say that." Olaf had a quizzical look. "You always said he owed more to Rasputin than to the German People."

"He did," Hegel said. "I don't know how he did it, but there was something about him that really got my attention."

"This is no time to speak ill of the dead!" shouted Karl. "Drachenblut's charm, magic, charisma, or whatever you want to call it, it's no longer part of Odinism."

"If that's all gone, how will you convince Himmler to do anything?" Olaf repeated his critique. "Him and deputy Heydrich swallowed everything Drachenblut said, hook, line and sinker. You can't do that. We all know they won't even speak to you alone."

"And Drachenblut wouldn't speak to you, either!" Hegel blurted.

It struck Olaf dumb. His bashful appearance irked Karl as much as Olaf's other attributes, but the silence in the room relaxed Karl's thoughts. This sensation is what he expected to experience when he ascended to the head of the religion, so the words coming from his mouth needed to show that.

"I'm not going to come down hard on you for that outburst, Olaf because we're all in mourning. You're shocked, and you'll think better of it tomorrow, surely. I'm the High Priest now, and I'll be more approachable than Drachenblut was.

"Let's take that back to what Olaf said, about the strength of Drachenblut's charisma. The first thing is to convince the German people that Odinism still has its magic, even if its High Priest has gone. I'd like to discuss that with you now, just to hear your ideas. What thoughts do you have about it?"

The disciples glanced at one another for several moments. Olaf opened his mouth first, but Rolf spoke more forcefully, and Olaf's lined forehead between the inverted eyebrows showed his irritation. Karl wouldn't cheer him up this time, so he turned to listen to his red-haired follower.

"Maybe there's other priests with those skills, then we could use them."

"Rolf, I know you mean well, but then we will be in the same situation again, with a different Svengali. Better the devil you know."

"We should focus on the Vestal magic," Olaf suggested.

"The Vestals are dead!" More tears erupted from Hadwin.

The thought of Vestal Helga ripped apart in an explosion pricked another tear in Karl's eyes. He blinked to hold back the onslaught. His long-gone pet quenched the flow.

"Everyone would soon find out that their skills are from sound and light beams in the Crypt. We don't want that."

Hegel put a hand up. "You should get a hypnotism tutor, High Priest."

"Excellent suggestion, Hegel." While praising his subordinate, Karl wondered how he had never thought of that himself.

Finding a hypnotism coach, or reading a book about it, wouldn't be too hard. Applying it in everyday life would take some practice, and he didn't know whether it would work on Himmler and Heydrich.

"Maybe we should all get one, or study it together. Yes, the notion of the 'five Highest Priests and their compelling stares' certainly sounds appealing. It wouldn't be good to lay this all on my shoulders, it might go wrong."

"So, you're not prepared to do something alone, High Priest?" Olaf's brow wrinkled. "Doesn't that show a lack of conviction?"

"It shows that he's not a stage act like Drachenblut was," Hegel shouted.

"You've tested my patience too often today, Olaf," said Karl. "Leave now before something happens that you regret."

Olaf stood, brushing a slab of blonde-streaked hair away from his face. Two steps and he reached the door, pushing Karl's loose papers into the air when he slammed it behind him.

"We don't hold you to that level of accountability," said Rolf. "Of course, it's better to do this as a group. I'm not enthusiastic about flopping alone in front of a crowd, either."

"How can we replace him?" Hadwin held his head in his hands and sobbed.

Karl glanced at Rolf for support. Rolf shrugged. "How can we replace the Vestals?"

Karl pictured Vestal Grimhilt, her full curves, welcoming bosom, and bottomless, blue eyes. Without warning, Karl's vision blurred, warm droplets ran down his face, and he squealed. He wiped his tears and tried to think only of his new job. Happiness returned, but he still didn't smile.

The memory of Karl's dead dog stopped him getting that far. "We're all emotional, Hadwin. New Vestals are about to be trained, and we can't do it without them. It was hard enough the first time." Agreement bubbled through the room. "I thought that we should abolish the Vestal position as soon as we could, anyway. It's nothing to do with Odinism. Romans didn't copy it from us Germans. That's only state propaganda."

"But the public love the Vestals. Won't abolishing them be a difficult thing to do?" asked Rolf.

"Drachenblut would use this to push his own agenda. Perhaps we should too. Maybe the Vestals' popularity means there's honour in not continuing with it. I mean, because they were so loved, replacing them after their death's, well, it's in poor taste."

"Good point. Logic like that works on Himmler and Heydr -"

The door swung open, hitting the wall. In the portal, Olaf's v-shaped eyebrows had inverted. Their a-shape lent him a dumbfounded appearance.

"They're alive! They got away! Drachenblut and the Vestals are on television!"

Hegel and Rolf shoved Olaf out of their way. His newest and best followers lost in the blink of an eye.

"Don't just barge in here like that, screaming!" Karl responded without pausing to think.

"But it's great news." Olaf appeared mystified.

"Not for everybody."

A long, slow, breath exuded from Karl. His shoulders sloped. Now he didn't need to put in so much energy to Odinism, he could coast again until time handed Karl another chance to reach the top. Unless something happened to Drachenblut before then. Karl ran past him and down the stairs. When he reached the television lounge, the crowd seemed bigger, but many of the faces were there earlier. He felt their eyes on him, judging him.

"Told you that you were too quick off the mark."

"Ambitious prick. Drachenblut'll want blood out of you now."

"Aww, what's he gonna do? Are you scared?"

So many castle staff stood in the room that their number gave them biting anonymity. The crowd didn't move away for Karl this time, and anger flushed his face. Karl pushed his way in, palms out and venom in his eyes. Covered in dust and debris, Drachenblut and the Vestals were being interviewed by the Popular Observer television show. The High Priest snatched the microphone, and the camera focused on his face. Sparks flew from his grey eyes and spittle from his mouth as he spoke.

"How could a missile have been lost?" Drachenblut's eyes opened wide in disbelief. "That is the question being asked by the grieving mothers of the Reich as we speak. Gothengau, the so-called Eastern

Defenders, have brought death and destruction upon the innocent people of the Fatherland."

He handed the mic back to the presenter and returned to comforting the Vestals, their faces still covered in makeup, dust, and tears.

"You said it was his fault before, but he's saying it's Gothengau."

"Keeping the rocket is Gothengau's responsibility, not High Priest Drachenblut's."

"Too quick off the mark by a long way!"

Every anonymous comment behind him bent Karl's mouth down even further. He had to force a smile, turn around and walk out. The events of the day suddenly caught up with him. Sleep beckoned, and the opportunity of the new day it promised. Perhaps Drachenblut would not be as angry as Karl feared.

Chapter 7

Berlin, Sunday, May 2nd, 1965.

The banging on Petra's door dragged her from the nothingness of deep sleep into a cushioned world of pillows and duvets under the harshly perpendicular angles of the bedroom's ceiling. She peered around at her alarm clock. Both hands pointed to twelve. She could hardly remember going to bed after taking sedatives to soothe the pain of the day away. It took her a while to figure out her location and the reason for Max's absence. Whoever was knocking must have been hammering for some time to wake her from the drug-induced slumber. They showed no intention of giving up. Nothing short of answering would halt the incessant thumping on the entrance, a thought which prevented her rising as much as it motivated. Finally, the noise breached her patience and forced her head from the pillow.

Sliding out of bed, Petra switched on the light to reveal the clothing-strewn floor and her pyjama clad body. Illuminating the room stopped the assault on the door. She opened the bedroom window and looked down into the darkness. Void, except for the sheen of the Porsche in the drive and the cream uniform of a Luftwaffe General.

Resting herself against the sill, she leaned out. "Fritz, what are you doing here?"

"Wanted to make sure you were alright. You know, after everything you went through."

"Thanks, but you needn't have bothered. I can take care of myself."

"There was something else."

"I thought there might be." She even guessed what it was.

"Could I come in?"

Not just like that he couldn't. "What's it about, exactly?"

"The Generals are meeting tomorrow at Wernher's base, and we need your help."

So Fritz came to put the Reich back on its feet. Petra knew Fritz too well to put her suspicions aside. Konrad would be interested in this opportunity.

"Hold on. I'm coming down."

It didn't matter how she appeared in front of Fritz, he would chase her whether presented as a frumpy wife or playful sex-kitten. Petra barely glanced at the mirror as she slid into her slippers, threw on her pink quilted housecoat and trudged down the stairs. Fritz didn't wait to be invited in when she opened the front door, and he barged past in his usual fashion.

"We've got to do something about what happened today. We've all had enough of the SS and their failures. The Wehrmacht has taken too much of their blame, and now they let this disaster slip through. Eastern Defenders, my eye!"

Though only a teenager at the time, Petra could remember being taken from the street by an SS man, Drachenblut specifically, not a Wehrmacht officer. Never buying into that Final Solution cover story herself, the news didn't surprise her. She never shared her doubts about the genocide. Such things were best kept private.

"And this meeting's the first step. We need Gothengau's assistance, but not from the top, from the inside. None of the leaders are trustworthy. We need a good man, somebody with a track record. There's only one of those in Gothengau, and it's your friend Konrad."

Fritz needed her contacts. Petra loved networking, and few possessed one that stretched to Gothengau. Petra also wanted to go to the meeting, as well as return to bed as soon as she could.

"Let me call him." She picked up the phone. "It's a bit late in Gothengau at the moment."

"The defence of the Reich has priority."

When Petra finished dialling, she got the engaged tone. "I remember, now. He leaves the phone off the hook at night. I'll ring him in the morning. Tell me about the meeting you're having."

Petra's lethargy ruined her charm, as Fritz's facial expression reminded her. Now she wanted something she couldn't help but be the kitten. She donned a seductive smile despite tiredness aching through every joint of her body.

Fritz smiled and leant toward her. "Can't I stay here?"

Petra knew men like Fritz, and their desires made them easy to manipulate. A hint of cleavage showed when she let her housecoat slip.

"Wouldn't it be lovely if I sang to you men after your talks?" She pouted. "An intimate concert for the troops."

"Having you perform would be fantastic."

Now, Petra had an invite to the meeting. Getting to the Baltic rocket centre would, though, be a bigger problem. Petra reached out and brushed Fritz's hand.

"So, I can get a flight with you?"

"I don't know off the top of my head, I have people for that sort of thing. You'll have to call me in the morning."

Petra let her hand slip inside Fritz's jacket. "Please?"

"Honestly, I'm not sure. Everything's crazy at the moment with flights." Fritz gently shook his head. "I'm not kidding. You'll have wait until tomorrow before I can be sure. Wait at Tempelhof in the morning, though, in case something can be arranged."

"I will do. See you tomorrow." Petra nudged a reluctant Fritz through the door and closed it.

She went back upstairs and got into bed. Sleep didn't come quickly, though, and her mind ran through her worries about her marriage. She returned to Lothar's death, guiltily aware that it should affect her more.

Petra woke, and the excitement of the day's activity cut through the groggy after-effects of the sedatives. She assuaged the excitement when she lifted the receiver to call Konrad.

"Konrad, It's Petra."

"Hi, Petra. How do you feel today?"

"I know how I should feel. Lothar and all those people killed, right in front of me. But I'm invigorated, change is coming. You and me, Konrad, we're going to be a part of something huge."

"Woah! I didn't expect that. What's happened?"

"All the things we know the Nazis did. Von Hohenzollern wants to do something about it."

A pause fizzed on the line. "About time. I'd love to help him out."

"That's great because he wants to meet you today!"

"Where?"

"It's at the rocket base in Peenemünde. Von Braun wants to speak to you as well. Do you have a pen and paper?"

"Always do. It'll be a privilege, speaking to von Braun."

Petra gave him von Braun's contact details, and they ended the call. Now she needed to go to the airport. If Fritz had told the truth a plane would be waiting to take her to the meeting.

A parking space opened in front of a towering entrance hall punctuating the sweeping convex arc of Tempelhof Airport. Petra slipped the Porsche in it while another car dithered. The blue Volkswagen honked as it drove away, its driver shaking his fist. She didn't care. Famous people got better things, and that was just the way things were.

Hidden at the back of the building, the Luftwaffe bureau housed an officer and his adjutant. Their guard, a tall fellow whose cap made him appear eyeless, stood at attention outside. Even Petra, so petite that she practically showed no signs of pregnancy when heavy with Wieland, found difficulty in squeezing through the cramped quarters. There were too many filing cabinets for the guest's seat to fit between the two desks. Petra stepped over the tubular chair to sit on it. After some shifting and squeezing into place, she sat before Captain Weiss, his moustache and his nameplate.

"Sorry about that, Petra." Weiss loosened his tie, revealing some red chest hair. "Only we're not used to getting your calibre of visitors here, are we, Hess?"

"No sir." Narrow-faced Hess's puppy-eyes lingered on Petra.

"Thanks for dropping in on us, what a lovely surprise." Weiss sat back and unfastened his top shirt button. "But, how can we help you?"

"General von Hohenzollern promised me a flight to Peenemünde today, and he wanted you to arrange it for me."

Hess shifted something. Weiss shot upright.

The captain precisely straightened his shirt and tie at double time. "Well, we can't just go handing you a plane on your word, much as we'd like to." Petra's calves clenched. "Let me contact his office. It may take a while, so if you could wait outside it would be great."

Captain Weiss stood, which seemed as close to showing her the door as the space allowed. Again, Petra snaked through the gap between chair and desk before reaching the door.

"I don't know how long this will take. Please, get some refreshments. Sit nearby, and we'll come over to you as soon as we're done."

As she went to sit, Petra reflected on what she could achieve today. Mostly, she would stay busy to keep her mind from wandering, and changing the Reich left little time for navel-gazing. Now, though, waiting for the next step, gave grief the opportunity to gnaw at her. Immediately she planted herself on a chair, her thoughts arrived at Lothar, Max and Eva. A heartstring snapped. Petra sprang up straight away. When she acted with purpose, she avoided breaking down, regardless of whether attempting involvement in a coup or grabbing a coffee.

Smiles of recognition from strangers differed from those she received before yesterday. More of them had sympathetic eyes, probably because of the tears she shed on her already iconic performance seconds before the attack. They might even expect or want her to weep. Being there for the German people also kept remorse at bay. Before the staff served her coffee, she held eye contact with an unshaven, middle-aged fan, and he spoke to her in a broken voice.

"Thanks." He covered his mouth with a tattooed hand and grunted. "I was there yesterday, you saved me. You saved so many of us."

"I just had to help the people of the Reich."

He held her hand, with that tattoo of his. It made her cringe a little more than normal. After looking at her for several seconds longer than she wished, the man tightened his grip on her and turned his pock-marked face to the rest of the cafe.

"Petra Hellfeier!" He raised her arm with his, despite her resistance.

Everybody turned to stare, and she did her best to smile despite wanting to scream.

"She saved me. She saved so many of us! Please, give her a round of applause!"

The stranger dropped her hand and clapped enthusiastically but alone for an uncomfortable time. The ordeal appeared over, but another pair of hands joined in, and within a few beats, the café patrons and the foyer passers-by outside rhythmically chanted her name.

"Pet - ra! Pet - ra!"

Worse things happened than being adored. Petra knew that getting back into show business would ease her loss too, but she had tried entertainment before and found its appeal vacuous and short lived. She held her hands to her lips and blew kisses as tears trickled to her mouth.

"Sing!" one of the onlookers yelled. The cry rolled through the spectators, gathering participants as it did until it became an avalanche. At least this took her mind away from Max and Lothar.

"Sing! Sing!"

Petra patted the air with her palms down to indicate they stop. When everyone held silent, she began a rendition of 'Where Have All The Flowers Gone?' much to the crowd's delight. When their applause subsided, and long before she expected, Captain Weiss struggled to get to her from the back of the crowd. She cut to the last verse to hasten their conversation. While performing had its uses for her, she so wished to be making a difference to the direction of the Reich at Peenemünde with Wernher, the Generals, and Konrad.

"Thank you so much for your good wishes," Petra said when the recital ended. "And good wishes for us all, after yesterday's horror."

A cheer went up, and Captain Weiss wriggled through the impromptu audience to her. Petra longed for the coffee waiting on the counter. From the Captain's straight lips, she expected little.

"I'm sorry, but we haven't got any flights."

A tear stung Petra's eye. She lifted the cup and sipped the hot drink.

"There might be one later, though, so General von Hohenzollern suggested you wait."

Weiss rubbed his hands together and lingered. He wanted to help but couldn't. Fritz would have her sit in public and wallow in memories of the missile strike. Although it diverted her thoughts, she couldn't just hang around in the airport singing all day, but if she didn't then she would sit around crying. A dam burst inside. Salty water dripped from her eyes, her hands covered her face, and the mug shattered on the floor. Arms embraced her. She heard whispers from the passers-by.

'Lost her little boy yesterday.'

'Nobody's seen Max. Or Eva.'

'Wasn't her boy.'

'She should be at home, resting.'

'Her real boy died years ago.'

'Needs to chase that husband of hers, not the public eye.'

What vapid, fickle, judgemental, gossip mongers civilians could be. That's why she wanted to help the Reich. But no, they don't need a singer's help. Whoever held her guided her to a chair.

"Everything is going to be fine." Petra knew that woman's voice.

Surprised that Captain Weiss didn't cling to her, Petra dabbed her eyes and opened them. Hanna Reitsch, wearing her famous blue flying suit and careworn smile, sat beside her. Witnessing a singing star being comforted by a flying ace forced the public back behind a psychological barrier of celebrity-sized personal space. She and Hanna had a cubicle alone. The onlookers carried on with their days. Releasing the tears made Petra feel spring fresh. She smiled and Hanna smiled back.

"My dear, you are getting known for these public displays of emotion since yesterday, aren't you?"

They giggled together, Hanna's short curls bouncing in time.

"I need to get to Peenemünde soon." Petra dabbed a tissue to her eyes. "General von Hohenzollern said he would arrange a flight after I did him a favour."

"What do you expect from Fritz, though? If you lead him on, he'll do the same to you. Why did you want to go there anyway?"

"There's a conference I helped arrange. I need something to occupy me, and this should be it. Now I'll have to stay home singing and crying."

"Is Wernher von Braun going to be there?" Hanna raised her plucked eyebrows and grinned.

"Yes, he's leading it."

"You know, I haven't seen him for ages, he's been so busy with the space programme. Perhaps it's time I paid him a visit."

"Yes." Petra wondered what the connection could be.

"I've got some time to spare today. Heinkel gave me a new passenger plane to put through its paces, and with all this disorder after yesterday no schedule's been set." Hanna stood and tugged Petra's elbow. "Come. I'm going to fly you there myself and see my old friend again. I bet he and Fritz are up to something interesting!"

Sun reflected from the polished metal of the flying wing, condensation dripping from it as refuelling ended. Walking under the aircraft into its shade, Petra flicked the water droplets from her jacket while the ground-crewman disconnected the tank. Poker-faced, his black eyes coveted her while his thin lips blew a cold kiss. Shuddering from the intensity of the workman, Petra followed Hanna up the steps to the aircraft's belly. Aisles between three wide rows of seats led to the cockpit's open door. Hanna sat in the pilot's seat, patting on the co-pilot's chair. "Come, strap yourself in next to me."

Petra buckled herself in while the engines thrummed to life. Their noise increased when Hanna pushed the power levers forward, and the plane trundled down the runway. Tarmac noise stopped when the wheels lifted off the ground, and a pensive silence reigned as the aircraft climbed to cruising altitude. Hanna concentrated on the flight controls while Petra's mind jumped from the explosion to Lothar, to Max, and to the Peenemünde meeting. Once the autopilot was set, Petra's thoughts returned to Max. Hanna could help her with that.

Petra grew tired of holding her tongue. "Where is Eva?"

"I've not heard from her. It's a long while since she lived at my house; the space program takes all her time."

"Max is always at the training camp as well. No wonder this happened between them." Despair swirled in and around Petra. "I should have seen it coming a long time ago."

"Don't blame yourself." Hanna patted Petra's knee. "That's how the Fatherland makes girls now. Sex is encouraged. The Reich wants their babies. It's not your fault."

"I don't want to blame the Reich. We've both done well out of Germany. But I feel sorry for the women that choose raising a brood of kids. There's no going back to work after that."

"They didn't choose motherhood. That's just what women do unless they've other skills. You and I are lucky to have that, but it's not what every woman dreams of. It's a man's world, but things change."

"They've already changed in America. Women aren't just cooks and mothers, and they go to work with the men if they want. You've been there, you know."

"Yes, I saw that too. Not many in the Reich know anything about that, and I can't see Steffi and Sebastian running a special."

"Perhaps we could start it ourselves." Petra sat up and it brightened her outlook. "We could be a double act. I arrange the meetings, and you take me to them."

"Yes, next time you need to go somewhere give me a call."

The women stayed silent for the remainder of the short flight. Hanna took a path that gave panoramic views of the Peenemünde facility, showing rockets of varying size lying near or sitting on launch pads. The runway was the biggest Petra had ever seen.

"Why is the landing strip so big?"

"They have to move rockets from here to the launch pad in Kazakhstan, look over there." Hanna pointed to her right at a bulbous, delta-winged craft. "Those are the transport planes."

After they landed Hanna parked the aircraft outside the small glass and steel arrivals terminal, where they disembarked. As soon as the doors opened, the scent of jet-fuel enveloped them getting stronger the further they descended the steps.

"I'm coming with you. Strength in numbers, and all that."

"Thanks. I'm glad of your help."

"I couldn't let you face a bunch of men on your own!"

They opened the hall doors, where Fritz waited for them, his eyes tracing the outline of Petra's skirt and cropped jacket.

"He must have heard you were landing." Hanna's elbow gently tapped Petra. "He's like your lapdog."

"Only when he's close enough to smell me!"

Petra knew that man's motivations increased the nearer together they were. Now he could catch her scent he became less Rottweiler than Chihuahua.

Chapter 8

Gothengau, Sunday, May 2nd, 1965.

Mounted cowboys galloped towards Konrad through the wheat fields. The riders were still distant when they shouted and waved their hats in what appeared to be greetings. Konrad didn't ease off the gas. The arrangements to meet von Braun couldn't wait. Despite holding his hand on the car horn, the horses didn't move aside until he came worryingly close to them. He swerved off-road, passed the traffic, then steered the vehicle back on the drive.

"Sturmbannführer Lapp!" one of the men shouted as his horse reared up and turned. Looking in the mirror, the horseman now faced Baer's ranch. "Come back!"

No horse could keep up with the Reich's standard issue army vehicle, but the vocal cowboy tried briefly anyway. "Stay away! Come back!"

Clouds of dirt kicked up by the horses coated Konrad's fatigues with dust as the open-top car raced through the billowing soil. He wiped his face clean. Richard Baer's usual riding companions made up the posse, but without the Gothengau leader. No horse could manage Konrad on its back, many even bolted at the sight of him trying to mount them. It meant he had a reason to decline the invitations Baer proffered.

Gauleiter Baer lived and ruled from this huge wooden house with two wings and four floors. Konrad parked in front of it, jumped from the car and took the eight steps to the porch in two bounds. A pair of sentries generally paraded along the patio that ran the width of the building. Maybe Baer had stopped the display out of respect for the deaths in the previous day's attack. Konrad reached the front doors as the sentries burst through them. The black-uniformed, jackbooted, jodhpur-clad men dragged a body, not that unusual for this colonial leader. But the lifeless form wore the faux-cowboy outfit that signified membership of Baer's inner circle.

Many stories circulated about Baer's twisted delight in violence. Normally he reserved murder for slaves, locals, or the odd low-ranked soldier. Such people were not invited to his cowboy-themed outings. After yesterday's attack and the television reports, Baer's fury had taken the life of an officer.

The guards dropped the body to salute Konrad. This blocked his way, so he waved his hand in response and stepped around them as nimbly as a giant could. He headed for Baer's office at the end of the corridor. Konrad hoped Baer would be open to the proposal he brought to him.

Only Guest Workers clad in striped uniforms were present in Baer's open office. On hands and knees, they scrubbed blood from the wooden floor. Behind Konrad, a man coughed gently: Konrad turned and saw Aurelian standing in the doorway of his office. The deputy Gauleiter's blonde hair had receded in the decade since he and Konrad first met when Aurelian became deputy Gauleiter. Nonchalance worked best in these situations, although it left Konrad feeling uneasy. He nodded towards the slaves.

"I saw a body being taken outside."

"You mean Otto? He broke the 'no spurs indoors' rule." Aurelian knitted his brows.

"Where's Baer now?"

"He went back to bed with his wives."

Konrad repressed a shudder, but bigamous marriages were still easier to acclimatize to than the offhand killings. It helped him to picture his own idyllic farm and his wife and children on these occasions.

"He's in an appalling mood after last night's Popular Observer. Tell me your news, and I'll think whether we can risk disturbing him. It's a dark day for the Reich, someone must pay. The likes of Drachenblut can't make us into scapegoats. Falling under his sway will cost Berlin."

"Wernher von Braun has a plan. When I told him how the Reds took that rocket, he had a solution right away. They won't get another, not with his idea. He's holding a meeting, and I need to be there, but I won't make it in time without Baer's help."

Aurelian made a sound of interest and rubbed his chin. "That's worth calling him down for."

He walked to the wall by the heavy wooden z-door and buzzed the intercom. There was no answer from the Gauleiter's bedroom. Aurelian buzzed again.

Baer's voice growled from the device. "What is it?"

"Konrad's here. He's got something important to tell you."

"I'll be right down."

Aurelian headed to his desk and indicated that Konrad should follow. Konrad dredged his mind for a topic of conversation.

"So . . . Drachenblut."

Aurelian threw his hands up. "The Führer is easily persuaded by that charlatan. Because of Drachenblut, Himmler ordered us to get closer to Japan."

"Why Japan?" Konrad replied. "Didn't you warn Himmler about the dangers? When I take my men into Siberia, we're on high alert. It's essential. Anything less and the Reds attack. Driving missiles around there is . . ." Konrad divined the most diplomatic term. "Unwise."

"We should have sent your men, but Baer was having none of it. 'Send the Barrier Boys', he said."

Konrad heard something jingle-jangle on the floor behind him: Baer's spurs. Konrad and Aurelian stood, turned and raised a salute. Baer stretched his arms wide.

"Enough formality! Come, put your arms around me".

Konrad anxiously approached and put his arms around the unpredictable gauleiter. Baer's hair didn't move; the remnants of his locks were securely fixed in place.

"Come, big guy, sit down over here. It's good to have real, true friends like you around, especially at a time like this. Your battalion should have been sent first, then this wouldn't have happened. Of course, Aurelian insisted the Barrier Boys would handle it just as well as your Outlaws."

Baer walked to the meeting area, beckoning Konrad to the darkened spot filled with shadowy, bulky wooden furniture. "Have a drink!"

Konrad nodded as he squatted on a chair near the conference table. He had to move the seat back, or his knees would tilt the black wooden surface. Baer clapped twice, and an orderly appeared, serving bourbon and beer. The pale, wide-eyed waiter moved as nervously as a lemur. He trembled so much that the bottles and glasses rattled on the tray.

After he took a beer, Konrad sat opposite Aurelian. Baer sat at the head of the table, rubbing the arch of his Roman nose between finger and thumb.

"I'm taking a lot of flak because of this rocket. Those bastards on Popular Observer said I missed the Berlin parade because I'd planned this to happen. Said straight out that I must have fucking planned it, I tell you. I hope it was good news that brought you here so early."

Konrad believed even his preferred status would not save him announcing something below-par or mediocre. "Well, sir, I've been invited to a meeting in Peenemünde today." Baer raised an eyebrow. "Wernher von Braun organised it. He's invited the Wehrmacht chiefs too. Wernher's invented something -,"

"Nothing new there, the man's a genius. What's he come up with now?"

"He's invented a machine, and no matter where the machine is, Wernher can find it. It works like this: something about the size of a shoebox sends a signal to Wernher's satellites, and those satellites tell Wernher where the signal came from. He can put these machines in our rocket launchers, and then he'll be able to tell us where they are. We won't lose one again."

"I wish he'd told us about this before. Did Aurelian say about these damn fool orders from Drachenblut?" Konrad nodded. "The High Priest's intuition has done enough harm to the Reich already. Perhaps now's the time for Odinists to take some of the medicine the Jews had." Baer slapped the table. "Well, it's good that we at least have something to work with. How did you find out about this gathering?"

"Petra Hellfeier told me, sir."

"I love Petra! That song of hers, what's it called again?"

"You mean 'Where Have All the Flowers Gone'?"

"Yes, that's the one! It's a beautiful tune, so suited to her. How do you know her?"

"We met on the boat coming over from America. A few years later I ran into her again at Hamburg Station. I stopped Drachenblut from putting her on a train East: he thought she was a Jew."

"He was wrong about her then like he's wrong about the Japanese threat now." Baer offered his hands up to Konrad and nodded as if giving irrefutable proof. "It's your chance to protect everybody from that charlatan." Baer pointed at him. "You get yourself to Peenemünde for that meeting. Take my jet. I give you full authority to do whatever you see fit."

"Thank you, sir. I shall give it my level best."

"Of course you will: you know what'll happen if you don't." He turned to address his second-in-command. "Aurelian, we should have a gathering: Konrad's family, my family, your family, the whole gang at your place. I've hardly ever been to your ranch."

Silence heavier than a velvet curtain fell across the meeting. The dearth of chatter meant that Aurelian's trembling heels squawked his jackboots louder than a flock of geese.

"We'll all be over tomorrow night, Aurelian. It's settled."

"But I need to progress the Drachenblut plan, sir. Doesn't that take priority?"

"Yes, of course. So we'll make it Saturday, evening then."

"But, sir, that's still only the day after tomorrow." Aurelian stood, waving his hands. "I won't be able to finish my wheat harvest, and then Gothengau won't make the quota." Calmed somewhat, Aurelian put palms up like a supplicant. "Can we risk any more trouble with Berlin?"

"You've got all that land, and the workers to go with it," Baer shouted. "What's wrong with you that you can't get it done on time any harvest season?" Baer rubbed his chin. "Konrad can help you. How many times have you won the Harvest Trophy? Is it four times?"

"Five, but I can only spare an hour. I must get to that meeting."

"Get over there and tell him how to do it, give him some inside information."

"How many hectares do you have to mow?" Konrad asked Aurelian.

"A bit more than five hundred."

Aurelian had been allotted much more land than Konrad. He made some mental calculations before answering.

"Sir, I really don't think we could have that done in two days. Even with my methods, applied by my men, that'll need another week at least."

Baer tapped his fingers on the desk. "We'll get together next Saturday then. You should both leave now, and Aurelian can return when he's finished reaping. There's plenty for him to get on with here."

Konrad followed Aurelian outside to the cars at the front of the house, then drove behind Aurelian's open-top Mercedes back to the public road. They passed local workers, more Guest Workers clad in striped uniforms, and mounted Stormtroopers in the fields.

Eventually, their vehicles drove between the totem poles supporting a wrought-iron arch proclaiming that "Work will set you free". Their convoy continued along the main road for ten minutes before reaching the driveway to Aurelian's ranch. It was humble, when compared to Baer's palatial home, but still befitted his status in the colony. Gothengau's second-in-command had residential blocks for workers, barns for animals and harvests, the latest agricultural equipment, and a large house built around a quad. Konrad expected that Aurelian would have these perks. Baer put Aurelian under pressure, and this compound was the reward that Baer mentioned at the rodeo.

They parked before the front door, and Aurelian dashed from the car to his house, slamming the door after him. Konrad was unsure whether to enter, so he hovered close to the door before going to knock. Konrad struck the door, rattling the steer skull and generating shrieks from inside, but Aurelian kept him waiting. He struck the door again but heard children screaming as well. Konrad waited so long, he wondered what excuses he would give Baer if he took the jet without helping Aurelian at all. Like a Gestapo agent, he beat his fist on the door one more time. It made him imagine what Aurelian's explanation of this could be. Konrad paced to the car and back, reflecting on whether he had waited enough to justify disappearing. One more try and that will have to do. Konrad battered on the entryway while picturing a bailiff.

Aurelian opened up, panting from exertion.

"Sorry, the house was in a frightful state. The wives wouldn't let you in before they'd tidied up a bit."

Given the dusty floors of the hallway and the clutter he saw of the salon, the story didn't hold up. When he stood nobody could see Konrad's eyes, so Aurelian didn't notice the suspicion in them. Other than the skull on the entrance, Karl May had less influence on Aurelian and his wives than on the rest of Gothengau; the cranium the only nod towards local fashion. The interior lacked any decoration; the furniture, a mish-mash of laminate, bare pine, and Victorian pieces, stood disordered and worn.

A curtain-less patio door overlooked the untidy garden around which Aurelian had built his home. It illuminated the open-plan salon, and two platinum-haired beauties sitting on folding chairs on either side of a plain white table. The women sat with their arms folded and legs crossed and struggled to appear relaxed. They were at different ends of their thirties. When they spotted Konrad, their faces suddenly took on exhausted smiles. Konrad didn't buy it.

"This is Tereza." Aurelian gestured to the older woman on the left.

"It's wonderful to meet the Gentle Giant." Tereza spoke with a sophisticated Slavic accent.

"And this is Helene."

"Yes, it's so rare that we get visitors." Helene had a thick French lilt. "And they arrive after yesterday's terrible attack!"

"We'll be getting more visitors. Baer and his family will come a week from Saturday. Konrad is bringing his family over as well."

Tereza counted on her fingers. "Is that a dozen people? That's three adults and seven children. Konrad's lot make another five." She turned to her husband and grabbed his hand. "Aurelian, you have to help us. Helene and I can't do this ourselves."

"You both know I've got a lot on at work. And I have to finish the harvest so the Reich can have bread."

That sounded like a moment at which Konrad could interrupt the conversation. "Yes, that's why I'm here. Shall we get on?" His question went ignored and unanswered.

"Oh, it's all about you, isn't it? You trapped me here with her and your kids, and now I have to get the place ready for guests," droned Helene.

"Where are the children?"

"They went on a school trip," answered Tereza.

What a lie, thought Konrad. He definitely heard young voices in the domestic cacophony as he waited to enter.

"So you have less work. Do you know what I have to do? I have to bring in the crops, get Berlin off our back, deal with your domestic bullshit, and keep Baer happy. I wish I had your high-pressure lives. He killed Otto right in front of me before!"

"But you don't have the fear we have, locked up here all day, every day looking after those freaks," Helene screamed.

Konrad had heard about the dysfunction in the Tausendpfund household. Something deeper ran through this than the miserable ménage-a-trois enmeshing Aurelian. It could be the reason that Baer dominated his Second-in-Command. The three-way argument reminded Konrad what a good choice only marrying one wife had been. He didn't want to watch the shouting-match escalate further. Unnoticed, he backed out of the salon, into the vestibule with the door and the stairs. Purely from luck, he guessed that the corridor on the right would lead him to the harvest more quickly. When he reached the corner, the light became dim, and the disorder further belied their excuses. Daylight shone through a door where the hallway next turned left, so Konrad followed it.

Konrad trod carefully through the darkened corridor, trailing his hand on the wall to guide him through the dishevelled passage. In front of him, the floor moved, and Konrad froze, foot raised with his weight shifting between floor and finger. His hand rested on a light switch. Shaking his head and squinting didn't help resolve the scene of his freak-show buddies. Limbless Ed harnessed to Ink's chest who climbed from the cellar. Excited, he stopped himself greeting his old friends. When he realised they were probably dead by now his mood fell back to earth. The Tausendpfunds said their children had gone on a school day trip. Not all the offspring, though. Aurelian hid these youngsters. This was crueller than letting Dr Mengele have them. Konrad couldn't tolerate this.

A boy spoke. "Let's go to the barn."

A girl, her voice younger, voiced her opinion. "I want yard. I got legs."

After only a brief time resting on the switch, Konrad's arm became tired.

"He'll see us from there. We're going where I said".

The girl traipsed to the yard.

"He'll see, he'll see, he'll see!"

Konrad's arm dropped slightly, flicking the light switch and stopping the youths in their steps. Now illuminated, they turned to face him, and when they did, the girl's hands shot up.

The boy's head, covered in a mop of sandy hair so uncut it covered his eyes, bobbed left and right. "Don't kill us!"

With a jaw more prominent than her cranium and a thick brow, the girl looked darkly simian. "He made me do it." Tears washed down the floodplains of her cheeks.

"I'm not going to kill you. You can put your hands down." Ink gaped in terror. Her arms trembled but didn't drop. "You should do what your father said, though." That, currently, was the limit of Konrad's thinking. Play the emotional card. "If you aren't in the cellar when he comes for you, how do you think he'll feel?"

"I don't care." Ed shook himself to uncover his resentful eyes. "We always have to be down there!"

Ink stamped. "I want outside."

Noise like that's going to distract their parents from the screaming row. "He keeps you down there for something, right?"

"Dad said they'll give us to the doctor if they find out." Ed trembled and his hair fell back over his eyes. "The doctor does things to people like us. You aren't going to tell, are you? Please don't tell!"

Konrad stepped towards them and lifted up the trapdoor.

"Come on. It's the best thing to do for now. I won't tell them if you don't tell your dad. I'll get you out one day soon."

"We can't escape. They gas freaks like us."

"You'd have to go to America. I knew people like you when I lived there, I'll be able to get you there somehow."

Konrad puffed out his cheeks when the kids moved towards the door. The girl's eyes almost disappeared in the liquid streaming to her bulky chin. With knowledge of Aurelian's secret came power. When the time came to tell Aurelian about the deep knowledge of his family tree, Konrad could gain advantage. If Aurelian wanted, Konrad would spirit the kids away. Right now, though, Konrad needed someone watching his back. Van de Beek will bring Schink and Mayrock to Peenemünde with him so Konrad had eyes at every angle.

Chapter 9

Peenemünde, Sunday, May 2nd, 1965.

Petra almost envied Fritz' collection of jewellery. He wore a medal on a ribbon around his neck. The flamboyance of the award's precious metal, its attachments of swords, oak-leaves, and eagles, matched the Luftwaffe General's pompadour and cream dress uniform. His fair hair fluttered in the breeze blowing through the open arrival gate at the Peenemünde airport.

Hanna reached the bottom of the steps first. "Look at him, with that Knight's Cross. He must be really important to receive one of those."

"Not as important as he likes to think." When Petra's feet touched the ground, Hanna linked arms with her. "Otherwise, why did I need a lift from you to get here?"

For this trip, Petra had made a few phone calls and performed a singing routine, but she had made it from Berlin to the Baltic despite the Luftwaffe Supremo's broken promise. Her conversation with Hanna dwindled then stalled.

"Petra, I'm so glad you came!" Fritz' smile, when this intense, formed a perfect bow which enhanced the laugh-lines and crow's feet.

"Just not glad enough to fly her yourself, eh?"

"Hello, Hanna. The same goes for you, of course." Fritz kissed Petra on the cheeks. Never missing a chance for some handling of the goods, his hands lingered on her hips. "Thanks for getting Konrad to this meeting." She lifted his mitts with a knowing look and pursed her lips. "It's going to be one of the most fruitful, productive days since the Soviets' still had air power, I can feel it. Wernher is an incredible person: a genius and born leader."

After walking through the arrivals hall and down a corridor, they entered the dining room. The diners turned to see Fritz escorting Petra and Hanna. Wernher stood to greet them, prompting the other men to stand and bow. A staccato rhythm echoed from beneath the table when heels clicked in greeting. Fritz walked behind them. Petra tried to shrug his hands from her shoulders. The guy always mauls me every chance he gets.

"Ladies, how delightful to see you. I did tell you, didn't I, about Hannah and Petra being sure to arrive?" The other attendees burbled pleasing noises in agreement. "Please sit down and drink some coffee with us. Konrad Lapp will be here shortly, and your Max is on his way as well. Maybe Petra will even sing for us? For the troops, as it were."

Petra turned to Hanna.

"Perhaps my Eva will be with him." Hanna stared at the floor. Petra stared at the floor too, a flush of heat burning her cheeks.

Wernher waved his hand, indicating that Mannteufel and Geissler should move along their bench. He, Petra, and Hanna sat at the table. Wernher continued addressing the leaders of the armed forces.

"So, this location system needs to be attached to an object, and our satellites pick up its signal. We then know where it is by pure geometry, and we have its exact position."

"An astounding achievement, Wernher." Fritz clapped his hands. "We'll be the Eastern defenders ourselves soon enough, and that will be down to you." Fritz's clipped voice gleamed with sharpness, and his eyes glinted.

A jagged welt ripped Mannteufel's cheek. "We'll show Gothengau, who's boss."

Petra turned, only for Konrad to fill her whole range of vision. He picked her up, and she kissed his ruddy cheeks. "This is the man who saved so many lives on May Day, not me."

"If Baer had sent my boys and me in the first place, then perhaps we'd have saved them all."

"The 500th!" Soldiers behind Konrad - one beefy and pockmarked, the other impish with a mischievous glint to his eye - stamped their boots and stood proudly, shoulders back. They each wore the inverted red and green triangles of convicts. Their good looking, lithe Dutch officer stared them down in muted admonishment.

"After Hitlerstadt, we all knew we were in charge." Fritz put his palm out. "They'd have lost more than a battalion if it hadn't been for the Luftwaffe and your Panzer divisions."

"And no thanks to their ground troop, either. They practically let a unit of Reds into my tent." Mannteufel made a throttling motion. "I had to kill two of the Bolshies with my bare hands." His scar flushed pink. Petra avoided eye contact. "I can see by the cut of these convicts of yours, Konrad, that it wouldn't have happened on your watch."

"Careful, Mannteufel." Fritz winked at Petra. "You're scaring the filly. It'll take time for Petra to get used to the Reich's toughest man."

"Take no notice, General. I'm not scared. Not when you're here to protect me." Petra giggled to hide her nerves.

"We'll protect you, Petra, don't worry." Growling reassurance from the pizza-faced convict made her fidget around the sharp, angular discomfort his tiny, prying eyes brought.

She needed to play her part at the meeting, although she wanted involvement in something vital, not just another chance for a song-and-dance routine. An adjutant approached Fritz, passed him a note, and walked away. When Fritz looked up from reading, he glanced at Petra with a frown.

"A message from the control tower: Max should be here in a few minutes. He's bringing Eva with him as well, so that means two of our first astronauts are on the same flight." He tutted. "Not just that, though: they're flying an experimental plane too." Fritz peered over his spectacles at Wernher. "Wernher, if that plane crashes, how long will the space program be set back?"

"A significant amount. But you can't tell Max anything when it comes to flying."

A chance for Petra to get noticed in this group of alpha-males must be grabbed with both hands. "You can't tell Max anything, period."

"Yes, we've all seen that in him, but you've got the best view." Fritz chuckled before recognition spread across his face and his bow of a smile crinkled the skin round his eyes.

Wernher stood, stepping towards them. "The tracking device will make it a lot easier to find any rocket patrols they lose."

The impish prisoner brought a foot down on the floor. "Decoys won't work now either, sir."

Their officer hissed. "Watch it, Mayrock!"

Pizza-face shoved an elbow in his abdomen. "Smart-arse."

"You too, Schink."

Konrad took a sharp breath. "The Reds built a dummy missile, and the Barrier Boys fell for it."

"I'm surprised they did." Fritz shrugged. "Didn't they see the missile deflate every time they shot it?"

"Maybe they missed!" Wernher slapped his knee.

Beside Konrad and Petra, everyone in the room burst into laughter. All those eyes twinkling with joy forced Petra to join in. She looked at Konrad's stony face. Everybody else must have acknowledged his absence of mirth. Chuckling ebbed until it became a slew of sheepish grins, then respectful silence.

Deep crevasses sunk into Konrad's brow when he explained. "I don't know the full details, but most of the soldiers they sent were killed in action, so we'll probably never understand what actually happened. That trick wouldn't have worked on my boys, though: they'd have seen it was no rocket when they landed. The important thing is that it never happens again, so, on Petra's word, Richard Baer gave me a free hand in this matter. He leant me his personal jet as well. How can I help you to help Gothengau?"

"Straight to business, eh?" A smile revealed Wernher's crooked teeth, some of the guests laughed. "Why not have some refreshments after your journey?"

Konrad folded his arms. "Not with Baer's jet outside. He wants it back as soon as possible, and it's very unwise to take any liberties with Richard Baer's property." Konrad shook his head. "He killed an *obersturmführer* for scratching his floor this morning."

"Then I understand your haste!" Wernher's charm had little effect on Konrad. "There is always a place for you here if things get too difficult in Gothengau."

Konrad's reaction surprised Petra, but nobody else noticed the edges of his mouth soften. Nobody else understood him well enough to give the small gesture any meaning. She had first noticed that on the passage to Germany. It signified his deepest appreciation.

"I also discovered something. Something so grave it is never spoken of. The Final Solution was not down to Doenitz. Himmler and Heydrich planned it, and Richard Baer carried it out."

Petra's face flushed. She knew of Himmler's involvement, but those convictions were kept in a dark, inaccessible part of her consciousness.

"You didn't know?" Admiral Geissler with surprise put his head to one side. "Did you never wonder how a submarine commander engineered all that?"

"There were others involved, and he used them. There were many others involved. They hanged them all."

"None of them had much, if anything, to do with it." Geissler shook his head. "They were just people that Himmler and Heydrich wanted rid of."

"Then I've been lying to myself." Konrad scowled and shook his head.

"We've all been lying to ourselves. They made a huge lie and repeated it often. Who wouldn't start to question their own experiences?"

Wernher broke the sudden silence. "We would very much like to remove that stain from the German soul. That means weakening Gothengau. Getting control of these missiles has to be our first stage. Will you help us?"

"Yes, of course. But I need my family to leave Gothengau. There's too much danger there - who knows what Baer would do to them if he suspected betrayal? If Mengele got hold of my twins . . ."

"I understand your concern." Wernher cradled his chin and nodded. "Perhaps they could stay here at Peenemünde?" His eyebrows slanted quizzically. "Then, should Baer call in some favours to help find them, they'll still be safe. It's completely beyond the reach of the SS."

"That takes a weight from my mind." It looked like something had been lifted from Konrad's shoulders when his chest swelled.

"But we digress, and you are conscious of time, so let me tell you about the process." Wernher lay open his palms. "The installation is quite a simple procedure. We need access to your rockets to install the devices. It doesn't take long."

"That's good. I wanted to avoid any interference between Gothengau and the outside world. But how do we know where the rockets are after that?"

"I'll tell you where they are in regular reports. There'll be a team of trained operators monitoring them. That can, however, only be done from Peenemünde at the moment."

"We want that too." Konrad used Baer's authority with confidence. Petra pictured him as Hercules, holding the roof over the Reich.

"That takes time and effort. And a lot of money as well."

"Don't worry about that, just consider it approved. What start date can you give?"

Wernher blinked rapidly, and a little colour came to his neck. He soon regained his poise.

"Well, it's never too early. I can spare myself and the team right now, we already have some of the tracking devices."

"Excellent." Konrad shook Wernher's hand to set the deal. That handshake and the trust behind it bound Konrad to his deed. "But you still haven't got Germany off the hook by watching Gothengau's rockets. To purify the Teutonic soul, you'll need to lop the head off. Himmler and Heydrich must be replaced."

Petra admired Konrad's bravery. Raising the subject of regime change had risks, even here.

There was a way in for Petra. "Those missiles are patrolled on Drachenblut's orders. Konrad and I know the second priest. A real ambitious type, he is, and we have enough on him to force him to kill Drachenblut."

"Yes, dear." Fritz patted her forearm.

Convicts Schink and Mayrock nudged each other and shook their heads. The room hushed, at least they sympathised with Petra, but heat still flushed her cheeks and her calf twitched because of Fritz's condescension.

Konrad came to her rescue. "It's a great idea. Himmler and Heydrich would be at his funeral. Once you know when and where then they can be attacked. Wernher would make a far better leader than those two murderers."

Raising Wernher to be the Führer filled Petra with excitement. She couldn't help but clap. Without caring whether she applauded alone, she looked only at Wernher. Konrad, then Schink and Mayrock, joined her, then everybody expressed their joy. Wernher raised his hands, a bemused smile on his face.

"I take it I have been elected Führer? I am humbled by your choice. It will be a difficult course for the Fatherland to take, filled with guilt and regret, but I am sure that we can go forward. This genocidal stain shall be removed. I humbly accept your nomination."

"Konrad for Gothengau leader," Mayrock shouted.

Schink looked around and glowered at Mayrock before repeating. "Konrad for Gothengau leader."

Now they chanted in unison. "Konrad for Gothengau leader!" Their officer shouted to no avail, continuing even after the Wehrmacht Chiefs joined in.

Konrad waved his hands. "No, no, please. I have enough on my plate already." His eyes falsified the modesty.

Wernher stepped forward. "Maybe they have a point, Konrad. Perhaps you should lead it after our changes are made."

Mannteufel smiled through his teeth. "Having a man of honour run that cowboy show would mean better food and fewer rocket attacks."

Schink and Mayrock clapped. Mannteufel smiled at Schink and tugged his ear. Schink's chest expanded proudly, and he cast Mayrock a sideways glance. Beaming, Konrad stared at his men.

Petra tugged Konrad's sleeve. "We need to put Karl to work. I'll call him later."

"I believe he often visits the Gothengau breeding clinic. I'll pressure him next time he's there."

Konrad turned to face the gathering. "Then we shall be off."

"So soon?" Notes of dismay raised Wernher's pitch. "But Max Hellfeier and Eva are arriving, don't you want to say hello to them? You can't be cleared for take-off until they land."

"Sir, I would love to meet Max and Eva, sir." Schink stamped his foot and stood straight.

"Then I'll greet them, and Baer'll have to wait a couple more minutes for his jet to be returned. It will be a privilege to meet Max and Eva. Thanks to Schink for reminding me not to waste this opportunity."

"Come, everybody. Let's make our way outside to welcome the astronauts." Wernher led them to the tarmac.

The group moved towards the runway doors. Petra dragged her feet. She had the most involvement in this surprise visit, but only had a supporting role because of the illustrious company she had helped assemble. Being peer-pressured to greet the pair with happiness and excitement fostered the opposite feelings in Petra. She would be there when the lovers arrived, but in the back row. They would know she was there. Let it take a little of the sweetness away from the lovebirds fluttering in to see their fans.

Those at the front staggered back. May Day came to mind when a blast of air forced Petra on a back foot. She crouched with everybody else, hands over ears. The sight of Lothar flying from her hand filled her mind's eye. The pressure wave tore the branches from the trees, and glass smashed elsewhere in the building. A barrage of shocks resonated through her torso. Windows rattled all the way from the woods past the end of the runway. Petra covered her face. Glass was sure to fly. Lothar's shattered body slithered down concrete and into her memory. It almost made Petra happy to feel guilt over her lack of mourning.

Even though Max had hurt her, Petra realised he must now be dead. It halted Petra's tentative pleasure. People struggled to get back on their feet. Beyond the terminal's walls, orange and yellow anger raged from the air crash.

Tears rushed to her eyes. Filled with mourning, now Petra hot-footed to witness the unexpected end to her marriage. Before even stepping twice, the lament for Max tore down her resistance. She let out an anguished scream, covering her face with her hands. Arms wrapped around her shoulders, stopping her from dropping to the floor and curling into a ball. Turning to her saviour, she smelled Fritz's aftershave and saw the distinctive colour of his uniform in her blurred vision. Her knees gave way, and his arms caught her.

Chapter 10

Gothengau, Wednesday, 24th August 1960

Amongst the dried grey petals and black husks, some heads of compact, white buckwheat flowers remained. They swayed in the warm breeze. Konrad planted that crop closest to the house purely for the view as the cereal was one of the few Reich-mandated plants that bloomed. He and Diana sat on the swinging bench under the back-porch's shadow sipping glasses of lemonade watching the insects and birds the field attracted.

"Most of these are withered now. I'll harvest it this week."

"That's a shame." Diana took in the scene. "It's lovely to see the wildlife."

Modernity - the telephone ringing in the house - forced itself on Konrad, pulling him from his bucolic stupor.

"I'll get it." Konrad strode through the white wooden door.

The phone sat on its own table by the front door. Konrad walked through the plain, utilitarian kitchen to the hall.

"Siegfri-"

"Yes, I know who I'm calling," snapped Gothengau leader Richard Baer. "I'm sure you know who this is."

Konrad's mouth turned dry. He sucked on his teeth.

"I've had the Agriculture Minister on my back all morning about buckwheat production targets. Doenitz runs a tight ship, and I'm getting pretty bloody sick of it. The minister was all 'fines' this, and 'energy restrictions' that. Never got that when Hitler was in charge. What are you doing about it?"

Konrad rifled through his agitated mind to pick out the 'it' Konrad had to do something about. Well, the only thing under Konrad's control was the buckwheat. "I'm bringing it in this week."

"Make sure you do, big fella. If we do get any power cuts here, it's down to you. Do you know what I mean?"

Konrad knew Doctor Mengele coveted his twin daughters. "Of course."

"Right, then I expect to see your consignment note on my desk when the crop's brought in."

Konrad trotted back out on the porch and motioned at the field. "I'm bringing this in as soon as possible."

"Was it the phone call?" Diana asked.

"Yes. Baer talking about quotas. I suppose the Reich has to eat." Konrad stared into the distance. "There are a lot of harvests right now."

"You seem troubled. Is something bothering you?"

Diana read him so easily. Konrad clutched her hand and smiled.

"I don't know where I'll get the men and machines to do it. I might have to do it with some help from Yuri."

"Aren't you getting a bit old for that?"

"At thirty-three? You're only as old as you feel, and you've got me down as an old man already."

"I just worry about you."

"Look after the girls. Let me do the worrying for all of us."

Konrad hid the terror of the Reich from his family as much as he could here on their farm, but Diana and the girls mixed with other wives and children. Spouses and offspring here bore the same ranking as the father although with fewer insignia but, very often, more ceremony.

"You can't worry about everything. We have our own lives with the women. You needn't concern yourself with every little nick or scratch me and the girls get."

"I have to go to the Agricultural Committee and make an equipment request. Without another couple of combines most of this will rot in the field."

"If you're going there then you should ask for some Guest Workers, like everybody else has."

Konrad shook his head, wondering how she didn't know. "Those men aren't guests. They're prisoners on a life sentence. Luckily for them they don't live long. I won't use that kind of labour."

Diana turned her eyes to the floor, then to Konrad. "But why do you work so much, anyway? If you ploughed the whole lot back into the field, you'd still be the best farmer in Gothengau." She lay her hand on his. "Have a rest. Spend more time with the girls and less with your soldiers."

Konrad shifted and drew himself straighter. He couldn't not be the best farmer in the colony. He felt his life depended on making the Nazis think him the superman of their dreams. Any slack with the buckwheat yield had to get picked up somewhere else in his life and that would most likely be with his convict regiment.

"I want suspicious eyes dazzled by my achievements before they look too hard. Now I'm not the Führer's Giant anymore, I get less special treatment."

"You notice it already?" Diana's eyes opened wide. "But Doenitz has only had the job a few months."

"Doenitz is a strange choice for Führer. He doesn't seem sold on the Nazi ideal at all. All the senior ones ask to meet me, but not him. Not sure how he got to be the chief. Seemed Himmler was the natural choice."

"It puzzled everybody." Diana threw her hands up. "Baer's wives were happy with it, though."

"Baer and Mengele were pleased too." Konrad let a scowl slip and sucked his teeth. "I don't know why, when they complain so much about the new religion."

"Why would Doenitz approve of that mumbo-jumbo?"

"Baer asked the same thing." Now Konrad shrugged his shoulders. "He thinks Himmler's behind it."

"What makes him suspect that?"

"Himmler was the driving force behind Wewelsburg becoming the SS spiritual centre. They bought the place because of him."

Diana frowned and shook her head. "If Himmler's calling the shots on Odinism, then who's really in charge of the Reich?"

"I don't know." The last drops of lemonade drained, Konrad stood. "I'm going to try and get more equipment. I should be back in a few hours."

"It must be a lot more comfortable driving now they took the front seat out."

"That's not even the best thing about it." Konrad grinned. "Nobody ever mistakes it for a pool car!"

Konrad walked around the house to his customised army issue vehicle. On the way through the buckwheat down the dirt drive to the road, he wondered how he could avoid using forced labour. The route took him through countryside that teemed with Guest Workers toiling in striped uniforms, overseen by cowboys and stormtroopers. Eventually, the white, low-rise suburbs of a town went by, punctuated by roundabouts until he reached the grassy square in the city's heart. The Agricultural Committee resided in the Reich Ministry of Agriculture, a building adorned with its golden sword and wheatsheaf symbol. Since his last visit, a rune-covered structure had appeared beside the government office. Its doors stood open and two long haired, bearded priests lingered half-in, half-out. Odinism's highest temple in Gothengau provoked more debates and discussions than it received visitors. Konrad parked in front of it. The black clad clerics, wearing rough-hewn black tunics and pants laced over with boots, approached.

"Excuse me, sir?" The blonde priest waved his hand.

Konrad looked over.

The raven-haired cleric stepped in the middle. "Have you heard the good news?"

Strange of them to use Christian gambits for the Norse Gods, thought Konrad before he bolted to the Agriculture Ministry. He had no interest in how they wove the resurrection narrative back into the religion of the Vikings. When Konrad reached the Ministry, he turned. Both priests had retreated back into the temple and closed its doors. He pushed through the Ministry's entrance. The ripe, hot, crowded office could use conditioning. At the counter, a cowboy banged his fist.

"Aren't you here to help us with that?" He took off his hat. "We grow the food and keep our borders strong. What the hell do you do?"

A murmur of approval swept the crowd.

Konrad turned to his nearest neighbour. "How long have you been waiting?"

The man removed his straw cowboy hat and looked up. Everybody knew the unfortunately named Berndt.

"I've been here since ten this morning." Scar tissue covered his hairless head and face. "These pencil-pushers are worse than useless. If I don't get these crops in on time I might get shot! Is that why you're here?"

Konrad nodded. "It doesn't seem worthwhile waiting."

"Seems like you wouldn't need the help, not with a battalion of convicts."

The obvious idea drew a smile to Konrad's lips. Why, he wondered, hadn't he thought of that himself?

"You're right. Thanks."

Konrad went to the car. The priests had reopened the temple doors, but they had their backs to him, carefully studying the ground. He wasn't approached again. After reclining and twisting the ignition key he pressed the gas pedal. Konrad revved the car for the journey to the 500th's base near Crimea's isthmus then put the car in gear and got moving. Some of the convicts under his command were completely unsuitable to be around women. Their rota would be restricted to work off the farm, away from Diana and his daughters but under the eyes of Konrad's trustworthy assets. With this deft use of manpower, Konrad near guaranteed he would win the Harvest Trophy again. More dazzle to blind witnesses to any good deeds Konrad might perform.

Rolls of barbed wire surrounded an aircraft hangar, plain brick mess hall, and rows of barracks. The 500th's base, Konrad's second home, where many of his men marched on the parade-ground. Before Konrad cut the motor, he heard their 'hup' and the single stomp of many boots.

"Attention!" ordered the sergeant.

Konrad had only just set foot out of the vehicle when van de Beek's long frame trotted into view.

"Heil Gothengau." Van de Beek winced. "Yes, sir, I know . . ."

"Worse things happen." Konrad had more serious issues than a greeting. "There's something I need from the men."

"How can I help?" Van de Beek cocked his head.

"Arrange fifty of them, just the well-behaved ones, no rapists, and have them report to my ranch. As part of their punishment, they're to help feed the Reich."

"I heard there's a shortage of materials for the harvest. Good thinking, sir."

Konrad chose not to say where the notion originated. Since arriving in the Reich, he hid information carefully. Revealing as little as possible kept him alive.

"I'll get on with it immediately." Van de Beek marched off.

Shouting stopped when Konrad entered the mess hall. Heels clicked and hands met brows in salute. Let them calm down. At the water fountain he soothed his throat, parched from the open top journey through the arid countryside. Once satisfied, he turned to the convicts standing in salute. Some of these guys, Konrad deliberated, are coming with me. He could see the strain of standing at attention showing in the tightened jaws and squinting eyes of the weaker soldiers. They weren't invited. Beefy and pockmarked, 'Sandface' Schink showed only strength. Hoechst, the oldest, displayed no feeling. Weedy, boyish Mayrock had a lot more fight in him than his size showed. Konrad saluted and the men stood at ease with a sigh.

Van de Beek's lithe figure entered the mess hall. "Schink, Mayrock, and Hoechst. You're all on a detail -"

"Excellent choice, van de Beek. You read my mind. You three are to harvest crops on my ranch."

Unabashed joy showed on their faces, a hint of envy in the eyes of the unselected. Good, thought Konrad, this annual incentive might help bring some of them out of their delinquency. Something for them to aim for in their daily duties.

"Report outside immediately," van de Beek ordered the men. "Come on, don't keep the vehicles waiting."

Schink, Mayrock, and Hoechst marched out at the double. Konrad walked back to his car and started home.

Shortly after Konrad disembarked, the men arrived in five armoured cars. Guns poked from bulbous turrets on the roofs of jagged-angled metal boxes suspended between six huge wheels. Blue exhaust billowed out behind them. Konrad cringed against the fumes when they blew toward him. Seeing their commander's grimacing face when they disembarked, all chatter between the men stopped. The hush let van de Beek organise the men into rows.

"Okay men." Konrad paced along them. "It's harvest time, and you might have heard that Gothengau is running short on men and machines to do it. Too many ripe fields at once.

"That's where you come in. Behind the house is a field full of buckwheat. You might not know what buckwheat is, but you do like eating pancakes and blinis, and drinking beer. Schink, especially." That got the usual laugh from the men. "Those are a couple of things the people in the Reich need. You can see the flowers behind the house are mostly grey and dry. I want you to take a bag and fill it with the seed pods at the flower's stem."

Many eyes wandered. This didn't hold the men's attention as much as Konrad required. They needed more motivation. Fear for his family's safety drove Konrad. He knew what drove a lot of the convicts.

"There's two days leave and a bottle of schnapps for the man who picks the most."

A cheer came up from the ranks.

"That's all. The sergeant has the things you need, form a line."

"So, which of you losers wants to come second?" Schink asked.

"You, crater face." Weedy Mayrock scowled.

Once the men had a bag each, they began picking from a row of plants. Mayrock eyed Schink intensely while he filled the sack. Schink occasionally turned his slit-eyed gaze on skinny Mayrock. Hoechst stayed quiet and focussed. His hands flew up the stems of the plants, dried petal confetti fluttering to the ground. Konrad couldn't only supervise. The crop needed to be harvested and the paperwork for it put on Baer's desk. Slinging a bag over his shoulder, Konrad started an unpicked row.

Mayrock looked up from his work, shifting aside the plants to catch Konrad's attention. "Hey, that's not fair, sir."

Konrad looked over at the rustling vegetation. "What isn't?"

"That you're in the competition as well, sir."

"No, I'm just helping, not playing."

"It's not much of a prize for van de Beek, though, is it, sir?" pock-marked Schink asked. "What would he do with a bottle of schnapps?"

"I would sell it to you, you drunk," van de Beek snarled. "Get on with it. You want to be in with a chance of winning, don't you?"

Konrad watched the men. "Look at how much further Hoechst has got than you others. He's coming up to his second furrow already."

"He's a sly old one, Hoechst is," said Schink. "Bet he could down a bottle of schnapps in one."

"Don't stand next to him when it comes out, though." Mayrock laughed and imitated a waist level hosepipe.

"Yeah, he might be a crack shot with a gun, but he ain't with his trouser snake." Men around Schink smiled and glanced at each other.

By now Hoechst was so far away, he might not have heard the banter. Pushing ahead like a machine, he reaped the buckwheat like he hadn't caught a word, his sincerest look upon his inscrutable face. He had already filled three sacks.

Hours later, as the sun touched the horizon, the bins near overflowed with buckwheat seed. Enough, thought Konrad, to get the consignment note in front of Baer today. Baer appreciated targets being met ahead of schedule. Time for Konrad to shine bright and dazzle. Crops had been reaped early, and he needed Baer ignorant to the absence of Guest Workers on his farm.

Konrad approached van de Beek in the adjacent furrow.

"Tell the sergeant to stand the men down," said Konrad. "We have all the buckwheat needed for now. I'm going to Baer's to tell him the news."

In the yellowing twilight, Konrad motored through to Baer's ranch, anxious to inform him. The dirt drive to the grand homestead was too furrowed to race the vehicle along it. Then Konrad noticed the reason for the damaged path. Baer's house was brightly lit, decked with streamers, and surrounded by cars. The extra vehicles had ploughed the road up. Music wafted over the note of the engine into Konrad's ears. Baer hadn't mentioned anything about a party.

Lack of space forced Konrad to park his kubelwagen far from the porch, where two black clad SS troopers stood guard. He leapt up the steps. Some of the guests, dressed in dinner jackets and ball gowns, applauded Konrad, then drank a champagne toast to him. Already, some of them were being held up or even carried from drunkenness. Konrad entered the house. Baer, his gut spilling from a mock cowboy outfit, an arm around each of his twin wives, had an ecstatic look on his face as he fondled their breasts.

"Konrad! Heil Gothengau."

"I've got the paperwork for the buckwheat, sir."

"What? What paperwork? Oh that, yes, well the Ministry of Agriculture is under new management from tomorrow. Have you heard the good news?"

Had Baer turned to religion? He was too drunk for preaching gospel, whether Odinist or Scripture.

"That's why all my old work colleagues are here." Baer swept his arm to encompass the room. "Had a great time with this lot in Auschwitz. Anyway, the news has come to me today that there will be an end to all this final solution nonsense the British and Americans have been pushing. The answers have appeared. It's not official yet." Baer touched the tip of his nose on the second attempt. "Nudge, nudge. Wink, wink.

But the evidence all points to Führer Doenitz misinterpreting Hitler's opinions.

"Have a drink," Baer thrust a bottle of champagne at him. "All our worries are over, big fella. Over."

Konrad shook his head. "It's not something that worried me, sir."

Whatever had happened at Auschwitz, however many these so-called people had murdered, had nothing to do with Konrad. No guilt for his actions shrouded him. How can I drink with these people? How can I even be around them, acquitted murderers all? He turned and ran to the car sitting apart and alone under the black sky.

Chapter 11

Peenemünde, Sunday, May 2nd, 1965.

Jet engines, torn loose from their wing mountings, screamed past the terminal building. Their fuel exhausted, they bounced along the runway gouging chunks from the tarmac. Shrapnel careened in every direction, shattering windows at the Peenemünde airport. Konrad and his men ducked for cover. Excepting gallant Fritz everyone else followed suit. Fritz shielded Petra from the blasts. The rest of the plane turned cartwheels on the ground behind its engines, a screaming cacophony of clashing metal. Its inverted flaming carcass slammed on the runway and blocked Konrad's view of the space centre.

Between the last metallic din of Max and Eva's air crash and the first notes of the fire and rescue sirens, only Petra's weeping could be heard. Fritz's hands travelled south to Petra's bottom.

Schink nodded towards the wandering hands. "What about that, sir?"

He had a point. Konrad hadn't seen a man as brazen as the Luftwaffe Chief, exploiting Petra's vulnerability. From Mayrock's scowl, it bothered him as well. The perfect time to offer gentlemanly assistance had arrived. Tapping Fritz on the shoulder, Konrad cocked his head. Fritz got Konrad's drift and left the old friends together. Schink glowered at Fritz as he strode away.

Petra trembled with tears as Konrad comforted her. The revelations about the Final Solution had changed his priorities. He wanted the real perpetrators to pay, their bloodthirsty hijacking of the German people shamed him. They had royally fooled Konrad, but no more. He would set them straight, but that needed alliances. Schink and Mayrock had won Manteufel over. Petra knew most everyone else. Konrad needed to cement the relationship between him and Wernher.

Wernher stared vacantly into space, his broad shoulders drooping. Shock stippled every face with slack jaws, wide eyes, and wrinkled brows. Apart from Wernher, all the men had a soldier's familiarity with death.

Konrad eased himself around so he could see the fire crew working, but shielded Petra from the harrowing sight. No benefit would come from seeing her husband cremated. Petra's shoulders heaved with grief. Hanna shuffled over. Her face now more careworn than usual.

Hanna craned her neck to look Konrad in the eye. "Go to the other men and help Wernher. We girls will take care of ourselves for now."

Konrad could let go of Petra. Wernher unified all those present, just as he unified the people of the Reich with his technological vision. Wernher's lips opened and closed noiselessly, but his ashen face appeared to look over some high edge. Konrad placed his hands on Wernher. Squealing brakes almost drowned out the klaxons, and all the noises together obliterated Konrad's words. Wernher's eyes begged to hear the words again. Konrad repeated them at the top of his voice.

"It's done now. Snap yourself out of it." Barbed wire lined Konrad's throat from shouting.

Wernher didn't respond, so Konrad shook Wernher's shoulders. Now, the rocket scientist looked at Konrad until a small explosion from outside pulled his glare away. "If the launch doesn't go as planned, they'll kill me."

"They can't do that with us behind you, but we need your leadership, Wernher. Can you give it?"

"Yes, yes. Himmler and Heydrich cannot overcome the forces in this room."

Wernher's confident poise returned, and he stood elegantly, chest out with his shoulders straight. Removing a kerchief from his pocket, he wiped his brow. The sirens outside abated, only the hissing of the fire and the pumping of foam remained audible.

"We need to hear your response. We need to understand your vision for the Reich, not just for space."

Wernher strode away from the crash towards the opposing wall, where a corridor led to the dining hall. He clapped his hands, and even Petra and Hanna broke from their mourning to turn and listen. Fritz's head moved from ogling Petra to focussing earnestly on Wernher.

"My condolences - surely, gentlemen, all our sympathy - go out to the ladies." Wernher looked sympathetically at Hanna and Petra. The other men made noises of agreement and sympathy. "The Reich has lost two great heroes, and we gentlemen are strongly affected, but it is Hanna and Petra who are suffering the brunt of the loss. I am sorry to cut the tribute to our friends short, but this is a matter of national importance. As we discussed earlier, the loss of our leading astronauts may set the project back substantially. This brings enormous danger for me, personally." The military men nodded and whispered. "Perhaps it is time, gentlemen, that we acknowledged the threat we all live under in the Reich. Any of us could disappear, despite our position in Germany, and the SS are the ones to blame. They have been the Nazis' real muscle since 1934. They will not be the instruments of our destruction, they shall be disarmed, disbanded, and sent into the footnotes of history." Guests threw in an 'indeed' and a 'hear-hear'. "They took Doenitz, a good man and one of us, and pinned their guilt on him. Who should have the strength to challenge the power of the Wehrmacht? Who in the Fatherland should reign supreme over us?"

Admiral Geissler fidgeted, clenching and unclenching his fists. His face, usually placid and inscrutable, transformed into a vicious snarl. "Nobody!"

"Nobody!" Fritz adjusted his tunic.

Mannteufel punched the air, the scar around his eye pink and engorged. "Nobody!"

Wernher raised his fist, almost hitting the corridor's ceiling. The three defiant military chiefs stood before him in the glass-strewn arrival hall, making the same gesture.

Energy ran through Konrad. This was his first inkling of the Wehrmacht's true opinion about Himmler, Heydrich, and the SS. Konrad's convict regiment followed him over all others. He looked forward to using them to change the regime. Wernher von Braun made a perfect leader for the Fatherland, and now the pieces came together for it to happen. "Nobody!"

Even Petra managed to call out her support through her tears. Konrad worried when he saw Hanna so stony-faced. Only time would tell if she could be trusted in the inner circle of this new movement.

"Let us plan our strategy." Wernher took a step toward the cafe. "If you don't mind, ladies, we will leave you here while we discuss the details."

Hanna's absence from the talks pleased Konrad. It would be easy for her to pass information on to Himmler or Heydrich since she moved amongst them in the highest circles. Wernher led the men back to the cafeteria.

Konrad held back by the entrance and blocked his men's way. "You three make sure nobody comes in. There's a door over there you need to watch, as well."

Everybody gathered around.

The putative Führer stood at the head of the table. "Konrad, why don't you come over and sit with us?"

"Just a moment." Head shaking, Konrad wanted to keep an eye on things. "I'm setting my men to watch. Anybody close could hear us."

"Good thinking, although Petra and Hanna are old friends of mine and I trust them."

"This room is very accessible and insecure." His hand pointed the through route. "So any of the rescue services could walk in. Somebody has to stay here, and the 500th are the ones to do it."

"The 500th!" Schink and Mayrock brought their heels down on the floor.

"Good man." Fritz's pompadour shook with sincerity. "It's a shame there aren't more like you in Gothengau."

"There are more, and I command them." Konrad pointed at the three men he brought with him. The Outlaws obey me over anyone else."

"The ones you fail." Mannteufel put up his hand. "What happens to them?"

"There's only been one failure, and they sent him to the suicide squad. I don't reject anyone now. There's jail for those that need it. Others are shunned, something my Amish people do back in America. Now there's a place for everyone in the 500th. Some just need longer, that's all."

"Then we have a hero inside our enemy's stronghold." Fritz turned to the leader. "Wernher, what are your plans?"

"You four are the military planners, and I am only the scientist. I have no plans, just a goal: to colonize the stars without having Himmler and the Nazi's put their bloody prints on it." Wernher squinted lopsidedly. "Have you never given thought of getting rid of the Nazis?"

"Yes, we have." Mannteufel's bitter expression seared his face. "Did you think that we would just let our friends and colleagues hang for

Himmler and Heydrich's wrongdoings? Doenitz was one of our best men, another visionary like you, Wernher." Mannteufel pointed at the scientist. "His ideas on naval warfare with submarines are still years ahead of anything the British have. They stitched him by making him the Führer. Him and a lot of other good men besides. The plans for a coup are old and need updating. Now we have Konrad's offer of help, we need schemes that include his men."

"You also have me on the inside, don't forget." Everybody looked at Wernher. "They forced me into the SS. I am a major. I command nobody but can give them bad guidance. They rely on data from my Space Agency. What are your strategies? Perhaps this is the best time to review them."

May Day's attack sparked the fire. An excited buzz of whispering filled the air. Without the Outlaws' oxygen, though, the plans didn't catch light. Konrad kindled the flames, so the blaze burned fiercely.

"Well, you all know me." Fritz's nose raised. "and how I've always detested the lower sorts that National Socialism appeals to.

"So the plan I've long cherished is the one where we get Himmler, Heydrich, and Drachenblut in the same location," Fritz continued. "We bomb them, and then occupy the Reichstag and the Reich's TV station. If we do it quickly enough, then the SS will be in their barracks with no time to respond. I'll stop any tanks leaving Gothengau. They have to pass the isthmus, but a few squadrons of ground-attack aircraft will put paid to that, and then we'll be the only ones with heavy armour."

"I'll have my men stop them leaving their barracks, make sure we have tanks on the streets and Autobahns. We can do this virtually unopposed." Mannteufel clenched a fist at his side.

"But how can we get the three of them together at a time of our choosing?" Geissler pumped his heels up and down.

"I know how." All stopped and waited on Konrad.

"Remember our inside contact at Wewelsburg? He's going to arrange for Drachenblut's funeral soon. It will be held at Wewelsburg. Himmler and Heydrich will be there."

"Do you know when this will happen?" Mannteufel asked.

"Not yet. The insider is doing this against his will, but when we've asked him favours before, he's always come through."

"Favours? You're asking him to do you a favour? What does he owe you that you can make him into a murderer?"

"We know something about him, Petra and I, and it's the last thing we'll make him do. It's the last time we'll use it against him." He felt their stares burrowing into him. A blackmailer, despite all his good deeds, that's what they thought. No, that couldn't stand. "It isn't even for us, though, really. It's a favour for the Reich."

Mannteufel shrugged. "I can have artillery flatten the whole castle. Give me a day's notice."

"Hah!" Fritz threw up his hands. "Given ten minutes' notice my bombers won't leave you anything to fire at."

"Gentlemen, please. Let's not turn this into a pissing contest." Wernher scowled at the pair. "We have only just gathered the nerve to start."

Fritz shook his head. "Now that we have the 500th we can also drop soldiers at the Reichstag and the TV station."

That's the planning that Konrad wanted to hear. "Even if I split the 500th into four divisions, we'd still have double what we need to secure both places."

"When everything is under control, we broadcast that Wernher is the new Führer."

"Why wait?" Mannteufel made a grabbing motion for an imaginary throat. "If we have the TV station and tell people that everything's under control, then it's under control."

"We will have a few days' notice before Drachenblut's funeral." Wernher tapped the table with the side of his hand "Enough time to put our ideas in place."

"No pressure, but it all hinges on you, Konrad." Mannteufel's scar still blushed crimson. "When you deliver the goods, when Drachenblut is dead, we can all do our bit."

Drachenblut must sacrifice his life for the Fourth Reich's birth. "It's a shame this has to begin with a death."

"Start as you mean to go on." Mannteufel's justification of more killing struck apprehension in Konrad. "Drachenblut, Himmler and Gothengau are asking for it anyway."

"Now we've talked it through." This meeting had gone as far as it could. "We should re-join the ladies. It seems wrong to leave them alone in their grief."

"Yes, yes. You're quite right," Wernher agreed. "Let's get back to them."

Wernher stood and led the group back to the arrivals area. Schink and Mayrock saluted as they passed. Green-uniformed, soot-covered rescue staff pushed broken glass out of the conspirators' way.

Konrad's three men led, once Mayrock had scarpered from the far doorway he guarded. Max and Eva's aircraft burned no more, and foam covered its metallic sheen. A rescue vehicle approached the aircraft chassis, an arm extending from its roof. After the projecting grip had entered the foam, metal snapped loudly. A motor on the truck groaned when the arm lifted the top of the wreckage from the lather covering it. The spray remaining on the aircraft fragment hid the inverted bodies hanging there. A hosepipe played on the suspended part, clearing away the fire retardant.

Petra and Hanna started screaming behind Konrad. He turned, glad to be relieved from watching the charred corpses appear from the foam. The women ran to the door at the far end of the building. Alarmed, the others looked around before chasing Petra and Hanna. Konrad's extra-long stride got him there first, and he reached the women as they left the building. Schink and Mayrock passed them a moment later.

Outside, at the forest's edge, stood a sight that made Konrad shout with joy. Petra needed no consolation because, stepping from the woods, Max held up a limping Eva. When Schink and Mayrock barrelled towards him, confusion swept across his eyes and mouth. They didn't slow down, grabbing the astronaut under his arms and lifting him up on their shoulders. Eva leaned on Mayrock for support.

Both their faces were scratched and bloody, and Max held his head at an awkward angle. Their flight suits were covered in leaves and twigs. When the four were close enough, Max's feet delicately approached the floor. Schink and Mayrock released their grip. Petra embraced Max and sobbed. Hanna held her adopted daughter so tight Eva struggled for breath.

Wernher von Braun's smile spread joy, and it infected Konrad. The rocket scientist stepped back when he met Konrad's eye, a shadow flickered across his happiness.

"You put the fear of God in me with your smile." Wernher patted Konrad's arm. "I thought it was your kill face!"

Chapter 12

Wewelsburg, Sunday, May 2nd, 1965.

Beside the delicious aromas of scrambled eggs and toasted muffins, metallic bangs and much florid language emerged from the kitchen hatch. Karl stopped talking for the time it took the two long tables of breakfasting priests to realise that their eyes couldn't feast on the calamity going on in the cookhouse. On his table, next to the windows away from the noise, Olaf and Hadwin presented the back of their heads to Karl. Between the stone wall and the glass pane, a spider circled around his web to reinforce its silken cross beams. A little longer passed than Karl's patience and schedule permitted before he rapped his knuckles on the table and recaptured his disciples' attention. Now, Karl needed to remind his followers of his point. Early meetings stressed people, sensitive Hadwin especially.

Hadwin's eyes were cloudy, with a good chance of rain. "Did you see Drachenblut and the Vestals?"

"They're being served in their rooms today. You won't see them in here, but it's my 0800 with the High Priest soon."

"Waited on hand and foot." Olaf scraped the metal plate with his fork. "There'll be no more of that when you're in charge."

Of course, the fawning service would continue when Karl became High Priest. After drawing the wrong conclusion about Drachenblut's death, if, and not when, best described Karl's succession. Despair ripped purpose from him. He forgot the point of this meeting, thinking only of his advancement. The photographs of the High Priest and Chief Vestal might not end Drachenblut's career. Karl's surprise at the strength of the High Priest's forbidden carnal relation increased every time he employed it: whatever he said, the affair continued. Only killing

Drachenblut would ensure Karl's ascendance to High Priest. The spider, maintenance of his web complete, sat in its centre.

"Will there, Karl?" asked Olaf. "No more being waited on hand and foot?"

"Why do you insist on my acknowledgement for every groan, burp, or fart that comes out of you? No, of course not, I mean, of course, that will end." The pampering would increase, if anything. "Are you satisfied?"

Olaf's inverted eyebrows voiced his concern, and Hadwin again appeared close to sobbing. Not the best way to keep his coterie loyal, though. Karl joined the group silence, a lull before his next appointment. He polished the last of the egg from his plate with a piece of rye bread, and the only sound was that of eating.

Karl slurped the last of his coffee. "I won't see any of you for a few days."

"Your girl's fertile time at the breeding clinic again?" Olaf attempted to return to favour. Karl liked grovelling.

A fly landed in the cobweb. The spider dashed towards its prey.

"She's like clockwork, your one." Olaf nodded and winked. Banter often brought him out of his funk.

"Well, that's the good part. But it's not like here. There's no fruitful ground for Odinism in Gothengau. I hate going there."

"Banging Scandinavians must be of little consolation!" A smile ingratiated itself on Olaf's lips.

"I take some comfort from that, I admit!" Karl couldn't resist grinning, either. "I'll see you when I get back."

At least Karl would arrive at the High Priest's chambers with cheer now. Soon after leaving the canteen, he banged on Drachenblut's studded door.

"Enter."

It took some effort to move the thick wooden door. Drachenblut stood in a windowed alcove at the other, bare-stone end of the wood-panelled room, his back to Karl. Daylight streamed through the blonde mane that reached his waist. On the approach to his daily head-to-head with Drachenblut, Karl passed medieval weapons hanging from the walls between shields decorated with runes. A broad desk sat between Karl and his superior, its black wood supported nothing except a human skull. By maintaining his stance in the niche after Karl's arrival at the guest chair, Drachenblut carried on trying to pull the mystical nonsense on Karl. It never worked on him. Excitement nibbled at his confidence, not doubt. It certainly wasn't fear, either. Karl wasn't scared.

"You were too quick with your assumption of power yesterday."

The High Priest must be ballet trained. Only at a choreographic performance had Karl seen somebody half-rotate with such measured pace. Even without seeing Drachenblut's feet moving, Karl knew it as another part of an act that he didn't buy. After the High Priest snaked around the imposing wooden chair and sat, he motioned for Karl to take a seat. In a moment of arrogant forgetfulness, before taking his place, Karl responded. "It didn't look like you could get away."

"Your decorum did!" Drachenblut's eyes braised Karl. "Didn't it? How dare you speak before being asked? And to make it worse, you yammer on while you sashay around the room! Remember your place and don't let your eagerness to fill my shoes blind you to reason.

"Besides, if you wanted to sit on this side of the desk, you would have played your hand with the pictures. You don't want this job. You love complaining and plotting and feeling short-changed too much to exchange it for happiness and contentment."

Never allow Drachenblut to perceive something as an interruption to his flow of wisdom. His denouncement's cutting insight would slice your soul to reveal the parts you never admitted, the parts that kept you awake denying. His smirk revealed a brown incisor. In Karl's American eyes, that required immediate remedy, not decades of festering neglect. A bite from Drachenblut's impure cuspid meant poison needed to be sucked from the wound.

"Your career and reputation would end if the Führer saw you regularly defile at least one of the Vestals. What would the public think? Would they still love Vestal Helga, knowing she is not a virgin, but a concubine?"

"If you thought that, then why not put them out there already? You fear failure too much, you believe you are weak, and if you believe that, then so does everybody else. Even your little schoolyard friends you always plot with know you can never overcome me. I will always be here.

"It makes no difference anyway. Vestal Helga will be marrying Richard Baer when her service is finished. Vestal Grimhilt will wed the Gauleiter of Memel-Narev, and Edda, the leader of Ingermanland. That should keep the colonies bound to the Reich, they've been very troublesome and independent minded, especially Gothengau.

"Go, now. Go to Gothengau and make them comply with Odinist Law, tell them to observe the feast days and holy days. Tell Baer to get divorced. Sow your oats at the breeding centre, while I guide our great nation in mourning."

Karl parted his hair with his index finger. "Lead the mourning that you caused." Flames rose from his belly. "The attack was your fault! You ordered the Führer to send those rockets because you're terrified of a Japanese invasion!"

"Gothengau lost the missile. The deaths are their responsibility, and their hands were soaked in blood before that. Leave, go to Crimea, and enforce their worship of the Norse Gods. And go alone!"

"Expect no progress if you send me without my team."

"I expect no progress from you whatsoever."

The High Priest's refusal to accept one shred of blame for the May Day fallen made Karl's eyes bulge. He fought back the urge to lunge at Drachenblut with one of the maces or axes adorning the room. Karl resisted slamming the door when he left. Infuriated, he pounded the corridor to the North Tower's spiral staircase and descended to the Crypt of the Eternal Flame. Though his temper cooled, the temperature increased as he trotted down the two flights. One of the Virgins had left the torch on too high, and only they could correct the problem. On either side of the stone doorway, two guards sweated away in full SS uniform. Karl climbed the stairs, in search of a Vestal to correct the situation. With a little luck, he would find his lover Grimhilt, not Drachenblut's whore Helga, or half-witted Edda. Secrecy meant Karl and Grimhilt had not seen each other since her return to the castle the previous evening. He left the North tower and entered the triangular courtyard. After the heat of the dank Crypt, Karl savoured the fresh air blowing through his beard and hair. It felt like freedom from the ominous next duty in Gothengau and blew away the lingering burning of Drachenblut's remarks.

Before Karl reached the archway opposite, he saw Grimhilt walking towards it on the other side. They both picked up their pace discreetly, Grimhilt from beyond the castle walls on the bridge over the empty moat. They met inside the tunnel under the castle's east wing.

Grimhilt's eyes appeared moistened with dew. "You must have been so worried."

"About w-." Karl realised that his primary concern on May Day should have been for Grimhilt. "Of course! I wept, ask anyone!"

"Liar." A fist emerged from her silk robes to thump Karl's chest. "You just want me out of the way."

"I'm not your father. Stop putting what he did to you on me, and just admit you like being a celebrity. Worse things happen to youngest daughters."

"There are so many girls, though. You have your choice, don't you?"

Karl shook his head. He wished. Karl thought he got little better than any other man in the Reich.

Grimhilt's face shone brightly. "Can we meet tonight, then?"

"I can't. I must go to, I must go somewhere-"

"Go to Gothengau and have your way at Ostara! That's what I meant about you having your choice, and you denied it."

"You're still shaken after the May Day attack. You should go and rest."

"I don't know whether you are concerned or condescending, but you're right." Grimhilt turned away.

"But, the Eternal Flame is running very hot. Can you turn it down?"

"No." She neither stopped nor looked back.

Dejected, Karl trudged to his office. It sat almost exactly above the tunnel where he and Grimhilt had stood. He needed paperwork for his trip. As he packed, the phone rang, its single tone signalling an outside line. Not expecting any external contact and concerned about his flight to Crimea, the call piqued Karl's curiosity.

"Hello?"

"Hi, Karl."

Karl recognised Petra's famous voice, even more readily since her pleading to the May Day attendees became the defining symbol of the attack. This was a call to make demands.

"Yes, who is calling?"

"You know who it is. I can hear it."

"What do you want now?" Karl's question admitted Petra's accuracy.

"That's more like it. We would like your co-operation on a rather big request. It's something that you want, too."

"Oh yeah. What is it?"

"We know who's to blame for the Berlin attack. We want you as High Priest and Drachenblut gone. Push him off something, like you did on the voyage here, remember?"

He recalled a dark night, the briny sea air, and hands pushing him on his knees to face a partially-inflated old cock. A rough jerk backwards, in a kneejerk reaction. That natural, youthful response released too much energy for a portly man with his pants down. He cried out, there was a splash, and then the silence of the ocean.

Guilt from that recollection forced Karl to lower his voice. "There was a reason for that."

"And there's a reason for this too. We all know how ambitious you are, and because this is such a big thing, we'll call it quits afterwards, okay?"

"But you've told me that before. Quit yanking my chain. You can't guarantee that with only your word."

"You believe Konrad's word, though, don't you? Everybody does. Say I get that for you?"

Every word Petra said fired Karl up for his promotion to High Priest. This would show Drachenblut that he had bravery, that Karl had the right to be High Priest. Karl visualised the look in Drachenblut's eyes as he killed him. Konrad's guarantee held more currency than a Reichsmark.

"Okay. I'll do it, but I want to hear Konrad's promise."

"He'll see you tonight."

Petra said something else as Karl put the phone down, it sounded vaguely like thanks. After reaching his decision, her words rang hollow. The dressing down that Drachenblut gave Karl fired the second priest up for revenge. Petra's call came at the best time. Her pressure to depose Drachenblut catalysed the reaction of his bitter experience and thwarted ambition. National treasure Petra Hellfeier blackmailed him, making it more her fault than his. If Karl could abstain responsibility for the crime, then he could do anything.

Pool cars, almost always kübelwagens, were kept outside the south wing of the castle. The rear-engined army vehicles had their baggage compartment at the front. When Karl opened it, he fought against the screech of the rusty hinges. Should he choose another car? They all looked equal on close examination, and the airport only lay kilometres away on the autobahn. A breeze cooled his face when the car moved.

Seconds later, the forest cover's verdant shade felt like diving into a mountain pool.

The kübelwagen's tyres screamed when it sank into the first bend on the hill's winding road, and Karl eased off the gas. Gravity gave him enough speed. The Gothengau flight would not leave without him, so he had minutes to consider how to trap Drachenblut. Women tempted the High Priest, so perhaps Grimhilt could be Karl's honey trap. If Karl got Drachenblut to the top of the North Tower, the chances of him falling to his death increased exponentially. Karl pushed someone to their death before. Stabbing and shooting, though, were too personal and messy. Karl winced at being drenched with blood. Guns had the same problem, but louder. There were tests for poison, but not for hitting the ground from a push. Karl believed his long tenure as Petra's stooge was nearing its end.

At the foot of the hill, the car emerged from the forest. Karl shielded his eyes while accelerating to join the autobahn. Once on the freeway, the engine screamed as Karl floored the gas pedal. His hair and beard flew around, sometimes tugging at the roots producing jolts of near-pain. On Karl's left, the stark metal and glass of the Wewelsburg Centre. Only one junction later, and the airport exit arrived. The brakes squealed, the gearbox whirred into its new speed, and Karl resisted his torso's lunge forward as the vehicle descended to the speed limit.

After parking the kubelwagen in the pool car lot, Karl extracted his luggage. There would be a three-hour flight to Gothengau, best used to further the plans to push the High Priest from a tower. Few others boarded the 12-seater aircraft with him. Karl plotted more until his eyes closed. The next thing he knew, the plane was bouncing from its touch down. There was little hope of getting Odinism to take hold here, and the feeling dragged his shoulders down. At least he would be visiting Ostara, and that nimble Swedish partner he'd been enjoying for the last four months. The aeroplane taxied towards the arrival stand as Karl's member hardened.

Chapter 13

Berlin, Sunday, May 2nd, 1965.

When Petra had buried Wieland, the boy's beautiful mahogany coffin didn't mitigate her sense of loss. After she saw it, tears burst from her eyes. Lothar had no casket. She gazed down at his remains, wrapped in fabric ready for the Teutonic funeral, and the scene made Petra hollow as if eviscerated. Her torso echoed, her consciousness a chamber scorched of feeling. It hurt even more that these feelings weren't for the boy's death but pity for herself and for the Reich at being dragged backwards with Odin and the Nordic Pantheon.

Petra pulled her jacket around her, but it didn't relieve the icy coldness crystallising along her skin. Thor's Hammer Mjölnir, the black sun and other icons were carved into the stone walls at the altar of the chapel of rest. Statues of Norse Gods popular with youngsters conveyed its function as a children's Valhalla Temple. Lothar's corpse lay before her on the stone table like a biblical offering. Her parents had died several years earlier, thankfully. Although her fame had resurged after the May Day attack tears, her husband running off with Eva had compounded her solitude. Even though Max's extra-marital activities went back way before Eva, and he had just left his family to face the Berlin rocket attack alone, she needed to be with a man. Potential lovers always waited for her, but she needed someone familiar, a man that knew her in the way she did him.

The front door squeaked open, then banged shut. A single guest arrived, but a foyer between her and the front door blocked the view. Petra stood and dusted down her black suit skirt. She gathered herself for the coming onslaught of emotion that the sympathies from this first visitor would bring, then turned. Max stood before her. His closeness sparked desire in her straight away. He pulled her towards him, she fell into his arms, and they kissed. Now she felt less alone. They embraced for a moment before the events between Max, Eva, and Lothar came to haunt her again. Droplets spattered the sleeve of Max's silver uniform.

Petra dabbed at her eyes. "Thank you for arranging this. I didn't have the strength."

"I didn't want you to worry about that, after all you've been through."

"They could have at least let him have a coffin."

Dark blotches stained Max's uniform where it soaked his wife's tears. Petra looked up.

Max wept gently. "How can they make us have funerals without caskets? Haven't they put us through enough already?"

"I don't want to be part of this experiment either, but we just have to go along with it. If we don't they could lock us up or worse."

The door squeaked open again. Petra left Max's arms but held his hand to face the new arrival, and the sour, jealous look on Eva's face warmed Petra's heart. Maybe Petra could get him back from this siren. Possibly her song compelled Max more than Eva's did.

"You soon got back to being her caring husband. What about us?"

Max turned abruptly to face his interloping lover. "It's our son's funeral. What did you expect would happen?"

"I came here as a friend in your hour of need! Obviously, your needs are more than satisfied. Please accept my condolences for your loss." Eva's blonde locks flicked when she turned. Then they flicked again. "And by the way, he doesn't love you."

Eva turned and left. The door banged shut behind her.

"Did you tell her you don't love me?"

"No."

She didn't believe him, and his face either reflected her doubt or showed his guilt. Footfalls from the front door signalled a new arrival. Fritz wore one of his muted uniforms, topped off with some of his more sombre medals. A black armband bisected his sleeve near the shoulder.

Max let go of Petra's hand. "You didn't invite him, did you?"

Fritz scowled. It enhanced his cragginess, showed his age.

"I am here as a friend of the family."

"That's what I thought. I'd heard that about you."

Max's jealousy aroused Petra. He still had feelings for her. Provided Max finished the affair with Eva, this burial could symbolise its dissolution. Perhaps she could use Fritz's arrival for her own advantage. "Have you had enough of Eva? Come home."

Petra touched Max's behind to show appreciation. He didn't have to stay on the punishment step this time. The May Day attack separated his fling with Eva from his previous transgressions. The ghosts of Lothar and Wieland swirled around the empty house with Petra. Without company, the isolation made her vulnerable to Fritz's carnal attentions.

Wernher appeared, dapper in his narrow lapelled black suit. He put down the planks under his arm and the toolbox in his hand to embrace Petra. Max shook Wernher's hand.

"Strange day for household repairs, Wernher." Max nodded towards the items.

"I will not have the May Day attack smash the feelings of the survivors as well." Wernher picked up two planks. "The rockets that hit Berlin were my creations. My God, they were practically my children, and that is where the damage will end." He opened the toolbox. "We will make a coffin for Lothar. We can stand together on this. It might be overlooked."

Joy cut through Petra's melancholy. She touched Max's hand, and their fingers entwined. This German funeral, an act of oppression against her and the rest of the Reich, could be resisted. She and Max had powerful friends. Lothar would take a final, perpetual slumber in a wooden box, not wrapped in linen.

"That is an excellent idea." Fritz wore a smug grin. "Is there anything you can't improve?"

"Yes, of course there is. I can't make the Reich better alone, not with Gothengau and Odinism ruining everything."

"I can help. You and the Wehrmacht can do it together. Unity is strength. We rule the West, the sky - you even rule the stars."

Max opened the tool box and brought out a hammer and nails. Wernher positioned five of the planks together to form an open casket. Nails held between lips, Wernher looked like a beautifully-dressed artisan. An eye for detail showed when all the snugly fitting pieces matched Lothar's size.

Fritz moved the base and one side of the box to the foyer wall. He picked up the hammer and nailed the wood together at the base, using the wall to steady the pieces against the rapid pounding the nails received.

The door swung open. Petra looked up, expecting another mourner, but an Odinist priest arrived, premature grey streaked through his hair and beard, boots laced up over his shins. He stood in the centre of the room, surveying the activity with folded arms. One of his hands had the smooth skin and uniform pigment of a prosthetic.

"What's going on here?" He looked in every eye. "This is a place for the Aryan dead to rest quietly before they enter Valhalla, not a carpenter's workshop."

Nobody responded. The priest stamped his foot. Petra almost repressed a laugh, and the priest turned his full gaze on her.

"Petra Hellfeier." Sometimes, Petra wished people didn't know her name without her knowing theirs.

"I expect better behaviour than this from you. Aren't you a holder of the Cross of the German People?" Petra didn't answer the question. "Well?"

The priest angrily prodded Petra in the chest with his plastic hand. Max came to Petra's aid. He moved between the priest and his wife.

"What's the problem? This is our child's funeral. You, you of all people, should know how to conduct yourself on these occasions. You are failing, royally failing in your priestly duties. Do your job, man."

The priest calmed. "The funerals of the May Day martyrs are to be Odinist. That edict came from the Führer himself. That's why all the burials were arranged for you so that this new German way would be easier for the Aryan people."

This was Himmler's doing! She threw Max's hand from hers in disgust.

"Stop making that box now!" hollered the priest.

The hammering continued unabated. There were now two sides to the coffin. Fritz reached for the third.

"I said stop!"

Getting no response at all, the priest marched over to Fritz and grabbed his arm. Fritz snatched his hand back and stood, almost knocking the priest over. His teeth clenched, he lifted the hammer ready to strike. The priest cowered under his prosthetic.

"Fritz!" Wernher grabbed the Luftwaffe Chief's arm. "Control yourself, man!"

Fritz dropped his hand, and the priest rebounded from his defensive posture.

"If you continue with this offence, I will have no choice but to report you to the Gestapo."

More hammering pounded its way into the chapel.

Max shook his head. "Just ignore him. Let him go and bother someone else. It sounds like Wernher wasn't the only one with this idea."

"You haven't heard the last of this!" The priest's false arm slipped, his other hand grabbed it. "No such disrespect of Odinism will be tolerated by the Führer. I don't care how famous or influential you are. You'll pay!"

The man backed out and left. Before the door shut behind him, Petra heard him shouting the same orders to those outside as he had to them.

Petra turned to Max. A droplet stung its way from a tear duct from the shame she felt at believing him. "You told me that you organised the funeral."

Max made no reply. Petra's earlier desire for familiar company came back to mock her.

Fritz carried on putting the last side on the pine box. The room stayed silent as Fritz went about his task until he lacked only the body and the lid to seal the coffin with. He carried the improvised pall and its cover to the dead body lying on the altar.

"I think that you should do the last part, Max." Fritz approached the astronaut. "You were the closest to him."

That angered Petra. Max hadn't been closer to the boy than his adopted mother. Nobody could be. She stepped forward.

"I deserve that honour. I was his mother!"

Petra never used a hammer before, and this was no time for practice. She turned to Wernher. "Can you help me?"

Petra placed Lothar's body gently into the coffin. When he lay straight, she opened the linen to see his face for the last time. She looked away from his crushed nose and shattered teeth. That's not how she remembered him, not the last image she wanted to see of him. He could have grown to be a great man.

She picked up the lid, placed it on the box and stepped aside so Wernher could play his part of the task. He held her left hand on the nail and wrapped her right around the hammer. With a few gentle taps, they sealed Lothar in the casket.

Petra lifted one end of Lothar's coffin, Max the other. Together, they walked out, Fritz and Wernher following them. They passed Hanna and Eva waiting outside. Hammering filled the air and came from all around. Hanna anxiously grasped Eva's arm, and they joined the procession. Heads lowered, they silently walked to a grave lying open in a new section of the cemetery dedicated to the May Day fatalities.

Another priest greeted them. "My condolences, Mr and Mrs Hellfeier." Evidently, they had given up insisting on the Odinist funeral rites.

Max and Eva walked past without acknowledging him. The priest hurried after them.

"Your boy will be safe now, guarded by the wolves in Valhalla. May he fly there with Valkyries."

All around them, graves were being filled with jerry-rigged coffins. It surprised Petra that people allowed the priests to conduct the occult ceremony on their departed. Perhaps the burial in linens had been a step too far. They reached a grave, separated from two other burials by several pits. Wernher produced the sashes that had been tied around Lothar. He threaded two of them under the box, and then Petra, Max, Wernher and Hanna suspended the coffin over the open grave.

"Cattle die, kinsmen die, the self must also die; I know one thing which never dies: the reputation of each dead Aryan," droned the priest.

Petra barely heard the Odinist dirge. It looked like nobody else listened either. She and Max held different ends of the same sash. Wernher and Hanna Reitsch held the other ribbon. They met each other's eyes and began to slowly let the material slip through their hands. Lothar's coffin touched the ground, and the attendees threw in handfuls of dust. A gravedigger appeared with a spade and finished the job, shovelling in dirt from an adjacent, communal pile of soil.

Hanna approached Petra, leading her daughter by the hand.

"My dear friend. Eva told me that she sincerely came here today to honour your loss. That the affair between her and Max was a mistake. The attack had only just happened; she wasn't herself. You know how it was."

That Hanna and Eva came specifically for this curled the corners of Petra's lips into a smile. Petra saw happiness on the horizon. Then, recalling where she was and whose burial she attended, a freezing blast of guilt blew through her. She froze in front of the contentment she sought since Wieland's death. Her only born child's fate eclipsed any feelings for Lothar's demise and pushed bliss further into the distance.

"I have to hear those words from your lips." Petra looked straight at Eva, and Eva spoke.

"My mother's wrong." Eva's blue eyes shimmered with hate. "You can't even make him a baby. All you do is wallow around feeling sorry for yourself."

Hanna gasped, her eyes opening wide. "That's not what you said to your own mother just now. You told me you were going to do the right thing."

"You're not my mother, I'm adopted. And I'll do what's right for the Reich, and good for Max and me."

Eva tried to fling her arms around Max, but he pushed her aside. She came back but his palm against her chest stopped her advances.

"You know we're meant to be together. We have to have babies. You can't do that with that barren bitch."

"I don't want you." Max looked like he had just stood in something.

Eva's brows knitted, her fists clenching and unclenching.

"Yes," said Petra. "Don't worry, though, you're hardly the first to feel that way. Is she, darling?"

Eva sprang towards Petra. Petra saw it coming and used Eva's speed against her, stepping aside and throwing Eva over her extended leg. Eva fell on the ground face first, cursing. When she got up the tears muddied the streaks of earth on her cheeks. After staring at Petra for a few seconds, she ran. Hanna, her damp-face grimacing, held out her hands, then turned to walk away.

Only Petra and Max remained from their mourner acquaintances, though they were being observed by strangers who buried their loved ones.

"At least nobody asked us for autographs." Max walked to the car park. "Shall we go home now?"

"You aren't coming with me." Petra remained reserved. The public had seen enough of her personal life.

"But you said!" Max spread his palms, putting on the wounded boy act.

"That was before you lied about the burial." Petra brushed hair from her face. A little more of a push and this part will be over. "How can I believe you about anything else?"

"You saw me reject Eva just now, how can you not believe me?"

"It's not only that. You can have her back any time, and we don't have any kids now, so what's the point in us being together at all?"

"You know they'll make us get back together when they realise we've split, don't you? They'll have us sleeping in the same bed, just like after Wieland."

The mention of Petra's departed only child pushed out Lothar. Even today, moments after covering the adopted boy in earth, she felt a hook bury itself in her gut and drag her down to the agony of Wieland's final hours. It was all she could do to stay on her feet. Guilt tugged Petra one way and mourning the other. She tasted the salt of the tears rolling down her cheeks to her lips.

"Until then, please stay away." She walked to the Porsche.

"Hey, how am I going to get home?"

Petra opened the door. "The same way you got here."

In the side view mirror, Max's reflection approached the Porsche. Petra dabbed her eyes and started the car. Max waved from behind her as she sped away.

A firm sofa welcomed Petra when she got home. She fell into it after switching on the television, and once the set warmed-up she watched Popular Observer. Steffi and Sebastian narrated sombre Odinist rituals at the same graveyard that Petra had buried her boy. The mass compliance, enjoyment, even, on the show differed from anything she had witnessed.

Chapter 14

Gothengau, Sunday, May 2nd, 1965.

Sunlight scorched Karl's retinas when he emerged from the aircraft. He blinked, then squinted to protect his eyes. The soft soles of his boot touched the passenger stairs and rattled them against the fuselage. On the first step down, an itch in his nose increased until it consumed his entire being. He stopped, screwed up his face, and breathed in. The nasal irritation peaked. He bent double to sneeze, hands covering his face. Afterward, he opened his eyes and stood. At the same moment his bags landed, ejecting his underwear and toiletries on the tarmac in front of the Gothengau airbase gate.

Laughter ran through the crowd waiting at the door. Grinding his jaw and glowering, Karl trotted to the ground and got on his knees to put his items back. Every time he heard more laughter his shoulders tensed. Their giggles became whispers. Stay calm, he repeated to himself. Finished, he stood again and strolled through the sniggering onlookers with eyes front. Stares, mumbled commentary, and chortling accompanied the start of Karl's journey across the steel and glass building. At least he didn't have to wait for his bags at the carousel. He just had to pass it with measured pace and shoulders straight. Between the desks of the check-in area, the mockery stopped. Pride salvaged, he stepped through the doors to the car park.

Something dropped on Karl's shoulder and his knee almost gave way under the pressure. A giant hand rested on Karl, and combat fatigues were all he could see when he turned. How had a man this size appeared from nowhere?

"I'm here to remind you of your duty to the people of the Reich."

"My duty to the people of the Reich? So that's what you and Petra are calling it, then. I see it as blackmail and murder, but it's a nice way of twisting this around to make you two feel good."

"You have my word that it's the last we'll ask of you."

"At least it's your word! Petra's commitments haven't been worth the air she spoke them into."

"Keep your voice down. Petra told me you wanted to hear me promise it, and now I have. She'll catch up with you again when you get back." Karl was manhandled to face the other way. "That's your driver over there. I'll leave you to it."

Konrad disappeared as mysteriously as he arrived. Karl walked to the car park, and the chauffeur, a smirking, blonde, high cheek-boned Aryan in his early twenties, approached him.

"Second Priest Dietrich, I am Trooper Lundquist. Please come with me, and I will transport you to your appointments." The young man had a Scandinavian lilt.

Karl smirked, pleased that they sent a driver. Hopefully, they had also sent a decent car, like a Mercedes, and not the ubiquitous kübelwagen. Lundquist's shoulders shook with mirth.

"What's funny, trooper?" Karl suspected Gothengau's usual mockery of Odinism.

"Nothing, sir."

"Then stop laughing and wipe that smile off your face, or I'll have you on a charge."

The white stubble on the back of Lundquist's head held Karl's attention until they reached the far side of the car park, when the Second Priest saw the vehicle. After a momentary disappointment, Karl seethed. The filthy, lopsided automobile sagged on one side. They drew closer to the car and it became increasingly obvious that the dirt prevented all the damaged bodywork being seen. Being driven around in the least-loved kübelwagen in the lot didn't give Karl a feeling of spirituality. Locals would laugh at him more than usual. Lundquist held the door open for Karl.

Karl slammed it shut behind him, almost catching the chauffeur's fingers. "Where are we going first?"

"The main temple." The driver started the car.

Karl moved the hair away from his eyes with his index finger. "The last time I was here, I left a list of instructions for it to be cleaned up and visited at least daily for prayers."

Lundquist didn't respond. Karl studied the back of his neck again for any signs of mirth, but only saw damaged skin. Lundquist needed a hat. His cracked, sun exposed dermis had fractures so deep it resembled rhino hide. A few minutes later, the brown grass gave way to an avenue of uniform, cubic white concrete houses. Crossroads intersected the street at monotonous intervals, Karl gripping the door handle tightly when Lundquist slowed down at the stop signs. Banners with Swastikas and SS runes hung from lampposts. Posters proclaimed Gothengau as the true Aryan homeland. People strolling by wore SS uniform or cowboy-casuals, most of them not acknowledging his passing. One old cowpoke, though, sauntered across the road, forcing Lundquist to slam on the brakes. The denim clad gaucho stared at Karl, spat, then shook his head with the same lazy rhythm that his moseying hips described.

The car sped on to the junction with the main square, passing more residences and a solitary dental surgery that stuck out like a missing incisor. While Lundquist waited to turn right, a charred newspaper blew across an ill-tended patch of grass adorned with a couple of lazy bushes and an idle willow. It smelled like there had been a barbecue. A pair of narrow, red Swastika banners ran down the two storeys from the building's roof to their fastenings on the ground. They framed the colonnaded portico whose grandeur contrasted with the rest of the dusty monochrome, functional Nazi party headquarters, its sealed windows flush with the walls.

The scorched broadsheet tumbled past the Reich's Ministry of Agriculture, which was so coated with ashes that the black on its sign merged with the white. Only the gold sword and wheatsheaf of the Ministry's icon showed through the soot.

"What the hell caused this?" Karl asked.

Lundquist's shoulders began bobbing up and down again, but Karl didn't feel a shred of pity. He knew the driver wasn't sobbing. The car turned a corner and revealed the origin of the cinders - the charred frame of the Odinist temple. Children played cowboys and Indians on the sacred smoking timbers. Angry thoughts squeezed through the gaps in Karl's reason, flushing his face and pushing his mouth open. He felt like he might breathe fire, but heat exploded from him as kinetic energy and his fist banged into the back of Lundquist's head. Emotional momentum stopped Karl from ending the assault, even though the chauffeur's skull injured Karl's knuckles a little more with each strike.

The driver covered his head with his hands before he leaned forward out of the path of Karl's fists. Karl stopped battering his assistant and sat back, exhausted, breathing hard, and nursing his fresh-scraped knuckles. The playing youngsters stood watching the fight, eyes wide.

Still Lundquist hadn't answered Karl, reigniting his rage. "So what happened here?"

"Looks like it burned down last night."

Karl held his fist to strike Lundquist again, but his calm side won the internal battle to keep punching. "What are you talking about?"

"I think there was a little disorder yesterday, and most of the temples caught fire."

"So why didn't you say that before we got here? Why didn't anybody tell me before I flew?"

A young man, blonde and barely shaving, wearing a ten-gallon hat stopped and stared. Karl simmered with anger at the lack of respect for Odinism in Gothengau, but his fury had ebbed. Now, Karl didn't really care enough to do something about it.

"Take me to Ostara, if it isn't a pile of ash as well."

"Ostara's still there, sir, don't worry about that. You have a new girl, sir, but the appointment isn't until this afternoon."

Electricity coursed through his member and shifted his attention from the conflict between Gothengau and Wewelsburg. If they had supplied him with a new partner, then the last one must be pregnant.

"It doesn't matter whether it's my turn or not, drive me there. Obviously, none of the Odinist practices have been observed. Now there aren't even any temples. I always end my day at Ostara when I'm here, and my day has definitely ended now. If I'm too early, then I will just make sure they follow the Odinist protocols. What's this new girl like, anyway?"

"Compelling."

Rage flashed from the riddle of an answer. "What's that supposed to mean?"

The driver didn't respond, but Karl lacked energy to press his point. Excitement quivered through the Second Priest's loins as they arrived at the clinic's antiseptic, white two storey buildings. Moistened pudendas at the top of toned thighs filled his mind's eye. How Pavlovian, Karl thought, that this everyday location fuelled his libido so much. When he got out of the car, Karl shifted his tunic to cover the bulge in his trousers.

His tumescence deflated when he walked into reception, until he looked at the magazines on the table. The woman on reception, wearing the purple satin folds of an SS Vestal, saw what caught his eye.

"Fancy some of that, do you?" When she winked, it emphasised the closeness of her blue eyes. "I'm Freya." She walked from behind her desk. "Follow me, Second Priest". Freya took Karl's elbow. "Your new girl awaits you."

Karl tugged his tunic over his crotch again. The woman went upstairs where the administration and surgeries sat. That's not where he normally went.

"Why are you taking me up here?"

"You are very privileged today. You are being treated to a new, experimental environment designed to increase conception rates."

"My fertility is more than good enough, though. I got the last girl pregnant, didn't I? Why not save this for the men that don't perform so well?"

"We want to study the results from our best men."

Karl rubbed against his cock. Well, that explains it. He was a better performer and got special treatment. Reassured, he went to the door. He'd show them how to shoot and hit. They reached the room at the end of the corridor. Usually, the chambers lined the hallways. Something about this nagged him. Nothing ordinary had happened. This could be some trap. He resisted taking another step.

"I'm not going in there. Something's wrong."

Freya stroked his penis through his pants. "Are you sure? Maybe I could join in as well, like in the magazine."

Oh yes, if that was on the menu then they could do anything. Whatever they did, wherever they took Karl, it didn't matter. Having two women doing what they did on that magazine cover meant all bets were off. He'd deal with his suspicions after the only pleasurable meeting of his trip. Karl took the Vestal by the hand and entered the room, where his almond-eyed new partner, a rope of brunette hair pillowing her head, lay naked on the bed. There didn't seem to be any difference in the chamber, despite it being an experimental environment. Once again, no Odinistic icons, perhaps because of the allegedly new surroundings, but that could wait until later. Nothing mattered for now, except increasing the Reich's population.

"I'm Second Priest Karl Dietrich."

"I'm Margarethe Zelle, but everyone calls me Mata."

Introductions over, Karl stepped forward and loosened his pants. The belt loops rested on his hard cock, before he tugged the fabric over it, and his rigid shaft sprang back up. No need to pull the tunic down now, my mast can fly free. Whose hand touched him? Masculine fingers pressed his shoulders. He should be the only man present. The world turned black. He had been right to suspect something. His lungs filled with the desiccated smell of sackcloth and old warehouses. Rough fabric scraped his face. A kick to the back of his knee pressed the bag to him when his head hit the ground. His buttock stung. Karl's eyes drooped, he forgot his bruised cheekbone, and drifted back to a childhood snowball fight in Minnesota. His father and the Church Elders looked down their noses at their simple games so close to the church and on the Sabbath. Thinking became too involved. Everything faded to black, then stopped.

Starting from a tingle in his feet, nausea crashed along his body. When Karl went to move forward, a head restraint kept him still. He was nude. A chill crawled across him. Vomit projected out across the floor and up into his nostrils, filling his nose with its acidic stench. The leather straps around his wrist and ankles stopped him wiping his mouth. Looking down, shock blasted any worries from Karl's mind. His balls were clamped. Pincers pulled his cock to an uncomfortable level of tension. A needle inside the apparatus touched his urethra. It whirred and moved forward. Agony forced its way out of Karl's screaming mouth. The device pushed further inside him. Tears poured down his cheeks. It didn't stop the burning, nor douse the fear bulldozing reason from his mind. Karl didn't know what he would do without his best friend. He had no idea what they were doing to it. Please don't cut it off. Please, I'll do anything you want. Please!

It must have gone the whole length. He felt something around his pubic bone. Suddenly, the device sprang back. He screamed. His member was still there. He panted a few times.

In front of him, a wall blazed in colour, completely filling his field of vision and stinging his eyes. A man, in the same chair as Karl, struggled against the same procedure inflicted on Karl. The camera panned back. He sat there, bemused until a small bang flashed between his legs. That got him screaming. It got Karl screaming. No longer a film, but a terrifying vision of Karl's own near future. The torn crimson root of the penis mocked its owner from the floor. They were going to blow his cock off.

He could not move his otherwise free hips. He trembled from the fear of something happening to his member. Stomach acid burned his lips and the odour of half-digested meals filled his nostrils. Karl spat but stopped when the drool ended up running down his cheek and matting his beard. His shoulders shook from a repressed sob. Drawing long, slow breaths took effort. A long groan emerged from Karl's bowels, wormed its way through his stomach and made contact with the outside world.

Levers clunked. His eyes shot left in search of the sound. Hinges squeaked. Hairs stood all over Karl's body. Slow, delicate footsteps approached. When they stopped, he heard breathing. Something squeezed and splashed. He screamed in terror of being abused with damp sponges and electric shocks. Fear didn't stop them. A cold, wet cloth wiped his last meal from his face and chest. Light movements like a woman. Floral smell like one, too. Occasionally, a flash of white uniform caught his eye. After leaving his field of vision the nurse tinkered with glassware. Karl smelled something antiseptic, then something cold dabbed his arm. Another injection to add to the others he couldn't rid himself of. Ankles and wrists again scraped against their bindings, but nothing Karl did could stop the needle puncturing his skin, nor prevent the syringe pushing deeper into him. Terror disappeared when she pressed the plunger. Agony ripped through him and eclipsed his fears. By the time she put stinging drops in his eyes, he didn't care how much they hurt. He whimpered, but Karl couldn't tell if tears accompanied the action. The painful liquid coating his eyeballs prevented it.

After the door opened, firm and purposeful footsteps approached Karl. The nurse and a man whispered about something. After a long pause they both laughed. The man paced toward the Second Priest again, breathing heavily just out of Karl's vision. Fear gripped Karl so fiercely that he only noticed his bladder emptying when his legs cooled down again. Accompanied by chuckles, the tips of a bolo tie dangled into Karl's face. Karl blinked, shifting his nose and lips to avoid the irritation. When the intruder backed away Karl saw Baer giggling at him.

"We at Gothengau have a favour to ask you. Our requirement will become apparent to you shortly. For what you are about to receive, we are truly grateful. If you do it and return here in three days, we might let you keep your tiny cock."

Baer and the nurse paced away from Karl and the door closed. Lights went out. The room remained dark and silent. Besides his pounding heart and rasping breath, Karl heard and saw nothing. Trying to remain tranquil, Karl counted his breaths. His panting slowed down, and by the time his inhalations numbered 117, the wall became a giant screen that filled his entire field of vision. Strong white noise played on it, the brightness and contrast punishing Karl's eyes. A low hum reverberated through his torso, and the urine-drenched chair vibrated against his clammy skin.

Anticipation of coming events turned to impatience when nothing changed. The terror of losing his penis returned to haunt Karl when nothing else occupied him. He swallowed several times to rid himself of the feeling in his neck, but it only increased his awareness of the object's presence.

Dots on the screen coalesced to form moving images. Swirling kaleidoscopic visions that occasionally revealed severed penises and their screaming owners. He closed his eyes, but they burned until he reopened them. The low hum that resonated through Karl became a discordant clash of agonizing commotion, filling his ears and eclipsing his thoughts.

"Kill Drachenblut." A woman whispered the order.

Between the pain of the pulsating, discordant noises she repeated herself.

"We will call."

Despite his discomfort, something compelled Karl to concentrate on the distressing beat. He picked out many voices in the rhythm. A legion of inflexions urging murder. Karl just wanted to hear the woman's voice again, in the same way that he had wanted mother as a child. He needed it more than anything. Karl almost begged to hear her command him again.

"When the images end, you will only remember to wait for the call."

A relay clunked, the screen went blank, and the room flooded with fluorescent light. Karl's eyeballs seared from the pale, flickering illumination. Two pairs of footsteps paced to him – the nurse's and Baer's.

"How did you like that, Karl?"

Karl shivered with fear and couldn't answer. He just had to take that call.

"We're giving you some delayed action strength for your task."

The nurse reached underneath Karl. His rectum felt a clammy touch. Answer the phone. He winced when a bony finger went up there. Strain and get it out. Most importantly, wait for the call.

"That Pervitin will stay up there before it starts working." Baer laughed. "No way can you push that out. You've shat yourself enough for a week!"

Even through the hypnotism Karl felt shame at the brown mess on the floor beneath him. At least the seat had a hole through it. He didn't wallow in his own filth.

"If you're back in three days, with the job done, we might let you keep your pride and joy. Now get dressed and go."

Once Karl had tied up the last laces on his uniform, the room went dark. A beautiful scent of flowers accompanied the loud hiss. A pasture appeared beneath him, and he lay down on it to better inhale the luscious aroma.

Karl found himself standing in the departure lounge standing next to his bags. He had a large, new case holding the telescope to give Drachenblut. All he needed to do was stay calm until they called.

Chapter 15

Gothengau, Monday, May 3rd, 1965.

Morsels of apple strudel remained on the Lapp family's plates. Apart from Konrad, nobody else had quite finished their Sunday lunch, but the meal's only formality was the clothing. He would speak. Sitting around the white, country table in the dining room was the safest place for them in Gothengau. Konrad tapped the table. The other four looked up, their raised eyebrows and wide eyes demonstrating surprise at the interruption.

"Thank you for the lovely food, Diana. I can't be quiet though: I will not lose this family."

"What's the matter, dad?" asked Mary.

Diana's pupils dilated. "Are we in danger?"

He had to be honest. "We always are." Now, however, it was clear and omnipresent, the threat higher than normal. "This time it's different. You and the girls must leave Gothengau in the next few days."

"Where? My parents don't have the room for all of us now the kids are so big, and we don't have the money to stay in hotels forever." Her eyes darted around the room before they focused on the napkin twisted in her clenched fists.

Konrad put a hand on hers. "That's not a problem, really. You'll be safer in a Wehrmacht base, anyway."

"Me and the girls, on an army base?" She snatched her hand back to carry on wringing the cloth. "How long will that go on for? What will we do all day? Why's this happening? Konrad, what have you done?"

"It's because of the May Day attack. And that's all I can tell you."

A loud rap on the front door made Diana jump. Konrad faced the window, and he'd seen nobody passing. His whole family seemed to cower in fear. Maybe they were right. Perhaps this wasn't any knock on the door. It could be *the* knock on the door, the one when nobody ever saw them again. A bicep flinched uncontrollably.

"Is anybody expecting visitors?"

"No," answered Diana. The children shook their heads.

"Then I'll go."

Plates and cutlery rattled when Konrad stood. Although butterflies fluttered in his solar plexus, Konrad strode to the dining room door, confidently entering the hallway. Biting his lip, his fist pulled the door wide open.

Konrad interrupted Aurelian mid-knock, his Bolo tie flying up. A reason for the colonial second-in-command's visit escaped Konrad. Maybe Aurelian's secret children had told him of their encounter with the paratroop commander, and Aurelian needed help.

"Has something happened?"

"Baer wants you to come over to his house. There's a visitor there who he insists you meet."

"Who is it?"

"Doctor Mengele."

Mengele's attention to Konrad disturbed him. The doctor's curiosity had stood the test of time. Mengele had been prodding and poking at Konrad since he arrived in the Fatherland.

"He likes you, doesn't he? It's written all over your face. Mengele loves specimens like you."

"He's taken a interest in me since I joined the SS."

"I know." Aurelian nodded. "It's obvious if you look in the right places."

"What do you mean?"

"I can't say, but you'll find out soon enough."

Even though Aurelian goaded him with crumbs of a story, he affirmed Konrad's lingering suspicion about Mengele somehow using Konrad for experiments. His eyes rested on Aurelian, who shifted his weight from one denim-clad leg to the other.

"I'll follow you."

The Gentle Giant only turned for a moment to don his black shoes and jacket, but by then Aurelian drove away. Konrad bade his family farewell, took the car keys and got in the kübelwagen, already some way behind Aurelian.

Konrad parked next to Aurelian's Mercedes and bounded up the patio. He reached Baer's office, but only Baer and Aurelian sat under the chandelier at the conference table.

"Konrad! Glad you got here so fast."

"Where's Mengele?"

"Should be here now, really. Mengele said he would be, but these intelligent types can be absent minded now and again. I'd forgotten how he is."

Behind Konrad, the door opened.

"Speak of the Devil!" Baer stood to greet Mengele.

Only the doctor wore the SS uniform, and he carried a doctor's bag and a varnished black wooden box. The cap hid his eyes, helping its skull and crossbones emblem defeat the innocence of the man's gapped incisors.

Mengele craned his neck to look Konrad in the eye. "Heil Gothengau, gauleiter."

"Enough with the formalities, Josef! Imagine it's like the old days back in the camp." Baer's jowls moved slower than the rest of his face, producing a wave of flesh when he shook his head. "Such times we had! What have you brought with you?"

Mengele sauntered over to Baer and Aurelian. Konrad followed.

"It's such a long time since I visited your house, and I didn't get you a wedding gift either. I present you with this to help rekindle our old friendship." Mengele placed the box before Baer.

"You shouldn't have." Baer unbuckled the clasp holding the front half of the trunk closed.

"I believe these are considered a high honour by many." Mengele smiled proudly. "This might be the first time I've had the pleasure of supplying you with one."

Baer gently opened the coffer. The contents, a gleaming white human skull with pearly teeth, besides one gaudy yellow incisor, grinned back at the room.

"Ah yes! One of your famous heads."

"I love the gold crown," said Aurelian.

"Yes, it did it for me too." Mengele grinned. "The moment I saw the gold tooth with otherwise perfect dentition, I knew you had to have his head. He was a big Russian brute, the size of a gorilla but half as intelligent. He came into the clinic complaining about his feet. Fallen arches aren't a problem for him anymore."

Baer stood and shook Mengele's hand. "In return, I present you with Konrad Lapp for your perusal."

Konrad coughed. He wasn't a possession to be offered to friends. Recent events had brought Baer and Mengele's true nature to light, regardless of Konrad's former aversion to such details. Konrad's head felt like a pressure cooker. These monsters passed him around like a box of chocolates. It pushed him closer to bursting out of his self-imposed restraint.

"Konrad, it's good to see you again." The doctor's head leant back to look Konrad full in the eye.

Mengele stuck his hand out, but Konrad looked away. The doctor opened his bag and produced two sacks. Konrad's neck bristled with fear of the contents. Holding Konrad's gaze, the doctor stretched the elasticated opening of each one until it snapped back in place. Konrad's forearms clenched, straining his white shirt's cuffs. A button popped off. Everybody chuckled, but Konrad forced his laughter.

Konrad's mind relaxed after Mengele put the bags over his shoes and stepped to Baer's desk, back ramrod straight. Konrad followed, getting there after Mengele stood on it. He looked Konrad in the eye with a light while he issued sympathetic clucking noises and spoke notes into a voice recorder. Konrad could only tolerate Mengele's presence if he closed his eyes and imagined himself far away, on a Minnesota winter's morning knee deep in fresh powder. In this part of the examination he couldn't. At least the red light shining into his pupils blocked his vision, and Konrad fancied it as snow blindness in his fantasy world.

"I've never understood why the doctor pays me such detailed attention."

"You are an incredible specimen of humanity." Mengele had a nasal voice. "You hark back to ancient giants of the Teutonic forests. I dream of making a race of men like you."

"Could you imagine that Konrad?" asked Baer. "A race of super-humans with enormous courage, just like you. Mengele is a visionary. He has a dream like your friend Wernher von Braun."

"That is your dream, but now you are awake." There had to something concrete for Konrad to hang his guess work on, not just Mengele's vision. "What are you going to do about it right now?"

"An academic paper: Choosing the Attributes in Descendants. It's about inheritance, and how the better features of parents can be forced into their offspring."

"Will I be able to read it when you've finished?"

"No, it's classified. Most of my work is."

"Even I can't see it," Aurelian said. "I know where it's going though, if you look hard enough you'll find out yourself."

Baer glared at his underling. "I'm cleared to read it. Believe me, you'd love it."

Doubt nagged Konrad. Cloning wasn't yet possible, although he had read stories filled with similar far-fetched possibilities.

Mengele got down from the desk. "Please sit on the desk, Konrad."

"We could use men like that to take over the Reich." Baer said. "The Fatherland's gone adrift. Nazi ideologies aren't being followed by Berlin. Himmler and Heydrich have been taken in by the pagan bullshit that Drachenblut peddles."

"Yes." Mengele tapped a mallet on Konrad's knee. "It should be up to men of science to take our country forward, not some hairy heathens in an old castle."

"Surely we don't need to wait for these supermen to appear." Aurelian scowled. "We have the armour, the artillery and the rockets to do it tomorrow!"

Mengele found the right spot on Konrad's leg, and Konrad's foot flew out. "You have an excellent patellar reflex, Konrad. One of the strongest I've seen."

"Ach." Baer waved his hand. "We have no air cover. We'd need an all-out rocket assault on all the Luftwaffe bases in the Reich."

Aurelian dovetailed his responses to Baer and built a solid discussion. Neither of them seemed remotely surprised by each other's treachery. Konrad recognised the practised parries and returns of a well-worn conversation.

"That is a commitment to civil war!" Mengele hadn't heard this topic before. "Under what circumstances would you do that?"

Mengele stuck a swab in Konrad's mouth. Thank God that the doctor hadn't injected anything into Konrad. He had a mouthful of healthy teeth, made better by American dentistry, and he didn't want his skull to end up as someone's ornament.

"It's funny you should mention it, Mengele. But we reached the last straw earlier. The so-called Führer wants me to divorce my two beauties and marry Helga Goebbels."

"That's taking Roman traditions a bit far." Mengele's unction oozed out through his smirk.

"Well, we're kind of sure it's an Odinist idea. And plans are underfoot to rid us of that bloody heathen for good. If that doesn't stop this marriage nonsense, then there will be consequences."

Both Gothengau and the Wehrmacht had the same idea: get Drachenblut out of the picture and use his funeral as cover for a takeover. Konrad and Petra set Karl on the case of killing the High Priest, so Konrad racked his brains to figure out Baer's scheme. He and Petra only had persuasion and blackmail to direct Karl. With the likes of Mengele at his disposal, Konrad feared what they had done to Karl. It looked like Drachenblut's days were numbered, and the Reich would be safe from his delusions. Having Baer's mad urges replace them would be worse.

Mengele pressed Konrad's palms against his own. "Push back against my hands. Good progress. Almost identical."

That irked Konrad enough to ask a question. There was only so much prodding and poking a man could take. "What progress? Almost identical to what?"

"Oh, typical progression of ageing, identical to an average adult male." Mengele became straight-lipped and less sincere now he had his back to Baer and Aurelian. Offset against the skull he wore on his lapels, Mengele's penetrating gaze, delta hairline, and sneering mouth scared Konrad. "It's nothing for you to worry about."

Getting told that always made Konrad concerned. He hadn't worried about what had gone on in the Final Solution because he hadn't asked. He had helped people, though. Those days hadn't gone yet: Baer and his cronies kept them alive. The skull, on such open display, represented something that had been hidden from him before. Mengele ordered Konrad to hold each arm outstretched and then touch his nose. The Baer wives entered.

"Please meet my Domina Heidi and wife Irma."

"I'm Heidi." The senior wife cocked her head to one side with a strained smile.

Mengele turned to face the Baer twins. He bared his teeth, the smile hiding his eyes. Konrad took it the nose touching part of the programme had ended and let his arms rest.

Baer raised an eyebrow. "What brings you two here?"

"Please don't let me stop them from joining." Mengele rubbed his hands together. "I don't believe we've ever met."

"There's a reason for that. Your thing with twins back at Auschwitz."

"Oh no." Mengele waved his hand. "That was for science! I'm a seeker after truth."

Some of the truths that Mengele sought were nothing more earth-shattering than changing the eye colour of one twin but not the other. The siblings used were disposed of cruelly afterwards. Those with healthy teeth would be decapitated and have the flesh removed from their severed heads in the crematorium.

"I can prove nothing with your wives that you aren't aware of. They are beautiful, strong Aryan women." Mengele oozed over to the sister-wives and kissed their hands. "Excellent breeding. I can tell by their scent. You will have no problem with your offspring, not with these genes mixed with yours."

"I have heard of genes," Aurelian said. "They determine what our children will get, yes?"

"That is one thing they do." Mengele nodded. "They do much we still have to learn."

Konrad understood Aurelian's line of questioning. He skipped something his children in the cellar hadn't. Aurelian risked revealing an unhealthy amount about his circumstances.

"Worried about your new arrival at Ostara, Aurelian?" Baer asked. "When's the baby's due?"

Aurelian took risks. Having children in the Lebensborn programme shoved the deputy Gauleiter into the limelight. The risks were clear to Aurelian, who had a role in disposing of such progeny. Konrad wondered why he made himself an easy target.

"Soon." Aurelian's voice broke. "Less than a month, I believe. I just want to be sure that they get the best part of me."

Konrad couldn't work out why Aurelian swam in such dangerous waters.

"What about traits that skip a generation? My father was left-handed, and so are my kids, but I use my right hand. Always have."

"Ah yes. That's just rolling the dice. I intend to make the dice less fair so that the best features come through every time. If they don't come through, then the results work well for experimentation."

"You're asking questions like there's more to it than the hand you write with." Baer tapped the desk and leaned forward. "Is there something bigger worrying you?"

"No, of course not. My lineage was approved years ago."

"Then you must be worried about what your wives will bring to the table," said Mengele. "I don't know how thorough research into a Czech or a French woman can be, but that's an old-fashioned method anyway. Soon, I will be able to tell from body tissue what an individual's actual background is. After that, the methods we use now will be thought quite stone age!"

"So why would you be worried about your partner at Ostara?" Baer asked. "Isn't she Swedish? She was checked out thoroughly before she joined the programme, but you can tell how pure she is just by looking at her. You pulled the long straw with that one!"

Whether Baer bantered threateningly or not, Konrad watched Aurelian carefully. The edges of his mouth trembled. If Konrad hadn't been examining him so closely, he wouldn't have seen it.

"I studied her myself," said Mengele. "A beautiful specimen. My nose found no fault with her scent, only aromas of fecundity and the Nordic Subgroup of the Aryan race."

Where Mengele got the scent samples, Konrad resisted asking once he realised. "These are things that any man would worry about." The other three looked around at Konrad. "With the complexity of nature, how can anyone predict what will happen?"

Aurelian looked over, eyes wide. "Yes! It's so complicated, how can anything actually be predicted? I just worry about my kids. I always have."

Mengele had no more studies to make of Konrad. The doctor's interest had been piqued by Aurelian's home truths.

A good time for Konrad to make his excuses. "If you've finished with your examination, then I'll make my way home."

"I should go too," Aurelian said. "I have plenty to be getting on with."

Both the guests returned to their cars. When they stepped off the patio, Konrad turned to Aurelian.

"I know why you asked Mengele about skipping generations."

The corner of Aurelian's mouth went into a larger spasm now they were outside.

"I can help you."

"I know something about you, too." Aurelian winked. "Mengele has done something with you, and I don't think you're going to like it."

Konrad returned to his cloning nightmare. Mengele couldn't do that. Nobody could do that.

"What's he done?"

"I can't say, but you're going to find out soon enough."

Chapter 16

Wewelsburg, Monday, May 3rd, 1965.

Wait for the call. Rubber screeched on tarmac and the seat under Karl shuddered. Keep your manhood attached. Through the window, Wewelsburg castle slowed to a standstill. Karl clasped the seatbelt buckle and tensed his calves ready to spring. He aimed to be first out of the plane, hence his seat next to the door. Once the aircraft approached taxiing speed, he flicked the metal flap on his safety strap and stood.

"Please remain in your seat." The stewardess facing him scowled.

Orders from beautiful women normally received near-instant compliance from Karl, but not today. If Karl didn't answer that call, he would be no use to any woman again. He had to stay a man. Nothing else mattered but answering that call. Karl got his bag from the overhead compartment and rested his hand on the door release.

"Sir, please!"

Karl didn't move.

"Sir, please remove your hand from the exit." She repeated this sentiment several times before the aircraft arrived at the stand, each time edging her closer to tears.

She no longer existed for Karl. Miraculously her beauty blended into the walls, her pleading merged with the engine noise. The air-stairs clunked against the plane and Karl pushed the handle down. He raced down and across to the terminal. There were stares from other passengers when he ran through the baggage area, but that didn't matter. Only keeping his manhood mattered. They would tell him how when he got the call. Karl saw the parking lot through the front windows. No shortage of kübelwagens, so no holdups getting to the castle now.

On reaching the best-looking car, Karl threw the bag on the back seat and hopped in. The keys were in the ignition. At the third attempt, Karl felt impatience bubbling up, but before he cried out in rage, the engine caught. Less than a minute later, the wind of the autobahn streamed his long hair behind him. Wind pulling at his hair and beard fired him up for the doubly-booked task ahead. He left at the next exit, hardly slowing down. At the first bend, the car's tyres screeched. The machine slipped along the road, back wheels faster than front. Karl steered into the skid, stopping the vehicle spinning. He avoided flying off the highway and pressed on the brakes heavily, fighting the steering wheel, until the car stopped.

Karl didn't know if he had waited for two seconds or two hours. With clarity, he put the car back in gear and rejoined the highway. Confident again, he paced himself around the winding forest lanes up to the castle. The scents of pine and elm filled his nostrils, infusing him with more vigour. The kübelwagen leaned into the corners snugly, dividing its ascent into sections with metronomic precision. Its slow rhythm lent momentum to Karl and imbued his deadly purpose with more potential.

On the final bend, the light at the end of the verdant tunnel shone through the forest's edge. The castle's south facing side appeared. Gravel shot from under the kübelwagen's tyres when Karl slammed on the brakes. The sentry shielded his face from the flying stones before approaching the car.

"Fetch the bags from my car and take them to my quarters." Karl got out, leaving the engine running. "Be careful. One of them is a telescope, a valuable gift for the High Priest. Keep your hands off it."

Karl ran into the castle and up the spiral stairs to Drachenblut's first-floor chambers. The sprint from the kübelwagen hardly raised his pulse at all. He rapped on the studded wooden door to Drachenblut's office, astonished but unsurprised by his complete lack of breathlessness.

"Enter."

Karl pushed the door aside and strode into the room, shoulders thrown back. He marched to the desk, where Drachenblut stood looking away from Karl. Should Karl wait, as usual, or state his business and arrange to meet the High Priest on the North Tower? Karl would wait on the High Priest no more. He opened his mouth to speak.

"Go back to Gothengau." Karl almost flailed his fingers out when the High Priest beat him to it.

Karl's mouth hung open. His Gothengau programming couldn't compute this new input. On the desk, the phone rang. Answer the call! Karl's arm shot out automatically, but Drachenblut's hand hovered over the receiver.

"No time for gawping. Go right away!"

Drachenblut picked the phone up.

"This is the call?"

Karl knew which call.

"You have the wrong number."

No, they just had the wrong person.

"Why would I kill myself?"

Drachenblut winced, shoved a finger in his ear and slammed the phone back down. Karl caught the noise, and it reminded him of something, but he could not place what that was.

"Why are you still here?"

Karl fished around for other important news to relate to Drachenblut, maybe that would change the High Priest's mind. "They burned down all the temples."

At last, Drachenblut turned to face Karl, but he didn't appear shaken by the revelation. Karl parted his hair with his index finger. Surely that information would compel the High Priest to give the colony space to breathe, relax, and think? Some time to calm down. Doing nothing could sometimes be the best option.

"All the more reason to return, then. You must show them that we mean business, that Odinism will increase in strength. Why ever didn't you tell Baer and his wives that we need their divorce certificates?"

"Because I didn't have it in writing, and I don't have a death wish."

"You should have used initiative. If I didn't tell you, it's because I didn't need to. It was implied. Come now, you are my right hand." Drachenblut chopped the air with outstretched palm. "You, of all people, should have faith that the gods will protect you from the terror of Richard Baer and his cronies. Are you not my closest and truest disciple?"

Did the High Priest have any supernatural knowledge? That question stood an indeterminate distance from the truth, but a short distance from Karl's lips. He opened his mouth.

Drachenblut got the first word in again. Karl hopped with rage without moving a muscle. "Don't worry, though. Your team are available now, and you may go armed if you feel the gods' protection is inadequate."

"But I have a gift I must present to you. And we need to discuss a new portrait of you, one where your prescience and stellar knowledge are displayed."

Drachenblut stared at Karl. "Are you drunk? Have you been at the mushroom tea? You heard my orders, now carry them out."

The hypnotism and Pervitin that Karl received in Gothengau withstood Drachenblut's strength for now, but Karl's confidence eroded under the radiation streaming from the German religion's leader.

"Of course not, High Priest. The idea of performing those services for you, it filled me with so much honour, and I'm disappointed it will not happen today."

"It will happen when we both have time. It will be difficult to get up there alone with me, though."

Without mention of the tower, Drachenblut knew Karl's plans. The High Priest's lofty glare ground Karl's self-possession down. Karl stood to leave before the High Priest scrubbed through the veneer and uncovered the truth.

"I'll get the men together and return to Gothengau as soon as I can."

"Good thinking." Drachenblut never complimented his underlings.

Normally, such praise from a superior would have Karl reading into each word for hidden meaning. Not this time. Karl didn't look around when he marched to find weapons and his crew of priests. Maybe he could encourage Hegel and Rolf to come along. Drachenblut left Karl's mind the moment the High Priest left his sight. Karl walked down the corridor to his office and picked up the phone. Armed or not, Hadwin quaked nobody with fear and Olaf could barely fight his way through his clothing. Hegel had to come along with them. Karl dialled his number.

"Hegel, it's Karl."

"What do you want?"

"Wondered if you'd like a sunny vacation." Karl played his hand straight away to counter the tone in Hegel's voice. "I'll be visiting the breeding clinic. I can't guarantee any action for you, but there's a very good chance you'll get some, too."

Hegel didn't reply, and Karl let him think about the offer.

"It's in Gothengau, isn't it?"

"Of course."

"Can I bring Rolf with me? I don't fancy Olaf or Hadwin's chances if there's any, you know, trouble or anything."

There will be trouble, but Karl had to keep his tail between his legs. Not on the floor.

"That would be alright. We're going right away. Get your things and meet in the car park."

"Give me five minutes." Hegel put the phone down.

It had been a while since he'd seen Grimhilt, and they hadn't discussed the weddings that Drachenblut proposed. Karl turned to look from the window. The Vestal House opposite looked occupied, so he trotted through the corridor and over the moat's bridge. When he reached the Vestal House, Grimhilt appeared. She ran over before regaining her calm and pacing delicately towards her secret lover. Her poise, so elegant, drove pangs of love into Karl's heart. They couldn't speak here. Karl turned and led Grimhilt back over the bridge and into the tunnel where they were less easily seen and less likely overheard.

Grimhilt turned. "Drachenblut's making me marry the Memel-Narev gauleiter."

"I know." Karl brought a layer of dew to Grimhilt's eyes.

"If you knew, why didn't you tell me?"

"Because I'm working on changing it. I have to go to Gothengau soon, but when I return things are going to change. You are going to be my High Priestess."

"Not if you still go to Ostara so regularly. Why can't you just want me?"

Before Karl could think of an answer, he saw he didn't have to. A detachment of guards marched across the courtyard, heading in their direction.

"Well, of course there will be ramifications from these political marriages."

"What?" Grimhilt's perplexed expression eased when she heard the soldiers' boots getting closer. "Yes, things will never be the same for us. Our hopes, dreams, everything's been pushed back since we were told about this." She could be such a whiner, given she had everything on a plate. "I feel for our replacements. At least we hoped of a normal life afterwards." Grimhilt never wanted a normal life. She didn't even know what one was. "The new virgins will know better, but that will make them resentful and bitter. If they act up, then the public won't love them like they do us."

The guards halted. Their sergeant spoke.

"We are your detachment for your Gothengau visit, Second Priest Dietrich. Drachenblut ordered us to accompany you."

"Are you blind?" Outrage flared Karl's nostrils. "Can't you see I'm in conversation with Vestal Grimhilt? Wait for me in the car park, my accompanying priests are yet to show themselves."

"With all respect, sir, I'm afraid that's wrong. The other priests sent us to find you. Everybody is ready to leave now."

There were no more excuses. Persistence would bring suspicion to their relationship.

"Good day to you, Vestal. Follow me, men."

They strode through the corridor and around the castle to the car park, where Hegel had the passenger seat while Hadwin, Olaf, and burly Rolf squeezed in the kübelwagen's back seat. Karl took the empty driving seat. The guards took the next vehicle, and Karl drove his entourage to the airport in a silence which he found comfortable. Icy, pained expressions on the others' faces didn't disturb his inner contentment.

Four hours later, Karl touched down in Gothengau again. Karl let his guards and entourage exit the flight first where his escort formed an honour guard at the foot of the steps. Descent into that warmed Karl's self-image. He waved aside the guard's salute like Caesar. Head tilted back, peering imperiously down his nose, Karl imagined himself to look like an Emperor as well. Wearing his Odinist uniform made him look more like a Vandal, there to sack Rome. Karl didn't know which fantasy suited the situation best, so he took the vain option and imagined himself Roman.

He led his men through the arrivals' hall, where everybody stopped to stare. They emerged into an area where many drivers waited in their vehicles. Karl quickly scanned them, finding all but one inadequate for himself and his crew. A black, twenty-seat bus seemed perfect for his use. He turned to the leader of the guard.

"Requisition that." Karl pointed to the jalopy.

Immediately the soldier turned to his colleagues. The four of them talked rapidly then ran to the bus. The two junior guards pulled the driver from his seat by his armpits and he sailed out of the door. He shouted then hit the tarmac. While Karl and his men boarded, the vehicle's former keeper kept his mouth shut and let his bloody, grazed face and waving fist speak for him.

"Take me to Baer's ranch."

The driving seat's original occupant had got up by the time Karl's contingent drove away and his voice had returned. They ignored the man's sacrilegious cursing. Karl had orders to obey. Karl had strength. But he wanted more.

When they drove under the "work will set you free" arch to Baer's ranch, the mounted soldiers overseeing the field slaves stared at the busload of Odinist priests. Some shook their heads at the charabanc. Others spat. Nobody saluted.

Karl nodded at Rolf and Hegel when he got off the bus. They had rifles. Karl wouldn't go in there on his own, unarmed. Baer might do anything. Rolf and Hegel accompanied Karl up the patio steps past the goose-stepping sentries and into the ranch. Karl marched to the end of the corridor. Aurelian already peeked through the crack in his door. He swung it open and blocked their way.

"Why are you here?" Aurelian raised both palms and an eyebrow. "This isn't a drop-in centre for Occultists, you know. You have to arrange it beforehand."

Baer's door opened behind Aurelian. The gauleiter stepped into the middle of the corridor, hands resting on pistols like a black-clad gunslinger. Karl heard rifles being cocked behind him: his new acolytes had his back. Aurelian stepped back into his office. Its lock sounded immediately he closed the door. Baer paused for a second more, and then took his hands slowly from the revolvers.

"Let's talk in here." Baer showed his palm to Karl's new followers as they moved forward. "Alone."

Baer closed the door. Karl ignored the deep, wide mahogany desk, and strode to the conference area. The furniture and the décor would suit a bordello on the American frontier: the red and gold walls were festooned with cattle heads and ornate mirrors, and the illumination came from a chandelier. Karl sat in a chair without waiting to be invited.

"What are you doing here?"

"I missed the call. When it came in, Drachenblut answered it himself. He suspects something. I need more men for my plan to succeed. You need to do what you did to me to the two priests outside. Three of us can easily overpower the High Priest."

"Is there anything else you'd like, your holiness? Should I kneel and kiss your ring?"

Mockery angered Karl enough to seek vengeance. The time arrived to tell Baer how things were.

"Himmler ordered you to divorce your wives and marry Helga Goebbels."

Baer scowled. They both looked around when Baer's desk banged. A petite blonde woman stood from under it, rubbing her head. The action of her hand shortened her denim dress, showing she only wore cowboy boots beneath her frock. She rapidly dropped her arm and tugged her dress down when she met Karl's eyes.

"That's Domina Heidi." Baer introduced his senior wife.

Heidi curtsied, but Karl neither bowed nor clicked his heels. An identical woman crawled from under the desk and stood next to Heidi.

"And I'm Irma," she announced with a curtsy.

After seeing Heidi's bush, Karl's erotic imagination started working overtime. Baer had it all.

"You want me to divorce these two and marry that red-haired bitch? Helga's always had an awful reputation, and I never thought much of her cripple father, either."

That comment stopped Karl. Even though his back-up stood outside, Baer still had the temerity to crudely denigrate one of the Reich's most senior figures.

"I wouldn't call Goebbels a cripple." Karl manoeuvred around the truth. "He needs a leg calliper occasionally, that's all."

"And he's the size of a rat, a weedy little thing. Not a good example of Aryan manhood, I don't care how he paints himself."

Heidi flared her nostrils and curled her lip. "Ugly, too."

"I bet it's like a maggot." Irma wiggled her little finger.

To Karl, pot-bellied, balding Baer hardly matched the physical characteristics of an *übermensch* either. Not exactly a gift to the opposite sex. Tall, broad, handsome Karl fitted the description of an Aryan much better than many of the senior members of the Fatherland. It was Karl's turn to get some action.

"Himmler decreed the colonies be bound to the Reich by marriage with the Vestal Virgins. You were chosen to marry the Chief Vestal. It's a great honour."

"This is too much. Himmler can decree anything he wants. I'm not giving up these two treasures." Baer swiped the air with his hand. "Those antiquated marriages can stay in the past. It's only given me more reason to get rid of Drachenblut."

Baer got up and moseyed over to the phone on his desk. "Aurelian can handle the new brainwashings." He dialled one number and immediately received an answer. "It's Baer. Arrange three more indoctrinations. The Drachenblut plan needs more manpower."

Strength ebbed from Karl after Baer ordered three reprogrammings. Who the third one applied to, he couldn't work out. He could hear Aurelian confirming the request from the room next door. Baer set the phone down and came back to Karl.

"It's done. But the process lasts at least twenty-four hours."

"We were planning to stay overnight. Is it still set up at the breeding centre?"

Baer confirmed with a nod.

"Then we should send those two over there." Karl strode towards the door.

When Karl put his head into the corridor, Hegel and Rolf straightened their slouch. Now he had respect.

"Two of the lady volunteers at the breeding centre are at their most fertile today, but their partners are unavailable. The Gauleiter's offered you their place at Ostara."

Hegel smiled and winked, nudging Rolf with his elbow. "Just like you told us, boss. Never got anything like this from Drachenblut."

Aurelian struggled to unlock the door before he opened it. "I'm arranging this treat for you. Please, follow me."

Aurelian stepped toward the door, followed closely by Hegel and Rolf. When they left the building, Karl returned to Baer.

"After you've disposed of Drachenblut, will all this marriage nonsense be off the table?"

"I don't know." Karl shrugged, but nervously, not like earlier. "These weddings are his idea, but he has a hold over Himmler and Heydrich. Even with Drachenblut gone, they might still be under his influence."

"Then this idea has had the opposite effect to the one Drachenblut intended. It has cleaved the Reich in two. I'm not playing along with stupid ideas, not if they spoil my family's happiness."

His wives both stood behind him, rubbing his shoulders and gazing at him and each other. If their smugness were sunlight, Karl would be tanned mahogany brown by now.

"Look at what we three have here. Himmler can go to hell: there'll be no divorce so there'll be no wedding!"

The opportunity to tell Helga the Chief Vestal that she'd been rejected brought a smile to Karl's lips. Karl wouldn't pass that message along to Drachenblut, though. Not until he saw him toppling from the North Tower of Wewelsburg castle. By then it would be too late for him to do anything about it.

"Someone is outside to show you to your room. You need rest for the task ahead of you."

All-powerful feelings ebbing, Karl also knew he could use a breather. He stood and walked to the door, touching the handle.

"Is it in this building?"

"No."

Nowhere else possessed the luxury of Baer's ranch. Other locations in Gothengau showed more Spartan cleanliness and order than elsewhere in the Reich. Gothengau resembled Sparta, but in Gothengau the soldier-lovers had different genders.

In the hall, Karl thought that four people were a little excessive to show him to his place. Until they pounced - then it made sense. They had him held by each limb and seemed immune to his struggling. Incomprehension on his face, he cried out.

"What's this? What's this?"

"The brainwashing only lasts another day. Yours is wearing off right now. I can see it." Baer wagged a finger. "Don't worry, though. We booked a refresher course for you."

Chapter 17

Gothengau, Monday, May 3rd, 1965.

Konrad arrived at the airfield first. When he drove with the roof down, the breeze relieved the sunburn but now that the car stood motionless his exposed skin's discomfort intensified. Minutes after parking at the end of the runway, humidity plastered fine hair all over his scalp. Two hours' drive inland from the Crimean Peninsula the still air gave no respite from the sticky heat. The adjacent landing strip's black tarmac radiated the fieriness it had spent all morning absorbing. Air shimmered above it. In the distance, the low, parched hills danced and on the runway pools of liquid appeared. Konrad smacked away a fly biting his arm when he reached into the glove compartment for a pair of field glasses. To escape the tarmac's torrid warmth he put distance between himself and the car.

The sun burned his neck where his collar rubbed the skin. Some steps away, he put the binoculars to his face. After scanning the western sky for a minute, Konrad found his target: a speck that carried Wernher and his technicians here for their rocket-tracking assignment.

A bus and two staff cars drew up. The long, graceful Mercedes waited for Wernher and his senior officers while the charabanc for the technicians idled. None of the chauffeurs bothered getting out, the flying wing plainly visible a few kilometres away. Rubber squealed when it finished its descent on the landing strip's other end. The bus driver opened his door and his slight form hopped to the ground.

Brakes screamed as the aircraft raced towards the vehicles. Drivers leapt from the three machines. The plane's rear lifted up when it came to a halt, tilting the nose close to the soil beyond the runway. Konrad got ready to spring away. The booming when the back wheels slapped back down again eased Konrad's worries and he relaxed. After the chassis stopped shuddering, steps descended from the plane's belly. Moments later, Wernher's tall, elegant form walked down to the tarmac, followed by his team. All wore the Reich Space Agency's silver uniform. Konrad strolled towards the rocket scientist.

"Great that you could come here so soon. Baer is up to something."

Wernher turned and waved in greeting. "Great to see you again, Konrad! Thank you for meeting us."

"I had to, really. Feelings against the Reich are running quite high. It wouldn't be wise for you to be here without an escort, The media keeps on putting out such negative Gothengau stories, everyone around here's on edge."

Wernher's smile evaporated. "Will we be in contact with the public today?"

"We'll only be travelling to the depot, that's where the missiles are stored, but there might be some vocal opposition from the staff there."

"Aren't there any rockets on patrol at the moment?"

"No." Konrad shook his head. "Baer suspended the patrols, and now all the launchers are back."

"Then at least the Reich is safe from the Reds. I worry about Baer controlling the missiles, though. The Fatherland isn't safe from him or Berlin."

Konrad and Wernher waited near the bus until all his staff had embarked. As the last few did so, a six-wheeled armoured vehicle came to a roaring halt beside them. Its engine shattered the air into a thousand pieces and tinted it grey-blue with exhaust fumes. Konrad tried not to inhale the stinking, noxious smoke. Twin cannons in a screeching dome on the camouflaged roof twitched while they scanned. Its bug-eyed weaponry and sharp angles gave it the look of a mantis at prayer. Few dared hold its gaze.

Wernher nodded to the troop carrier. "Expecting trouble?"

"Insurance. You never know what might happen. Popular Observer blaming Gothengau has upset a lot of people around here, and that could make you into targets. There's a long day ahead, we should get to the cars now. I'll lead the way."

"How far is it?"

"It's close. About a ten-minute drive along the rail lines."

Konrad pointed out the tracks running parallel with the road perpendicular to the runway, then strode to his kübelwagen. Business took his mind off the heat after the flight arrived but approaching the airstrip's roasting concrete forced droplets of itchy sweat to his brow again. After backing the car up, the flowing air cooled him and eased the pain of his reddened face, reducing the salt sting of perspiration on his parched skin. He pulled over to the side of the road until the convoy caught up with him. When the armoured car's engine bellowed it took the rear position, and Konrad put the car back on the highway to direct them to their destination.

Along the road, all the parched soil lay untilled. No people lived here. They passed no other building or car until they reached dozens of empty missile launch trucks parked around a raised mound, shoulder high to a horse, which spread over the area of several soccer pitches. Cupolas occasionally interrupted the flat surface, and a sunken road and a train-track appeared to run through the centre of it. The silo lay near a railway junction, and the facility's camouflage neared perfection but for the vehicles abandoned in its vicinity.

The convoy arrived at the car park, and von Braun's driver pulled-up next to Konrad's car. A pang of jealousy flashed through Konrad. Why couldn't he have a Mercedes instead of this generic old piece of scrap? Putting it from his mind, he got out of the kübelwagen. Envy returned when Konrad's eyes skimmed over the deep black lustre of the limousine's paintwork, then the stone-chipped olive drab of his own vehicle. Wernher von Braun gathered papers together in his monogrammed briefcase.

"Nice bag." Konrad couldn't help a little coveting, a victimless sin, now and again.

"Thanks. It's hand made."

Jealousy then shame sizzled through Konrad. Okay, coveting isn't victimless. Konrad was the casualty. Behind them a door clanged, and they turned to a nearby entryway. From its sunken stairwell came the crunch of many boots. A sergeant's head appeared above the parapet, then a dozen more marched behind their leader. The man's vacant eyes never left Konrad as he stormed toward him. Wernher's measured steps halted beside Konrad.

"What's this?"

"We are here to meet and deal with any and all intruders." Dead-eye snorted. "There is to be no sabotaging of Gothengau's defences."

"What intruders? What sabotage? This is a contingent of the Reich Space Agency here at Richard Baer's request. Who ordered you out?"

Konrad eyed the sergeant's epaulettes with disdain. "You don't have the authority for this."

"The senior officer present ordered me, sir. Lieutenant Himmelsman is inside, should you wish to speak to him."

"I certainly will talk to the Lieutenant. He has seriously overstepped his bounds - much more of this, and he'll be serving under me in the 500th! The Outlaws have plenty of red and green triangles to spare for recruits."

Downturned sceptical lips ended the sergeant's deadpan expression. "Aren't you a little outnumbered to start calling the shots?"

"Where do you get your confidence? I outrank everyone here and von Braun is the head of the Reich Space Agency. You will obey my orders, or you will join my unit. I will make your life hell!"

"You and whose army? I only see space cadets. They look like oven-ready turkeys!" The sergeant laughed, looking around until his followers joined in. Even his jug ears raised and fell with mirth.

Konrad bristled at being the laughing stock, but then he heard the armoured personnel carrier's mighty rumble. Konrad knew the sergeant saw the menacing vehicle when the smile wiped from his face and his men abruptly stopped giggling. The NCO looked aside to check on his platoon as Konrad paced to the bunker, forcefully pushing the bully from his path. Stocky, pockmarked Schink and another dozen of Konrad's most violent offenders ran from the back of their vehicle to follow him into the rocket silo. The sergeant picked himself up exactly when Schink, idle malevolence written all over his cratered moon face, delivered a boot into the Sergeant's head. The bunker's detachment of troops stepped out of Konrad's way, showing fear and apprehension at the sight of the convicts' red and green triangles. The soldier-prisoners of the 500th barged past them, and down the stairs from which the sergeant's men just appeared. Konrad and Wernher followed into the musty lair when they pulled the armour-plated door open. Low, neon lighting flooded pulsating, artificial daylight to the metallic right angles, nose cones and rocket nozzles jutting from the racks that held the weapons three high.

"Lieutenant Himmelsman! Get out here and explain yourself."

Rows of missiles disappeared into the greying distance, only a line of portable buildings standing against the wall disrupted the chamber's symmetrical layout. Lights in the cabins were on, so Konrad marched to them with a formation of his convicts close behind. As he reached it, one of the doors opened slowly. The lieutenant gingerly poked his head out. Konrad nodded in pockmarked Schink's direction, then to the nervous officer. Schink stepped forward, reached out and grabbed Himmelsman's neck with both hands then pulled the lieutenant's head towards him so hard that Himmelsman came off his feet. Schink's delivery of the officer to his commander looked graceful, almost effortless, until Schink broke the illusion and threw Himmmelsman to the ground at Konrad's feet.

"Explain the greeting party you sent out." Himmelsman got up. "What do you think you're playing at, interfering with Baer's instructions?"

Himmelsman dusted himself down and squirmed. Konrad squinted. Did Himmelsman have a hare lip? That explained the weak moustache.

"The radio, sir. Haven't you heard?"

"I've been driving a car without a stereo since the crack of dawn. Tell me what they've cooked up now."

"The news said that Gothengau is more of a threat to the Reich than the Reds, sir."

Konrad repressed a wince. He took that slight personally, despite its veracity. "They're wrong. We are here to help prove it. After von Braun's upgrades to these missiles, the Reds won't be able to fire at us again."

Himmelsman smiled. "I knew you wouldn't put anything before Gothengau."

Konrad shook his hand. "I'm glad you can see that now. Please excuse Schink for the way he ushered you over. Oh, by the way, we also need your office, so I want you to leave right away."

"But sir, there's somebody -"

"Will nobody listen to me today?" Konrad had no more patience left, only a squirming, selfish beast wriggling in his torso. "Just leave!"

Himmelsman skipped around Konrad and his people before he opened and slammed the door as noisily as he could. Himmelsman reminded Konrad of many new arrivals to the 500th. Not impressive on their first meeting, but the potential to be a real soldier by the time Konrad had finished with him.

The rocket scientist ended the briefing with his technicians and watched them start their task. Next to the lowest rack on the nearest row, the first team of four engineers fell to their knees by the missile. They opened the cases with skill and alacrity then began removing panels. Von Braun faced Konrad.

"Shall we sit?"

"Let's use Himmelsman's office."

Konrad ushered Wernher into the cabin. A desk and chairs sat before a door to the next cubicle.

"You know that these locators have a dual purpose, don't you?" Konrad cocked his head. "Yes, they're not just for pinpointing valuable items. They're a self-destruct that halts an attack the moment it's detected."

"That is an excellent defence against Gothengau. They've got no air power, rocket attacks are their only advantage. Now they can't make the first strike."

"It's really a question of keeping it secret from Richard Baer, and then you will be the Gauleiter."

One of Konrad's men appeared at the door, his pitted face peering in.

"What is it, Schink?"

"Richard Baer has arrived, sir. He just pulled up outside."

"Show him to us."

"No need, sir. He's showing himself in."

Schink left, and Konrad met Wernher's eye. "We'll just keep this self-destruct thing between you and me, then."

The door behind Konrad opened.

Aurelian stood silhouetted in the doorway. "I might just let Baer into your little secret."

Konrad jumped so hard that he pushed the door closed on Aurelian's arm. Gothengau's second-in-command yelped in pain just as Baer stepped into the room.

"What happened?" Baer nodded toward Aurelian doubled in pain, grabbing at his elbow.

"Aurelian got caught in the door."

Aurelian nursed his limb, grimaced and eyed Konrad suspiciously. "They're planning something."

Wernher, brow lined, glanced at Konrad too. Konrad stepped smoothly into the pause that Aurelian had left.

"Yes, Richard. We were planning a surprise party for you at Aurelian's. We were thinking of having it in your basement, weren't we Aurelian?"

Suddenly, Aurelian stopped rubbing his arm and dropped his hands to his sides. Daggers flew from his eyes, his jaw dropped, and his mouth opened and closed like a dying fish. Konrad wouldn't protect Aurelian's offspring at the expense of everybody else in the Reich, no matter what afflicted them. Aurelian could reveal Wernher's news, if he were prepared to pay the ultimate price.

"Is that true, Aurelian?"

Aurelian averted his eyes from Konrad's and became animated again.

"Not entirely." Aurelian giggled. "The basement is being used for storage at the moment. Not sure why Konrad thought otherwise."

Wernher smiled and nodded to Konrad approvingly.

"So how are the installations going?" Baer asked Wernher.

"There are no problems so far. I expect that it will be completed before tomorrow."

"Then I shall let you get on with it. Aurelian, are you coming back to work?"

Aurelian obediently followed Baer before they both left. After the silo's door had closed, Wernher turned to Konrad.

"I thought it was all over for us when Aurelian appeared. How did you manage to shut him up?"

"I visited Aurelian the other day. He and his wives had an argument, so I slunk off and bumped into some of his children. The ones he doesn't want anyone to know about." Konrad looked around to make sure nobody could hear, then leaned close to Wernher's ear. "He hides his disabled kids there. They used to call them freaks, and they remind me of two I knew in my days as a carny hand." Konrad thought it best to avoid mentioning his own freak status.

"Really?" Wernher cocked his head. "That's useful information. Maybe it could bring him over to our side."

"I don't know about that, he's very secure and well-liked by Baer." Konrad thought harder. "As far as Baer could actually like somebody." Wernher's head bobbed up and down. "It does make an excellent leash though. I've got it in mind to save his kids, so perhaps he can protect mine if the time comes. There's something I want to know about, though. Maybe I could use Aurelian's kids to find out about it."

"What is it?" Wernher opened his palms. "Can I help?"

"Something has been getting under my skin about Doctor Mengele."

Wernher nodded. "There's a lot to dislike about him. What's bothering you?"

"He is too interested in me. He might be trying to do something with me that I don't know about. I'm no scientist, I don't know. Maybe you could tell me. Can humans be cloned?"

"No, no!" Wernher laughed. "That can't be done yet! I think you can ease that worry from your mind. Come. Let's see how the work's going."

Wernher patted Konrad on the shoulder and walked out of the office into the cool, grey air of the missile bunker. Konrad followed him. In the rest of the building, Wernher's men climbed around the rockets while Konrad's paraded up and down. Wernher spoke with one of his senior technicians for a moment and then returned.

"They've made excellent progress. It'll be finished by nightfall."

"Fantastic news, but we still need more assurance." Konrad turned to his nearest men. "I want you to patrol outside. There are no threats in the silo. Check what Himmelsman and his men are up to."

"Yes sir."

"Follow me." Konrad led them out.

The metal doors creaked as he pushed them open. He trotted up the staircase, but before the doors slammed after them, the 'pop-pop-pop' sound of shooting reached his ears. Terror's familiar sharp, bright feeling ran from his sternum to his throat. He quashed the fear before it took his senses. Konrad dropped to the floor. Whistling bullets thudded into the soil covering the silo, the impacts spraying him with earth. Before the firing had stopped, his men had retreated down the stairs.

"What are Mayrock and van de Beek doing?" Anger was one emotion Schink didn't repress. "There should be covering fire already."

"Mayrock can't take orders." Konrad expected his right-hand man to fix this. "So van de Beek must be on his case."

"Yeah, van de Beek won't let him shirk."

A prolonged volley of shots came from Himmelsman's squad. Konrad put his face to the floor. When the shooting finished, he looked up again, relieved: the armoured car's cannon scraped from left to right. The barrels spat fire. Konrad stood, drew his pistol, and ran up the stairs. Explosions burst around the feet of the Himmelsman posse. They dived. Konrad's men roared behind him as they charged, taking pot shots at the opposition. Himmelsman's team stayed down, until Konrad stood over their cowering bodies at the next entrance to the bunker. Schink arrived with the others as their opponents stood, with their eyes down, hands up and guns on the ground. Konrad's men guffawed at their unworthy adversaries.

"It's not a joke, fellows." Konrad pointed at the vanquished. "Arrest these men."

The convict troops stopped laughing. With teeth bared, they screamed and stamped before they sprang forward and ran to their opponents. Konrad, irked that his violent soldier-prisoners punished their opponents with knees and fists, still didn't command them to stop. Himmelsman and his crew had asked for that treatment. Konrad expected them to reprieve themselves under his command in the 500th.

Chapter 18

Gothengau, Monday, May 3rd, 1965.

This time they didn't drug Karl. Once bound at the ankles and wrists, the snatch-squad gagged him. The bag on his head smelled like the one they used when they tricked him last. It took a while for the vehicle to get them to Ostara, a good ten minutes of bumping on the hard metal floor of a truck. There was no point in resisting. It would achieve nothing, so when they carried him into the clinic, Karl just acted like the plank he felt. After transferring him to the seat, Baer pulled the bag off. Rolf and Hegel were still unconscious in the neighbouring chairs. They started to salivate and work their jaws. Karl knew the surprise they were in for. It looked like Hegel had a lot to lose in this endeavour and envy almost jostled terror from its pinnacle. Rolf groaned first.

Hegel jolted and screamed. "Karl's dead when I get hold of him."

"Karl's right here next to you." Baer laughed.

"You knew about this, didn't you? Might fix you up at Ostara, you said, and all the time it was gonna be this. What are they doing with my dick?"

"Relax, you'll find out when the film starts."

Rolf found words through his saliva-matted red beard. "Why haven't you clamped Karl's tiny cock?"

"He's already had one put in."

"Wait 'til I get out of this. I'm gonna slit your thro -"

"No, no, no. You will obey the mission's orders. Get back here in three days with the job done, and we might let you keep those tails of yours. That's enough information. Relax and enjoy the show."

The lock's heavy clunk showed Baer had gone.

"You're dead, Karl. I don't care what he said, you're dead."

Hegel didn't know how he'd feel after this. Karl did, so the intimidation meant nothing. Kill Drachenblut. That's all they had to do.

"I'll shoot you in the -"

Hegel's threat stopped when the screen started.

Footage of their penile operation shut everyone up. Until Rolf and Hegel had the explosive inserted into their urethras. Though their agonising howls tore into his eardrums, Karl relaxed a little knowing that he didn't have to endure that again. It almost made Karl happy that Hegel would probably lose his big schlong.

Under the swirling images and breathy commands, time meandered to a stop. Only when the abrasive light of the fluorescent tubes eclipsed the hypnotic images did Karl realise where he was and what was happening. That, though, wasn't important. He must kill Drachenblut and keep his manhood. Hegel and Rolf had shut up. They would be thinking the same.

A door creaked open and several footsteps approached. Karl recognised Baer's gait.

"Did you sleep well?" Baer had a recognisable twang. "All rested and ready to go back to Wewelsburg for your new project? I know he's going to die on his own, but you three are going to make that a day in the near future."

Baer's allusion to the High Priest caused adrenaline to course through Karl and his team. The chairs vibrated in response to their sudden tension.

"Who am I talking about?"

Fury rose in their breasts. They ignored the pain and discomfort to pound their bodies up and down on the metal.

"Can you tell me what he's called?"

"Drachenblut!" they screamed.

"I didn't hear you. Who did you say?"

"Drachenblut!"

At his name, their anger and rage focused on the High Priest like a laser. Baer chuckled.

"The synchronised assassins are funny, but it draws attention to them, and this is a secret mission. Can you fix it, Mengele?"

"We've never programmed a group before, these results are fascinating."

"Fascinating's better for another time. For now, they're a pain in the ass. What are you going to do?"

"Five milligrams of sedative should calm them down enough. Nurse! Give each of them five mils of Relaxatin."

A pretty woman's face filled Karl's field of vision. Wincing, he squinted against the manipulation of the line in his throat. It hurt as much as expected. Seconds later, when she moved to the next bed, Karl felt less anguished but also aware of jealousy. Rolf and Hegel would soon feel the same way as Karl. His escorts were next for treatment.

"Take things easy." Mengele said. "If you try too hard then you'll all move as one and everyone'll see you are up to something."

"Don't mess it up again, Karl," said Baer.

Karl couldn't say so, but he hadn't botched anything. Drachenblut sent Karl back from his previous mission the moment he got back to the castle, just as the promised call arrived.

"You don't want to find out how disposable you are." Baer scoffed. "You're as disposable as your tadgers." He giggled and increased Karl's discomfort. "Wewelsburg can't protect you, and Gothengau's arm is very long."

Under normal circumstances, a threat from a Gauleiter would terrify Karl into immediate submission, but intimidation from the Gothengau leader would make him tremble even more. Now, with Karl augmented by his entourage, the Second Priest had the strength and fortitude of three men. Three men terrified of castration.

"So, what's the name on your lips?" Baer asked.

Karl had less anger now. Others answered first. "Drachenblut."

"That's better. They're not a barbershop quartet now, eh, Mengele?"

Despite what Baer had done to them, Karl, Rolf and Hegel's frenzied aim could not be moved from the Drachenblut target to their real Gothengau threat. No ire could be directed to the Gauleiter. All strong feelings stayed honed on the High Priest. Karl ached to find him. He hoped Hegel diverted his thoughts to that from revenge for Karl's subterfuge.

"Now it's time for your flight back to Wewelsburg," Baer said.

"Nurse!" Mengele ordered. "Open the restraints."

Around his temple, wrists and ankles the steel flipped back, and it struck the table with a deafening clang. While they endured the agonising clamour, the lines in their neck and crotch were pulled out and the wounds dabbed with a solution which brought tears to Karl's eyes. He covered his modesty with his now-free hands.

"Your clothes are on the floor beside you," said Baer. "Get dressed and go to the airport. You should make it in time to meet the rest of your party. Don't worry about them, though. They've been occupied all night, and we made sure they were too entertained to think about you three."

Worries about Hegel's revenge kept popping into Karl's mind. Wait for the telephone call. He daren't look at Hegel in the likely event that the same conflicting thoughts raged inside his skull. Kill Drachenblut.

After the door clanged shut behind Baer, the lights went out. A hissing sound accompanied a sweet smell, and Karl found himself dreaming of lilacs in a pasture. So lush was the meadow, that he had to lie down in it and gaze up at the clouds.

Karl woke in a stretched car as it pulled up to the airport. The sedatives made Karl and the others droop at the shoulders, and their half-closed eyelids peered from slack-jawed, hangdog expressions. Karl kept quiet. So did the others.

The stopped outside the airport entrance. Overcome with lethargy, nobody moved. Moments later, the driver shook his head and sighed before he stepped out to open their door. His fawn uniform had stains under the arms. Karl didn't like his stink, it put him in mind of school gyms. "We're there, get out. And hurry up with it, too. The plane's going in a minute."

Nobody moved. The chauffeur stepped out and opened Karl's door. If this wasn't the expected call, then it could wait. Even when the driver pulled Karl out by the scruff of the neck, he wasn't bothered. Hegel, though, sprang out and around. Karl was set free after Hegel punched their escort to the floor. Karl dusted himself off and got the bags to the rhythm of the grunts and thuds Hegel kicked from his victim.

That Hegel could so easily be drawn from his task of waiting for the call worried Karl. Hegel's ire could easily be turned on Karl to exact retribution. No time to dwell on that now. Think about it after the call. When a telephone rang on the airport loudspeaker, the three of them stopped what they did and looked desperately around for the source of the call. When it stopped, they carried on as before.

Karl passed the melee. "Leave it now. Let's get the flight"

Still calm, Hegel joined Karl and Rolf and walked to their comrades by the boarding gate. All chatter stopped before Karl reached earshot.

Everybody looked at the floor, the ceiling, the aeroplanes. Anywhere but at Karl and his associates.

"Where were you lot last night?" Olaf broke the tense silence. "You missed all the fun. I notched up three." His eyebrows became less inverted and face animated. "How many did you have, Hadwin?"

No jealousy affected him from hearing of his colleagues' nocturnal romp. "We had a private room at Ostara." Although Karl wondered whether he had actually been at the breeding clinic.

"Sowing your seed for the Fatherland, eh?" Olaf winked.

"Something like that. What we did there will be great for the Reich."

The public-address system announced the flight to Wewelsburg. All three marched out of the gate and up the aircraft's steps. They occupied the front row seats nearest to the door. Everybody that passed glanced at him and his entourage. Suspicion arced from their focussed eyes, across flared nostrils, to their pursed lips. Two free rows of chairs buffered them from the others. It gave them space to conspire.

During the 2-hour 27 minute flight, Karl, Rolf, and Hegel held a vibrant, compelling conversation. They whispered while almost rubbing faces against each other. Such proximity to other men disgusted Karl. But he must answer the phone call and kill Drachenblut. Otherwise, he would be singing falsetto.

"They bought a telescope for him. I gave it to Drachenblut yesterday, before he sent me back here. We make him use it. Get him up the North Tower to survey the Paderborn countryside, and then throw him off."

Rolf's revolting breath invaded their shared space. "If he resists, we'll walk him up there at gunpoint."

"He might need a bit of softening up first." Hegel liked a punch-up.

"As long as he dies, I don't care." Karl began to drift off to sleep.

A bump brought the trio back to earth when the plane touched down. Leaning forward with the aircraft's deceleration caused them to resist the inertia. Rigidity returned to their spines, and they pushed their bodies back into the chairs while the runway-noise was highest and well before the vehicle reached a canter. The stewardess glanced imperiously at the simultaneous clicks from their seatbelts when the aircraft reached its stand at Wewelsburg airport. Karl, as the closest to the exit, reached out to the handle. The air-hostess no longer felt inhibited.

"Sir, I insist that you leave the operation of the door to the cabin cr-." The door hydraulics sighed, cutting her short. She exhaled and shook her head.

Now the stairway connected the passenger exit to the ground, the three marched down to the asphalt with Karl in the lead. Like a religious procession, Priestly Karl led his clerical acolytes through the terminal building. They drew little attention, neither clerks, nor porters, nor passengers paid them much mind.

In the car park, a bus waited for the entourage. If the Second Priest and his guards used that to reach the castle, then they would need to wait for the rest of the party. Instead, Karl went straight for the row of kübelwagens. He took the driver's seat of the first vehicle they came to. When Rolf and Hegel sat behind him, Karl turned the key in the ignition and the gruff air-cooled engine coughed to life. The first of their fellow travellers stepped through the airport doors just as the kübelwagen's throaty exhaust roared past. Its noise prevented Karl understanding what they shouted at him. All three minds focussed on the mission that Gothengau had implanted in them as the acceleration whipped the priests' hair and beards back and they joined the autobahn.

The moment Wewelsburg Castle came into view Karl took the autobahn exit and raced towards the forest canopy where cool shade welcomed them. After they entered the woods, Karl drove onto the first bend, his leaden foot weighing the gas pedal down. The rear end of the car began to swing out faster than the front. Panic rising, Karl turned into the skid and pumped the brakes. All heads turned towards the tree-trunk approaching them, tyres screaming against the road surface. The moss infesting the trunk loomed large, but a ridge of soil slowed them to a trot. The kübelwagen's rear wheel arch struck the oak with a bang. The car shuddered, alarming Karl, but he calmed when realised its cause. The motor had stalled.

Karl twisted the ignition keys again, and the engine sprang back to life. This time, though, Karl knew to slow down for the contours of the winding uphill route. A couple of bends later and they emerged from the copse to the car park in front of the castle.

The sentry on duty saluted them as they paraded past and crossed the bridge over the dry moat. They saw nobody else on the way up to Drachenblut's chambers on the first floor. Karl took shallow, rapid breaths before they stopped in front of the High Priest's door. There was no answer. Karl looked at Rolf and Hegel, then the phone rang inside the office. This could be the call! Karl barged in, Rolf and Hegel pushing him forward.

Drachenblut's chambers were empty.

The phone hadn't completed its second ring before Karl's hand became the first of the frenzied trio to bring it to their ear.

"This is the call." Excitement straightened Karl's spine. "Kill Drachenblut."

After the familiar voice, the agonising cacophony from their brainwashing started. Now Karl knew what to do. Determination clarifying his stare, he allowed Hegel to hear the command.

Enlightened, Hegel passed the phone. "Where else would he be?"

"He hasn't left the castle." Karl reassured them. "He's often in the Chamber of the Eternal Flame. Or maybe he is with the Chief Vestal."

Karl and the others turned to leave. They halted before even taking the first step in their quest for the High Priest.

Drachenblut bowed to them as he passed through the doorway. "How did Baer . . ."

When Drachenblut met their gaze, his eyes darted like those of a cornered animal. He snapped back from the door and ran down the hallway. The trio burst out of the door after him. Karl saw the High Priest's foot entering the stairwell, but nobody determined which way he went. They squeezed into the landing on the steps, silent and listening for clues. None were heard.

"We're going downstairs." Karl held seniority in this team. "He could be in the crypt."

They marched across the courtyard gravel towards the base of the North Tower, the excitement of the chase replacing the disappointment of Drachenblut's rapid escape from his chambers. When they entered the Chamber of the Eternal Flame, the sentries' salutes went unanswered. The pair of soldiers stood at either side of the door with their arms out.

Seeing the circular chamber empty, they ran around the sacred flare hoping that the High Priest had hidden in one of the alcoves set back from the wall. He hadn't, and when they were furthest from the door, Drachenblut's form filled the arch. The trio jumped over the low wall around the flame, the heat singeing Karl when he leapt through the fire. Burning hair overpowered any other scent. After the High Priest returned the guards' salutes, the sentries readied their rifles, preparing to aim at Karl and his followers. Hegel ran to them, fists flying. When Rolf joined in, his punch to the other sentry got a hit in kind to his nose. There was no room for Karl to get out and chase Drachenblut. Both watchmen had a grip on Karl's loose vestments, forcing him to witness the High Priest disappearing behind the staircase's spiral. Drachenblut's footfalls ascended the tower at a pace.

Fist clenched in frustration, Karl punched the sentry still keeping him back. Now fighting two men, the soldier buckled after a few strikes, falling to the ground holding his bloodied face. The other trooper turned and ran. He kept running, but Karl and his men stopped at the ground floor, checking for the High Priest in the courtyard. Drachenblut's absence turned them back to the tower, and after they reached the next floor, they pushed open the Hall of the Generals' gate.

Bathed in blinding light and framed by colonnaded windows on the other side of the round table, their quarry paced back and forth. The strong sunshine and white walls made it difficult to see, but Drachenblut wore black. Eyes easily followed his movements. From the left, Hegel approached Drachenblut alone, while Karl and Rolf padded towards the High Priest in the opposite direction. The High Priest faced one way for a second, then the other, never for long enough to know where he might go. As Karl's party passed the table's diameter, Drachenblut leapt up on the huge piece of glass covering its centre. A crack appeared in its surface.

The High Priest skidded across the top. He arrived at the other side when Karl, Schmitt and Hegel dropped on the table. More fractures appeared, but they were not superficial and when Drachenblut bounded from the glass, a huge snap rang out from the clear facade. Karl and his companions dropped to the tiled pattern on the floor below, fearful of being opened up by the sharp edges forming all around them.

When they hit the mosaic floor, the thick pieces of jagged, vitreous threats almost obscured the circular patterns beneath them. It didn't obscure Drachenblut racing away. Each of them carefully manoeuvred around the spikes and edges that the breakage created.

"Let's rest." Karl had to think. "Before we kill ourselves."

Chapter 19

Berlin, Monday, May 3rd, 1965.

Shades and a headscarf, contrary to Petra's expectations, helped strangers to recognize her. Perhaps her desperate need to be hidden drew strangers' eyes to confirm or deny their suspicions of the concealed identity before them. Despite firmly burying her head in the stupendous array of silk stockings in one of the department store's quieter corners, she felt eyes exploring her. Petra only wanted to get out of the house. It took her mind from the death of her adopted son and the end of her marriage. Shopping helped. Sometimes. But here she bristled with a reticent expectation that complete strangers would descend on her begging for a singing performance, as they had in the airport. The woman crossed Petra's invisible boundary, invading her personal space. Petra turned her head to examine another piece of hosiery, hoping to put off the inevitable stuttering conversation that followed. Her fan missed the hint.

"H-hi. It's Petra, isn't it?" The enthusiast interrupted Petra before she opened her mouth in confirmation. "You moved me. Well, you moved us all. When you cried."

Every time Petra left the house this happened.

"Thank you." Petra stepped away.

"We wish you and Max good luck in overcoming the boy's death."

Petra winced. How could that woman speak for everyone? Why did she think it was her business to comment on?

Hunger poked at Petra's stomach. She kept next to the walls to stay out of the public eye but couldn't get to the top floor restaurant that way. The stairs were the most discreet route to take to lunch, but the five-flight price tag was too much to pay for privacy. Petra peeled away from the wall and headed for the elevator bank in the middle of the floor. The racks of skirts and blouses hid Petra's miniature frame from all but those lofty enough to see over the merchandise.

The forest of garments ended before the elevators. It left an area barren of commerce sparsely populated by staff with clasped palms, sombre uniforms and name badges. Customers loitered with the intent to explore higher reaches. Heads turned when Petra pushed the button to go up, and she sighed in frustration. A tall, dark assistant approached her first. Although barely past midday, the hirsute floor-walker had a five-o-clock shadow and the blue-black stubble made his cheeks glossy. He opened his mouth to speak and Petra turned. The hint was not taken, so the lift arrival bell let her step away without appearing too rude.

In the lift, the attendant did a double take as Petra walked past his perch by the controls. Petra supposed the lad could always be a jockey if this line of work ended.

"Any floor you want, Petra."

"The top, please."

A murmur rose and when she reached the back of the lift car, she turned around. Everybody faced her, but their glass-eyed stares and inscrutable expressions fixed on her in such a small space made her gasp and step back. When they advanced towards her in return, she felt the walls close in. The concertina metal frame of the lift's inner doors shut. Petra thought of barred prison windows.

"Hold tight, going up."

Petra and the gawking fellow travellers juddered with the elevator box when it started its ascent. She looked past them, but the view of the shaft going by through the grate compressed her chest in a vice. Their silent examination lasted until the second floor. Finally, one of them took their eyes from her.

"Hey, I wanted that floor!" The man complained.

"Catch it on the way down, sir," the attendant replied. "We're going all the way to the top first."

Petra knew he did that for her. Her buttocks clenched in embarrassment as the other passengers realised it too. No longer comfortable staring at the passing levels, Petra stared at the ceiling for comfort. The tutting and clucking from the other passengers accompanied the rattle of the elevator car in its shaft.

'Alright for some, isn't it?'

'I never thought she was that great.'

'Wish people went out of their way for me.'

'What about the tenets of National Socialism?'

With a loud clunk, the lift jarred to a halt. Relieved, Petra pushed through the line of gawking, hostile fellow-travellers. She breathed in their silence but exhaled their glare when she walked toward the restaurant. She strolled out of the elevator lobby to the open-plan, brightly lit, garishly coloured café, and obeyed the instruction on the sign. Wait to be shown a table, but Petra couldn't see any available. Already she wasn't the only one in line.

After a short pause, a waiter arrived. "You are alone?"

The penguin suit that he wore combined with the half-moon rimless spectacles which he stared at Petra over, made this little man appear a lot bigger. He barely exceeded Petra's height, and his hooded eyes looked smaller because of wrinkles. His question cut Petra like a hurtful comment. Why didn't she have a close friend to be with?

"A table for one, Madame."

She followed him to the table closest to the bathroom. Much as she hated to, Petra would have to tell him her identity to get a decent place to sit. People craned their necks for a better look at her face.

"The place is suitable, Madame?"

"Not really. Haven't you got a better table?"

Petra pulled her sunglasses down in case that reminded the waiter of her identity.

"No, not even for you, Petra."

Her eye stung from a newly created teardrop. Fame wasn't always sweet, and she had forgotten how bitter the public could be. Either sit and eat by the toilets or go somewhere else. Too exhausted to leave, Petra dropped her things on the floor and sat. The waiter handed her a menu.

"Would you like something to drink while you make up your mind, Madame?"

"A glass of water, thank you."

As she looked around, Petra realised that the restaurant was too full to accommodate her celebrity anywhere but by the bathroom. A group at the next table turned to her. Petra gave them a timid, nervous smile. Without her meaning to, the wan simper gave them the green light.

"You're Petra, aren't you?" asked the grey-haired patriarch.

Petra nodded. The steely patrician turned back to his group, who rapidly mumbled a conversation, making the man face Petra again. He fingered his Bavarian collar before speaking.

"If you're on your own, come and sit with us. It's awkward sitting alone, isn't it?"

There seemed to be no comfortable place for Petra. The neighbouring group's well-meaning intentions forced her to wonder whether she could still leave and have a sandwich. She had only ordered water.

"Oh." Petra stood. "I've just remembered I must be somewhere else right now!"

Reaching into her bag for her purse, she left a tip on the table for the server. This time, taking the stairs meant no exertion and less exposure. With fast paces she dodged between the backs of chairs to the stairwell next to the lift. She let the heavy door close. Its echo reverberated through the musty column of still, cool air surrounded by iron-grated marble steps. Goosebumps rose from her skin when her footsteps resounded back like those of a giant. Gingerly, she leant against the wall and padded down to the car park.

On the driveway, the sight of the house dragged her thoughts back. Early afternoon on a weekday, and Petra had nobody to spend time with besides her philandering husband. She prepared bread and cheese in the kitchen before she switched on the television and settled in for the evening.

Popular Observer's bombastic theme opened Petra's eyes. The setting sun meant only the light of the box illuminated the salon and when she glanced at the set, she groaned. In the studio background, behind Steffi and Sebastian, hung a huge photo of Petra in tears as she begged the crowd to leave before the May Day attack. If Petra was so wonderful, why did she fall asleep on her couch with nobody for company? With a solitary evening in front of the TV to look forward to, her mind raced through any female who she could call a friend, or even an acquaintance. Only Hanna Reitsch remained after the anguished sifting of the unspoken words and uncomfortable pauses she had shared in the company of other women. For the mother of Max's latest conquest to be the only woman she could think of speaking with spoke volumes. Petra's time in the Fatherland had not been spent trying to make friends, and now she paid. She didn't even have parents or siblings. Desperate, she picked up the phone to ring Hanna.

"Hello, Hanna Reitsch speaking."

"Hi Hanna, it's-"

"Petra, it's so lovely to hear from you! How have you been since the . . ."

Hanna meant Lothar's funeral but neither she nor Petra could bring themselves to say it.

"I've been fine, keeping myself busy."

"What did you do today?"

"I went shopping in the AWAG in Berlin. It was lovely. I found some great things and had a little lunch." Petra didn't have to make everything sound like the agonising drama that it was.

A pause, no longer than the blink of an eye, hung on the line.

"Are you sure you're alright?"

Hanna's perception shone a light on Petra's terror of loneliness. Tears dripped on the handset and a sob burst through the dam Petra had built for the rancour and grief that had flowed her way.

"I've been so lonely. There's nobody around me at all and I don't know how to cope."

"So Max didn't come back?"

"No, I never want that lying bastard here again."

"Would you like me to come over and keep you company?"

"It's too far. You live on the other side of town. I wouldn't make you drive all that way only for my benefit."

"What will you do then? Not just tonight, but every night. I'm alone all the time since Eva joined the space programme, being famous doesn't keep me company."

Petra chewed her lip, puzzling over what to say.

"Have you thought about having Max back?" Hanna asked. "You sound in dire need of company, otherwise I wouldn't suggest it."

"No way!" Petra reflexively blurted. "He's so full of lies. You know, he told me that he arranged Lothar's funeral himself!"

"That's silly. How did he think you wouldn't find out?"

"I don't know, but that was the last nail in the coffin."

"That's terrible, but won't they make you get back together like after," Hanna paused. "After your birth-son died?"

"They might, but I'm going to have to take that chance. I'm not letting him come home this time – he wasted too many chances already. Let him carry on being the playboy."

"I think Eva is losing interest in him. After the scene you had with her, she doesn't really believe what he says anymore."

"If he's anything like the last time he went off the rails then she is the latest of many."

Car tyres on the gravel drive distracted Petra, stopping her hearing Hanna's response.

"I'm sorry, Hanna, but I've got to go. A car just pulled up."

"Look after yourself."

Petra replaced the receiver just as the visitor beat the front door. The banging raised the tension around her sternum; she almost vomited and opened the door wearing a bitter, bilious expression. A wall of a man faced her. Petra's eyes ran up the Gestapo agent's full-length leather coat to his lipless face and frameless glasses magnifying his hooded eyes. A leather trilby covered his shorn scalp.

"Good evening, Petra. I am agent Wilhelm Stern. My friends and I are here to mend your relationship with Max."

Stern pushed past her followed by Max and two more Gestapo men clad in biker jackets. One was grizzled, the other clean-shaven. Both of them had the cut of burly street fighting skinheads, the whiff of the football terraces lingering around them. Petra's heart jumped, then it fell when she realised what the impromptu marriage counselling meant for the rest of the evening. For the rest of her life. Her uniformed husband kept his eyes down as they led him home. He walked with his hands behind his back because his wrists were cuffed, but the silver restraints blended into his Space Agency clothing. Max stood in the centre of the room with the Gestapo agents either side of him.

"My orders are that you two will live together in this house," Wilhelm said. "It's unbecoming for a national hero like your husband to be seen running around behind your back, Petra."

One of Max's guards thrust his elbow into Max's abdomen. Petra stepped back in shock. Max crumpled to his knees, head moving to the floor. The agents tried to grab the scruff of his neck before his nose hit the carpet. Would she get that treatment as well?

"Not his face." Wilhelm gritted his teeth.

They pulled Max up from the floor. The carpet had burned his eye and forehead. Wilhelm turned to face Max.

"So, mister spaceman, are you going to keep your wife happy?"

Max shrugged. "Yes."

"You don't sound like you mean it! Let's hear it one more time with feeling, a bit more gusto!" Wilhelm's lifting hands ramped up the enthusiasm. "C'mon Max, you know you can do it!"

Petra's hands trembled, and her right eyelid moved under its own will.

"After me. I promise . . ."

"I promise to remain faithful to my wife and to live in the house with her." Max held Petra's eye.

"We will ret . . ."

"We will return to our former appearance as the Fatherland's happily married, leading couple."

Petra averted her eyes from Max's. Letting Max look in the window to her soul would reveal the visceral hate for him that took up residence after Lothar's burial. Wilhelm turned to Petra.

"And what do you say? Will you, Petra Hellfeier, take this man Max as your lawfully wedded husband?"

An offer Petra couldn't refuse, but she didn't react immediately. Wilhelm strode over to her, standing too close. She smelled his beer breath. Her eyelid went into spasms of fluttering.

"I do." The words grazed her throat. Wilhelm squinted. Her mouth less dry now, she could make a better attempt. "I do." Wilhelm nodded sagely.

When Wilhelm slapped her on the back heartily his eyes held no joy.

"Good, good. Well men, we shall leave these two love birds here on their own, then, shan't we? Let's be having you, gents. Take his cuffs off."

Max rubbed his wrists after they removed his handcuffs. The door slammed behind the Gestapo men, then a car engine barked to life and its growl receded. They were alone. If the day's events taught her one thing, it was that she needed companionship. Max flopped down on the sofa, rubbing his stomach.

"Where did they get you?"

"At the base. They knew where I was."

"That's more than I knew. Hanna just told me that this would happen, but I didn't think she meant this soon."

"You know where I am now."

"You're sleeping in Lothar's old room. This pretence at marriage ends when we walk through the front door. I don't care what the Führer says. He can stay out of our bedroom, at least."

Max sat up. His hand rested on his thigh and a smile schmoozed across his jaw. "Come and sit by me."

"Your charm isn't going to work on me again, so you might as well give it a rest."

"It's still working fine."

"That's what your girlfriends think, but I know you."

"Would you like a drink?" Max got up and faced the kitchen.

"There's white wine in the fridge. Don't get me a drink. Don't even ask me - I don't want anything from you."

Max didn't look at the ground anymore. He ambled towards Petra in the middle of the room. Something about his movements seemed different. With feline grace, he edged a little too close to Petra than required. She shook her head at this pathetic attempt to get back in her esteem. Max dived on her.

His familiar scent smothered her when she hit the floor. Something twisted in her ankle, and her arm fell awkwardly behind her. Max pinned her down with all his weight, clawing at her skirt. His finger hooked in her knickers and he pulled them down. They tore from her when he ripped at the silk. Petra liked these panties, too. She pushed at him, but he pinned her arms to the floor. No way was she having this. Her forehead sprang up and slammed into Max's nose. It cracked. He roared. When he reached up to his face she got away into the kitchen.

Grabbing a knife from the block she returned, brandishing the weapon.

"I'm sleeping in the bath. Don't bother me. You know I'll use it."

Max lay on the floor groaning when she took a blanket and pillow to spend a night in the home's only lockable room.

Chapter 20

Gothengau, Monday May 3rd, 1965

Blood trickled from Karl's palms and scarlet drops followed him from the broken glass in the Hall of the Generals. Crimson handprints on the wooden table edge showed their path. Shards had penetrated the supple leather soles of his shoes, splashing red footprints on the white floor's black circular mosaic. Rolf and Hegel bled, too. The laces over their shins hung loose and lacerations showed crimson through their torn uniforms. Karl ignored the pain. Better his shins than his manhood. He returned to their mission.

"He ran up the stairs."

"He could be anywhere by now." Hegel's stare burrowed into Karl.

"Where should we start looking?" Rolf had the right idea.

"We'll go to his office and take something. Something that will get him on our tail."

Karl's bloody footwear squelched through the Hall of the Generals' gate. The door of the North Tower framed a wing of the castle, but they weren't going that way. Agony cut into Karl's feet but he didn't limp or wince. He got through it and raced up the stone staircase. Their movements still echoed from the stairs behind them when they marched along the corridor to Drachenblut's chambers.

Karl twisted the wrought handle and they tumbled into the High Priest's office. Drachenblut's absence did not change the plan, so Karl grabbed the skull from the High Priest's desk and span around. They ran to the North Tower's stairwell. If Drachenblut wanted to keep his treasured gift from Mengele, symbolic of his acceptance into the elite of Nazi society, then he had to follow Karl's tracks.

Vestal Helga stepped out of the spiral, touching her deep red curls absent-mindedly. When she saw the trio, her hands fell to her hips and her facial features sharpened to a sneer.

Helga pointed at their feet, disgust contorting her mouth. "Why are you covered in blood?"

Hegel broke ranks and ran to Helga. Her face dropped.

Air rushed out of the Vestal when his shoulder hit her stomach. The impact set her eyes wide open while her jaws opened and closed in total silence. Her face turned pink before it took a blue tinge. Now her fingers pleaded for help. Karl's calm indifference to her suffering surprised him. He had neither the inclination nor knowledge to assist her. Her life concerned him much as a worm on the end of an angler's hook. The fish would come whether the bait lived or died. With a guttural wheeze, she took another breath.

"Put me down." Helga's hands and legs beat up and down, but Hegel held her fast.

"What's wrong with you? Get your hands off! You're not allowed to touch me!"

"Drachenblut does, though." Karl got her attention. Helga stared at Karl until Hegel climbed the stairs and its central column eclipsed the pair.

"You're no angel either. Do you think I don't know about-"

The voice became a muffled cry. When Karl got to the first floor, Hegel had his Vestal prisoner in an arm lock, shoving her mouth full of silk from her voluminous robes. Satisfied, Hegel slung Helga over his shoulder again. Helga's eyes burned almost as red as her hair, and without the brainwashing her stare would have singed Karl's spirits. After the mind-control, though, the piercing gaze energised him.

"What the Hell are you doing?" asked Grimhilt.

Helga's moans increased. Something grabbed Karl's robes, pulling him back. He looked around as tears burst from Grimhilt. She dropped to the floor at a bruising speed, taking him with her. The trio couldn't proceed. Karl knew she would keep them at a standstill. He held her hand, but she snatched it away and rubbed the blood off on the stone floor.

"Didn't you always want to be the High Priestess? You know, the two of us, leading the spirit of the Fatherland to Valhalla"

Grimhilt scowled, scepticism and disdain spewing from her. "Why are you talking about it in front of them?"

"I'll be High Priest soon. Gothengau are making us do it."

"Why do they want Drachenblut out of the way? The attack was Gothengau's fault."

After such a short time apart from Karl, Grimhilt already took the government line. Karl parted his hair. How could she be so dense?

"Are you stupid? Drachenblut ordered the rocket patrols," Rolf said.

"He thinks what you think, doesn't he?" Tears rolled down her cheeks. "If you think I'm stupid, why do you want me as High Priestess? What am I to you anyway?"

Warmth filled Karl's breast when he reflected on her question. Their rushed passions in closed spaces entered his mind.

"You are my true love and confidant. Without you I would be lonely at the top."

Hegel snorted. "He only likes you because you're hot in the bedroom."

"What? Hegel can't know that." Her blonde hair shook out of phase with her head. "I'm a Vestal and shouldn't even have got close to you." She pled with her hands, palms up. "Nobody can know! You've ruined everything! You're right, I'm stupid. Stupid to ever believe in you." When she sliced the air with her hand, her panting, pouting lips were almost irresistible. "You're nothing but a scheming dreamer. I'll never be the High Priestess with you!"

In a flurry of silk and tears, Grimhilt jumped to her feet and ran down the east wing. Her footsteps and caterwauling faded, but the vision of her abandoning them burned in Karl's mind. They turned to climb the stairs and continue with their assignment, the atmosphere in the stair well warmer than before. Karl focussed his mind on killing Drachenblut. Before Karl reached the second floor, his ears filled with Olaf's screaming.

"Hey, you! What are you doing with her? Get your hands off her, Hegel, this isn't Siberia!"

Thoughts about the blonde priest and his vexed eyebrows sprung into Karl's mind. Rolf reached the second floor first.

"Why don't you go and tell Drachenblut, then?" Rolf asked.

"What do you know about it?"

Rolf leant his weight on his front foot. He leapt down into the corridor, running when he landed. Karl stepped up after him. Rolf blocked Karl's view of Olaf until Rolf jumped and grabbed Olaf's knees. Olaf stuck out his arms to break his fall. Rolf swam along Olaf, grabbing at his pants and tunic until he held Olaf's head by his blonde locks. Karl sauntered over while Rolf growled in Olaf's ear.

Olaf took Drachenblut's side too often for Karl. On May Day, after Karl had banished Olaf from the room, he had run back in and announced Drachenblut survived the attack. Rolf stopped growling and stood up. He landed a swift kick in Olaf's abdomen.

When Olaf rolled on his knees, Rolf galloped and stuck a boot in his behind. Olaf flew sprawling along the corridor but scurried back upright and ran along the wall until only his golden locks remained visible.

Helga still jerked and shook over Hegel's shoulder, wordless yet far from silent, her fiery eyes screaming vengeance. Rolf returned to the staircase. His boots clomped to the third floor accompanied by Helga's grunts and rustling silks. At this level of the tower, the clean scent of the outdoors mixed with the stagnant air of the castle. It cooled the stairs, hot from the light of the Eternal Flame. Karl took a deep breath and turned the fresh draft into a waft of stagnant, two-day halitosis. Helga retched.

Hegel stepped out of the staircase to the penultimate level of the tower. "Shut up with your indigestion,"

Drachenblut was certain to be alerted by now. His imminent arrival completed their use of Helga as a lure. Hegel dropped one knee, sloping to the right. The Chief Vestal tumbled from his shoulder to the floor in a sprawling mass of pastel silks and copper hair which emitted an increasingly loud, nasal whine. How could Drachenblut not answer the siren call of his lover?

"Wait 'til I tell Drachenblut about this. He'll have your guts for garters, and that's before I even tell my father!" She wagged her bony finger from her extended, spindly arm. "Karl, you'll never be the High Priest after this. You won't be alive!"

Helga didn't know whether Karl would become the High Priest or not. Nobody knew that, although Karl felt he would get that promotion, and soon. Helga's thin, white wrist protruded from the pile of fabrics covering her and she put her weight on her slender, beautifully manicured hands to push herself off the floor. Blue veins swelled from the glistening ivory skin of her forehead and forearms as she trotted away into the gloom of the castle's top floor.

Karl returned to the staircase, Hegel and Rolf following him as he ran the final few steps to the roof of the tower. A bass voice climbed the stairs, drowning out the stomp of ascending boots.

"This is your date with destiny." What nonsense the High Priest broadcast through the North tower! If anyone were to meet their destiny today it was Drachenblut. In a short while, Karl knew that Drachenblut would plummet from the roof.

"You're going be taking flying lessons soon, Drachenblut," shouted Rolf.

"Of course, that's what I expect to happen."

Why the High Priest now ran to his demise puzzled Karl. Earlier, he had run away from Karl and his guards. "Have you got a death wish?"

Rolf didn't announce that because Karl gave him no time. With reflex, mindless actions the key to keeping Karl's intentions private, he dwelled on nothing, jumping to action instead.

"I wish only to meet my destiny, as do you."

"Always coming out with this mystical bullshit! What does anyone know about the future?"

"You only speak of it that way because you can't explain it. It's fear talking. We both know what's going to happen next. It's what occurs after that scares you, isn't it?"

"Your death's next in my diary," Karl shouted. "Why are you running to it now?"

"You will praise me!" Drachenblut's booming voice reverberated around the stone of the spiral staircase.

"What are you talking about?"

Silence reigned until Hegel opened the trap to the roof and the clunk of the door and rattle of the ladders echoed. Karl felt Rolf's impatience like an itch in his brain, which he relieved by turning to climb the final stage of the journey. The cool metal of the step ladders soothed his wounded palms, but Karl's blood-soaked boots slipped when he put his weight on them. He focused on the top of the castle, carefully planting his hands and feet until he felt the wind across his face and grit under his palms. Karl pushed himself on the carapace, expecting soon to be the High Priest. An ember of anxiety glowed in his abdomen where Drachenblut's enigmatic message had ignited.

A cool breeze blew, assuaging the apprehension that grew in Karl. The tower's parapet, so low it only prevented rodents from falling, forced all three to huddle in the roof's centre. Karl felt Rolf's fear.

"I'm not a paratrooper. Nobody ever asked me to work at a height before."

"You could have let us know earlier." Karl shook his head. Rolf was almost as useless as his usual disciples. "Lie down by the trapdoor. When he arrives, you attack first."

Trembling, Rolf took a step forward then dropped to his hands and feet, scrabbling to the open door. He lay down and popped his head into the castle.

"I don't see h-"

Both Karl and Hegel jumped in surprise. Rolf's feet flew forward and his body flowed through the trap door. When he reached his hips, the legs flew up in the air and vanished. There was a thud of breaking bones, then nothing. Two deliberate paces rattled the ladder before Drachenblut's mane rose through and his fingers curled on the rim of the trapdoor. The High Priest threw himself up and raised a knee, placing his foot on the roof. He thrust his whole body from the hatch, his calico vestments raced past until the shin laces of his boots appeared.

"You will praise me!"

Karl worshipped nobody but the Norse Gods. Though the High Priest's build was impressive, Konrad and the Gods had legendary size.

"No he won't. You're talking nonsense again," said Hegel. "Nobody will praise you. They will forget, nobody remembers your predecessor."

"Taubert was nobody. I am not. Karl will carry my torch for me, and he will be my agent on Earth performing my orders from Valhalla."

"Where do you get these ideas?" Karl screamed.

"From a place that is beyond your knowledge, where the Valkyries fly and the Gods sing ballads of glory."

"Warm up your voice, then. You are going to sing with them now." Hegel bolted towards the High Priest.

The pair joined where Hegel's shoulder met Drachenblut's stomach. The High Priest doubled over, grabbing handfuls of Hegel's uniform, pulling Hegel up. Drachenblut fell centimetres short of the parapet, Hegel's head hit the low stone wall and his legs flew up and over the balustrade. Hegel opened his mouth silently screaming. His vestments disappeared beyond the tower's walls. Karl clenched his jaw and stretched out his hands to break Hegel's fall as Hegel flew to the ground. When the caterwauling stopped Karl felt nothing except pleasant surprise. He didn't want to experience someone's death.

Drachenblut looked up at Karl and smiled when he grasped the High Priest's ankles. With a surge of might from the Gothengau brainwashings, Karl thrust Drachenblut's knees up and threw them into the Wewelsburg air outside the North Tower. Drachenblut's hair and beard were the last to fly below the edge. The High Priest's long limbs flailed each meter they fell. Karl thought they beat out a rhythm when they pounded the stone of the fortress with a series of damp thuds and cracks.

"You will praise me!"

A final crack of flesh-wrapped bones breaking against rock, and then a long groan as life took leave of the outgoing High Priest. Karl sidled towards the edge and looked over at Drachenblut's limp, ragged body laid in a cross over Hegel's corpse. He looked dead to Karl. Drachenblut's prophesy meant nothing.

Karl placed a foot on the step ladder. The cuts in his feet hurt him now, and his arms and abdomen ached with exhaustion. When he stepped on the floor below, he found it difficult to release the ladders. Leaning on them eased his burden.

"What happened?" asked a feminine, dozy voice.

Edda, the junior Vestal Virgin, had finally arrived to investigate the source of the disturbance.

Karl parted his hair. "I'm the High Priest now." If Drachenblut were burned to ashes, then he couldn't come back. "Start organising Drachenblut's funeral pyre." She couldn't do it on her own. "Tell Hadwin to help you." The pair of them might be able to make a start on the task.

Chapter 21

Berlin, Tuesday, May 4th, 1965.

The Hellfeier's on-suite bathroom windows blocked none of the morning light. No arrangement or combination of the pillows and duvets helped Petra to sleep in the tub. It felt like she had been awake all night, remembering only vague patches of dreams here and there. Her thoughts turned to a long-term solution to her newly violent husband. Deep in her inner world of locksmiths and handguns, the sound of engines dragged her back. Who or what brought cars here, at this time?

Maybe the Gestapo were about to check their sleeping arrangements!

Petra jumped from the bath and coiled the duvet loosely over one arm. Completed, she leant over to grab the pillow. She unlocked the door and ran for the stairs, throwing the bedding on Max. Outside, car doors slammed and voices chattered.

"It's the Gestapo! Get up!"

Max's feet thudded on the bedroom floor. As Petra landed on the bed, the visitors hammered on the front door. She arranged the bedclothes.

"You answer that."

Max attempted to tie his robe closed.

The callers banged on the door again, so hard it rattled in the frame. Max finally managed to tie his dressing gown and sped off. Petra followed, hovering on the balcony to peer over the stair rails at the welcome mat. He thumped down the steps, landing with a bang.

The door squeaked when Max opened it. "Hello, you two! This is a lovely surprise. What brings you here?"

"What happened to your nose?" a familiar voice asked.

"I hit my head on something at the rocket base."

Petra drew closer to the stairs to see better. On seeing the unexpected arrivals, she ran down, as excited as when she descended the steps to take the title 'Voice of the Reich' in 1950. Steffi and Sebastian, presenters of Popular Observer, stood in her hallway dressed in tailored suits and exuding self-possession. Steffi idly fingered an ornament on the telephone table, but Sebastian puckered his lips to kiss Petra. His facial expression reinforced the effeminate vibe Petra always sensed from him. He pecked her cheeks.

"Petra, it's wonderful to meet you again. We should get together more often."

Steffi drew breath before speaking. "Yes, that's what we're doing now, isn't it?" She ran fingers through her auburn locks and drew her cheeks in.

"How can we help you?" Petra asked.

"We received a message from the top." Sebastian pointed both index fingers up.

"The Führer said, 'let there be singing'." Steffi directed her blue eyes to Sebastian's satisfied smirk, emulating his grin.

"Yes, he wants you to make a special comeback performance tonight in Gothengau." Shock pushed Petra a step back. "Max will accompany you."

"The Führer insists that you two," Steffi ran her paws down both of them, "can close the rift that opened up between the Reich and Gothengau since the attack."

In a practiced move, Sebastian stepped in with more concrete information. "There will be a concert this evening at a wonderful, fairy-tale location overlooking the Black Sea. You will travel from the airport in an open top motorcade. You have many fans in Gothengau, especially after May Day."

"Of course, Max is always welcome," said Steffi. "The greatest Hero of the Fatherland can turn up anywhere unheralded and still draw a crowd."

"It's a really exciting offer, but it's too short notice." Petra shook her head and touched her chin. She didn't want to perform. "I haven't done any voice exercises for months."

"Now come on, Petra." Scepticism lapped over Sebastian's expression. "Everyone's heard about your impromptu concert at the airport the other day. Lack of practice isn't going to wash with the Führer."

Max tapped Steffi's elbow. "I'm also due at the training base tomorrow."

A condescending smile and shake of Steffi's head disagreed. "That's been rescheduled."

"So you have no excuses." Sebastian grinned and lowered his head. "Everything has been taken care of for you, and your carriage awaits." Max shook his head and looked away. "Please take a little time to pack your requirements for an overnight trip. Max, wear your Space Agency uniform and all your medals. We'll wait in the car."

Steffi held the door open and raised an eyebrow at the three Gestapo men who beat up Max the previous evening. Max clenched his fists and moved from their view before Petra slammed the door and stomped to the living room.

"This romantic getaway is the last thing I need." And it could even be avoided. Hanna Reitsch had offered to fly Petra around the Fatherland. "At least I don't have to travel there with you."

The time to call in the favour arrived quicker than Petra expected, but she needed speed to pack for the trip and also speak on the phone. On the way to the bedroom she sat by the telephone and looked up Hanna's number. It rang and rang. This forced weekend away might be irredeemable. Petra returned the handset to the cradle until she heard Hanna's greeting and jerked the receiver back to her ear.

"Hi, Hanna. Petra speaking."

"This is a surprise! Is there something I can help you with?"

"Well, yes. You remember you offered to transport me around the Reich?"

"Of course! Where do you need to go?"

"Gothengau."

"Oh dear. That doesn't sound very nice."

"I know, but the Führer's forcing me to make a comeback concert to promote unity with Gothengau. Max is going too, but I want to spend as little time as I can with him."

"When do you need to get there?" Hanna asked.

"Now! Steffi and Sebastian are waiting to take us to the airport the moment we're packed. There are three Gestapo agents with them in case we disagreed."

"I'll wait for you outside the airport. See you soon."

Petra replaced the receiver and rushed upstairs to choose an outfit and a change of clothes. She tried not to pamper herself in the shower but panicked, water going up her nose and in her mouth. The visitors pounded the front door. It had taken too long. The Nazis wouldn't even let her have a decent wash. A spring coiled inside her. Patting herself down with the towel eased the tension. Changed but unrefreshed, she trotted down to the living room with her overnight bag. Max, in his silver uniform with medals around his neck and on his breast, cast her a black stare. The clean-shaven Gestapo agent bent over, pushing Max, then picked up Max's bags for him.

"We'll carry Madame's luggage, won't we chaps?"

His stubbly colleague's shoulders trembled. "Mustn't have our precious little snowdrop break a sweat if it's not space related, must we?"

"Enough with the ribbing, now boys." Wilhelm slapped each of them on their shaven heads. Both appeared resigned to the manhandling. "Get him in the car."

Max flinched when the thugs grabbed his shoulders, his pupils dilated almost to the edge of the iris.

"You get in the car as well, Petra."

The Gestapo shepherded them to the vehicles on the drive. Max looked at his beloved Porsche as the senior agent steered him away from it. After the Gestapo threw Max in the stretch limousine, they retreated to their kübelwagen. The standard vehicle stammered to life and rumbled away.

In the limo, Steffi and Sebastian sat on the back seat, facing away from each other. Petra sat opposite, sliding along the leather to the window, as far from Max as possible. When Max sat, the dejected look on his scuffed face belied the honours spread across his chest. The driver started the engine, and the stretched car took them down the drive. Soon, they reached the *autobahn* and the chauffeur hit top speed, flying down the inside lane of the highway. All gazed out their own window at the telegraph poles whizzing past accompanied by the drone of the Daimler engine and rumbling of vulcanised rubber on the road surface.

Petra fell off her seat when the car swerved violently. Fear of the speed at which they raced along smashed into her. She stabilised herself instinctively, hands on door handles, careful not to grab too hard.

When the motion steadied, Petra found her hand around Steffi's slender ankle. Steffi reached down to brush the hand away, then snapped open the glass panel to the chauffeur.

"Driver, what the Hell was that?"

"Sorry, madam. The car in front braked."

"Then stop tailgating! Are you trying to get us all killed?"

"Won't happen again, Steffi."

"It better hadn't, and it's Madam to you, not Steffi. So bloody familiar, the staff these days!"

After slamming the driver window shut, Steffi turned back to face the joyless travelling party once more. She flicked the hair from her face and glanced at Sebastian.

Sebastian brought his knees together and leaned forward. "You two don't seem to be enjoying each other's company. I hope you don't mind my asking, but what's the problem?"

"I do mind, actually." Petra's internal spring wound tighter in her abdomen. "We're being pushed around like pawns by the Führer, and now TV journalists want to discuss our marriage. As you can see, it's in a trough at the moment, and this weekend away isn't helping."

Steffi turned to Sebastian. "Why not make this a feature for the show? The headline could be 'Tough at the Top - Max and Petra Hellfeier tell all'. Sebastian and I would interview you together and separately to get both sides of your story."

"Aren't you listening?" asked Max. "You don't seem to be letting go of the idea. We're not interested."

"I know the Führer's interested. I mentioned it to him yesterday, and he got quite enthusiastic."

"You know that they'll only force you to do it if you refuse." Sebastian nodded sagely. "Why not welcome it instead?"

Petra's eye stung. A tear, plump with frustration, tumbled down her cheek. When Wernher became Führer, this would cease.

"Okay. We'll do it but give us a little time. We've been through a lot."

Steffi and Sebastian looked at one another. She pouted and he jutted out his chin.

"Of course. The next time we're in contact with Himmler, we'll let him know what you said."

The road noise changed when the car slid to the left and the driver slowed the vehicle down. Petra stared out the window again, keeping an eye out for Hanna while the car curved around the slip road to the airport's wide, concrete fascia.

On the pavement outside the entrance, the public turned their heads to follow the distinctive extended car. All but one: Hanna Reitsch stood apart from the morass of the gawkers, beaming with happiness and standing proud in her navy-blue flight suit. Recognition's smile curved Hanna's lips when she noticed Petra and Max in the limousine. She stuck her hand up and waved.

"What's she doing here?" asked Max.

"I called her when you were getting changed. She offered to fly me to Gothengau herself."

Steffi and Sebastian glanced at one another, then Sebastian leaned forward.

"I'm afraid that won't be possible. You must travel together."

"That's fine. He will sit in the back. Hanna and I will sit up front."

"Oh, no. No, that's not possible. I mean, you could fly off and be heaven knows where. No, no. That's not happening."

Anger flashed across Petra's sternum, tightening her solar plexus. The coil in her abdomen creaked. After she clenched her buttocks, the moment passed. The car pulled up near Hanna, who helped Petra open the door. They embraced when Petra stepped on the sidewalk.

"I'm afraid there's been a misunderstanding." Petra dabbed her eyes. "Max and I must fly together, to a known destination. Sebastian said that you might fly off anywhere."

"Utter nonsense!" Hanna threw her hands up. "If he can't trust me, who can he trust? I might have to have a word about this with the Führer myself. The cheek of it!"

The three Gestapo men lingered near the entrance to the departure lounge. Wilhelm glared at Petra.

"Why not have our minders come along?" Petra nodded towards her Gestapo stalkers.

"Are you being watched?"

"Yes. They've been with us since last night. Let's go and tell them."

Petra strode towards the agents, and Hanna scuttled after her. The Gestapo men stared at them casually, then looked at each other in silence.

"How can we help you, ladies?" Wilhelm fingered the buttons on his leather coat.

"Could you accompany us to Gothengau?" Petra asked. The agents all burst out into loud, hearty laughter.

"That's what we're going to do! No need to tell us twice - not after Himmler ordered us, anyway."

"Yes, but we want you to fly with me," Hanna said.

"So? As long as Max and Petra fly together, our job's done."

"That's great." Petra pointed back at the limo. "So we can grab Max and all board Hanna's aircraft?"

"Sure, whatever."

Petra led Hanna by the hand. They marched back to Max by the limo.

"Now we just have to get Max to agree."

"How are you going to do that?"

"Those agents beat him up last night." Hanna gasped and brought a hand to her mouth. Petra thought that would shock Hanna from her blindness to the Reich's dark nature. "The stick's been used on Max already. Maybe we can offer him some carrot."

"What can we offer him?"

"He loves his toys, and you are giving that new Heinkel its flying trials." Hanna's mouth formed a circle. "Why don't you offer him a go? I doubt he can resist flying the latest aircraft."

When they got back to the stretched car, Max looked up from putting the bags on the luggage trolley.

Hanna waved. "Hi Max." He only grunted in reply, barely meeting her eyes.

Max stood and leaned on the baggage cart, peering into the distance. "What do you want?"

"We want you to pilot the new Heinkel that Hanna's been testing."

Max's eyes came back to near focus.

"What's it like? I suspected it would slew around because it has no tail fin."

Hanna nodded. "It might. I may put that in my report to them, but I would love to hear your opinion before I do."

"What about Steffi and Sebastian?" Max hopped up and down. "They insisted that we go with a known pilot."

"Your Gestapo friends offered to put their minds at rest and accompany us to Gothengau." Petra's revelation knocked the thrill from Max.

"They were going there anyway." Hanna shrugged.

"They won't be able to share the cockpit?" Max's concern revealed a scared child.

"It will be just me and you there, at most."

Something on the ground caught Max's eye, and he spent the next moments examining it and poking the ground with a toe. "As long as they aren't all over me."

Petra needed to sell the idea harder. "It's a big plane, isn't it, Hanna?"

"Yes, it's got thirty seats so there's plenty of room. Just sit on the other side from them and read a book, if you want."

The presenters strolled over to them. Sebastian's brow showed concerned furrows and Steffi looked everywhere but at her fellow travellers.

Petra faced them. "Max is flying with Hanna and me."

A sigh hissed from Steffi and she rolled her eyes. "What do you think you're playing at? We told you that you can't just fly off on your own somewhere."

"The Gestapo agents are coming along. You said that'd be okay."

Steffi folded her arms and turned away.

"Yes, that will be fine, then," Sebastian said. "We will follow you, once we are airborne."

All three walked to the terminal, Max behind Petra and Hanna, pushing the luggage. The Gestapo men erupted in smiles when they saw Max.

Wilhelm nudged the grizzled underling. "Smart bell-boy you've got there, Petra!"

Max threw his shoulders back and planted his feet solidly on the ground with each step. He showed his brave face to the world, but this might not be such an easy journey for him. As they walked, passers-by turned their heads. There were mutterings and the occasional cheer for one or all of them, but the hall was silent as they walked through to the runway. When Petra pushed the door open, a wave of applause washed over her. Hanna, Petra, and Max turned and took a bow.

"I'm getting a bit tired of this fawning adulation." Petra turned to the planes. "I'm glad you two were there. It's like everyone is urging me to break into song everywhere I go."

The silver flying wing that Hanna used stood next to the conventional aircraft that Steffi and Sebastian had chartered. A ground-crewman let down the steps from the belly of Hanna's plane, and as they entered Petra watched the television personalities climb the air stairs. Sebastian turned and waved before he stepped inside.

At the front of the aircraft, Max's head moved from side to side as he inspected every surface of the previously unseen plane. Hanna stood in the cockpit doorway.

"Come in here," said Hanna. "It's much more interesting than looking at the passenger cabin!"

Max hopped into the cockpit and buckled himself in the co-pilot's seat next to Hanna. Hanna pressed a couple of buttons and the engines began roaring. On the map, Max plotted the way to Gothengau. Behind Petra, the door rattled as the Gestapo men lifted the steps up and sealed the plane. The aircraft's wheels trundled along the apron and Petra strapped herself into a seat.

"We're going to play cards to pass the time." Wilhelm deftly proffered a fanned deck of pornographic pictures, winking. "Why don't you join us?"

"I packed a book." At least she had it in her hand, so fighting off the gorilla proved easy.

The Gestapo chief shook his head. "Whatever." He returned to his comrades.

She tried to ignore their staring and chattering. How would she handle close contact with the Gestapo for the next few minutes, let alone the next 24 hours? At least the noise of the plane racing along the runway muted their mumbled taunts. If being escorted to Gothengau by the Gestapo was the height of her success, she worried what the nadir would be and when it would come.

Chapter 22

Gothengau, Tuesday, May 4th, 1965.

Konrad's head snapped up from the newspaper - blatant falsehoods about Gothengau's role in the rocket attack - at the clip-clopping of hooves, revealing a black-clad cowboy framed in the sitting room window. White foam dotted his black stallion's veined coat. Its rippling, jaw muscles pumped up and down as it swallowed huge draughts from the trough in front of the farmhouse. The weals on the beast's haunches demonstrated Baer's ample use of the whip. Konrad galloped to the door. By the time he stepped out on the porch, the dismounted gauleiter faced away from him. The sound of a roaring engine also drew Konrad's eye to the open-top car gunning down the drive.

"Hi Richard." Tension spread across Konrad's pectorals. Why had Baer come now?

"Konrad, I've got a surprise for you!"

Konrad's stomach revolved. "You've already startled me enough by coming here, what more could I hope for?"

"I don't know what you hope for." Baer tensed his mouth and stared. "But your friend Petra is flying over with Max as we speak."

"That's good news, and this car looks like I'm in for another shock."

"That's Aurelian with a surprise for me." Baer threw his hands up. "Why the bloody hell can't he leave me alone to enjoy a moment to myself now and again?"

The horse paid no attention to the vehicle pulling up beside him. Its shoulder twitched a fly away and the animal continued vacuuming up the contents of the watercourse. Uniformed Aurelian rushed out of the car.

"Great news! You've been invited to a funeral. Drachenblut is dead!"

"Then we must enact the plans. Better get ready Konrad, because you're going to have a lot to get on with."

"Yes. Especially with Petra coming. When is Drachenblut being buried?"

"He's not being put in the ground. He'll be cremated on a pyre at Wewelsburg Castle the day after tomorrow," Aurelian answered.

"Will Himmler and Heydrich be there?" Baer's expression flickered on the cusp between hope and disappointment.

"The guests of honour."

"Ha!" Baer made a little dance. "Then I won't be going. My rockets will take my place! Konrad, you take your men and secure the TV studio and central Berlin. Well, not all Berlin. The government areas around the Volkshalle will be enough."

"I already had that in mind."

"Excellent, so it won't take you long to get the details worked out. Leave it to your second in command, come to the airport with me and see Petra. She and Max will drive to the coast for tonight's concert. It's at the Swallow's Nest. We'll go to the airport and meet them now."

"I'll get the car," said Konrad.

"Forget your car! I'm not being driven around in a kübelwagen, I'm the Gauleiter. We'll take Aurelian's wheels."

Aurelian's shook his head. "I can't drive you there. I've got too much to do!"

"Relax, you're not taking us. You're taking my horse back."

Now, the deputy Gauleiter's shoulders sunk. He sauntered to the horse, and the animal lifted its head, banging Aurelian in the face. Baer bent over, hands on his leather chaps, chuckling heartily. The deputy held his head in his hands, shaking his head. He freed his face, and tears streamed down it.

"There's nothing broken." Aurelian caressed his nose. "Don't worry."

By that time, Baer sat in the driving seat of Aurelian's car. Konrad joined the Gauleiter and they backed away while Aurelian tried to swing a leg over the saddle. When they faced the right way, Aurelian still hadn't mounted Baer's horse. Pit-props in Silesia's deepest mines endured less pressure than Baer's lackey did.

"How long is it since you saw her, then?" Baer asked.

"Petra? She was at the meeting in Peenemünde the other day. That was the first time I'd seen her in years, except on the television."

"Haven't you ever been to one of her concerts?"

"Strangely, no. Tonight will be the first time."

"Wonderful!" Baer said. "You shall sit with me at the front."

"I have to ring my adjutant when we get to the airport. He can start with the preparations for the drops."

"You should take a page from my book. Aurelian is an adequate number two, so I put most of the burden on him."

Everybody knew that. Konrad didn't reply to the unhelpful advice but considered his duplicitous position. They continued in silence through fields of ripening wheat that swayed in the gentle breeze. The ears bunched together in waves under the wind's fine touch.

Jets roared overhead, and the flying wing Konrad saw at Peenemünde passed them. Its wheels yelped when they kissed the ground. It touched down parallel to the car. A minute later, another plane landed.

"That will be them now," said Baer.

They came to a junction and turned right. Baer parked the car and they hurried across the road to the terminal.

"Come on." Baer waved overarm to the airport. "They'll be out by now."

"You welcome them. I have to call my base."

Baer held a door open and Konrad marched over to one of the phone cubicles. By squeezing in his shoulders, he managed to get in and pick up the phone. After he dialled the number, it only rang twice before the cool Dutch tones of Konrad's adjutant answered.

"Obersturmführer Joost van de Beek speaking."

"Joost, there's something happening in two days, and I want you to prepare the men for it because I can't be there."

"Yes, sir. What will that be?"

"We are to make two drops over Berlin. The first will be at the Volkshalle, the second at the TV studio."

"How many of us will be on the team?" Joost asked.

"Two hundred. You'll need four planes to fit everybody."

"Of course, sir. May I ask what this is about?"

"No. I'll tell you when we're on the way there. I've got to go, Baer ordered me to welcome Petra Hellfeier and go to the coast with her."

"I heard she was coming," Joost replied. "I'm not a fan. Have a good time tonight."

Konrad replaced the receiver on the wall-mounted public phone before he eased out of the booth. He barely fit inside the structure, so getting out involved sharp edges digging into his shoulders, back and thighs. In the duration of that call, the terminal had filled up considerably, and the arrivals spoke excitedly of Petra and Max, space rockets, and missile attacks.

Konrad trotted to the windows. The stairs on Hanna's flying wing had not yet come down and Baer peeked and poked at the fuselage and wheels, peering up and crouching down to examine details. Konrad barged through the door and marched over to the plane. The doorway beneath the flying wing opened and Baer looked up at the source of escaping air.

Steps slid down the platform until they nudged against the ground and rattled. Max appeared first, the crowd in the terminal building cheered when they saw his face. The volume increased when Petra descended with a wave, but Max's smile became a frown when the audience's response changed. The couple scanned the ground, but their wandering gaze halted when it reached the unmissable Konrad. A beam spread across Konrad's face and his raised hand waved greetings. Both Max and Petra returned the salutation and the smile. When they reached the foot of the steps, Konrad received them first. He stooped to embrace the diminutive singer, then shook Max's hand.

"I only heard about the concert just now."

Baer's elbow touched Konrad.

"We only heard about it this morning," laughed Petra.

Max eyeballed his feet, and Baer cleared his throat. The Gauleiter stepped forward.

"It's a pleasure to meet you." Baer stretched out his hand. "I'm your biggest fan. Not forgetting, Max, of course. Why, your actions in the Battle for Russian skies gave me what I have today!" Baer opened his arms in a wide sweep.

Petra's eyes lacked any sparkle and did not reflect her smile.

"You're going to love your concert hall tonight. It's a beautiful miniature castle on the cliffs overlooking the sea, the audience will be on the meadow. Afterwards, you and Max can rest in a palace nearby. Its last owner was the Czar! You're going to have the most romantic working weekend ever."

The Gestapo agents exited the aircraft and padded behind Max and Petra. Wilhelm's nose flared when he breathed in sharply.

"Yes, they are, Gauleiter Baer. My men and I will ensure it."

Max touched the red marks around his eye and the lofty agent fixed his stare on the astronaut. His two smaller companions grinned at each other. The Gestapo leader caught Konrad's eyes, then his gaze darted away.

"Come, the cars are outside," Baer said.

When Konrad and Baer turned and stepped forward, the crowd erupted. Cheers and applause accompanied their passage through the building, with well-wishers touching Max and Eva as they strode through the throng.

A silver Mercedes with three-colour tail-lights in its exaggerated tail-fins waited by the door. Behind it sat Baer's car, and both chauffeurs jutted out jaws over expanded chests. A flunkey opened the doors for the celebrity couple, and the moment they sat, men appeared on the airport roof and rained tickertape on the Hellfeier parade. Baer grabbed Konrad's arm and dragged him to the following vehicle.

"This way, big fella. You're coming with me."

When the door clunked the procession eased forward, and the spectators broke into a round of applause.

"Listen to that." Baer raised a hand to his ear. "They love her everywhere after the tears. It's great she's back in the public eye. She has such a wonderful voice."

"Max has plenty of fans, too."

"Pah." Baer shooed that claim away with a wave of the hand. "They could send a monkey up there. It's not Hellfeier that matters with space, it's von Braun. Just like Mengele is important in our project, he could use a monkey for that too but the results wouldn't be as good as using . . . a fine Aryan specimen."

Konrad scratched his jaw. Shards of doubt shattered to stiletto fragments within him. "What project are you working on with Mengele?"

"Nothing for you to worry about, but you'll find out soon enough. You're going to be taken aback, I can tell you."

Reassurance from Baer silenced Konrad. The paratroop commander got no relief from his concerns from the Gauleiter's pep-talk. Baer gave the Nazi salute as the convoy slid through the spectators. His arm returned once the crowd thinned. The cortege took a higher gear, and the wind blew through Konrad's fine hair.

When the cars reached the coast, cobalt and azure met at the horizon and the sea breeze dragged the brine scent with it. They drove up a slope. Baer turned.

"Have you been here before, Konrad?"

"No, I haven't even heard of it."

The car reached the brow of the hill. Before them lay a natural bowl that focussed on a miniature, three storey ivory castle at the tip of the headland. A group of workers in striped pyjamas finished constructing a few rows of seats close to the building.

"Stunning," said Konrad. "Why is it even here?"

"It's a folly. An Englishman designed it for one of the Czars."

"Such luxury, and with their people owned as serfs as well. No wonder the Bolsheviks killed them."

"And we killed those Bolshies for being subhuman. Such is the progression of history. I mean, next we are going to strengthen National Socialism by getting rid of this Odinism twaddle. We've already started on that. Drachenblut didn't die of natural causes, know what I mean?"

Good, thought, Konrad. It wasn't his fault that the High Priest had died, Baer had applied more pressure. The convoy pulled up in front of the bridge leading to the little redoubt, and Konrad got out first. Petra approached him when he stretched, expelling the tensions that built up during the journey with Baer. Baer slammed the door when he exited the vehicle.

"Well, Petra, what do you think?" Baer's arms indicating the Swallow's Nest and the clifftop location.

"Spectacular. Perfect for the little castle."

"You'll feel like a princess, singing up on the top there."

"A princess trapped in a tower," Max said.

Petra answered silently, nodding sedately but with her face free of expression.

"You should start getting ready," said Baer. "The sun's going down, and the technicians and musicians are almost done."

Max began unloading their luggage from the car, but a nod from the chief Gestapo man forced his underlings into action.

"You have a rest." The grizzly agent shouldered Max away.

"Let us do the hard work." The hairless one lifted a bag over his head.

Max stared daggers ahead of him as he and Petra ambled over the walkway to the tower. Rounded balustrades defended them from the precipice on either side. Konrad followed, stepping carefully along their path. The banister came to just above his knees and offered no protection from falling.

Chairs, instruments, and music stands occupied the lower two of the tower's three levels. They walked through the string section to the door. Inside, the place was a changing room for Petra.

"This is a gorgeous location, Petra," Konrad said.

"Isn't it just? I'm hoping for a memorable night."

"Then we will leave you to it," said Baer. "Break a leg! Come, Konrad. Let your friend prepare. It's the night of her life."

As they walked away, Petra began opening her bag and removing the clothes. After Konrad squeezed through the door, he and Baer waited for Steffi and Sebastian to cross the bridge before they did. Both presenters screwed their faces and stared ahead as they navigated the chasm, arms firmly on the guard rails.

In the west, the sun neared the horizon and groups of people gathered on the hill. One of the cowboy-themed cliques fired revolvers into the air and whooped.

"We'll be sitting here, on these chairs." Baer pointed to the seating. "The show starts in another hour."

Stars twinkled above and the breeze blew cool sea air over the large crowd assembled on the hillside. On the folly, the musicians tuned their instruments and increased the anticipation of Petra's first concert in several years. Gradually the caterwauling became more harmonious, until the last violinist put the right tension into his strings. The silence lasted a moment, until the audience began cheering for Petra's appearance. At the back, the shouts, whistles, and applause of encouragement from the rank-and-file Gothengau residents were peppered with celebratory gunfire. Muzzle flashes impersonated fireflies.

When Petra appeared between the four spires around the ultimate tier of the Swallow's Nest, the cheering equalled the rattle of shooting. Smiling serenely, Petra waited patiently for the excitement to subside. When the band hit the first notes, she joined in.

Nobody heard because of the rancorous adulation. The revelry faded, until they recognised the tune and increased their loudness to signal approval. Baer began singing along to "Where Have All the

Flowers Gone". Obviously, people feared telling him about his voice and Konrad didn't broach the subject.

From this distance, Petra's facial expression was unclear. She most likely couldn't see him well, either.

"This next number is for those who lost their lives at the May Day attack."

This time, the gunfire didn't just come from pistols. Machine-gun rapid shots dominated the audience response. Konrad tensed up straight and his seat dug into his lower back. She began the minor notes of "Now the Sun Wants to Rise as Brightly", and the crowd fell silent at the dirge. When she had completed it, a gentle round of applause went up. Konrad shifted to get comfortable and managed to wipe the tears from his eyes with discretion.

"The tempo's going up a gear now. It's going to get more Country and Western." The audience whooped. "We can't mourn all the time, can we? Let's drink some of my pappy's White Lightning."

The band launched into a refrain on the slide guitars and the audience whooped. Konrad turned when the automatic gunfire rang out again. Scowling Hanna faced the same direction.

"Who brought a machine gun?" Konrad asked. "That's a bit dangerous in a crowd."

"Ahh, let them have their fun." Baer waved a hand in their direction and shook his head. "This is their heroine returning just for them, and they all love this song."

Baer passed Konrad a bottle of Schnapps.

"Here, have some of our White Lightning."

Konrad threw his head back with the alcohol to his lips. It burned before, during, and after he swallowed it. He passed the bottle along the row, a warm glow of pleasure spreading across his face. In moderation, drinking had its merits. Petra neared the crescendo, and the guns rattled their lead out in celebration. Something muffled the noise and the crowd broke out screaming. When he proffered Hanna the alcohol, she shook her head and immediately handed it to her other neighbour.

The crowd rippled on the hillside. They escaped a point somewhere near the back, but the momentum they gained pressed those standing too near the cliff edge. Lines of Gothengau's future dug their heels in to the precarious turf. Mouths ripped open with screams before they dropped.

The trickle became a flood. Caterwauling faded and ended with a series of bone-cracking thuds. Somebody needed to do something.

Konrad jumped up and ran past the walkway to the Swallow's Nest. A row of young people stared into the chasm, their eyes and mouth wide with horror. Konrad swung his arm across two of them and dug in his heels. Another pair were held by the other arm. Two or three rubbed their faces in his chest and tickled his chin with their hair. Grunts squeezed out of him as he leaned into the burgeoning crowd. These people will not fall. He ground a foot into the rock beneath and drove forward with every fibre of his being. The effort became gargantuan, dimming his eyesight. It must be. He would save these lives. Konrad planted one foot in front of the other and cantilevered his strength against the push to the crevasse behind him.

Chapter 23

Gothengau, Tuesday, May 4th, 1965.

Blinding stage lights stopped Petra locating the source of the gunfire. Her vision ended at the four white spires marking the edge of the tower, the Crimean night beyond its boundaries made opaque by the searing beams. Though they represented only irrational exuberance, the shots made her tremble with fear. The shaking spread to her abdomen. She missed an out breath and struggled to vocalise a line. It didn't spread to larynx or lungs. Pushing the nerves back down, she kept belting out the tune. The playlist contained a lot of crowd pleasers, and this song about home-made hooch hit the Gothengau spot more accurately than the two maudlin tunes she opened with.

As Petra sang the closing lines, the note of the shooting dulled, followed by a chilling, thousands-strong scream. Her spine quivered. Shading her eyes with her hand, she saw nothing but the glare of her limelight. Then the illumination shone on her no more but highlighted the tragedy unveiling below. Waves of bodies plunged over the cliff-edge to the blackness beneath. She dropped the microphone. From her throat to the end of the digestive tract, everything twinged and clenched. Despair twisted her stomach when she surveyed the carnage.

On the ground beside the turret Konrad brought forth strength unwitnessed since Samson pushed the columns apart. How could she or the Reich do without this man? Like a rock in the river, the concert-goers flowed around him to their doom, but his steadfastness caught many before the pressure of numbers swept them over the precipice.

Not wanting to witness slaughter again, Petra turned and descended the stairs to the Swallow's Nest. In the next level, the three Gestapo agents played cards around a low table.

"Your set isn't over yet. Is that what all the crying's about?" asked Wilhelm

Petra stammered. It amused the agents. "Something outside, on the cliffs. Lemmings." She sobbed.

Eyebrows raised and faces tensed, the Gestapo team clattered up the stairs as Petra ran to ground level. Max sat outside her dressing room, drumming on the chair with his fingers. After he saw the expression of grief on Petra's face, he shook his head, shot up and ran out. The door swung open. Mournful wails gate-crashed the room. She staggered behind her husband but straightened when she reached the bridge to the headland.

Max brushed Hanna out of his way and stomped over to Konrad. Hanna opened her arms and Petra dropped into them, buckling Hanna's knees a little.

"Oh my, Petra." Hanna staggered. "Give me a warning before putting your weight on me. I am too small for that surprise, even from you."

"Why do these disasters keep happening to me?"

"Relax, this is nothing to do with you. It's not your fault, you only happened to be here."

"Just like the attack." Lothar's splayed and fractured torso slid into Petra's mind.

"Exactly. Like that, but this time you didn't lose anyone close." A salty, translucent pearl tumbled down Petra's cheek. "You've shed enough tears for a lifetime this last week. Be good to yourself. We're all staying in Livadia Palace tonight. Go there now. Sleep. In the morning, have a long lie in."

The cars sat where they were parked earlier, and Petra returned to the tail-finned, silver Mercedes convertible she arrived in. It sat too close between two other vehicles to manoeuvre it out, but the limo behind it wasn't blocked in. She slipped into the driver's seat, and cold metal brushed against her leg. Instinctively pushing it away, she caught the keys dangling from the ignition. She turned them, and as the engine caught and she slipped the car into gear, a hand grabbed hers, wrenched it anti-clockwise and pulled the keys away. The engine cut out, and the chief Gestapo agent peered down at her, shaking his head.

"I'm afraid you going home on your own is more than my job's worth, Petra."

Behind him, the other two secret policemen stood either side of a deflated and dejected Max.

"You take the spaceman, and we'll follow."

The keys flew from the Gestapo Sergeant's hand and the sharp edges stung Petra's palm when she snatched them from the air. After putting Max in the passenger seat beside Petra, the agent slammed the door. Max looked away as she backed the vehicle up and turned it around. One of the Gestapo agents blocked her path once the car faced the other direction. He only cleared their way when the Gestapo's ride turned around and he joined his comrades. Petra put her foot down. The breeze temporarily relieved them of worries but burned a connection between the pleasant sensation of fresh, salty air and the screams of senseless deaths. No future trip to the seaside would be complete without replaying tonight's events.

The palace windows reflected the cars' headlights. Palm trees waved in the breeze, and the building's white colour gave the impression that it far exceeded its two-storey frontage. The convoy halted in front of the colonnaded porch and Petra jumped out on the path. If she got in the place first, they may not be able to find her to force her into bed with Max. Her soles slipped away from her and she grabbed the nearest door handle. It didn't move, leaving her upright but firmly outside. The Gestapo caught up with her.

"You'll need the keys for that, Madame," said the Sergeant. "Is this you just running to bed? You must be very tired."

"Yes, quite. It's been exhausting, emotionally speaking."

"You're not as drained as some others, though." Scepticism drenched Wilhelm's face. "Are you?"

"Somebody else having it worse doesn't make me feel any better." Petra attempted to stop the inner spring from being overwound. "How dare you make my suffering out to be less than the next person's?"

A deep belly laugh from the Sergeant stiffened Petra's jaw. Her resolve against this police intrusion drooped, though. When could they be rid of their unrequited chaperones? The other two agents brought Max with them. His uniform and medals broadcast pride and vigour, but his sluggish, adolescent movements and slouching posture gave no credence to the clothing and accessories. Max dawdled when the Gestapo escorted them to their room.

They weren't even near the stairs the second time the troupe stopped for Max. The sergeant turned and stomped over to Max.

"Grow up and get a move on! Schicklegruber, get behind him and make sure he keeps up." The grizzly skinhead took the rear of the convoy.

Petra wanted to take Hanna's advice and sleep. Exasperated, she turned to Max. "I'm tired. I've been through so much. Can't you hurry up so that I can get some rest?"

"Stop being such a drama queen. I've been through everything that you have."

"So, you don't think that dragging your feet is making a scene?"

Max responded by stopping dead. He grunted when Schicklegruber shoved him in the back, and his right foot sprang forward to prevent his face hitting the ground again. Max stared at Petra. His downturned lips mouthed the words 'just you wait'.

"I don't want to wait, I want to sleep. Do whatever it is now, in front of everyone. I'm not running around the bed all night to get away from you."

All the Gestapo agents guffawed at Max and Petra's public domestic disturbance.

"You two are great," said Wilhelm. "We never usually have an assignment this funny, do we, lads?"

Schicklegruber and the other minion chuckled in agreement. "No, boss. These celebrities really take some beating."

Max flinched at Schicklegruber's remark, standing ready for a blow to fall. None landed, however, and Max scampered away, his face twisted into a snarl. They climbed the grand main staircase to the next floor and marched to the first door in the corridor. Schicklegruber opened the room, his arm describing the path Max and Petra needed to follow to enter their chamber.

"Goodnight, everybody."

Petra sauntered in. Max got pushed. He hit the floor as a collection of splayed limbs, but immediately transformed back into a dapper state. By the time he regained his elegance, though, the door slammed shut.

"What's up with them, kicking and punching me like that?"

"They're jealous, and this is their chance to feel like they're better than the fastest man in the world. Once we're back home we'll see them a bit less."

"Thanks for your deep psychological assessment."

"I'm only trying to help. There's no need for the attit-".

Max twisted around so fast that Petra barely saw a silver flash reflected from his clothing. Pain burned from her scalp when Max pulled her to the bed by the hair.

"If you want sex, try better foreplay!"

All Petra wanted was sleep, and she had almost got there. Enduring the rape, she held her silence and stared at the light fixture on the ivory ceiling. Fine silver ornamented the light's ceiling shackle, its engraving detailing plants and flowers, as far as Petra could perceive over Max's bobbing head. The chain suspending the apparatus still referenced the double-headed eagle crest of the former owners, the Romanov dynasty. More excited, thankfully, Max shook, irritating Petra's nose with his fine hair. She sneezed, and that climax was the closest she would come to an orgasm from this repeated, unwanted coupling. Max grunted and thrust at her hips, deeply but without feeling, relieving himself of tension and freeing Petra from her marital duties for the night. He rolled over and snored.

A helicopter's continuous droning and images of limbs frantically grasping the air stood between Petra and a good night's rest. Every time she turned to find slumber, she found jealousy. Max just did his thing, closed his eyes and was out for the night. All Petra's pharmaceuticals sat at home in her bathroom's medicine cabinet, and she knew that that by sunrise she would still rattle the gates of the land of nod. Only wandering the halls could help, so she rose and donned her robe and slippers. Max grunted, but she didn't care about his disturbed nap. She pushed his shoulder to reduce his comfort.

"I can't sleep. I'm going for a walk."

Thinking of only herself, she let the bedroom door fall closed and its latch pushed into the socket with a thud. In reaction, the chandelier above her jangled its crystals and precious metal in a gentle alarm call. The next room's door opened. Hanna put her head around it.

"Petra, what are you doing?"

"I'm trying to get to sleep."

"By waking everybody up? How will that help you? Don't you have any sleeping pills?" Petra shook her head. "Then come in here. I always carry a few. Getting to sleep's been hard since, well that's no matter."

Before Petra had chance to take up Hanna's offer, the door opposite them opened. The Gestapo sergeant even wore black silk pyjamas embroidered with the SS runes.

"Is this musical beds? Get back to your rooms."

"I can't sleep."

"And I have sleeping tablets," Hanna said.

"Alright then. But don't have me coming out here again, okay?"

Wilhelm remained watching while they stood there. "Go on, get your drugs."

Petra entered Hanna's room. She heard the Gestapo sergeant's door slowly brushing against the plush carpet as he shut it. Hanna hurried to her bathroom, rooting around in the cabinet above the sink.

"Here!" Hanna held a medicine bottle. "I told you I always have some with me."

Hanna took a glass from the sink and filled it from the tap. Petra palmed the tablets and swilled them down with the liquid. She felt tired the moment she swallowed the two capsules, although she knew that was wishful thinking and it would take ten minutes before she drowsed beside her husband.

"I know it's a little personal." Hanna patted Petra's knee. "But are the Gestapo making you sleep together?"

The tension that the rapes built up boiled over her emotional barrier, and sobs hurled briny droplets from her eyes. Hanna opened her arms, sympathy personified, and Petra slumped into them.

"They humiliate him every chance they get, but he takes it out on me when nobody's looking. And he keeps making me have sex with him."

"Oh, well. It's hardly the same as a stranger jumping out of a bush, is it?"

"No, it's not." Petra shook her head in agreement. "But that doesn't make it right."

Somebody gently tapped on the door, and Hanna held Petra's stare. A slightly louder knock ensued, and Hanna rested her hand on the doorknob. On the third request to enter, she swivelled the handle and peered through the gap between door and jamb. Tension rose from Petra's sternum, sliced along her chest and shut down her throat. All she wanted was sleep. Why couldn't she be left alone for a moment?

"What is it? How can I help?"

"You don't want to listen to the stories she's spinning for you," Max said. "She is such a cry-baby lately."

"Why are you worried about what she said? Are you guilty of something? Do you think my daughter Eva would like to know what Petra said?"

"Don't say anything, Hanna, please."

"Tell her, Hanna," Petra said. "If she knows who he is, then it's over for them. Do you want your daughter playing around with a wife-beater?"

Petra slurred her final words, the medication removing her alertness. She put her weight against the wall and closed her eyes.

"Go to bed before you collapse." Hanna's voice existed somewhere in the dreamscape growing around Petra. "Here, let me help you."

When Petra leaned on Hanna, her knees buckled. Max's fragrance met Petra's nose as a hand grasped her other arm.

"Make sure that you have a lie in tomorrow morning." Hanna said. "A bit more rest will do you the world of good."

The floor covering changed when she entered the hallway, then it returned a few steps later after they entered Petra's room. The door clunked closed behind her. Petra's side imagined the feathered luxury of the royal beds. A few steps later, their softness hit her and absorbed Max's throw.

"What are you doing?" Hanna tapped Max's arm. "She is not to be hurled around like luggage. I am so disappointed to see this side of you, Max. You are becoming a disgrace to the Fatherland, not a Hero."

"This is our private business, and I've had enough interference to last a lifetime. Keep your nose out of it!"

"Take your hands off me, I'm going!"

Another door slam and then the mattress responded to Max lying down. Petra sloped towards the unwelcome arrival and wished it to be the last disturbance before she slumbered. Her head jerked back and pain scorched her scalp. He exposed her buttocks.

"Not again."

Max overestimated his potency. He couldn't manage another one so soon, despite all the provocations he suffered. When she laughed, it barely rustled the sheets, but Max still noticed. His fist rained down on the back of her head before he twisted around, pulled the sheets away, and put his back to hers.

Chapter 24

Gothengau, Wednesday, May 5th, 1965.

Light streamed over the eastern horizon, illuminating shattered young bodies at the foot of the cliffs below the Swallow's Nest. Night's passing brought birds to scavenge the pickings from the corpses. Those at the bottom had hit the ground first and absorbed their followers' impact. Now that Konrad's handiwork had revealed the older corpses, there was much loose flesh on which the vultures feasted. Further away from the food chain's peak, crows cawed waiting their turn and seagulls drank from the rivulets of blood flowing along the boulders before muddying the sand. It stank like a butcher's shop.

The sun made the artificial illumination unnecessary for cleaning up the fatalities, and the superfluous arc lighting switched off with a heavy clunk. Almost all the corpses were laid out on the headland. Konrad's sparse hair splayed flat across his scalp from energetic down-drafts. The helicopter reappeared. It floated seaward until its blades cleared the cliffs and then repeated its paced descent, stopping and hovering before its wheels touched the water. Foamy manes waved away from the powerful blast forcing the massive aircraft aloft.

After holding the human tide back, then spending all night loading cadavers, Konrad barely possessed the strength to hand one body at a time to the chopper crew. He kept his gaze down alongside his spirits when he lifted the body of a young man in uniform whose spine snapped unnaturally back. The girl after that was a case study of compound fractures in cowhide and leather boots. By the time he loaded the third carcass, so pummelled that bile and blood eclipsed its costume, somebody in the aircraft grabbed both his arm and his attention. He looked up. Baer shouted something at him, but Konrad heard nothing against the cacophony of rotors and engine. Indeed, it was the first Konrad had seen of Baer since the stampede. Konrad cocked his head and squinted, to which Baer answered by pointing up, and pulling Konrad in the cabin. Once Konrad stepped up from the rocks, they rose beside the limestone precipice. He flopped down on one of the side benches, head in hands. His eyes were closed when something landed in his lap - a microphone headset. Konrad looked up and Baer gestured at the pair he wore, then Konrad donned his too.

"Good work." Baer's voice crackled through the apparatus. "You might as well grab some sleep now, there's plenty to do when we get back. We're going to organise our little tribute to Drachenblut. The cliff-top crew can finish off gathering the last dead when they've unloaded this batch."

Konrad nodded and removed the headphones. Any two metres length of horizontal space suited his immediate, pressing requirement. He lay on the form, clasped his palms under his head, and closed his eyes.

A heavy landing bumped Konrad from his disturbing, tortured dreams. The surrounding landscape lay flat until the horizon, save for Baer's three-storey ranch. Blades chopped the air with decreasing speed the instant that the motor cut out. Konrad followed Baer to his house. He stooped to stand in the cabin and then get through the door. His final reserves of strength ebbed away after he leapt to the ground. Konrad fell to his hands and knees, and the gruesome thump of flesh and bone pounding against the earth forced Baer around.

"I've something that will help you with your exhaustion."

Konrad knew himself and his needs. "If I eat something and sleep for a few hours everything will be all right."

"You can sleep when you're dead! There are plenty of things to do today, so I need you sharp and agile. My medicine cabinet's got the perfect thing for your weakness."

"Do you mean those Panzer chocolates? One of my men killed himself after that. I banned them."

"Yes, you might feel it tomorrow, but they'll have you up and running in minutes, don't you worry."

"Are you sure?"

Baer waved his hand dismissively, his mouth downturned. "Don't let a few weaklings put you off something so useful, man! You're the size and strength of Atlas! I'd be surprised if the normal dose even affected you."

They took the back stairs to the ranch's patio into the government wing where Baer's twin blonde cowgirl-wives stood scowling in the hallway together with a buttoned-up butler sporting a morning suit, wing-collar, and bow-tie. Senior wife Heidi stepped forward.

"Why didn't you take us to the concert?"

Baer walked to his office without even glancing at his wives. "You don't even like Petra. You would have hated it anyway - there was a disaster. Hundreds died."

Heidi shrugged and turned away, but sister Irma's eyes opened wide. "What happened?"

"People were shooting in the air. Somebody dropped their gun, but it kept firing when it hit the ground." Baer had moved so far away he had to shout. "The crowd ran over the cliff getting away."

"It must have really affected you, Konrad." Irma's eyes met his, and she stepped forward to touch him. "You look like you've got the world on your shoulders."

Before Konrad could reply, Baer butted in the way of her hand and small talk.

"No, no. Not our Gentle Giant. He was up all night helping move the bodies to the top of the cliff. That reminds me." Baer faced the servant. "Schmitt, bring the Panzer chocolates and two glasses of water. And a jug of coffee to keep us awake for now."

"If I take those, then I'll be hyperactive today but tomorrow and the day after I'll be half dead," said Konrad. "We need me to be totally alert the whole time. I suggest that I eat something now then sleep for a few hours, it's still early. That will keep me alert for today. Tomorrow, on the mission, I'll use the amphetamines if needed."

"That's what you say now, but you should see how you look. Like an inflatable Odin with a puncture." Baer laughed. "You need some edge, some vitality! Be modern. A plate of food and forty winks won't do what German scientists can. I know you can be a stick in the mud with your Amish nonsense, but you're dismissing science by ignoring it."

Schmitt clicked his heels, bowed and left.

"You ladies amuse yourself for the rest of the day. Konrad and I have plenty to be getting on with. Aurelian should be here soon as well."

The Baer twins skipped and slunked from the room. Stooping, with shoulders slumped, Konrad collapsed into the chair in front of Baer's desk. Soon after they arrived, Schmitt came carrying the tray of coffee, water and a tube labelled Pervitin. The butler poured coffee from the can, Konrad took a cup and sipped the strong, hot fluid. It made him feel better after the first mouthful, but he knew it wouldn't last more than ten minutes. Baer grabbed a dose of speed. Konrad swilled a pill into his mouth and grimaced at the tablet's sharp edges under his tongue. Coffee got rid of the astringent, chemical taste it exuded from its hiding place. Baer smiled and put his share down.

"I don't need one. I spent last night sleeping in the palace next door."

Konrad resisted spluttering at Baer's dissembling and his dereliction of the previous evening's duty. Soon, however, the mere trace of Panzer chocolate dribbling down his throat would have him running his mouth, blurting opinions, and making fantastic predictions. His men did that when they took it.

The office door opened and in scuttled Aurelian. "I have Drachenblut's funeral arrangements."

"I must use the bathroom." Konrad stood and made for the exit.

"It's the third door on down the corridor on the left," said Baer. "Save me the details until Konrad gets back. I don't need to hear it twice."

When Konrad got through the door, he brought his hand to his mouth and spat the tablet out. The time resting in his palate made its edges less defined, but even the tiny amount he swallowed affected his movements. His jaw turned into a mill, his teeth millstones. In his mind's eye, a tennis pro returned rapid shots from a machine firing thoughts and ideas from multiple angles.

A few long, quick paces down the hall and Konrad pushed into the bathroom. Like the building, its plumbing harked back to the 19th-century frontier. While he drained his bladder, every breath infused him with power. Buttoning himself up, meth-induced suspicions rose in his mind. A stealthy return to Baer's office might reveal the Gauleiter's reason for his reckless attitude to Konrad's battle-readiness. Konrad cushioned the bathroom door closing behind him, padding back to the Gauleiter's room with his back against the wall and an ear toward Baer's office. Aurelian spoke.

"I'm sure Konrad's plotting something with Wernher. I don't know whether to trust him so much. If he doesn't take the TV station and the Reichstag, then we'll have no foothold in Berlin at all."

"What do you suggest we do? He's the only airborne unit we have, and any armour we send into the Reich's going to get destroyed."

"He isn't the only airborne unit. What about the Children? Mengele said they're old enough now."

"Yes, there is that. Mengele insisted the Children were combat ready. I've laid the groundwork for using them - I hear him coming. Quiet."

Konrad discovered a valuable nugget of information. Whatever the Children were, his cloning fear still loomed large despite the protestations of innocence from all quarters. Too massive to be inconspicuous, Konrad opted to break cover and plonk a foot down. He strolled into Baer's office. Aurelian shuffled papers in his hands. Baer drummed his fingers on the desk.

"Good, he's back now. So, when is the funeral, Aurelian?"

"It's going to be tomorrow."

"Then we only have today to prepare. Aurelian, order the missiles out on patrol again with the new targeting details. I've changed my mind about firing them, though. Why destroy our own air fleet, when we'll conquer the whole world with it? The plan's changed. Konrad, you should take your men and occupy the easternmost Luftwaffe bases. You won't even need to jump. You'll only have to land there and block the runways."

Aurelian stared at Konrad. Those rockets had Wernher's own self-destruct mechanism. They both knew about the kids Aurelian kept in the cellar but revealing that to Baer now served no purpose besides revenge. Konrad knitted his brow to stare back at Aurelian, attempting to remind him that the tragic offspring in the cellar were no longer secret. Aurelian averted his gaze. Konrad's orders from Baer ran counter to those he'd received from Wernher. He sighed. This would be the first time he went against a direct command. Konrad served the German people and their future, a future that Wernher already led. Baer represented every shocking past crime made by Nazi Germany.

"He's not being buried he's being burned on a pyre in the castle courtyard." Aurelian nodded at Baer's grunt of surprise. "Himmler and Heydrich will arrive there at 11 am for the ceremony in convoy along the Autobahn. When they arrive, the rocket attacks will start against

Wewelsburg, and our tanks will race to Berlin to consolidate our position."

"So, plenty for you to get on with today, Aurelian."

Konrad fought the boiling vat of aggression that his mind had become in the last few minutes. Staying around here meant revealing the truth. He danced over to the door.

"I have plenty to get on with myself. I'm going to get my men into order."

Konrad knew the helicopter hadn't left, so he ran back outside. With his car not here, he would find it difficult to get around. Konrad's adapted kübelwagen sat at home. Despite feeling like he could run back to his house in a few minutes, he still knew that no man could run so quickly. He popped his head into the cockpit. The pilot's jaw muscles rippled as he chewed a sandwich. His other hand nursed a coffee. Cheek's bulging, he shrugged.

"Take me back to my house. Baer's orders. It's ten kilometres in the direction you're facing."

Shaking his head, the pilot set his meal aside and started the rotors. Konrad got in the back. Shortly after fastening his seatbelt the aircraft rose, tipped forward and flew. He would be back home in minutes of finger and foot tapping, of staring wildly from side to side.

Konrad undid his seatbelt buckle and leant forward to the pilot. "It's this one. Put me down here."

Konrad ended up with his face against the back of the empty co-pilot's seat when the aircraft decelerated rapidly. Resisting the urge to punch the chair out of the helicopter, he stood and braced for landing. The chopper came to the ground with a gentle bump steps away from Konrad's front door. Konrad mumbled thanks to the pilot and ran to the house.

The telephone sat on a table next to the front door. Konrad dialled a number and waited for the answer.

"Wernher, it's Konrad. I've come from a meeting with Baer, and they have made the same plans as we have for Drachenblut's funeral."

Over the next two days, Konrad intended that his actions would shape the future of the Reich.

Chapter 25

Wewelsburg, Thursday May 6th, 1965

Light flooded into the High Priest's office through the recessed window behind Karl's new seat. The broad, squat desk lent him a sense of security. He would attend to the Reich's religious affairs in this office for many years to come. Two guards packed Drachenblut's items away in boxes under Karl's supervision. They hadn't started on the bureau, and Karl grew weary of seeing the empty eyes of the skull resting on him from his working area. Only the holy texts of the scriptures, the Eddas, would sit on the new High Priest's desk. There would be no distractions at his workplace. Karl occupied this venerated position now and had waited long enough to see the last of the morbid ornament. He pointed at the polished bones and turned to a guard.

"Get rid of that."

Banging and crashing came in from outside, drowning out Karl's senses of order. Building the funeral pyre started after dawn, and it could take the rest of the day to make so this disturbance must continue. He shouted the command again, but the noises from outside ceased at the exact moment he opened his mouth. The soldiers turned and stared, alarmed at his raised voice. They were scared, and Karl liked it. Some respect from the men was long overdue.

"Well, what are you doing sitting there? I gave you an order!"

"Of course, sir." The guard caught Karl's eye as he stood and padded to the desk.

Karl had hated the cranium since Mengele had presented it to Drachenblut. The blank stare from the eye sockets saw into his psyche, into the brainwashing and its effects. The skull knew. Karl would show the nameless head: he stood and opened the window then picked the head up and held it to his face before throwing it outside. A second later, it hit the pavement between the castle and the Vestal house, and the sound of it shattering filled the room. Both the men stared at him wordlessly.

"Don't just stand around, get on with it!"

No eagles, weapons or shields hung from the walls now, nor did any of the runes that had formerly been displayed there. Karl's favourite icons had replaced them, and the primary theme would be the Norse Web of Wyrd: nine staves arranged in an angular grid, in whose matrix all the runes could be found. It represented all actions of the past and future connected on the middle line to show the present. On the opposite wall, the Web's three-leaved knot form showed the same connections with curved arcs. Life's complexity summed up in such simply constructed diagrams.

That's how Karl would have Odinism. "Make it quick. The Heads of the Army and Luftwaffe should be here in a few minutes, and I want this place looking like my office, not Drachenblut's."

Drachenblut never received these leaders when he'd been in charge. A wave of confidence, an echo of the Gothengau brainwashing, forced his thoughts from his mouth.

"They'll see that they have a High Priest they can deal with in me."

Anxiety replaced self-assurance when the men looked around at him, then looked at each other.

"There are only these two runes left, sir. Where would you like them?"

"Put the Hrungnir's heart close to the door."

"Which one is that?"

Sometimes, the lack of basic Odinist knowledge frustrated Karl. That symbol denoted a warrior lost in battle, meant as a tribute to Drachenblut.

"It's the three triangles. Put the Helm of Awe on the wall opposite."

"This one, sir?

"It's the only other one left, you fool!" Where could Karl get good staff that actually knew something? He would have to set up some kind of school.

That rune protected against evil. Karl included Drachenblut in that camp, it occurred to Karl that Drachenblut might even return from the dead. That's why Karl would cremate Drachenblut, just to make sure he didn't get up to come looking for the new High Priest. Drachenblut's last words would be meaningless. 'You will praise me', Drachenblut had said before Karl pushed him off the North tower, but it wouldn't be easy to do that with no marker of his grave or shrine to his passing. Karl had been so cool, so detached, when he'd dispatched his former boss. Those feelings would be imbued into his new role.

On the desk, the phone rang, but Karl let it ring several times before answering.

"High Priest Dietrich speaking."

"Your visitors General Mannteufel and General von Hohenzollern have arrived to see you, sir. Shall I escort them to your office?"

"Of course."

Karl hung up.

"Okay, you two, it's break time. The visitors will be here in a minute, so take the boxes with you. I don't want it looking like a storeroom in here."

Unfamiliar voices wafted into the office as the guards left. Karl couldn't quite hear what they said, but one had an aristocratic accent and the other the rough, hard tones of Saxony. Their escort tapped on the open door.

"Please come in." Karl stood. "Hail Odin, and welcome to Wewelsburg, Generals."

Fritz and Mannteufel, both wearing formal uniforms, marched to the desk, clicked their heels, and bowed.

"Thank you for asking us, and please accept our condolences," Fritz replied.

"Also, let us congratulate you on becoming the High Priest." Mannteufel's scar flushed a frightening pink. "We were a little surprised at your invitation." He dusted down a chair with his hand before he sat.

"I asked you here to assist us in the funeral ceremonies. High Priest Drachenblut, beloved of all true Germans, will be burned on the pyre tomorrow." Karl steepled his fingers. It made him appear sagacious. "To properly honour him would, in my opinion, require a military fly past and a 21-gun salute. You are the Western defenders and are the only ones with that sort of power."

Fritz frowned and cast a sideways glance at Mannteufel. It triggered a spasm of paranoia. Karl tried to reason with the fear, knowing it must be a hangover from the brainwashings, but that didn't stop the flood of worries. Karl didn't know why Fritz knitted his brows. Obsessive concerns penetrated his consciousness like an insect larva. He had enough control to push the maggot out but the hole it left oozed persecution.

"We'd love to perform this service for our late religious leader."

"Yes." Fritz spread his knees and leaned in. "What's the timetable for the cremation? We can fly from the closest airbase and be here in minutes."

"Bringing artillery requires more than minutes, of course." Mannteufel waved a hand. "We will move the pieces here overnight and have them in place by sunrise tomorrow."

Ready co-operation from the Generals threw Karl into confusion. Maybe this new-found enthusiasm for Odinism was because of Karl's accession to the top of the German religion? Maybe they had another reason, something more sinister still? The Wehrmacht were to surround the castle with cannons and fly over it with combat aircraft - they could have a more destructive motive. He didn't know whether their allegiance lay with the Reich or with themselves, or if Petra and Konrad were connected to the generals. Petra knew everyone; she could easily have that fealty. Karl felt sweat prickling under his arms and hoped that it wouldn't show through his tunic. His thoughts were scattered, panicky; convictions made and broken every second. Who could he trust if he couldn't trust himself?

"Do you have a schedule?" Mannteufel tapped on the desk.

Karl twitched when his mind returned. He hoped they hadn't noticed.

"Are you okay?" Fritz cocked his head.

The generals looked at each other again. How would they think Karl a High Priest they could deal with when they saw him so easily distracted? He must focus.

"Yes, yes. I'm all right. My thoughts are with Drachenblut and the speech I'll give for him. Back to your question about tomorrow's agenda, Field Marshal Mannteufel, we obviously do have one already."

Karl opened a drawer and removed a notebook. He leafed through a few pages before reaching the right one. His finger trembled as he pointed to the line.

"Here it is, Führer Himmler and Deputy Führer Heydrich will arrive at the airport at one, then they will be driven in a motorcade along the autobahn to the castle."

Fritz produced a pen and notebook, jotting down the details. "And what time will the cremation begin?"

"I will light the pyre at two. That gives plenty of time for the leaders to drive from the airport at a stately pace, and for everybody to settle into their seats."

Fritz scribbled on his notepad as he qualified the time that his aircraft should be overhead. "And we should aim for the flypast as you light the fire?"

Karl envisioned torching Drachenblut, the flames engulfing him as a dozen jets screamed overhead. Some advanced, fast, powerful and striking German aircraft.

"Yes. An excellent idea. Make it twelve aircraft in a chevron formation. I think the Messerschmitt 1000 would be the perfect match with its wings swept forward; such a magnificent aircraft."

"Yes, that's the plane we were going to use." Fritz's chest puffed out.

Karl's suspicions were aroused. He wondered if it could only be that the Luftwaffe chief found this plane as appealing as Karl did, or did he have some ulterior motive. The doubt leached suspicions the more he dwelled on it. They could attack the castle. They could destroy the German religion. Could this be an attempt to annihilate everything he aimed to do?

"High Priest Dietrich!" Mannteufel clapped his hands.

Once again he'd drifted away. Karl shook his head.

"I'm fine. It was nothing."

"It didn't look like nothing," Fritz said. "Are you sure you're okay?"

A slew of suspicions swam into Karl's stream of consciousness. What did they know, and what did they want? He blurted out his fears.

"It's Gothengau. They worry me."

"Why?" asked Mannteufel.

Fear breached the dam where Karl stored his dread. "Gothengau engineered Drachenblut's death."

Fritz stared at Karl.

A vein throbbed in Mannteufel's temple. "How?"

Karl couldn't tell the truth about this, even to himself. "They drugged him. Or someone." Karl parted his hair with his finger and the digit glistened afterwards. "It doesn't matter how they did it if they did it. And they are behind this, don't worry."

"This is a serious concern to us, indeed to the whole Fatherland, and we sincerely thank you for informing us." Fritz nodded. "But don't worry, we have everything under control."

Perhaps Karl's best protection from Gothengau lay with the Wehrmacht Chiefs. He needed to get them on his side, and his rumbling stomach brought the castle kitchens to mind.

"Are you hungry? We have an excellent chef, and a cellar stocked with the finest wines."

"That's a very good idea," said Fritz.

Karl walked to the door.

"Lunch will not be ready for a short time but allow me to give you a tour. This is the only Seat of the German Religion."

Until the trio reached the tower, there were no windows into the courtyard, and even in the tower's spiral stairway little could be seen through the arrow slits. After they descended from the first floor, Karl led the Generals into the courtyard. Logs filled the shoulder-high framework of the triangular pyre. Drachenblut's bed for the night. Karl stopped before it.

"Cremation isn't the customary funeral in Odinism, is it?" Mannteufel asked

"Generally no, burial is far more widespread. Drachenblut, though, was neither common nor general. He deserves a more distinguished ceremony."

Four priests carried Drachenblut's shrouded corpse on a bier from the North Tower. Karl had no idea who ordered them to do it. Each had a corner on their shoulder, and some grimaced in discomfort and exertion. Rage popped and fizzed. Karl had esteemed guests. His underlings should only pay him respect, not display their mistaken initiative.

"Halt right there." Couldn't these people use their own mind to see that this was wrong? "Why are you placing him on the pyre without my orders, without even notifying me? I am the High Priest now!"

Karl marched to the head of the bearers. Why did everybody have to work against him?

"We thought the time had arrived." The priest shifted his weight-bearing shoulder. "We meant no disrespect, High Priest Dietrich."

"I certainly hope you didn't! Do not presume to know my orders again - not on this or any other matter."

Karl held the priest's gaze for several moments, while he blinked nervously and averted his eyes. Maybe they had a point, though. This could be just the moment, with his important guests here, to spread some of the Odinistic faith.

"Follow me." Karl turned, taking a half step and pausing. The pall-bearers followed suit.

He had always pictured Drachenblut's final journey accompanied by a verse that Karl had composed years before.

"Odin, prepare yourself,
Asgard is to receive a new inhabitant,
Valhalla will have new blood."

Slowly and purposefully they stepped towards the opposite end of the bonfire.

"The blood of a dragon,
The High Priest Drachenblut will feed purity to
Nidhogg as it devours the cast-out Neaths at Yggdrasil's roots."

As they reached the end of the pyre, they turned a vertice of the triangular heap before they resumed their slow parade. Panicked joiners sprayed perspiration, hammering the final touches to the log pile steps that led to Drachenblut's final resting place.

"Drachenblut will become a new
Blood red ring in Yggdrasil's trunk,
Unifying the Nine Realms."

They turned to climb the new stairs, and Karl went to the rear of Drachenblut's litter. Frantic battering accompanied the party's first paces towards the steps before the carpenters stepped back from their fast work.

"Lay here to rest tonight,
Before you feast in Valhalla tomorrow."

Already the front of Drachenblut's bier had ascended the steps to his funeral pyre, the rest of his body sloped down with the stairs' thirty-degree angle. When the trailing bearers stepped forward, Karl placed his foot on the first step. He put his weight on the log and brought his other foot forward but a loud, wooden snap emitted from the bonfire. Underneath him, the log rolled, and Karl teetered on it, trying to regain his balance by swinging his arms. It didn't work, and Karl fell on his back with the other steps rolling around him.

Drachenblut's litter shot up into the air as its bearers fell to the floor. His shrouded corpse seemed to stand unsupported for an age, but not for long enough for Karl to escape Drachenblut's new descent. Drachenblut succumbed to gravity, toppling towards Karl, and landing on him so that he and Drachenblut were face to shrouded face.

Karl struggled to get free, pushing the stiff body away and squeezing from underneath it.

"You will praise me." Drachenblut's disembodied voice repeated his last words before Karl threw the corpse off him, screaming.

Chapter 26

Gothengau, Thursday May 6th, 1965.

Someone, or something, cleaved Konrad's head in two. Though the Pervitin had merely rested in his mouth yesterday, the hangover it inflicted today sparked thoughts of a brain tumour. He didn't recall taking to bed last night but feared looking around because of the pain daylight might bring. After summoning the courage to peep, he squinted at the bed above him and the bunks around him for a few seconds before remembering his location. He had to prepare for today's drop on Berlin at the 500th's barracks.

On the wall, the clock ticked towards seven. Time for roll call. Konrad scrambled from the cot and placed his hands over his ears just as it sounded. The strength of the alarm almost made Konrad scream out. Hollering would only make it worse. Keeping his mouth shut, though, took as much strength as holding back hordes from the cliff edge. He panted. The bell must be nearly finished, it had to be by now.

A coffee aroma opened Konrad's eyes. He reached out automatically to the tin mug being offered to him. The acrid, bitter brew improved Konrad's sprits enough to scrutinise his surroundings and assess his status. First, he needed his uniform; offices of state could not be captured when wearing only underwear. As an obstetrician attending the Fourth Reich's birth, Konrad needed to be properly attired. He reached for the uniform that he threw on the bunk above him the previous evening.

"It's best to shower first."

Konrad jolted in surprise.

"You know, Sir, to get rid of your hangover." Near invisible, Hoechst always had a way of being there without being noticed.

Perhaps it was his sloping mouth. Maybe his downturned shoulders. Either way, everybody overlooked him and it shocked Konrad that he occupied somebody's attention so deeply that he had a Court Martial.

"I'm not letting the men take those pills again. I've never felt this bad in my life."

"You already banned them, Sir."

The after-effects impaired memory as well as thinking. Konrad grunted acknowledgement of the reminder and shuffled to the bathroom.

Warm water dripped on Konrad's, face, shoulders, and then the fluid spread the heat across his whole body. To wet his scalp, he stooped. The tingle made Konrad human again, breath rushed through his nose, his chest expanded. Leaning against the wall with one hand, he enjoyed the liquid's heat traversing him, increasing its intensity by massaging himself with the soapy sponge. He rinsed off, wrapped a towel around him and padded over to the line of sinks on the wall. When he brushed his teeth and shaved, he improved more, although his eyes were now so tiny that he could barely make them out in his reflection.

The flights would take off at eleven hundred hours. Konrad put on a fresh uniform and returned to the bunk room where Hoechst sat polishing his boots.

"Hoechst, bring Obersturmführer van de Beek."

Van de Beek could organise the men, Konrad had too little energy to rush around making sure the 500th had dotted all the 'i's and crossed all the 't's. That's what junior officers like van de Beek were for. Five minutes later, Hoechst returned with van de Beek, and the cool Dutch Obersturmführer stood at attention awaiting instruction from Konrad. "At ease. We're flying at eleven hundred hours." Konrad rubbed his hands down his face. "Make sure all the men are ready to board in the next thirty minutes. And fetch me some aspirin."

Van de Beek saluted and turned on his heel. His barked commands were easily heard from the next room, as was the men's resulting activity. Hoechst returned with a glass of soda and the headache pills. Konrad swilled the tablets down. They brought immediate, if psychosomatic, reduction of the pounding in his skull. As the pain subsided he remembered to call his wife.

Konrad went to the Sergeant's office and closed the door. After he dialled the number, Diana answered quickly.

"Konrad? I've been so worried. Petra called. She was really upset about something to do with you."

The roar of a landing helicopter drowned out his voice when he spoke. He reached to close the window as Aurelian and Baer stepped from the chopper. Now Diana could hear him a little better.

"Baer is here. Something is up with the mission, I know it. I have to go. You and the kids have to go."

Diana might have said something other than goodbye as the receiver arced to its cradle.

Konrad met the new arrivals on the lawn. Both of them wore SS dress uniforms and broad smiles revealing their happiness and jagged teeth.

"Today Gothengau builds the Fourth Reich!" Baer held his arms up. "How are you feeling, Konrad?"

Baer stood on his toes to give Konrad a hearty pat on the shoulder.

"I'm weathering through the Pervitin I took yesterday."

"Good, good! You'll be okay when you're on your new mission, take my word for it.

"We decided you don't need to focus on the Reich Broadcasting studios or the Chancellery anymore. You remember we spoke of the secondary targets last night? You are to take the Eastern Luftwaffe bases."

"What?" Konrad couldn't believe his ears. "That's a significant change at the very last minute. How are we supposed to plan a different mission when we fly so soon?"

"Don't worry, it's okay to forget after taking Pervitin," Aurelian said. "That's why I didn't take any."

"I know we talked about the importance of the Reich Broadcasting studio and the Chancellery last night, but I've changed my mind about it now. That's all show, all bluster and bravado. A tank invasion at the earliest opportunity, that's the way to do it. And we don't need a reminder of their air superiority, so you should capture all the eastern Luftwaffe bases."

"That's a massive change in plan, sir. We don't have the locations of the targets, and we take off soon."

Aurelian handed Konrad a folder.

"The details you need are all in here. I'm sure it will come back to you when you read it. There shouldn't be any resistance, should there?

Just landing on the runway will stop them. By tonight, Konny will be famous."

Suspicions dug itself from the grave Konrad had buried it in, soil tumbling from its fingers. "Who calls me Konny?"

Nobody answered. He sucked on his teeth to keep his opinions inside when he browsed through the sheets detailing the air bases most in need of capturing. Clones pushed from their quiet mental corner.

"Hand the locations to the pilots and let the commanding officers read up on it during the flight," Baer said.

"Why aren't you firing rockets at the air bases anymore?"

"Those aircraft are valuable resources," said Aurelian.

"And we need them for the next stage of our plans." Baer rubbed his hands. "Our dominance won't be limited to the Fatherland and the lebensraum anymore. Look at what England has - it has the whole world, and we have only Europe. The globe will be ours, but if we have to rebuild our air power, it won't happen soon enough."

"So, if I'm not to go to the TV studio, why will I be famous tonight?"

"Aurelian is convinced you will be seen as the saviour of the Reich." Baer shrugged. "Of the whole world, even, because of your capture of the air bases. That's what will allow our forces to take over the Fatherland. You are Gothengau's avenging angel, descending on Germany from the skies."

A bicep twitched, flickering like a light. More likely Konny was one of his copies. This pair of liars had used his own body against him, he was near positive. Now Konrad's stand against these murderers hardened. No way would Baer oversee the Reich if Konrad had anything to with it, and Konrad sat centre stage of the whole operation. Disobeying orders be damned, Wernher will be Führer of the Reich today. National Socialism executed the Final Solution. It was time they accepted the stigma, crawled under rocks, curled up, and died.

"Yes, that's totally what I meant." Aurelian nodded his head too emphatically. Did the deputy Gauleiter wink at Konrad?

Konrad had to arrange his family's safety, and he could do without these two scoundrels blocking his path.

"That's great. I'm very reassured by that, but I really have to be getting on. The change of plans you gave me means I'll have to address the men again before we fly."

"No problem, we completely understand." Baer nodded in sympathy. "No mistakes, though. I've waited on this day for years, and later the Reich will be mine: soon after the whole world! We also have our change of plans and the need to speak to the . . . the . . ."

"The other details," Aurelian said.

"Yes, absolutely. We must see that those other details have their orders too."

Baer and Aurelian turned on their heels and trotted to the door before Konrad could ask about what that meant. Almost straight after it closed behind them, the helicopter's engines revved back to life and they flew on to their next appointment. Konrad dived for the phone.

"Diana, you and the girls have to pack your bags and get over to the base. I'm sending some of my men to escort you."

"Right now?"

"Sooner, if you can. You'll be going somewhere else after that."

Konrad put the phone down and turned to van de Beek. Van de Beek organised the flight for the drop. They still travelled to Berlin, so van de Beek needed no new instructions.

"Something's happened. My wife and girls need to be kept safe from threats - threats in uniform. You're not coming with me anymore, because you're going to get my girls and bring them here. Arrange enough men to fill four Hanomags and head for my house. Just take political prisoners, not the rapists. Place my girls under the highest protection, and trust nobody."

"Yes, sir." Van de Beek saluted and turned.

Before the adjutant got anywhere, Konrad grabbed his shoulder and handed van de Beek the documents.

"Have the kitchen staff set fire to these."

While Konrad tucked into a plate of Bratwurst and potatoes, pockmarked Schink appeared at the table. The meal had improved Konrad's mood and substantially improved his hangover. He looked up at the pugilist.

"How are the preparations going?"

"Everybody is ready. We are only waiting on your word."

Konrad nodded and returned his attention to the remaining morsels of food on his plate. After he had swallowed the last mouthful, he swilled down the rest of his coffee and stood.

"First, though, gather the men."

Steadier on his feet, now, Konrad took huge strides towards the parachute rigger room. He took his parachute from the locker and slipped it on his back, then went to the runway.

Two hundred paratroopers stood to attention and saluted as Konrad strode outside. Behind them, the four aircraft transporting them to Berlin waited, engines already turning the propellers. Konrad returned the salute, and the sergeant ordered the men to stand at ease. The sound of their heels stamping in unison briefly drowned out the turboprops.

"Today, you will be redeeming yourselves and the Reich. You men of the 500th will change the whole world."

"There are two groups. My team will jump over the Reich Television studios, and the other will take the Chancellery. We will secure them for a change in the government of the Fatherland. Later today, Wernher von Braun will become our Führer."

"If it sounds easier than our forays into Siberia, don't be fooled. What we'll see there, whether there will be an opposition at all, is a mystery. I know it sounds crazy, but Mengele has got me worried with his prodding and poking. Any opposition you do see may, I fear, be familiar to you. You might see others that look like me, but they are not me."

Schink stared at Konrad, an eyebrow cocked.

"Take pride in what we do today, be proud of tomorrow's Reich for you will be its builders. Now, board those planes, and we will take Berlin!"

Sergeants ordered the men to the open rear doors of the aircraft. Once the planes were the men's backdrop, it became difficult to see them as clearly because of the matching camouflage of the uniforms and the flying machines. Konrad boarded the lead plane. He sat at the back, between pockmarked Schink and invisible Hoechst, whose helmet rested so low Konrad could barely see above the tip of his nose.

Motors whirred until the back door latched shut, leaving the interior of the plane dark and dingy. Konrad's eyes adjusted for a moment before he could see the row of men sitting against the wall opposite. No sooner had that happened than the engines started in earnest, drowning out any other sounds.

A few minutes later, the craft levelled out letting Konrad and the men effortlessly sit perpendicular to the bench. The turboprops quietened enough for a conversation to be heard over the roar. Schink turned his head to face his commander.

"Sir, what did you mean in your speech about the 'familiar opposition'?"

"I have a fear that I've been cloned by Doctor Mengele."

"What? That's crazy!" Schink's shaking head, fleshy and heavier with armour, ran through his body and the peak of the wave touched Konrad. "How did you get that idea?"

"Before we flew, Baer and Aurelian visited me with new instructions." Konrad raised a finger. "I mean, entirely new, nonsensical instructions to change our destination." His wife's possible message over the phone came to mind. "And a phone call I had!" Excitement subsided. "For a while now I've suspected that they were up to something, Mengele has been too interested in me and my ways. Baer's reasoning sounded, to me, like my clones are going to take the TV studio and the Chancellery. We're supposed to take the Eastern air bases to prepare for a Gothengau land invasion."

Schink's cold eyes held Konrad's unblinkingly for several seconds. The brawler's fierce stare made him almost inscrutable. Konrad hoped that his admission had been the right thing to say. He had gone off a bit.

"What do you want us to do if that's the case?"

"I don't know. But I think that me killing the clones would be, well, killing myself. Hold fire until they start shooting us."

From the other side, Konrad felt Hoechst nudge him.

"I speak for all the men, Sir, when I say that none of us would wish you any injury. If it happens, we'll try and capture them."

"If you're right," said Schink. "What do you think the clones will do when they see you?"

"We'll know soon enough."

For the remainder of the flight, there was silence in the plane. About an hour later, Konrad felt his body leaning with the aircraft as it made a rapid descent. The rear doors opened, giving the vista over Berlin. Above them, the lights changed from red to yellow. They stood in two lines looking out over the dome of the Volkshalle and the crater on the Avenue of Splendours where the rocket struck less than a week earlier.

The plane banked, slowing down to turn, and the light changed to green. A familiar feeling of fear and excitement spread from the pit of Konrad's stomach as he stepped forward into the draft at the back of the aircraft. Air rushed past his ears and into his squinted eyes. His parachute deployed and straps around his torso dug through the uniform so hard he felt them chafing his skin. Soon after the deceleration, he floated like a petal ceding to its fruit, relishing the view of the antenna threaded through the courtyard of the twenty-storey cylinder. He steered to avoid the cables staying the transmitter, but a gust of wind pushed him back.

Wrist thick bound wire rushed toward him. Beneath lay over ten meters of air between Konrad and the ground. Tugging one of the parachute's guides made him drift away from the hazard, but a breeze put him back on path for disaster.

Konrad was so close to the danger that he could reach and touch the stays. He looked up. The parachute grazed the metal. It folded in on itself. The floor no longer ambled in his direction. Grass rushed towards him. He reached out instinctively, trying to stop hurtling to his death.

Chapter 27

Berlin, Thursday May 6th, 1965.

Several years had passed since Petra last graced the Reich Television studios, and it brought baby Wieland to mind. The cylindrical building, its sheen, and the antennae soaring above it had the poor boy's eyes open almost as widely as his cherubic mouth. She had taken him there the last time she visited, shortly before he departed the world. Waves of memories - Wieland's awe at the cameras, his smile that still shone through his agony - washed over her, and her foot didn't take the step it should have. Standing there, Lothar's death, the rocket attack, the calamity at the Swallow's Nest, put her mind firmly in the shadows. Getting through this public appearance took strength, and she did it alone. Max had it so easy. Wernher ordered him to the training camp the moment they were back from Gothengau. Her fists clenched recalling the happiness shining from his dilated pupils.

Steffi stopped beside Petra and turned. "Come. It's not much further."

A hand clasped Petra's. Sebastian looked down at her with a tender smile, her hands in his. Jesus, this guy. He drew her towards him. Muscles around her lumbar clenched then fluttered.

She shuddered when their faces brushed together as his breath molested her ear. "You look so pale. We know how you must feel." The nonsense this guy spouted - he didn't even know how much he repelled her. "You've been through so much this week, but we have some pills to help you when we get to the studio. Steffi and I have very busy lives, so we often use them."

The walk from the car had been a struggle, but Sebastian's smarmy encouragement made it worse. Only the promise of pep pills kept her going. Petra's next leaden steps carried her toward her appointment to co-host the broadcast of Drachenblut's cremation with Steffi and Sebastian.

They entered the building through the glass-walled reception area. A ten-meter high ceiling covered a room the dimensions of a football pitch. Faux-Doric columns decorated the walls all the way to their peak and between them, monochrome murals of Aryan figures competed in sport and experimented in science. The transparent walls at its far side showed the courtyard, with the focus of the whole structure: the base of the antenna that lashed the Berlin sky.

A grey-haired man in his late fifties emerged from the lift bank with an entourage following him. Staring at Petra intensely, he strode over to them and extended his hand out to greet her.

"I'm Florian Siegler, head of Reich Television Broadcasting. This whole thing is my circus." Florian's hand described an arc. "And I want to make sure that you have everything you need to get through this. If you want anything, ask me or my assistant Jürgen."

Florian nodded towards Jürgen's youthful, lean figure before leaning towards her, his cologne filling her nostrils when he whispered.

"I know what you've been through, I heard all about the incident at the Swallow's Nest."

Florian stepped back, and he smiled at her open mouth. Bodies bounced off rock and into Petra's memory. Florian was on her side, and it eclipsed the painful events of the Swallow's Nest concert. Unseen strings tugged at Petra's face, turning her gape to a grin.

When they entered the green room, a young male assistant handed her a cup and a white tablet on a saucer. Petra gladly took the pill, washing it down with her first sip of coffee.

"It hasn't changed since you were last here," said Steffi. "Do you remember what happens now?"

Petra nodded. They would all go through to make up, but she still didn't feel like talking and left her communication to a nod and a knowing smile.

"Bring your drink through with you." Steffi led her to the next stage of the process.

Each of them sat before a lightbulb-framed mirror, where the make-up girls waited in their extravagantly fashionable mini-skirts and Day-Glo colours. Having to look at her own face so brightly illuminated, especially after her recent misfortunes, made her feel self-obsessed. Blotches blemished her skin, and she couldn't be the only one to notice those crow's feet. Not until she had finished her coffee, and the make-up girl finished applying the first coat of stage-paint, did the tablet take effect. The previous week's tribulations merged with the wall-paper of her waking mind. Sebastian, sitting in the chair to her left, caught her eye and smiled.

"You look like you're feeling better."

"I'm starting to. What's today's schedule?"

"We're going to narrate the progress of the Führer to the castle after his plane lands, and then the progress of his cortege to Wewelsburg Castle."

"There are more cameras at the castle," Steffi said. "We'll be cutting back to them regularly to comment on the situation there."

"Oh good." Petra shifted her weight from one side to the other. "I can't wait to get started now. Is there anything that you'd like me to focus on?"

"If you could talk about Karl Dietrich, the new High Priest, that would be great. Nobody knows much about him, but we discovered that you and he came to the Fatherland together."

"Well, we were on the same passage, but I wouldn't say we came together. I was a girl at the time."

"That's still more than most people know," Steffi said.

"Oh, I know something about him, alright." Euphoria spread out from her sternum across Petra. "The flypast and the hundred-gun salute are going to change the Reich for good." The edges of Steffi's lips curled, and her eyebrows moved closer together. "I mean, they're going to be good for the Reich." Good save, it stopped Petra's trembling before anybody noticed. "Showing this level of respect to Drachenblut can only enhance Odinism for the German people."

The drugs loosening her lips worried Petra.

The make-up brush stopped against a cheek. "Could you relax you jaw, please Petra?" After Petra sighed, some relief came to her strained muscles. Concern started to show through her skin in tingling sweat beads.

The make-up artist applied a little more brushwork, her throat-length bobbed hair bouncing in rhythm. "Hot in here, and then there's the nerves."

Petra's self-consciousness struck her dumb. She nodded but occupied her tongue with an examination of her teeth until her prep had finished, then straightened her shoulders and strutted through the beige double-door with a green light above it. Entering the studio of *Popular Observer* again her solar plexus hummed with nervous joy. A smile wavered on her face.

Inside, lights hung aloft illuminated the vast black space. They were so bright Petra had to raise a hand to block her eyes before she acclimatised. When she looked again, *Popular Observer*'s set, familiar to everybody in the Reich, sat in the centre of the chamber's activity. All the cameras focused on the three metal and leather seats arranged around a low glass coffee table and a bank of television monitors. Sebastian guided Petra into the middle chair. They made themselves comfortable as the studio and make-up staff put the finishing details to their appearance. Petra oozed confidence. She was ready.

A man pushed his camera toward the trio, and their make-up artists hurried with the last touches of powder before they scooted back. A floor manager used his fingers to countdown from five. All three presenters took their seated positions and straightened their clothing. Hush fell when the supervisor held only a thumb aloft and the light on the closest camera turned green. Excitement burned Petra!

Sebastian straightened a sheaf of papers. "Greetings on this most sombre of days."

Steffi cocked her head slightly. "Today, our great High Priest Drachenblut is to be cremated." She turned to Petra. "Back from her retirement, we are honoured to have Petra Hellfeier as our companion in presenting this solemn event to the Reich."

Petra beamed in response, perhaps inappropriately for a funeral. She couldn't fight the artificial happiness now – the medication had knocked her depression out with a hammer blow.

"Thank you for the invitation."

Steffi laid a hand gently on Petra's knee. "Quite a difference from your comeback performance in Gothengau the other day, isn't it?"

Petra's mind's eye instantly saw the crowds going over the cliff. "This is only one death, so it is very different."

Steffi smiled, but Sebastian stared at her, lips straight. Petra had revealed that secret on live TV. Troublemaker Steffi set traps for Petra. She needed to engage her brain before her mouth.

Sebastian leaned over. "There's a thirty-second delay before broadcast." Petra's throat felt coated in goose bumps when Sebastian's breath whistled into her ear. "But watch yourself."

Petra's skin burned, but whether from indignation or shame she didn't know. Sebastian held his earpiece and turned to the active camera.

"I've just been told that the Fuhrer's aircraft is coming into land at Wewelsburg."

In front of them, but out of the camera's view, the bank of monitors flickered between test card and white noise before displaying images from different cameras. A half-minute old image of Petra and the two presenters filled the largest screen, marked 'on air'. An aerial view of the airport near the castle became the broadcast picture: above the Paderborn plain, a flying wing, silver but for two red circled black swastikas, made its final descent.

"That is the Führer's plane coming on its final approach," Steffi said.

Sebastian leaned forward, spreading his legs. "Luftwaffe One has been recently updated to the latest Heinkel jet. A reminder to everybody, when the Führer visits, that German technology is far and beyond the best in the world."

Pride surged through Petra's chest. Wisps of smoke came from the aircraft's tyres as it landed on the runway then it decelerated to walking pace.

Steffi gazed at Sebastian. "Appropriate, isn't it, Sebastian, that the Führer visits the site of the world's most modern religion in the world's most modern aircraft?"

Petra almost choked as she sipped from a glass of water and the presenters looked around at her. What could be modern in the religion of the Vikings? Worshipping Odin made as little sense as praising the Jewish god.

"Was there something you wanted to add, Petra?"

"Does modernity come into any religion?"

"Of course it does." Steffi's shoulders lifted to ear-level for a second. "If a religion is newer, then obviously it's more modern!"

"Anyway," Sebastian said. "The Führer is walking to the motorcade, and what a beautiful convoy it is. The open-top Maybach's elegance and solidity are the perfect complement to the Fuhrer. Deputy Führer Heydrich is taking the Mercedes just behind him."

Heydrich's gangly frame folded to get into his vehicle. Both he and Himmler saluted as the cortege moved away. The small crowd waiting for the Reich's leaders stuck their arms out in response.

"This event has been brought to us by the saddest of circumstances. Look at the faces, though, and the pleasure that this visit has given the ordinary German people today," said Steffi.

Sebastian perched his fleshy backside on the margin of his leather chair. "Here are the planes!" Sebastian looked at Steffi with the excitement of a child on Christmas morning. "It may, as you said, be a sad day for the Fatherland but not as far as our technology's concerned. Just look at the wings changing configuration from Delta to conventional, a completely amazing ability but not just done for appearance. These planes, Messerschmitt 1000s, manoeuvre well whatever speed they're doing. Look at them break formation - they've slowed down to branch away from each other like that. Excellent flying from them, twenty of Germany's finest pilots. But what am I saying?" Sebastian shrugged and motioned his hand towards Petra. "We're sitting here with Mrs Max Hellfeier. What do you think of their piloting ability, Petra?"

Petra left flying, and any discussions of it, to Max. She had no opinion, but the drugs directly connected her brain to her mouth. "They haven't hit the ground yet, so I suppose they're not that bad."

"Ha ha." Steffi laughed without conviction. "You are so witty."

Biting her tongue and looking away stopped Petra responding the way she wanted. Slapping Steffi would be good television, but bad publicity.

"Now the Führer's convoy has entered the autobahn," said Sebastian. "Traffic has been cleared by the police so that the Führer has easy access to the next exit, the exit to Wewelsburg. The distance between the two autobahn slip roads is so short the Führer's cortege can't even fit on it. The leaders are already getting off the autobahn for the winding road up to Wewelsburg Castle."

"Look, Petra," Steffi said. "The planes have turned around. Impressive flying, too. Just look at the way that the planes hug the ground as they approach the head of the convoy."

Petra thought it looked more like an attack than a display.

Sebastian knitted his eyebrows but carried on, but with hesitation couching his words. "Like Steffi said, those Messerschmitts are flying directly back to roar above the Führer at low altitude."

Sebastian blinked when flashes burst from the first aircraft's guns. "That looks like an unplanned fireworks display . . ."

Around the front of the convoy, explosive rounds shook the vehicles. The cars swerved to avoid the ordnance but burst into flames when they failed. Their burning metal and fabric carried on moving until hitting the side of the road and scraping along the barrier. They lay at rest, the scorching occupants jumping from vehicles and rolling on the ground to extinguish the blaze that engulfed them. Hush fell on the studio staff. Only machines could be heard. Steffi and Sebastian held their faces in their hands, mouths open in horror. Nobody believed what they saw, except Petra. Her heart beat excitedly.

The Deputy Führer's ride followed Himmler's car onto the pasture next to the road, dodging the block that the now-burning first vehicles made. The staff in the studio screamed. All the cameras' lights shone red, and the 'on-air' screen showed the fluttering Nazi flag while the attack carried on, unknown to the world outside Wewelsburg and the studio.

Shouts from the staff dragged Petra's attention from the events at the castle. A pair of men fought one another near the doorway. The trouble spread quickly, and when Petra next looked around the room, fists settled many differences.

From the helicopter, the cameraman followed the attacking jets as they flipped over to momentarily face backwards and fire a few more shells at Himmler and Heydrich's swerving cars. By the time the planes had managed to turn around, their targets had entered the road through the woods and presented nothing to the aircraft's gunsights.

Florian Siegler, a coterie in his wake, strode through the room to Petra and the two presenters, but the silence broke before he opened his mouth. Even in this soundproofed chamber, the drone of aeroplane engines could be heard. Florian nodded to a cameraman who came over to him. Afterwards, the man trotted towards the door and opened it. Not only did the volume of the aircraft increase, but the sounds of machine gun fire and smashing glass eclipsed the engine noise.

Petra looked around her surprised and concerned, but Florian's firm grip on her shoulder gave her comfort.

"Looks like a new government has been chosen. It couldn't come soon enough." This revelation from Florian filled her heart with hope for the coup's success. Florian spread his arms in the direction of the technicians. "Why is this not being broadcast?"

Muttering and mumbling ensued as the staff around the studio shuffled in response to their boss. A few seconds later the 'on-air' screen stopped showing the Nazi pennant. It displayed the swarming jet fighters turning in the distance to fire a third volley at the Reich's leaders. Florian whispered to Sebastian, then the commentary resumed.

"Excuse us for that break in transmission."

Steffi straightened her jacket. "We are back now with our narration."

"It appears that the fly past attacked the Führer, pitting the Luftwaffe against the government of the Fatherland."

Petra tapped her foot. "It's not just the Luftwaffe. It's all the Wehrmacht, and they've had enough of Berlin."

Petra's timing couldn't be improved, and her location was the most useful for the cause. Reich Television was on the side of the Wehrmacht and the Space agency. That alignment enhanced the rebels' strength considerably.

Loud gunfire sounded from the studio door. Petra looked over to see a familiar, huge figure entering. "Here's Konrad - the other passenger with Karl and I on the boat to the Reich."

Chapter 28

Wewelsburg, Thursday May 5th, 1965.

Pacing freed Karl from worries. The rapid steps drew his concentration from other issues, freeing space in his mind that gave him room to think. Karl favoured the triangular courtyard of Wewelsburg for such strolls: its high sides protected from the wind, some rain, and most noise. Drachenblut lay on the pyre, rigid and swaddled in linens. On the third orbit of Drachenblut's wood-pile, though, Karl stopped loping and listened. Car doors slammed, and voices brayed while staff marshalled visitors. Karl rushed into the arch through the east wing to greet them. Once on the bridge, the voices became clearer. In front of Karl, red-haired Helga poked her head from the top floor of the Vestal house to face the source of the noise. Streaks of mascara darkened her alabaster complexion.

"Shouldn't you get ready, Chief Vestal?"

Helga scowled and closed the window.

Karl rounded the corner of the castle. In the area normally reserved for the pool vehicles stood a two-sided, triple-tiered set of wooden bleachers. It faced out over the countryside. A camera crew took position facing the seating. An outside broadcast truck sat nearby, its side shutters rolled up with fawn-overalled men standing before them. New arrivals, the celebrity great and good of the Fatherland, found places to rest. All rows were occupied by the socially and politically ambitious when Karl arrived at the focal point of the seating. The carpenters worked well, Karl liked the results: all eyes naturally fell on him, and the camera crew pointed their lenses at the new High Priest. He relished their optical caresses for a moment. He held the eye of one audience member after the other while his feet took him along either end of the seating. Satisfied everyone watched him, Karl stood in the line of sight again. He allowed himself a smug grin as the audience paid him tribute with their minds.

A bit of grandeur, Karl. Make them listen. "The service shall be given here."

People kept settling into place. Karl parted his fringe with his finger. Arrogance's machete slashed a path through his confidence. Nobody had heeded Karl or his words. His temper climbed to his collarbone before he remembered the television crew recording him.

"Since there is insufficient space in the courtyard, the service will be held here."

Audience distraction fed back into Karl's patience. He brought his hands together in two measured claps.

"Now that I finally have everybody's attention, we can begin the day's sad duties." Muscles in Karl's leg twitched and fluttered but he had the mourners with him now. "Drachenblut's reputation carries on into Valhalla, where the halls are filled with the Gods, who hold a great feast to welcome the glorious new arrival to the high table."

A whisper ran through the audience, and each face that turned from Karl raised his internal mercury. It neared the top. The German people needed Karl's speech, not some rumour. How dare they talk amongst themselves when he hadn't finished? Karl glanced to the left. In a cloud of pastel silks, Grimhilt appeared from behind the seating and the crowd sighed, then applauded. The German people loved the Vestals, but they would learn to live without them once Karl settled into the new High Priest role. His secret lover strolled to him. Grimhilt turned her mouth down when she meant business. Karl parted his hair with his finger. They had not reconciled since Drachenblut fell from the North tower, and she definitely marched to battle. Hubris pushed the quicksilver inside him closer to its limit.

"Thank you for your greetings." Grimhilt nodded her head. "Our new High Priest Karl Dietrich brought this event together in a very short time."

"Thank you, Vestal Grimhilt, but I only gave the orders." Karl had to take back control of the situation. "Others did the work."

"I disagree with your false modesty." Grimhilt's head shook. "You performed the difficult, essential task that brought everyone here today. The part without which a funeral is incomplete."

The audience applauded Karl. They loved him again. Surprised, the High Priest bowed in appreciation and unexpectedly received more adulation. When Karl stood, the reason for the extra praise became clear: Helga's arrival next to him. Irritation straightened Karl's mouth, but when the camera crew focused on him his lips softened into a knowing smile. Think sagacity, High Priest Karl.

"Which essential part of the funeral was that?" Helga asked.

"The death." Grimhilt strutted between Karl and the camera. "Don't you remember him and his priests chasing Drachenblut up the tower on that fateful day?" The crowd cooed.

Karl fumed, red rage mixing with his sight, time obeying different rules. He stopped the words 'that's enough' in his mind just before they formed on his lips. Cameras still pointed at him. Karl looked around rapidly and couldn't help but wipe at the sweat seeping from his brow. Nobody would notice. He had to carry on with the events of the day.

"When the Führer and his deputy arrive they will address you from their vehicles before we enter the courtyard. There I will light the bonfire that shall take Drachenblut to his rightful place with Odin, preparing for the battle of Ragnarök."

Grimhilt came to him and stood so close he smelled the fruitiness of her hair treatment. "You."

Karl ignored her. "The Führer and his deputy -"

Despite her small size, Grimhilt's punch to his shoulder forced him on the back foot.

"You pushed him."

"Have you been drinking the mushroom tea?" Karl forced a laugh out. It strained his throat and the muscles around his smile. Best the audience think this some kind of amusement.

"You pushed him off the North tower."

A flash of silver passed over their heads, then the low-flying aircraft shattered the air around them. Their vibrations resonated through Karl, turning his ribs into chimes. Everybody ducked and covered their ears. The cameraman dropped his equipment. In a second the noise rescinded.

A sweating technician at the broadcast van looked up from his screen. His face was almost as red as his Nazi badge. "The planes are attacking the Führer and his convoy!"

A series of rapid explosions filled the air. Flames shot from under the attacking planes when they fired on the Reich's leaders. At least the firefight distracted the guests from the Vestals' accusations. Again, the jets roared overhead. Their cannons spat explosive rounds. Karl's suspicions of the Wehrmacht's motives had been correct. He praised himself for seeing it. Then the present situation forced its way past his imagination and shame dragged his feelings low again. Karl's suspicions had done nothing to prevent this.

The technician mopped his brow. "They're out of danger!" He looked back at the screen. "The cars are in the woods now."

With the air-display over, gazes fell on Karl once more. Discomfort rose, heating his face and shortening his breaths. At least the cameraman repaired his equipment, so no permanent record of his visible stress existed. Best change the subject now.

"You killed Drachenblut!" Helga screamed at the top of her voice.

Better get a retort quickly, Karl. "You slept with him!"

Helga's face turned red as her hair. The audience gasped. With her jaw hanging open, Edda joined the other Vestals.

Grimhilt's alluring stare belied her motives. "You slept with me!"

"Why am I the only real Virgin?" Tears sprayed from Edda. "Why does everyone hate me?"

Everybody fixed their stares on Karl. If the conversation couldn't be changed, best leave it. He paced back around the seating, running to the bridge once behind it and out of the sight of the funeral guests. Their laughter followed him over the moat, each guffaw pushing his inner thermometer to the limit. He was High Priest no longer. Never again would he hold any post at Wewelsburg. Not after Helga and Grimhilt's public bombshells. Once Karl cleared the tunnel, he rushed to the pyre and cradled his sobbing face in his arms. The mercury dropped. Drachenblut's corpse the sole, impassive, witness to Karl's uncontrolled emotions.

After a few moments, light footsteps tapped the cobbles, slowly approaching Karl. The Vestals spoke gently amongst themselves.

"Feeling sorry for yourself, are you?" Grimhilt asked.

Karl found the energy to turn and face the Vestals. As he lifted his head to look at them, a blur of silks and red hair pummelled his shoulder and torso.

"Murdering bastard!" Helga wailed.

Karl wrapped his fingers around Helga's reedy wrists and quiet fell. As they stared wildly at each other, panting, a great cheer came in from outside. The cadence and rhythm of the shouting clarified into chants of 'heil Himmler'. Scrabbling his forefinger on his hairline, Karl let Helga go. No matter what just happened, he must face Himmler now.

"We have to go back and greet the Führer."

Grimhilt opened her eyes and pursed her lips. "You want to face the crowd after that?"

"We have to."

Accompanied by the continued cheers for Himmler and Heydrich, Karl led the Vestals to the bridge over the moat. When they reached the other side, the deep, bass thud of the 21-gun salute boomed. The vibrations resonated through Karl, nudging his thoughts to a realisation. That sound honoured nobody.

"Get down!" Karl threw himself on the ground.

High pitched whistles accompanied the incoming ordnance. Himmler had only cleared the aircraft. The Wehrmacht had another means to dispatch the Reich leaders. The Wehrmacht's other chess piece had checkmated him. The Vestals dived on the floor and the world turned a deafening shade of orange.

Under Karl, the ground shook with each detonation. There were only twenty-one cannons, but the explosions seemed endless. Glass and masonry showered the earth around them. If the assault went any longer the castle might fall. Karl brought his knee up, ready to run. Then silence. He stood and turned. Windows were smashed, and some of the features needed replacement, but both Karl and the castle escaped serious damage.

Glass crunched under Karl's feet. Ignoring the still recumbent Vestals, Karl rounded the corner to assess the audience situation. Trees burned in the forest by the chapel. All that remained of the visitors and their seating was a crater filled with a pile of charred timber and burning flesh. Himmler's cortege consisted of the skeletons of two smouldering car chassis. Karl's humiliation before the guests had been boiled by the firestorm and now simmered over glowing embers. No evidence of the downfall remained. Karl wondered whether it had actually happened.

Apart from the crackling of the flames, nothing could be heard. Karl paced to the road for a closer inspection of the Führer's remains. As he passed the place where he had addressed the guests, something tugged on his boot. On the floor, digits appeared from a bunch of scorched, bloodied rags and attached themselves to the laces around his pants.

"Help."

A witness to his disgrace remained. Karl snapped his ankle away from it. There could be nobody to remember this event. Although the chances of the wretch seeing the sun rise again were low, Karl wanted no risk. Determining the supplicant's vital parts proved difficult, and the High Priest put a finger to his lips to ponder the matter. Karl didn't want to be pressing his foot on this bloody mess all day. Then he found the martyr's throat. Though he looked away, Karl still heard the body's final rattles and felt its last movements. Now, none but the Vestals knew what happened.

Karl picked up a burning piece of wood. Drachenblut must be rid of immediately, and the available flames were better than the torch preparation that he planned. There need be no ceremony after the attack, there were no witnesses. Keeping the flames away from his hair with arm outstretched, Karl strode to the courtyard. The Vestals sat where he left them, dazed and idle.

"I'm lighting the fire. We mustn't let this attack stop Drachenblut's funeral."

"In a hurry to burn him after you killed him?" Helga asked. "It's not like he's going anywhere."

"Grimhilt lied. It wasn't me that killed your boyfriend. Gothengau did. There's a reason you didn't see anyone from there around today."

"I saw you push him off the tower," Grimhilt said. "Why are you lying to a witness?"

"They made me do it! I wasn't in control of my own mind. They brainwashed us to make sure we got him."

"Like you never wanted his job for yourself." Grimhilt waved a dismissive hand. "Bringing back true Odinism is all you ever talked about, you never respected our virginity because it's not really a part of this religion"

"Drachenblut didn't respect it either - he was banging Helga from the start. He only brought the Vestals into this to set up his own harem, I'm surprised he didn't sleep with all of you." Karl's head shook in disbelief at their lack of awareness. "Enough of this. I'm lighting the pyre before this torch burns my hand."

Karl stomped into the tunnel. Sonic booms echoed through his chest. He crouched. When he looked up to the source of the calamity, vapour trails criss-crossed the sky, overlaying the swirls left by the air assault. Rockets hurtled towards them. Gothengau attacked. Wewelsburg faced imminent destruction and Karl was powerless, cowering on the cobbled floor with the women.

Dozens more shock waves blasted the castle. Each new report dispelled Karl's belief that the last missile struck home. When the explosions started, they were distant. No glass shattered, no ramparts fell. Curiosity wrenched Karl's survival instinct behind his back. Up in the sky vapour trails ended prematurely where clouds of flames and smoke rained debris.

"We are saved!" Karl stood. "The Space Agency protected us!"

The Vestals pushed themselves up and watched the skies.

"What's happening?" Edda asked.

"Gothengau and the Wehrmacht are trying to take over the Reich. Gothengau's rockets are useless." This was what the visit from the Generals had been about, and Karl knew who he sided with. "Their missiles can't do anything. The Wehrmacht just took them down. World class German technology, right over our heads."

"So which of them will win?"

"We'll have to wait and see, but it's not looking good for Gothengau."

Karl stooped and picked up the still burning piece of wood. Gently blowing and fanning his hand encouraged the incandescence to stand confidently from the timber. Satisfied, the High Priest funereally paced forward to the pyre. When he arrived, something vital was missing. The torch left his hand and clattered on the floor. Instead of the linen-wrapped corpse, only logs and splinters remained atop the bonfire.

"He is risen! He lives!"

The Vestals ran to the woodpile. All of them shared Edda's expression of gaping jaw and vacant eyes.

"Where could he have gone?" Asked Grimhilt. "I didn't see anything."

"This is what he meant when he said 'you will praise me'. Come, everyone. Let us praise him. Praise Drachenblut!"

"Now you can worship his magnetism and charisma to keep you in his old job." The hair on Karl's neck stood up. Grimhilt's divination of the truth bridled him, and he scowled at her before his mission returned.

"Hear the good news. Drachenblut died that we may live!"

Chapter 29

Jefferson County, Alabama. July 1946.

Two things made this railyard memorable for Konrad. Not much over a couple of years ago, on his first night with the circus as Hercules the Giant, Cleopatra the trapeze artiste made him a man. Here, in this very sleeping cabin.

"What ya thinking about, big boy?"

"The last time we were in these parts."

"Why's that on your mind?" Cleopatra pursed her lips and moved a hand toward his crotch. "You feeling frisky?"

"Isn't it a bit soon to come back?"

She snuggled around him, nimble despite the limitations of the bottom berth, and caressed his upper thigh. He tingled.

The second cause to make this train yard stick in the mind, Ed, hollered outside their door.

"We're here again. I told them not to come, but they took no notice."

"Oh yeah." Cleopatra's wide lips curled up. "Something happened to Ed." She burst out laughing and rubbed her palms together.

Such a terrible event being the source of her amusement hit Konrad like an alarm in a peculiar dream. This couldn't go on. Surely this morning was a sign he had to wake up and return to Pennsylvania.

"I'm quitting and going back. Today."

That confounded her. "Was it something I said?"

"This is where I started. Seems like a good place to call the end. Full circle."

"Stick around. There's good money coming my way tonight." Cash held no interest, so he shook his head. "But how will the tents be put up without you?" Now she appealed to his duty.

"Okay, but only this last time before I go." How had he only just noticed her scheming?

Cleopatra's long scarlet nails dug into his arm. "I'm a few days late for my monthlies."

"What's that supposed to mean?" He rose, his head touching the carriage roof.

"Maybe you're gonna be a daddy."

Konrad put on a robe over his pyjamas. "You've said that for years. You sound desperate."

Cleopatra's shoe flew his way. "I'm not desperate. You go if you want to." He dodged another shoe. "Get out now, you freak! Go be with your freakshow buddies, you Amish asshole."

He opened the door and squeezed through to the corridor, glad to escape. Limbless Ed, mobile only by being harnessed to Inca's chest, continued walking up and down, wailing to the occupants of the open section of beds. Pointy-headed little Inca rocked back and forth.

"You back with us now, Hercules?" Ed's backside thumped Inca's abdomen. "Turn around, ya moron. Look at Hercules when I'm talking to him!" Inca shuffled around and wiped tears from his eyes. "Cleopatra never looked at us till you showed up." His eyes rolled back completely. "Never, not until she decided to take you and the room in our compartment. Get to Cleopatra's door, ya moron. We're gonna make you one of us, one day, Cleo. You'll see. Oh yeah, you'll see."

"Well, it won't be you doing it, nor that numbskull you're strapped to." Cleopatra barged past the pair and headed to the carriage door. "I'm going back to be with the real humans."

Ed screamed and shook his pelvis so hard that Ink had to grab on a railing.

So, Cleo thought Konrad subhuman? That smarted. "I'm going back to Lancaster County." His feelings needed a timescale. "Tonight." There were cries of disbelief.

Those sleeping in the open section of beds, Texas Pony Girl, Ed, Inca, Tiny Hans, and Legless Jonny Eck groaned. When the alabaster Martian brothers knelt and whispered to the tiny Wild Men of Borneo, the Martians' matted slabs of white afro hair almost blocked the little people from sight.

"This is it for me, I'm going to be Amish again. For good. I'll farm and get married. Raise some children. Thanks to all of you for letting me see some of the world while I thought it over."

"So, all this time with us was just you moping about your future?" Hans' whistled. "Lucky for some. We ain't got nothing outside of sideshows."

Jonny hopped up and down on his palms. "If you got legs, you got plenty."

"Hell!" Ed's tongue stuck out and wagged. "He's got all his fingers and toes. And he's rich, too!"

Texas Pony Girl held up the leggy appendages dangling from her waist. "I wish somebody would take my spare hooves."

"Whatever happens, Hercules." Ed jutted out his chin. "You'll always be one of us." His eyes rolled, exposing bulging red veins. "God bless you on your new way. May the Lord cast his eyes favourably upon you. Touch my head. Touch my head."

Through thin, brown hair the Braille of scabs told Ed's story of laying anywhere anybody cared to put him. Ed's blessing gave Konrad little comfort.

Doors banged and Cleopatra's voice raised loudly enough to be heard in their carriage. "Okay, okay. If you're trying to welch out on it then I'll, I'll . . . you'll find out!"

"It's your idea, you go finish the deal."

Once more Cleo appeared. She edged her toned hips around Konrad and touched Ed beneath his navel.

"You're coming with me to drum up business in town."

"With you?" Ed turned almost ashen. "What makes you think I'm gonna do that?"

Her fingertips caressed his pelvic bone. "You might get something you always wanted."

Greyed pink tones returned to Ed's complexion. "We'll think about it." His face twisted up. "Won't we, Ink?"

Little Ink hopped up and down, cooing.

Disgust at such sexuality tightened Konrad's shoulders and stomach, almost bringing up vomit. "I'm going to do the tent."

He ran down the corridor and tumbled out on the track ballast, panting. After what he witnessed, he could barely wait to get away permanently. But he had promised to help one last time. The tent was stored in the last carriage, right next to the sideshow.

With moustache unwaxed the Ringmaster still looked intimidating. Much like a withered and distressed walrus he'd seen once at a zoo.

"Heard you're leaving."

"Cleopatra must have run and told you herself."

"She gets around. I'll say that for her." Ringmaster's chins glinted twice when he turned his head to look both ways. He beckoned Konrad to stoop. "She's managed to get some money, but Ed might pay the full penalty. Be careful of her. She's . . . she's got us to stay here, but you were too strong for her. We - you - can still save Ed."

Pebbles scrunched nearby when Cleo leapt from the train. "What story is he telling ya, big fella?"

Konrad threw her a glare. "He's saying goodbye. What else would he be doing?"

"Yeah, you just make sure that is what he's tellin' ya. I got money for ya if ya leave right now, on the next train through here. Get yourself good and far from us carny sorts. Go back to Pennsylvania and tell stories about the wild ways you saw in the circus."

"You tried bribing me to stay, but now you're paying me to go."

"You win either way." She paused while a train passed.

Looking down the line revealed boxcars and flatbeds going on for miles.

He drew a large breath to shout over the freight's rumble. "I'll make the tent."

The Wild Men tumbled from the train and skipped over. Without catching Waino's long, dark, combed back hair, Plutanor jumped on his shoulders, then slid the wagon door open. Plutanor leapt in and passed a few boxes to Waino before Plutanor hopped aboard. He climbed to the top and began making a Konrad sized hole. They beckoned him and pointed to the alternative route across the train. Konrad jumped into the trailer and squeezed into the new gap.

But he got stuck fast in the mid-point and no number of physical jerks freed Konrad's forward movement. No shuffling took him back. Plutanor scurried away. Dust and cotton filled his nose. Konrad sneezed at least five times before the door facing him slid open and the Wild Men grabbed a hand each and tugged him free. Two steps and he stood outside again.

"Thank you, little men." Konrad offered his hand.

Waino leapt out and shook. Plutanor did the same.

Konrad ran to the sideshow's carriage. "Where are Ed and Ink?"

The Martians, Eko and Iko, blocked the door. "Cleo took them into town." Eko told him.

Iko completed the conversation. "They wouldn't hear anything against it once she'd promised them -"

Startled when Konrad dived to the door, they sprang from his path. He caught sight of Cleo and Ink walking to town just before a train, another leviathan, blocked them from view. The three of them would be well ahead of him by the time he could follow. Shortening that wait, he walked against the train's direction. Although mostly drowned out, the Carny folk waved and shouted. Some mouthed the words 'big top', but saving lives knocked raising the tent into second place.

By the time Konrad could cross the rails he caught no sight of his prey. Most vehicles, such as there were on this dusty highway, honked their horns as they passed. The rest swerved or stopped to get a better look at him. As he neared the riverside city limits, a car slowed then prowled along just over his shoulder. Before he stepped on the bridge a siren wailed for a moment. Then again. Konrad stopped and let the policeman pull up alongside him. The driver door opened, and the cop got out. They stared at each other, disadvantage Konrad, whose eyes weren't hidden by mirrored sunglasses.

The star pinned to his fawn shirt read Sheriff Poulson. "I know you."

They had become acquainted last time, in a way. "Yes, sir."

"You stopped our fun with that limbless friend of yours." Poulson shook his head and spat. "I hear he's due in town. Head back where you came from and stay away, now." A hand jangled the cuffs that hung from his belt. "Otherwise, I might have to lock you up in the interests of public safety. You and those other freaks on the road behind you."

Who else could have come along after him? He would find out soon, but first he had to show good manners and follow orders.

"Thank you, sir and goodbye." Konrad turned and began returning to the train.

Not looking back took effort. A short way ahead, the Wild Men trotted, and the Martian brothers sauntered towards him. Watching them eased the pressure to find where Sheriff Poulson gazed.

"Is the police car still there?"

The Martians leaned around Konrad and squinted their milky blue eyes. Their heads shook.

"What about Ed?" Eko's jaw hung open waiting for an answer.

"If I go to town, they'll arrest me. But they're not using him as a football again. I'm taking another way in."

"Where will you go?" Iko took his turn speaking for them.

"The bridge, like the last time."

"We'll come along the creek with you." Eko nodded at his brother.

"Are you sure about going? They're keen on people being White around here."

"We're White, but we ain't people." Iko shook his head.

"We're Martians." Eko turned to the Wild Men. "Are you coming?"

Waino and Plutanor glanced at each other's near identical long, bearded faces, faced the Martians and nodded.

"I've got to run for those trees over there." Konrad pointed to a copse by the stream. "To be sure nobody sees me. We'll meet under that bridge."

Scrub tugged at him until he clambered down to the brook's edge. When Konrad stooped, the road became hidden. He splashed through the reeds and shallows, disturbing mice, lizards, and terrapins before arriving in the shade beneath the river's crossing. Taking deep draughts of moist air, he tasted the meandering river.

Vegetation crunched under a new arrival. Konrad put his fists to the floor, ready to run. The Martians appeared by the stream and he relaxed.

"It's the next bridge along, isn't it?" Eko pointed along the creek.

Iko took his turn. "Where it happened, right?"

"I think so." Everywhere around here looked the same to Konrad. "But it was two years ago."

"The bridge had stone railings." Eko nodded downstream.

"This one has metal." Iko pointed up as a motor vehicle sounded overhead.

"And there was a football field next to it." Eko rubbed his temples.

"They were gonna play a game." Iko nodded.

"With Ed being the ball." Eko made like he held an American football.

Plutanor held Waino's hand, then reached up to tap Konrad's forearm. Waino pointed to the next bridge and nodded. Silent but for rustling of reeds and splash of footfalls, everyone followed Konrad's first steps.

Once they cleared the bridge, Konrad looked up and caught sight of the goal posts by their destination. There were people there, too. And voices.

"Hey, there's something goin' on up ahead." Iko pointed.

Ed's voice stuck out, but Ink's scream split the air.

"You gotta help him, Hercules." Eko began lamenting.

Hearty laughter drowned out the screaming. Iko joined his brother's keening. Plutanor and Waino stared at each other, then Konrad.

Konrad's voice stayed low as his posture and his hand patted the air. "Keep it down."

He moved forward, taking advantage of the commotion. Quiet now, his four assistants tagged along. They caught a view of the bridge. Konrad took cover behind the rushes and so did his men. Cleopatra stood alongside Ink and Ed opposite a group of middle-aged men. Two stood at the front, one in a light-coloured suit and the other overalls. Sheriff Poulson was there too.

"Come on, hand over the money." Cleopatra stuck out a hand.

A billfold appeared from the besuited man's jacket. He grandly counted out the notes.

It made Cleopatra smile and nod. "That's more like it."

"See to our side, Roscoe."

"We'll take care of you, now that's sorted out." The man in the overalls reached out towards Ed and gently lifted the screaming, writhing bundle of despair. "Got him, Dale."

As soon as Dale heard that, the billfold returned to his pocket. Such total disregard for life, even for the honour of his own words, exploded through Konrad's mind. Body now under its own control, he ran to Roscoe.

"Now ya all leave as soon as possible, ya hear." Poulson stepped into the fold, hand on holster. "And by that, I mean don't pitch your tent here tonight." He looked towards the river. "What's that racket?"

Soil and grass ran through Konrad's fingers. Gritty stone grated his palms when he pushed down on the parapet. He leapt over and landed on the road. Instantly, he sprang back up, leaping toward Roscoe and Ed. Roscoe's jaw slackened, and he put his arms out between himself and Konrad. Foam hid Ed's mouth. Deep wrinkles focused on his manic eyes. Roscoe's grip opened. Ed screamed as he fell. Konrad's fingers grabbed Ed's green leotard and pulled him in. Even under Konrad's arm, Ed still raged.

Turning on his heel to leave, Poulson stood in Konrad's way. Arm raised to push him aside, the gun pointed at his chest halted Konrad. It didn't stop Ed's racket.

"Put a sock in his mouth, Roscoe. He's driving everyone crazy. Told ya not to come back around here, boy." Poulson's free hand reached for the cuffs. "Get rid of the freak and put your hands behind your back now, ya hear?"

Roscoe snatched Ed away and shoved a rag in his mouth. Steel bracelets in hand, the policeman shuffled around, his gun almost touching Konrad.

When Konrad's arms slowly reached Poulson's gun, the Sheriff jumped back. A dry swallow almost made Konrad cough, making a muted roar boom from him. That firearm didn't make the lawman confident.

"Keep putting those hand behind ya, nice and slow."

Arms at the level of Poulson's neck, Konrad tested the Sheriff's resolve. He stopped moving. Poulson stammered several times before managing words.

"Okay Roscoe, I got a better idea. Go get rope from your truck. We're gonna hog tie this giant."

"Yes, sir." The oil-covered man put Ed on the ground and ran to his vehicle.

Poulson cocked his head. "Dale."

The well-dressed man raised an eyebrow. "Sheriff?"

"Get his arm ready behind his back."

"Sorry, big guy." Despite the apology, Dale leapt up to grab Konrad's wrist.

Behind the backs of the crowd the Martian brothers scraped up the bank to the road, pale faces smudged with mud.

Dale faced the albinos. "Hey everyone, look what I found over there!"

"String them up!" The mob stampeded.

Konrad shook Dale's grip from his wrists, turned, picked up terrified Dale by his lapels and threw him to the ground. He scurried away to join the lynching posse. Sweat poured down Poulson's brow and the gun shook in his trembling hand. Konrad stepped back until he reached Ed's heaving torso and gathered him to his chest. For now, the Martians had to help themselves.

"You're gonna have to put our little friend down there, mister." The Sheriff's gun arm drooped. "The deal's . . ."

Taking advantage of the Sheriff's condition, Konrad stepped forward. No reaction, other than drooling and squinting. Konrad grabbed the gun dangling from Poulson's hand. It snagged, pointing at the floor. The mob cheered. Pulling harder got a shot, a screaming ricochet, then the revolver. Poulson clutched his arm and fell to the floor. Konrad turned just as Roscoe did.

"The giant shot the Sheriff!" The throng stared. "Get him."

Konrad backed away. Against his upbringing, he had a gun in his hand but lives still had to be saved. They moved toward him silently, a lazy wave along a gently sloping beach. When he pointed the gun at Roscoe's chest they quietly stopped approaching. Only Konrad saw, behind them on the bridge, the little Wild Men pulling up Eko and Iko by the ropes round their necks. Bent over, coughing and gasping, the Martian brothers drew attention away from Konrad.

Waino picked up a loaf-sized rock like it were bread and hurled it at the man in the suit. Dale fell back and stayed down. When Plutanor ran in to take his turn with the granite the crowd backed away, keeping a good distance from Konrad. The carny folk followed Konrad back to the creek. Ink emerged from the undergrowth arms outstretched. Konrad passed Ed to him, removing the rag from his mouth. Ed gasped.

Ed returned to Ink's papoose. "You gotta get outta here, Hercules. We all gotta get outta here, but you gotta go alone."

Waino fished Dale's money from his waistband. Plutanor took it, looked at his brother, then handed it to Konrad. He shook his head

"You're gonna need that." Ed reminded him. "You've gotta go far. Go to New York, maybe nobody will look at you there."

After he took the billfold, Konrad halved it and passed one part to Ink. He did not know where he would end up, the cash would be important. When he reached the yard, he hopped on the first freight train passing through. Konrad couldn't go back to Pennsylvania. The righteous had no quarter for murderers.

Chapter 30

Berlin, Thursday May 6th, 1965.

Konrad's fingers grabbed the antenna's cable. Already descending fast, the grip around the fastening scorched his hands. He couldn't let go. His abdomen screamed with the effort of lifting his feet to the rope. Once his feet hooked around the stays, the huge blocks pinning the aerial to the ground slowed. Besides the pain, this now felt like a day at the fun fair. Squeezing his limbs tightly, his feet bumped on the clamps, and he could hop down. He inhaled the recent mowing and unclipped his harness. The backpack fell. Somebody else could gather the 'chute, Konrad's hands were bloody. No need to brandish the rifle. A line of his men all now packed up their kit and drew towards him.

When they assembled Konrad faced them. "Right men." Some of the guys were too keen. "Schink, and the others, shoulder your weapons. This is a television studio, so we don't expect any resistance. Now we will enter and make the announcement."

Schink raised a fist. "We're gonna be on the telly!"

Maybe letting van de Beek look after Konrad's family had been a mistake. Now Konrad had to control all the convicts on his own.

Best go along with them. "Make sure you smarten yourself up for the German people. They'll all be seeing you soon enough."

"Squeeze some of your zits, Schink." For that, Mayrock got laughs from his colleagues, but an elbow in the ribs from his spotty neighbour.

"That's it now, men." Konrad had extended their leash enough. "Attention!" Heels struck the ground in unison. "Left turn." Lack of practice hoarsened Konrad's throat. "Forward march." Luckily, his voice didn't falter.

Behind the plate glass windows of the foyer, well-dressed, good-looking people stood and stared at the advancing troops. Two long-limbed, navy-uniformed concierges raced through the bystanders towards the door. They paused to dust themselves down before swinging both the huge doors open. The aging gentlemen held up their hands to stop the procession, anxiously looking from side to side and each other. Their lined mouths opened and closed like mute puppets. Konrad didn't mind. He brushed them aside. Behind him, Schink grunted and one of the porters hit the deck, his hat flying back to the building. Schink could always be relied on for muscle, although he hadn't needed to.

Mayrock laughed. "No, he won't sign the guest book." The rest of the men chuckled over the rhythm of their heels.

Inside, the beautiful people of the studio retreated to the lift bank and through the swing doors to the area marked 'broadcasting'. Glad it was so clearly signposted Konrad led his men to the cameras they craved. All the remaining civilians clung to the cathedral-high walls as if they, too, were part of the murals depicting Aryans playing, acting, and experimenting. Awed, they silently watched the convicts march through their domain. Shouldering the guns was a good idea.

Wolf-whistles blew when Konrad led the men through the makeup room. It was rare for the convicts to encounter women, even rarer for the ladies to be so beautifully made up. The tallest woman met his eyes once she had given him the once over. Konrad couldn't betray Diana or the girls. Well, maybe wouldn't was a better term. At least the men kept in line through this temptation.

Through the next doors were the last barrier to being broadcast. 'Live-on air' was lit up in a box over them.

"We're gonna be famous!" Schink had hit the right spot. All the men cheered.

Pushing the door open revealed a black void, whose brightly illuminated centre hosted the Popular Observer set. Petra reclined on one of the three chairs next to the two presenters. Once Konrad's eyes adjusted, he made out the cables linking the shadowy figures nestled around monitors and behind cameras with the three celebrities in the chamber's glowing heart. The eyes of the world would be on them all soon. Konrad shared his men's excitement. Even Hoechst bared his teeth in joy.

After marching ahead a few paces the gloom revealed a smiling, grey haired man in a dapper suit leading an entourage of pretty secretaries and yes-men. The two groups met halfway to the set.

"Florian Siegler, head of Reich Broadcasting. Konrad, commander of the 500th, I presume." Florian offered his hand.

Konrad stooped and they shook.

"Until you got here, this whole thing was my show." Florian winked. "I have good sources that Wernher von Braun is behind this, and I completely approve. Couldn't happen soon enough. How can I help?"

"Change your programming to support us over Gothengau. Their hands are in this, too."

Even in the isolated, protected studio, a huge boom rumbled. Konrad turned to share Florian's view of a screen. Outside, parabolic vapour trails headed their way. Before they reached ground, their trajectory stopped short. The trail transformed into grey, orange nebula billowing flames and smoke while precipitating debris. Everyone looked up when it rattled on the building.

"That's Wernher's doing, destroying Gothengau's rockets." Konrad gestured at the images. "If it weren't for his work, we'd be dead now."

"Then we owe you our lives. All this studio's output will be on your side."

Schink elbowed his way between them. "Sir, when are we gonna be on telly, sir?"

Florian waved a hand and shook his head, lips pursed. "Only Konrad's going to be on the camera. This is too important for you to share it."

Rage seethed from Schink. "He's gonna be the next boss of Gothengau, Mister Siegler." Schink thrust his shoulders back. "Wernher von Braun promised us."

Schink had stepped over Konrad's line. He patted the air with a palm and glowered at the convict. Things were in play. No need to push.

"Why don't you go up and meet the presenters?" Florian's arm showed the way. "I believe you know Petra. You'll be in the heart of the Popular Observer studio, and in the eyes of the Reich. Tell the world. That's going to help your cause enormously."

"You're right. We'll take you up on that offer."

"I'm sure you would with or without my permission!" Florian chuckled. "You two already know each other, don't you?"

Petra smiled. "Yes. He's saved my life a couple of times."

That was something Konrad would do for all but the monsters back in Gothengau.

"We came over from America on the same voyage."

Florian nodded. "It would be fantastic if you interviewed Konrad for Popular Observer."

"Are you offering me a job?"

"Of course."

Konrad flexed a bicep. "She can't interview me now. I'm making the announcement and then we're going to the Volkshalle."

There wasn't time for all this. He barged into the limelight between cameras and presenters. Effete Sebastian and austere Steffi cringed back in their chairs. The cameras pointed at Konrad. He was on the screen now. No time for nerves. He was here making a public service announcement, and he'd done that hundreds of times back at the circus. Straighten yourself up. Dust yourself down.

"People of the Reich." Deep breath. "There has been a change of government." Exhale. "I represent the Wehrmacht and the Space Agency. Wernher von Braun is to be made Führer at the Volkshalle within the hour." Take a few breaths. "That is all."

Trembling now the show had finished, Konrad strode away past Petra and Florian. "Steffi, take Petra and a film crew along with you."

Time worked against Konrad. He checked his watch. According to the plan, the Wehrmacht transporters waited for the 500th outside the studio.

"You'll have to catch up. We're leaving."

"But sir, we weren't on TV!" Mayrock whined.

"You should have said you were the new Gothengau leader, sir." Schink's pleading reminder forced Konrad to question himself. He forced him down a track he preferred to avoid.

"It's not important. Follow me. Our lift to town should be waiting outside by now."

Returning to the girls in the make-up area did nothing for the men. They trudged through silently, watched by gorgeous mutes. In the foyer, Schink muttered with Mayrock and Hoechst. If only there'd been time to bring van de Beek along, then Konrad wouldn't have this nagging at him. "Keep it down and behave yourselves."

Outside, Wehrmacht Hanomags exuded smoke while they waited for the 500th's next move. No need to secure the TV studio. The boss himself had promised allegiance. Konrad would bring all the men to join their colleagues that had landed around the Volkshalle.

"Everybody board. We're going to make Wernher von Braun the Führer."

The cheer the men returned fell short of Konrad's expectations. He could do without this, but van de Beek did what Konrad should have done. Protect his own family. A quick field promotion was in order. Who did the men listen to the most?

"Schink, you're acting sergeant."

Schink raised a fist. "Yes!"

Which of the men had most sense?

"Hoechst, you're the acting obersturmführer."

"What do I get?" Mayrock grumbled.

"You get nothing," shouted Schink. "Keep moving and keep quiet!"

Little could be seen in the transporter. The lights were too low. Konrad sensed something unusual from the men's posture, their astute silence. Blinks and hand gestures made Konrad suspect they silently communicated with their nearest comrades. The stand-ins were no substitute for van de Beek. He trusted his family with him, though. You can't have everything.

The throbbing engine quietened, and the door Konrad leaned against lifted. Muted daylight filled the transporter's interior again. After the opening reached halfway, Konrad recognised the multi-storey colonnades that fronted the Volkshalle. He disembarked and looked at his watch. The plaza before the dome was empty, but according to the schedule Wernher and the Wehrmacht Chiefs should be here now. Men of the 500th guarded all the key points in the administrative complex. Konrad turned from the grand entrance and stared at the Arch of Total Victory. Trucks filled the Avenue of Splendours, tipping loads into the gaping hole. Workers in striped pyjamas flattened the aggregate that filled up the crater. Windows along the road were boarded up. Only the feet and plinth of Hitler's statue remained. Debris from the recently destroyed rockets littered the otherwise clean streets.

Hoechst nodded at the damage. "Really made a mess, didn't they, sir? Still, they've got the Guest Workers to clean it up."

Konrad took a sharp breath. "There'll be no more of that soon. Wernher will see to it, once he gets here."

"Good, sir. I knew you wouldn't let that carry on."

"I want him to release political prisoners as well. You could be back in a normal regiment or a civilian again if you wanted."

"No, sir." Hoechst folded his arms. "I'll stay with you."

A convoy of vehicles navigated around the crater. Some of the trucks had the insignia of Reich Television along their grey sides. Once past the bottleneck, the leading car revved its engine and raced to Konrad. It screeched, but its tyres slipped on the smooth stone pavement. Konrad and the men jumped back for safety. Petra grinned sheepishly in the passenger seat, her shoulder rotating as she opened the window.

"Sorry."

"That's okay, I've seen worse. Your crew have time to get ready. Wernher isn't here yet."

Horns blared, and Petra turned. Wehrmacht armoured cars waited impatiently around the abyss in the boulevard.

"This will be him and his escort."

Guest Workers scrambled up to the pavement when the tippers reversed to clear the military's path. Metal screeched against metal when the Hanomags squeezed through the gap. The convoy spread across the avenue. Armoured vehicles sandwiched the four open-topped limousines. Besides Wernher, each general had their own vehicle, and they drew closer together to fit through the narrowing before the dome's plaza.

Wernher, garbed in a black SS ceremonial uniform, leapt from the car and ran to Konrad.

"Great work, Konrad." Wernher pumped Konrad's hand with both his. "Your television announcement was perfect. And you've brought your Petra to help film. Wonderful."

Schink stepped forward. "Now Konrad's gonna be the Gothengau leader."

Wernher looked aside. "Listen, there's something I have to tell you about that." A balloon of relief floated up in Konrad's sternum. "We'll have to put that off for now." That's what Konrad wanted to hear.

Schink scowled and shook his head. "Until when?"

"Schink, it's not your place to ask." His behaviour flabbergasted Konrad.

Konrad turned to Wernher. "Are you ready?"

Wernher nodded agreement.

"Forward, march." Konrad and the 500th strode to the Volkshalle. "Why are you wearing an SS uniform?"

"Since the SS are a massive part of the Reich, the generals and I thought it best not to totally alienate them. I was made a major in the SS some time ago. I rarely ever use the title or uniform, but if it unites the Fatherland, then I'm all for it."

"What will be your first act as Führer? Did you notice the slaves repairing the damage from the rocket attack? Freeing them would be a great gesture for any new leader, but especially one appealing to the better side of German nature. Nothing can undo the Final Solution, but the shame of slavery can be wiped away right now."

"Yes." Wernher let out a long sigh. "Without forced labour, though, my space program will cease straight away."

"Why is that?"

"It's very dangerous work at the rocket factories, no Aryan would put up with it. The labour is taken from Siberia."

"Oh. I understand." Konrad started to get it.

"You could free the ones on the Boulevard." Hoechst piped up about slavery. That's why he served in the 500th.

Wernher waved a hand. "Of course, but then they'd all expect freedom when they see it on the television."

"My middle name is Abraham." Konrad had been fooled again. "Being named after the President that freed the slaves gave me a lot of pride. Surely you could be the Abraham Lincoln of the Fatherland?"

"I will be. But be patient, it won't be today."

"When will it be?" Konrad didn't stop the frown rampaging across his forehead.

"I'll have to see when I get the job. These things aren't as simple as they seem at first sight."

"Then make it simple. Make the rocket factories safe for all, not just the Aryans."

Wernher sighed. "Konrad, I am really grateful for your help, but idealism won't help build the Fourth Reich." Wernher held up a hand. "Your dreams need to wait their turn. We have a lot to do if we want to push Britain out of the way and rule the world."

Konrad seethed. Wernher just wanted to go to the stars and didn't want murderous handprints all over the project.

When they stepped through the columns and approached the two-storey gothic brass doors, the scent changed. The musty note combined with Volkshalle's darkness and the low, echoing hum bouncing around the structure, blending into a sound suitable for the edifice. A few wisps of cloud lingered hundreds of meters above them, caressing the ridges of the building.

The marching resounded across the concrete span arcing way above them. At the far side of the cupola, cameras stood beneath the enormous niche housing the Nazi eagle statue. Powerful beams illuminated the area from many angles. Technicians frantically adjusted the broadcasting equipment. A procession of scarlet-robed judges ascended both stairs flanking the sculpture's base.

Konrad looked down at Wernher. "How did you arrange all this so quickly?"

"It's easy with lapdogs like the judiciary. They saw the writing on the wall. You know, it would be great if we split in two groups. One going up the right steps, the other the left. Good for the cameras. That's one thing I've learned from the Nazis. Make it look great."

Schink listened in. "Every second man, take the left stairs."

To give that order, Schink must have been monitoring everything Konrad and Wernher said. If only van de Beek had joined the coup, then he would at least only have been betrayed, not that plus overworked.

"We'll go up together on the right-hand steps." Wernher peeled away, Konrad followed.

On the platform, the judges stood beside each other before the raised swearing-in throne. Cymbals crashed, horns blew, and strings scraped when Wernher set foot on the stairway. Jubilant sounds reverberated around the vast covered space when the musicians played 'The Flag on High'.

A scowl pinched Konrad's face. "Who chose the music?"

"A joint decision really. I know it's very strongly associated with National Socialism, but we want a smooth handover of power."

Konrad squinted, trying to peer through his disbelief. "Are you going to change anything?"

"Of course!" Wernher's head bobbed emphatically.

Somebody behind Konrad tutted.

"When?" Despair's tendrils ripped across Konrad's abdomen.

"We haven't come up with a schedule yet, but don't worry. Everything is going to be put right. Have some patience, big guy."

Mayrock must have been the one tutting because now he exhaled and shook his head.

They climbed to the platform in silence. The band finished their tune, so near hush fell when they arrived at the top of the steps. Reverberations of the attendees' cleared throats and the dying notes of the performance rebounded from the concrete, filling the air with an ominous rumble. Konrad pictured storm clouds over the flat Midwest.

Schink glanced at Mayrock who nodded to Hoechst. Apprehension grasped Konrad's chest so tightly that he drew the shallowest breaths he could. The dozen red-robed judges stood in a row before the swearing-in throne.

Konrad and Wernher led their troops to meet the others. Spotlights blinded them when they entered the floodlit area, five storeys up. When they uncovered their eyes, the Reich Chief of Law stepped from his place in the centre of the line and faced Wernher. His eyes were close to his mouth. Wernher and Konrad returned the judge's straight-arm salute and clicked their heels.

"Are you Freiherr Wernher von Braun?"

Wernher nodded.

"Then please be seated for the ceremony to begin."

The smug expression Wernher had before sitting down became shock as his jodhpurs touched the throne. Konrad shared the confusion. His men suddenly presented arms. If a gesture of respect, it hadn't been ordered. A moment later, imperiousness returned to the rocket scientist. Schink and Mayrock wouldn't want to be his honour guard. Konrad almost stepped back when the men cocked their weapons and aimed them at Wernher. What were they playing at now?

Schink stepped forward, his rifle pressing against Wernher's jacket. "Stand up."

Wernher's pleading eyes darted between Schink's gun and Konrad. Konrad couldn't tell him what was going on, either.

Mayrock clarified the proceedings when he levelled a gun at a Chief Justice. "This is Konrad Lapp. We in the 500th have decided that we'll have an honest Führer next, and Wernher's been fibbing to us the whole time. Swear Konrad in, or you die."

The judge nodded with vigour and an unctuous smile that nearly edged past his eyes.

No way could Konrad be the Führer. "Just being Gothengau leader was too much for me, men."

That's not what scowling Hoechst thought. Backed by several others, he jabbed his gun's barrel in Konrad's midriff, apologetically edging him to the throne. Hoechst! For that guy to come out of his shell he had to be committed to the cause.

Suddenly, they all leaped at Konrad. Surprised and outnumbered, he stumbled back, falling into the chair. Many arms pinned him down.

Punched in the shoulder by Mayrock, the judge produced a leather-bound text from inside his red gown and brandished it at Konrad.

"Do you, Konrad Lapp, swear that you are of pure Aryan blood?"

"I swear that I am of pure Aryan blood." This couldn't happen.

"Then by the authority granted in me by the Fatherland of the Greater German Reich, I pronounce you Führer of all Germany and the German People."

Well, if you insist on my being the Führer, then I'll have to do the best I can. "In my first act as your leader." The hands pinning him loosened. "I decree that all slavery in the Reich is to end." Konrad threw his shoulders from their grip. "Men, free the slaves on the boulevard outside." There's enough to put right for a lifetime.

Wernher shook his hands. "But Konrad, I explained why we can't do that . . ."

"You had your chance, Wernher." Schink waved his hand as he passed. "Now for somebody that keeps his word."

Mayrock laughed. "Quite a few of us are in the Outlaws for thieving."

Forced to the top because of the mistake back in Alabama. This is not what Konrad wanted. Even coming to Germany was something he'd been tricked into. Please, just let me get back to my farm and my girls. Maybe it's not too late to try for a boy with Diana.

Schink punched Mayrock's shoulder. "We're the king makers."

If Konrad's own convicts manipulated him into such responsibility, then he didn't know why.

"No more of putting up with the bosses' lies." Mayrock rubbed his bruise. "We're the bosses."

He had to make the best of the situation. If these put him here, then they could also take him away.

Hoechst raised a fist. "The hidden hand of quiet power."

Konrad doubted that such a thing existed.

This time, Schink beat Hoechst's arm down. "And from a grown man that can't even piss straight."

As they raced towards the doors, they rattled in their hinges.

"There must be a lot of people outside to try and open that door." Hoechst's demeanour hadn't been altered by Schink's abuse. "Only you've done that own your own, Sir."

The cloning fear returns. If only Konrad could open that door alone, his copies might well be outside. Ready yourself. "Hold fire, men."

One - just one - Konrad-sized figure stood in the daylight streaming through the opening. As only Konrad had done, the newcomer pushed the doors wide apart. Nobody in the Fatherland wore blue jeans tapered at the waist. This individual was his size but couldn't be a Gothengau clone. Not on its own. Not dressed like an ordinary American.

Mayrock pushed beside Konrad. "Who's that, sir?"

"Is he a clone?" Schink shoved Mayrock out of the way.

Hoechst avoided his colleagues and sidled up on Konrad's left. "Are any of your family that size, sir?"

There weren't. Konrad had always been the oddity.

"He doesn't half look like you, sir." Mayrock got back in the lead.

"Hey, sir!" Schink started chuckling. "Maybe he's one of the kids you don't know about."

Solving this mystery couldn't wait. Konrad picked his feet up, running to the door. His echoing boots were almost drowned out by his men's laughter. It did look like Konrad's reflection. Although Konrad couldn't keep bafflement from his face, the interloper held his arms open, a beaming smile baring his teeth to the gums. Did Konrad look that frightening too?

"My name's Hercules. I'm your son."

Now the terrifying grin spread across Konrad's face. Cleopatra had given him a son all those years ago. A son, at last, a son!

The End.

Thanks for getting here.
Please show your enjoyment by sharing, liking, or reviewing!

blink-182

THE BANDS, THE BREAKDOWN & THE RETURN

Joe Shooman

Published in 2010 by
INDEPENDENT MUSIC PRESS
Independent Music Press is an imprint of I.M. P. Publishing Limited

blink-182 – The Bands, The Breakdown & The Return
by Joe Shooman

British Library Cataloguing-in-Publication Data.
A catalogue for this book is available from The British Library.
ISBN: 978-1-906191-10-8

Cover Design by Fresh Lemon.
Cover photograph courtesy of Paul Bergen/Getty Images.

Printed in the EU.

Independent Music Press
P.O. Box 69,
Church Stretton, Shropshire
SY6 6WZ
Visit us on the web at: www.impbooks.com
and www.myspace.com/independentmusicpress
For a free catalogue, e-mail us at: info@impbooks.com
Fax: 01694 720049

blink-182

The Bands, The Breakdown
& The Return

by Joe Shooman

Independent Music Press

CONTENTS

A long, long time ago in a city far, far away …

Episode IV: A New Band

It is a period of international conflict, where nation invades nation for oil and tainted glory. Worst of all, the USA bans breast implants. Everywhere, small groups of rebel musicians are beginning to pop up, wearing big shorts and playing barre chords with melodic lines on top in order to defeat an empire of evil that has been dominant for too long. There is a battle of ethics brewing between grunge musicians with droopy hair and greasy introspective songs and those who have secret plans to create an ultimate weapon: a band of skate-punks with tunes so powerful, jokes so stupid and farts so obnoxious that they could infect a whole planet with smiles again. Chased by nobody in particular, Californian-born bassist and skateboard custodian Mark Allan Hoppus races from his Washington D.C. home toward San Diego, with plans to save music and restore pop-punk lunacy to the galaxy …

Chapter 1
First Steps

Thomas Matthew DeLonge Jnr was born on December 13, 1975 and raised in Poway, California. It's a town of just shy of fifty thousand inhabitants in San Diego County. A nice place to be, if a little on the slow side in comparison to the bright lights of bigger cities nearby. Poway is an ancient Native American settlement with the name meaning 'the two little valleys' and many spear points and arrowheads have been excavated along Poway Creek, making it a valuable and historical place. All of which was probably known by a teenage Tom who got expelled from Poway High for turning up at a school basketball game drunk. Not a good thing for his high school career; eventually brilliant for his musical career. Necessarily, DeLonge had to subsequently register for another school and that was Rancho Bernardo High. In 1992 it presented Tom with a second chance and an opportunity to indulge in his growing musical appreciation, which at that time had expanded toward punk rock (Descendents being a particular favourite at the time). The best thing about Rancho Bernardo, however, was their propensity for arranging Battle Of The Bands competitions. For a kid with a growing anti-establishment attitude – and a brand new, brand old guitar as a birthday present – it seemed a gift from heaven. He immediately set about writing some material to play on his acoustic, and when show day came around he was ready to rock, as were many other young bands at the school.

"My band, The Necropheliacs, played a cover of Metallica's 'Creeping Death'," recalls local musician and original blink-182 drummer, Scott Raynor, exclusively for this book. "Tom played an original song called 'Who's Gonna Shave Your Back Tonight?' which was just him and his guitar, to a basketball auditorium filled with people." This performance – which may have been under the temporary moniker Big Oily Men – made an impression on the crowd, and also on Raynor, whose own group was soon to be destabilised by the departure of founder member Paul Scott, who was moving out of the state. But not before Paul introduced Raynor to DeLonge at a party where the two found they had plenty in common. Tom explained he was a guitarist/vocalist looking for a more permanent band and so he and Scott decided to get together and jam.

"We started writing songs at my parents' house," recalls Raynor of these very early sessions, which at that point didn't have any ambition other than having a blast and playing some loud music for the hell of it. Scott William Raynor Jnr was born on May 23, 1978, was keen to develop his drumming chops even further, having been brought up on a steady diet of metal in a succession of youthful groups.

"I had been playing the drums for about three or four years before I met Tom," continues Scott. "Mostly my friends and I playing cover songs. The first song I played was with my friend Ryan Kennedy; we were both eleven and had recently been inspired by Metallica to pick up music. Metallica was far too technical, so we learned 'Twist of Cain' by Danzig and 'London Dungeon' by the Misfits. We played those songs at school in a kind of 'show and tell' thing. The first song I played at a real show was 'Vlad The Impailer' by Gwar. But I hadn't been in any bands that I would have considered 'serious' in the sense of successful."

Raynor and DeLonge's ad hoc sessions with a variety of bass players (as legend has it, there was even one called Derek, although this could be a subsequent in-joke reference to Spinal Tap's Derek Smalls, of course) weren't getting anywhere all that fast, aside from a lot of joking around and skating. But that was soon all to change.

Enter Mark Allan Hoppus, older than the other two guys, born on March 15, 1972. Hoppus had been living in Ridgecrest, California, which was brilliantly once named Crumville. Mark had been playing bass since being bought one as a gift for his fifteenth birthday, and by the time his family upped sticks to move to San Diego, he'd already played in a series of bands including Pier 69 and a group called The Attic Children, who in 1988 recorded some demos of their act – largely based round covering songs by UK goth grin-avoiders The Cure. Another band was Of All Things, which by 1992 was going so far as to play actual mini-concerts at friends' parties and The Oasis venue in Ridgecrest, albeit mainly covers of tracks by Descendents. But a gig is a gig, and the experience left Mark with a thirst for live performance. For a time after the move to San Diego, Hoppus would head back to Ridgecrest on a weekend to continue rehearsing and playing live with Of All Things, but after a while it became too much distance to bear so that band inevitably fizzled out. Also a good thing, because otherwise he wouldn't have had time to spare when his sister, Anne, introduced him to Tom DeLonge through her beau of the time.

"Tom and Scott met at a party a long time ago and started talking and decided that they wanted to start a band," recalled Mark later. "At that same time, my sister was going out with one of Tom's best friends, so she introduced me and Tom and we started writing songs together, and it just began from there."[1] The banter began immediately: one of the pair's early meetings was at a local skate park where Hoppus, in trying to out-trick his new buddy, managed to spectacularly crash and burn, falling from a lamp-post and cracking his ankles, an injury that put him in crutches for three weeks. But bass players are nothing if not fearless, and the pairing of DeLonge and Hoppus was a comedy duo who hit it off from the first moments.

Scott Raynor for one was delighted at this development in his musical world. "I really enjoyed their company. I thought they were hilarious although I was only fourteen or fifteen when I met them. I mean, I didn't even have a driver's licence yet, so I gained a lot of agency through hanging out with them and their group of friends."

Tom and Mark also, crucially, instantly found each other's musical muse a real kick, easily meshing in with each other's riffs like they had played together for years. "We started out practicing in my room," says Raynor. "My parents even stuck up for us when the neighbours complained. I'll never hear the end of it from my family though. It was hard enough to listen to the band live when we were practiced, let alone when we were just starting out."

That summer, the new band-mates hung out together, playing music constantly and goofing around as much as possible. "We went to a lot of punk shows and movies," continues Scott, "and ate a lot of fast food. We did stupid stuff like prank calls and practical jokes. I remember the first night I went to Mark's house, he and a bunch of Tom's friends told another friend who had never been to Mark's to come over, but they gave him the address of the house next door. Then they went and put a sign on the neighbour's door that said, 'Don't knock, just come in.' We all waited outside in the bushes for him to arrive, to see what would happen. He walked up and tried the door, but lucky for him it was locked."

The love for hi-jinks may have been based round simply having a great laugh, but the pranks were also inventive. "Tom used to call local businesses posing as a pest control salesman," laughs Raynor. "He tried to convince the owners of a local pizza hut to pay him to spray their property with 'synthetic coyote urine' in order to keep rodents away. Just stupid stuff, but [those guys] were a lot of fun to be around." Occasionally, they'd even play music, too.

Chapter 2
Steppin' Out

Even at this exciting nascent stage, the new band could have eroded when Mark Hoppus' girlfriend of the time asked him to essentially choose between hanging out with her or continuing with the band. Even though he'd only just bought a new bass amp and despite his initial protestations he decided to make a go of things with his lady. So reluctantly he left Tom and Scott to their own devices. But in the same way that the split with Of All Things hadn't stopped his musical pulse beating, the brief time away from his buddies (and their music) quickly became unbearable.

"We did record a couple of demos on a four-track with the aid of [friend and occasional musical collaborator] Cameron Jones," recalls Scott Raynor. "One was Tom and I, and I think maybe Cam on bass. However I don't really remember the chronology of their completion."

Before too long, Hoppus heard that Scott and Tom were recording their songs in a rehearsal space in Scott's bedroom and Mark was tempted back into the fold. When he returned, the three made a vow to get things moving properly at last. First port of call – find a name for their project. The three were toying with the names Duck Tape and Figure 8 at this stage, but hadn't decided on anything concrete yet. When I asked him, Scott Raynor said that at one particular rehearsal, DeLonge came armed with an idea.

"Tom came with the name 'blink' one day," explains Scott. "He said he liked it because it was a fast action verb." The others agreed. Newly christened Blink, there was a need for another demo tape to celebrate the return of Hoppus. As with the original Cameron Jones/Scott Raynor/Tom DeLonge tape, it was recorded on a four-track – a strangely anachronistic piece of gear in this computer-based, Pro-Tools age, but at the time it was an essential part of any budding band's armoury (in 1992 computers ran on bits of string and hope, and the very idea of recording multiple tracks of audio on a PC was as preposterous as, say, Arnold Schwarzenegger becoming the governor of California).

For those born after 1990, a four-track used a regular audio tape as its recording medium, recording across both sides of the tape and therefore allowing for multiple tracks of bass, guitar, drums etc to be laid down separately on to the cassette. It was and is a resolutely analogue medium, in which noise levels increase with every pass through the machine and degradation and distortion of the music is an inevitable (and sometimes a creative) part of the process. But on the other hand, in common with today's digital recording practices, it was a relatively cheap way to reproduce your music and for a band at the start of their careers it was essential to produce a tape to send round to promoters, venues, journalists and even record labels.

This new demo was dubbed *Flyswatter* by Blink, and comprised the songs 'Reebok Commercial', 'Time', 'Red Skies', 'Alone', 'Point Of View', 'Marlboro Man', 'The Longest Line' and 'Freak Scene'. It was a mix of covers and bedroom originals but with a terrible sound and a performance quality that is at best naïve. Blink have subsequently been rather keen on distancing themselves from it by pointing out precisely what it is – youthful and raucous first steps. The tape, which was 'released' by the band on their made-up Fags In The Wilderness Records (complete with cover drawn by Mark), captures a certain excitement but also includes one heck of a lot of bum notes and muddy recording standards. It sounds as unfinished as you can imagine, and though of historical note in certain regards, you wouldn't necessarily want to put it on the stereo. Indeed, Mark told an interviewer in 1996, "Trust me. We sucked way worse then than we do now."[2]

Another tape, cunningly dubbed *Demo No.2*, was invaluable in assisting the band in their live aspirations as the Blink name started to spread. An early supporter was Mark Hoppus' boss at his record store job, one Patrick Secor.

"The store [we worked at together] was called *The Wherehouse* – Where? *The Wherehouse*!," Secor explained for this book. "They're a chain that back then was like Tower-lite, a regular record and video store in North County San Diego. I'd been assistant manager at another location and got transferred to the store where Mark was, so that I could be the manager there and that's where I first met him. It was the coolest job you could have compared to what everyone else was doing and all the people who worked there had an interest in music. I was just out of high school so it was great as far as jobs go because you could order things in and get discounts! Every day you had exposure to music, you were right in the middle of things."

The guys hit it off straight away, despite Secor's seniority of post. The manager recalls that his first impressions of the young Hoppus were good ones. "Mark was very charismatic, funny, easy to get along with and we hit it off right away. He was a good worker and we never had any issues as far as that went. We had a lot of similar interests. He'd just got together with the other guys and started the band and at the same time I wanted to start my own record label."

The youthful, can-do attitude and shared excitement about the possibilities in music was one thing but in the early 1990s getting gigs was another matter entirely in a town with very limited options in terms of venues. "The first Blink show was at a high school," recalls Secor. "They played at a lunchtime concert. Frankly, San Diego was very conservative and there weren't many places for underage people – at the time two thirds of the band were too young to play a real club. There were benefit shows, one with Bad Radio which was Eddy Vedder's first band. It's so different from today and the Bay Area where there's tons of places to play. It was absolutely DIY – when you were small and starting out there was a limited amount of clubs and places to play, so you had to be creative if you wanted to get your band out there, [find] places where you could get an audience together. Obviously after a while they could play anywhere they wanted but [initially they] had to create [their] own audience."

Early Blink appearances are recorded at San Diego's Spirit Club – their (non-school) debut – and the influential local shop, Alley Kat Records. 1993 saw the band consolidate and begin to perform at The Dungeon, a side stage of the city's biggest club, SOMA, where on April 9, 1993 they were on a bill with fellow local hopefuls Papillon, Product, Grip and Loophole.

"SOMA was just getting started and it was a small basement of a building," explains Secor. "It was kinda raw, and the only place that was all ages in San Diego. There was a lot of good energy. You could either go to SOMA or to [Mexican border town] Tijuana if you were underage so it was nice to have that kind of a place in San Diego."

Secor's part in the tale at this point is that of facilitator; he was into Blink's music and also wanted to start his own record label. Soon the idea came into focus: to get Blink into a 'proper' studio with a view to releasing material on Secor's brand-new label, Filter Records.

"If you could get one good microphone in those days you were far and above everybody else," remembers Secor. "These days anybody could probably get some free software and a coupla cheap mics to hook into your computer and get good results but back then I had an old 386 computer that I used to type out college papers on. There was no real public internet. The problem was, 'How the hell do I get people to listen to my band?' Whereas now you can just upload it to MySpace for people to listen to. But in those days you'd spend hours every night recording tapes to give to people. My thinking with Filter Records was to start small, get the band out there, get people to hear it, start getting reviews which would kick you up a level and start sending those tapes out to get gigs. Also to play anywhere you can as much as you can and that's how the word would spread. It was very local."

"I'd go to Scott's house to their practices. I'd hang out with them; they were fun and catchy and I thought this would be a great band to start a label with. The whole purpose was to sign them, put out a record and keep going. They got a bunch of songs together, Mark and I talked about it so I said, 'Let's put out a record'. At that point they'd played around enough to get their chops up so I took all the money I had in savings and we went into the studio for two days." It was understandably a time of great excitement in the camp.

That studio was Santee, California's Doubletime, where the engineer was Jeff Forrest. "They were playing a lot at SOMA and drawing a lot of people," Forrest explained for this book. "They were still in Poway High School but they drew really good crowds. The idea with the demo, like with every other band, was that they needed it to go out and get other shows. So they'd hope to widen their audience and get shows out of town, stuff like that."

It was already working; the group had branched out to places like Soul Kitchen in El Cajon. Tom himself had returned to Poway High and was selling copies of *Flyswatter* at lunchtime to get kids into liking his band, as well as putting up flyers wherever he could. And the crowds were increasing steadily as a result.

"I went to a few of those shows," remembers Jeff Forrest. "It was crazy; when they would play they would pack the place, there was probably about six hundred kids there going nuts. I believe they were all skaters at that time."

Six hundred fans? More than enough to justify that frantic studio time. The project would be dubbed *Buddha*. "The *Buddha* tape was basically a collection that represented almost all of the songs that we had written up to that point," explains drummer Scott Raynor. "Mark had a friend that put up the funds for recording and we went in to Doubletime and put them down. It was factory pressed. I can't remember now if we hand-made the covers and packed them ourselves or if they just came that way. We started selling them at shows and at school, and it helped us get some people out to see the live show."

In fact, the tapes were manufactured at a professional copy house, but the insert sheets for the tapes were photocopied then cut and folded by hand. The band would then drive round to local record stores and persuade the owners to sell copies on the counter. There was also a screen-printer to hand where the group would run off all manner of daft Blink T-shirts which have, of course, become collectors' items. The *Buddha* sessions – such as they were – were being scheduled round work and school commitments but unfortunately at the time Mark was suffering a little from illness. Undaunted, however, the band carried on like any good punksters should – testament to their excellent attitude, according to Forrest, who says that such short sessions are commonplace.

"A bunch of bands came through the studio," he muses. "A lot of them in the same vein of music as Blink. But Blink seemed that they weren't pretentious; they were just kids having fun. *Buddha* was cut live then we added the vocals. Two days and they were done – including the mix. It's quite standard for a young punk band to do that. They sold a lot of the tapes at their shows."

Rock music was in the ascendancy at this time; guitars were firmly in fashion as was being a little different, alternative, out-of-the-loop. From 1991-1994, the charts had been infiltrated by bands such as Nirvana, Soundgarden, The Smashing Pumpkins, Pearl Jam, Mudhoney and Alice in Chains, all of whom, to a greater or lesser extent, would find themselves pigeon-holed as part of the dominant movement: grunge.

Grunge had been brought into the mainstream by a collection of groups in Seattle and the surrounding area, and its blend of sludgy, fuzzed-up guitar choruses and clean verses appealed to a generation of kids who thought heavy metal was preposterous and yet were also too young to have been punks the first time around. Grunge's rawness was in fact directly influenced in spirit and musically by both punk and elements of metal, and lyrically it spoke of apathy, rejection, downbeat alienation and disenchantment with society.

The charts of 1994 were filled with such themes but alongside the grunge bands, somewhat more of a positive-sounding note was being sounded by the likes of The Offspring, Rancid and Green Day, the latter two of which were arguably more politically-minded than their grunge counterparts as well as more enamoured of the high-energy, major-chord punk style of Descendents, Ramones and so on. Californians Green Day in particular had blasted into the musical consciousness and sparked a whole new generation's interest in punk rock. Although signing to a major label had brought them criticism from punk purists, the move was also a massive success – their third album *Dookie*, released in 1994, sold 15 million copies throughout the world.

But everyone has to start somewhere. Billie Joe and his boys kicked it all off with tiny shows and an independent label, giving them street smarts as well as punk credentials. They were a massive inspiration for bands throughout the world – and for a trio of musicians from just a coupla hundred miles down the road, Green Day's ascent was simply a blueprint to success.

By contrast, San Diego in 1994 was hardly a hotbed of activity; there were gigs to be found but, according to contemporary musician AK Skurgis, getting ready for said gigs was a tricky proposition.

"There were never enough rehearsal spaces," he declares. "Bands would rent storage units, garages – whatever they could to save money and time and the inevitable hassles from landlords and the authorities. My favourite place to rehearse was Nestor studios in El Cajon." There were, however, a surprising amount of venues in which to cut your teeth as a live act, continues AK. "There were a few really cool venues: The Casbah, The Spirit, The Velvet, Crowbar, Bodies, SOMA – and a couple of coffeehouses had live bands as well. I know that Café Chabalaba did ... as well as The Ché Café at UCSD. Blink were a tight little power pop band."

Thanks in part to their ability to rehearse at Scott Raynor's house rather than chase down the very limited spaces elsewhere in town, plus their demos' success in getting them live gigs, blink were becoming part of a circuit that also included the likes of Ten Foot Pole.

"As an outsider coming in to play shows," explains Denny Jegard of that band, "it was all about playing at SOMA, which had a big stage where we could open for big bands, such as Pennywise, or headline when we were doing well, and a small stage where we headlined a few times playing with local bands or touring support bands. I don't recall having a bad show there, and I remember having a lot of respect for Len, the owner/promoter and his staff. Then later that building was shut down and a new building was opened, also called SOMA (I think), where we played with Millencollin on an Epitaph *Punk-O-Rama* tour."

"San Diego is rad," Tom DeLonge told John Robb. "It's very suburban. Lots of beaches, lots of surfers ... lots of movie theatres. It's the suburbs. San Diego seems to have more nicer areas than any other city in America."[3] 'Nice' or otherwise, there had always been a fascination with punk in SD, something that the growing trio were happy to go along with.

"It's a huge punk population," continued DeLonge. "It's bigger in Southern California than anywhere else, apart from Quebec. It's because South Cal has so many skateboarders; the music scene is so big there because you are right next to Los Angeles and San Francisco – the centre of the entertainment industry. All these kids surfing, skating and snowboarding are into alternative lifestyles. They don't want to listen to the radio, they want to listen to edgier things. The Sex Pistols opened up the doors and the next wave of bands came along ... and were even angrier. That was very much a New York/East Coast thing; the West Coast scene was not so angry. Every new punk band had a new angle and got more poppier and learned to play. Bad Religion started the *oohs* and *aahs* and the real crazy vocals. The Californian middle-class suburbs have nothing to be that bummed about. New York is gloomy, dark and cold. It makes different music."[4]

Blink, thanks to their ever-growing fan-base and momentum, had by now moved up to the main room at that newly-refurbished SOMA, something that was pleasing them immensely whilst simultaneously scaring them half to hell and back.

"SOMA shows were a lot of fun," says Scott Raynor. "Eventually we started headlining. It's difficult to describe, in words, the nauseous mix of fear and excitement that would hit me when I first started seeing lines of people waiting to hear us play."

The *Buddha* album was now out on tape on Filter Records and was clearly getting the band noticed amongst the kids as well as further afield. For the band and the new label boss, it was an exciting time where everyone was on the same gloriously unfettered joyride. Meanwhile, the band themselves had to try and support themselves by any means possible. San Diego may have been a relatively affluent area but that didn't mean that anyone was given a free ride, either. DeLonge had possibly one of the most taxing jobs possible, working on his musculature day by day.

"I lifted concrete for drillers," he explained of his work, which also involved driving and lifting hundred-pound bags by hand. "[It wasn't] just bags, [they were] pallets. After the forklift broke, I had to lift pallets of concrete and sand by hand."[5] Never let it be said that he's afraid of hard work.

Dreams of making music a full-time occupation were lifting too and by 1994 the band were on the verge of the holy grail – a record contract with the established label, Cargo Records.

Chapter 3
Grin To Win

Cargo Records was the biggest indie label San Diego had to offer and for any aspiring band – particularly a punk band – it was an ideal home on which to continue to develop. There are several versions of the way that the deal came about, the predominant one being that Cargo owner Eric Goodis' skater son Brahm was a major champion of Blink and pestered Goodis the elder about them so much that he eventually came to see the band play live. Also instrumental was the efficiently-named O, guitarist for Fluf, one of Cargo's best-selling bands. Pat Secor, who had recently relocated to the Bay Area, says there were also other people pulling for Blink's move onto Cargo Records.

"When I moved," Secor explains, "my roommate at the time knew a lot of people in magazines and newspapers and also people on Cargo, so I pushed him to get Blink heard. The concept was to get a band, put out a record, get them signed up and you'd keep putting out their first record and get a solid base. Once they got signed to Cargo they wanted to use some songs from *Buddha* and I thought that would be great because it'd just bring more attention to the Filter tape." Any group selling out SOMA was bound to sign a record deal sooner rather than later and Blink were no exception.

"The son of the label's president pitched us to his dad," says Scott Raynor, "and then O helped convince him to sign us. I remember all of us being ecstatic about it. There weren't any other offers at the time but that was the top label in San Diego so it wouldn't have mattered if there had been."

Recording sessions were soon set up to celebrate the deal, with Westbeach Studios in LA the first port of call for the band, a venue that was very famous for the likes of NOFX, Face To Face and Bad Religion having all recorded there. The story has it that Tom DeLonge actually recorded some guitar parts through Bad Religion guitarist Mr. Brett's own amplifier, further cementing the similar sonics that the young Blink were keen on creating.

"It was our first recording with a budget," says early blink drummer Scott Raynor. "Westbeach was where all the Epitaph bands had been recording at the time. I spent the whole time thinking, 'Greg Graffin probably sat in this chair', 'Brett Gurewitz probably stood in this doorway,' etc. We did the record in three days fuelled by some great, terrible Chinese food."

The engineer was Steve Kravac, who was also just embarking on a sonic career. "I was then the house engineer at Westbeach," he recounted to the author. "I had no choice but to work with the little so-and-sos! Really it was a case of showing up for work. Thank God I did, I may have never made it in the business otherwise."

Blink made an immediate impression on Kravac with their boisterousness and sense of fun; the sessions scheduled were not the most forgiving in terms of length, though, so it was very necessary to get down and dirty almost immediately.

"When I met the guys it was obvious that they were young and a little green but they made up for that with a rambunctious enthusiasm that became their trademark. I was based in L.A. at the time so it's hard to say exactly what was going on down there in that scene, probably not too much. The music scene I was exposed to from San Diego was more art-core stuff. Obviously Rocket From The Crypt and Drive Like Jehu were pretty big acts but there were other cool bands like Three Mile Pilot going on that were not part of the punk or skate scenes. It was pretty diverse around that time."

Although Blink were now in possession of a contract with the biggest indie label in San Diego, Cargo were still not in a position to offer more than a few days' worth of finances to record Blink's first efforts for their new home.

"It was over pretty fast," remembers Kravac. "Cargo had sent the band to Los Angeles to record and mix the seventeen tracks in three days. There was no time to really think about anything except just 'start playing and I'll hit the record button'. Basically the band had little-to-no equipment, and that didn't help the situation. I set them up live on the floor and they blasted through the songs. We may have done a couple of retakes here and there. However, there wasn't much time for any development of the songs or getting good sounds. In retrospect that may have added to the final version of the record having a raw appeal."

Kravac says he wishes that there had been a little more time to establish a working relationship beyond the blink-and-you're-gone 100mph approach that was a financial necessity for all concerned at the time.

"The entire time we were doing the record I kept saying, 'Let's call Cargo, rent a couple of good amps for you guys and book a little time to do some overdubs,'" sighs the engineer. "I could see that the path we were going down wasn't going to work for the record that the band felt they needed to make." One man's opinion, of course, but borne out of frustration at what may have been. "We basically worked together to get on the right track. I tried to guide the guys in a direction to get some credible performances in what little time we had. Mark really tried to make the best of it, but I feel that Tom was frustrated."

However, after the Westbeach sessions, according to Jeff Forrest the band decamped to the more familiar surroundings of Doubletime which was booked once more – not for three days but one whole week, unprecedented in Blinkland.

"There was no pre-production; they already had all the material together and they always wrote really catchy and fun songs," recalls engineer Jeff Forrest. "They would come in, we'd do the drum and rhythm tracks, overdub the guitars and do the vocals. A lot of it was almost mixed as we went along, it was pretty fast. There's a big benefit to working at that pace because when you're restricted by time and money I think you go in with a different attitude. You don't second-guess yourself so much, which can happen a lot. People get so caught up in thinking a lot that they'll take something home and decide they'd better re-write all the lyrics, re-do this and that. I've had it happen where it took somebody two years to do a record because they kept changing their mind! But when you're under pressure I think you get a higher energy level and you're not second-guessing so much. You're focused."

Quite so: even if a number of the tracks were recycled from their Filter Records debut, it's still some achievement to bang out sixteen tracks in six days or so and to have them sounding coherently energetic. The songs would make up an album to be called *Cheshire Cat*, named by Tom DeLonge after "my favourite character"[6], the continually grinning pussy in Lewis Carroll's infamously gory monster thriller, *Alice's Adventures In Wonderland*.[7]

"O was here with them," concludes Jeff Forrest. "He was the producer … they had a lot of jokes, a lot of fun. They were funny guys. At that time they were still in high school with girlfriends and all that stuff, nobody was married yet and they were just typical teenage fun kids. [Bands like that] still come to the studio, it's always fun working with those kind of fun kids."

Fun sessions or not, things weren't simple for Blink by any means. For one, Scott Raynor's parents had upped sticks and moved to Reno, Nevada. A fine town in itself and the inspiration for one of Johnny Cash's most famous songs, 'Folsom Prison Blues', but hardly convenient for the nascent Blink who were attracting plenty of good old fashioned interest in their activities.

"Just after signing the [Cargo] deal, my family had to move," explains Raynor. "I stayed one last summer, living with my sister, in order to rehearse for the *Cheshire Cat* recording session which, at the time, was to be my last performance with the band. At this point we were playing in Tom's parents' garage. I remember [us] writing 'M&Ms' in there."

As it turned out, Blink did briefly get a stand-in drummer – school friend Mike Krull – but it wasn't the same vibe as they had with Scott. After some negotiations it was decided that the youngster was an essential part of the band and as such it would be excellent if he were able to hang out for just a little longer.

"So the band asked me back," Scott explains. "Mark's family was kind enough to let me live with them. And my parents were kind enough to allow me to drop out of full-time school, move back to San Diego and play in the band. The catch was that I had to finish my diploma by taking a home schooling curriculum, which I completed by often doing homework while out on tour. Anyway, the night I moved in I was carrying a box off stuff into the house from my car and Mark's step-dad asked, 'You planning on staying for a while?' I thought he was joking. It turns out they didn't tell him – until I was moving in – that I was moving in! I think Mark and his sister Anne and I stayed up watching old TV shows until morning that whole summer."

Cheshire Cat was released to a fan-base eager to hear the results of Blink's latest adventures in the studio and it remains a breathless, energetic and fun romp through the songs that had served the group so well on their two-year apprenticeship on various San Diego stages.

The album starts with 'Carousel' which also had opened the Filter Records debut cassette *Buddha* in 1993. It is a track that had its genesis in the very first jam session between Tom DeLonge and Mark Hoppus back in 1992. It begins with a mid-paced riff and some nice undistorted jangling guitars before smashing into a satisfyingly fast-assed punk song in the vein of NOFX with some very adept dynamic breakdowns. Even at this early stage and in a relatively rough recording, it's clear that this is the work of a band that not only loves tuneful US skate-punk sounds but also know what it takes to create a very catchy song.

'M&Ms' is another instantly-recognisable Blink track that's based round power chords, a playful lead figure and insistent guitar chops, plus Mark singing about getting away from it all – a song featuring immortal words about making love with your hand. 'M&Ms' is Blink in microcosm, in less than three minutes they nail their sonic colours to the mast, with speedy bridges, tuneful vocal melodies and insanely danceable beats hammering away behind it all.

Another recycled song from *Buddha*, 'Fentoozler', ambles along nattily enough with some decent call-and-response singing, although Tom's nasal vocals get a little lost in the mix as the album takes a slightly modest breather after the comparatively brilliant first two tracks. 'Touchdown Boy' is even faster, a sonic assault that deals with wanting to be like the hero who always gets the girl (and questioning if, indeed, he is a hero at all). It's based around a real school friend of theirs and originally the lyrics actually featured said guy's name before the band thought better of it and toned it down a tad. There's also a middle-eight where Tom and Mark exchange some innuendo-loaded banter that echoes the band's growing stage-craft. Their onstage ability to make each other and the audience laugh with ever-more outrageous statements about sex, farts and boobies had by now become a vital part of the Blink live experience.

'Strings' is another classic Blink moment wherein a rampant-riffed verse structure all about girls and wanting a life free of complications is surprisingly slowed down by the brilliant and simple chorus. The breakdowns and intertwined guitar work is surprisingly sophisticated for an act whose technical ability may not quite yet be on a par with their undoubtedly fertile musical imaginations. 'Peggy Sue' – no relation to the Buddy Holly classic – is all about holding off from being aggressive when other people are telling you what to do, no matter how much you feel provoked. Do anything else, including running in the street barefoot, but don't rise to the bait. As a slab of teen angst it's as authentic as they come, although some of the boomy feedback on one of the guitars is horrible. The incredibly short and snappy 'Sometimes' carries on the theme of those strange girl creatures, love and running away, before another album highpoint – 'Does My Breath Smell?' – where Tom manfully singing some self-searching lyrics over a subdued riff whilst in the background assorted Blinks basically rip the piss with some distinctly odd sounds. Quickly, however, the mojo is regained with the track slamming into mosh-melting territory, a great little drum break and one of the most economical lead guitar counterpoints to the layered vocals so far on the LP. 'Cacophony' also begins in mid-paced mode, this time Mark's bass leading matters before a heavier riff begins to insinuate toward the lyrics, all about a relationship in which confusion reigns due to the imbalance of enthusiasm between both involved. The lyrics are unguarded and show a sensitive side of Blink that's quite often been somewhat obfuscated over the years by the popular perception of the band as goons goofing off.

'TV' is another high-paced number that, possibly in a loving tribute to Scott Raynor and Anne Hoppus' aforementioned summer spent watching the box, observes that television is absolutely a vital part of life. It's not just entertainment, it's *needed*. Another old track from the Filter Records debut, 'Toast And Bananas', starts with the spoken word explanation that his pants are 'off right now' before embarking on a feast of stomping drums and playfully fluid guitar lines. Again, Tom sings of a girl, to the point of not really caring what she says because essentially she's out of his life and he'd rather be alone. 'Wasting Time' meanwhile, takes on the challenge of trying to get the attention of a girl, Mark's vocals surfing on top of waves of guitar chords as he contemplates the best way to get through to the object of his affections, to the point of writing a song about her.

'Wasting Time' is notable for a line having been suggested by Jeff Forrest. "He came up with it while we were recording Mark's vocal for the song," smiles Scott Raynor. "It's a very 'Blink' line. Jeff never offered any further insight into what may have been the source material for this pro-active free association, and we never asked." Fair enough. Another classic teen anthem in the making, 'Wasting Time' is the precursor to another Blink-type builder, 'Romeo And Rebecca', also a re-recording of a track from *Buddha*, and one that says definitively that the fairer sex are a waste of time. At least, in the somewhat miffed view of the victim of a presumably failed relationship.

All of which would already go toward a more than decent second album, but there's more in the form of three 'joke' songs under the thrall of which the listener is left somewhat open-mouthed. First off, there's 'Ben Wah Balls' – a song that variously talks about an old man farting, Chinese love eggs (hence the title) and a generous hint toward incest to boot. 'Just About Done' commences with a satisfyingly metallic set of riffs atop which unearthly squeals abound. It's both daft and musically incredibly different from the rest of the album and as such makes a welcome break, although repeated listens fail to really unearth any significant content. Which is probably the point, of course. Finally, 'Depends' rounds matters off in as much of a juvenile way as could be imagined with lyrics about pissing on yourself and other people. What it does do is give both vocalists the chance to sing lead on the same song, albeit in the silliest way possible, particularly on the messing-about spoken nonsense of the outro. As it turned out, the trio of daft tracks were a big hit with the fans. "Those joke songs are more popular than some of the others," laughed Hoppus, "which I think is rad!"[8] It's a fun end, though, to an album that is heavy on fun, growing musicianship, ace nippy songwriting and sprayed with exuberance. Given the incredibly fast way it was recorded in two separate studios, it isn't half bad at all.

Chapter 4
What's My Name Again?

Blink is such a great name for a band that it was pretty much inevitable there was going to be some kind of issue somewhere down the line. And, as it turns out, as Blink started to get out of the blocks down in the So-Cal sun, there was another group also starting to make a few waves with the same moniker. Over the years the tale has become such an integral part of blink-182's history that the story, such as it is, has been somewhat obscured by the bigger picture. It's worth a quick look at this to set the record straight once and for all.

Here's how it played out.

In June 1991, several members of an Irish act that had in a previous incarnation in the late '80s gone by the name of Rex And Dino were invited to contribute four tracks of their new band to a CD for release during the *CMJ New Music Seminar* music biz conference/live event over in New York. The guys decided they may as well get some songs together, but obviously in order to do so they'd need to call themselves something different as it was a new project.

"We had yet to come up with a name for this band," chuckles the affable Dermot Lambert of the Dublin group. "This was a very funny time. There was no band. If we'd wanted to gig, we weren't even sure if the material could be played live, by us at any rate. Barry Campbell, our drummer, suggested the name Blink so we could call ourselves something. He got the name from his favourite song of all-time, 'Ice Blink Luck' by The Cocteau Twins. I simply thought it was a great reason for the name, although I did express my opinion that the name itself sounded like a cabaret moniker." To everyone's astonishment that CD appearance started off a bidding war amongst several labels, the upshot of which being that Blink (the Dublin version) signed to EMI in 1992. Now the eagle-eyed amongst us might notice that June 1991 is some months before Mark, Tom and Scott started jamming over in San Diego. So the first Blink were the Irish chaps, whose debut album had as much punk credentials as you like, having been co-produced by John O'Neill of the quite wonderful Undertones[9].

With the Irish band's name starting to get around, including tours during 1993 and 1994 with the likes of Carter USM, Ned's Atomic Dustbin, Power Of Dreams, and Crowded House, and heavy radio and press support in the UK, it was inevitable that their 'fame' would reach San Diego at one stage or another. It is beautifully ironic that during this period there was a certain San Diego indie label reputedly interested in the Dublin electronic-tinged act's future career.

"[Then] either late 1993 or early 1994 at a gig in Manchester," continues Lambert, "a girl called Donna used to come to all our shows, and she arrived one day, all huffing and puffing, asking us what were we going to do about this American band called Blink. The American Blink had released *Cheshire Cat*, I think, on Cargo Records, a label we were talking to in the US. I think we just thought it was no big deal, but it wouldn't be likely that Cargo records would want two Blinks. I suppose we thought that if it ever became such a major problem, it would be only if we were getting huge, or they were getting huge, and I honestly don't think anyone in our immediate circles saw that that would be a bad thing."

Although nothing came of the Cargo interest as far as Dublin's finest were concerned, it was a bit daft to have two bands with an identical name just starting to break through into the wider musical consciousness and on both sides of the Atlantic it was seen to be probably a good idea to get this matter sorted sooner rather than later.

"Gradually," continues Lambert, "we began to be asked so often what the story was by our fans at gigs that we just said, 'Why don't we just see who had the name first?' Don't forget, this was 1994, and I personally knew that neither band were sure they could qualify, as both bands were relatively new. We were happy enough to go along with this, quite frankly expecting to be told we'd be changing our name, and the sooner the better too. This actually led to a list of names being drawn up and considered."[10]

In the dark days of 1994, communications across the pond were a little less instant than in the email age. One consequence of the coincidentally shared name was that it led to the Dublin act checking out their American counterparts. "It really was just a minor pain in the arse, and at one point we thought it was funny. We got to listen to them, and liked them, so we felt like we were on a strange kind of compadre buzz with them. There was no internet to speak of, so we didn't realise they were slightly more serious about it than we were. Another irony."

Contact was eventually made between the two camps and to sort it all out there was one particular piece of incontrovertible evidence that proved who was there first (and that only by a matter of months). These themes are fairly commonplace in music – anyone who's ever looked for a name for their own band will be familiar with how incredibly hard it is to find a cool one that hasn't been taken yet.

"The facts, plain and simple," concludes Lambert, "were that we had released a CD in October 1992 for the CMJ which is currently selling, or not, as the case may be, for $2,000.00 on a certain website. This CD was the first Blink release in the USA. There were four tracks on it and it's great! It's called *Blink CMJ 1992*. That's it. End of story."

A legal agreement was drawn up to establish naming rights. Lambert – a sterling chap who runs a company called Garageland which is instrumental in supporting unsigned bands and getting them gigs – explains: "We understood that everybody was so relaxed about it, that when it came to drawing up an agreement, we actually agreed to allow them to retain the Blink in the name ... as part of the legal agreement, we were also consulted on the 182 [that the San Diego band wanted to add], which, for the record, we were told is the number of times the word 'Fuck' is used in *Scarface*[11]. Whether or not they were having a laugh at our expense, that was the reason we gave the go ahead to the name blink-182 ... so like it or not, that's official. One of the final ironies with the whole thing is that after all this Blink business, a stupid band name that I for one never valued, we are now stuck with the name."[12]

"This shitty techno band from Ireland called and said, 'We're called Blink and you have to change your name,'" Mark Hoppus stated in 2000. "So we added the 182 for no reason. It means nothing. Tom always makes up stories about what it means, but I'll rat him out right now. It means nothing."[13]

"It was Mark's suggestion," offers Scott Raynor. "He just blurted it out in Rick's office when we were deciding to change the name. It's supposed to represent a random number but I think it has unconscious relation to the film *Turk-182*."[14] It has also been noted that there was much 'confusion' amongst fans of the San Diego group now called blink-182 and the Irish band called Blink; apocryphal tales exist all over the lovely internet of kids being hoodwinked into going to gigs by the wrong version of Blink, or even buying a Blink (Dublin) CD and complaining to blink-182 that their 'new direction' sucked. The links between the two Blinks have in fact continued over the years, with Lambert's outfit taking to the road with one of the San

Diego group's compatriots.

"We toured the USA in 1998 to 2000 with Samiam, who are mates with blink-182. At that point we were aware that blink-182 weren't loving us too much but we were great buddies with Samiam, and often inquired if anyone in the audience expected to see Blink or blink-182. They agreed with us that this was not the case."[15]

One thing that is undeniable is that there exists artwork for early copies of *Cheshire Cat* crediting it simply to Blink. Notably, the upper case 'B' was used on this sleeve's artwork, although later issues were altered to the standard lower case presentation, blink-182.

Chapter 5

Out On The Road With A 182 In Tow

With a lower case spelling of their new moniker and that 182 suffix in tow, plus some vibrant recordings in the bag, it was time for Mark Hoppus, Tom DeLonge and Scott Raynor to specifically look to expand their fan-base outside of their relatively comfortable status as growing stars of the San Diego circuit.

"Our first national tour was with Seven Seconds and Unwritten Law," explains Scott Raynor. "Leaving the state felt like going to the moon. Everything ahead was entirely unknown to us." During this period it was imperative to keep the bandwagon rolling, particularly after the band's first foray on vinyl hit the streets; a split release with Cam Jones' band, The Iconoclasts, on the superbly-named, off-shoot Big Weenie Records. It was a relatively low-key release but had the added benefit of being on exceedingly cool red vinyl. The blink-182 tracks were strong – 'Does My Breath Smell?' and 'Wasting Time' – and the record served to spread the group's name further afield. At first the band were travelling in a small convoy of cars (being too young and/or far too broke to afford a van) and making some serious mileage between dates. But the San Diego scene was ever-helpful and on one particular occasion blink-182's good mates Unwritten Law saw fit to lend them their own van for a gig up in Reno, Nevada. The name of the vehicle says it all: The Cock (Scott himself had a lucky escape from the crowded and freezing trip as his folks already lived up there). The gig was a great one with the audience getting off on blink-182's set but the drive back was almost a total nightmare with The Cock deciding first not to start and then, after some input from the roadie of headliners Face To Face, started up but wouldn't turn off again. The Cock was even left running whilst being filled with petrol.

All this zipping around the US and the growing buzz about the band drew the attention of Mike Halloran of 91X FM, who became the first person ever to play the band on the radio (the track was 'M&Ms'); then, crucially, within a short space of time, the San Diego trio were taken on both by a manager, Rick DeVoe ("a great manager, super talented,' Scott told me. "He was our Colonel Parker.") and Rick and

Jean Bonde of the Tahoe booking agency. The two Ricks were a massive asset for blink-182, taking responsibility for spreading the name of the band far and wide and getting the group as many gigs as was humanly possible.

1995 was an excellent year for blink as activities ramped up to include more releases including the (clear blue) vinyl single entitled 'They Came To Conquer ... Uranus!' which featured older tracks 'Wrecked Him', 'Waggy' and 'Zulu' and, crucially, the release of *Cheshire Cat* properly. With the momentum growing apace, the band were able to shoot a video for 'M&Ms', directed by Darren Doane and Ken Daurio. It is a video that entirely encapsulates the fun and energy of a band at the start of their career, and in the words of Scott Raynor, had them "doing skate-tricks without skateboards and being shot to death all in the same day. Fantastic!" Rick DeVoe's connections were also to prove instrumental in tying the group into lifestyles and vibes that they held very dear to their hearts: the skate, surf and snowboard scenes. Specifically, a contact of Rick's by the name of Taylor Steele was looking for rad new groups to include on the soundtrack of his latest surf video, *Good Times*. It was one hell of a breakthrough for Hoppus, DeLonge and Raynor: this was entirely their marketplace – cool young kids interested in tricks, blasting music and having as much fun as possible. Blink's future was beginning to look incredibly rosy; and the good times literally were to continue with the *Good Times* tour of October 1995, also featuring Seven Seconds, Unwritten Law and Sprung Monkey, dates which both introduced the south and east to blink and conversely inducted blink-182 into the curiously addictive world of touring.

"It was a blast," confirms Scott Raynor, "although it was rare at that point to have any blink fans at the shows. Nobody really knew of us yet. Unwritten Law and Seven Seconds got the big reactions. It was play, pack, travel or play, pack, sleep on someone's floor. Sometimes we got pancakes in the morning, sometimes I had to wear earplugs while I slept to keep the cockroaches out of my ears, sometimes I had to wear earplugs so I could sleep while people came and went buying drugs. It was a shifty business sometimes, sleeping on floors, but like in most things, blink was lucky with that and we never had any real trouble. Honestly, the shows went well. We always got a good reaction, and the next time we came around we had more fans and better floors to sleep on – some with carpet!"

The tour, as you might expect from a bunch of young musicians thrown together in close proximity to boredom, booze and bad smells, was not without its incidents. One example was when Tom DeLonge was caught drinking a beer in the street on Halloween night at a Jacksonville date and arrested (he was underage for the state). It wasn't an experience he wanted to repeat in a hurry. Elsewhere, there were rather less savoury incidents, as Raynor explains.

"There was a small riot on that tour. Tom and I had just walked into the venue ..." recalls Scott. Concerned by the level of force used by bouncers against the fans, tension had quickly spiralled between security and the crowd, words were exchanged and soon after fighting broke out. "[Another band's guitarist] launched himself Superman-style across the stage at a bouncer ... then the whole place broke out. The bass player from [this other band] was hitting another bouncer on the head with his bass. It was crazy ... that kind of thing happened a lot. Not always to that degree but there is an underlying tension at punk shows between the fans and the bouncers who signify authority."

On a lighter note, and for reasons lost to history, it was deemed necessary for one of the blink team to apprehend a life-size cut-out of Lenny Kravitz from a concert in Dallas. Lenny remained the perfect, silent, fart-less tour-mate for several dates.

"Sometimes we put him up centre stage with a mic," laughs Scott Raynor. "He didn't say much though; just stood kinda stood there caught in a poise of pure rock *jouissance*."[16]

The more they played, the better gigs got and the more experienced blink-182 became in terms of handling an unfamiliar crowd. Every night was both a challenge and a delight and by the time the US leg of the *Good Times* tour came around, the group were bang up for continuing the party with the planned Part II. Unfortunately, despite their growing reputation, the opportunity to continue touring on this particular ticket was looking completely out of reach. Had the gigs been in the same country then that would have been probably just about manageable but the problem was that Part II of the tour was to take place in the latter days of 1995 ... in Australia. And even with sales of *Cheshire Cat* starting to lift, the band simply didn't have that kind of money to hand. It looked like, for the first time ever in their history, blink-182 were about to fall off the radar.

Enter Pennywise, a band who had already exerted a sonic and attitudinal influence on Mark, Tom, Scott and the rest of the blink camp. Having been formed in the late '80s, their subsequent 1991 debut *Pennywise* had been released on the mighty label Epitaph –

where so many young hopefuls aspired to sign (blink-182 undoubtedly included). Pennywise's planned presence as headliners on the Aussie leg of *Good Times* was of major interest to everyone concerned, making it all the more heartbreaking for blink to be on the verge of dropping out. Pennywise, however, were made of defiant punk rock credentials, having reputedly turned down several offers from major labels to sign with Epitaph, and their all-for-one attitude also extended to holding out a helping hand to a broke young band by buying the blink boys' plane tickets. Thanks to Pennywise's amazing generosity of spirit and financial help, blink-182 were off to Australia.

"I was freaking out," recalls Scott Raynor. "They had been one of my favourite bands for years and one of three major influences along with Bad Religion and NOFX that got me into punk. I loved it. That tour was insane, literally. There were some pathological personalities that dominated that whole trip. But that's what makes punk rock, punk rock to a certain extent. Pathology is one of its most endearing qualities and also one of its greatest fictions." Pathology being in this context something like the study of human nature through its diseases or imperfections. Which seems entirely apt for a punk rock band on tour of the magnificently odd and gnarly continent of Australia. "The crowds were also wonderfully pathological. Each show would end in either some kind of small scale riot or an exodus of fans still chanting Bro-hymns into the Australian night."

Aside from the pathology there was, as ever, a burning need to have as much fun as possible. The tour passed without too many major incidents, at least until the final Melbourne date, where Mark recalled one member of the band's team drinking rather a lot and running around the city completely naked. It was only the start of the fun; the band decamped to a house party.

"It was packed with people and everyone was dancing; which was weird because every party I've ever been to, people just stand around and nobody dances. Tom comes in and he's super drunk, so I ask him why he doesn't get naked and start dancing. So, Tom gets full on naked and starts dancing. It was one of the funniest things I've ever seen. The whole room just cleared out. All these Australian people got up and left."[17] These days, of course, they'd be taking pictures on your ten megapixel camera-phone first. Wobbly bits or not, it was a quite wonderful way to round off a fantastic year in the lives and careers of the musicians known now as blink-182. Surely 1996 had a lot to live up to ... and it wasn't to disappoint.

Chapter 6
Sign Here

The trio entered the new year with a joyous trip up to Alaska, not only playing alongside Pennywise and Unwritten Law but also getting a chance to be involved in the *King Of The Hill* snowboarding contest. A few hi-jinx later, involving water, fire extinguishers, Pennywise, Rick DeVoe, Unwritten Law and blink-182, and it's fair to say that their hotel manager was rather less than stoked to have the band around. Still, it was a blast – being on the road suited the utterly energetic guys and the pattern continued with the band booked on a mammoth February set of dates that were notable for their terrible weather. It has since been dubbed the *Shitty Weather* tour but despite the horrendous wind and rain, devilish ice and snow and freezing venues, it certainly served to spread the name of blink-182 around even more. There were long drives filled with boredom, including a seventeen-hour trek to Quebec City which certainly kept the group's attention due to the unbelievably harsh conditions. When they finally made it to the gig, all was forgotten – it was the *Sno Jam* festival where the crowd went wild to blink-182's every move. Sometimes the hardest journeys are indeed the most worthwhile.

"[Our] 'entourage' was really just either Cam Jones plus Mark's sister Anne or maybe just Cam to help us drive and load equipment and sell T-shirts," says Scott Raynor. "I think we wrote a few songs while on the road. We were touring so much we didn't really practice much when we were home." When they did get a chance, the group would chat about their growing fan-base and the occasional inability of fans across the country to get hold of *Cheshire Cat* in their respective local stores. With a genuine buzz starting to roll around blink-182 as far as the music industry was concerned, thoughts began to turn toward perhaps talking to other record labels with a bigger infrastructure than even Cargo Records. Cargo were massive in San Diego but when it came to places like Quebec their reach was less wide.

Blink-182 were, and are, a punk rock band in the sense of an alternative lifestyle based round looking at the world's skewiff corners, asking questions, having fun, drinking beer and talking about girls.

There are complex ethics involved in defining punk at the best of times, but suffice to say that the San Diego trio had no qualms about trying to spread their music to the largest amount of fans possible. One way to do that is by signing to a multinational record company – anathema for certain punk purists but on the other hand punk was always about thinking for yourself too. So it came to pass that around March 1996 something of a bidding war began. Labels looking at blink-182 at the time included Epic, Atlantic, Interscope, Columbia and the ultra-credible Epitaph, with whom the band felt a great affinity due to many of their favourite acts – including Pennywise – being signed to that label.

"We met with Brett from Epitaph," remembers Scott Raynor, "and took a nice walk through the cactus garden there ... we met with some other labels too, ate some Chinese food." Presumably without ordering Ben Wah Balls by accident. When it came down to making a decision, there was already a path mapped out which would enable all concerned to continue working more or less as they had done, as MCA had begun working with Cargo Records. Chinese food or not, the deal offered was the best both in terms of dollars and potential for growth.

"I always had aspirations for the band that went beyond the independent paradigm," explains Raynor. "I didn't measure success in terms of oppositional credibility. I loved being on the radio and MTV. We were certified products of pop culture, born and bred in suburbia. I was happy for the band when we got signed. It was like setting a lobster free in the ocean: 'There you go little buddy, you're free now, swim, swim, and never ... look ... back.'" A typically thoughtful approach.

"Our take on punk is really just fun," Mark said in *i-Zine*. "It's fun to offend people and do what we want to. But it isn't that offensive. We make music for ourselves and everybody else who gets it. It's a lifestyle scene. If you don't get it you don't have to listen. I'd like to make a lot of money and fuck credibility. If I did it doesn't make me any different. Just richer. People make so much out of something that's just the band trying to get ahead and get its music to as many fans as possible."[18] And you can't get a clearer mission statement than that.

MCA label representative Darren Wolf was also very impressed with the group's hard work in building up a fan-base by touring, writing great songs and making their own T-shirts. Those T-shirts sometimes featured a punk rock bunny which had been designed by Tom DeLonge and drawn up by one of the roadies in the blink camp (prename-change). It was an early foray into merchandise which was to develop into rather an interesting sideline one day. The bunny even started appearing on their fans' bodies as a tattoo – lasting proof of the genuine affinity that kids all over the US had already started to feel with the band.

Whilst contract negotiations went on, blink-182 were delighted to be part of the rolling blast of extreme sports and punk rock that was the *Warped* tour. Other acts included Beck, The Deftones, Down By Law, NOFX and Dance Hall Crashers (which was the only other group that didn't have a plush tour bus). DHC and blink-182 members were often seen wandering around various towns in the early post-gig hours of the mornings searching for their salubrious accommodation for the night. It was an absolute blast: the sun was blazing, there was skating to be had and plenty of new friends with whom to party.

"It was awesome," agrees Raynor. "Yah, it was great. It was relatively small then. A lot of fun. It was routed for buses and we were in a van so we had a hell of a time keeping up. But we managed. I was never much of a fan of playing outside, myself, but I really appreciated the whole festival vibe. Good clean fun in the summer sun. It was just about one of the most unequivocally positive experiences of my time with the band."

"*Warped* is the best tour I've ever been on," smiled Tom DeLonge in *Anonymous* magazine. "And I mean it. It's so much fun. We'd probably do it all year if we could!"[19] Partner-in-crime Mark Hoppus echoed the sentiment, telling one interviewer that, "None of the bands had rock star attitudes, and everyone, including the athletes and skaters, were very supportive of each other. In fact, after the shows on a few occasions, everyone had these huge barbeques where everyone came and hung out and drank and had a great time. The tour was a lot of work, but well worth it."[20]

"We're like all the other has-been kids who used to skate in high school," explained Mark, "but we still bring our boards on the road and fuck around in parking lots when we have the time. We also like to go snowboarding when we get the chance."[21]

There was the odd down moment, though. At a show in Canada a thief ran off with $6,000 of blink-182's cash – a huge amount for any band on tour and living out of suitcases but something that the group quickly shrugged off because life was too fantastic to let money troubles impinge on the serious business of having fun and developing a musical career. 'Wasting Time' had, by the summer, been released by

Cargo/Grilled Cheese to keep matters moving along nattily, the final throw of the dice from the *Cheshire Cat* sessions before the group decamped to DML Studios in California for some serious pre-production and rehearsals. It was time to get cracking on a new album.

Sessions started in late 1996 at the world-famous Big Fish studio in Rancho Santa Fe. The facility is in one of San Diego's most affluent areas, and in a former life it served as a guesthouse. For the tour-hungry blink-182, studio work was fun but a necessary evil that anchored them to one place for a specific period of time. And for the first time in their career, they weren't watching the clock in terms of hours, but instead the calendar in terms of weeks. It wasn't the greatest of winters, making the atmosphere a little duller than the excitement of the summer, and the recent fires that had swept the area had left a trail of devastation. That said, the new songs were starting to be honed to perfection and the usual jokes and daftness had reached a new level. Unfortunately, and in an echo of Mark's initial meetings with Tom, someone did actually get hurt. This time it was Scott Raynor, who contrived somehow to break both of his ankles when a stunt didn't go exactly to plan. "[It was] stupid drunken shenanigans," says Scott. "I tried to fly but fell instead. That sucked."

A number of dates over Christmas were scheduled but with Scott out of action, they were in danger of being pulled. That is, until stand-in drummer Brooks Wackerman sat in the hot seat briefly – at that time he was also a member of The Vandals, the legendary punk band featuring Joe Escalante. Wackerman went on to play with Bad Religion so a sticksman can't get better credentials than that. But the stand-in, great drummer and all, wasn't a member of blink-182 so was never likely to record the album. No problem; Raynor worked hard and soon got himself as fit as possible for the sessions at Big Fish, albeit with some difficulty.

"I had to record and practice in a wheelchair," he explains. "The studio was nice as far as studios go. Somewhat remote; luxurious." Which helps things immeasurably; there is an uniqueness to the recording process that can be a little long-winded at times.

"Being in the band, the studio is the first time one ever hears the songs without performing them," continues Scott. "It's fun to hear it all pieced together. I always felt that mixing day far surpassed any glee I ever experienced on any Christmas morning. The day-to-day is pretty banal though. A lot of incremental steps not worth recounting. There is a lot of rock lore around the studio session but I think for blink it was about as pro-active as a dentist visit. You sit there and wait, read magazines, until it's your turn to go under the drill. Except when you leave the studio you have a new record instead of a new toothbrush."

The band were listening to a lot of music, notably Jawbreaker, Bad Religion and Lagwagon's *Double Plaidinum*, setting the backdrop for the recordings under the watchful eye of Jimmy Eat World producer Mark Trombino. There were long days of work interspersed with blink-182's trademark hilarity, but Trombino's more studied approach to his work meant that he wasn't one to join in with the banter.

"He was a good guy," says Raynor. "I am not sure if we ever won him over to our cheap sense of humour, but if we irritated him he never let it show explicitly." Ever the professional. As Christmas approached, the recordings were nearly complete – aside from vocals, usually the last piece of the sonic jigsaw. One track in particular, 'Damnit', had put quite a strain on Mark Hoppus' vocal range which was exacerbated at a show with The Vandals. The bassist subsequently lost his voice completely, forcing the sessions to run over somewhat.

Trombino's excellent production had taken the group to literally unheard-of heights. One interesting aside was that it was noted how Donnell Cameron of Track Recording Studios seemed to have his own drum sound, one that had already been in evidence on the latest LP of one of blink's great heroes. "So the band asked Fletcher from Pennywise," recalls Donnell, "if he knew anyone who could remix it and he suggested me because I worked on the Pennywise record. We went into Track [to] record and when the drummer hit slightly off-centre it had a ring, a sustain to it [that they liked] so I ended up gating and compressing it, processing it a little. The album had been mixed already by Mark Trombino and it sounded amazing ... trying to beat those original mixes was difficult, they were really good to start with!"

Cameron remembers the additional sessions as being a lot of fun, not least for blink-182 who were busying themselves with a brand new project at the time. Namely, who was going to be the champion of the Playstation game, *Crash Bandicoot*.

"Those guys played it the whole time, like *constantly*! And they were really good at it, man, I mean, when I tried to play I could never get anywhere. But these guys were *into* it. Blink had already mixed the album once so maybe they were kinda over it by then but I didn't get a feeling that they were aloof – they were really just having a good time playing video games. They'd come in, listen, say they liked it and go back out but they were just pretty cool, it was a lot of fun. They didn't take it seriously in the sense of planning their careers – they didn't have attitudes or anything, they were just good guys. Really funny! Like, constantly cracking up. I was pretty much obsessed with mixing the album so it was me and the assistant in there but they were really humorous to be around and it was pretty cool."

Representatives from MCA would drop by from time to time and even if the trio were downplaying their latest musical adventures, those who were about to release it certainly had an awareness of the possibilities that the new collection of songs would engender.

"The label was excited about it, for sure," muses Cameron. "When we were in there mixing, the A&R person would come by. The label was pretty excited by the album. I don't think the band really knew what they had but certainly the label knew that they had so many good songs on the record."

After a couple of stutters, then, the new album was finally complete. It was time to see just how far this band could rock with it.

Chapter 7
Warp Speed, Part 2

With the new album finished, and after a short spot of R&R for the walking wounded, blink-182 headed back out on the road, most notably once more joining up with the *Warped* tour in June 1997. Having by now picked up sponsorship and endorsements with the likes of Billabong, the group looked and sounded better than ever before. June of that year was particularly excellent, with the extended line-up of *Warped* rolling through the US in an absolute blaze of glory, bands this time including Sick Of It All, Snot, Lagwagon, Social Distortion plus saviours of blink, Pennywise, and none other than the mighty Descendents, without whom none of this would have been possible, etc. Not a bad line-up at all and for blink-182 to be holding their own in such company speaks absolute volumes for the status of the band.

The 'ethics' of signing to a major label are endlessly debated but for blink-182 there was no such thing as 'selling out' because they'd never been anything other than honest about their ambitions. MCA's deal would enable them to have a career in music and get their songs to as many people as possible, a fact that they knew resonated with their audience because some of the punk rock originals had been in a similar position over the years.

"I try and tell kids, 'The Clash, Sex Pistols and the Ramones did it, so how come we can't?'" Tom offered, quite reasonably, to John Robb. "If people are bummed, we don't care. It's normally critics. Older critics."[22]

Again the band were absolutely ebullient about the travelling *Warped* roadshow, Mark telling an interviewer for *Circus* magazine that it had been growing in stature since its inception, with bigger venues and more vociferous crowds.

"Obviously the kids that were there from the beginning who were involved in the scene," he began, "knew all about it from the get-go. The kids who are just starting to get turned on are understanding what it's all about now. They are really starting to support the shows which is awesome. They are learning about all of these different kinds of music which is involved in the whole punk rock thing. Ska punk, ska, hardcore and power punk. So they see how it all comes together with the board sports. I think it's almost like educational for the kids."[23]

The band's collective views on the brilliant *Warped* tour were similarly gushing, particularly the organiser and co-founder Kevin Lyman, who was responsible for launching many acts. Lyman was one of the good guys with a big heart, as evidenced by his turning down of potential sponsorship from a major US cigarette company. There's *Warped*, and there's *warped*.

In the period between recording and releasing the new album, the boys found the time to contribute the track 'Dancing With Myself' to the compilation *Before You Were Punk: A Punk Rock Tribute To '80s New Wave*. The old Billy Idol track was typically high revved, as was 'M&Ms', which found its way onto an Alphabet Records compilation called, humourously, *Out Of The Bin*. And by August, 'Voyeur' had been included on a film soundtrack – *Godmoney* – a tale of urban survival in New York and California that had been directed by blink-182's mate and video director Darren Doane.

The new album – *Dude Ranch* – hit the streets in the US on June 17, 1997 and thanks both to the huge amount of touring the band had undertaken for the best part of two years and their knack of making people feel damned good, their growing fan-base absolutely loved it. Make no mistake about it, *Dude Ranch* was the moment that blink-182 went from being a promising, fun punk act to coming on strong as a serious proposition that could look to challenge everyone at the higher end of the charts.

The album begins at full pace with 'Pathetic', on which Mark and Tom fire lyrics back and forth about yet more trouble with girls. It's an insistent slab of fifth-gear punk-pop and classic blink-182. 'Voyeur' is a lust-filled and frenetic stomper with Raynor's double-kick getting a decent workout, and then comes the first genuinely great blink-182 song on the album, 'Dammit'. The track that nearly blew out his voice, it's a break-up song (sung by Mark), full of teen angst but also a swathe of hope that this feeling will pass. Its careful use of dynamics and excellent guitar arrangement somehow capture a moment in time that's obviously heartfelt, whilst at the same time also being universally-accessible. 'Boring', featuring some steady but also flair-filled bassing, is another short and sweet stormer; then we're into the humorously-named 'Dick Lips' which is all about that moment when Tom was kicked out briefly from Poway High for that basketball/drinking incident. The name itself has no further significance aside from being an insult that was being bandied around in Big Fish studios during recording. The band wanted to record said phrase for posterity and so the track became named thus. 'Waggy' is just over three minutes based around, so the story goes, the title – which Mark Hoppus managed to say whilst belching. 'Enthused' and 'Untitled' pass without standing out as anything aside from tight punk-pop tracks, before another highlight is reached with 'Apple Shampoo', as the LP starts to enter the final straight. 'Emo' is a tribute, in part, to the likes of Jimmy Eat World, and 'Josie' is yet another proclamation that blink-182 have well and truly arrived. Featuring references to great friends Unwritten Law and Dancehall Crashers, 'Josie' also has a guest appearance on backing vocals from the Law's vocalist, Scott Russo. The track's eponymous subject is bigged up to the max by Mark – some girl! She'd have to be to compete with the protagonist of 'A New Hope', who is none other than Princess Leia from the Star Wars films that the band love so much. 'Degenerate' is a new version of the by-now-ancient blink song that first appeared on the band's Filter Records cassette album debut, *Buddha*. The fact that it doesn't sound out of place on an LP of a band three years and several hundred gigs later is testament to the strength of the earliest tracks written by the DeLonge-Hoppus axis. Finally, there's 'Lemmings' and album closer, 'I'm Sorry', another pair of songs that feature melodic guitars trading off against full-throttle drums and bouncy bass lines before some typically playful hidden unsavoury silliness involving urination and dogs. The album is as cohesive as blink could have hoped for and hit the streets with a *bang*.

"We write songs about things that happen to people," said Mark. "We're obviously not a band that writes about politics or how you can vote. We write songs about us and our friends – just normal people. I can listen to a song about a guy who got screwed over by a girl, and relate to that more than a song about a guy and the insurgents in Nicaragua and stuff like that."[24]

Sputnikmusic.com were openly enamoured of its "raw pop-punk perfection. If pop-punk bands these days could consistently put out records like this one, the genre wouldn't be such an utter shithole. The band's sound is tight, the songs are catchy, and the lyrics are fun and well-written." *Allmusic.com* gave it four and a half out of five and websites and magazines everywhere began to raise their eyebrows a little more at the So-Cal trio. They even got a review in the mighty

UK rock magazine, *Kerrang!*, although the reviewer really put the boot in, awarding it only one K (of a possible five) and saying that there was "little depth, passion, soul or even vaguely memorable hooks."[25] Proof if nothing else that music is an entirely subjective art-form, music criticism even more so.

Regardless of reviews, blink-182 continued to tour heavily in preparation for the single release of 'Dammit' which was again to feature a video under the direction of Darren Doane and Ken Daurio. The track had already been picked up by LA radio station KROQ and many other shows across the US, and the crazy video that features Mark attempting to take a girl away from another guy at a cinema is also notable for having a snack bar attendant (who eventually gets said girl) – look closer and you'll see it's none other than manager Rick DeVoe. The blink-182 camp was nothing if not close-knit …

The amazing commercial success of 'Dammit' – the single reached Number 11 in the US charts – brought with it a whole bunch of other commitments to add to the hefty touring schedule. The trio soon found themselves being interviewed, reviewed, poked and prodded at every turn. 1997 was the year that blink-182 started to become public property, something that is inevitable for any band enjoying success in the music industry. It's also something they'd coveted since the outset – what's the point of being in a band if nobody's interested in chatting with you about your music? The boys, always generous with their time, were starting to realise that although it was amazing fun, the work could be incredibly taxing too. No matter; they were young, strong and had a bag full of dick jokes to dip into.

"We do not consider ourselves as having hit it big," Mark explained. "We definitely feel very lucky to be where we are, and the band has gone much further than any of us ever expected, but we still consider ourselves a small band from San Diego. I don't think that we ever want to think of ourselves as rock stars. [The best thing about the band is] being able to get paid for doing what I love and getting to hang out with my friends while doing it. Also getting to travel everywhere and meet cool people all over the place."[26]

'Apple Shampoo' was the second release from *Dude Ranch*, released in October 1997 with the band still out on the road with the Australian leg of the *Warped* tour. It's said to be about a certain girl in a name band and the specific brand of shampoo she used. Although it didn't have the impact of the mighty 'Dammit', it hardly mattered as the former was still getting serious play on radio and TV stations across the land. The tour rolled on, blink-182 pushed on and the gigs kept coming thick and fast. This was crunch time for a band seeking to kick up to the next level – a successful album was picking up sales like mad, making it all the more vital for the three amigos to get themselves seen by as many potential new fans as possible.

"The whole punk thing is suffering from overkill in the US," Mark remarked at the time. "And it's become jaded; it's much fresher in Australia and Europe. We're realistic and taking it a day at a time. This year's been great fun and next year's looking good at the moment. You know, there's a lot of bands going round now trying to make something out of the scene and it's really cluttered it up. So you have to be the best you can to keep on top. We've got our chance."[27] As 1997 came to a close, that chance looked good. But events early in the next year were to shake the blink-182 camp to its foundations.

Chapter 8
Man Overboard

The group had pushed themselves harder and harder, gigging constantly pretty much since the completion of *Dude Ranch*. No wonder that the pressure began to show; with very few days off, tensions began to come into play between even these three best friends. There is, undoubtedly, a natural limit of the time in which any one person can hang out with their very closest buddies without at least a couple of weeks to recharge and recuperate, even if your breakthrough album has just been certified gold to signify 100,000 sales. Regrettably, however, small things become huge deals without the chance to chill out properly and by early 1998 the blink-182 camp – locked into a seemingly endless succession of live dates, interviews and travelling – was hardly a happy one. Something had to give.

"We weren't getting along well," Tom DeLonge told *Kerrang!* "We ... were playing terribly and we were pissed at each other and all stuck on the same bus."[28] It got to a very low point in Nebraska when the whole band had a depressing fight. The *Sno Core* tour of February 1998 will not be remembered by any blink-182 member as anything other than a dark time for the band, although the fact that they were accompanied by the skilful Primus and the excellent Aquabats may have been of some consolation. There was a new single knocking about, too, with 'Dick Lips' having come out on February 28, although it failed to register on the radar of the charts as such. Following that *Sno Core* non-extravaganza, blink-182 went out on a short West Coast tour along with The Aquabats, who had become great friends by this stage.

"I remember Jimmy and I [from the band] ran into Mark Hoppus in a Wendy's in Ottawa and he bought us lunch," 'Prince' Adam Deibert of the Aquabats told the author. "[We were] waking up at the base of a mountain for half of the tour and snowboarding all day, then playing in the evening. It was fun and there were definitely jokes to be had. I think I have a photo of [Aquabats singer] Christian breathing fire in their dressing room."

Looking back on it now, drummer Scott Raynor is able to

philosophise about how things had unravelled so quickly from the triumphs of 1997. "At that point the band had gone really well," he told the author. "We had experienced consistent success. Tom and Mark wrote some good songs and I think, from my angle, I was just always trying to bring them to life in a way that was worthy of their quality. Which usually meant being able to play them with enough energy and endurance. Style was another crucial ingredient. I was always conscious of the tradition from which we drew our influence. I tried to pay homage to our hero bands while at the same time adding something new to the tradition by mixing in the style of my background. Punk rock was traditionally a very blue-collar expression; coming from a middle-class community I really liked mixing in pop styles derivative of the music I heard on the radio and MTV as a kid. I loved all the contemporary Fat and Epitaph stuff, along with their [forefathers] like Bowie, The Clash, and the Pistols. Primarily though, I listened to the Ramones and the Descendents. And most primarily the Ramones."

"The Descendents are the band that got us all into punk rock. They are the band that we really related to when we were growing up. They basically started the whole California scene," Tom has said.

"When you hear the music and look at them, they are nothing like what you expect," added Mark, before Tom continued the theme. "That's what's so rad about it – it's so unassuming. No look at all. They were these dorkish guys playing this fast, edgy music just because they wanted to be different. They sang about food and girls and were catchy and upbeat before anyone else did."[29]

Punk rock, in its purest sense, is meant to enable anyone to do anything they like, appropriating whatever comes to hand to destroy the past and then create something brand new with the ruins. Musically-speaking, the mid-1970s heyday of punk brings up familiar names: Sex Pistols, The Clash, The Damned. In the US, Ramones were vanguards of the movement. But this is a problematical context that ghettoizes a concept and reduces it to a small subset of influential musicians that operated for a very small period, rather a long time ago. As Stiff Little Fingers once said, they never did want to be anybody's heroes. Punk was never about that; inspiration can come from anywhere – and without Iggy there would probably have been no Ramones in the first place. The spiral is endless.

Nonetheless, this narrow definition of punk still permeated minds of journalists, particularly in the UK, and especially when bands like The Offspring, Green Day and later blink-182 came along and declared that they were exactly that, punks. This new breed of pop-sophisticated goons enjoyed life, smiled, sang about relationships and sex, and very rarely talked about anything to do with Situationism in interviews. The mid-1990s were the first time that the classic punk paradigm had been challenged, or at least fully absorbed into the mainstream.

Fans of blink or Green Day, rather than being pissed-off nihilists, were more prone to challenging authority by being a bit drunk, always up for a party, and loving guitars and extreme sports, or simply wearing green or pink hair. That both Green Day and blink grew up in the sun of California meant that inner-city introspection was unlikely. Coming from the tail-end of Nirvana's complex inner-space miserablism, the pop-punk reaction/revolution was an inevitability.

That it also inspired such repulsion in the ageing punks of the music press was a beautiful irony, particularly given the fact that Buzzcocks, Undertones and, of course, Ramones were heavily influenced not by politics and unhappiness but by confused relationships, beery nights and growing pains. What happened in the early to mid-1990s was that the sons and daughters of the Buzzcocks' songs became teenagers and started to find a voice of their own.

In the case of blink-182, they added something that had been long-missing from alternative rock and that was *a sense of humour*. Whilst Nirvana's era had been all about listening to the inner voices and battling inadequacy, blink's approach was all about listening to the inner voices that were clamouring to go try out a 720 at the skate-park, and if you crash and burn ... just laugh it off. Every musical movement has an inbuilt sense that there will be a subsequent reaction; blink, as the central figures in the tale, were the catalyst for hundreds of youngsters to get a smile on their face and start grabbing life for all it was worth. This positivity and inclusiveness was inspired by many bands, including Green Day, but mostly by the unique chemistry of DeLonge, Hoppus, Raynor and later... well, we'll come to that shortly.

That breadth of influences was crucial in forming the blink sound (182 or otherwise). Scott had certainly come a long way from the early days of listening to Metallica and trying to work out exactly how Lars paradiddled and flammed. And though blink-182 had pretty much scorched their way up to a certain level of success very quickly, it was a ride that wasn't as comfortable as Raynor had hoped. Indeed, since the very earliest days he'd been commenting that one day he would go back to college. A famous quote from back in 1994 was "I don't want to be 30 and still in a punk-rock band. That seems kind of scary to me."[30] Which is pretty unequivocal stuff even if it had been a tad tongue-in-cheek at the time.

In another interview, Tom and Mark pondered the future. "[Scott] wants to go to college. He's the only one who actually has goals beyond the band," began Mark before Tom continued: "We think we're going to be rock stars. He could get his GED [General Education Development tests]."[31]

As previously mentioned, Raynor had indeed often been taking homework out with him on tour to try and complete his high school diploma, even whilst preparing for that evening's gig. Still, post-blink plans of any nature seemed out of reach during the years up to mid-1997, as the drummer explained when he looked back at those times.

"At that age the future seemed so far, like something that would never come," he explained to the author. "I never thought about it. I was completely into what I was doing. I think though, after a while the direction the band was going was beginning to suit me less and less comfortably. It got to the point that I felt like I was trying to smile while wearing a really heavy wool sweater garishly decorated in a really hot room while people took my picture while demanding that I not complain. I felt bought up, shut up, and let down. The major label experience was nothing like I had hoped. Not long after we released *Dude Ranch* I started dreaming about a life outside my current situation."

It's not that uncommon for bands who rise swiftly to experience this kind of dislocation; something that started as a project between best friends suddenly starts to have differing demands and previously undreamt-of pressures put upon it. Where once it was *us-against-the-world*, suddenly the world seemed to own a piece of blink-182 and, cocooned in the tour bus with nothing to do all day but contemplate exhausting drives, there have been countless other examples of groups going off the rails. One thing that was always secure, though, was the fact that the gigs were a defiant release from those offstage tensions.

"Tours were always a blast," smiles Raynor. "I never got tired of playing live. No matter what was going on outside of it, once I got on the stage everything fell together. Music always has done that for me; transformed all the negativity of life into raw ecstasy. With something like that you really can't lose. The Australian tour [that year] went great.

Our momentum was really building down there. But I was feeling knocked out; internal. I was like lead boots on the band."

The band were by now barely speaking to each other and yet coming up was a date at Los Angeles' Palladium. That gig, on May 1, 1998, was something of a dream for any band. The Palladium meant an act had really, truly arrived and here were blink-182 readying themselves for the experience. But even as the guys looked forward to that mega-date with destiny, Scott Raynor's life took an awful turn.

"Just after the start of that tour I suffered a tragic loss," he recalls. "I had to fly home. I returned to the road after a couple days and finished the tour." Tom and Mark turned to the drummer of their support band, the Aquabats, to fill in for a few dates whilst their close friend Scott Raynor was away. That drummer's name was Travis Barker, and he was born on November 14, 1975 in Fontana, California[32]. After a few knockabout bands with such exciting names as Snot and Feeble[33], he found himself gainfully employed by The Aquabats in 1996 as they prepared to record a brand new album.

"The Aquabats started in the summer of 1994 with a bunch of friends in Orange County as a lark," erstwhile Bats band member Adam Deibert explained for this book. "They were just looking to have fun and created this 'band' that was definitely more theatrical than musical. I saw them when the band I was in played with them in Santa Fe Springs in September of 1994. I was blown away and thought it was hilarious. It turned out I knew the trumpet player Boyd from Aleeda Wetsuits. I saw them play a party a few weeks later and asked them half-jokingly if I could be in the band. They were looking to get a few people who could play in the band so they called me a few days later and I was in. The next two years we played a bunch of local shows and the fan-base grew. We released a few demo tapes and recorded *The Return Of The Aquabats* in the summer of 1995, released in the December. As time wore on we started to take being in a band a little more seriously, going on little tours, doing a demo record deal, and continuing to play. I was sort of half in the band through this time as I was going to school in Santa Barbara."

The multi-instrumentalist Deibert played, variously, trumpet, guitar and bass and he explains that by 1996 the 'Bats were firmly looking for new members for their rolling circus troupe. "Chad (Crash McLarson) played in a band that played with Travis' old band a few years before The Aquabats; I think the band was called Feeble. We needed a drummer quickly, Chad called Travis and he agreed. When he was with

Feeble they all lived in Laguna Beach and [he] worked as [a] trash man." Trash cans or otherwise, Barker's ability to work out songs at incredibly short notice was a rare one. His background had been musically broad, with his parents enabling him to take lessons on piano, guitar and vocals. He was much-enamoured of a variety of styles including military and jazz rhythms, but was most taken by the driving rhythms of hip hop and, of course, punk rock. He was a real asset to The Aquabats, then, as Deibert explains.

"His technical prowess is world class. He keeps impeccable time and plays very imaginative parts. He's a very hard worker. He didn't just fall into being a rock star, he worked super hard for years and years. Having someone in a band that's reliable and works hard is a huge plus." All the credentials anyone could ever need.

Famously, blink-182 and Barker jammed for only 45 minutes before the first gig, by the end of which he'd worked out the whole of blink's set. "He was a friend of ours anyway," explained Mark to MTV, "and he knew most of the songs. So when we needed a new drummer, it was very natural for us to call on Travis."[34]

For Barker's part, he had a driving ambition to make it work for himself but added drive was there as his incredibly supportive mother had tragically passed away the day before he started high school at the age of 15. This horrendous tragedy was something that focused him strongly. His mother had always dreamed of her son having a career in music, and though Travis had been formally trained for a number of years he – like a lot of teenagers – kinda rebelled against it, preferring to follow another dream of his: to be a pro skateboarder.

"I was taking lessons from this jazz guy named Ed Will," Travis told www.drumstuff.com, "and I studied with him for a couple of years. I just wasn't into it. I wanted to be a skateboarder. So, she passed away a day before school started, and I was just like, 'You know, I'm over skateboarding. I'm going to play the drums.'"[35]

Rehearsing regularly was key to Barker's growing mastery of the instrument, and he has often cited essential books such as *Advanced Funk Studies, Stick Control* and *The New Breed*, by Gary Chaffee as well as the David Garibaldi book, *Future Sounds* amongst others. No sooner had Travis hooked up with The Aquabats than they went into the studio to record a new album, entitled *The Fury Of The Aquabats*. At the helm was the legendary producer Jim Goodwin.

"The majority was recorded at Paramount Studios. Some overdubs were recorded at this place in the San Fernando Valley," remembers Prince Adam. "Jim was cool. We had recorded with him before the Fury for a Devo tribute [as well as] Fury demos so we knew each other. He was very easy to get along with, very low key, knew the methods he preferred to make a good record. It was a good experience."

"We recorded it in pretty standard fashion. Tracked all the drums, then bass, then guitars, then horns, then vocals and other various overdubs. Travis was there for those first three days when the drums were tracked, and I don't remember if he came in the after that. The day started usually between ten o'clock in the morning up to noon and went on until about eight to ten in the evening. Some days were shorter, some longer. Playing with a good drummer is so much different than playing with a poor drummer. I've been really lucky to play with a bunch of really great drummers in the bands I've been in, but Travis was definitely a different breed."

Travis' speed and accuracy meant that once his parts were laid down, he was free to head off and rehearse (and sit in with other bands whilst he did so, of course). He'd also picked up, in true Aquabats fashion, a nickname: Baron Von Tito, the reasons for which are largely lost to history although Deibert remembers some of Travis' buddies referring to him as 'Tito' on occasion.

Monikers aside, *The Fury Of The Aquabats* was released on Goldenvoice Records on October 28, 1997 and although it hardly had the commercial success of certain other bands, it was an artistic triumph. Steven Irwine of *Allmusic.com* called it, "an infectious collection of ska-punk. Although the group's songwriting is a little uneven, and they have the tendency to wallow in sophomoric, 'wacky' humour, they have enough hooks and energy to satisfy ska junkies."[36]

The album begins with the track 'Super Rad', which does exactly what it says on the tin; it has an insanely catchy hook and in just about three minutes sets out a joyous manifesto for The Aquabats' mission. The album is bustling with ideas, too, the likes of the ludicrous-but-memorable 'Magic Chicken' and 'Martian Girl' full of ska-punk magnificence. Humour and heavy riffing can, of course, go together extremely well – no wonder blink-182 felt such an affinity with their Batty counterparts. 'Idiot Box', meanwhile, is a couple of minutes of sax-heavy madness, whilst 'My Skateboard' takes a half-step back in terms of pace before ramping up to full throttle once more with some excellent horn work. The album closes with 'Theme Song' which is essentially a book-end to the opener's mission statement. There's even a hidden track, 'Playdough Revisited' which is a faster version of an old song by the 'Bats. *Absolute Punk* declared *The Fury Of...* an instant classic, "combining hilarious lyrics, strong horn melodies, and originality that only the 'Bats can muster, The Aquabats give it their all on this release, and they do a pretty damn good job of it."[37]

In the same way, Travis had done a good job filling in for Scott Raynor, who duly returned to play with blink-182 at that pivotal Palladium appearance. Things were back to normal again in the San Diego punks' camp, then.

Chapter 9

A Disturbance In The Force

Rewinding to April, 1998, Scott Raynor smiles at the memory. "I am wearing some really tacky black swim trunks, a black T-shirt, and a pair of black Chuck Taylors with no socks ... oh, and my hair is black too. I just finished a set, Primus is on next, and I am smoking a cigarette backstage after packing up my drum-kit ... reflecting. 'Gee, that was really great,' I am saying to myself. I am pretty sure what the rest of the night will be like. Usually I am tired physically, yet pumped full of adrenaline; a high from which I come down by drinking and listening to Danzig full blast on the back of the tour bus. When it's time for bed I climb into my bunk, put on my headphones, and listen to my Psychedelic Furs *All Of This And Nothing* tape (yes, I said tape. Back then personal CD players (yes, I said CD) ate up battery power too quickly). Then I stare wistfully out the window as the barren landscape slips past under cover of night, sigh a home-sickened sigh not unlike the protagonist in that song by Robert Clark Seger that Metallica covered so well[38], and drift off to sleep only too eager to awake and rock again once more."

Despite having returned to the blink-182 camp, things were still not right for the band. There were fundamental forces pulling in opposite directions at this point, and ones that the band were not unaware of. For Raynor, the unease had set in a year or more before.

"With an indie label there was less pressure and more creative freedom due in part to the relatively minimal financial investment on the part of the executives," he says. "At the major, the initial investment was a lot higher so there was more pressure and less creative freedom. Which is okay if you are happy with where the executives want to take you."

"However, I was always only half on board with the decision to go to the major. The fact that Epitaph wanted to sign us still stands as one of the greatest achievements of my life. I really wanted to go with them, but being in a band is about compromise. Looking back I mark the decision to go to a major over Epitaph as the point where I was only half-invested in blink. I mean, I was intellectually invested,

I recognised it as a smart move financially. But it's like that song says, 'I Left My Heart in San Francisco'; I left my heart in the office at Epitaph. After that compromise I found it difficult to make further ones, and I felt like I was asked to make a lot. Eventually, there was not enough of my heart in the band to justify my sticking around. I backed away. I was dead weight."

1998 had also been a very difficult year for various reasons for Raynor and he freely admits that it had taken its toll on his health and lifestyle choices. Put simply, those 'unwinding' moments had started to get somewhat out of hand on occasion.

"I was drinking way too much," he says, bluntly. "I was being irresponsible." There is a saying in rock 'n' roll that goes something along the lines of 'Do what you like but when it's show-time, it's *show-time*.' Mark and Tom had tired of Scott's excesses, and presented Raynor with an ultimatum: quit drinking and go to rehab, or be an ex-182 member. "They asked me to go to an in-patient rehab," he says. "I agreed ..."

Mark and Tom took the decision that a parting of the ways was still necessary. To their credit, Mark and Tom have been asked numerous times about the situation and always tried to minimise the impact of the question, preferring to be philosophical on the matter. You're unlikely to read more than Mark's 2000 quote to *Rolling Stone*: "Scott was kicked out of the band ... it was what was going on outside of [blink-182], but it was affecting his performances."[39] They had been through one hell of a lot together and despite the parting of the ways not being ideal, Scott's worldview and thirst for knowledge in a more academic sense may well have led to a similar situation somewhere down the line in any case.

"It's a major heartbreaker," concludes Raynor. "But I don't hold a grudge, toward them or myself. The band was right to fire me." Whichever way it may have ended, it is beyond doubt that Scott Raynor was, and thanks to the outstanding records of the era, still is an integral part of blink-182's story. From the very earliest days of having massive amounts of fun and occasionally remembering to play some music, through the early tours and certainly some of the fastest, most uncompromising punk-pop tunes around, Scott's drum sound and personality were a vital asset to blink.

Things change and people move on but the evidence is there in the *joie-de-vivre*, belief and excitement of the recordings. The parting of the ways, for whatever reason, will never change that fact – and if any further evidence were needed, just spin that copy of *Dude Ranch* a coupla times. Awesome drummer.

Mark and Tom were now faced with a huge amount of dates stretching out in front of them, a new album being planned, and no drummer. It was a no-brainer to bring back the guy who had filled in so manfully on the dates when Scott Raynor was away.

"I remember Travis rehearsing backstage for an hour or two, then playing with them during sound-check," says Prince Adam Deibert of the Aquabats. "A few of us were standing behind the stage and I vividly remember the feeling of *this is the new blink*. We should have looked for a new drummer right then because it was obvious what band he belonged in."

Raynor rates his replacement highly, in fact, telling the author that, "Travis is a very skilled drummer, with the discipline of a professional athlete." Later, Barker was very complimentary of the Aquabats, who to all intents and purposes had been a springboard for his future success.

"I was sleeping on my friend's couch, playing in his band and I was a trash man," he later explained to Bobby Gorman. "I was just going to fill in for The Aquabats for a couple days and I ended up joining the band. And that was the first band I ever got to tour with really. That was the first band I ever got to make real records with. It was cool man, like it was so different, I learnt so much. If I wasn't in Aquabats, I couldn't be in blink-182 right now. I would've never hooked up with Mark and Tom and I would've never filled in for them. I love The Aquabats ... I never had hard feelings for those guys. I'd always wish them the best and everything. I would do anything for those guys to this day."[40]

Back in 1998, without too much fuss, and no time to think about it as such, Barker – who had long been hanging out with the blink boys in any case – became a part of it all. And the jokes started once again; when asked by MTV about the change in personnel, Mark was content to pull the interviewer's leg in classic style.

"Right at the end of touring behind our last album, *Dude Ranch*, it just came time that we needed a new drummer. We kick people out when they get too old."[41] Typically playful given that Mark was the oldest and of course Scott by far the youngest member. Equilibrium was restored to the force; surely from here it would be plain sailing.

Chapter 10
Oh Buddha!

Blink-182 had already been chatting with some friends of theirs, Kung Fu Records – a label run by excellent and influential act The Vandals whose own DIY credentials were beyond question. "Blink were on Cargo and they were one of the bands who we would have open for us here and there," says Joe Escalante of both The Vandals and Kung Fu Records.[42] "We took them on the road for short trips. At that time I was working for CBS television so we couldn't go on many long trips. Whatever weekend trips we'd do they were one group we'd take with us. Some people in our generation thought that the new poppy punk wasn't cool or it was too much like NOFX. I didn't believe that at all; I thought they were just great. To me, punk rock was part-music and part-attitude and I mean, these guys were punks. They were borderline hoodlums, suburban maniacs! They could hold their own with Pennywise, Fletcher and that kind of stuff."

"They had our respect because they were fun, smart, hilarious guys – a perfect blend with The Vandals. We liked them and we did whatever we could for them. Other bands, like Pennywise, could do more for them but we did whatever we could. They were doing fine in California, but if we were going to Colorado or Utah, Arizona, stuff like that where the Vandals would have a name but they wouldn't, we'd take them. But in San Diego, the first time we played with them was an Unwritten Law record release party and arguably we should have been opening for them because they had more fans than we did at that time! They were more active there and we were just old guys but by playing with them that helped them and us. We had our second life then, playing with bands like blink-182, Lagwagon and the *Warped* tour – we couldn't have done that if we hadn't attached ourselves to bands like blink so they were helping us as much as we were helping them. We tried to help them, they tried to help us and everybody wins."

The punk community can be proud of their closeness on occasion and this concept of looking out for each other extended – as it had at the outset with Filter – to putting out each other's records. "They'd already sold 60,000 copies of *Cheshire Cat*," explains Escalante, "and

I thought, 'Man, if I can sell just 10% of that that would be great for the label,' and of course it sold a lot more because they went on to be superstars."

There was some considerable controversy at a later date regarding Filter Records' position in the selling of this first tape after blink had moved to pastures new; a lot of water has passed under a lot of bridges since 1994 – and for that matter, since 1998 – but it's a chapter in the blink-182 tale that invites the reader to make up his or her mind for themselves. Credit where it's due; both Escalante and Secor are important names in the tale of the early days of the band and it's probably time they're *both* acknowledged as such.[43]

Musically-speaking, the CD-version of *Buddha* cleaned up the tracks a little – where possible – and sharpened up the mastering, but essentially it was the same release as had come out on tape four years' previously. It is the utterly free sound of a band with everything in front of them, youth on their side and a clutch of songs that were just one whole thrill to play.

"It was our kind of music and we loved it," beams Joe Escalante. "It was like they're in the studio with limited time and experience and that was what came out. When you're making a record at that stage usually everything that you've written, even if it's half-finished, ends up on the album. Usually you get a few gems, too."

Opening with 'Carousel', one of the oldest songs in the band's oeuvre but still getting played at gigs to great response, *Buddha* – like *Cheshire Cat* – comes on strong with one heck of a lot of personality. Aside from the jangly-then-punky old track 'Time', from the *Flyswatter* first demo days, the next tracks – 'TV', the excellent 'Strings', 'Fentoozler', 'Romeo & Rebecca' are earlier, rougher versions of the *Cheshire Cat* sessions (which of course were frantically hammered through themselves). Then '21 Days' – another love story sung by Mark with some burbling bass – takes the tempo down a little momentarily. 'Sometimes', with its dancing lead line, is something of a race to the finish, clearly one for the moshers in a live arena, being just over a minute or so in length. *Flyswatter* cut 'Point Of View' sounds rather like something that cult band They Might Be Giants could come up with after drinking eighteen or so cups of coffee, 'My Pet Sally' features some pretty accomplished bassing and elements of skilful guitar technique though the same can't be said for the vocals, and 'Reebok Commercial', first seen on the *Flyswatter* sessions, retains its charm throughout the tempo changes, shrugging off the rather monotone vocals in the process. 'Toast & Bananas', another one that had made it through to *Cheshire Cat*, is rawer than its Cargo counterpart (though, it must be said, not massively so) and nods both to The Only Ones and Avril Lavigne's (later) awful 'Sk8er Boi'. A great cover of the Screeching Weasel song 'The Girl Next Door' and the jaunty 'Don't' close the album. In context with blink-182's career at this point, it doesn't hold up all that well to *Dude Ranch*, which was absolute galaxies ahead in terms of production, performance, sounds, musicianship and general songwriting. That said, the revamped sleeve notes do exhort the listener to share "a whimsical journey back to our humble beginnings."[44]

Back to more contemporary matters, and it was time to think about a new single to keep the momentum of *Dude Ranch* going strong. This time, the cut was the tale of 'the perfect girlfriend', the catchy song, 'Josie'. There were in fact two versions of this video undertaken. The original one, which was never released, had the band (including Scott) stuck in a basement which was quickly filling up with water. The trio weren't massively happy with the results so it was tackled again, directed by Darren Doane and Ken Daurio and featuring the extremely attractive actress Alyssa Milano who shrugged off both the hanging-out tongues of the appreciative band members (and crew, and extras, and some people passing by the shoot who were supposed to be at work...) to play the title role. The video, in typically anarchic blink-182 style, also features the funniest food fight since *Bugsy Malone*. It quickly followed the likes of 'Dammit' and 'M&Ms' as a video much loved by the kids, gathering MTV play and helping the single chart at Number 31 in Australia, where the group's fame was growing apace. The remainder of 1998 was spent on the road touring with Unwritten Law and Homegrown, a jaunt that the boys dubbed the *Poo Poo Pee Pee* tour in typical style before taking a well-earned couple of days to reflect on their crazy year. They'd begun 1998 down in the dumps and wondering what might happen next but ended it with a new drummer, new impetus and a couple of genuine hits on their hands. Their tracks had started to gain serious airplay, as *Billboard* Airplay Monitor Report (BDS) figures indicated. To put that into context, 'Dammit (Growing Up)', with 1000 plays, was the second most-played record on KROQ, had attained 900 plays on Seattle's KNDD and the same amount on NY station WXRK, making it third best played, and it gained Top Three status in terms of spins on KITS San Francisco, WBCN Boston, CIMX of Detroit and KWOD, Sacramento.

In Phoenix, KEDJ spun it no less than 1,400 times. That is *huge*.

"A lot of their success was timing," says Joe Escalante. "To me, what was going on at that period, the radio stations were all over NOFX who was putting out great records, perfect for radio when you could have a few punk songs on commercial radio and it would really energise the listeners. It was a good balance for the stations and NOFX was a good band to do it but they didn't really co-operate with radio. It looked to me like blink-182 was there saying, 'Look, our music is – to the radio stations – indistinguishable'. You and I could tell the difference but to the radio stations it was the exact same thing ... [plus] there was only three of them instead of four to argue and discuss what was cool to do or not."

"But then there was a big Christmas concert: *KROQ Acoustic Christmas* which isn't really acoustic but a huge radio show in Los Angeles. I forgot [which band] cancelled but it was someone huge and there was an empty slot. Someone at blink's label [Cargo] told me that the songs were [now] getting dropped from KROQ because it was dead. Its time was over ... but they then took that slot in the *Acoustic Christmas* show, they did their thing in front of the KROQ audience, they were funny, they were witty and they played their accessible, catchy punk rock whose time had come. And that boosted them back into KROQ airplay, put them back on the rotation of the most influential station for that kind of music in America, and by that time all the DJs had seen them play, plus the live audience in LA really got to see them. It was a lot of things, a bit of luck, these guys getting a shot, it wasn't automatic but they did it and they stuck with it. I mean, that's my take on what I heard being in LA and I was paying a lot of attention because I wanted *Buddha* to do well but other people might see it differently. But that was how I saw it."

As blink-182 prepared to go back into the studio with a clutch of new songs ready for another year and another assault on the charts, 1998 came to an end with Mark guesting on The Ataris' track, 'That Special Girl', whilst Travis stepped into some serious shoes, playing a few dates with Escalante's band The Vandals.

"[Josh, the usual Vandals drummer] couldn't come on the tour. We'd been using Brooks Wackerman but he'd joined Bad Religion and we needed someone. We knew Travis – it's not that hard to find someone to sit in Josh's shoes, they want that slot so it wasn't that hard to convince people – but we got on really good and he came on the tour and it was a lot of fun. We knew him as drummer for The Aquabats who we'd played many shows with. As a bass player I've had the luxury of playing with Josh [so] if I'm ever with other drummers I'm so in tune with the best drummer in the world that when Josh isn't there I notice *so* much. But with Travis he's a very similar kind of drummer, amazing sense of timing and a good memory which you need as you're memorising these parts of songs and the beats. I've played with other drummers and there's things you can't do with them, not that they're not great but there's just not enough time to practice. But with Brooks and with Travis, and with Derek Grant from Alkaline Trio – these are our 'rotation' as we call it – you can do anything that you can do with Josh."

You can't get higher praise than that. Things were once more rosy in blinksville, San Diego, California.

Chapter 11
Finn-land

Sessions for the new album began in the New Year with writing sessions up at DML Studios where, despite their growing fame, the band were relaxed enough to chat to the growing army of fans who gathered outside. A lot of groups would avoid the prospect of coming face to face with the fans like this, but blink-182 knew that the kids who watched them weren't anything except an extended bunch of mates who got off on pop-punk, cool T-shirts and extreme sports; the band would even let fans into their rehearsal studio from time to time. Demos were recorded[45] before hammering down to Mad Hatter Studios where – true to form – Travis played like an absolute beast and recorded his drum tracks for the new album proper in his usual phenomenally quick time, completing his parts in less than a week.

The album was recorded under the watchful eye of a new producer by the name of Jerry Finn. He was an up-and-coming studio genius who had already worked with a number of bands including Pennywise, Green Day, Rancid, Jawbreaker and The Vandals – credentials that made him an attractive choice. He also came with an array of amps, effects and equipment to enable the band to play around more with sounds than they'd ever been able to before.

"Jerry had like, thirty guitars and ten amps," explained Tom, "so it worked out good for the recording. A lot of times we'd have to rent the stuff, we wouldn't know what to rent. But he had such an array to choose from. So we did have free rein and it really made a difference this time around, I'm so glad."[46]

"[It] allowed us to do a lot of different things," Mark told MTV. "We used different ideas for parts of songs and for sounds, and that made a huge difference in the way the final record turned out."[47] He also said, "We were able to try out everything we wanted to try out, that's the most important thing about recording is taking the time to try different ideas, that's what makes the record cool. It's the extra shit that we add in."[48] Having a gold record with *Dude Ranch* gave more breathing space and adding Travis Barker to the camp also helped take things in a different direction. After some six years of working in their chosen genre, the boys certainly knew their way around a catchy melody and a raucous guitar line. Experienced enough to learn from their previous mistakes where applicable, but young enough to retain all of their exuberance and spark, it was prime-time. The band had already worked with Jerry Finn on a track called 'Mutt' which was scheduled to appear on a forthcoming film tentatively titled, at this time, *East Great Falls High*, described as a 'coming of age comedy' and due to be released in mid-1999. Initially, it was mooted that the group appear in the film but other plans prevailed and the music was considered the best option. Blink-182 and Jerry Finn, through the process, found that they absolutely bounced off each other's senses of humour and this made for absolutely hilarious studio sessions. Finn later told *Entertainment Weekly* that the sessions had a trademark blink-182 element to them throughout the process. "I saw them naked," he sighed. "More than I ever care to see anyone naked."[49] Between waving their bits about, the band began constructing by far the most complete set of tracks they'd yet committed to CD.

With recording sessions completed by the spring of 1999, thoughts turned toward matters not directly related to music. With blink-182 sponsored by the likes of Billabong and Hurley, with whom they felt a great affinity, Mark and Tom had an idea to bring together some of the cooler clothes and gear that they liked to wear into an online site similar to amazon.com, in order to make them available to all who had a computer hooked up to the net, which by the turn of the Millennium was just about everybody. That site was given the typically-irreverent banner of Loserkids.com – a one-stop shop for fans of skate, surf and snowboarding gear that was often tricky to get hold of in smaller towns. Because the worlds of skating and pop-punk were intertwined, the fashion and focus spilled over – being a fan of a band often means investing in a lifestyle and conversely it was possible to get into a band by watching a cool skate video, as the *Good Times* release had so eloquently proved. Anyway, Travis was a regular boarder and despite not necessarily being world champions (and breaking limbs aplenty, as we have seen), the whole band enjoyed skating and snowboarding when they had the opportunity.

Not content with setting up a cool webstore, Mark had also been helping a young band by the name of Fenix TX, formerly known as Riverfenix, a group from El Paz with a gnarly punk sound and a growing reputation. However, commitments with the new blink-182 album soon put paid to Hoppus' advisory role with Fenix TX who went on to have some success over the forthcoming two years with their LP coming out on MCA Records.

There were a few live gigs to take care of before the new album came out, including a quick nip back across to Australia for the Offshore Festival and a fabulous jaunt to the beautiful Bahamas town of Nassau to rev the group back up into live mode for the forthcoming *Warped* tour – which this year blink-182 would be *headlining*.

The new album – entitled *Enema Of The State* – was released by MCA on June 1, 1999. It is a record which takes the blueprint of their previous work and adds a maturity of songwriting and a new production sensibility to help the sound reach even more ears, be it the punk basement disco venues, much larger concert halls, or, whisper it quietly, stadia. What is remarkable about the LP is that even whilst it is polished, slick and obviously a band firing on all cylinders with a decent budget, it's absolutely and definably the same set of musicians who fizzed through the *Buddha* race-sessions in a previous life.

The album opens with 'Dumpweed', which in contrast to previous put-upon lyrical explorations takes the view that the protagonist needs a girl who he can actually train to be good to him instead of the nightmare of the present. Sonically it blasts in with a brilliantly warm-but-crunchy guitar figure before the first indication of their new drummer's undoubted talent leads into the jump-around, double-time and catchy chorus. As an opener it makes a massive statement that blink-182 are a force to be reckoned with – check out the surprisingly complex middle-eight. Next up is 'Don't Leave Me', another one from the tried-and-trusted downbeat-lyric boy-meets-girl, boy-gets-confused, girl-breaks-up-with-boy formula. The very last chord however has the protagonist saying that he'll be fine, though.

'Aliens Exist' reflects the group's fixation with outer space – Tom had only bought a computer to make sure he could catch up with the latest conspiracy theory sites, telling an interviewer in 2000 that he considered the net, "a huge neurological brain centre all over the world that ties in all the information that we read, everything we learn, everything that we buy and sell. It's all on this giant fibre-optic system tied into the Pentagon and they are monitoring everything we do and we're all gonna die. The only reason I bought a computer was to look up UFO sites and learn how to get probed. Anally."[50] As ever with the guitarist, there was a serious point amongst the scatology. 'Aliens Exist' can be read in many different ways but probably the truth is that it's more fun to play with the idea that just maybe these things are real despite all the nonsense that the internet had to offer. The anarchic nature of the web reflects a certain way of looking at the world, perhaps a punk one in the blink sense – *if it's fun, then why not?*[51]

'Going Away To College' is a track with a real tenderness and longing about it, the girl having gone away and the protagonist pleading for her not to forget the moments they'd shared. Quickly, though, the open-hearted stuff is slapped to one side with the absolutely fantastic 'What's My Age Again?', a song that takes on all the taunts and put-downs about being a grown-up and the brilliance of keeping young and not conforming to other people's expectations of what you ought to be doing with your time. Certainly, with Tom and Mark both having hit 27 during 1999, they were heading for the big 3-0 at some pace but without compromising for a second their love of life, prank-filled and fun. One of their favourite things to do on tour was to pretend to be the receptionist at their hotel, call up their tour manager and send him down to 'collect a fax' from the front desk. When he was on his way down, they'd call reception and say something along the lines of, 'Hi, I'm Mr Smith and I am coming to flirt with you – the codeword is *fax*.' You can imagine the consequent conversation ... 'What's My Age Again?' had a video featuring the band running naked through the streets, although in fact the guys had to cover the more dangling parts to avoid getting arrested by the local feds. Still, it was entirely in character and quickly became a highly-played video on MTV, whetting appetites for the album on every play. One heck of an introduction to their new drummer, too.

'Dysentery Gary' romps through weasels, slaggings of people's moms, transvestites and Slayer before the quite remarkable 'Adam's Song', a track that is the most soul-bearing blink tune to date. It deals with teen suicide and depression; feeling isolated and helpless but, ultimately, being able to stay strong and see hope even in the darkest times. It is an astonishing moment of on-the-button social commentary that proves the keen intelligence the band always had behind the jokey exterior. It's clear that this is written by someone who understands human nature, albeit usually through the prism of teenage-style relationships[52].

And in true blink-182 style, the thoughtful and slightly mid-tempo song is soon blasted away by an absolute stormer of a track which is undoubtedly one of the most iconic songs the band would ever write and possibly also one of the most memorable tracks of the late 1990s pop-punk explosion. It's called 'All The Small Things' and features some of the most heart-warmingly addictive sing-along vocals of all-time. You need to merely hear 'All The Small Things' once and the "na-na-na-na" section is burned into the back of your brain, via the grin-and-mosh muscles. A career highlight, no less.

Time to celebrate, and 'The Party Song' does exactly that, albeit its tale of drunkenness and trying to get with chicks is certainly not as straightforward as it seems; the protagonist also feels something of a dislocation from his surroundings and there's a definite sense of desperation to the whole set-up. 'Mutt' was by now firmly a part of the blink-182 live set, a tale of sexual relationships that are twisted by both of the damaged parties mentioned in the song. It's not exactly Hubert Selby Jnr, but it isn't exactly portraying either of the couple in a good light either. 'Wendy Clear' is another from the ever-fruitful tree of failed relationship songs before 'Anthem' rounds off a record which has the balls, stature and breadth of both musical and emotional vocabulary to take on all-comers.

Enema Of The State's artwork[53] features the adult film actress Janine Lindemulder dressed as a nurse whose suggestive pose in pulling on a rubber glove makes for what you might call one of the more arresting album covers of the decade[54]. The band – semi-nude, of course – are also shown on the back readying themselves for the nurse's next move which appears to be some kind of injection. Mark looks worried, Tom even more so whilst the heavily-tattooed Travis looks on with nonchalance. Perhaps they were wondering how many it would sell …

Chapter 12

Grinning Like A Cheshire ...

The new album soared to Number 9 in the *Billboard* Hot 100 with first week sales of 110,000, an absolutely amazing result. Nobody could have predicted this reaction, despite the band and Jerry Finn's excitement about what they'd produced. The reviews were unremittingly positive, too. *Rolling Stone* praised its party atmosphere, naming the band as masters of getting people up and dancing, saying that, "It's all harmless but still gnarly enough to foment the kind of anti-everything rebellion that spawned rock 'n' roll way back in the day. Sometimes feeling good doesn't demand more than a sense of collective ennui."[55] *Q* agreed, giving it a good write-up in general and were particularly enamoured by its way with the swift, three-minute pop tune. Rock, metal and punk weekly *Kerrang!* also got on board with its radio-friendly songwriting skill, calling 'What's My Age Again?' "ridiculously infectious" and noting that 'Adam's Song' showed "a rich, mature songwriting talent". The reviewer concluded that "there's enough energy, attitude and cracking songs here to ensure that blink will be remembered for more than just onstage nudity."[56] Not a bad review at all, to put it mildly.

The band was also, brilliantly, featured in the normally-staid *Newsweek* that June. In their underwear, of course. Meanwhile, the LP was 'Album of the Week' in *New York Times*. The guys were also delighted to comment on a particular story doing the rounds that *Playboy* magazine were interested in employing them as guest photographers with a view to taking some snaps of the increasing amount of chest-flashing female fans who came to see them on tour. Of course, this never happened but the story was picked up by both MTV and *Rolling Stone*.

With blink-182's career soaring as they embarked on the latest *Warped* tour, the end of June also saw the release of the film that had sparked off their creative relationship with Jerry Finn, as the track 'Mutt' was played in the background of a sequence where a young lady was enjoying what we might call a 'special solo moment'. The group made a small cameo in that scene, though the film was now retitled from *East Great Falls High* to *American Pie* which quickly became a gross-out booty-chasing movie franchise that had subject matter as varied as sex with apple pies and fantasising about your friends' hot moms. You could say that blink-182 were fairly suited to be involved in such a project. Equally, the *Short Music For Short People* compilation, a 99-track CD of songs each under 30 seconds, was released on legendary punk label Fat Wreck Chords and featured a ditty called 'Family Reunion' whose completely silly, remorselessly sweary lyrics are completely unplayable on any radio station at any time of day.

"I dunno how that song came around," mused Mark. "We were just fucking around on stage one time, and just did it, then Fat Mike said, 'Oh, we need a 30-second song.' So oh, we'll do the 'Shit Piss' song. And so we did it!"[57] Another comp, *A Collection Of Warped Music, II* – songs from the bands on the 1999 tour – was closed out by a live version of 'Apple Shampoo'. That year's tour also featured the likes of Ice-T and Eminem, ramping up the energy with some good, hard-hitting hip hop which would have pleased Travis immensely. The difficulties of the previous summer seemed far behind them and the band were back on a roll.

'What's My Age Again?' had been gaining mass airplay and video time throughout the summer of 1999 so it was an obvious choice for a single, released (over two CDs with slightly differing tracklisting) on September 20, 1999. It registered at Number 58 in *Billboard*'s Hot 100, and gained a placing of 40 in the US Top 40 tracks. Impressively, too, it peaked in the Top 20 over in the UK with a highest spike at Number 17 in the official UK Charts. Proof that the band's sentiments, attitude and music were universal indeed.

"I sit in my bedroom in California," Mark explained, "and write a song and people all over the world are able to hear it. Like we go to Germany or Italy and they know all the lyrics. That's mind blowing, really."[58] The kids knew where to find the good stuff although some of the rock press were still a little dismissive of the So-Cal punksters, such as the opinionated *NME* who sniffed that it was "more mindless, punk-pop guitar-thrashing from the world's current favourite American brats ... on the plus side, the song – again, much like blink-182's career, we hope – only lasts for two-and-a-half minutes."[59] The UK magazines were not quite on board with the concept of *fin de siècle* punk-pop at this stage and toward the end of the year *NME* put the boot in again by calling the band, "as bad, as meaningless as the cock-rockers and hippy wankers punk originally sought to destroy."[60] And one of those original punks, John Lydon aka Johnny Rotten, dismissed blink-182 as a "bunch of silly boys ... an imitation of a comedy act."[61]

It took more than a few harsh words in the press to drive down spirits, though, as news soon came through that *Enema Of The State* had turned double platinum – two million records sold – and that *Dude Ranch* had passed the million mark too.

Though the American audiences were completely on board with the blink-182 ethos of kooky fun songs making for a punk album, it seemed Europe still needed a little educating. As noted, the press wasn't overly enamoured by blink-182, *NME* in particular still seemingly on a mission to cut them down. Reviewing a gig in London on October 8, their unimpressed reviewer opined that he "might as well be watching Hanson ... it's so slick and polished that it lacks anything remotely linked to the concept of punk rock."[62]

This cultural difference is one of the main obstacles that blink faced in their breakout period. Whilst *Warped*, with its cool clothes, cool sports and cool bands playing beer-happy, fun-loving poppy rock was the epitome of modern punk rock over in the US, the dissenting voices of some people still alluded to events of 1976 in London, where a depressed population and fractured economy led to a roar of revolutionary dissent; the music of Sex Pistols, The Clash and others that literally was the voice of the streets. It was heavily politically-charged both directly and indirectly and shattered a complacent and uncaring '70s generation. The main problem is that, pure though that version of punk might be (and it certainly filtered across both sides of the Atlantic in the likes of Fugazi, Black Flag and Dead Kennedys), by the time of the late '90s those days were two decades past. The voice of youth in the relatively affluent end of the Millennium was a more worldwide one; the internet had brought influences together, in Western terms the likes of blink-182, Green Day and The Offspring were relatively well-off and – concrete lugging and trash-man jobs aside – these bands were more than able to buy themselves guitars and drum kits. There was no political struggle to speak of, as such, and since the early '90s when the grunge movement reigned supreme, the emphasis was less on introspection and street-scraping miserablist poetry than it was on having fun, chasing girls, drinking beer and enjoying life. The voices of the kids on the streets therefore at the latter end of the '90s were clear: politics was a turn-off. By contrast, chugging a few beers back and dancing like lunatics to high-energy, three-minute blasts of power-chord melodic rock was a massive turn-on. Blink and their contemporaries were not pioneers in the way that Sex Pistols had been, but in their own way they changed the world in the best way possible: by putting smiles on people's faces. And that is an achievement that ought never to be underestimated. The biggest problem for the dour elements of the UK press was in the terminology used. 'Punk' by definition means whatever you choose it to mean, after all.

"Politics and music should be separate," declared Tom. "That whole P.C., vegetarian, anti-drug, straight-edge, do-it-yourself ... all those weird things I'm not interested in. I'd rather be in a band and have a cool attitude and act in a way that the kids can relate to."[63]

"I understand why people have a tendency or a need to categorise bands," he continued on MTV, "because you want to be able to understand what they're all about. You can say we're a punk band, but you can also say we're a pop band. We're just the same."[64]

Anyway, *Kerrang!* got the idea, awarding four Ks out of five for blink's gig at Manchester Roadhouse on September 13. The reviewer considered the band the very essence of contemporary punk rock, summing blink up as, "Three cute Californian guys with hard-ass tattoos, an indulged fondness for mild scatology, a flair for memorable and melodic post-Descendents popcore and an easy, garrulous charm."[65] Bang on the button.

There were important shows to play, anyway: awards shows like the Teen Choice Awards in August and then the MTV Video Music Awards pre-show, an outdoor preamble to that television channel's shindig, plus the small matter of a clip of the band streaking in Las Vegas opening the 1999 *Billboard* Awards. There was also the job of supporting Travis Barker's own foray into merchandising with a show on October 21 at Riverside, California – the base for his clothing and accessories line, Famous Stars And Straps. Its range of hats, jackets, T-shirts and socks was complemented by belt buckles, bandanas and skateboard decks along with posters and all kind of merchandise.

The tail end of 1999 had the group returning to America for their *Loserkids* tour which was their first genuinely massive set of dates, being in arenas as headliners for the first time. Those enormo-dome concerts also featured Fenix TX and Silverchair, natives of the land that *did* get what blink were all about, Australia. The tour was sold out throughout and the banter was flowing between songs as ever, although a gig reviewed by *Rolling Stone* on November 13 at Roseland in New York City suffered from bad sound throughout. "The band sounded just awful," wrote the mag. "Feedback was a major problem and the vocals were almost completely washed away."[66]

There was also time for Tom and Mark to star in a television show, *Shake, Rattle And Roll: An American Love Story*, covering a song by Jan & Dean called 'Dead Man's Curve' – the show was a historic documentary about '60s music and if nothing else showed that the pair's songwriting *nous* was based on some strong foundations. It followed on from the April cameo that Tom had made in the movie *Idle Hands* – as a Burger King employee. He has a line of dialogue but it's fair to say that he's more comfortable with a guitar round his neck spitting banter with Mark onstage. The main small screen appearance, though, was their own video *The Urethra Chronicles*. Effectively, this full-length video gives the band's viewpoint on events in blinksville from the outset. It's chock full of humour and the usual messing around. Tom, Mark and Travis each have a personal five-minute segment as a biography and it also collates their videos to date: 'Dammit', 'Josie', 'What's My Age Again?' and the newest of the bunch, the forthcoming single 'All The Small Things'. The self-filmed home video snippets show the band bouncing off each other with constant joking and fun. It begins with Mark running naked over the waste ground near Big Fish Recording Studios to Tom's nature-film voiceover and pretty much carries on in the same vein from there, taking in the usual blend of sex, bodily fluids, nudity and having one heck of a ride with a smile on your face. To say it wasn't a contender to win many awards at Cannes is probably an understatement but it's also missing the point. *The Urethra Chronicles* was released at the exact time that blink-182 became megastars and what it did more than anything else was demystify the group entirely. No bunch of aloof rock stars these – one session watching the video places them firmly back with their feet on the ground. The interplay between Tom and Mark is that of two very close mates and Travis takes the group's quiet man persona with suitable cool. The video in a very real sense serves to bring the band closer once more to their audience by its unrelenting honesty. Even better was the fact that they didn't go with another title they had kicking around: *The Diary Of The Butt*.

Christmas 1999 rounded off a great year with the band performing at the KROQ *Almost Acoustic Christmas Concert* once again. The charity show had been good to the band and it was good to give something back – the band led a chorus of the salty sea shanty 'Silent Night'. The year, the decade and indeed the Millennium was rounded off in style with the trio performing at the *MTV 2 Large* event along with the likes of Christina Aguilera, Jay Z, Bush and Goo Goo Dolls. It was entirely fitting that the group would spend the last day of the Millennium with grins on their faces, in contrast to the doom-mongers elsewhere warning of Millennium Bugs that would surely lead to millions of computer chips[67] going haywire, traffic lights exploding and all manner of technological disasters.

Chapter 13
Small Things And Big Things

Of course, the year 2000, Y2K, came along without any trouble whatsoever and the world breathed a collective sigh of complete shrugging indifference. That the Millennium didn't actually *start* until January 1, 2001 wasn't the reason, either. Still, for the boys in blink a new year always meant a new set of releases and gigs to get their teeth into. January was the month that *Enema Of The State* went triple platinum whilst the three amigos unleashed the second single from the album, 'All The Small Things' which had become one of the more popular tracks in their armoury.

'All the Small Things' could be traced back to the DML sessions and was built on some riffs that Tom had brought in for the band's judgement. As a big Ramones fan, he'd long wanted to write a track with some "na na na's" in it and here it was: two minutes and forty eight seconds of pop-punk magnificence. The lyrics are about Tom's girlfriend at the time and the ways in which she made him happy. There are lyrics about an incident where she left him some flowers on their stairs when he came home, for example, and the line "work sucks" is constantly shouted out at high volume by audiences at shows. Obviously a sentiment shared widely.

"It was one of the last songs we recorded," Tom told *Kerrang!*, "because it was simple it wasn't that much fun to play. But once we put it all together and played it as a band we all looked at each other and said, 'This song's huge!'"[68] Add into the mix a video that parodies boy bands and one whole raft of contemporary pop videos – and gives the guys a chance to pull a few sweet dance moves and also send themselves up in the process – and you've got a massive hit on your hands. It became blink-182's first chart-topper, in the *Billboard* Modern Tracks list. It did well worldwide, hitting Number 2 in the UK and Number 6 in *Billboard*'s Top 100 as well as Top 10 in Italy, Austria, Sweden and of course Australia. Mark was particularly happy about the video shoot for 'All The Small Things' as it was the place where he met Skye Everly, whose job at the time included booking bands to appear on MTV. They subsequently got married during 2000. The video, directed by

Marcos Siega, went on to win 'Best Group Video' at the 2000 MTV Video Music Awards where it was also nominated for 'Video Of The Year' and 'Best Pop Video'.

"We never intended to insult anyone," director Marcus Siega commented in an interview later, "so I never expected any backlash, but I was a little surprised it went over so well. I thought maybe the fans of those bands on *TRL* would kind of react negatively toward it, but that didn't happen. I think we had the opposite effect. In some ways, I think that that video put Blink at that sort of pop level with those other bands. We were making fun of them, but it kind of became [what it was making fun of]."[69]

Q magazine loved it, for one, eschewing the whole 'ah-but-is-it-punk?' nonsense and merely commenting that it was, "one of those power-pop tunes that the Americans get soooo right ... [it] has more hooks than the Fishing Channel."[70]

The band meanwhile had headed out to Australia for January's *Big Day Out* before once more hitting the UK for some spring dates to boost their growing reputation. *Enema Of The State* sales had now jumped toward the four million mark and whatever some sections of the press said, you don't sell that many records without having a serious fan-base. There was also a chance to show their compassionate side once more, with a live version of 'Dammit' lent to the Mojo Records compilation, *The Solution To Benefit Heal The Bay*, with the profits from the collection going to an organisation set up in 1985 that worked to conserve the coastal waters round Southern California and Santa Monica Bay. The boys could have done with a little healing themselves, with Tom and Travis picking up throat infections during the March European tour which unfortunately led to seven gigs being cancelled across Germany, France, Holland Switzerland and Italy – the French and Dutch dates were rescheduled for the end of April. In a statement, Tom commented that the band "wanted to go on, but the doctors told us that the infection was only going to get worse if we didn't stop performing. It came to the point where we felt we couldn't get on the stage and give our fans anywhere near the 100 percent that we always give."[71]

The band were cheered up by the first of a raft of awards coming their way, being nominated for 'Outstanding Album' and 'Outstanding Single' ('All The Small Things') plus 'Outstanding Group' at the California Music Awards which were known as the Bammys and then, in May, winning a Blockbuster Award for 'Favourite Group – New

Artist'. Later that year, the guys went even better, snagging a surfboard each in the Teen Choice Awards for 'Choice Rock Group'.

Tom and Mark also found time – somewhere, somehow – to set up a clothing brand alongside childhood friend, Dylan Anderson. The vision was to create a fashion that would appeal to the youth of the new Millennium whilst retaining kudos. Atticus was therefore a clothing label that was intended to create clobber for musicians and kids who don't quite fit skate or surf scenes but want to have a choice of what to wear to look cool. In many ways it was the natural extension of the early home-made T-shirts that blink were so enamoured with. Atticus also released several compilation CDs featuring contemporaries of blink and some of their favourite bands. The clothing aspect became something of a badge of honour for blink fans who could identify each other not just because they were wearing a T-shirt with, say, Tom's face on it – but by their Atticus-labelled hoody.

Things were certainly moving at an incredibly fast pace, and it was time to look at recording a video for the third track to be taken from the wildly-successful new album. It was decided that 'Adam's Song' was to come out next, with a video directed by Liz Friedlander. After the high-octane previous two singles with their relatively light subject matter, 'Adam's Song' showed an entirely darker shadow to the band, and a very sensitive one. As a track that concerns suicide (or thoughts of it), it was a massive departure in many senses for blink-182 and certainly wasn't the kind of material that fitted in with the nakedness-and-goofball-humour persona that had grown around the band.

The track is massively hard-hitting which has led to various rumours that it was about a letter, supposedly from a fan, that Mark had read, or concerned an old friend from Rancho Bernardo High who committed suicide, or even a play entitled *Adam's Letter* which had the same focus as the song. That play was publicised online by a fictional suicide note by a boy named Adam Krieger. But despite the internet rumours, that play by John Cosper has no connection with blink-182 either as an inspiration for 'Adam's Song', nor vice versa[72]. For one thing, the play didn't appear until over two years after the blink song came out.

"The play was written in 2001 with a different title, *Final Word,*" confirmed John Cosper for this book. "It was re-named and released on the web as *Adam's Letter* in around 2005. The actual suicide note was written by me as a part of the play script. As it was written two years after the blink song, there is absolutely no connection whatsoever between the note and the writing of the song. By the same token, the naming of the central character was a coincidence. The name goes back to the original script; I had no knowledge of blink-182 or their music at that time."[73] Ironically, since the explosion of interest in *Adam's Letter*, Cosper has started to follow the band's activities. "I have become a fan of their music," he says. "I think Travis Barker is arguably the best drummer in rock today. I'm also more into their fast tunes, particularly the Star Wars-inspired anthem, 'A New Hope.'"

Whichever way you look at it, this was a glimpse into the wider world of blink-182. 'Adam's Song' connected with their fans deeply, as a clearly blown-away Mark Hoppus commented in 2001.

"Some fans wrote us mail and said that they wanted to kill themselves, they seriously contemplated suicide, but then they heard our song, 'Adam's Song' and it changed their mind. That really, really is great. I think that was one of the greatest moments ever in my life."[74]

Tragedy had struck in May when a student at Columbine High School by the name of Greg Barnes had taken his own life with 'Adam's Song' reportedly on repeat on the CD player. The seventeen-year-old was a very talented basketball player but had been traumatised by losing his best friend and a teacher in the previous year's Columbine shootings. The repercussions of that terrible incident were still being felt, and blink-182 were devastated when they heard about this sad story. The song undoubtedly discusses depression and feeling down but ultimately it actually has a very powerful message of hope, as Mark commented during an interview around this time.

"The heart of the song," he said, "is about having hard times in your life, being depressed, and going through a difficult period, but then finding the strength to go on and finding a better place at the other side of that."[75]

The band returned to the road along with the mighty Bad Religion and their good mates Fenix TX for a tour dubbed *The Mark, Tom And Travis Show*, based round a drive-in movie theme. The arena show was their most ambitious to date and the band were excited – in their usual tongue-in-cheek way – about the possibilities of it all, particularly the laser lights. "You know those lasers that you get for eye surgery?" Mark pondered to *Rolling Stone*. "That's what we're using. People will watch us, and we will correct their faulty vision."[76]

It was a great touring line-up and as a result the gigs were being very well-received. The band were happy and rocking on full power. That is, until an appearance at Cuyahoga Falls in Ohio on Sunday, June 4, where some locals began shouting comments to Travis and his girlfriend who were sitting in Taco Bell. The couple were then accosted and Travis ended up breaking his little finger defending himself. Although it could have been much worse, it meant that he was physically unable to perform that night – something of a problem with four hours to show-time and ten thousand tickets already sold.

Tom and Mark turned to a rather unlikely source – Damon Delapaz, who was actually performing with Fenix TX as their guitarist although he had been a drummer for many years. Nonetheless, the pair knew that he was a talented drummer and immediately drafted him in as temporary sticksman. Credit to Delapaz who was replacing one of the finest tub-thumpers in contemporary rock music, although Tom DeLonge was a little disconcerted to find, once more, that someone could learn a set in such short time. "That questions our ability as musicians!" he laughed, "that in three hours he learned our whole career of best songs!"[77] So it became the 'Tom, Mark and Damon show' until Travis recovered from his injury. Not that they were the kind of characters to look back with regret, there must have been more than a couple of pangs of longing for that summer's *Warped* tour – the first they'd missed in five years. Green Day were playing the slot that blink-182 would undoubtedly have filled usually and, by all accounts, having a whale of a time doing it.

Chapter 14

The Show Must Go On

August 2000 began in fine style with an appearance on the front of *Rolling Stone* magazine, that Teen Choice award and recording sessions for a brand new song, the first new material since the beginning of 1999. The song, 'Man Overboard' had been missed off the final set for *Enema Of The State* but was to feature on the next LP which for the first time in the history of blink-182 was to be a full-length live album. After some time being seen as a band of jokers who'd strip naked at the drop of a pair of Y-Fronts, it was probably time to remind the world that they were actually a fine pop-punk band who had the capability to get any crowd on their feet. The group had recorded two concerts on home territory in California – at Bill Graham Civic Center, San Francisco on November 4 and Universal Amphitheatre, Los Angeles 5, 1999 on the *Loserkids* tour – and after some nifty editing and selection of the track list, the boys were ready to go with *The Mark, Tom And Travis Show: The Enema Strikes Back*. It is a fantastic live album, full of all the energy and *joie-de-vivre* that the band had exhibited during their career to date. And though *Enema Of The State* was selling like wildfire, the live album also served to show people that actually there had been quite a back-story to the band and *three* full-length albums before the worldwide breakthrough. New blink fans rejoiced in this sudden realisation even whilst getting off to Tom and Mark swapping unsavoury insults about dog semen, playing with lyrics to get another dig in at each other and portraying the Devil himself in *South Park*-like fashion. The gig begins as *Enema* does with 'Dumpweed' and thrusts through a top notch 19-song set that has many highlights, but particularly the trio of terrors 'Carousel', 'All The Small Things' and 'Mutt'. The live element of the album (which was produced and mixed by Jerry Finn) is concluded with a hugely upbeat blast of 'Dammit'. The LP was initially meant to be a strictly limited-edition deal but given that 'limited edition' in this sense meant that 'only' a million were pressed, that's a moot point. Nonetheless, it's been a popular album which came back into print in 2006 thanks to the insane demand amongst the blink cognoscenti. Its cartoonish artwork is colourful and has all sorts of characters portrayed thereon; look out for sexy nurses, aliens, the dancing bunny and wizards for a start. The album was pretty well-received amongst the press and served its purpose: outside the relatively strict confines of the studio, this was purely and simply blink-182, with personality to the fore as they hammered through their catchy anthems.

Even the UK seemed to like it; *Melody Maker* (the now defunct weekly rival to *NME*) observed that the album, "obeys the First Three Laws Of Rock: have a good time; maintain the generation gap; keep it simple."[78] In the USA, *Spin* were similarly instant in their appreciation of the release, and weren't afraid to enjoy the "self-deprecating one-liners about boobies, boners and crooked wieners."[79]

'Man Overboard' was released online as streaming audio at the start of September, 2000 and very soon began to cause a stir amongst clued-in fans of the band. Its lyrics seem fairly unequivocally about a break-up: the protagonist expresses his sorrow that things are over and goes on to highlight times where the person who's left wasn't sober enough to be dependable any more, and that the excuses were running short. And in such a situation, with said person on the precipice, it proved impossible to talk them down; watching a friend drowning is excruciating and yet, in this context, inevitable. The song ends in a terribly sad fashion where the good friend is lost and the protagonist is resigned to the truth that after all the problems he just doesn't miss his old friend. To many, it seemed to be Tom and Mark's letter of regret that their old compadre Scott Raynor fell overboard just as the *Good Ship blink-182* was entering successful waters. It's difficult to read 'Man Overboard' any other way, but when I asked him, Scott had another view on the matter.

"I have never heard the song all the way through," he says, "and I don't know what the lyrics are. Besides, it couldn't possibly be about me. In all our years of touring together we only took one nautical voyage, it was a ferry ride from France to England, and that went fine." During 1999 and 2000, Raynor had been keeping himself busy with various musical projects including a group called The Axidentals. Rather than sitting behind a kit, however, he picked up a guitar instead.

"It was fun," he recalls. "We recorded twice at Doubletime. Once for an E.P. then later a full-length record. We never released the full-length because shortly after it was recorded Vagrant Records began showing interest in signing the band. Trevor from Face To Face met with us to discuss producing our first release. The deal went through, but due to a dispute ... I split from the band. They went on to release a full-length on Vagrant under the name Death On Wednesday." It wasn't the only way that Raynor was keeping himself busy; for quite some time he volunteered for a charity called *Stand Up For Kids* which is an outreach organisation that helps street and homeless youth. He also taught music to kids in trouble with the law under the *Street Of Dreams* programme (you can find out more about the charity at www.standupforkids.com). Scott went on to join a plethora of bands, many of which are excellent and more of whom in due course.

Back in the land of his former band-mates, 2000 drew toward a close with the release of *The Tom, Mark And Travis Show: The Enema Strikes Back* and talk of a feature film with director Siega. During the latter days of the year, a script had been completed but with the schedule crammed due to the group's runaway success, plans in this area were put on hold, as was the proposed movie that Tom and Mark were writing together (which was to be titled *Pranksters*, much in the vein of shows like *Jackass*). Unfortunately, also put on hold was the planned tour of Australia and New Zealand in November because Travis was struck down by a particularly gnarly flu. For someone with such great timing, it was terrible timing. So it goes; the live album would have to do for those Aussies desperate for a bit of blink action in the meantime.

The break gave Mark and Tom even more time to devote to loserkids.com which was starting to look like rather a smart move in the then-growing world of e-commerce. It was not only a shop where kids could buy cool stuff, it was also something of a portal where the guys could recommend other bands to their fans. And that meant the likes of The Vandals (of course!), Pennywise (heroes) and Jimmy Eat World (Trombino!) – three groups that would lead directly back to the likes of the Descendents. The popular perception may have been of empty-headed, naked dudes arsing around onstage and playing throwaway ditties whilst talking about having sex with each other's moms (and occasionally dads ... and dogs). But there was also a huge swathe of credibility about their influences that was sometimes missed, given the band's background with Pennywise *et al.* Kids were coming to blink-182 shows and going to the record store to buy something by Descendents as a result. The more serious, credible side of blink-182 may have been lost in the swirl of tits and turd jokes but there's a self-awareness about the band in nearly all their interviews that speaks of very bright individuals. Hoppus concluded that to take themselves seriously would be anathema to the group. "If someone came to you and said, 'You don't have to act responsibly and you can have a bunch of money and travel the world and hang out with your best friends and do what you love', you'd do it too."[80] Quite so.

The tail end of 2000 was spent preparing for a new full-length studio record, which would build on the great success of *Enema Of The State* and keep the momentum going for a group who were now becoming an established name in the charts. The working relationship with Jerry Finn had been so fruitful that the same team was largely engaged for the next record, which as ever had some fruity potential/tongue-in-cheek titles being thrown around: if rumours are to be believed you can take your pick from *Genital Ben*, *If You See Kay* and other typically silly puns. The truth is that blink-182's sense of humour has always been something of a release valve from the high pressure that there can be on bands. That pressure was only increased by the massive success of *Enema...* and so there was no real reason to suddenly stop kidding around. Music was fun, but it was hard work.

The tracks that started to come together in the Finn sessions of 2000/2001 were, however, a far cry from the frantic pace of *Cheshire Cat* or even *Dude Ranch*; the band had learnt that speed wasn't always the answer and Travis' multi-styled skills weren't always best served by hammering it out at five thousand miles an hour. He could roar along in fifth gear with the best of them, but his power and technique had started to get the boys thinking that there was a wider world of music to be explored – albeit within limits, for the time being.

With recording sessions at Signature Sound completed, there was an April, 2001 tour of Australia and New Zealand to contemplate. The blink boys were absolutely flying during the late spring-early summer and returned for a huge tour back on US soil during June, including an appearance on *The David Letterman Show*, just in time to promote their new album. It had eventually become entitled *Take Off Your Pants and Jacket* because of an off-the-cuff conversation after a friend had got drenched whilst out snowboarding. In a vintage moment, one of the cheeky chaps present had advised said soaked snowboarder to 'take off your pants and jacket'. Cue hilarity. What it also serves to do is highlight a glint of sharp intelligence behind the boys' humour as it draws oblique attention to the fact that, latterly, blink-182 had often been encouraged to get naked in order to promote themselves. It's a very self-aware album title in that context and a portent, perhaps, of what was to come.

The LP opens with 'Anthem Part Two' which is immediately

a complete opposite to the boobs-and-party fun-time-frolics that was synonymous with the group's presentation to the media during this period. Its lyrics are the most heavily politically-charged as on any blink release to this point – essentially it is a generational manifesto that exhorts the kids to be wary of the system that surrounds them. It's a call to arms to the teenagers who are feeling helpless and alienated by the machinations of politicians, parents and darker forces. 'Anthem Part Two' is not exactly a conventional opener to an album and shows that those days touring with the likes of Pennywise and Bad Religion as well as the musical influence of Pennywise are indeed a part of the band's approach to life and music. The facts are that these politics had rarely been displayed overtly on a blink record up until this point and opening an album in such a fashion can be only taken as a strong statement of intent.

To completely contradict that last point, 'Online Songs' is one of those girl's-gone kinda straightforward tracks, essentially a follow-up to 'Josie', that the band had made a staple of their lyrical content throughout their previous four albums; then 'First Date' is as upfront as you like, going through the emotions felt by the everykid-blinkster just before heading out on an adventure with a new potential girlfriend. Obviously, then, this is no heavy-politico record – 'Happy Holidays, You Bastard' is a classic sub-minute torrent about not getting enough presents. It's a typical rash of bad language, wanking, diarrhoea and shagging moms and one that the blink gang could whack off in their sleep with predictably messy results.

'Story Of A Lonely Guy' is another downbeat track, returning to the feeling of alienated confusion that is often but not solely the teenage human condition. In fact, these intimations of being helpless and somewhat useless are often also the mark of the artist. And with lines dealing with fleeting 'romances' with a procession of girls, fake smiles and falling behind, it's a short step to extrapolate that this deals with the touring life of a professional musician, at least on one level. Not everybody is suited to the hollow pace of the relentless touring machine; we're back in Bob Seger territory, filtered through the usual blend of tuneful guitar lines reminiscent, in fact, of The Cure, and hefty drum patterns. It's almost melancholy in approach, such are the feelings of insecurity.

'The Rock Show', however, is an entirely different matter, being an incredibly upbeat piece of music that harks back to 'All The Small Things' in both feel and lyrical approach. It's an effervescent celebration of love, life, music and perhaps blink-182 themselves as a band. Its tale of two teenagers meeting at a rock show is heart-warming because despite all the problems of disapproving parents, failing at school and all the rest of it, when they hold hands or sneak into each other's rooms, the world is complete and the future is entirely theirs. It's absolutely joyous stuff, which is once more flipped off as the album enters another regretful phase with the very sensitive tale of a parental break-up. 'Stay Together For The Kids' is essentially a piece of angsty poetry that sums up the horrible situation from the point of view of the kids themselves, who would do anything to stop it happening (it's based on Tom's experiences of his parents' divorce).

"I lived, ate and breathed skateboarding," he later recalled. "All I did all day long was skateboard. It was all I cared about. So I didn't notice too much [else going on]. When I got home [one] day, my dad's furniture was gone, my mom was inside crying and everything just erupted at that point. I was 18, sitting in my driveway when it all went down. So I just took everything from that day and put it into a song."[81]

It's testament once more to the affinity that blink-182 had with what you might call 'the teenage experience'; for good and for bad these feelings are in vivid technicolour and, as it was with 'Adam's Song', the trio were beginning to explore all aspects of life and delve into darker areas of material. *Take Off Your Pants And Jacket* has many indications that after four full studio albums and one live record these musicians were developing in more ways than may have been initially apparent.

'Roller Coaster' and 'Reckless Abandon' are standard carefree-ish tuneful summer-punk memories of looking for, and chasing, love and kisses in bathrooms before 'Everytime I Look For You' is another cut about a long-term relationship gone bad, all fairly standard stuff but sounding absolutely fantastic under the brilliant sonic direction of Jerry Finn (whose influence in shaping the stadium-sized blink sound was beginning to make itself very firmly felt indeed). 'Give Me One Good Reason' is a kind of younger sibling to 'Anthem Part Two' in talking about hanging with the misfits and freaks that the parents just don't understand whilst dreaming of sacking off school to just be with people who share similar tastes to the protagonist. The verdant territory of youthful/teenage woes is revisited once more in 'Shut Up', essentially a lament of being left behind whilst the old gang has split town. In the face of being told that he's worthless, the central character is not one to meekly accept his fate but quite justifiably shows two fingers at those who are decrying him and vehemently restates the fact that nobody can tell him what to do – it's time to strike out on his own. It's a fairly familiar rites-of-passage tale but only adds to the general themes of isolation, alienation and moving on to a new place that pervade *Take Off Your Pants And Jacket* as a whole. 'Please Take Me Home' closes the album proper in bewailing the problems engendered by dating someone who is also a friend – not the most upbeat of endings, it must be said.

"I don't think of them as teenage songs," Hoppus offered when asked about the record. "The things that happen to you in high school are the same things that happen your entire life. You can fall in love at sixty; you can get rejected at eighty. People are always going to give you shit and tell you how to live your life."[82]

The album was initially released in various forms, which each had numerous bonus tracks and various coloured sleeves with different designs. The red, 'plane take-off' version included 'Time To Break Up', another one that pretty much does exactly what you might expect from a song covering that theme. The other extra song is 'Mother's Day', one of the sweary blink ditties about fucking, sucking and touching. The incongruous chorus is classic blink-182. The version released in the green jacket enjoyed a pair of extras that began with 'Don't Tell Me It's Over' – familiar break-up territory once more – and 'When You Fucked Grandpa' which, quite frankly, is indescribable but suffice it to say that Grandma joins in at one point, too. The 'yellow pants' version of the album had 'What Went Wrong?' as its serious extra track, another break-up song but one where the protagonist, despite his frustration at the situation, is filled with a righteous sense of anger and as such is ready to kick out. This version of the record also includes the notorious 'Fuck A Dog' which pretty much bottoms out the depths of depravity blink were able to sing about and remains disgustingly hilarious. These ridiculously vulgar joke songs are an absolute counterbalance to the sensitive issues discussed elsewhere on the album and although a little incongruous in that context are also a part of the blink-182 oeuvre in their own right. It's just how they are.

At the end of May, 2001, Tom DeLonge married interior designer Jennifer Jenkins in San Diego Bay's Colorado Island. The happy couple were serenaded by Jimmy Eat World, that band playing as a gift from Jennifer to Tom – a gesture that moved him to tears of joy. Tom gave solid silver yo-yos to his groomsmen, including of course Mark Hoppus, on this very happy occasion.

The album came out on June 13, 2001 and rose rapidly in sales, scoring the guys their first Number 1 in the full *Billboard* charts. Everything up to now had been heading towards this absolute career vindication: the band had worked their balls off in the live arena to get people on board – the days of flyering the local high schools to try and get enough kids there to fill a SOMA side-stage were long gone, even if there were occasional songs on the album that made you wonder. Critical response, though secondary to huge sales of course, was mixed. On one hand, the UK in particular wasn't always on message with blink-182 and this new version of 'punk', but on the other it was undeniable that there was a whole generation growing up who absolutely felt connected to the So-Cal band and their ilk. The bad reviews and naysayers may have merely held a mirror up to the generation gap that had now appeared between some reviewers and what was important to the new generation of music fans for whom the first flush of 1970s punk was already ancient history. An odd position, no doubt, to be in: it's the age-old concept that the kids just *don't get it.* Meanwhile, the kids hate everything that has come before. Or, some might say, the older generation hold on to the past …

"The new punk rock sound," explained Tom, "is more of musicians trying to play their instruments and concentrate more on, if not their lyrics, then their melodies and harmonies and trying to integrate their music … we're just one band out of a very positive movement. We've never been an angry band and we never want to be. We want people to have fun and say whatever they want to say and offend people and run around naked and do whatever the fuck they want to do!"[83]

"This record is the hardest, fastest record that we've done," he continued. "It's way more punk-rock than our previous records, and we're excited about it."[84] A lot of people felt the same. "They bare their painfully adolescent fragility, confusion and vulnerability," wrote a reviewer for *Rolling Stone,* "without playing coy about their pathetic sex drives or their moronic sense of humour … as they plough in their relatively unself-conscious way through the emotional hurdles of lust, terror, pain and rage, they reveal more about themselves and their audience than they even intend to, turning adolescent malaise into a friendly joke rather than a spiritual crisis."[85] Pretty spot-on stuff. *Kerrang!* gave it a high-profile review and was more positive than not, offering the somewhat back-handed compliment that the album was "eminently hummable dummy-spitting tantrum rock for the emo generation; a golden shower of easily bleepable swear words and the kind of unshakeable tunes that will very probably haunt you to your grave."[86] Meanwhile, the band were in a spot of bother with the Federal Trade Commission, whose report rapped their team on the knuckles for marketing explicit material to children.[87]

The lead single from *Take Off Your Pants And Jacket* was the utterly catchy 'The Rock Show', for which the band had recorded a video that included them trashing televisions, trains, taking homeless dudes out for a spa makeover, handing out cash randomly to passing strangers and paying dancers to go and cut people's lawns. The relatively large budget for the video, reputedly $50,000, had to be spent somehow, so there were quite a few happy extras and bystanders on the set that day whilst the band merrily spread the wealth to all they encountered. Pro skater Jeremy Klein makes an appearance and the group delight in giving out some cool gear to kids. Although it only reached Number 71 in the *Billboard* Charts, it scored Number 2 in *Billboard*'s Modern Rock Charts.

"It's just a good, fast, punk-rock love song," Mark commented. "We tried to write it in the spirit of, like, the Ramones and Screeching Weasel. It's a really simple song. It's just three chords, and it's basic, but it's a catchy song."[88] Fitting tribute to the Ramones, indeed, and in particular Joey who had passed away to the great gig in the sky during April that year. The Ramones are often forgotten when the new punk bands are talked of, but their stripped-down limited-chord approach and frequent predilection with simplicity and love affairs is pretty much a direct influence on blink-182. And the Ramones predate the Sex Pistols, so go figure.

June and July were taken up once more with live work, the band taking the record on tour extensively for a summer jaunt sponsored by Honda. The band again came in for a little criticism about selling out (which often appears to be shorthand for 'being a success') but by way of mitigation their tickets were consistently lower priced than most groups of their stature, so by accepting corporate links such as this they were able to continue to give the most important people – the fans – a good deal. Tom DeLonge even commented that despite some groups selling hundreds of millions of records – like the Bee Gees, for example – nobody would admit to liking them because there would be some kind of credibility loss somewhere down the line. Frustrating, but pop was ever thus.

Perhaps appropriately, 'First Date', the second single from the album, paid homage to the Bee Gees in a great set-up that was based round the theme of the mid-'70s. The band had, of course, inordinate amounts of fun in playing long-haired, uncool versions of themselves and plenty of other bands along the way. This fun was amplified by being able to tap into the 2001 *Warped* tour's unique atmosphere, the band using a rare day off to guest at a gig in Somerset, Wisconsin on July 14, 2001. Their favourite rolling musical freak show was entirely an ego-less trip; anyone displaying rock star attitude would get brought down to earth incredibly quickly and quite simply excluded from the party with all its sweaty filth, fury, camaraderie and communal punk spirit. The fans were loving it too – so much so that the tour dates were to be extended to September, 2001.

As the summer shadows started to lengthen, it was time to shoot a new video, this time for 'Stay Together For The Kids', the next planned single from the album. The filming took place on September 9 and September 10, 2001 round the theme of a wrecking ball smashing through a house in which the band were performing. But the video would never be released.

Chapter 15
Reality and Extra Curricular

The events of September 11, 2001 – 9/11 – are beyond the scope of a musical biography; suffice to say that there is nobody alive who has not had their life inexorably changed by what happened that day. The numbness many felt made thoughts of music seem rather frivolous; but adversity often brings out the best in people. In the immediate aftermath of 9/11, the world seemed to be put on pause, but life goes on and so it is with music, too, with an added determination – even in these most shocking of circumstances – to carry on regardless of any threats to liberty from such provocative and violent attacks. It was across the board; the USA's infrastructure had been violated on many levels and strong decisions had to be made by everybody as to which steps to take next. In practical terms, blink-182, after much thought, rescheduled their planned September tour dates in the UK.

"We kind of got put in an awkward position because we had to make a decision pretty quickly," Mark told Ben Myers. "After the attacks the world kind of went into freeze mode and we didn't know whether to carry on with things or not, but it came to a head when America was just about to attack Afghanistan. It's hard to predict what's going to happen a month into the future, so we decided we'd rather everyone was safe and play the shows a little later instead. I could think of nothing worse than some kid getting hurt at a blink-182 show, for whatever reason. We'll be coming over in January now. It sucks because we want to play so much. Touch-wood, this is hopefully going to be the best tour in Europe that we've ever done and to have to guess what's going to happen with the world is definitely a hard thing to do."[89] But probably the right one. From September 18, onwards, there had also been instances of Anthrax spores being sent through the post to public figures and news stations, further heightening the tense mood Stateside.

"It's tense and scary," confirmed Hoppus. "It's all you see on TV … right now we're just taking it easy after all the touring, just spending time with our families, our friends, our girlfriends and our houses."[90]

On a personal note, there was exciting news for Travis Barker, who joined the ranks of the married on September 22, 2001, getting hitched to his long-term girlfriend Melissa Kennedy. There was also a new video for 'Stay Together For The Kids' which was very sensitively dealt with by a band whose intelligence was starting to reveal itself ever more overtly. Post-9/11, the band rightly felt that the video was just too close to the bone, despite the featured crumbling house actually being a metaphor for divorce. However, the shots of the World Trade Center falling had of course made the blink video more than inappropriate by association rather than design. The band re-shot a video with the same crew and production people – but in front of an empty house.

With the tour of Europe postponed (and then further postponed because of DeLonge suffering a herniated disc), there was a little spare time so blink-182 turned their attention to other projects. Tom DeLonge had long been toying with the idea that there was music to be had outside the relatively established sound of blink-182 and in the final months of 2001 he took the plunge and headed into San Diego's Signature Sound studio to crack on with some tracks that were a little more raw than the now-polished 182 sonic. The engineer on the sessions was Sam Boukas, who worked closely on the project alongside the legend that is Jerry Finn.

"It's probably the best studio in San Diego," offered Boukas in an interview for this book. "Size-wise and best-equipped. Blink recorded *Take Off Your Pants And Jacket* there. It's a great place with great equipment and Luis the owner is a great guy. A comfortable environment for the blink guys. They didn't want to go to LA and live in an apartment or a hotel while they worked on the album."

The new project would involve songs by Tom and, for the first time in collaboration, Travis Barker. It would look more toward the lesser-known but no less important influences of the artists. "Quicksand was a very big influence on all of us in the band," offered Tom DeLonge. "We're all very big fans of Quicksand ... they're such a great band. We just wanted to be able to experiment with music for the first time without any expectations. [91] There was even a name for the new act – Box Car Racer. The name comes from the plane that dropped the H-bomb on Nagasaki at the tail end of the Second World War, although in fairness DeLonge's hugely anti-war stance meant that the name was merely an appropriation rather than an endorsement of any kind. The WWII B-29 was called Bokscar (or Bock's Car) – spelled incorrectly as 'Boxcar' in many places and further altered to the three word Box

Car Racer for Tom's project. It wasn't in fact the first time that Travis had used the name in his musical career; it had been the name of one of his kickaround bands a few years previously. "My friend Alex [from that old band] told me that every time I left on tour, it was like his girlfriend was leaving him. We only played a couple shows."[92]

New name or not, it was catchy enough to stick (and there were no Irish bands knocking about with a similar name, luckily). As DeLonge said, the intent was to produce an album of not-really-blink but definitely punky and darker material that would never find its way onto a blink-182 album. Sessions began very quickly, with the ever-resourceful Jerry Finn having sent one whole load of equipment to Signature ahead of his arrival. It was the first time that any blink member had been moved to record outside the band to any significant extent. The fact that it was two-thirds of the group rather than all amigos together was at the very least, a surprise – inside and outside the 182 camp. It couldn't be blink because Mark wasn't there; but statistically 66.6 per cent of the band were involved. At the time it posed some interesting questions. But something fantastic had already come out of it – another welcome chance to work with Jerry Finn.

"Day One I walked in," laughs Boukas, "and they'd already delivered all of Jerry's things here. I don't know how many road cases were piled into the studio but we had to sort it out because half the space of the studio was taken up. He travels with so much gear; a hundred guitars, different amps, heads, cabinets and then also two huge six-foot-high racks packed with studio gear. It was great, I was really excited! It was all top-end stuff; there was nothing that was worthless in the rack just taking up space. Tom showed up first, came in and was checking stuff out. I remember Jerry was the last to arrive, he made an entrance. I'd never met him and they were all like, 'Hey Jerry, nice to see you!'"

"My first impression of Jerry was that he was just a normal guy and if I saw him on the street I wouldn't think anything of it. Casual in tennis shoes, shorts and T-shirt. Tom was relaxed too but he has more of an energy around him where Jerry is more reserved, as you'd expect from a producer compared to an artist."

The material was definitely on the road to being completed prior to the studio sessions, observes Boukas, with a definite statement that this wasn't by any means a blink-182 album. Guitarist Dave Kennedy was a good friend of Tom's, although according to the respected engineer, DeLonge was in control of the Box Car Racer songs to an incredibly hands-on level.

"Almost everything was done for the project," he says. "If anything wasn't finalised it was lyrical ideas, most of the musical ideas were already in place and it was a matter of putting things down. Tom had an itch to do something where he didn't feel locked in to what blink was. He wanted to have some liberties to do some stuff so Dave Kennedy came on board. All the drums were already recorded by the time we came to San Diego. They'd been into a studio in LA with a really nice room to do the drums but they came to Signature for Tom to lay down all his guitar tracks." DeLonge certainly had a strong idea of how he wanted each instrument to sound, explains Boukas, and as well as singing, the industrious Tom laid down his own guitar and sketched out some ideas for other parts too.

Dave Kennedy had cut his teeth in San Diego straight-edgers Over My Dead Body and had become good buddies with Tom DeLonge through the circuit. The two had chatted about bands, gigs, the underground scene and throughout the early years of the 2000s it sparked off more interest from DeLonge in exploring his more traditionally hardcore/punk leanings.

"We had been hanging out a lot last summer or whatever," said Kennedy in an interview with Bobby Gorman. "Talking about music or talking about different types of music we were kinda interested in, and coming together and playing ... it came about that we were talking about a type of music [with which] we were gonna experiment and do ... blink had some openings [in their schedule] and he said if we were gonna do it, that we had to do it now. And that's really how things evolved in the band. Just hanging around really."[93]

Boukas recalls the recording sessions being much quicker than blink-182 had been working of late, albeit that the guys were more than used to having limited studio time, harking back to the rough-and-ready *Buddha* and *Cheshire Cat* romps of a few years previously. But rather than spend months and months refining and polishing everything for a major label and international pop market, Box Car Racer's approach was a lot closer to the original DIY spirit.

"We were in the studio for not more than around six weeks which is relatively quick," continues engineer Sam Boukas. "They already had the drums done but I know it only took him a day. It doesn't take Travis long to lay down his drum tracks, what takes time is getting the mics set up to make it sound right. If everything's set up already it only takes him like one day to record his drums for an album. I think they spent a week in LA doing drums at most. When you're starting out and budgeting everything and paying for it all, things are much quicker, like their early recordings."

Although Box Car Racer was essentially an outlet for DeLonge's more esoteric leanings, it very quickly became obvious that this was an album that was destined for release. Blink-182 were smokin' hot and therefore any musical project with which any member was involved was very likely to fly off the shelves.

"I remember that a representative of MCA came in a couple of times," says Boukas, "to see how things were going and check on the tracks. He seemed pretty pleased with it. I don't think there was ever any doubt that it was gonna be released – you have a project with two members of blink-182 on it, it's pretty hard not to turn a profit on that. I guess if the record company wasn't going to foot the bill, they were quite prepared to foot it themselves for *Box Car Racer*. They just wanted to do it. My feeling is that it was not self-indulgent but much more that Tom felt like he needed to do something different from blink. He wanted an outlet, not to do something that was bigger than blink or to take it onto the next level. It was never that kind of thing where they were saying, 'We're here, let's take this up, and up, and up'. I got the impression they [just] wanted to do this album, Tom wanted to do the songs the way he wanted them and they wanted to play some shows and that was it. But at no point did I get the feeling that he didn't want to continue with blink-182."

There were however a few inevitable issues with the fact that whilst Travis was on the album, the other member of blink – Mark Hoppus – was not directly involved with matters. As Tom's best friend it was something of an oddity not to be around the writing and recording – they'd always worked together up until now and Box Car Racer was the first time that either one had struck out alone since the pair had met. Although Mark was not directly involved, there was time set aside for him to come in and do some backing vocals for the track 'Elevator'. Hoppus and DeLonge found some time to sketch out some additional ideas, too.

"Tom was there when Mark was in doing the vocals," says Boukas. "It was relaxed, they were fine and Mark was really happy that Tom invited him in to sing on this one song. It went smoothly, I think it took one day to get his vocals in place. At one point Mark picked up an acoustic guitar and said, 'I have an idea for a song for the next blink album' and he was playing that to Tom. It's really cool to have that kind of insight and see how they work. For me as a musician it made an impact in that those guys work the same way that all bands work. One comes in, says, 'I have an idea, let me play it to you' and they do and the other one will say, 'Yeah that's cool, I can think of some other ideas coming off that.' So it's not that different from any band. It's great. Because you think they're doing something so magical – which they are, of course – but at the same time anybody could do it."

In theory, perhaps, but in practice very few people could go from writing singalong fun-punk tracks that had become the blink-182 staple to an entirely different set of more reflective, heavier and more experimental rock material in a matter of months. DeLonge's need to explore other sides of his creativity was the direct motivation behind Box Car Racer, something that wasn't necessarily shared by his bass-playing buddy at that stage. "Mark was really interested in being involved in the project," notes Boukas. "But of course then it would turn into blink-182 and Tom wasn't interested in that happening."

With recording complete, there was just time to announce an intriguing rotating headline tour for the summer where blink-182 and Green Day would join forces for a series of dates under the banner *The Pop Disaster Tour*. Unsurprisingly, fans were pretty much foaming at the mouth at the prospect. Meanwhile, Box Car Racer busied themselves with arranging a set of their own dates and shooting a video for the track 'I Feel So'. Co-directed by Tom himself, the promo film has the band playing in a rehearsal room/basement, whilst in her bedroom a young girl is crying. It was successful with MTV as people started to prick up their ears with some interest. The self-titled album was released on May 21, 2002 and immediately achieved the kind of critical and credible success that blink-182 often found so elusive from some sections of the press. Allmusic.com loved its serious approach, paying particular compliment to the "lyrics that are retrospective and thoughtful – witness 'Watch The World,' which could fit on a Dashboard Confessional record, with a libretto that boarders on poetry. This is a far cry from the party-boy ethos DeLonge is best known for, and he wears the emotional depth well, with songs that are just as hooky as from his bread-winning main squeeze."[94] Old rivals *NME* even praised the record, commenting that it showed, "the sensitive, socially conscious and politicised Blink-18U2 ... BCR attempt to bury the blink schtick at the Joshua Tree."[95] Q magazine were a little less hysterical in their style but no less impressed by the album, writing in their June 2002 issue that Box Car Racer, "confound expectations with a very good record."[96] Which goes to show that expectations are nearly always a bad thing. "DeLonge's lyrics reveal a preoccupation with death and apocalypse that's totally at odds with blink's blithe juvenilia, and the explicit Christian overtones in 'Letter To God' and 'The End With You'" commented a very positive review for *Blender*, "suggests that DeLonge is eager to distance himself, not just musically but also ideologically, from the blink locker room."[97] Adding to the darker tone was the fact that DeLonge was experiencing back pain throughout the recording process; a nagging condition that was ever-present although it didn't actually stop him performing as such. Later, speaking to MTV, he attributed the music's sombre tone to this at times excruciating pain. For Travis' part, he was happy to plough on and let the music speak for itself; he wasn't bothered, he said, what music critics were going to say about it.

"Most of them are like fifty years old," he roared. "And they're not really educated in what kind of music we're playing to begin with! The overall response to this album has been ridiculous. We didn't have much push or anything, we didn't do a whole lot of promo before the album came out and it still did really well." He went on to comment that Box Car Racer really had nothing to do with blink-182 aside from sharing a couple of musicians. "It's neither of our side projects. It's just another band."[98]

The album has hints of U2, Fugazi and Refused, and inhabits largely the more serious and sensitive soul-baring tone of 'Adam's Song', and 'Stay Together For The Kids'. It opens with plaintive single 'I Feel So', a sad track about being young and feeling anger at the world, hardly new ground to tread from the songwriter but in contrast to the adrenaline rush of blink, the way that the theme is framed is crucial in setting up *Box Car Racer*. It's a great opener that leads into the high-octane 'All Systems Go', a punkier offering that deals with another familiar theme, that of rebellion. 'Watch The World' explores feelings of alienation, love and helplessness with a gravity that lets the listener know that this album really does mean business. 'Tiny Voices' could well be a blink track in another dimension but here is notable for the band's conversation during the bridge section. Tiny voices, indeed.

'Cat Like Thief' features guest vocalists Jordan Pundik of New Found Glory and Rancid frontman Tim Armstrong, both great mates of the blink lads and both happy to lend their distinctive voices to the project. 'Cat Like Thief' is a hip hop influenced track, Travis pummelling out a fantastically authentic rhythm whilst the singers exhort the protagonist not to leave his girlfriend. It's an excellent track that sits next to 'And I', another tale of an unsuccessful relationship. Next is the ambitious 'Letters To God', an acoustic-based song that ramps up the emotional content hugely. The album is somewhat confused at this point with DeLonge seemingly unable to entirely leave the dunder-punk vibe entirely alone and 'My First Punk Song' is the result. Though undoubtedly tongue-in-cheek and a direct tip of the hat to the hardcore punk rock bands like Black Flag that formed DeLonge's early listening habits, its juvenile lyrics and breakneck pace really are out of step with the rest of the album. It's not a bad song, *per se*, but its inclusion next to something like the sophisticated multi-tempo of 'Sorrow' is unfathomable. 'There Is' is another acoustic-based piece that again has a real sense of gravitas about its sentiment, before 'The End With You' picks up on the world-is-ending theme of 'Watch The World' (and, for that matter, 'Anthem Part Two' the opener of *Take Off Your Pants And Jacket*).

Were there any proof needed that Mark Hoppus was on message, musically at least, with the Racer, 'Elevator' is it. Of many skilled tracks on an intriguing and well-conceived record, 'Elevator' shines with personality throughout as Hoppus and DeLonge recount the tale of a suicide and a shrugging world. The chorus/hook lines talk of forgetting this and moving on. It could be about the end of a relationship; the question is obviously to which kind of relationship it refers. It also hints very strongly toward being a song about the events of September 11, 2001. The album ends with 'Instrumental' which on the cassette tape (yes, I said tape, again) was replaced with an instrumental version of 'I Feel So'. The video for that song is also included on the enhanced CD. In terms of artwork, the bleak burgundy brown and black silhouettes plus a graffiti-esque band logo set a certain feel, whilst there are plenty of hidden messages and points of interest in the insert. For example, "LN W 13 01 1" is printed on the case and those numbers and letters are longitude co-ordinates that point to Manhattan, New York being a huge influence on the stories that make up the album narrative. There was pretty much no getting away from the fact that DeLonge and Barker's main band was going to be uppermost in people's minds, though, as David Kennedy mused when talking to Bobby Gorman.

"We are only getting to do it because of them, I mean automatically at this level. So it's not that big a deal [when people ask about blink-182 during interviews]. Obviously, it's a Box Car interview [and] all four of us, even more so Tom and Travis, prefer to be referred to as Box

The original line-up: Scott Raynor, Mark and Tom backstage at the legendary Whisky A Go Go venue, Los Angeles, October 8, 1996.
Photo: Jim Steinfeldt/Michael Ochs Archives/Getty Images

Stopping to pose for a photo at the Board Aid Benefit in Big Bear, California, March 15, 1997.
Photo: by Jim Steinfeldt/Michael Ochs Archives/Getty Images

Blink-182 performing on the Vans *Warped* Stage at the Reading Festival, August 22, 1997. *Photo: credit: George Chin/IconicPix*

Hanging out backstage at The Borderline London, September 14, 1999. *Photo credit: Tony Woolliscroft/IconicPix*

True to form, Blink-182 find a novel way of introducing the *Billboard* Music Awards hosts at the MGM Grand Garden Arena in Las Vegas, December 8, 1999.
Photo: Frank Micelotta/ImageDirect/Getty Images

Tom displaying some classic punk rock moves, June 18, 1999.
Photo: Jay Blakesberg/Retna Ltd

Passing time at the *Big Day Out Festival* in Sydney Australia, January 26, 2000. *Photo: Tony Woolliscroft/IconicPix*

About to hit the stage at the MTV European Music Awards in Germany, November 8, 2001. *Photo: Frank Micelotta/ImageDirect/Getty Images*

With the indefinite hiatus looming, the band appear detatched, 2004.
Photo: Jim Ruymen/Corbis Images

Mark and Travis step out with new band +44, November 10, 2006.
Photo: Chris McKay/WireImage/Getty Images

DJ AM and Travis Barker join forces and perform at LAX Nightclub at The Luxor Resort in Las Vegas, USA, June 18, 2008.
Photo: Kabik/Retna Ltd/Corbis

Angels & Airwaves on the Vans *Warped* Tour at Comerica Park, Detroit, July 18, 2008 in Detroit, USA. *Photo: Paul Warner/WireImage/Getty Images*

Blink-182 cement their return by announcing a summer tour at the El Compadre, Los Angeles, California, May 18, 2009.
Photo: Jordan Strauss/WireImage/Getty Images

Now he's just showing off ... Travis at First Midwest Bank Amphitheatre, Tinley Park, Illinois, August 15, 2009. *Photo: Daniel Boczarski/Getty Images*

Tom back to his old tricks 'arsing around' while Blink perform live at the Susquehanna Bank Center in New Jersey, August 27, 2009.
Photo: Bill McCay/WireImage/Getty Images

Well and truly back to business at the Hollywood Palladium, Los Angeles, October 10, 2009.
Photo: Christopher Polk/Getty Images

Car not blink. So they might be even a little bit more quick to mention it than myself or Anthony [Celestino, BCR bassist] would. It doesn't really bother me that much as long as it stays relatively focused. But it's inevitable that people talking about Box Car will be curious about blink. Or vice versa."[99]

Were this an entirely new band rather than an additional project by a chart-topping new punker, it would have been heralded as a very promising debut indeed, but here it was a stand-alone project that ran its course during 2002 and DeLonge shelved it permanently in mid-2003.[100]

Meanwhile, events in blinkland continued apace in early 2002 with the release of *The Urethra Chronicles II: Harder, Faster, Faster, Harder* this time on DVD, which couldn't have been more different from the focus of Box Car Racer. Another home-movie-based bit of fun with the band and assorted mates joking and kidding around, it also features live performances and videos of 'The Rock Show', 'First Date' and the previously-unreleased house-wreck video for 'Stay Together For The Kids' (as well as the official one). Again, no Oscars are likely to be aimed at Travis, Mark or Tom for this one but the fans loved it regardless on its February release. 'Stay Together For The Kids' was also released as a single and an excellent EP that had plenty of live tracks and video extras to play with. Time to head out on the road once more, with blink's most ambitious project to date …

Chapter 16
Battle For The Empire

There were sessions in garages, short songs, happy songs and California sun-days. They were close friends getting together for the joy and effervescent life-affirmation of playing tuneful punk-rock rhythms together. The three-piece were instrumental in bringing a new kind of punk sound to the world having paid their dues on small independent labels, subsequently jumped onto a major label only to find accusations of selling out following their every move. During the 1990s, their fan-base remained largely unflappable and they were guaranteed to sell out venues of an arena size throughout the US and Europe. Their association with the *Warped* tour only served to cement their place as one of the greatest 'new punk' bands that the latter years of the Millennium had produced. As 2002 dawned, they stood at a crossroads in their career, seeking to develop in sound and vision without breaking away from the elements that had made them such a force in music.

Their name was Green Day.

Although the band had won multitudes of awards and plaudits, in the earlier days of the '00s, this trio had, in the eyes of some commentators, already peaked with albums like *Dookie*, *Kerplunk, Insomniac* and *Nimrod*, variously held up as classics of the era. *Nimrod* was notable for featuring an intriguing take on the Green Day sound, bringing in elements of surf music, ska and even an acoustic ballad-type hit in 'Good Riddance (Time Of Your Life)' which hinted at – gasp – a new maturity to matters in the camp as singer Billie-Joe Armstrong mused rather than raged. *Nimrod* was largely a bridge to *Warning*, the 2000 album that was another step into adulthood for a group who'd been seen amongst some quarters as purveyors of 'snot-punk'. It's an album packed with social commentary and themes of hope and faith yet this soul-searching approach wasn't necessarily leading to sales of the magnitude of previous hit records. Though Green Day had come through 2001 with a clutch of trophies at the California Music Awards, their November 2001 *International Superhits* greatest hits compilation looked like something of a book-end to at least phase one of a hitherto fabulous career. In early 2002, Green Day's star was fading a little, not least in the face of their Poway equivalent, blink-182. The two bands shared a sonic and attitudinal approach and the only real surprise is that the idea of a co-headlining tour had not been put forward previously.

For fans of hugely-entertaining, slightly-anarchic, fun-and-fuckery new punk madness, the *Pop Disaster Tour* of April to June 2002 was an absolute godsend. Not only would Green Day and blink headline, you would also get Jimmy Eat World fresh from the success of their own 2001 album, *Bleed American*, plus Saves The Day and Kut U Up. The line-up was formidable and anticipation was high. As it turned out, blink-182's new obsession with pyrotechnic set-ups made it very difficult for Green Day to physically go on last so the concept of a 'co-headline' tour was, shall we say, rather a flexible one.

"Well, it would be pretty impossible to play after because they've got all these shenanigans on the stage and all this fire and other crap that would take about two hours to remove," said Green Day drummer Tre Cool. "A set change would be impossible. And I don't think they want to do a show without that stuff. They're a big band ... right now, so it's appropriate to put them on last. I don't think anyone's having a bad time on this tour. We're all living it up."[101]

The tour had been conceived by blink-182 on an aeroplane jaunt to Las Vegas, and echoed the famous Monsters Of Rock tours; the idea was to have, effectively, a Monsters Of Punk tour. Green Day was approached, the answer was favourable, and their bassist Mike Dirnt came up with the typically tongue-in-cheek *Pop Disaster* label. It's probably evident from the music but just in case anyone was in any doubt, Green Day had, amongst others of course, influenced the blink boys from the outset both musically and subsequently in terms of what is possible in career development outside the indie-punk-DIY ghetto.

"The first day I met Tom," recalled Mark Hoppus, "I was playing a Green Day song on bass ... Green Day opened a lot of doors for bands like blink-182 and all of the pop-punk bands that have come along after them [by signing to a major label]. They took a lot of heat at the time but they really wanted to show people that you could still be on the radio and hold exactly true to what you believe in."[102] In the same interview Hoppus declared that there was no rivalry to speak of between the two enormous bands and that the tour was set up only to showcase their respective talents rather than compete for the unofficial title as Pop-Punk Kings. Apparently.

The gigs, at the outset, were absolute stone-cold classics, with Green

Day roaring their way back into the national consciousness playing a familiar set that included all their killer tracks. A reviewer for *Spin* was blown away by Billie Joe and the boys at the Dallas gig on May 9, 2002. "Shucking off their increasingly mellow public demeanour, Green Day seemed reborn. The super-hits shot out like streams of water from the water cannon that Billie Joe occasionally used to drench the crowd." In the face of that performance, blink-182 had a lot to live up to and in that writer's opinion they fell a little short on this occasion. "Pity the band that had to follow [Green Day]," the review continued. "Sure-shot singles … still sounded fresh but the infamous Mark Hoppus/Tom DeLonge onstage banter … seemed uninspired."[103] The double-whammy of GD and b-182 was perhaps, if anything, too much to handle as reviews continued to sing the praises of Green Day over the charms of the Mark, Tom and Travis show.

"Sometimes playing last at a rock show is more a curse than a privilege," began a *San Francisco Chronicle* review ominously. "Pity the headliner, for instance, that gets blown off the stage by the band before it. Blink-182 endured that indignity Saturday at the Shoreline Amphitheatre."[104] The reviewer was unimpressed by the pyrotechnics of blink-182's set, even when Travis' drum riser spun and lifted into the air during his solo spot. Not even Mark and Tom being taken offstage on stretchers was enough to impress the writer concerned. More of the same was hammered in blink's direction by the *Orange County Register*, too.

"After Billie Joe's seminar in showmanship, blink-182's tag team of Tom Delonge and Mark Hoppus seemed to suffer from charisma deficit disorder. Their shtick wears thin quickly … blink also had trouble measuring up in the musicianship department to Green Day (or, for that matter, Jimmy Eat World). The group simply didn't sound tight much of the time, thanks in part to drummer Travis Barker, who has yet to learn how many beats are too many."[105]

The tour was flawed from the outset; who could possibly ever follow an hour and a half of Green Day's full-on set that not only had punk-mosh magic but also featured a song in which members of the audience would be invited onstage to play with the band? Billie-Joe was handing out guitars here and there and by the time he'd encore with 'Good Riddance (Time Of Your Life)' the audience had already been taken on an immense and exhausting, journey. To come on after that and hammer through even an explosives-laden set of smirky humour was always going to be a tall order.

"No matter what the bands tell you, a co-headlining tour is a battle between two popular groups desperately trying to upstage the other," wrote a reviewer. "The one thing blink-182 lacked more than anything [was] a library of hits the size of Green Day's ... in the end, blink-182's momma jokes and toilet humour fell short in the battle against Green Day, implied or not."[106]

Speaking to *Kerrang!,* Tre Cool acknowledged that Green Day had come to view the tour as an opportunity to regain their status at the top of the tree. "We set out to reclaim our throne as the most incredible live punk band there is ..."[107] After three years of amazing success, blink-182's rise was impressive indeed but perhaps there was a lot more to be discovered about themselves and their own place in the pantheon of contemporary rock bands. The tour, from blink's point of view, had been put together as a show of unity in the face of consistent accusations of rivalry between the two bands. It had become tiresome, said Mark.

"For years the press has tried to make out some kind of rivalry between Green Day and us," he sighed. "Especially over in Europe. In every interview they were trying to start some sort of feud between us and it got to the point where actually I called a mutual friend and said, 'Hey, will you tell those guys we have no animosity toward them.' We put this tour together to prove people wrong."[108]

You can make your own mind up about how it all transpired; the 2003 movie, *Riding In Vans With Boys*, follows the tour as it roars its way around the United States. It was actuated by Mark and Tom's fledgling production company, Rising Bird Productions, yet another creative outlet. Watching the movie, regardless of band rivalries, despite all the talk of who-was-smokin-who, it's damned obvious that the dates were also one whole lot of fun. With sold out venues across the board and friends old and new made whilst playing music to thousands of kids, you can call it pop, but a disaster? No chance. After a quick appearance on the *American Pie 2* soundtrack, with 'Every Time I Look For You', blink-182 as a unit went their separate ways for some much-needed time off, although that has always been a somewhat flexible concept in their ever-busy minds.

Chapter 17
Surgery

The association with Jerry Finn had become very fruitful; he'd not only produced the two best albums of blink-182's career but also overseen *Box Car Racer* with good humour and a huge amount of skill. His contacts were also handy in getting Tim Armstrong's vocals for that album, the singer being a pretty unstoppable force as far as music was concerned. Armstrong's creativity and drive were not just confined to his main band, Rancid. In fact he had been sketching out songs in his basement studio for a number of years with no specific direction in mind. Meeting up with rapper Rob Aston (aka DJ Boss Hogg) and programmer/multi-instrumentalist Dave Carlock, the intent had been to release an album with DJ Boss Hogg on vocals but it didn't quite click together at first.

"We started meeting regularly in the mornings – the record started out as an 8.30am session a coupla times a week," explains Carlock. "Rob would come down, he was really into hip hop and had a mellow, easy voice at that stage, more a typical hip hop rapper but Tim wanted a more hardcore element so he kept saying, 'Scream, yell, make your voice really rough, hardcore!' And that's where the Skinhead Rob persona came from."

Carlock had been brought in largely to help Armstrong set up his new digital recording system, the now-ubiquitous hard disk-based Pro-Tools. It's a system that allows for great flexibility without any of the degradation or sonic restrictions to which analogue tape is prone. Soon, Carlock found himself collaborating with the punk rock legend – the best way to learn equipment is to have a reason to use it, and so a band of sorts was born.

"We'd meet, work on these tracks and get all the ideas down and Tim would write different track ideas and come up with strange sound-bites, different things that he'd take from the television if it was a cool sound effect, build a crazy sound around it, being extremely avant-garde to take advantage of this new type of recording. I'd come in the morning and help him build round those ideas, and eventually I played some bass for him as he was more of a guitar player naturally.

I sort of filled in the blanks, he said, 'It would be cool to put a piano part in' and he didn't really play piano so I'd throw something down."

"That's how the Transplants began; it was really just me and Tim in the basement with Rob coming over to write lyrics and do vocals and we continued that way through early 2000 and the full year of 2001." There was then a pause in momentum before talk of a new band line-up called The Silencers, which essentially never got off the drawing-board stage, but the tracks were pretty much ready to rock. It was felt that the collisions of beats, hefty guitars and aggressive lyrical delivery needed one hot and heavy drummer to beef the hell out of it. But who to ask? Armstrong's connections with a certain producer were to come in handy.

"Tim knew Jerry Finn, who'd produced blink-182," beams Carlock. "Word had got around that not only was Travis Barker an amazing drummer, [but that] he was also an amazing studio drummer which was a skill that a lot of drummers don't necessarily share. Travis had this reputation of being a guy who could sit down with a click track and no music and have the arrangement in his head and he could lay down the drum tracks in five, ten minutes for a song and then the band could play on top to him as if he was a drum machine. It's unusual: a lot of drummers want to hear guitars, hear bass, hear the arrangement but he would just go in cold with his click track and lay the whole thing down because he'd know it inside and out. So that was perfect for the Transplants because we needed someone to take the tracks which were basically finished but needed real power of drumming behind them."

"Tim contacted Travis in mid-summer – we were trying to finish the record in June, early July 2002. He came into Tim's studio and as we were recording in a residential part of LA, there was Tim Armstrong, punk rocker, recording in a house that wasn't really soundproofed so he had a gentlemen's agreement with his neighbours to cut out any super-loud sounds by 5pm when they'd get home from work! So Travis came in one day, set up the drums by eleven in the morning and cut the drums for the entire Transplants record – ten, twelve, fourteen tracks that got cut down on the final version – he cut everything in one sitting in one day except for one song. The reason for that was that about quarter to five we had this weird thing happen with the headphone system and we couldn't get it resolved by five when we had to stop to keep the peace out of respect for the neighbours. So Travis had to come back the second day to literally play drums for ten minutes. The next day the headphones miraculously worked for some reason and Travis came down the second day and nailed it. It's pretty much superhuman. He is one of the very best studio drummers I've ever worked with and I was always amazed. He's a massive star with blink, but my joke with him was that if he wanted to get serious about this music thing he could be a really great session drummer!" Always good to have something to fall back on.

Transplants was tailor-made for Barker, whose love of hip hop and punk rock come together on an album that has a definite edgy charm to it. As with *Box Car Racer*, it serves to show a side of Barker that was straining to get out of the relative straitjacket of blink's rampant beats. There were some summer dates with The Distillers, too, one of which was recorded for posterity by the ever-industrious Carlock.

"What's kinda cool about our fan-base," explained Skinhead Rob, "is that we get a lot of Rancid fans, blink fans, and Box Car Racer fans. But at the same time, we get a lot of people who aren't necessarily into punk rock, or who might not check out those bands. They're into us because they're into all different kinds of music. A lot of people's moms say they like the record. We basically made a record that sounds like nobody else's, so people can't say, 'Well, it's not punk.' We didn't try to make a punk record. It's more than that. We just do what we want, and fuck what everyone else thinks. We're happy."[109]

Transplants, as the culmination of all this work for Armstrong, Aston and of course the ebullient Dave Carlock, holds together very coherently as an album. It all kicks off with the provocative 'Romper Stomper', one of the more hardcore tracks on the record, somewhat akin to the cruel-paced likes of Sick Of It All. Its aggression and vituperative delivery pricks up the ears right from the outset. Coming hot on its heels is party-time classic 'Tall Cans In The Air', a gleefully wasted blast of a track absolutely jammed and rammed with frontline frenetics and a cracking hip hop beat from Travis. Next up is 'DJ DJ', before (not just album highlight but one of Armstrong's career highlights) the fantastically catchy 'Diamonds And Guns'. The piano loop was written by Carlock after a discussion with his band-mate as to what the basic track was lacking. It gives a real insight into the writing processes at work on *Transplants*.

"'Diamonds And Guns' was the big surprise of the record," Carlock told the author. "Tim was really passionate about it as a concept and there are early demos [... and] we kept adding things to it but it was his favourite song and he said, 'Try a piano track on it'. Because he's a gigantic Clash fan he asked if I could do a bluesy line like 'Rock The

Casbah'. We worked on some things and it didn't turn out like that song but it had a bluesy militaristic kinda feel which was much too straight to do a Clash thing so we worked really fast on a lot of things, we'd keep an idea going but move on very quickly. We would often find it funny, Tim would say something I'd done was perfect and me being the session guy would want it perfect and to do it again. He was very instinctive and hated repetition and I was always fighting to get it really nailed spot on – this was one of the few times that without too much bantering I got him to allow me to work the whole idea out, I spent ten minutes working out that lick until it was ready. Then we went and picked the best one which was the 'Diamonds And Guns' piano loop." More of that track in due course.

Davey Havok of AFI guests on the next track, 'Quick Death', keeping the testosterone up to the max, whilst 'Sad But True' bridges the gap to another track, the woozy, loose 'Weigh On My Mind' on which Armstrong's then-wife Brody Dalle of the Distillers lends her distinctive vocals. 'One Seventeen' is another speedy tale until the album gets to the reggae-tinged 'California Babylon' which is another fine track, although the vocalist's version of a kind of Jamaican accent is quite odd. That said, it is an absolute stormer of a song that holds up to repeated listens. 'We Trusted You' brilliantly blends Country & Western ole-boy singalong choruses with heavy-set spit-out politico-raps in the verses. An excellently-planned and joyfully-delivered piece of mischief that in many ways sums up the ethos of the Transplants. 'D.R.E.A.M.' appropriates the Wu-Tang Clan's 'C.R.E.A.M.' and spins it on its head before it all comes to an end with the down-tempo smoky ska of 'Down In Oakland', rounding off an experiment in cross-genre rocking out that mirrored *Box Car Racer* in attaining both underground credibility and press plaudits.

"Travis Barker has broken out as punk rock's first superstar drummer," declared *Rolling Stone*. "On this latest side project, Barker singlehandedly drags his old-school-leaning band mates ... into the future with some timely percussive tricks, incorporating frantic jungle beats into 'Romper Stomper' and hip hop rhythms on the wave-your-hands anthem 'Tall Cans in the Air.'"[110] Praise was also forthcoming from allmusic.com whose reviewer felt it an "inspired side project ... every time Armstrong's gutter punk-accented, mush-mouth voice appears, Transplants sound more soulful than rap-rock."[111] Even the usually august *USA Today* loved it, gushing that it stood head and shoulders above many other releases of 2002. "[It is] the year's most audacious and thrilling side project," they wrote. "The trio toggles from explosive instability to lock-step precision in a brash clash of punk, hip hop and drum-and-bass electronica … Punk purists may protest, but Transplants' reckless fusion couldn't be more true to that genre's rebel code."[112] Beautifully put.

"I don't know a band that sounds like us," said Skinhead Rob. "We get the punk police, whatever, saying, 'Oh fuck that, it's not punk because this, that, or the other thing' ... I mean for the most part the response has been really good. To be honest with you, even if the response was one hundred percent terrible, I really wouldn't give a fuck. I want to be successful and I want to sell records and I want to have billions of dollars and nice things, but you can't miss what you never had."[113] And as for whether the Transplants was a punk band or not, Rob was in particularly fine fettle.

"Who fucking cares?" he retorted. "I'm not a fucking punk rocker. I'm Rob and I sing for the Transplants. I'm no one special. I'm not the fucking idiot asking for change outside the show. I fucking hate those kind of people. Don't get me wrong, I love the kids, I love punk rock, but all these punk purists are idiots. They can suck a dick."[114]

It would take a while, but 'Diamonds And Guns' in particular became synonymous with the Transplants experience. The small amount of gigs in 2002 were more for kicks than anything else as the band members were, of course, all very busy people (one massive surprise was when a shampoo company were able to licence that track for use in its commercials).[115]

"It helps sell our records," said Skinhead Rob. "We get paid every time that motherfucker goes on. And people get to hear our band. People say, 'Oh, you're selling out.' Well, suck my dick, you know what I'm saying? We've got bills to pay like everyone else. There ain't nothing wrong with getting your song on TV."[116] And that song was getting on screens both big and small all over the place in short order.

"It was also in the Jet Li movie – as a remix – in *Bulletproof Monk*," continues Carlock. "A track was used in *School For Scoundrels* with Billy-Bob Thornton, but I never saw that one. 'California Babylon' was in *Tony Hawks' Underground* skater game which was quite appropriate."

Chapter 18

House Band

Aside from a September appearance at the KROQ *Island Invasion*, that was pretty much it for blink's live shows in 2002. There was finally time to take stock of how far they'd come and what was happening around them. At the outset of the band's career, the tail end of grunge was paramount, with a more reflective outlook and certainly one eye on the dark shades of life and music. Bands like Green Day, The Offspring and subsequently blink-182 had worked hard to pull guitar-punk into a much poppier, lighter approach. As ever with music, once blink and their compatriots had become assimilated into the establishment, their own effect on popular music became very evident with a new breed of 'bands', in the loosest popular term, being presented to the worldwide public. The fact was that blink-182 had sold several millions of records, based round largely having a fun time and presenting a side of life that was lighter, less stressful and generally much more compelling than the state of the increasingly-paranoid post-9/11 world around them. Unfortunately, however, this meant that every record label worth its salt was looking to pick up on a fun-time band that took elements of the skate-punk sound, some of its style but none of its depth and pull it into the pop arena. By the autumn of 2002, for example, in the UK a band called Busted was all over the media like a rash. Essentially, Busted were three pretty boys who could play guitar and sing, pull some heavily choreographed star jumps and tease their hair into 'faux-punk' spikes. The controlling hand of Simon Cowell and a massive PR campaign behind them meant that they'd fast-track through the charts like a dose of diarrhoea. Their debut single, 'What I Go To School For' talked about fancying their teacher; the band members were in their teens and connected with a whole new audience in a way that older rock stars could not.

"The shit that is coming out right now [worries me]," Travis mused when talking to Bart Niedzialkowski. "When I heard blink on the radio before I was even in the band, it didn't bother me. These kids [blink-182] have been around for six years. I have watched them be around for six years and they do what they do and they do it good. Before I was even in the band I said that. I appreciated it. I liked it. Even if I wasn't the biggest blink fan before I got in the band. These kids are good. They write good songs. That's the same thing with Green Day. Those kids are good! That's like when I hear new stuff that's influenced by bands like blink and Green Day, I'm beside myself the way they are doing it. It hurts me. It hurts me. It's like cookie cutter shit. It's like 'Awwww, man.'"[117] Quite.

But whilst Busted (and later another band by the name of McFly) could boast none of the punk credentials, sonic sophistication or keen intelligence about their material that blink-182 could, the odd situation had arisen that by 2002 Tom (who was 26, going on 27), Travis (age 26, going on 27) and particularly Mark Hoppus (who turned the unimaginably ancient age of 30 that year) had become a trio that was peering over a generational schism that, if not quite a parental gap, was certainly a grown-up-older-brother one. Tom DeLonge had celebrated the birth of his first child, Ava Elizabeth, during July, with Jack Hoppus cheerfully appearing to a delighted Mark and Skye in August. Meanwhile, Travis bought a couple of new cars to add to his ever-growing collection of Cadillacs, thereby taking his total of vintage motors to eleven.

"My dad had one when he was young," explained the drummer. "I never had the money for it. I bought my first Cad for six hundred dollars and I just kind of like fell into it. I just loved everything about Cadillacs. I love the logos … I don't know … there's something to be said when you see a Cadillac going down the street. Like a 66 is beautiful, or you see a 78 El Dorado and it's convertible ... I don't know, just the feeling you get when you drive it. Or a 84, like a Low-Rider. I don't know man, it's just *something*. You know how some people are into Volkswagens and they go buy those buses and bugs and shit, like that's how Cadillacs are for me. I'm just a freak. I love their cars."[118] The car had, of course, long been associated with rock 'n' roll success by everyone from Little Richard to Elvis Presley.

Travis had also been pretty much constantly busy appearing on other artists' projects, including the 2001 Puff Daddy video for 'Bad Boy For Life' which for a hip hop fan was immense, although he faced some odd criticism, he says, for that one. "I got shit when I played on the P-Diddy album and I did a video with him. I mean, hey, are you kidding me? Where did I ever say that I never liked hip hop?"[119]

Travis even allowed the MTV crew into his home for an episode of the series *Cribs*, which essentially was an entirely prurient delve into the homes of pop, rock and hip hop stars. "Cribs," he rightly noted, "is such a weird thing. You're kind of like sitting there, showing off what you have, which is kind of retarded, but at the same time, I didn't even think about it like that. I didn't feel like I was bragging or anything. It felt pretty much like, *Bam*, this is what I've got, this is what I do, and if you don't like it, screw off, you know?"[120]

The *Pop Disaster* tour is without doubt the last page of a certain chapter for blink-182, who were by now – whether they liked it or not – adults in the eyes of the Busted/McFly generation. Those two bands, of course, couldn't point to appearances on *The Simpsons*' three-hundredth episode as the blink boys could. But the world looked like it was at their feet.

The autumn appearance of the *Transplants* album and a Box Car Racer DVD were an indication also of the developing need for the blinksters to explore other musical avenues. The DVD featured interviews, live performances and the two videos to date – 'There Is' and 'I Feel So'. *NME* called the latter "over-earnest and cobblers" before opining that though Box Car Racer was better than blink-182 in their eyes, "so is getting your face chewed off by angry pigs."[121]

Certainly the live Box Car reviews had been positive enough; the audiences may have been intrigued at first by the blink connection but it was soon evident that the band was an entirely different proposition. "I was kind of unimpressed at first," wrote a reviewer, "thinking 'Tom just isn't the same without Mark standing next to him, but after a while, I got used to just Tom, as he busted out every song on their self-titled album."[122] At that particular show, Box Car Racer covered Barry Manilow's grappling wrestle-manic drill-core classic, 'Mandy', a wry nod to a great pop song even as they sought to distance themselves from the mainstream.

Following the end of the Box Car Racer tour in November, it was time for blink to think about exactly where they ought to head next. For sure, a new album was going to happen and Jerry Finn was already lined up to produce but for the first time in the career of the band, there would be an entirely new sonic approach. Having hinted at all sorts of new depths of darkness and light with Box Car Racer and the Transplants and wanting in part to stand outside of the pop-punk cage that had been built for them, the trio went into pre-production with no preconceptions. There were even suggestions that the new album may head in a much more electronic direction. The group were intent on taking their time to not just create songs rooted in the pop-punk tradition but to explore the possibilities of the studio and utilise new technology to achieve interesting sounds and songs throughout the writing and recording process (much in the vein of experimental punk rockers Bad Astronaut, who were a side-project of members of Nerf Herders, Sugarcult and Lagwagon – bands more noted for their pop-punk credentials but in this guise providing something entirely more challenging to their audiences and, crucially, themselves).

Mark Hoppus had been challenging himself, too, taking on a serious dramatic role in the TV series, *Haunted*, where he played a hermetical man of the mountains. A far cry from getting naked and running through the Hollywood streets, he'd enjoyed stretching himself and felt it was satisfyingly at odds with the persona he delivered as part of blink-182. "When you're in a band, you're just yourself," he told MTV. "When you act, you become somebody else or portray a completely different person, and I like that kind of creativity."[123]

Meanwhile, blink's creativity was going to be explored in a unique way. Rather than head into a studio for the new album project, the band decided to write and record one a whole lot nearer home, literally. "They actually started out in a house with this project," explains Sam Boukas, who was again employed as Jerry Finn's right-hand man on the sessions. "It was rented, not far from where their houses were, which is a very rich neighbourhood. They started demoing the songs in this large house, starting to rehearse and piece together demos. Nobody wanted to be in a windowless studio for hours per day and they wanted to be in a more relaxed, creative environment that was also a ten-minute drive from their houses. Tom and Mark were both married at this point, both with children and they wanted to be able to live their lives and also record in a relaxed place. It made perfect sense; it was a great set-up." The house was a lovely place to work, open and full of light.

Transplants producer/keyboardist/engineer Dave Carlock came in to help prepare the area during the demo process and was immediately blown over by what he found. "The house was extremely beautiful," he recalls. "A gorgeous house, just beautiful." So much so that the Pro-Tools expert expressed his wish to live in the area.

"Mark and Tom just smiled and said, 'This area is the single most expensive area of land in the entire United States … it's like a million dollars for an empty lot.' Maybe I won't move here then guys! It was crazy."

"The family to whom the house actually belonged owned another house over the water meaning that the guys had free rein for a good six months to do as they pleased – within reason. It was an open-house design that obviously wasn't set up for punk bands to record in, whether intending to produce a new kind of blink record or not," said Carlock.

"I had to find ways to treat and make the house useable because [I had] 'rock's quietest drummer', Travis Barker (!), and put him into this beautiful, sunny, glass-filled house with lots of doors and windows … so we put him in the middle of the house in this great room to record drums in. You could go out to the driveway, pull up an armchair, crack a pint and have this perfectly audible concert from Travis. We thought it could become a problem, the neighbours might complain, it could be a mess. So we needed to soundproof this gorgeous expensive house. One of the first projects there was getting the contractor who did repairs on the house (as the family trusted him), to build at my design these soundproof walls. In the centre of the house there were gigantic alcoves with nowhere to trap the sound and it'd get to the perimeter of the house which was all French doors. Nobody had to think anything about cold temperatures in San Diego so it was the worst sound leaking you can imagine. We created these gigantic walls to block out the alcoves and made proper acoustic walls which helped dramatically. We had to be really careful, doing major construction to the house without damaging these beautiful hardwood floors or messing up their walls so there were some interesting conversations with the family. But they were so cool – if someone'd come to me wanting to do that to my house I would have probably been a nervous wreck! Their daughters were blink fans so that helped an awful lot and I guess with the sizeable deposit they thought they would take the risk." Carlock, who had gone to help set up the Pro-Tools and demo studios prior to the arrival of Jerry Finn and his assistants, also had a real insight into the writing process as the album began to shape up in its initial, relaxed form.

"Tom and Mark were working on ideas separately then would get together to flesh it out," he recalls. "A lot of times it was Tom on the couch with an acoustic guitar and Mark with an acoustic bass on the other just working out ideas and arrangements of the guitar parts to get the demos together. Travis was always around, listening and getting his head into how the songs were and making suggestions in terms of arrangements and he might have offered up lyrical ideas too."

"Travis' natural musicianship was a massive help in speeding up the process; his almost-unearthly ability to zero in on a song meant that the amount of time needed to arrange the percussion was minimal. He was always around absorbing. So when the time came to laying down the tracks he would know the songs inside and out. He would go out and we'd figure out the tempo for the click track. He'd pop on the headphones and play the whole thing tip to tail in usually one or two takes, then we'd use that drum track – which was brilliantly executed – to build all the guitars and basses and vocals on. I mean, he was like the human drum machine. You go on, you press the button, he just lays it out and you build the tracks on it. It was awesome; a lot of drummers can't play with clicks but Travis practices with a click. Even when we were doing the Transplants' tour he had a Tama metronome, a fancy one, and he would sit there and kick out a tempo and warm up on practice pads, he would do it religiously. Like a boxer warming himself up to go out into the arena, Travis would warm up on the practice pads, get himself mentally prepared and he was always working with clicks, so in the studio it was a breeze for him."

"Travis is really into everything," confirms engineer Sam Boukas. "He's an astonishing musician. That was great; at one point I was able to stand in the room while he was tracking some drums and just to watch him play was amazing. It was cool. It's not like he's taking it for granted either and saying, 'I'm good, I don't need to do anything else.' You could hear him in one of the bedrooms in the back at times with his metronome going and doing his rudiments on his practice pads. Staying in top shape – and it showed."

"The band knew basically what they wanted to do but they were also open to changing things. One of the reasons it took so long is that we'd try different ideas out and it'd either be, 'That worked, let's move on to the next idea,' or, 'That didn't work, what else could we do?' Jerry really left it up to the band. Unless the band asked specifically, 'What do you think of this – better this way or that way?' he wouldn't push things on them. He wouldn't say, 'You need to do this here.' More like, 'You're the artist, you come up with the ideas and I can push you one way or another but you guys are the creative drivers.' Some projects are a lot more hands on. Jerry put the pressure on them to really perform their parts right. He'd say, 'You played that guitar part good, but it's not right, it needs to be done again because it could be tighter.' And he had that amazing ear for guitar tones and getting it all right. He was on top of that as well. Having a hundred amps and guitars doesn't hurt! To have that arsenal at your fingertips."

Indeed so. The house/studio was a great place to be but inevitably there came a time when the family wanted it back and so operations moved to the more conventional confines of a local studio in order to complete an album that had essentially grown at its own pace. They went to a studio called Rollin' Thunder but that didn't work out to everyone's satisfaction either.

"It's subjective as to how finished it was at that point – for the most part everything was there, there was a lot of stuff down but after all that they went to LA for a couple of months to work on drums, vocals, a few bits and bobs, just a little more. I think their goal was to not worry about time and just to do what they wanted to do. They had the opportunity to indulge themselves; the only thing I can think is that sometimes, I think Brian Eno said, 'If you have two weeks to do a project, it'll take you two weeks but if you have two years, it'll take you two years.' Things weren't going very fast sometimes in the house, the drum tracks were down in the first week and then the next three months were guitars, vocals, different little tracks. There were a lot of times where we were just eating lunch, getting coffee or just on some sort of nebulous break! It was pretty cool, really relaxed and those guys are a lot of fun to be around. A lot of joking around." Some things never change.

Chapter 19
All About The Drummers

On January 11, 2003, shocking reports came in that ex-blink-182 drummer Scott Raynor had been shot dead. The story spread like wildfire, amplified by the hysteria of the internet. As the tale went, there had been an altercation and/or dispute within his band du jour, a group by the name of Grimby, which had got nasty leading to Raynor's demise. The web was always going to take hold of this information and reproduce it 'til it was a Xerox of a Xerox of a Xerox of a story. Thankfully, it had absolutely no basis in reality. Raynor, who'd largely kept his counsel since splitting from the blink camp, was moved to post online that rumours of his demise were premature. "I woke up one day and found out I was dead," he told me, a little wryly. On a more serious note, the socially-responsible charity worker immediately emailed the sites in question with a press statement:

"Hello, this is Scott Raynor. I was not shot but I have a friend who was. She was a homeless youth living on the streets of San Diego. Thirteen children die on the streets of America ... everyday. I don't want this to happen to children; I volunteer for a national non-profit organization called *Stand Up For Kids*. We, as volunteers, go to the streets to rescue the homeless youth of America. It works: many are saved. If you want to help, go to standupforkids.org or volunteer at another charity for homeless youth in your area.

Thank you,
Peace,
Scott."[124]

The internet did not pick up on the fact that Raynor was not actually referring to someone specific. It wasn't the case that an actual friend of Scott had died. Rather, Raynor was wanting to make a point about the fragility and tragedy of homelessness: "I made the mistake of trying to use the internet as a social platform by using the publicity to bring attention to the fact that I wasn't dead but that [indeed] as many as thirteen homeless youth die each day on the streets of America. That comment got twisted into an anecdote about a homeless youth being killed in a violent skirmish that might have taken my life instead. But that's the sardonic beauty of the internet; its fun-house mirror effect. By default, it generates a topology of America's pathological obsession with death and celebrity." And as for the altercation with his band, Grimby, it had simply never happened. He was in action with that group between 2000 and 2001, having left at least eighteen months before this fictitious non-incident was reported. Raynor says Grimby is one of his personal favourites in terms of post-blink bands he was involved with.

"We recorded a three song E.P. at Doubletime," he recalls. "A one-day affair, three tracks, recorded live. A lot of fun. Very heavy sound. It was heavier, in terms of sonic tone, than anything else I have done before or since, but it was the lightest in terms of mood. It was dark comedy. Kind of like a Black Sabbath, Ramones, and Weird Al [Yankovich] milkshake."

Meanwhile, back on planet blink-182, Raynor's replacement had other things on his mind, namely quite an incredible tour planned for the Transplants. Travis, Rob and Tim Armstrong had already shot videos for both 'Diamonds And Guns' and 'DJ DJ' that January, but then the opportunity came up to play a set of dates in April and May 2003 as support to none other than rock behemoths, Foo Fighters. It was the Transplants' first opportunity to head out to support their self-titled album save those few dates with Distillers the previous summer. It was a fabulous opportunity although it brought with it more than a few technical problems, says keyboardist Dave Carlock.

"What was tricky was that so much of what made *Transplants* an interesting record was the sound effects, loops and that, so if you took the samples out it really wasn't the same band and so it was a case of how we brought it to life so it didn't sound like a Rancid guy, a blink-182 guy and a hardcore guy just trying to do a version of Transplants songs. Tim told me that a lot of folks said the live Rancid shows were different from their records and he wanted me to help present the Transplants record properly, bring it as it is to life rather than just playing the songs, which added a challenging technical component to it because there were all these random things … like when you move house and you start to pack and you realise how much stuff there is in random places and things in your space you need to pack but you've accumulated so much." The affable multi-instrumentalist, however, had other concerns about the tour too.

"How do I go out as keyboard player for a punk band? These guys are crazy! Tim is constantly moving, tons of energy, jumping off bass drums, then you have Craig Fairbaugh from The Forgotten to play who's a wild, amazing energy, and Travis too, Skinhead Rob *prowling*, then me, this guy stuck behind a keyboard! I devised a way of sample-triggering from crash cymbal triggers – I'd be punching cymbals with my fist, triggering samples to try and give it some energy, trying to look like the guy who wants to get out from behind the keys to keep up with these maniacs on stage. Lots of people were really intrigued by all that so I was able to hold my own in a stage sense."

"It's gonna be cool," remarked Skinhead Rob, in one of the understatements of the century. "I haven't had a chance to meet any of those [Foos] guys yet, but I heard they're really nice. It'll be cool to watch them every night, because they're a fucking great band."[125]

The tour also brought together three of the very finest drummers in rock at that time: Travis Barker, Taylor Hawkins and one certain David Grohl. Hawkins and Barker found lots of time to talk technique as the dates rolled around. "To be on the road with someone like Taylor who really cares about drums is just great,"[126] beamed Barker. Hawkins and Grohl were not just stupendous drummers but also great buddies; Dave Carlock remembers the Foos had unique ways of warming up before shows on the Transplants tour.

"Dave and Taylor would come in with bunches of CDs to the green room and listen to tons of music," he recalls. "They also had a ping-pong table which they'd set up and they'd play massive ping-pong tournaments – they were quite good! Champion drummers ping-ponging against one another ... it should be on the television: *Celebrity Drummer Ping Pong Death Match*." Technically, though, Taylor Hawkins was up there with the best of them when it came down to taking care of business, particularly in sound-checks.

"What a monster he was, he used to blow my mind – his warm-up started with a mid-tempo groove, he'd then double-time it without changing the tempo and then half-time it. One hundred to two hundred to fifty beats per minute but keeping the exact metre without speeding up or slowing down. He's such a great drummer." The Transplants dates with the Foos were generally well-received, with reviews considering them an excellent support act.

"The Transplants were well received among the youthful audience," felt a reviewer for *The Rip*. "While Tim Armstrong pumped out the Rancid punk-inspired songs, vocalist Rob Aston screamed out his raps which left the floor somewhat satisfied while others looked disaffected."[127] The date at LA's Universal Amphitheatre on April 18 was beset by a couple of technical difficulties but nonetheless the Transplants were still able to hammer out the good stuff, being joined onstage by none other than Lars Fredriksen of Armstrong's day job, Rancid. The show was a typically raucous one.

"Tim Armstrong was running from side to side with his enormous guitar looking like a caged animal ... he would periodically jump into the pit, guitar and all ... Travis beating the skins reminded me of Angus Young from AC/DC with his relentless headbanging and boyish looks. On full throttle they covered the Clash's 'White Riot' ... the crowd loved the energy they were throwing out."[128] The Transplants' word-spitter Skinhead Rob was full of energy himself, telling an interviewer post-tour that it was a fantastic period in his life and commenting that the Foos' crowd were open to a bit of punk-hop madness. "The response was good for the most part. Their fans were receptive to us. We definitely play a very different type of music ... we did what we did, and it was a good time playing in front of all those people. I think we walked away with a couple of new fans, and maybe even some new enemies. But it was good shit."[129]

Whilst in LA the Transplants also met up with a fan/collaborator whose given name is Alecia Beth Moore, but who is probably better-known to the world at large under her stage name: Pink. Her growling blend of hip hop, soul and punkish vibes had propelled her into the charts during 2000 and 2001 with debut album *Can't Take Me Home*, which had yielded two US Top Ten singles and the beginnings of a worldwide career. However, having experienced life in the pop-sheen world, the singer was keen to explore other dimensions of her creativity and in this she found a surprising supporter in Armstrong. Tim Armstrong, with his constantly-evolving ideas and new ability to quickly demo songs, had long harboured the wish to write for other musicians across genres. The Transplants were one manifestation of that but there was much more in the tank.

"Pink was someone he admired," explains Dave Carlock. "As well as being a punk rocker, Tim loves a great pop song. He admires the craft and loves great songs. She had great songs, a punk edge and real talent and he met up with her in the late summer of 2002, right before the Transplants record came out. It was at the KROQ *Invasion* – a big summer concert in Eastern Los Angeles where tons of working-class folk are and there's a huge Hispanic population. He met her backstage, said he had some songs for her and she said she'd always loved Rancid. So he played her some track ideas and they talked about doing some work together. Then in spring 2003 Tim started collaborating with her and invited her to join a Transplants show in the Gibson Amphitheatre in LA. They were gonna do some side by side writing then she said she'd come and meet us in Philadelphia where she'd been to see family, so she jumped on our tour for the last few dates and rode on the bus with us as we were about to finish in New York." The bus was kitted-out with a miniscule but serviceable recording set-up which in fact led directly to the recording of one of Pink's most-recognisable singles.

"I set up the studio in this tiny back lounge of the bus. It was tight, a tiny chair, racks of stuff, a monitor on one seat. Tim was working on ideas in the evenings and she'd come and write with him." One night the track that was being demoed was a bluesy, raucous rocker by the name of 'Trouble'. Pink pulled off a great performance in the back of the tour bus and the rest is history. "After we got back from the tour, they decided Tim was to produce tracks for [Pink's next album] *Try This* and we re-recorded some overdubs and extra takes but the main lead vocal for 'Trouble' was the one we actually recorded on the bus that night on tour with the Transplants in New Jersey. The sound Tim was going for in the back of the bus was an edgy, distorted vocal. A pristine vocal would have sounded rank but the distortion filter he used on her voice covered up any minor sonic quality discrepancies so it worked. Pink can sing a great performance if it's on a bus, in a bathroom or in an amphitheatre. It won us a Grammy certificate for 'Best Female Rock Vocal Performance' – testament to her great vocal. She's great." Proof that talent is the most important part of the recording process. Travis was later to add his considerable talents to her new album too, a worldwide smash on its November 2003's release.

Digressions aside, in June the Transplants found time to reconvene for a week to enable them to do the KROQ *Weenie Roast* (with guest vocalist Pink, of course) as well as appear on the Jimmy Kimmell show and then the next night, a TV appearance of quite spectacularly impressive note – The Snoop Dogg show, *Doggy Fizzle Televizzle*, which was less a series of music videos and more toward the comedy side of matters. Skinhead Rob was stoked to be in such company, says Dave Carlock.

"It's one of those moments where you ask yourself, 'Am I really jamming with Snoop on TV?'" he laughs. "It was the craziest thing

– I would never have said I would ever do that. Tim and Rob both love Snoop Dogg but Rob absolutely *dug* Snoop Dogg which is evident from his Boss Hogg days. So Rob was in heaven to have an opportunity to be onstage rapping with one of his idols. Personally, I couldn't feel anything other than marvel that I was there but I was proud of Skinhead Rob and watching this kid's dream come true was really exciting to me. It meant so much to him to work with Snoop – for me it was when I worked with David Foster[130] so I knew what it felt like."

The Transplants went their separate ways again in the summer of 2003 with vague plans to reconvene, sometime soon hopefully, as long as the wind was blowing in the right direction and as long as the members were all able to be in the same place at the same time.

Chapter 20

What's My Name Again (Again)?

In typical style, news surrounding the next blink-182 album was swirling around in the usual kaleidoscopic mélange of truth and silliness. There were rumours – often spread, it must be said, by the band themselves – that the LP was being finished off in Fiji; that the group would tour it in the Middle East to support the troops fighting out there; that it would take inspiration off Guns N' Roses' *Use Your Illusion I* and *II* by being called *Use Your Erection I* and *II*; collaborators on the album were, apparently, Dan The Automator, The Neptunes, DJ Shadow and Robert Smith, lead singer with The Cure. The truth was out there, as Tom DeLonge would say. What is for sure is that the summer of 2003 was spent working on the record at a slower pace than normal and that it would not be a 'mainstream' blink-182 album. Travis had time to contemplate becoming a dad with his new girlfriend, ex-Miss-USA Shanna Moakler, who gave birth to son Landon Asher in October, 2003 (Barker had divorced from Melissa Kennedy the previous summer). So the three guys had a new outlook on life as well as music, the first fruits of which were heard not on a single but as part of the soundtrack to a computer game, *Madden 2004*. The track, 'Action', follows a sexual theme but despite its up-tempo passages is more contemplative than many previous offerings from the band. It is wistful, regretful and considered in its sad reflection on fate, the fading of the summer and the ending of happier times. Although it is very catchy in a pop sense, its Latin-influenced rhythms and outstanding arrangement place it in a sonic space that blink had rarely previously visited – at least, not together.

blink-182 (the album either has no name or is self-titled, depending how you feel) begins with 'Feeling This', the actual name for 'Action' (as the name was still not finalised when *Madden 2004* was put into production). Though the group had been working on *blink-182* for some ten months, the latter weeks had been rather fraught with mixing, re-mixing and tweaking the album. In fact, several of the mixes were only completed with hours to spare before the final deadline, such is the near-obsessive attention to detail that the group had thrown into the project. 'Feeling This' starts with a sample from the *Captain America*

TV series exhorting the listener/protagonist alike to get ready for the action that is to come. Lyrically the near hip hop delivery of the verses on both vocals and drums is followed by a very controlled chorus/bridge, as it becomes very clear that in contrast to the roughneck pace of previous offerings, this is purely and simply a rock album. In fact, the dynamic control, counter-melodies and interesting drum patterns are oft-reminiscent of Foo Fighters. The production and engineering is similarly full of interest, with the sonic field lively as various effected vocals pip between left and right. It's recognisably from the DeLonge/Hoppus/Barker stable, but there's something deeper at work here, which is a band taking what they do very seriously. It may be a subtle difference, given that blink had always been very hard workers in the studio, but the eyes and minds are fully-opened here to what they can and perhaps *ought* to be doing. Sam Boukas offers his opinion on how the band came to this point.

"Once the door was opened by Tom and Travis with *Box Car Racer*," he says, "Mark started to be more on board with that concept. He was also more flexible and the next blink album was able to be a pretty big departure from the previous two. *Box Car Racer* opened the door in that sense and I think the three of them wanted to be more creative and have more creative liberty on that next album."

Travis Barker enlightened *Rolling Stone* as to the creative process and his part in it. Although a fine musician in a pure sense, Barker's not necessarily a multi-instrumentalist but his input into matters was very important as he mentioned as early as December 2000. "I don't write lyrics, I don't play guitar, but I arrange everything," he mused. "I decide what tempo a song will be, and I arrange how verses, choruses, breaks happen. When I first got in the band, I wanted us to write songs that were more clever and less repetitive. And that's what we did."[131]

Those words were already evident on the first track and they become more and more true throughout what is an extraordinary blink LP. Following from 'Feeling This' is the aggressive 'Obvious' which kicks into life with another tale about being used, relationships ending, frustration and a release of anger. The lyrics hold within them both disappointment and hope, making it another very human song from the trio. Next on the album is the magnificent ballad 'I Miss You', a song that is notable for Travis playing with a brush to contrast the harder edge of the more rock drumstick, duly creating a looped beat that is both jazzy and hip. The track features acoustic bass, plaintive string pads, piano and a host of bell-like samples round which Mark and Tom describe the protagonist's confusion between wanting the ex-girl to leave him alone whilst still, subconsciously or not, having to admit that he indeed does miss her. It's as naked as the band have been to date, in an artistic if not always a physical sense. When people talk about bands 'maturing', then this is pretty much a perfect example of what they mean. It's a fine piece of songwriting by anybody's standards.

As if to prove that they still could smash out one of those satisfyingly speedy numbers, the introduction to 'Violence' is pure blink-182 before the verses seem to morph into a Transplants song, then the choruses hammer in with pop-punk skill. The atmospheric nature of this flipping between genres and the use of space and absence of sound as a production and songwriting technique serves to make the power chords and distorted punk moments all-the-more blasting; Travis' heartbeat-kick drum in the verses makes the song a very internal and personal one. 'Stockholm Syndrome' is even more a personal eye on the world, beginning with lone piano underneath Joanne Whalley's reading of longing letters that had been sent by Mark Hoppus' grandfather to his grandmother during the Second World War. Its poignancy is undeniable; there was of course a very contemporary point being made here too as the post-9/11 world of paranoia and warmongering had utterly altered the atmosphere throughout the Western world. Nobody was immune to its pull and the so-called 'War On Terror' was already all over the media. 'Stockholm Syndrome' is a reminder that whatever the governments and rulers above may be planning, those charged with implementing the decisions and actually doing the dirty work are soldiers, people, husbands, lovers – powerful stuff. The lyrics are that of isolation in a relationship; being stuck in different rooms, where different dreams and only disappointment and bad communication abound.

'Down' is a three-and-a-bit minute blaster of the punk/relationship stable, with a theme of longing; the rain is flowing outside but the boy wants the girl to stay. Rumours abounded that it was about an ex-girlfriend of Tom's, but it's undeniably one of blink-182's excellently-observed relationship songs that had got ever-more sophisticated during their career, a theme which reaches a high point here. 'The Fallen Interlude', meanwhile, begins with an effects-laden dubby couple of minutes during which the band are able to play with ideas and minor-chord ambience. A Travis collaboration with Jack Gonzalez, his exemplary hip hop beat here is served well by the arrangement; swirls and sweeps run in and out and around the single plucked harp chord. There's a sense of inevitability and desolation to the repeated, mantra-like lyric that is incredibly powerful. 'Go' sees the band back on more familiar territory with a stock, catchy blink-182 punkerama, then 'Asthenia' borrows some spacey imagery with heart-pulling lyrics about loneliness. The title is a term coined by NASA and relates to a breakdown in space. The track is on the face of it about an astronaut waiting to return to earth but also wondering whether it will actually make a blind bit of difference on what he perceives as being a negative, bruised planet. But when he sings of the room's boredom with rehearsals and being sick with boundaries, it's easy to read into it a frustration with the band's own status in the media as fun-guy custard-pie naked punks. He even says his memories are delusional and useless – there are lines about wanting to go back but being unsure as to the wisdom thereof. Is this a comment on the band too? Certainly the LP had been the culmination of a few years during which several seismic events had taken place both within music and in the wider world. Hidden a little within a catchy pop-punk number is a thread that says much about the state of the creative minds within blink-182. Half the fun of music is in speculation, but needless to say it's about hope, or the absence of it.

'Always' begins with a riff reminiscent of The Only Ones' 'Another Girl, Another Planet' and soon becomes layered in multiple synths, making it both the thickest-textured blink track of all-time but also nodding heavily to a more '80s kind of pop approach. 'Easy Target' harks back very strongly to the sound and feel of much of *Box Car Racer*, a minor-key tale based on one of the band's roadies' first crushes back in So-Cal. As the story goes, said future member of the blink crew is enticed to girl's house; off he duly runs to get there as fast as possible; when he does the object of his affections jumps out from behind a bush and sprays the hell out of him with a water gun. The riff is slowed a little, re-arranged somewhat and re-contexted. What's notable about the next track, 'All Of This', aside from the spacious arrangement, is that it actually features one of Mark Hoppus' greatest influences, Robert Smith of The Cure.

"Robert Smith was sent the track and he did it wherever he was in the world at that time rather than in the studio with blink," remembers Sam Boukas. "The Cure is more of an influence on Mark and in fact during that session he went out of his way to purchase a six-string bass because it was the same bass that they used on *Push*. Mark finally got this Fender six-string bass, he'd found a broker and told him to find him one and the price wasn't that important – I remember him playing that riff on the bass. He was a big Cure fan." The Cure's frontman himself was happy to be asked to contribute to the album, although initially he was a little bemused as to how he might fit into the blink-182 sound. "I'd heard a couple of singles," he told *Blender*, "but I couldn't really see how I could sing on anything or write any words. But the demos for the album that eventually came out were fantastic. I think they suffer in a way that we [The Cure] suffered in that people weren't allowing them to become something else. If another band put that new CD out as their first album, people would go crazy."[132] High praise indeed, and a more than valid point. "We said, 'Wouldn't it be awesome if we could get Robert Smith from The Cure to play on this song? Let's try!'" Hoppus later told *Rolling Stone*. "So we called him. Talking on the phone to him was an amazing experience, like a dream come true."[133]

As the album winds up toward the end, 'Here's Your Letter' talks of needing more time to get a problem fixed – another track about isolation, feeling dislocated, loneliness and despite the upbeat musical framing it's another powerfully introspective moment. It all comes to a close with 'I'm Lost Without You', which is the longest track that the band ever recorded. In many ways, the song takes the theme of 'I Miss You' both musically and in terms of subject matter. It's a very downbeat note on which to end an album, albeit that it is also a track that's full of love. Again, there are sounds and techniques at play here in the arrangement that are of a distinctly '80s bent as the song undulates and builds round a mid-paced and somewhat wistful feel. The piano returns for a quiet middle-eight before the repeated lyrics talk about being scared to be alone. The album as a narrative ends here but various international, tour and updated editions include a couple of bonus tracks. The UK edition, for example, tacks on 'Not Now' which certainly could have been an album track and there are unclear reasons why it was initially left off the track list. 'Not Now' is all about fading away, dying, but not being able to communicate this to your girlfriend. You can't even say goodbye because she doesn't know you're there at all. It's about life, death, God and love. Heavy stuff. Musically, jangly guitars and tom-heavy drums from Travis introduce a Descendents-y riff which is interspersed with church organ verses. The UK edition then features a live version of 'Anthem Part Two' complete with intro dedicating it to a guy in school who endured the embarrassment of an erection whilst wearing jogging pants. Perhaps it's intended to give the fans a little light relief after the heavy themes of the rest of the record. The lengthy recording sessions and, surprisingly, the move out of the lavish house, had been vital in the creative process, as Travis explained.

"I think the second half of the record being written in LA was key," he told Bobby Gorman. "[In] San Diego, there's not much going on. It's very beautiful and rich and everything I don't want to see when I'm writing a record, not a punk rock record or any kind of record. Being in Los Angeles, the heart of fucking street bombs to drug dealers to pimps to fucking gang bangers, that gives you inspiration. Like me sitting in fucking San Diego seeing rich people drive their nice cars and go to their nice houses doesn't do shit for me."[134] Nonetheless, the unique gestation of the project had been directly responsible for *blink-182*'s sophisticated sound and material; it was, according to the drummer, an album rather than a collection of short, sharp, shock potential singles. After *Take Off Your Pants And Jacket* had, essentially, given the public what they wanted and expected from blink-182, it was time to take back creative control for themselves.

"We would take some time off, like a couple months [to record previous albums]," he explained. "We'd get together to do the record. We'd write the whole thing in two weeks and then we would record my drums in a day and we would record guitars, bass and vocals over the next month. This record, we recorded over a year. We wrote a song and then recorded it, took as much time as we wanted. We've never wanted to spend that much time on a record in our whole lives. But it was just like we felt like a band again, man! When you go in and you do things and you don't care what people expect from you or what you've done in the past, I think you do great things. I think so many people live their lives, whether at work or in their relationships, doing what either their partner, their girlfriend or their employees expect from them instead of what they really want to do or how they feel at that time."[135]

Listening habits had also moved on a little, Travis explaining that every member of the band had expanded their horizons considerably. "Up until last year," laughed the sticksman, "Tom didn't listen to anything but punk rock. He didn't know Pink Floyd. He didn't know who the fucking Who was! The Who's one of the greatest punk rock bands of all-time."[136] The fact that the band's deal with MCA had ended and that they had a new label in Geffen only added to the sense of a new beginning.

"blink-182's protracted adolescence has finally ended," wrote an impressed *Rolling Stone*. "There is nary a goofy moment on the San Diego punk-pop band's fifth album, which is more experimental and harder-hitting than anything else it has done."[137] Meanwhile, in the UK, *Kerrang!* was bang on board with matters, reflecting that the group's efforts in growing and developing their sound were unexpected but welcome. Going on to praise Travis' outstanding drumming, the reviewer also expressed the thought that it was difficult to believe that this was the same band who recorded 'All The Small Things' a mere 'blink' of an eye previously. The writer was unsure as to whether their fan-base was ready to join the Tom, Mark and Travis show on their new adventure but concluded by offering that "this foray into a new world of enthusiastic experimentation feels something close to a genuine triumph."[138] *Blender* reflected that the band sounded angrier than they ever had before, having replaced Bart Simpson-esque posturing with a more focused fury. "Obsessive attention to detail and smell-my-finger goofiness have been jettisoned," the review ran, "giving way to charged, chewed-off refrains … blink have been twenty-somethings struggling to keep their childhoods from slipping away – when all else fails, they've found the fountain of youth between their legs, railing off dick jokes. Here they stay wistful, but their smiles have turned to glares."[139] The coverage was similar across the board. "Any of the (female) teeny-bopper pop-punk fans that make *BLINK ME* T-shirts when they go to concerts probably won't like this one,"[140] mused IGN.com, whereas *Entertainment Weekly* declared that, "Despite their newfound earnestness, [blink] seem incapable of pretension."[141] In a nod to the outstanding production on show, *Spin* advised a thoughtful approach to listening to "a dark, emotionally intense record, best experienced on headphones."[142] Satirical website *The Onion* reviewed it as part of its straighter section of the site, and was on the whole pretty impressed. "The disc does meander in spots, and its most achingly sincere love songs become cloying," it mused. "But it's easy to both enjoy and appreciate blink-182's effort and evolution, especially when hooky pleasures continue to function as its primary stock in trade."[143] It wasn't all one-way traffic. *Mojo*, a magazine aimed primarily at an older market, was never really going to get the idea anyway but nonetheless felt it necessary to add its opinion that, "The heart of the album sticks closely to their well-tried formula: sing-song melodies and puerile lyrics set against a steady backdrop of numbingly bland riffage."[144] *Q* were more succinct, their review pretty much boiling down to saying that, "the majority of material ... is forgettable."[145]

The album hopped up to Number 3 in the *Billboard* charts on its November release and hit the top in several countries worldwide, including Canada. It was never going to sell at the pace of *Take Off Your Pants And Jacket* but it still shifted 313,000 in its first week, as opposed to 350,000 for the previous effort. The artwork featured a new logo, too: a smiley face with five arrows to the left of it.[146] It'd been inspired, Travis noted, by pop art during a session at his company, Famous Stars And Straps. "Me and my two designers at Famous came up with the idea," he told Bobby Gorman. "We basically just wanted an icon. I hated all the last blink ones. We didn't really have anything that our band stood for. There was never a symbol, you know what I mean? With Famous I made up the badge of honour, the *F* that you see everywhere. It's like with Chevy. You don't need to see the word *Chevy*, you know the Chevy symbol and it's branded in your head. And that's what I wanted. I wanted to brand an icon. It just had to be a cool kind of happy face but I wanted arrows. The Jam were my favourite band, they always had arrows in their logos and stuff. It was just kind of inspired by pop-art."[147] It has not gone unnoticed that the logo pays tribute to other bands' graphics: Nirvana, Social Distortion and the Weirdos have all sported or incorporated similarly inspired pieces of art over the years.[148] Punk as a concept and a genre is by nature ever-morphing, and *blink-182* is a fine example of a band freeing itself from self-created musical or genre ghettos.

Album duly released, statement duly made, November saw another set of dates that would set blink-182 further aside from their peers whilst also re-affirming their punk credentials. And it is a punk album, in a real sense: playing with expectations and being creative, exploring new boundaries and confounding preconceptions; preconceptions of media, of fans, even of their own. To tour it with a series of gigs in soulless enormo-domes somehow didn't sit right, and so the idea came up to go play small-sized venues, divested of the accoutrements of fame, explosions, flying drummers and just rock the fuck out with their people. A tour was set up with support from The Kinison and, intriguingly, rapper Bubba Sparxxx. It was in stark contrast to the recent dates, which had included an appearance at the Reading/Leeds Festivals in front of tens of thousands of ecstatic punters and that trip over to Bahrain to entertain troops stationed out there. Travis Barker's dad had served in Vietnam and Tom's brother was a member of the forces so it was particularly close to their hearts that the band contributed to morale.

"We didn't get paid," explained Travis. "We didn't go for press for it. We didn't stay in hotels. We stayed with the troops. It was cool to go on a plane that was for our soldiers. They didn't think anyone would come play for them. There were grown men and women crying. It felt weird too. When we went to Kuwait, the living conditions ... you can't take showers and it's over a hundred degrees. You could just tell their spirits are really low. And we talked to people who have been scarred mentally. Part of it was rad and part was depressing. I really support our troops no matter what, I'm not sure they should still be there. I feel we started problems. Working their ass off under weird conditions."[149]

The *DollaBill* Tour was organised round a series of clubs – including SOMA in San Diego – that had been good to the band. Initially, the intention was to make tickets free (blink absorbing all costs) but in practical terms actually charging for tickets meant that numbers could be controlled rather than having a mad rush for the few spaces available in the venues. Travis was stoked about having Sparxxx on board as he was one of the drummer's favourite acts, whilst Tom DeLonge mused on the touring line-up as a whole. "We love punk rock, we love hip hop, we love drum 'n' bass music,"[150] he said. "People gotta grow. They gotta open their minds and listen. I really like Bubba. You can't discount him just because he's a white rapper. He's not talking about bitches or cars. I'm not really into rap. Listen instrumentally, there are some amazing things going on. I think Timbaland did a great job producing that album."[151] The smaller stages enabled the band to reconnect with their fan-base more directly, as Travis Barker had told interviewer Ben Myers in 2001.

"It's ridiculous," the drummer mused. "Not just punk bands, but any band. Two years ago we were playing to four hundred people. It's super-cool. Playing those little intimate shows are great – I'd rather play to a thousand people a night for ten nights than an arena show [where] we're so far away from our fans it's hard to feel the energy, but I think we pull it off a lot of the time. We've done shows where the crowd stretches [so] far and it's very weird – all of them there to see a stupid punk rock band." Or, in this case, a rapidly-maturing rock outfit with roots in punk. "This record is kind of like a rebirth of blink and we feel like a band again; we wanted to go back to playing small venues again and we wanted to do something cool so our fans would come watch us play,"[152] he also said. Mark Hoppus took up the theme. "We've been lucky with our band and our fans have really supported us," he smiled. "So it seemed like a fun thing to go out and play shows for a dollar. We're really stoked because all of the venues on the tour let us use the rooms for free for the night."[153] Travis had a more inventive comparison for the whole idea of bringing The Kinison and Bubba Sparxxx on tour. "When you go to a museum or you go to a place where art is, you see different styles of art," the drummer began. "You don't see the same artist over and over again or you don't see a bunch of people who look like Picasso. Or you don't see a bunch of Andy Warhol stuff and then imitators. You see such a broad spectrum of paintings and styles and that's what touring should be. That's how I think. I think you should be able to go to a show and you should learn. Like you should see the coolest indie rock, punk rock band like The Kinison and then see like the coolest white rapper in the world, like Bubba Sparxxx and then blink-182. You know what I mean? And it's for a dollar. I think it's just opening kids' ears and eyes to other styles."[154]

The Kinison were so impressive to Travis that he made them one of the first bands to come out on LaSalle Records, which was the label the ever-moving drummer officially set up in 2004. Typically, LaSalle was named after Barker's beloved Cadillac, being a budget model released by that car manufacturer for a mass audience. Travis' eclectic musical tastes meant that LaSalle was never going to be confined to merely punk bands; he's expressed his wish to find hip hop, country & western, any kind of music as long as, of course, it was *good* music. It was all a manifestation of a burning energy that forbade his standing still, even for a second.

"I thrive off being busy, that's my thing," he explained to Bobby Gorman. Now, I spend most of my time that I have that's free with my son. I have my record label I'm launching; The Kinison record comes out in March. I have my clothing company. I design usually at night or once a week I'll get together with the rest of the designers there [at Famous Stars And Straps]. And I have good people who run that for me. Designing shoes is painless for me. It's the best thing in the world, it's awesome. Another way of expressing myself. Then the bands I play in, I love and I never think of it as work, I always think of it as playing. In my free time I box, I love boxing. I just like to stay busy, I like to be constantly learning something or improving; it makes me feel better."[155]

2003 came to an end with the release of 'Feeling This', which featured a typically blinkish video that started with the boys playing in a cage outside a correctional establishment; the kids rebel, take over the prison, the girls storm out of school and the kids fire out to watch the band. By the end the ladies in question, who are all of course over eighteen, have stripped down to their white bras and panties. *Plus ça change, plus c'est la même chose.*[156]

Chapter 21
2004

The New Year began with news that Travis and Shanna were getting engaged, with plans to marry later in the year. It was to be twelve months heavy on the air-miles as the group set up a huge amount of dates in support of their new album, commencing in the United Kingdom where by now they were starting to turn a few heads with a more thoughtful approach that was also something of a catharsis. The band were into *everything* now, and felt that the doors of creativity were open wide. This new approach was well-received – the Wembley Arena show was a particular highlight as the old and new blink rubbed together nicely. Then it was time to head back out to Australia, one of the group's ever-supportive markets. Lady luck was hardly on the band's side, however, and after an accident following the Melbourne show, Travis broke his foot. Being the dogged and highly-skilled performer that he is, he managed to somehow soldier on through the next night's gig in Adelaide by using his left foot on the kick drum and playing his kit in reverse. Astonishingly skilful and a bit like cleaning your teeth by holding the brush with your toes, but necessarily the remaining three shows of the tour plus the Japanese leg and the Hawaiian portion of the dates were postponed. There was consolation on the other side of the world when tours were announced first with rap-meisters Cypress Hill that April and then pop-ska-punks No Doubt as touring partners throughout June. A new single was also out, 'I Miss You'. The video, which references the film *A Nightmare Before Christmas*, has the band playing in a haunted mansion. It sold well, peaking at Number 8 in the UK Charts and in America topping *Billboard* Modern Rock Tracks, although only hitting 42 in the Hot 100. It showed a much more considered and vulnerable side to blink which brought them more on par with the likes of Green Day's output. There comes a time in every band's life that they are able to pull off a ballad and stay credible; 'I Miss You' wasn't the first introspective song they'd ever released, but it was perhaps the one that resonated the deepest.

Outside of the band, Travis busied himself with the release of The

Kinison's debut album for LaSalle Records, *What Are You Listening To?*, which attained a few decent reviews, including *Music OMH,* who thought it had "a listenable consistency, though the album's stand-out tracks are scarce ... hopefully their non-stop touring ethic will prove as useful to The Kinison as it did for such bands as At The Drive-In."[157] The reviewer also noted that the group had been given rather an excellent leg-up by having been taken out on the European dates of blink-182's tour.[158] Further into the left-field, Barker also embarked on a new venture in April, buying into the Wahoo's Fish Taco franchise with a restaurant at Norco, California. The surf-themed eaterie had branches all over So-Cal and parts of Colorado, and the Norco site's opening featured Mark and Travis greeting guests, as well as professional skating (from the likes of Eric Koston and Andrew Reynolds) and motocross demonstrations. Proceeds from the opening went to a Cystic Fibrosis charity. With all this going on, it was remarkable that he had any time for music but there was the small matter of a new Transplants record to be getting on with.

In contrast to the several years of sketching out ideas, playing with sounds and almost organically constructing the Transparents' well-received self-titled debut, the band members' respective schedules had become so incredibly full that a new approach was essential. Tim Armstrong had been working on a number of ideas along with a solo record for Skinhead Rob. Writing was patchy at this stage, and continued to be so off and on throughout the summer of 2004 on any days off from the Cypress Hill and No Doubt tours – not that there were many in blink-182's exhausting gig schedule. The band released the single, 'Down' in May, complete with a video that featured several actors who had formerly been members of gangs. Some of these actors were signed to Suspect Entertainment, an organisation founded by one Manuel G. Jimenez in order to try and provide a legal, cool and decent living for such guys. The video itself centres round a house party performance by the band whilst the attendees bump, grind and dance to the great chagrin of the cops (the main policeman is brilliantly played by actor Terry Crews), who look for then chase one particular guy (called Trouble) on foot, in cars, helicopters and the rest. He gets away. The single again made decent progress, briefly bothering the Top 10 but only peaking at 24 in the UK charts. The tour dates with No Doubt were as successful as anybody could have hoped, the bands meshing in together incredibly well.

"With childlike abandon," went one review, "the trio ... offered snippets of playfulness and lyricism that's helping to change the definition of their sound. While founded in the school of nu-punk, the boys seem to be trying to stretch out. The band is still in-your-face, fuck the critics, let's party 'til we drop, SoCal punk rock cool while at the same time trying to find new maturity in their music."[159] Another reviewer was impressed by a show on June 23, 2004. "No Doubt and blink-182 were fully energized for Wednesday's sold-out show at Phoenix's Cricket Pavilion," they wrote, "turning the summer shed into a giant, pogo-hopping free-for-all."[160] The reviewer went on to note that Mark and Tom's stage banter was much more subdued and divested of the more juvenile humour that had marked the band's past appearances, and the article also contained a quote from Mark Hoppus who during 'Stay Together For The Kids' commented that whilst once they would have asked their audience to hold up lighters for the duration of the song, now everyone should hold up their mobile phones instead. As with the whole tour, and with Travis now fully-recovered, it was a great gig. The band then returned to Australia and Japan for those rescheduled dates before going their separate ways for what was ostensibly billed as 'time off' throughout September and October. Their former drummer, Scott Raynor, was busy too, fulfilling a long-held ambition to work with Nirvana producer Jack Endino, as latest project The Spazms revved up for a recording session.

"I love that band [Nirvana]," Raynor says. "It was always a dream of mine to record with Jack Endino. I am a huge fan of a lot of his work both as a songwriter/guitar player and producer. Joining up with [The Spazms] was the closest thing to fate I have ever experienced. I saw lead singer Majenta's band, the Apocalypstics, in San Diego and right away wanted to jump in the van and go on tour with them. Maybe a year or so later all of a sudden [I] got the urge to move to Seattle. The next morning I threw my drums in my truck and moved up there. The day after I arrived, I saw an ad in the local weekly that former members of the Apocalypstics were looking for a drummer. I went to the audition and Majenta was the singer. I played so hard I almost puked. They let me join. Some of them were friends with Jack so when it came [to be] time to record we asked him to produce." Endino remembers the sessions well, and is very complimentary about The Spazms' ultra-credible punk rock.

"I remember that the EP actually was pretty much a stormer," he told the author. "They raged. I think I saw them live maybe twice too. Singer was this remarkable chick named Majenta who is a huge girl with fluorescent pink hair and her entire body covered with tattoos ... she actually owns a tattoo shop ... but she had a killer voice much like Mia Zapata of The Gits, really good. Nothing much happened with them though, it seemed they fizzled out and I never heard why."

"I am really happy with that record," philosophises Raynor. "It's well rehearsed and with Jack's expertise in the studio, the songs turned out as close to perfect as can be. It was a one-day affair so a lot of the tracks are first takes. Jack liked that. I asked him to set me up with a metronome and he basically told me off. The language of the whole record really speaks for me. It's deskilled, nihilistic, and posits, by default not intention, a Franco-feminism."[161] Quite some feat, that, but shows an inherent and very typical thoughtfulness behind the (quite brilliant) brashness – two qualities that blink-182 members past and present certainly share. Seek The Spazms out: it's well worth it.

By this stage, Tom DeLonge had developed real ambition outside music not to mention a huge social awareness. 2004 happened to be the year that America was to find itself a new president, and there were two main candidates. Sitting Republican president George W. Bush was running against Democrat John Kerry, whose camp DeLonge was firmly in as the musician became involved with an organisation called Punkvote.com. DeLonge was very outspoken in his support for Kerry and spent time in the campaign headquarters. "As I started making money," he told *Blender*, "I started paying attention to who was in power and how they got there, which got me obsessed about politics. Long before he ran for the presidency, I had a collage of John Kerry on the wall of our studio."[162] Along with musicians such as Serj Tankian of System Of A Down, John Mellencamp, Alicia Keys, Adam Horowitz, Chuck D and others, he laid out his reasons for supporting Kerry in an issue of *Rolling Stone*. DeLonge was very critical of Bush's reasons for going to war, noting that the president's pre-administration career had hardly been sparkling whilst John Kerry would be a respected figurehead who was understanding of other cultures. "Bush is like someone's old dad who just doesn't get it," roared DeLonge. "A person who's not able to grow or change. Among musicians, no one is backing Bush. Except for Ted Nugent, the guy who wears loincloths."[163] He also said, "I'm a big supporter of change. If people aren't into change, it's a question of whether they can read. That's what I think."[164] Forceful words, spoken at the Teen Choice Awards, at which blink-182 picked up a gong for 'Choice Love Song', for 'I Miss You', and 'Choice

Tour' for their dates with No Doubt.

Politics and punk rock have always mixed, of course, with the UK version of the movement being firmly based in non-denominational left-wing righteous anger and, subsequently, over in the US, the likes of the Dead Kennedys' Jello Biafra even running for governor of California. DeLonge's forays into lending his voice to the campaign for change was based in personal politics but also an awareness that as a nationally and internationally famous figure he had the power to get a message through to millions of young voters. The election was close; Bush won in a cloud of confusion. The final total – after hundreds of millions of votes cast – was 50.73% compared to Kerry's 48.27%. On such margins empires truly rest. DeLonge's optimism, along with nearly half his country's, took a huge hit. For them, the latter days of 2004 felt like a hangover, a missed opportunity, a disappointment. Tom's passion for helping drive change had been somewhat consuming, as he was later to acknowledge.

"There was a while when I actually thought I was going to be doing stuff in politics," he admitted. "If Kerry would have won, I was pitching all these different initiatives to his administration, y'know? There was a good chance I would have bought a place in D.C. and been more involved than I probably would like to admit."[165] He also said, "Kerry knows why he didn't win. It was because he truly believed he should win being the better candidate, not by playing dirty – and the Republicans play as dirty as they can."[166] Elsewhere he said, "Being that close to someone you really, truly believe is going to change the world is electrifying ... you really feel for once that anything is possible."[167] And so there was a hint of hope amidst the gloom, nonetheless.

With the band finishing some European dates, the year was rounded off by the release of the fourth single from *blink-182*, the '80s-tinged 'Always'. Because of the fact that it features one whole load of synths, it had only ever been performed twice in the live arena, making it perhaps a surprise choice for many. The inventive horizontal split-screen video also features the extremely attractive Australian singer, Sophie Monk. Essentially, each member of blink acts out the part of the guy who's trying to apologise/fix a fracturing relationship. The fights, the arguments and the occasional making-up/making-out (handled here by Travis) are all part of the end of a relationship. The guy in the suit is all the members of blink-182 collectively and individually but tellingly they're not ever in the room together as a band. It's a very, very clever video that shows the dislocation and problems in harnessing several parts of the same personality (the band) whilst keeping it together enough to function properly in a relationship. There's a massive underlying tension at play here in the song that director Joseph Kahn (who had previously worked with Nelly and Eminem) perfectly delivers with his excellent video. It was a hit on many music channels but didn't really trouble the charts too much. DeLonge himself had dipped his toes into the fast-paced white-water raft of video directing, being at the helm for Taking Back Sunday's promo movie, 'This Photograph Is Proof'. He put his heart and soul into the two-day shoot, and although the band said that they didn't really know what the concept behind it was, it was certainly cool.

Travis Barker was also to return to the small screen, having invited the MTV cameras into he and new wife Shanna's[168] home for a reality series called *Meet The Barkers*, which detailed the ups and downs of being a rock star and Playmate respectively and trying to make life work with kids, bands, interviews and the attendant pressures of it all. The series was scheduled to air during 2005. Barker had clearly forgiven the channel for his appearance on the notorious prank show, *Punk'd*, in 2003. That previous storyboard went a little like this: Travis and Shanna go out for dinner, an ex-boyfriend of Shanna's shows up and starts bigging up how great he was as a boyfriend, Travis gets more and more wound up and looks like he's going to finally flip before the film crew come in and reveal it's all a set-up.

"There's never ever another guy. So it was way out, it was way out all the shit she was saying. She kept laughing, you know? You don't see this in *Punk'd* because they edit it. And I'm drunk basically. And the lighting is really, really lit up and there's weird people that look like actors in the restaurant with me. You know what I mean? I'm kind of putting two and two together but then I was just like contemplating, 'Should I hit this motherfucker or should I just be the bigger man and let this go?' Like what should I do?"

Ashton Kutcher, the *Punk'd* host, did show up and Travis says he almost hit him too, but in the end the drummer had no option but to see the hilarious side and laugh along at himself. He had mixed feelings about it, finding himself still wanting to deck the guy for ruining his date whilst also wanting to laugh his head off to acknowledge having been suckered quite so spectacularly. It was also Travis' birthday and after the *Punk'd* incident, Shanna had something quite spectacular lined up as a present. "We went and she had a huge party for me in Los

Angeles with all my friends and there were belly dancers, it was amazing. But I think *Punk'd* is rad. It's real, like you get people's honest reactions. Which I think is rad because with a show like that you can see how people really are."[169]

"My old lady watches that stuff," he continued. "I watched *The Family* when that was on and that was rad. I would like to go to the *Newlyweds* with Jessica and Nick and knock out Nick Lachey. He's such a pig to his lady. As much as I've been with lots of girls, you know he just makes me angry."[170]

Travis then duly decided to show how it should be done with *Meet The Barkers*. During filming, Travis had been working with Tim Armstrong, Rob Aston and Dave Carlock once more on new material for a planned second album by the Transplants. "Travis had a label, Tim had a label," explains Dave Carlock, the technical wizard and keyboardist for the band. "The first Transplants album could be on one label and the second on the other guy's. It was all cordially worked out as a concept. It was one of those things we'd had in mind since the 8.30am sessions and the fact the first album did so well was really surprising. It seemed more like a project, an exercise to see what could happen, and it ended up doing great. The second record took on a whole different approach as it was now a group [that] toured and had a concept and Tim and I wanted to step up the sonic quality from the first one so we wanted to bring everything up a notch on the second record. Tim was always working on ideas." Barker joined up with the guys briefly in August, to bang out demos at Conway Studios in LA. It was soon evident that there was plenty of material ready to be knocked into shape – but also that it would take rather a lot of knocking. Barker's drum tracks, of course, were as near as finished in a very short time.

"During the Fall, specifically October 2004," continues Carlock, "Tim and I took all the tracks he had for the Transplants' second record at that point – about thirty – to an undisclosed mountain hideaway where he had a little place he could go to when he wanted to create away from Los Angeles. We were there for two to three weeks with ideas, banging out tracking, editing, trying out ideas in this little cabin he had out there. We were bringing in wood for the stove as we got snow up there because of the altitude, and we banged out as much as we could, then sat on it for a while before saying we'd be picking it up again in January." With talk of getting the Transplants onto the 2005 *Warped* tour line-up, it looked like it was going to be one hell of a year.

Chapter 22
Implosion

On February 18, 2005, ostensibly during the band's time off, blink-182 were scheduled to appear at the *Music For Relief: Rebuilding South Asia* benefit concert in Arrowhead Pond, Anaheim Park, California. The charity gig was to raise money for victims of the devastating December 2004 undersea earthquake and tsunami and featured the likes of Linkin Park, Jay-Z, No Doubt, Ozzy Osbourne and Jurassic 5. Ozzy Osbourne had pulled out with sincere apologies due to "a family emergency" but the big shock of the moment was unfolding when blink-182 announced they would also be withdrawing. More seriously, reports began swirling that this was a potentially terminal situation. Dave Navarro of the group Jane's Addiction (and, of course, Camp Freddy) fuelled the fierce internet crucible of rumours by posting on his blog that blink-182 had apparently split up.

"The big shock came when blink-182 pulled out. Evidently they broke up yesterday. I know how it can get when it's just not working anymore. Anyway, best of luck to those guys."[171] As it turned out, Navarro later posted a retraction; but, of course, essentially his words were prophetic. An official blink statement was released on February 22 that emphasised that the band had not broken up, but would be on what they called an 'indefinite hiatus' for the foreseeable future.

"For over a decade," read the official statement, "blink-182 has toured, recorded and promoted non-stop all while trying to balance relationships with family and friends. To that end, the band has decided to go on an indefinite hiatus to spend some time enjoying the fruits of their labours with loved ones. While there is no set plan for the band to begin working together again, no one knows what tomorrow may bring."[172] The next day actually brought more clarification. Whilst Tom and Mark remained tight-lipped about matters, Travis was moved to phone the ever-supportive LA radio station K-ROQ to explain what was actually going on.

"I love those dudes; they're my brothers. I wanted to clear up the rumours of us fighting with each other or hating each other. It's just not true. Right now, everyone's life is calling for something else …

there was so much going on in the band at that time [that it wasn't] healthy time for us to be playing shows. We needed that hiatus to start right away. We wish things could have been different."[173] He went on to claim that the break was designed to allow people to explore their own creative endeavours, and that once these separate projects and other interests might allow it, the band could regroup and return as a coherent unit.

Observers suggested that had the group collectively wanted two years off, contracts permitting, they would surely have been able to. And with clothing companies, restaurants, families and other bands on his plate, Travis certainly was living proof that a full and varied life was possible without necessarily cracking under the strain. Hoppus was interested in producing records and DeLonge in directing videos, two occupations that could conceivably be slotted into their schedules alongside blink. There was surely more to it than met the eye?

For now, there was nothing more forthcoming from the blink camp. Release-wise blink-182 appeared on Atticus' third *Dragging The Lake* compilation release with 'Not Now', something of an ironic title but not anywhere near as ironic as the tracks they'd contributed to 2003's *Dragging The Lake Volume Two* ('Don't Tell Me It's Over') or 2002's *Dragging The Lake, Volume One* ('Time To Break Up'). If Dan Brown was writing this book, there'd be a quality conspiracy theory in those three titles alone.

"I'm not surprised to see any band want time away from each other," old mate Denny Jegard of Ten Foot Pole told the author. "As a band is like a multi-partner marriage, except that before you get married you usually date for a while and have criteria used to judge potential partners. In a band, you typically come together based on random factors, such as your brother knows a guitar player, or there's a guy with a van who also has a drum set, so you start playing music together with little thought about how your philosophies, hygienic styles etc could affect your ability to work together for decades." Joe Escalante of Kung Fu Records and The Vandals, both of which were vital in helping the San Diego trio back in the early days, wasn't overly astonished to hear about the indefinite hiatus. "I wasn't sure how long it was gonna last when they became superstars," he says. "Because when punk rockers become superstars they've gotta deal with so much of, 'Why did we start this band, is it becoming mundane, I'm not sure what we got into this for?' I've never had to face that problem [myself but I can imagine] what they went through. It can't be easy."

"I was around Travis' studio right when the blink break-up happened which I thought was crazy," says Dave Carlock. "Because those guys together were such a great team. The most fun I had making a record [2003's *blink-182*] was with [them] – those guys are hilarious. There weren't even all that many dick jokes – they were just bloody funny in general and would crack each other up. Tom and Mark are very smart, that whole bathroom humour they did was sort of aiming for an audience but all of those guys are really smart and their sense of humour is too, at least in private. Their sense of humour had me laughing constantly. They'd crack each other up – we had such a good time making that record and when they broke up I thought it was such a shame because the chemistry between those good friends was just *so* good, so creative and certainly if there were any stresses during the making of that record I didn't see them." Evidently they were there; a year on the road is a real test, particularly if you have a young family as all the members of the band did by 2005. And despite the fact that they were able to afford a luxury tour bus each and therefore bring their families out with them, the constant feeling of having to be somewhere else meant that chilling out properly just hadn't been an option. Blink-182 was paused. There were other things to be getting on with in life.

Chilling out, of course, is not a phrase that you hear Travis Barker use very often in his professional life, and with blink on the back burner (or completely finished, depending on what your viewpoint was) it was time to turn his attention once more to the Transplants, whose debut album had been so excellently-received what seemed like a lifetime ago.

"Rob wanted to do some vocals in a big studio to raise the levels a little bit and raise the bar so we went into AmeRaycan Studios, that used to be owned by Ray Parker Jnr, it's the house that Ghostbusters built! We did vocals there as they did lots of hip hop and his energy resonated from there. We were really pushing to finish because they really wanted to go out on the *Warped* tour that year. Tim was tentative and there were some strains in the band around that time, trying to figure out where to parcel up their time and everything else."

With deadlines looming, the album was completed in Carlock's own studio. Mixing was another matter: after the surprising success of the band's first release, there was a drive to step up a few gears and to that end a superstar mix engineer was engaged: Neal H. Pogue, who had enjoyed huge success with his work on Outkast's massive hit, 'Hey Ya'.

"We had a music factory going on to finish the record," remembers Carlock. "I was cranking it out daily on a tight schedule and we were really behind as we needed the record to get turned in by March. It was stressful, we were like two months behind and we just needed to get the record finished. Neal was booked to mix at a certain date for big money and we didn't have that pressure before because we could finish the first record at Tim's studio. I was just, every day, cranking as fast as I could, getting ideas ready for Tim to come over and he would come over, stay over, write lyrics, we'd do vocal tracks at nine in the morning just pushing and pushing so songs could be completed and turned over to Neal. At one point Neal was working faster than we were so we had to say, 'Hey I think you need to take your wife out for a date this weekend man, I think she misses you, she deserves dinner and a movie, why don't you guys go to the coast?!' So me and Tim would work really hard just to get it turned over and finished." Eventually, they did. The new album was called *Haunted Cities*.

"It's not punk rock," explained Travis to writer Bart Niedzialkowski. "It's hip hop and punk rock. That's what the Transplants are doing and that's what I was trying to get across when I went into the P-Diddy thingy. Or that's what I get across when I do a Black Eyed Peas album. We are crossing boundaries. We are crossing lines that shouldn't be crossed, but we need to cross because it's so lame for kids to grow Mohawks or wear a leather jacket and safety pins and pierce your face and say, 'This is cool and nothing else is cool' and once everyone likes it, it's not cool anymore. You can't live your life like that. That's weird, ya know. Some kids get it and some kids don't. Everyone has their own preference. I don't like certain bands, you can't do anything for me to make me change my mind about that. There are some bands that I just don't like. I'm not a huge Good Charlotte fan. There is nothing you can do to change my mind and I understand that. If kids don't like the Transplants or they say, 'Fuck the Transplants. I don't like Rancid', I can't change their minds. [Some] kids are not liking the bands for the wrong reasons, because we talk about drugs or girls or money. Those are real things. The world revolves around that shit, whether we like it or not. The Transplants talked about it. We get a lot of heat from that. 'I got the most money, the most girls, the best cars', like Rob said: fuck that. We're doing it and it's real, it's not fantasy. My girlfriend listens to hip hop and R&B. She loves the Transplants. She loves the Clash and she loves the Transplants. That says something. My dad likes the

Transplants. My dad likes jazz music. There is something about the Transplants that is refreshing. Anybody in this world – if you listen to hip hop, R&B, reggae – I think you could find something about the Transplants that would make you say, 'That's the shit. That moves me.'"[174]

There was more to it than just music, of course. The facts were that Rob Aston, Tim Armstrong and Travis Barker clicked on other levels too. To even countenance taking the Transplants out on a gruelling (albeit fun) tour like *Warped* meant that there was a necessary tightness to them as a unit. A chemistry, according to Barker. "[The chemistry is everywhere,] from us three talking. From me and Rob hanging out, getting in a fight at a bar, not literally a fight but it almost happens and we have gotten guns pulled on us, me and Rob, to me and Tim sitting down eating dinner talking about music. We have the best chemistry ever. You know. We have fun together. It's like when you meet a girl. You know within the first five minutes that you are going to fall in love with this girl. It's the same feeling. You know when things are right."[175]

Haunted Cities opens with 'Not Today', featuring guest vocals from Sen Dog Reyes. It announces the album in typically hard-hatted fashion, punk guitars, brambly beats and urgent vocals although sonically it's already much smoother-edged than the first release. 'Apocalypse Now' follows, a not-so-amazing track with heavily political lyrical ruminations on the current war and conflict in general as Armstrong and Skinhead Rob swap vocal duties. Next up is the outstanding 'Gangsters And Thugs', full of keyboards, samples and an insistent dubby bass line underneath ultra-catchy lyrics straight from the sharper edges of the streets about how tight an extended crew of mates can be, whether they sell records for a living or make their money by drugs. It's raw stuff and not exactly what you might call politically correct, but as Travis says, the lyrics are only talking about things that happen every day in the city's darker underbelly.

'What I Can't Describe' features Boo Ya Tribe, and is a more soulful, funkier number than some of the rest of the album, laid-back in delivery and oozing with a kind of hybrid NYC/California sun hipness that, were it not for the dark lyrics, could easily be on the soundtrack of any number of feel-good buddy movies. And just to put the cat amongst the pigeons, it's followed up by 'Doomsday' which is full of insistent jazzy shuffle as Armstrong takes a stroll through an industrialised wasteland, encountering a character who duly robs him; the song is intensely political in a wider sense and takes in government corruption and societal control along the way. It's immediately followed by another excellent track, 'Killafornia', on which B. Real guests. 'Killafornia' is another reggae-tinged piece of skilled hip hop – the title is fairly straightforward and gives an indication of the subject matter but what it can't put across is exactly how strong the main hook of the song is. If that little run of great tracks wasn't enough for the listener, the middle section of the album has another gem to offer and that is 'American Guns' which taps right into Armstrong's obsession with The Clash. It's a top class hip hop punk rock (and roll) song with another ultra-catchy chorus and channels the spirit of the likes of 'Train In Vain' musically to excellent effect. 'Madness' comes next, a song which keeps the pace up both in its gnarly lyrics and also with the guitar-heavy arrangement. This is followed up by the dark ska of 'Hit The Fence' which comes at the listener insidiously with tales of scrapping to survive, drugs, violence and all the rest of it. The album title was never more appropriate than within the confines of this slice of urban claustrophobia, for sure.

Haunted Cities starts to wind up toward its end with 'Pay Any Price', a fragmented song full of bravado and demo-fuzzy guitars that sounds basically inebriated from start to finish, with Travis showing off with some out-of-this-world rolls. 'I Want It All', meanwhile, flirts with ravey-baggy beats and scratches and brings elements of Madchester to LaSalle. It hangs together pretty well, mostly down to the brilliant bass line that nails the constituent elements to the floor. 'Crash And Burn' ends it all in style, the bossa-nova rhythm of the song having Rakaa as guest and another of Armstrong's tales of self-destructive parties. It's a track that looks again at the world situation with some despair but hopes that soon all will have its cycle and things will come back into a much better state. The Japanese version of the album has 'Red Dawn' as a bonus at the end but for the rest of us, 'Crash And Burn' ends the album niftily.

Reviews were once more positive, *Rolling Stone* particularly impressed. "[It] is less songful than its predecessor," they wrote. "Put on propulsive winners such as the flamenco-flavoured 'Crash And Burn,' [and] Armstrong's snaggle-toothed choruses make for a soulful counterpoint to his mate's swagger."[176] *Blender* also liked it although they felt it was, "more tuneful and less experimental than their debut."[177]An *All Music Guide* reviewer said that, "The whole package ends up having this strangely alluring glimmer. It's like discovering California Babylon after being lost in suburbia."[178] *The Onion* weren't entirely convinced, however, finding it a little hit and miss. "Transplants make a splattery mess of modern music as often as they stumble over something new and exciting."[179] It was a sentiment echoed by UK magazine *NME* who once again put the boot in. "As if the macho posturing wasn't bad enough, *Haunted Cities* is also a mess musically,"[180] they sniffed. Possibly the most evocative review came from *Spin*. "While Transplants' self-titled debut caught the trio at that moment when the third-beer buzz kicks in," they wrote, "the new record seems to have picked up several pints and bong hits later, when shit starts to get grisly."[181] Luckily, *Kerrang!* were a little more understanding of what it was all about, giving it three Ks out of five and calling parts of it "raucous slabs of punk rock."[182] What was undeniable was that there were no other bands around doing what Transplants did, so as far as Travis, Tim, Dave and Rob were concerned it was a good job well done. Plus they looked forward to the summer's *Warped* tour feeling that two albums were starting to look a little bit like a musical career.

The album was later given the chopping and screwing treatment by one DJ Paul Wall. To be chopped and screwed (in a musical context, anyway) is to be remixed in a specific Houston style that emerged in the 1990s. Slowing down the music to about 60 or 70 beats per minute enables DJ techniques like beat-skipping, record scratching, stop-time and FX to come into play, a very creative process that distils the musical spirit and brings it into a hip hop context. *Haunted Cities* is also available to buy in this form and the reworked 'Killafornia' in particular sounds notably good.

"*Haunted Cities Chopped & Screwed* was about Rob being really into Houston," says Dave Carlock, who knows a thing or two about sonic manipulation. "He loved all that underground hip hop and the stuff Paul Wall was doing down there. It came up that it was a good idea to bring in lots of hip hop records, they'd been chopping and screwing the scene down there and someone – Rob or Tim – suggested they should chop and screw the Transplants record and it would be the first rock record to be chopped and screwed. There was talk initially to get Paul Wall to make an appearance on a song and the label hooked them up but they were having trouble time-wise so what ended up happening was that he chopped and screwed the whole record and it was released again so it was interesting and unusual to have it re-released for a whole new genre."[183] Absolutely. For Travis Barker, also, it was an exciting development to be on the cutting edge of one of his favourite genres.

Barker wasn't finished there; he'd also taken time to first meet up with and then declare his intent to work with DJ AM, who was at the time dating Nicole (daughter of Lionel) Richie, for a project that would occasionally play clubs – innovatively, the performance would be essentially a DJ versus a drummer. The more experimental side of Travis Barker was itching to come out during mid-2005 and it was no surprise that, even whilst final preparations for the Transplants record were underway, there was welcome news that he was again collaborating with Mark Hoppus. Now *that* was interesting, for a number of reasons …

Chapter 23
What's Your Number?

Mark Allen Hoppus had been the only blink member not directly involved in Box Car Racer, but he harboured no grudge to Travis whatsoever. It was very telling that the two would also work together, without Tom, in the aftermath of the blink-182 'hiatus' statement. What it seemed to say is that there was still music to be made, even if that didn't involve DeLonge. If it were merely the case that Hoppus and Barker were pushing for a new direction, musically-speaking, surely they had already proved that their fan-base would absorb fairly experimental material, as had been the case with the 2003 *blink-182* album? And wouldn't it have been great to see them tackle something completely different as a trio? There was obviously slightly more to it than met the eye; that chestnut/euphemism of 'musical differences' was clearly not the whole story. Nonetheless, Barker and Hoppus announced in April that their new project would be called +44, a reference to the telephone dialling code for the UK. +44 at this stage also featured the vocal talents of Carole Heller, previously of the band Get The Girl, and the sessions that had started in Travis' basement were on-going during April 2005 in the window before Barker was due to head out on tour with Transplants. It was to be a much more experimental, electronica-tinged affair where drums would be electronic pads and Barker and Hoppus would both play keyboards, pianos etc. At this stage there were no more than three or four tracks in production, but the blend of hip hop breaks and decidedly '80s sonics brought together elements of the Transplants and even Hoppus' early-days Goth-ish band, The Attic Children, to form something both familiar and, hopefully, excitingly new. Hoppus, speaking in 2006, told interviewer Trevor Baker of *Rock Sound*, about the way that the initial idea to collaborate with Barker on a separate project had come about in the first place. It was, he said, connected to the last tour with blink-182. After Tom had announced he needed time off touring, "we said, 'Well, we're not going to stop playing music.' And they were like, 'Of course. We'd never expect you to stop playing music.' And Travis and I were talking in very general terms about writing songs."[184] Which they of course were always going to pursue. +44 would have to wait, however, due to Travis' *Warped* tour commitments. Summer did have time for there to be several internet rumours about the reunion of blink, one of the more plausible but obviously untrue ones being that they were lined up to play at K-ROQ's September 17 *Island Invasion* concert. In actual fact, Mark Hoppus busied himself by collaborating with the band MxPx, co-writing the track 'Wrecking Hotel Rooms' from their *Panic* LP.

Hoppus also threw himself into an excellent production job on Motion City Soundtrack's new album, *Commit This To Memory*. The project had been mooted after an Atticus employee had played Mark a previous MCS LP and Hoppus had been so taken with it that he raved about the band in *Rolling Stone*. The sessions were scheduled at a rented house that had once belonged to Jeff Porcaro, the drummer of the band Toto. It therefore sounded great, particularly for drums, and the pool in the garden helped matters along considerably, too. As a producer, Hoppus was firmly from the Jerry Finn stable of not forcing his own ideas on his charges, preferring to suggest possible ideas and allowing the group to decide ultimately which they would implement and which they would ignore. He'd learnt from the best, after all: why mess with a winning formula? Motion City Soundtrack frontman Justine Pierre was generous in his praise of Hoppus' approach to recording, which involved a lot of watching and listening.

"Mark kept telling us, 'Your name is going to be a lot bigger on the front than mine is on the back.' So he would throw suggestions out there but always say, 'Feel free to turn these down.' And we would!"[185] The results are a nicely polished album that to some listeners sounds a little like latter-day blink-182 although without the retrospective undercurrent of internecine tension to it. As summer faded and the leaves of the trees began to change from green to a golden hue, it had become more than obvious that Hoppus and Barker were both going to keep busy in music in one form or another. When Travis came back off tour, he and Mark once more set to writing tracks for +44's album, which was intended to be released in spring 2006. In the meantime, that pesky MTV show was being aired. It's an interesting and often-compelling insight into the rarefied atmosphere that's created when a superstar punk rock/hip hop/teacher drummer[186] marries a very famous former Miss USA-turned-actress. Episode One is all about the stresses and great moments associated with a house move, handled in decent spirit by Shanna Moakler due to Travis actually being out on tour at that time with his band. The second episode has Travis looking after the kids whilst his better half organises a video shoot elsewhere, then in Episode Three the drummer throws a surprise party for his delighted fiancée. Thereafter Travis and Shanna both come across as genuine people who may inhabit lovely properties and have no financial worries but who definitely do find joy in the same things as everybody else: kids, togetherness and love.

At this stage Mark and Travis were firmly of the opinion that +44 should be based round loops, samples and female vocals. The pair had added a studio to their list of real estate in order to further explore their muse (Hoppus and Delonge also moved to sell their shares in Atticus). The bassist was also keeping busy with his new podcast and blog, 'Hi! My name is Mark,' which featured downloadable interview and audio content in the now-and-again series, *The Morning Zoo*. It introduced new bands and gave Hoppus an instant outlet to jot down his thoughts and feelings about life, music and the rest of it. Having turned 33 that summer, there was no messing about but plenty of time to reflect on events and the podcast was named *Best Of 2005*.

Tom DeLonge had been keeping a little quiet during the year but he hadn't faded away into oblivion either. Come September, he was more voluble than ever, taking the opportunity to enlighten the world about his own new band. They were to be called Angels & Airwaves, and according to DeLonge they were out to change the way the world saw music in general. His feelings boiled down to the fact that blink had produced, with their latest album, another masterpiece of pop-punk but that was as far as that band went and so Tom's sights were now set on a kind of neo-prog outlook based round melody, larger-than-life in the way that Pink Floyd, Led Zeppelin or Rush had been but from a uniquely American perspective. It would be full of dynamics and drama.

So having conquered pop-punk, DeLonge was in full roaring ready-for-it mode on prog rock. Punk and prog are two genres that have never, ever rubbed along together ever since John Lydon wore his famous 'I Hate Pink Floyd' T-shirt thirty years previously. "This is [going to be] the best record of my career," DeLonge continued when speaking to Trevor Baker. "It took twelve years and all those millions of records we sold with blink to make something this good. During [the writing of] this album I was looking back at WWII, which was the last great war which was clearly a battle between good and evil. And that was followed by a great time of prosperity for America in the '50s.

I could see an analogy with what was going on in my life. There was a personal war that I went through with the band breaking up. That was something that I had to do for me and my family, and I hope that with this album I'm coming into my own great era."[187] You can't accuse the man of lacking ambition, at least. The plans didn't end there, however, with the promise of a movie to coincide with the Angels & Airwaves album on its release, which was scheduled tentatively for the spring of 2006. DeLonge was hugely excited by the possibilities inherent in making a film.

"It's one third a documentary about the band, one third a love story and one third CGI," he told Trevor Baker. "It's very Pink Floyd but Pink Floyd wouldn't have been able to do this just because the technology wasn't available. People are going to wonder how we did it. I wonder how we did it!" There was also a huge emphasis on using technology with light shows, the internet and all kinds of futuristic stuff coming together to bolster the band's music. It was intended to be a cross-discipline, all-powerful art project working in as many media as DeLonge and his new band could think of. The group's MySpace page originally had a statement from DeLonge (later taken down) which showed that Tom was looking to the future but not yet ready to forget events of the recent past.[188]

Angels & Airwaves would listen to the sounds of bands such as U2, The Police, The Cure and Pink Floyd, he planned, and take the music to an entirely new level. The documentary movie to accompany it would track the break-up of blink-182 and present the brave new world that incubated AVA[189] to replace it.

The band line-up was completed by Box Car Racer guitarist David Kennedy, plus Offspring drummer Atom Willard and Ryan Sinn from the Distillers. But it wasn't a supergroup by any means, said DeLonge. "The last thing in the world that I wanted was anything about this being, just, marketing value, y'know?," he said. "I actually had people calling me from bands who've sold millions of records, but I wasn't into it. I needed this to be a very organic thing because of the message and because of what it is we're trying to accomplish."[190] In putting the band together, he said, he'd had a very specific set of factors in mind, and although he had loved being onstage with Hoppus and Barker, it wasn't what he was after for this new project; the persona angle, the banter and the humour were far from his mind. And whilst the vast majority of the time with blink-182 was spent in a nihilistic, anti-message fug, Angels & Airwaves' approach would be the exact opposite.

"With Angels & Airwaves, its absolute message [is] absolute … positivity. I needed something that was organic. The first [rule] was respect for the band members and respect for their families. And the second rule was the ability to grow into a really hard, predestined friendship."[191] As September 2005 rolled on, DeLonge admitted that he hadn't spoken to his erstwhile blink-mates since the split that February. And details began to leak as to exactly what had happened.

"Our priorities were mad, mad different," he said. "My priority was my family, and my life had to be structured in a way where I had to be around for my daughter. She was two years old at the time. And they wanted to keep touring."[192] Later, Mark Hoppus was to give his own version of events. He obviously deeply loved his family too, that was a given, and he was simply acknowledging that it was never a chore to be a member of blink.

"There was no pressure in blink-182. We never felt any pressure to do anything, other than what we wanted to do. Really, we were blessed. We got to do what we loved. It wasn't like it was a pressure job. It was just write music and tour." The fact that DeLonge wanted time off wasn't necessarily the problem *per se*, he said, but more to do with the timing of the announcement and the way that it was handled.

Hoppus was also less than impressed by DeLonge's methods in informing the band, via his manager, that things weren't A-OK. If the anger was palpable, it was also based on the fact that brothers always did tend to have the harshest fights. There was also an issue about how the next blink-182 record would come together.

"We rented a rehearsal space to get ready for the [Tsunami] show," Mark told Jason Tate, "and while we were there we started arguing about the break, and the next blink record, and Tom told us he would only record it in his house. So, at this point Travis and I were like, 'Wait dude, we're three people in a band, and we understand that you needed your time off, and that's cool, but now it's like you're saying when we can and can't tour, when and how we can record.' He was talking about us mailing Pro-Tools files back and forth and he would record stuff at his house and Travis could record drums in LA, and that's not a band. That's not blink-182. We were a band for thirteen years before, and this is just not right. And, we're a band when we're all in the studio together, not this separate thing, you know? And he said, 'Well, that's the only way I'll do the band now.' And I said, 'No, this isn't right, we're a three-piece, this has always been a democracy; we vote on things, we respect one another."

"I don't know what the changing point was, but slowly it became [that] we weren't a band, it wasn't the three of us working together for a goal, it was like me and Travis having to pull him along, and be like, 'Come on, let's go, let's do this that we all created and that we love,' and we wanted to help Tom. We were like, 'Dude, if you need your family bring them along, get your own tour bus, we're so lucky that we have the opportunity to do this, and take your family all over the world, show them everything,' and we seriously did everything we could to keep the band together."[193]

Mark gave a very interesting and revealing interview in *Ultimate Guitar*[194] and elsewhere, Travis was clearly very angry. "When one of your dearest friends," raged Travis, "who you've known for twelve years, doesn't have the balls to personally call you and tell you he doesn't want to be in a band anymore, it's pretty easy to write that dude off. It's not hard to never think about a guy like that again. That's how it was for me. I realised, 'Ah, okay. That's how you are! ... from then on it was very easy for me to dismiss him … for Mark to say what he said about Tom proves how bad it was."[195]

There was little chance, then, of a reunion any time soon, although DeLonge was complimentary about his former band mates as musicians and pals. For him, blink-182 had run its course and he was desperate to find a release in another outfit as well as spend time with his young daughter.

"I'm going to let it be for a while, but I definitely want to talk to them again obviously," Tom mused of Travis and Mark. "I would love to rebuild my friendship with those guys, they're amazing people. It just wasn't the right thing for all three of us to be doing [blink] together forever."[196] As if to prove the point, Geffen released a *Greatest Hits* album that seemed to be the definitive last word on the matter.

Chapter 24
The Race For Release

Back with Travis and Mark, the +44 project was still at something of a confused stage. Barker was planning all sorts of guests to appear on the forthcoming album including, at one stage, the producer Danger Mouse. Travis then announced the formation of yet another group, this time featuring Paul Wall and Skinhead Rob – the band would be more traditionally hip hop than the Transplants and already had a name lined up: Expen$ive Taste. Travis was also starting to make inroads into becoming a producer, meeting up with people like Bun B and T.I. Things in the world of +44 were changing rapidly, however, and by the start of 2006 there was a major line-up change when Carol Heller parted from the boys, the official reason being that she wanted to start a family. Musically, too, the plan to make it a solely electronic project had morphed somewhat once more which had also been instrumental in Heller's departure. It was largely down to the fact that the initial creation of the tracks was programming/keyboard-based. This different approach had become more of a straitjacket and the latest news was that the electronic tools had merely been a vehicle that would lead to wider creative climes. Along with the new approach there were also two new band members to replace Heller[197], first guitarist Shane Gallagher of The Nervous Return (who were signed to LaSalle) and then bassist Craig Fairbaugh who had been touring latterly with the Transplants. Gallagher had come in around a month after things had kicked off and after inputting some great ideas was asked to join the band. The same applied to Fairbaugh and so a four-piece was born. For the early part of 2006, it was all hands on deck in terms of recording at the new Los Angeles studio which had been a smart purchase as it enabled the band to pick up wherever they'd left off without any pressure of having to move gear in and out for other bands to take over. It also enabled them to crank up the live instruments and was central in morphing the +44 sound into more of a rock direction than had originally been planned. The studio had been bought originally just for +44, but later Mark was to acknowledge its value; his podcasts were recorded there and Travis was also working with beats and hip hop projects there, too.

"In the beginning, we were hoping it would make sense to buy a studio and now we don't know how we existed without owning a studio. If I had an idea right now, Travis and I could be there in an hour and recording. Having a studio now is the best thing in the world." [198]

Season Two of *Meet The Barkers* was broadcast throughout January and February of 2006, giving fans another insight into the Travis and Shanna sideshow. The two-series run finally came to an end with the finale 'An Alabama Christmas', where Shanna's baby shower yields loads of presents, she and Travis debate possible names and somehow Travis manages to score another brand-new Cadillac along the way. And that, as they say, was that. Both series will definitely go down in the annals of reality TV history.

The first ex-182 to get some music officially out into the wider world was Tom DeLonge, the man who was repeatedly saying in interviews that he was aiming to change the world with his new band. There had been an early leak of five songs from the DeLonge-produced record that were then distributed throughout the internet. The demos had a completely different aesthetic to even the Box Car Racer days, with little of the aggression of guitars and none of the lyrical light-heartedness of blink-182. The lyrics were earnest and dark, amidst themes of wars and hurt. The first official music to be released (May 18, 2006) was the single, aptly-titled 'The Adventure'. It's a massive, anthemic track with programmed beats and hammering riffs – the vocal harmonies are great as Tom sings of wanting to wake up from a dream and he's reborn. It's about love, rebirth and new hope – easy to read as sentiments expressed in the wake of what had happened in his recent musical career. By now everyone was awaiting the final version; there had been a net version as early as February 2006 as the soundtrack to a grainy short film that had been recorded on the resolutely analogue 8mm film, a science fiction-themed piece of work that was reminiscent of George Lucas' earlier work with the likes of THX-1138. Part 2 of said short film was pushed out via AVA's official site in April, a continuation of the narrative but this time with 'It Hurts' as the music behind it. The song is muscular but growly with an enormously emotionally-charged chorus where the title is repeated over and over again; it's a song about being manipulated and cheated on by your partner and how this can eat you up from the inside out. Relationships are such fertile ground for epic slabs of post-modern electronic progressive rock, and Angels & Airwaves had firmly set out their stall in that area. The official promotional video for 'The Adventure' was directed by The Malloys and has the band getting onto a spaceship to play the song, cuts to Tom alone in a field, employs footage from World War II and ends with Tom walking off as the sky is illuminated with planets. It feels a little bit like the closing sequence of *The Incredible Hulk*, but that's probably not entirely overtly designed. It peaked at Number 20 in the UK charts, a more-than-decent opening result.

Just a week later, Angels & Airwaves' debut album, *We Don't Need To Whisper*, was unleashed to a very interested public. It starts in cinematic style with the expansive 'Valkyrie Missile' which has more than a hint of 'Thus Sprach Zarathustra' about its intro; resonant of new birth, drama and complexities to come. It also effectively lays out the band for all to see, in that despite the fact that things hurt, and hurt badly, everyone will come to hear the message: take a chance, hang in there, I will be here and the good will out. It is, in essence, a six-and-a-half minute '80s prog opera and is suitably serious and yet full of hope. 'Distraction' has heavy war imagery that talks about the fall of cities in a destroyed landscape but still having love to see you through. If the world was feeling out of control in general at this point, politically and aggressively, there were still some things that were to be valued and AVA get to the point via keyboards, handclaps and heavy melodic chorus. 'Do It For Me Now' is a love song which DeLonge had originally written for a rapper on a project that never came to fruition. He certainly shoehorns in one heck of a lot of words into the verses, which are a stream of consciousness about being frightened, being hurt, remembering good times and yearning for forgiveness. The protagonist has one last wish and that is to be loved once more in the way that was now presumably lost. He repeats lines about holding on, and wanting to be held. The track bleeds from teary eyes. It's a very powerful moment indeed. Next up is 'The Adventure', rounding off a four-song opening salvo that answers every question the listener had as to what the album is all about.

There is a huge religious theme to 'A Little's Enough' which talks of a *deus ex machina* coming down to make everything OK again; perhaps this is God talking but the narrator of the song says that essentially everything can be fixed with a touch more love. Depending on how you look at it, this is either DeLonge's alleged (and highly criticised) messianic complex writ large or a classically ambitious piece of timeless storytelling. Either way the guitar riff is lovely and Tom sings with real passion. 'The War' is the band at their most anthemic, massive military drumbeats and powerful lyrics about oceans on fire, soldiers on beaches, death and the pointlessness of it all. It's another song wanting resolution from a situation, desperate for communication and asking, exhausted, why this situation is being allowed to turn his brain inside out. 'The Gift' is nothing to do with the Velvet Underground track of the same name, but is instead a very upbeat and excited song about new love. If it rains, says the song, then he can make storms cease, he can light a dark path, he can melt away fear and make the world disappear. Tom has never been more eloquent on the subject of love and 'The Gift' has a certain poetry to it that is clearly rooted in deep honesty. 'It Hurts' is the absolute flipside of this in every way, before 'Good Day', with its confusion but ultimately upbeat message that today is probably good if only he could start to work out how he felt. Then finally comes the fantastic album-closer, 'Start The Machine' which features a pink toy piano that DeLonge had bought from a toy shop he found when out getting an ice-cream with his daughter. The lyrics are all about leaving destruction and apocalypse behind, not apologising but looking for a new future; he feels he's escaped just in time and it ends in satisfyingly circular fashion with repeated lyrics about listening to a word, a message, of love.

The critical reaction was bound to be mixed due to its founder and frontman imbuing it with such pre-release significance but on both sides of the Atlantic magazines queued up to give their opinion which in itself is probably an indication of the importance that AVA had taken on, for good or for bad. *Alternative Press* considered it fantastic and entirely contemporary. "*Whisper* encompasses everything a rock band should be in 2006,"[199] they gushed, whilst elsewhere *Kerrang!* said it had "some stunning moments of perfection" and commented that it showcased Tom DeLonge's songwriting and musical abilities whilst it "puts a lid on his past … and moves forwards."[200] The review also expressed a worry that they may have boxed themselves into a sonic corner with their themes and ambitions, though. *Entertainment Weekly* thought they probably liked it but they were less convinced by Tom's singing. "If only DeLonge's nasal vocals were more suited to the Robert Smith romanticism of tracks like 'It Hurts,'"[201] they wrote, a little uncharitably. *Spin* referred to the band as a unit rather than a glorified solo project as others may have seen it. "Here, his three sidemen elevate his emo tendencies to something grander and more timelessly romantic – though somewhat less exciting."[202] Over in the UK *Uncut* remained somewhat unconvinced. "Coming from a former punk goof ... all this sentimentality feels somewhat po-faced."[203] What was that about preconceptions again? "With Angels & Airwaves," wrote *Rolling Stone*, "former blink singer-guitarist Tom DeLonge expands on his old band's recent heaviness with epic love songs that pack as much arena grandeur as they do forward momentum ... cathartic choruses over loud-soft-loud rushes, synth washes and fussy guitar parts ... evoke U2's *The Joshua Tree*."[204] That U2 comparison was one that was to appear again and again. DeLonge expressed his thought that the album may well be best listened to in a darkened room by the light of a single candle, only adding to the drama and portent around matters.

The band had already appeared live, their debut gig being on April 12, 2006 at Glass House, Pomona, California, an hour-long set that also included run-throughs of 'There Is', from *Box Car Racer*, and a few bars of blink-182's 'Down' which was reappropriated as an introduction to 'The Adventure'. The band toured throughout May, June and July, the latter two months being as part of a touring package that also included Taking Back Sunday and Head Automatica. The *Boston Phoenix* reviewer was ambivalent about what he had seen. "Their performance played out much like their debut album," he wrote. "Lots of samples, DeLonge's voice filtered through robotic reverb, a back-up vocal track. The stage was lit up like a space station ready for lift-off to match the music's desolate mood with different backdrops dropping in for the album's subtle shifts in tone ... efforts to connect with the crowd by walking through the audience with a spotlight and a wireless mic, surrounded by security beefcake, came off as cheesy. If you wanted a re-enactment of the A&A CD, you got it; some of us wanted a live show, and what we got, mostly, was a flashlight in the eyes."[205] Over in England, the *Birmingham Mail* was a little more forgiving of Tom who was in a thoughtful mood that night. "Tom Delonge also took time out to share with the audience the origins of the band, as well as touching on other subjects such as his childhood, September 11 and his brother's military service in Iraq ... [it was a] highly enjoyable evening which also promises a healthy future for Angels & Airwaves."[206] Tom DeLonge's new band sold 200,000 copies of their debut album in the first week; not a bad result although not quite the world-changing effort that he had planned. And no sign of that movie either ... still, it was a grand old start.

"My honest opinion of that Angels & Airwaves record is that it didn't really do anything for me," mused Hoppus later. "After I heard the first single I thought that the verses were really good, and then it got to the chorus and for me it just fell apart after that. I felt there were a lot of ideas that were trying to work their way out, but none of the songs got to that part where they just opened up, you know? ... when I heard the actual execution of them, I was kind of disappointed. But, with that being said, I want to say that I've always respected Tom as a songwriter, and I know that he has the ability to write really good songs. But that record, just, well, didn't do anything for me."[207]

Travis and Mark were by now fully in the flow with +44 and had called in the services of Dan The Automator to help out with their album, which was eventually to be co-produced and mixed by good old Jerry Finn. The fact that the track, 'No, It Isn't' had found its way onto the internet as a download through their own site in late 2005 may have preceded DeLonge's efforts, but it was also made available on December 13 – the day that Tom was originally due to release some material of his own and also, non-coincidentally, DeLonge's own thirtieth birthday. Mark and Travis denied this was their design. The song in this form was also briefly available on a now very sought-after limited CD release of five hundred that came free with purchased merchandise from the band's site. The track is apparently called 'No, It Isn't' as a pre-emptive strike against the inevitable questions as to whether it is about Tom DeLonge. +44 denied that it was, although its lines about it not being goodbye but being a message that I cannot stand you, burning down beautiful things, cashing in on dreams and so on were surely so obviously about the break-up of blink-182 and DeLonge's part in it that eventually Hoppus was forced to concede the point.

"Originally I was going to hide behind something else when people asked what the song was about. Obviously they'd ask if it was about Tom and I was going to say, 'No, it isn't; it's about a girl I used to date,' or something. But we all love the song so much and I thought, 'Why would I hide behind anything other than that's the way I feel?' So it was actually way more meaningful and liberating to say that's what's the song's about."[208] "[The song is] a classic case of something bad happening and everyone around you not telling you what the deal was," Travis added.[209] It's pretty vicious stuff, even in its earlier form with Carole's backing vocals sweetening it up a touch. 2006 had not been great for Travis, having filed for divorce from Shanna that August, with various Myspace posts from each party on the subject.

Travis threw himself back into the music as he always had and soon +44 were ready to rock. Their first show took place at the Roxy Theatre in Hollywood on September 7, 2006 with a second appearance following at London's Astoria. That London date was reviewed by most of the rock magazines and though the performance was adequate, first impressions of the +44 sound, at least in the live arena, were that it was close enough to blink-182 to be an addendum to that band's career. They weren't exactly leftovers from that group, because the subject matter had been written around the break-up, but although +44 were clearly great musicians, it was very nearly as if blink had carried on with two new members in the band to replace Tom. In contrast to AVA's obvious break away from the old and expected sound, +44's oeuvre was familiar enough to be linked to their recent past in a more organic way. One can speculate as to how things may have turned out had Mark and Travis not bought that studio and gone back to the rockin' together that they did so well. Given Barker's experimentalist tendencies and Mark's growing need to bare his darker side, the results could have been very intriguing indeed. As it was, the original 37 ideas that +44 had for tracks were distilled into a more manageable array of songs.

The first release was 'Lycanthrope', another vitriolic and dark track about things ending, loneliness, hollow words and feeling broken. The protagonist in the chorus says he's going to set the other person free and to just let things happen without being afraid – if they would only just stop talking. Despite initial protestations, it's another track that is surely directed toward DeLonge, despite cover stories that Mark and Travis may have felt moved to offer along the way. It was released first through the website in September to both give the fans a taste of the forthcoming material and presumably to make their feelings on what had happened as clear as possible. There was also a bit of business to be taken care of, on September 9, with +44 filming a video for another confessional song (were there any other kind?), 'When Your Heart Stops Beating'. The video is a pretty stock shoot of a group playing in an abandoned warehouse whilst all around people dance and couples are seen arguing. That track also gave the forthcoming LP its name, after some speculation that it would be called *Little Death*, which in French – *Le Petit Mort* – is a colloquialism for orgasm. Not entirely appropriate for an album that was borne on the dirty, oily wings of a band break-up, so the heartbeat theme was taken up instead. The band embarked on a promotional tour of the UK directly after the video.

However, Travis felt that there was something wrong; he was drumming in constant pain but soldiering on through it, night after night, even altering his kit set-up to accommodate. "He is now using his left foot as his right arm, Def Leppard style," confirmed Mark.[210] A doctor cheerfully informed him that in fact he had broken a bone in his arm on that video shoot. He was told to immediately rest and not to take any part in +44's live dates including the early 2007 visits to Australia and Europe. It was time for the album to be released, and by November the music was finally ready.

When Your Heart Stops Beating kicks in with 'Lycanthrope' before launching into 'Baby Come On', notable mostly for having the rather excellent lyric that states that the past is just the future, except with lights on. The album clearly has more in common with the likes of 'Dammit', musically-speaking, than it does with *blink-182* although lyrically you could say it was vice-versa. The drummer-breaking 'When Your Heart Stops Beating' is up next, a track of heavy pop-punk that is about little deaths of all kinds. It's got 'single' written all over it and is the first true highlight of the album so far. 'Little Death' is another one, a sensitive song that is about love, strangers, death by information and all of this making life a much more meaningful experience as a result. It seems to say that some experiences are timeless and memories never fade. It's a track about communication in a digital age with a whole lump of sex thrown in.

Hot on its heels is '155', another song about conversations not making sense and the fact that things are much harder now that the subject of the song has been proven to be a liar. It's not the time nor place to talk about things, says the song, to a distinctly synthy backdrop whilst rich guitars undulate powerfully underneath. The middle-eight is pure '80s pop, another moment of inspiration from The Cure and their ilk. It's a very catchy song that's sometimes been swamped by the more obviously targeted compositions on the album.

'Lillian', with its arpeggiated acoustic guitar figure, is a very effective ballad with Travis providing some really interesting shuffling, shimmering beats behind lyrical tales about dead hearts and being emptied of everything. 'Cliff Diving' with its nearly-naughty title, is a straightforward poppy punk love song that frankly could have been written at any time over the previous thirteen years. It's a decent effort, but nothing groundbreaking by anybody's standards. The chorus takes inspiration from The Undertones' excellent hit 'Here Comes The Summer', a truly fantastic track that blended pop music with jangly distorted guitars to perfection. There's a short, vocal-less track, 'Interlude' which despite good intentions (probably unconsciously) takes its cues from a rather less obvious source: that's The Carpenters' 'Close To You', and it's difficult to listen to it without thinking of that track which is a shame because it breaks up the pace nicely. In the aftermath of that downbeat moment, the even-more down-paced 'Weatherman' is a regret-filled emo track about not saying sorry but hardly being able to hold it together now that the world has crashed down. Its rather droney ambience and tom-heavy work from Travis conveys a satisfyingly claustrophobic atmosphere and there are some genuinely excellent touches to the song's arrangement as layers of vocals and guitars play around the rather static melody.

'No, It Isn't' does its inimitable thing next, before 'Make You Smile' taps into the darker side of Mark and Travis' psyche for a piano-led duet that utilises the undoubted vocal talents of Carol Heller. It is an all-too-brief window into the more loop/beat-based efforts of early +44 and it is an excellent slice of mature pop songwriting. Clearly it was important for Mark and Travis to let loose and rock out but their initial instincts to create something different to the norm had resulted in tracks like 'Make You Smile' which is so unlike the rest of *When Your Heart Stops Beating* that it actually feels like an entirely different band. Which in many ways, that track could be said to be, of course.[211] The album sighs to its weary end with 'Chapter 13', another post-break-up song that has excruciatingly personal/self-analytical and frustrated lyrics. Musically, it's got a lot in common with 'Lycanthrope' and those two tracks book-end the album fairly neatly. There are two bonus acoustic tracks for the UK disc, versions of 'Baby Come On' and 'Weatherman', both of which it must be said sound great in that format, the latter absolutely lovely with a lone cello in counterpoint to plaintive piano and Mark's defeated vocalisations. It wasn't all downbeat stuff; there were other tracks that didn't necessarily make the cut including an indie-country track that was a very positive number sending a message to their respective kids that the world is indeed a beautiful place despite some of the darker moments of what was a cathartic album.

"A lot of the record," said Mark, "is about finding strength in hard times and finding strength in people that you love. In a lot of ways it has been a very downer [these] past two years, but it's been a very great last two years [too]. Obviously we would never have wished for blink to end, but it did and we were dealt a hand of cards that we picked up.

We formed this band and have made some music that we're all very proud of."[212] The record was co-produced by Jerry Finn; once Travis and Mark had got the process underway of getting ideas down, his expertise had ensured the album's completion.

"Jerry Finn came in and guided us in the home stretch, just to make sure," confirmed Hoppus. "We did want that outside opinion. We did want Jerry's input. He knew how much we wanted to push ourselves as musicians, and, at the same time, he keeps us very grounded. Having his input was definitely necessary."[213]

The album was released that November and sold 66,000 copies, notably much less than the AVA debut. What +44 shared with Angels & Airwaves, though, was the fact that they divided the critics. *NME* were typically so-so about the record. "There are more ideas here than blink-182 had in an entire career," they wrote. "It's just that they're the same ideas that Jimmy Eat World had on their last LP."[214] That publication thought 'No It Isn't' was a high point and compared 'Weatherman' to the band Sunny Day Real Estate. *Rolling Stone* bemoaned the fact that Mark and Travis had turned away from their initial electronic direction and turned out, instead, an album that was essentially full of blink-182-style tracks. "On gut-punch punk-pop numbers such as 'Baby Come On' and the title track, the keyboards and mechanized beats feel more like an afterthought than an operating principle,"[215] they wrote, before praising 'Make You Smile', 'Weatherman' and 'Little Death' as introspective tracks on a par with blink's 'I Miss You'. *Entertainment Weekly* loved the record, considering that, "downbeat but still catchy, tracks like 'Baby Come On' or the New Order-ish '155' could easily have featured on blink's bleakly impressive last CD."[216] *Blender*'s thoughts could be distilled to the telling, "blink-182 without the humour,"[217] and *Alternative Press* found it rather flat in general. Q magazine were spectacularly underwhelmed by the record, particularly disliking Hoppus' voice. "Hoppus, whose flat vocals once dovetailed deftly with Delonge's nasal whine," they declared, "is sorely exposed as a sole frontman."[218]

Things were a bit more serious these days. There was just time left in 2006 for Tom DeLonge to completely steal the media spotlight by announcing that AVA would make another record of their lives the next year. Oh, and of course there was going to be a full-length mind-blowing movie to coincide, too.

Chapter 25

Absinth Makes The Fart Grow Honda

Travis Barker had busied himself by heading into the studio with Rob Aston and Paul Wall for the Expen$ive Taste debut, 'Slidin' On That Oil,' which was to released on Wall's forthcoming album. Also in early 2007 Barker was starting to fiddle about with remixes and production techniques for many other people, preparing some loops and beats for Juelz and looking to open two new boutiques, one in LA called Fast Life and one in Venice Beach by the name of Rogue Status. Meanwhile, early 2007 saw +44 out in a cold and rainy Europe. The band members themselves were suffering from colds but managed to crack on with a visit to Berlin where they were astonished and delighted to find there was a signed caricature of David Hasselhoff on the wall of the local MTV studio.

"We all love our families and want to be home with them," Mark grinned, "but, we just wanna tour the world and be supported by the most amazing fans in the world. And play music, and that's it, we love playing music, and we're very excited about our new record. And it's forced us to do shit that we never thought we could do – and it was like the best thing being born out of the most ugly situation we were put in. We can't help but all be ourselves. Fuck, we love to tour, we love to play, we love to have a good time. So I think we're going to be ourselves."[219]

The Tommys, who were on tour with +44, enjoyed the opportunity to play alongside some of their favourite musicians. "Mark was totally cool," Stevie Shepperson of that band told the author. "He really welcomed us onto the tour and didn't make us feel uncomfortable or out of place. He went out of his way to say hi, or stand and chat. He actually gave me a few tips on stretching my hands before I go on and gave me tips on my singing."

"The atmosphere backstage was hard to describe at the gigs. It was well scheduled but not in an overly stressed-out way. Everyone was busy doing their own jobs but once the show was over it completely changed. Everyone was chilled out and just relaxed." Not words you can use to describe the crowds, however: there was a noisy and enthusiastic hardcore fan-base there desperate to see what Mark and, for the first two shows at least, Travis would come up with next. Travis' arm was still troubling him though and following an excruciatingly painful Amsterdam gig, Gil Sharone of the Dillinger Escape Plan and a good mate of Barker was drafted into the live line-up. As legend has it, he was able to learn the whole +44 set on the plane journey from America to Europe. Actually, Sharone, Barker and Hoppus had run through the set over and over again on the tour bus using practice pads for most of the night. The tour was back on.

"The first show we actually played, at Paradiso in Amsterdam, was insane!" recalls Stevie[220]. It seemed like thirty seconds and I was so nervous I could have passed out. I just remember looking down the stairs and at the bottom stood Travis and Mark looking up at me. The lights went down and the crowd screamed. Some crowds were sceptical with us being an all-girl group but once we kicked a few songs out we won them over. And the same went for a few girls, they were giving us funny looks but once we started playing they were soon moshing with the rest of them. Europe was also a lot more lively than England." There were no mentions of 'the old band', however, although Shepperson observed that a lot of the audiences were, like her and band mate Fran, also long-standing fans of Hoppus and Barker's work. "I think the crowds were mainly blink fans," she concludes. "If someone wasn't wearing a blink shirt they were wearing a +44 top, although they never played any blink songs on that tour." +44 got on with hammering out exciting rock shows, Mark in particular relishing the jump back to smaller-sized venues rather than the massive arenas of latter-day blink; the kind of places where sweat drips down from the ceiling and there's an intimacy with the crowd that's only possible in 'proper' gigs. The tour rolled on to Australia and Japan, where the band busied themselves with press and well-received live appearances. Travis, meanwhile, was getting himself fighting fit again with the aid of a medical device known as a 'bone stimulator'. He would need all his strength: he was going to be out on tour for the whole of April, May and June on the Honda Civic Tour of the US and Canada alongside Fall Out Boy, The Academy Is... and Paul Wall – another tour that blink-182 had pioneered, of course. Meanwhile, +44's music was getting out and about. WWE wrestler, Ashley, was a major fan of the band's debut, gushing that she loved *When Your Heart Stops Beating* and calling for her followers to all go out and buy it. "I've been waiting for the culmination of this project since blink broke up," she wrote. "The band is now comprised of Mark Hoppus (in my opinion one of the more interesting humans on this planet), Shane Gallagher and Craig Fairbaugh (who was also the touring guitarist for Barker's other project, Transplants). Give it a listen."[221] The end of March 2007 had the band participate in a great exchange of cover versions, heading into the studio to perform a version of Wir Sind Helden's track, 'Guten Tag' – WSH reciprocated with 'Wenn Dein Herz zu Schlagen Aufhör' ('When Your Heart Stops Beating') on the ace exchange set up by iTunes. +44 also covered 'I Am One' for a Smashing Pumpkins tribute project through MySpace and contributed 'Baby Come On' in acoustic form to the cleverly-named second instalment in that series, *Punk Goes Acoustic 2*.

As it turned out, Fall Out Boy were forced to delay the start of that Honda tour, which was a bonus for Travis' recovery. He certainly had a full schedule lined up during 2007, drumming for Idiot Pilot on the song, 'Elephant', The Federation ('Black Roses'), and creating well-received remixes of '(Crank That) Soulja Boy' and Rhianna's smash hit, 'Umbrella'. As the Honda Civic tour rolled around the US, fans were able to grab themselves a copy of Expen$ive Taste's mix-tape, *DJ Skee Presents Expen$ive Taste*, at the merchandise booth. It was also made available online through the SkeeTV site. Rob Aston was in typically brutal/honest mode, making it clear that the subject material would be as gnarly as ever.

"I speak about subjects that I deal with, things that go on in my life and experiences I've been through," he said. "Maybe my stuff is not always the friendliest of subject matter or the most radio friendly, but fuck it. I've never been worried about getting no airplay before, so I ain't trying to tone nothing down now. If anything, I'm going harder than ever on these motherfuckers 'cause there is still shit cracking off on the daily."[222] "Mix-tapes are really the only way to break or get a hip hop artist bubbling in the streets that can carry over to the mainstream," explained DJ Skee, pointing out that Li'l Wayne and even Kanye West had dropped mix-tapes before their albums came out. It was almost like a sampler for what was to come; you had to get the interest rolling before you could hope to sell records. "In hip hop today, you can't just come out of nowhere with a big single and no street/mix-tape presence and expect to have a career." [223]

DJ Skee Presents Expen$ive Taste begins in moody, minor-key flavour, with guest rappers B-Real, Too Short, Damu, Eddie Rap Life joining Rob and Paul Wall on 'Famous Anthem Part 1', which with Skee's interjections and mixing skills is just over five minutes of typically self-referential, raw hip hop. It's miles and miles away from Rob & Travis' previous encounter and distances Expen$ive Taste from the Transplants project completely. 'I Can't Fuck With It' follows, sounding a lot like Eminem has been on the same page. It's raw and straight-up in its flow. 'Trunk Full Of Boom', as its title might suggest, is all about Cadillacs, old skool and bass, whilst 'I'm The Shit' has more crunk influences and all the braggadocio you'd imagine. 'Them Are Gs On That Bitch' features also Rich Boy and Topic. Skinhead Rob/Damu's collaboration, Warfare, provides the following track, 'Smoking Kush Blunts' which is full-on and in your face in its street aggression. 'Same Ol Routine', billed elsewhere as 'Everyday', draws on the skills of Slim Thug, as the mix-tape ramps up the claustrophobia even more, with a tale of being sick of the same old routine of chasing money, breaking bread and getting green. 'We Some Go Getters', billed as Lil Spank Booty featuring Damu and Skinhead Rob, ramps up the action via insistent verses and wonky-ass chorus then 'Powder And The Danrk' showcases the not inconsiderable talents of Milano with a screwed backing woozing along with a party-power reaffirmation of the power of expensive tastes, musical and otherwise. 'You Know Me' fires Bun-B into a violent haze of unfettered linguistic play where the sheer weight of the amount of profanity renders it entirely creative. It's about being cool, hustling and never standing down for a second. 'Gunplay', with Damu on board again, is delivered in a nifty, low whisper with a descending b-line underneath a tale that does justice to the title. The Boo-Ya Tribe pop up on 'Memory Lane', a typically tuneful piece of laid-back soul-hop, which is both excellently conceived and masterfully delivered. Paul and Rob are back in doom-ridden mode on 'Ride To The End' which can also be found hiding in dark corners under the name 'Motherfuckin' Fool'. Of all the tracks on a mix-tape that introduces many great artists that were inspiring Expen$ive Taste and its members at the time, this one's the closest to Transplants material, both for its subject matter and its musical approach. You can imagine it with punk rock guitars sheering over the top of the tale of regret and destiny. Warfare are back on 'What Them Hos Wanna Do', another cut from the streets, full of guns, money and retribution. The last track of the mix-tape sees Cashus, Hayes, Lil Spank Booty, Mitchy Slick, Krondon, Chance Infinite and Skinhead Rob round it off with

'Famous Anthem Part 2'. The mix-tape went down well on the hip hop underground, Barker's credibility gaining another boost for his obvious immersion in and love for the genre.

Expen$ive Taste even played a show in Houston after the Honda Civic gig; Mark Hoppus wrote on his website about how much he enjoyed the six-song set, calling it awesome and noting that people were singing along and dancing. "Bun B and Slim Thug both came out for guest appearances. The entire show was filmed. Everyone had a great time."[224] As indeed had everyone on the Honda Civic Tour. It wasn't the headline madness of previous years, but it was a good chance to connect with the fans in the live arena. +44 were enjoying themselves so much, indeed, that they even started slipping old songs into the set. 'What's My Age Again?' began to reappear. This was after many interviews in which they'd been rather adamant that they would never play blink-182 songs again. But, as Hoppus shrugged in a blog post that was reported by old 'mates', *NME*, "Travis and I *love* our history with blink-182, and it seems a shame to let those songs sit dormant forever because of what happened two years ago. And that song is *so* much fun to play. So why not? It was awesome to play that song live again."[225] And it was awesome for the crowds to hear it; +44 were on a roll and so launched into 'The Rock Show' at their Cleveland appearance. Toward the end of June, after one of the +44 band had to rush home for a family emergency, Mark joined Panic! At The Disco in an acoustic run-through of 'What's My Age Again?' for the delighted crowd. Hoppus and Barker were back in their natural domain, but rather than keep the show literally on the road with the planned dates later in August 2007, further live work was being postponed by +44 for slightly unclear reasons; one that was given was that they wanted to go back into the studio to start work on their second album. "We want to start writing new songs and we are really excited about the direction we have planned," ran a press statement. "So we're going into the studio instead of playing these few dates. We hope that our fans will forgive us for the cancellation; in the end, this will make for an even better live show when we come back."[226]

Mark was now much in demand as a producer, and the final work with Idiot Pilot (whose track, 'Elephant' had drums courtesy of Travis) had been praised by much of the music community. His project during July 2007 involved Ohio band Socratic, who had sent some demos out purely speculatively to Hoppus. The bassist and producer loved it and immediately emailed the band back to get them down to his gaff.

It was so quick, vocalist/guitarist Duane F. Okun told the author, that the group hardly had enough material ready. "We didn't have all the songs at all for the record. We wrote a lot of the record during pre-production out in California. It was quite odd at first [meeting Mark] since we have all seen him on TV and had posters of him when we were younger. But he was such a nice guy right away and we quickly thought of him as a friend and not some famous dude. He is very opinionated but that was because he wanted to do the best record that he thought. I had a fun time in the studio." The hours were more in line with Transplants recording hours, says Okun, working from nine to five-ish daily. The experience was a good one, the singer says, and Hoppus as a producer was very good to work with.

"He didn't severely change any songs we had," concludes the Ohio musician. "It was more a rhyme change here and there and making certain parts shorter, to keep it all more pop-oriented. I consider 'Spread The Rumors' a tight little package – almost like one of those airtight pouches. It was pretty intense due to working on songs very quickly and driving out across the country and back." But worth it. Hoppus' production career continues to be an important part of his musical adventures.

Chapter 26
The Empire Bites Back

Angels & Airwaves had been beavering away on new material, but the first serious news of 2007 came out in April, when it was said that due to difficulties within the band, bassist Ryan Sinn would not be appearing with AVA at the Free Earth Day on campus at MIT. The reasons for this were shrouded in relative mystery and remain so at the time of writing with neither party elaborating much on the subject. Significantly, on Ryan Sinn's official site discography at the time of writing, there are photos of records by bands with whom he's played including Distillers, The Innocent and other acts but there is no sign of *We Don't Need To Whisper*. What is verifiable is that Sinn was replaced by Matt Wachter of 30 Seconds To Mars fame. By the autumn of 2007, Angels & Airwaves were ready to build on the relative success of the full-length debut. They were all inputting: whilst Tom was recording, Matt would be editing video and Adam would be sorting out mixing gear.

Tom told an interviewer that David Kennedy, a motorbike obsessive, rode up to meet Harley Davidson reps at a recent meet to discuss how that company may be able to help with an idea the band had relating to album artwork. "While I was recording," he continued, "David was trying to figure out how we can make more partnerships with people who can help us communicate the ideas that we're singing about. Bands wouldn't normally do stuff like that. We have the skill sets to make the music we want to hear, to create visual art for the sleeves, to make them and [then] we look at the whole thing and say 'It's fucking good.'"[227] And on the seventh day, they rested … the ambitious nature of Angels & Airwaves was directly related to Tom DeLonge's drive to push the boundaries of music, technology and expectation, which was pretty much directly in contrast to +44, whose album had slipped back into a similar aesthetic space as previous bands. Credit to DeLonge, then, whose full-on pronouncements of how the new act was going to change the world were a notable part of his interview schedule throughout 2006 and 2007. His seriousness had come from a deep dislocation from his situation; he was also beginning to reconcile some of his more *outré* statements although hardly backtrack. The relentless promotional confidence and deep self-belief was, he said, rooted in his utter conviction that what AVA was doing was peerless.

"We feel like we're the best thing since sliced bread!" an obviously relaxed Tom continued. "I don't even think about failure. It's impossible to fail, if you stay true to your idea of what's good. The music will find its audience. Everything I write, people can whistle it, people can sing along. My music's immediate, melodic, universal. The truest art-form is creating something that can speak to the masses ... when I don't address my ambitions I get depressed." He went on to say that the band felt terrible when not expressing their energy because if you love what you do, it really doesn't seem like 'work'. Which is, indeed, a universal sentiment. The new album was to be called *I-Empire*, an allusion of course to Star Wars but also, DeLonge explained, another call to arms – that the world was 'yours', and that rather than being some figment of the imagination, if you live in the moment you will understand. He felt that the group was, "about the advancement of the human race, rather than being pissed about where you came from. Because the only thing that truly exists isn't yesterday or tomorrow, it's today."[228] Living in the moment but not being bound by it; a philosophical idea that has resonated through the millennia in many belief systems, but in the case certainly of AVA, an entirely positive one. Despite some of the darkness and melancholy of *We Don't Need To Whisper*, Tom said that his lyrics were always very positive. It's very clear that in the latter months of 2007 Tom had a way more upbeat and together vibe about him than the somewhat more prosaic figure of the previous eighteen months or so. And although there was an obvious reason for that, DeLonge revealed to the world that on top of the events surrounding blink's break-up, he was not wholly facing the world alone. The long-awaited movie/documentary, *Start The Machine*, would lay it on the line, as he told *Absolutepunk*'s Brad Streeter.

"The documentary was meant to first be about what this project [AVA] was. But then it turned out to be how I had to turn this message that was so outward around and apply it to myself. I didn't realise it till halfway through. You know I was losing my mind, I was on thousands of painkillers, and I almost killed myself."

This situation had obviously impacted on his relationships within blink-182; although it's difficult of course to separate each strand of the situation out simply, the fact that Tom was not feeling himself only exacerbated his feelings of isolation within that group. "I didn't quit that band because I wanted to," he revealed. "I quit that band because

I had to ... There was no communication, there was no friendship left, and there were arguments for about a month. For weeks and weeks of it in Europe and we would never solve anything."

"But I never really went on to the public and talked about it much and said I needed to make a major life change ... I wanted to go out and do really positive good things with my music that can really affect people. And I can't do that with people that you are not talking to. I mean in blink we didn't hang out, we didn't share dressing rooms. We never rehearsed; we never got together because we were just not friends anymore. We are totally different people. They are amazing guys and amazing musicians and we had a really brilliant time at the beginning, but it got to a point [where] personally I wasn't getting anything out of it. It wasn't about money at all. It was about [the fact that] I had a family I had to raise and I had to spend 90% of my time on the road with people I never talked to, and we had totally different goals of what we wanted to do. Travis wanted to go more and more into the hip hop area, Mark wanted to stay around where we were, and I still wanted to be the biggest band in the world at the time, but I knew I had to go home. It was sixth months to a year without me seeing my daughter and I was trying to be a dad for the first time. It just really didn't work."[229]

That this only came out a couple of years after the event was part of the problem; Hoppus and DeLonge had been so close for so long that when things changed, each was struggling to come to terms with the new relationship. Outside the band, the world had also changed: surfing, girls and booze still existed, but so did paranoia, death and war. It's interesting to note that blink-182 went on hiatus entering their thirteenth year ... growing up is hard to do and teenage years are the hardest of all. Just to answer all questions related to the break-up, Tom admitted that he hadn't talked to Mark and Travis at the end because, simply, there was nothing left that they could say to each other.

"Absolutely they were pissed about it," he conceded. "But that was after we argued for weeks and weeks and there was nothing left to say. Like nothing. If we would've started arguing about it again it would be like the movie that you have seen for the seventy-fifth time in one month. It was like, 'What are we fucking doing?' I guess we feared to talk about the same things again and again. I mean we are talking about arguments with tears and screaming backstage in Europe for days and days, then we got home and they wanted to start talking about it again after we agreed to take a break, and I could go home to my kids. [After we announced the hiatus] they all wanted to go out and tell everybody, and they went out and they were mad. I mean they had every reason to be angry. I took away from them something they wanted to keep doing, but I told them. I don't want to quit this band. I started this band. It was me. It wasn't like that. I didn't want to do that. But it just came to that situation ..."[230]

The saddest possibility of it all was that DeLonge, having come through his darkest days perhaps, perhaps felt a huge hole in his life? Angels & Airwaves was of course his top priority and the new album plus all their other plans was a source of great excitement, but there's a heart-aching vulnerability about his admission that suggests he missed their company the most that's upsetting in its honesty.

"They are awesome guys," he sighed. "I wish I could be friends with those guys, but it really isn't a reality right now. We just have totally two separate lives and ideas on how we want to live our lives."[231]

The first taster for AVA's new material had come at the end of July, when the band presented four new tracks to the audience: 'Secret Crowds', 'Sirens', 'Lifeline', and 'Everything's Magic'[232], which were soon leaked onto the internet somehow. By now the feeling in enlightened sections of the music industry was that early, live or acoustic versions of forthcoming tracks swirling around webspace does nothing to harm the band, but rather only creates more anticipation for the 'proper' record. *I-Empire* was the first album to be recorded at Macbeth Footwear's new Jupiter Studios, produced by Tom himself and mixed by Tom Lord-Alge, who had worked with blink for many years. By October, there was a short pre-release and unwelcome album leak to contend with but the single, 'Everything's Magic' had been getting out and about, first played on K-ROQ on August 25 and soaring up the iTunes chart during September. It was officially released on October 29 and brought a far more upbeat set of emotions to the world. DeLonge always saw *I-Empire* and *We Don't Need To Whisper* as two halves of a larger whole, much in the vein of William Blake's *Songs Of Innocence And Experience*, and 'Everything's Magic' seemed to burst with positivity. It had a much more upbeat short film associated with it, too. It didn't trouble any of the mainstream charts but it made one heck of a statement. Reviews were mixed too, *Soundfile.com* pretty much summing it up for many. "It's a little like U2 meets McFly but with a good extra dose of pretension and the slickest of slick production."[233]

"I honestly think we are going to create world peace," DeLonge told Shane Richardson. "And I believe everyone is going to have one more baby because of this record. Even people who can't have kids will have one baby because of us. That's how fucking great it is! I do think as far as what is happening in music and what we have done previously in our careers, this is the best work we have ever done. Angels & Airwaves have absolutely the ability to compete with anyone. We came up with this sound. This very epic atmospheric music built on a crescendo and [it] has a sonic lift. The lyrics are very optimistic and describe a world you want to be involved in, and that definitely had to come after something tragic in my artistic career."

"When the last record came out and I said it was the best band in the world everyone gets so angry when you say that. Like, 'How could you be so fucking pompous?' But music is totally subjective. Like how can you say one piece of art is better than another? And that's what I thought was so funny about it. Because people start arguing and get pissed that you say that, but I'm basically just going out there and saying red is the best colour and everyone says you can't say red's the best colour, how dare you. And that's what so funny about it all. I do think we will eventually be the biggest rock band, but it might take twenty years or two years or somewhere in between. I think two years is a tiny bit ambitious to say that. It is an on-going work of art."[234] A slight repositioning of attitude but a crucial one. Tom had got the world to pay attention but the project had hardly begun; he'd started the machine but he needed time to ramp it up to full power.

I-Empire, eventually released on November 1 through the AVA site and a few days later throughout the world, opens with 'Call To Arms', which, like 'Valkyrie Missile' is an opening salvo full of belief and rabble-rousing lyrics. In contrast, though, the punchy 'Call To Arms' is all about trusting yourself and reaching for the stars – the band's message is much more hopeful than the claustrophobic, earnest ache that had pervaded *We Don't Need To Whisper*. The uplifting single, 'Everything's Magic' rolls along next, verses coming across like an '80s-pop version of Jimmy Eat World's song 'Your House' filtered through The Cure's 'Close To Me' and even blink-182's 'Anthem Part Two'. There are resolutely optimistic lyrics about getting ready for the best to come because everything is, indeed, magic. It's like Tom is singing to his 2006 AVA incarnation; now he's come through it all, he can reach back, extend his hand to the lonely, lost and depressed and show that the world is at his feet. 'Breathe' is a more thoughtful rumination on love, eternity and hope. It's also the most blatantly U2-esque moment of AVA's career to date, the interplay between the guitar and heartbeat drums creating a cocoon of sincerity. Here, Tom's hand is reaching out to another – he loves her, but sometimes it's hard when she's near. But the union and connection is so deep to last until time ends. 'Love Like Rockets' has more of that shimmering, heavily-reverbed tinkly end-of-the-'80s sonics before launching into a song that for a second feels exactly like it is going to fire into 'Pride (In The Name Of Love)' but, slightly disappointingly, doesn't. It's a moment that detracts from a decent enough track. Maybe when DeLonge said he wanted to change the world with his music, perhaps he meant that he actually wanted to turn into Bono? And there's barely enough room for one Bono as it is. Nonetheless, his songwriting skill is absolutely undeniable, a point that's proved with the excellent 'Sirens' which has some ace singalong backing vocals and a driving pop sensibility. After the bombast and indulgence of Angels & Airwaves' occasionally-pompous debut, there's a lightness of touch here that, rather than washing the listener away on a sea of sonics, allows the songs to float on their own pop currents. 'Secret Crowds' opens with a Barker-esque drum-loop and atmospheric introduction before the band cut loose from the '80s to get stuck into a great crunchy riff. The verses are controlled, the dynamics impressive and the choruses an album high point. If he had a world of his own, he sings, he'd build an empire for you, and it would be one of love which would spread like violence. It's slightly messianic but in a unifying way as the power of love will carry all. The breakdown near the end is reminiscent of the breakdown toward the end of 'I'm Feeling This'; 'Secret Crowds' is the sound of Tom DeLonge reclaiming his intelligent, punk-pop side, and the album is all the better for it.

'Star Of Bethlehem' is a very interesting instrumental track, all fresh morning synth pads and mid-1990s rave-scene ambient soundscaping and filter sweeps. That it's only two minutes long is a surprise; it feels like it could have been a ten minute psych-dance epic. What it does do is serve as an extended introduction to 'True Love', which kicks in with a pleasing tightness after several minutes of what can only be described as aural foreplay. The hook, when it does come, is absolutely irresistible after all the preamble – another fine, mature pop moment. 'Lifeline' has a flute/bass interplay that is excellently delivered, Tom's voice sitting somewhere in the middle with a song all about making mutual wishes come true; the birth of a dream, reaching for the sky. But chasing the dream should be together, if both parties want it to happen then it will. We all make mistakes, he says, but here's forgiveness and a lifeline. There's more singalong yo-ho-whoas here that lift the track considerably. 'Jumping Rooftops' is more Josh Wink-esque higher-state filtered interplay, the euphoria just getting set up in a (interesting bit of numerology here) 44-second close encounter; this and 'Star Of Bethlehem' hint toward a pure dance music side of DeLonge that perhaps he will one day pursue. But to rid anyone of those kind of heretical thoughts, back comes old-school Tom with the resonant 'Rite of Spring' in which the protagonist traces his family life, first dates, his father leaving him and his mother. She's crying, yet the kid is determined to make a better life. He says that if he had the opportunity he would not change a moment because all that has gone before has come together to make him the man he is today, and this is a realisation that has freed him to understand who he is at last. He's even free to, as he says, delude himself that the whole world is at his feet. It's absolutely coruscating self-awareness and with this song the slate is entirely wiped clean. He knows, ultimately, that success is relative in context with happiness, which is another nebulous concept in itself. The machine-gun bursts of energy (and snippets of tracks from the first album) that shoot through the introduction to the brilliant 'Heaven' are a fine way to herald the coming of the end of the album and the end of the double whammy of *We Don't Need To Whisper* and *I-Empire*. The song itself is as epic, ostensibly meaningful and gloriously contradictory as anything DeLonge had written for some time.

Reviews as ever were interesting to read; despite the highbrow conceptual basis for Angels & Airwaves' work in general, most magazines took the songs on face value. *Rolling Stone* weren't hot on the album. "In blink, cheesy year-book scrawl lyrics ... were balanced by bratty guitar. Set off by poppy, twinkling synth rock here, they're painfully earnest. It all sounds like the soundtrack to a *last-party-of-the-summer-bro!* flick."[235] An IGN reviewer felt that *I-Empire* was essentially a transitional album in AVA's development. "They seem torn between the realm of creating truly epic songs and keeping a large chunk of the streamlined pop element intact. The result is that some songs succumb to epic, neo-prog sensibilities and others crumble into somewhat derivative 'modern rock' territory. There's a lot to like about this disc, especially when the group goes for bombastically epic soundscapes."[236] *Blender* hated its ambition and what that magazine saw as unnecessary pompousness: "DeLonge is hungry for the vast truths of the universe," they scratched. "But there were more of those in one bar of blink's 'First Date' than on this whole record."[237] *Billboard* appreciated the concept a little more, praising the new rhythm section of Wachter and Willard, and noting that the album was a, "sweeping conceptual piece with a message as big as its sound and just a bit more enigmatic."[238]

This time around, *The Onion* was impressed. "'Magic' isn't the sole highlight," they declared. "'Sirens,' an earnest new-wave throwback, may even encourage DeLonge's sternest critics to sing along."[239] DeLonge's fiercest critics, *NME*, weren't going to take that advice any time soon, though. "Angels & Airwaves labour under the illusion that 'mature' equals 'worthwhile,'" they contended. "And that means long, directionless songs swathed in echo pedals and factory-set keyboards."[240] *Kerrang!* were as ever a little more charitable, awarding it three Ks and finding it a better record than that which had come before. "There are some impressive qualities ... the band has a sense of control over the music that is at times anthemic ... *I-Empire* is a patient record, powered by a sense of mood rather than a band attempting to break the world record for the number of drum rolls to be found in sixteen bars."[241]

The artwork – which in one place misspells Matt Wachter's surname as Matt Watcher (although, of course, that may be deliberate) – was conceived as a blend of astronauts, motorcycles, a desert and spacey imagery. DeLonge's interest in UFOs has been well-documented over the years, regularly musing as to whether there was life on Mars, whether the Ancient Egyptians hadn't known about starmen all along, and other nifty bedtime topics. Given this fixation with space, aliens and future-past timelessness, there was only one person to go to with a concept for artwork that ambitious and so the group made contact with Drew Struzan, the genius artist who had been responsible for the iconic posters for the *Star Wars* movies.

"A number of emails begun negotiations on the project," Struzan explained for this book. "Between myself and Tom's secretary. I recall she was very kind. I don't recall ever speaking with Tom or members of the band; it was all through emails. Once we agreed to do the artwork I received some photos of the band and a shot of Tom on his beloved motorcycle, a few shots of the guys in the desert, the flags and that's all the materials I received. From those shots began the concept and design stage. I was to include portraits of the members, Tom in the middle and the cycle on a lonely road. Yes, they wanted a more period look. Am I old fashioned? I designed with the elements provided. I didn't listen to the new album [whilst I was designing]. I tried to make them powerful and at the same time approachable and beautiful. Sci-fi, I guess. Gave it a bit of mystery in the atmosphere." Struzan says it was a great job to be asked to do and he is humble about the way that the album artwork came to pass.

"They were good to me. After giving me the materials they trusted me to design according to the intent they wished. An artist's dream is to be allowed to create with my own spirit and my own take on the assignment. I felt very free which gave me power and confidence in the creation. I sent them a comprehensive design which they had opinions about and from which they gave me direction; the spirit they gave me was one of freedom and that is how I warmly recall it." The artwork is, needless to say, fantastic and given the album's title the concept is put across very eloquently as a result. The band loved it; Angels & Airwaves was all about a multi-media experience, utilising technologies and techniques of great skill to kick rock up to another level.

One new technology that had been in development for much of 2007 was something that DeLonge had repeatedly said would shake up the way that the music industry operated. It was testament to the AVA manifesto, he told Brad Streeter. "We instantly wanted to be as ambitious as we could and start doing things that we really could set standards for what other bands could do. I have access to a lot of different resources that others don't because my company makes films and a lot of powerful people work there that are bright and intelligent. So we have access to doing other stuff. I wanted to show what would happen if bands try; I know I was the first one doing it ... and I was going to have to involve my friends and company to try and pull it off ... to clearly set a mould for what bands could do. That's why we are in the middle of building this huge piece of technology and operating system for bands to use and athletes to use. We have the movies coming out, and we are working on all these artistic performance and broadcast stuff."

"I mean kids and punk rock kids and critics don't really understand it. But it is all going to make a huge change. This is what I was talking about a few years back when I was coming out saying I want to revolutionise rock 'n' roll. And people kind of took it the wrong way ... but the thing was we were really working on these things. We were spending millions of dollars on this operating system called Modlife, and it's revolutionary! It's really, really amazing. We are spending money on these films. But then I get these calls from companies all over the world that want to work with Angels & Airwaves. Like huge ones! Like the biggest media companies in the world. They see that one band is doing all this, and I am trying to explain to everyone if no one does it then music is going to fail. So we help push the limits on what we can do, and what bands can do. If CDs are going to be free, we have to learn how to communicate our art on different mediums. So what sparked my interest is there is a crisis in the music industry and I have an overambitious soul that wants to do something good with my time here."[242]

Modlife takes the social networking concept with which we are all familiar by now, utilising the concept of a self-selecting (fan) community and such tools as live video, interactive conversations with bands, audio, video, artwork, blogs and text chats. It's easier to dive in than to explain, to an extent, which is always the case with sites like that, but imagine a blend of Facebook, MySpace, MSN chat and Youtube and you're halfway there. In November, 2007 the site went into a beta (draft) release with Angels & Airwaves its sole signee at that point, which since then has developed into a wide-ranging communications tool involving many more artists, products and people working in other fields. There are three levels of site access: free, registered and premium, with a sliding scale of tools at your disposal. It's a way of bands finding a new solution to the constant problem of recorded music having become synonymous with free music thanks to the ability of everyone connected to the internet to be able to copy songs and send them around instantly. Album sales are not the force they used to be; another way of putting value back into bands' activities has long been sought by a music business in flux. For bands, Modlife is an operating system enabling close contact with fans and giving a level of control back to the artist, who would now not need (theoretically) the bloated structures of the old-school distribution chains, media campaigns and all the rest of it. Maybe one day we will all live our lives entirely digitally, *Lawnmower Man*-style, but not quite yet. Modlife is an excellent and visionary tool, nonetheless. In practice, Modlife has become a part of the strategic marketing, promotion and interactive approach of the technologically-aware new breed of bands and fans, but it hasn't yet replaced the physical act of buying a CD.

Musically, and in terms of having a lot more fun, 2007 had been a much more positive time for all concerned. Travis and Mark spent the remainder of the year in discussions with record companies before announcing that the planned next +44 album would come out via Interscope records. Hoppus was also busy recording with Fever Club and Our Lunar Activities, and bigging up the potential in Chris Holmes' solo project. Engineer/occasional co-host of *Morning Zoo* Holmes had also remixed the +44 track, 'Little Death' during the European tour and co-mixed the Socratic stuff.

There was a scare in October when the homes of Hoppus' family and DeLonge were affected by the devastating fires sweeping through Southern California. Mark's family were amongst the first evacuated from their San Diego home, but thankfully no-one was hurt. Big Fish Studios was at one point very close to being totalled by the blaze, but the wind changed direction in the nick of time. Scary stuff, nonetheless.

Chapter 27
Politics And Mixtapes

DeLonge was enthusiastically supporting the Democrats once more as another presidential election loomed and because of his new clarity of thought, there was more hope than desperation on show. America had a real choice to make; did they want to, as *I-Empire* had suggested, believe in their own power to make a change? It was certainly a sentiment expressed by potential candidate Barack Hussein Obama, who was becoming one of the more interesting politicians in living memory. Young, handsome, intelligent, cool and with tons of charisma, Obama's campaign, based on the catchphrase 'Yes We Can', resonated with all generations. Despite the growing warnings of imminent world recession, the message of hope was clear for all to see. Optimism was back on the agenda. Obama's knack of connecting with all ages made him a very popular candidate, particularly with DeLonge.

"I think Obama sees the world of change. Absolutely. I think he is probably the best bet ... he is the closest thing we have to JFK. Obama in his young adulthood grew up with the internet and was connected to the world in some larger degree. I think he will think about how to solve problems on more of a global level. For one he has a family member from Kenya."[243] The United States couldn't elect an African-American president, though, could it?

DeLonge took AVA out on the road in January-March 2008. The announcement that Angels & Airwaves would appear on that year's Vans *Warped* tour shocked many people, although of course past line-ups had been eclectic. Were AVA 'punk' enough to fit in? (the relentlessly unpunk bubblegum singer Katy Perry was also on the bill). The dates began in June and ran through July and August. One of the support bands on AVA's short UK tour in April 2008 was You Me At Six.

"I was a big blink fan and still am and how I thought Tom was gonna be was the Tom on their DVDs," said Josh Franceschi when I interviewed him for this book. "Having fun, playing around, playing pranks on the other bands and having a laugh. We weren't expecting it from all of AVA but we thought we might get a bit of that from Tom. It didn't really happen, obviously he was a lot older than when he was doing all that stuff with blink. The whole motivation behind AVA is completely different to blink. It was all very casual, basic conversations like you'd have on the first day. He said he was really enjoying watching us and we reminded him of Taking Back Sunday. Tom's maybe a different person when surrounded by different people and the vibe and jokey set-up of blink, the non-stop jokey atmosphere is one thing but maybe him and the rest of AVA don't want to surround themselves with that kind of thing. They want to be more serious and do the music that's meant to be completely different to blink. A U2 compared to New Found Glory. He did make a few fart jokes which is always great, though as a blink fan it wasn't quite what I was hoping from the experience, but I thought it was great."

YMA6 were happy to be playing the London Astoria, a venue that for a rising band was something like the holy grail. "For us it was a huge, huge thing but I got the impression that for AVA it wasn't because Tom was used to playing huge arenas. Before the last show I went on and asked Tom if he was going to the after-party and he said, 'Nah, I'm gonna go back to the hotel and get some spaghetti.' When you've been in the game for a long time maybe playing the Astoria is a club show, but for us it was the best thing we'd ever done."

"The crowds – I'm not sure if this is bad – you could tell it was a sixty-forty split. Forty percent are there for Angels & Airwaves, they're passionate fans of that band. And sixty per cent of the crowd are there for any kind of taster of blink. When I walked around the shows there were kids in Dickies and Macbeth and when AVA whacked out a few blink snippets here and there, that's when people went absolutely apeshit. The big AVA songs were big as well but you felt that some were there for the Tom DeLonge show. I think once you've been in such a huge band like blink, who've had a huge impression on things and such a huge impression on other people's lives, it's then hard to go and do another band that's not gonna get an audience there wanting to see your old band."

"I knew that the kids were there at the early parts [of my career]," said Tom. "So a way for me to tip the hat and make a nod to them is to play a verse of a blink song then I would lead into an Angels song. Except we played 'There Is' [from *Box Car Racer*] whole because it is just David and I and we were both in Box Car Racer together. I wouldn't say we would never play blink songs in their entirety but it's still to be determined. I'm super proud of what I achieved with blink. We sold thirty million records which is a feat in itself. The whole thing was based on rebellion and doing what you want, when you want, and not caring. Therefore as far as being in a rock band and having that tag, it's probably the coolest one you can have. It certainly gives me a lot of heritage and it plays into where I'm at now. But the coolest thing is that Angels is the polar opposite. This band is about caring for every little detail and has so much message, when blink had so little message."

"It was sad the way it ended, I think after so many years we found ourselves in such different places in our lives and with different priorities. We just hit a wall and wanted to go on different paths. I think we will come back and rekindle our friendships, but I think we need time to go off and be ourselves first."[244]

His continued conciliatory tone was justified, in many ways: 2008 AVA's sound was firmly established and they went onto the *Warped* tour with much confidence. June, 2008 also saw the release of the much-awaited movie, *Start The Machine*. As intimated by DeLonge, it was a very naked look at the blink-182 breakup and the subsequent work toward Angels & Airwaves' debut album, *We Don't Need To Whisper*. Directed by Mark Eaton, the movie worked so well because of DeLonge handing over control entirely and not asking for final approval of any sequences for any reasons. This honesty comes across extremely well in a part-documentary, part-album-companion and all-invention.

"I met with a film grouping in LA, Lionsgate," DeLonge told Brad Streeter. "We were just talking, and the guy who runs the company is a friend of mine. I was asking his advice about this documentary. He instantly said, 'You have to submit this to Sundance Films'. I was never planning on it going to film festivals. So when I called up my friend Mark who was making the documentary I said, 'Mark, just finish it, and make [it] as true as it can be.' And he said, 'Do you want to include everything in there [including the stuff about painkillers]?' I said, 'Just make it true!'"[245] Mark Eaton did just that, it was sent to film festivals and gathered lots of praise for the brilliant production and direction as well as the classic nature of the story. It was always intended as more than just a rockumentary, though, as DeLonge mused.

"It has beautiful CGI footage that shows the conjunction of war and love which is what the whole record is about. A war with yourself, the drugs, losing your best friends, the previous band, and starting a new band. Then finding your way out of it. It was very much a human story. So it very much seemed to connect and resonate with these film critics. It's not a normal documentary with a hand-held camera. Everything is filmed beautifully, artistically. It is quite a tremendous arc of a story … you know, it is definitely something for other people to watch and see what other people go through, digest it and communicate back to them and hopefully learn something from it. That's what art is all about."[246] It's one interpretation. The movie did justify some of the anticipation for it, albeit that it hadn't changed the world. Together with the album, it makes some clear and very human points about relationships, war, technology and confusion in a very skilfully-edited and often breathtakingly visual manner.

Mark Hoppus kept himself busy too, hosting a raucous Honda Civic Tour launch, the bands being Panic! At The Disco and Motion City Soundtrack and The Hush Sound this time around. Production-wise, Mark was now in the studio with All Time Low, with whom he was also co-writing. There was also talk that Hoppus would be collaborating with an as-yet-unnamed act on yet another album project. As for +44, there had been months slipping by with no real work on that one aside from writing snippets here and there, although there were also reports flying about that the next tour would take in a lot more of the world including South America, a territory that blink-182 had never toyed with in any tangible form. Hoppus then worked with the band Koopa, voiced the part of an elephant for an animated series, then headed into the studio with New Found Glory. A pacy first seven months of the year for Hoppus, who'd turned 36 in March.

Travis had hardly been a slouch either, first releasing a hip hop remix of Flo Rida's 'Low', which followed on from the great critical reaction to the previous year's similar work on Soulja Boy's 'Crank That'. The videos of Travis hammering the drums along with the revamped tracks were very popular when they were posted on Youtube. Barker and Soulja Boy had also appeared on *The Jimmy Kimmel* show doing that track, with the drummer now firmly in demand in hip hop remix and production circles. He was to produce tracks for Paul Wall's forthcoming album, whilst finding a little time spare to record – with Mark – a cover of The Adolescents' 'Amoeba' for a forthcoming Vans *Warped* tour compilation album. Barker was hoping to collate his growing arsenal of remixes with a bunch of new tracks on which he was working. It started to germinate into the idea of making a solo album, producing it all himself and calling in hired shots to spit and spin over his hip hop cuts. As the spring turned into the summer, it became more and more likely that this project would supersede +44 for the immediate future, though that band would return, by all accounts, once everything was in place for the solo record. Guests so far on his own tracks included Young Dro, Too Short, the Federation, E-40 and Keak Da Sneak, with later contributions from huge names Willie Nelson and Damian Marley. Barker was also looking a little further into the future, too, contemplating a time when he hit fifty years old, a fine age, he reasoned, to be the leader of a big jazz band. He enjoyed the swiftness of the hip hop process, noting that whilst with traditional rock bands the writing and recording of new material could take up to a year to complete, it was entirely possible to make beats, get some samples and vocals, and finish a track a day in the hip hop arena. His continuing unique collaboration with DJ AM was interesting more than a few people too. Essentially, DJ AM would mix a set of classic tunes (dance, funk and anything he fancied) live with two turntables, then Travis would match the beat with live drums. An odd concept but one that crowds absolutely loved, and when the pair played on stage at the MTV Awards, the audience went wild. DJ AM and Barker released a downloadable mix-tape called *Fix Your Face* through their website in all its inventive glory. By August, Barker was even commenting on blink-182 in a much more relaxed manner.

"To be honest with you," he mused, "I haven't spoken to Tom in five years. I speak to Mark every day, he's one of my greatest friends, so ... that's the status of that. I think everyone would have to be friends, and I think we'd all have to want to do it in order for it to happen."[247] As DeLonge had put it the previous year, chasing the dream should be together, if both parties want it to happen then it will. Sounds a little like a lifeline. The three ex-amigos' relationship – or lack of it – may have been thawing by the start of August, 2008, but they would also be brought together by not one but two awful, devastating events.

Chapter 28
Farewells

Jerry Finn's influence on blink-182's greatest moments was absolutely crucial: his skill in bringing the band toward the music that they had the potential to make was instrumental in their crossover from the cultish and rougher punk-pop of the *Dude Ranch* days through the massive success of *Enema Of The State* and *Take Off Your Pants And Jacket*, when the band truly conquered the pop arena; subsequently Finn helped blink push back their own personal boundaries with the 2003 self-titled album as well as Box Car Racer, +44 and many other projects. Jerry Finn had also been the mixing hero behind Green Day's *Dookie* and *Insomniac* as well as much work with Pennywise, Rancid, The Vandals and many more punk bands over the years.

For Tom, Mark and Travis, as it was with all of the bands with which he'd worked, Jerry Finn was a friend, a sonic mentor, and a production genius. During 2008 he had been working with English fop Morrissey on a new album, *Years Of Refusal*, to stunning effect, after the pair had worked together very successfully on the bequiffed vocalist's 2004 return-to-form, *You Are The Quarry*.

Shortly after finishing the Morrissey record, Jerry Finn suffered a brain haemorrhage. Rushed to hospital, he spent a month fighting for life but tragically he was finally taken off life support and left to work with Strummer and Hendrix in the great studio in the sky on August 21, 2008. It was a truly shocking moment: a man who, at the young age of just 39, had become one of the most influential forces on modern punk rock, but had been taken long before his time was anywhere near up. Engineer Sam Boukas, who worked with Finn for years, recalls hearing about Jerry's passing.

"I found out from the owner of Signature Sound. I was shocked; I couldn't believe it," Sam says, before remembering the ultra-talented producer with a smile. "Jerry did some great things and he was a really fun guy to hang around with; he had a lot of energy and he was really smart. He was more of like a guide in the blink-182 sessions, saying what was good and making a few suggestions, very vague but gently pushing in this or that direction. Being also like a vessel, allowing them to do what they really wanted to do. Kinda paving the way for them and allowing them to say what they wanted to do, then giving them options but technically and sonically saying, 'I can make this happen for you.'"

"Jerry was a big part of their success and what happened was awful," Dave Carlock says. "Such a talented producer in seemingly great health at the age of 39. He was a very talented guy." Mark Hoppus was in a state of shock, and in a post on his site himynameismark.com, wrote of his devastation at losing a man he considered to know everything about recording and production. A guy who was true to his love of music, a fantastic friend and a quick-fire wit. "Jerry Finn was one of the most talented, funniest, coolest, smartest, and honest people I've ever known ... Jerry loved life. He was happiest when quietly making music he loved, and loudly making fun of everything he didn't. When I think of times spent with Jerry, all I can think of is us laughing. So much laughter."[248] No words could describe the sense of loss or how fantastic a person Finn was; Mark had learned so much from him about recording and about life over the years but above all he had lost a treasured and dear compadre, an individual that Mark was proud to call his friend. A clearly devastated Tom DeLonge heard of the news whilst on the Vans tour and dedicated a song to him; earlier in the tour, DeLonge had been exhorting crowds to send out good vibes to the hospital where Finn was receiving treatment. Mark Hoppus may have been the one to write the words on his blog, but it was a sentiment shared by all who'd worked with or met Finn, particularly those who'd been as close as Travis, Mark and Tom. Mark's words spoke for them all, as well as literally millions of others whose lives Finn had touched with his music, including Morrissey.

"His death was astonishing because it was very quick," Morrissey said. "A few weeks earlier to this we were at his house, listening to the album playback and everyone was very happy ... I was with him for the last few weeks of his life and it was terribly sad. But the lesson for all of us is that this doesn't last forever."[249] It was a horrible August. Life had to go on, as it always must, but unbelievably there was more devastation to come.

On September 19, 2008, Travis Barker and DJ AM had just played at a free T-Mobile show in Five Points, Columbia, where other acts included Perry Farrell and Gavin DeGraw. Barker and AM, along with Travis' long-time friend and bodyguard Charles 'Che' Still and the drummer's personal assistant, 'Little' Chris Baker, headed to the airport to catch a private Learjet 60 home. A few minutes before midnight, according to witnesses, the aircraft over-ran the runway, hitting some antennas and lights. Sparks flew as the plane skidded through a fence, crossed a road and crashed into the opposite embankment, catching fire on impact. Tragically the pilot and co-pilot, plus Chris Baker and Che Still, lost their lives in the incident. Travis Barker and AM managed to miraculously escape, as reported to one of the first officers to arrive at the crash, Lieutenant Josh Shumpert.

"They slid down the wing on the right side of the plane; they said they were on fire, and that they tackled each other and put each other out. When I got there they were on the side of the road ... pacing and in shock. Travis was very shaken up. Travis was wearing some kind of shorts and no shirt, one sock on. And a black hat on his head."[250] Barker, who had suffered second and third degree burns to the lower part of his body, and AM, who had suffered facial injuries, were both taken to Joseph M. Still Burn Center in Augusta, Georgia, where it became clear that both men would survive but recuperation would take quite some time. From his hospital bed, Travis announced that a fund would be set up in honour of Little Chris and Che through his Famous Stars And Straps website. The cause of the crash is still to be verified at the time of writing.

Shanna Moakler summed up the feelings of many in a statement. "We can only ask for prayers as we heal and mourn the loss of our dear friends who we considered part of our family," Barker's ex-wife said. "Our lives will be changed forever."[251] Mark Hoppus and Tom DeLonge respectfully kept their counsel for several weeks following the crash which had shocked the world of music. It wasn't until weeks later that DeLonge referred to the tragedy during a transmission he made live on Modlife. It had totally freaked him out, he said, and it blew his mind when he found out about the incident, which was infinitely more monumental than any arguments that had ensued from their musical activities. He also commented that it was surprising that people were asking for his own thoughts.

"Everyone wanted to know what I think, but it's not about me and it's not about blink at all ... it's about Travis and his family, so stop worrying about what I think, and what I feel, and what I'm going to say, because it doesn't matter."[252] By October, Barker and AM had recovered enough to be released from hospital and Travis travelled back to Los Angeles by bus in order to continue his treatment at a facility closer to his home. He had said it was his greatest fear to be involved in an aeroplane crash, and that he was grateful to still be alive.

"I am doing the best I can possibly be," he told *US Weekly*. "I'm so anxious to get out of here. I've just been in surgery after surgery. I have third-degree burns basically from my feet up to my waist and both hands. One of my hands has second-degree burns and one has third-degree burns. I'm trying to have a quick recovery and play the drums again, and be able to hold my kids again."[253] It wasn't until November that Mark broke his respectful silence. It had been an awful time, first losing Jerry Finn and then this crash in which his great friend Little Chris and Che had been called before their time. In a blog on his website, Hoppus paid tribute to Chris and the way that he would instantly make friends with everyone he met, be they rock stars or kids just starting out, everyone was treated the same, with love and respect. Chris had been around the blink/+44 camp for a long time and would be hugely missed. Commenting that Travis was like a brother to him, Mark also expressed his gratitude that the drummer and DJ AM had managed to make it out of the crash. He talked of his amazement at the speed of Travis' recovery because Barker was born to play drums and it was amazing to see him so quickly take his place once more behind a drum kit.

The tragic events had also put something else into perspective: old friendships would start to be rebuilt between Mark, Tom and Travis in the aftermath of the tragedies of the autumn of 2008. Mark said that the three had started talking again, noting that initially it was on the phone, then in early November the trio had hung out in person for an hour or two, simply re-establishing their friendship after several years without talking to each other. Hoppus was aware that the first question people were bound to ask was whether this meant that blink-182 would be getting back together. He said that it just hadn't been a subject for discussion because what was more important was that the once-inseparable threesome were all simply enjoying the opportunity to be together again as mates because the last couple of months had shown them all that life is too short to be hung up on what had previously happened. The past was the past – it was the future that was important.

By the end of 2008, Travis had recovered well enough to declare that he and DJ AM would be performing for the New Year Nation's *Los Angeles Party* at The Wiltern on December 31st. The gig would also be streamed live on the internet. In fact, AM had already been able to return to action as early as October, with an appearance in Avalon, as well as DJ-ing for Jay-Z, an artist to whom Barker had given the remix treatment on the track 'Jockin' Jay-Z' which had spread throughout the net with help from a debut on DJ Skee's radio show. When asked whether blink were getting back together, he was firm about the matter. "No [we're not getting back together]. We're friends, though, everyone's getting along pretty good."[254]

Meanwhile, Mark had spent November in the studio with Our Lunar Activities and recorded a project for Richard Gibbs that was intended for use in a movie, appeared on a TV show giving advice to aspiring bassists and guested on a track at the behest of Ace Enders, of the band The Early Novembers. The track was released under the label of Ace Enders And A Million Different People, and also featured many other guests. It was in aid of a charity called *VH1 Save The Music Foundation*, which was set up to ensure that every child would have access to music education. As 2009 dawned, Hoppus was in good form about musical matters, revealing that for some time he had been working on new material that was destined for a planned future solo album. Travis of course would be playing on some of the tracks, as well as working on his own solo stuff. Reading between the lines it's not difficult to see that as an entity it seemed that +44 had probably reached the end of the line, although Mark was later to indicate that he enjoyed working with Shane and Craig so much that it couldn't ever really be said to be the end. Hoppus was also really happy that he and Tom were talking again three or four times a week or even more often. The three amigos were stoked that they were invited to the Grammy Awards, on February 8, 2009. The trio would be presenting an award together. But speculation was rife that there was also an announcement ready to be made, too …

Chapter 29
Family Reunion

The trio strode onstage to the sound of 'All The Small Things' and made a quip about how good it was to see the Jonas Brothers and Stevie Wonder "playing together again". Which of course had never happened before, but it was pretty much just a preamble to enable them to drop one hell of a bombshell. "We used to play music together, and we decided we're going to play music together again," revealed Travis Barker, arm in a sling after some surgery to his fingers. Mark Hoppus yelled, "blink-182 is back!"[255]

It sent the web into a frenzy; an announcement of some kind had been expected since AVA guitarist, David Kennedy, had implied on Modlife that blink might be working on an album during 2009. Fans of the band descended on the Poway pop-punks' official website, where a simple statement read that blink were back, writing songs, friends again and making plans to tour the world. Mark Hoppus told *Alternative Press* that the idea for the reunion had been in the trio's minds for a few weeks, but didn't come to fruition until Tom DeLonge had broached the subject of a possible reunion.

"I remember he said, 'So, what do you guys think? Where are your heads at?' And I said, 'I think we should continue with what we've been doing for the past seventeen years. I think we should get back on the road and back in the studio and do what we love doing."[256] Once decided, it was only surprising that it took so long for the secret to come out.[257]

"I didn't get the feeling they were gonna come back at all," mused engineer Sam Boukas. "At the time Travis was getting involved in other projects, like the Transplants and gigs with other groups and they were all busy living with their family lives and being separate and being happy about that. Tom was also talking about what eventually became Angels & Airwaves, also with Dave from Box Car Racer, feeling he wanted to do something that had that '80s feel. That's what he was trying to do with AVA and kinda tried to do on that 2003 blink album, some of that energy he liked so much from some of the '80s stuff he heard. And Mark was doing +44 so there was never a strong feeling that they were going to come back with a blink album any time soon. But I'm glad blink is back, that's great. We always need a bit of joy and fun. I guess [that's] true more now than ever. But then again in the States we've just switched over to Barack Obama so we feel upbeat."

Josh Franceschi of You Me At Six sums up a long-term fan's viewpoint about blink's somewhat unexpected comeback. "I think they just realised that, God forbid if Travis had died, the whole blink-182 vibe would never be the same. They could get the best drummer in the world and it wouldn't be blink. It was just a huge wake-up call. They just realised they should get on with it and do it and everybody's more than happy it's all happening." One of those who's stoked is Kung Fu kingpin/The Vandals' Joe Escalante, who has an interesting take on the concept of groups coming back. "I have a theory that every band in the world will get together sooner or later," he told me. "It's just a matter of time but eventually every band finds some reason to get back together to play a few shows and I think we're all looking forward to that."

Back in San Diego, Doubletime Studios' Jeff Forrest muses on the past few years with the authority of a guy who's seen many bands before. "I thought Angels & Airwaves was kinda crazy," he recalls. "You know, when someone goes from being the funny guy to really serious and talking about politics and all that stuff, I'm watching Larry King and they're on it and I'm going, 'Dude, what are you doing?' He was good at sitting in the studio farting. Then I read about [the painkillers] and it was, 'Oh, well'. With Angels & Airwaves I always tell people I liked them better when they were U2. They did some serious stuff on those later blink albums that was good stuff. The serious moments are great. But in the world we're living now we need blink-182's sense of fun. That's for sure!"

By February there was songwriting going on, Tom and Mark showing each other ideas and jamming them out. The fact that they had their own studios was a big help, and though Jerry Finn had passed away, they still felt his presence in everything they did. Hopefully elements of the talented Finn's mastery of production would rub off on the band when they actually set to producing the planned new album. Oh, and by the way, it wasn't a reunion: they'd never split up. It was a continuation after the 'indefinite hiatus' had turned out to span four years. And now they were back there was no need to rush into recording something that was going to be unsatisfying. The new album would not be coming out in 2009 after all, but rehearsals had gone superbly well nonetheless. There was soon an announcement that blink was to tour with Weezer and Fall Out Boy that summer; melodic sounds to the ears of fans. During April, blink were spotted shooting a video in front of a green screen, a system that enables other footage to be subsequently dropped into the final version, placing the band in any context other than just a studio situation.

Angels & Airwaves had also reconvened at the start of January 2009, to start work on a planned new album under the simple but always vital banner of 'Love', although the return of blink-182 inevitably had led to speculation that AVA would now split. However, the project is more than just dependent on the musical whims of its members and as such the multimedia project continues to be very active. In May, it was announced that the band's third album and new movie would be released simultaneously on Christmas Day, 2009, in the name of 'Love'. The *I-Empire* movie had morphed into *Love*. It's said to be a modern version of Pink Floyd's famous movie *The Wall* and anticipation was high to see what the pinnacle of several years' work might be. There is also talk of possible link-ups with none other than NASA to broadcast live events as Tom continues to try and push boundaries in all directions both in and out of blink-182. DeLonge's company, Macbeth, was also going great guns; set up some years before to provide footwear designed by and for musicians, it had expanded into an entirely vegan range as well as being very active in the charitable field. It was important that Macbeth were aware of their social responsibilities, and they were proving just that.

Travis Barker's remixing skills were much in demand during 2009, when he had time to work with another one of the heavyweights of hip hop, Eminem, on a track called '3AM'. It was the first track on which he'd worked since the crash and it was instantly a Youtube hit, as all his mixes have always been. He was also lining up to play on an album by ex-Guns N' Roses guitarist, Slash, later in 2009, two typically diverse projects from the hardest-hitting and hardest-working drummer in showbiz. For Mark's part, there were remixes of Peter, Bjorn And John, work with New Found Glory and others as he continued to be an in-demand studio guy.

Blink appeared live together for the first time in four years on May 14, 2009, hammering through a three-song set at a T-Mobile party. The tracks were all old classics, though perhaps not the most obvious ones: 'The Rock Show', 'Feeling This' and 'Dammit' went down a storm and the band was absolutely delighted at the response. The forthcoming tour was going to be very interesting, and a whole lot of fun. In true blink-182 style, there was even a name for it that was almost certainly a leg-pull: *One Way Ticket To Boneville.* Appearances on *The Tonight Show With Jay Leno* and *Jimmy Kimmel* cemented the great news once and for all. Tight, fun, excited and just a little older in looks but not in spirit, it was like a weight had been lifted from each man's shoulders as they rocked, rolled and smiled their way through their performance. The Kimmel show was only intended to be run-throughs of a couple of tracks, 'What's My Age Again?' and 'Dammit', but the band were having so much fun that they carried on playing – despite prompting the ecstatic audience that as they'd not played most of the tracks for several years they may well screw them up. But they didn't, and blink jumped their way through eight songs in total, including 'Dumpweed', 'Reckless Abandon' and 'Josie (Everything's Going To Be Fine)'.

Back in full flow, blink also playfully suggested they'd be covering songs by New York popstrel, Lady GaGa, at some point. As the summer beckoned, excitement was at a high level. The new songs that the band were planning were apparently heavier than before, more serious almost, although the 2003 album had certainly be leaning in that direction anyway. There were rumours of demos being knocked out like 'The Night The Moon Was Gone', about how everyone shares fears, desires and wants, and how everyone, no matter who they might be, just wants to find a way of making it all make sense, a sentiment that surely everyone shares. Other tracks in the planning, pre-production and rehearsal stages were the likes of 'Up All Night', a mix of Pink Floyd, blink and Rush that was rumoured to become the flagship single for the new album. Any new songs would start to be filtered into the major tour that begun in July.

It all began in Las Vegas on July 23, where anticipation was quite simply through the roof. When it came down to it, the show blasted the roof right off. The scene was set from the moment that Tom DeLonge uttered the first words of the tour, and the comeback, through his microphone: "Motherfucker shit fuck!" Welcome back. Tom and Mark swapped insults and stream-of-silliness banter about getting dirty with Lance Armstrong, The Rock and Shaquille O'Neal – and each other's moms. Like they'd never been away, in fact. The merchandise on sale that night had a knowing, typically playful, smart-alec air to it: the T-shirts were labelled 'blink-182: crappy punk rock'. As MTV observed, it was just like old times. The difference between this and their previous gigs was that this time they all wanted to be there; a happy band of brothers firing out their songs to create an atmosphere of fun, warmth, stupidness and some more serious stuff too. Travis had his solo, spinning riser and all, and he blasted out a host of rhythms including accompanying the Jay-Z track 'Dirt Off Your Shoulder'. The set smashed through their hits and ended with encores of 'Carousel' and 'Dammit'. Vegas was the perfect place to kick it all off again. It was all being filmed by HND$M*RND$M who had been given full access to the rehearsals and preparations for a forthcoming 'Blinkumentary' that would track the progress of what Mark was vehement in refusing to call a 'reunion'.

"That has the stigma of a band that's riding on its own coat-tails," he told *LA Times*. "This is a continuation for us. We want to make an album, do what we love and continue where we left off." [258] But as for that new song 'Up All Night', the ever media-savvy band said that they'd not be playing it on the new dates in order to avoid the inevitability that the first exposure many fans would have to it would be a cruddy phone-video recording on Youtube. It would be far more preferable for the completed studio version to hit the streets first, but with their schedules full both with blink and other projects, the band had not had the chance to head into the studio and record it as yet.

"It's not so much that we were concerned that it was going to get played somewhere where we didn't have control of it," explained Tom. "We were just concerned that the first impressions weren't going to be the beautiful hard work that we put into recording the song and the way we recorded it. At the end of the day there's only three of us onstage, but in the studio you can really twist and turn the audio signals to do something special. It's two different mediums, one is creating the art, the other is communicating it. I always feel you should communicate it after you've created it."[259] The song was scheduled instead to be recorded and released following the tour.

What was definitely the case was that 'Aliens Exist' would be one of the first tracks confirmed for the awesome next generation of the popular *Rock Band* console games – *Lego Rock Band*. The kid's toy was a feature of summer life – Hoppus and DeLonge had contributed mosaics in the plastic brick that were themed round the ocean and displayed at Legoland California Resort throughout August in a charity auction for the Surfrider Foundation.

The band were in top gear and by the time the tour hit Vancouver there was enough room for Travis to unveil his full flying kit schtick ... where he would play his drums entirely upside-down. As August dawned, the blink-182 camp revealed what had been much-speculated since the comeback announcement – that they would tour Europe in 2010. All three of the band wanted to make it happen and so it was quickly pencilled into the schedules. Meantime, Tom DeLonge announced the next stage in the Angels & Airwaves adventure with a three-minute trailer for the *Love* film. The trailer juxtaposed images of war, shooting, explosions and soldiers with typically meaningful statements from Tom about how he intended AVA to have an impact on music, the industry, how music was marketed and delivered. Blink may be back but AVA weren't getting pushed aside as a result. In the past, DeLonge had found the sides of his musical, personal and artistic leanings somewhat difficult to reconcile but these three minutes blew that all away. There was, and is, room for everything and Tom was not going to compromise anything in his quest to both change the world – and have some fun too. *Love*, the album, would be released for free on Valentines Day, 2010. At gigs, too, Tom'd been wearing his *Love* T-shirt as well as playing through his AVA-logo amplifier. As had become increasingly clear even before the hiatus, it was important that there was substance and statements below the silliness. As for Mark, he'd announced that he was to work with Panic! At The Disco on at least one song of their new LP. Mark, (by now producer for All Time Low and Motion City Soundtrack), was becoming a very in-demand 'man in the chair'. Nonetheless he was super-delighted to be asked to remix the iconic Jackson 5 track, 'ABC' – giving it a sensitive treatment that nonetheless was noticeably different enough from the original mix as to be somewhat fascinating. It was a project driven by Motown, who had asked fifteen different producers to contribute their own remixes for a possible album *Michael Jackson: The Remix Suite* to be forthcoming as a tribute to the recently-departed Jacko, who had shockingly passed away in June on the eve of his own comeback – an ambitious 50-date run at London's O2 Arena.

"[It] was huge for me," he said. "Just being asked to be a part of the Michael Jackson tribute was so amazing. I thought to myself, 'Are they sure they called the right guy?' It was really fun to do. I was glad to be a part of it and I hope it did justice to the song."[260]

Cadillac-lover Travis Barker, meanwhile, had other plans: to give away one of his custom-vintage cars to a lucky fan. The 1966 DeVille Convertible is a stunning piece of lastingly beautiful workmanship, something that anyone would be proud to have in their collection. Also included in the prize was a round trip for two to the blink gig on

October 1 in Charlotte, North Carolina and accommodation. Some prize! Barker also kept interest high in his solo album and Twitter was awash with news that those who had heard the work in process were suitably bowled over with the sonics so far. But Travis' world was about to be blown apart once more with yet another tragic event.

Since Adam Goldstein – DJ AM – and Travis had walked free from the plane crash the previous year, it had seemed that their individual and collective acknowledgement at being spared had given them both a new outlook on the world. And of course it led indirectly to the return of blink-182 in the first place. Tragically, however, at 5.22am on August 28, 2009, DJ AM was found dead by a friend in his New York apartment, following calls from pals who had not seen him for a while. He had just finished filming for a fly-on-the-wall MTV series. Though Goldstein had understandably been prescribed medication for pain following the crash, it was shocking when the New York medical examiner reported that the 36-year old had died from "acute intoxication" listing several prescription drugs and cocaine. However, the NY medical examiner also reported it was an "accidental overdose."[261]

Blink's show at Hartford, Connecticut the next day was a sombre one as news filtered through of the ultra-talented DJ's passing. Mark said onstage that it was a very difficult night for them all. "We lost a dear friend yesterday," began Hoppus, speaking on behalf of all that knew the musician. "His name was Adam Goldstein. You probably know him as DJ AM. He was an innovator and a genius and he loved music more than anything else. Above all he was a very dear friend."[262] As the band played 'Down' in tribute, the tears flowed. Travis, subdued, held his head in his hands at the end of the set. Subsequent dates in New York, St. Louis and Cleveland were rescheduled over the next week in order to allow this awful news to somehow sink in.

During the tour, whilst the band were preparing for a gig in Atlanta, Georgia, Travis visited the burns unit at Doctors' Hospital, the Joseph M Still Burns Centre that had treated him following the plane crash. He spent hours there meeting patients, signing autographs and most of all thanking the staff who had been so very instrumental in his recovery. "I'm here to say 'thank you' to everyone who took care of me after the accident," a statement by Travis read. "I was sort of unconscious the last time I was here, and I felt like I owed them a big 'thank you.'"[263] The band pledged $100,000 to the centre before heading off to resume what they do best: playing a storming live show to tens of thousands of rapt fans. Healthcare was firmly on the agenda, Mark writing a piece for the *Huffington Post* that discussed the huge amount of his countrymen and women who were currently unable to afford health insurance. It was an issue that was being debated far and wide across America and it had hit close to home when one of the catering crew had been forced into hospital with a condition that would go on to cost her over $40,000. Said employee had started a website where people could donate to help her predicament, Hoppus said he'd match every dollar, and the editorial piece that followed put the issue right in the minds of an often politically-bored youth. Such is the power of music; anyone who claimed that it was all dick jokes and farting around had got the guys way, way wrong.

The blink-182 tour ended in October with Travis for one saying that it had been the best tour the three had ever embarked upon. They felt closer than ever before and this rediscovered intimacy on a musical and personal level had been of vital support during those horrendous low days following what had happened with DJ AM. Musically, he said that he was going to squeeze in as much studio time as possible on his solo record and tour plans were mooted for April 2010. There was just time to start the excellent process that led to the reissue of the band's back catalogue one by one on limited-edition and lovely vinyl; also for Mark to work with a few people including Leighton Meester, and for Tom to head back into hospital for more surgery on his troublesome back, before blink-182 headed back into the studio in January, 2010 to complete work in earnest on the long-awaited new album. By now, the anticipation was as high as for any previous blink record.

The new year started in much the same vein with each member of blink continuing to work incredibly hard. First off, Mark Hoppus and Pete Wentz announced they had written and completed a track, 'In Transit', that was to appear on one of the movies of the year – Tim Burton's gothic take on *Alice In Wonderland*. And though Wentz and Hoppus denied that it was the beginning of yet another offshoot supergroup, they did admit that they planned to record more together, schedules permitting. Hoppus also teased fans by saying that the new blink-182 material was going to be poppy, catchy but weird. The various influences of the members, he said, pretty much dictated that would be the case, from hip hop, indie rock, stadium sounds and the

'80s epic stuff that Tom DeLonge was really into. Hoppus said he was going to do everything in his power to get the new blink LP out in 2010, displaying an urgency to get the ball rolling that was shared by Travis Barker.

The drummer's own year began with a performance at the Grammys along with Lil Wayne, Eminem and Drake, hammering their way through the Drake track, 'Forever' and 'Drop The World' by Lil Wayne. Barker had remixed 'Forever' previously, and commented that he'd run into Eminem in Detroit and the pair did a track together for his album. That long-player was rumoured to be called *Can The Drummer Get Some?* Guests and collaborators also included Weezy, Swiss Beatz, Rich Ross and Lil Wayne. Amidst regular get-togethers with Hoppus and DeLonge for pre-production and recording for the new blink LP, Travis also teamed up with Kanye West's tour DJ, A-Trak, for a set of gigs in March. The pair had jammed in the autumn of 2009, with Barker playing atop A-Trak's scratching. The live shows included an appearance at the South-by-Southwest new bands festival as well as Miami's Winter Music Conference. The pair said they would be performing versions of remixes as well as new music they'd recorded at Travis' studio in LA. More guests on the album included Corey Taylor of Slipknot and RZA of Wu-Tang Clan as the Barker solo album continued to be refined and stacked with musical gods from all genres. Keeping his hand in with his teaching, just in case this rock 'n' roll thing didn't work out, Barker made time in his schedule to spend some serious hours with Rihanna, showing her some tricks. She proved to be an adept pupil.

Tom DeLonge had been more circumspect about the appearance of the new blink album, commenting that it was more likely that it would come out, possibly on Interscope, in 2011. He could hardly be blamed, however, for wanting to concentrate on one thing at a time: Angels & Airwaves had released their third album, *Love* on 14 February, 2010, and fans could download the record from the Modlife site in return for an optional donation – in return for which they'd receive the Mark Hoppus remix of 'Hallucinations'. The band had partnered with many businesses and sponsors on the release as they continued to try and find a new paradigm for the dissemination of music. Fans didn't care as long as they had some new music to listen to, and it was good stuff too. As ever, there was a film promised to coincide although it didn't appear on Valentine's Day. DeLonge had said that the album was a blend of Radiohead, U2, Pink Floyd and that the movie was a circular narrative about human life, destiny and space. The plot, said the singer, involved an astronaut, Lee Miller, stranded on a space station as the earth collapses, and realising he is the last person alive ... until many years later he discovers something out there with him. The plot, as had become the norm with AVA, was a typically ambitious one where there was an underlying theme – this time that of hope and the fundamental requirement of humans to connect with each other, and perhaps with God. A kind of mix of Bowie's 'Space Oddity' and Kubrick's seminal *2001: A Space Odyssey*, except with added '80s synths and pedal-delay guitars all over the place.

The album opens with an upbeat instrumental track, 'Et Ducit Mundum Per Luce', the title of which translates to 'lead the world by light' or 'by light lead the world' in Latin. Quite a jump from joke songs about sex with dogs and grandparents. 'The Flight of Apollo' follows, a lengthy story soaked in string sounds, lyrics about positivity and some great chugging guitars. The dynamics of the arrangement and the grooving guitar riff are AVA at their best – a somewhat wistful, semi-orchestral track with eyes toward the future and a sonic that acknowledges the past, all anchored by Tom's vocals that are earnestly pleading. 'Young London' has a familiar-sounding, fast-fretting piece of pure U2 in its main riff, as Tom talks about the weekend, dancing with your friends, picking up girls, pheromones and, well, young love, before it ends with Atom Willard seemingly falling downstairs together with his drum kit. 'Shove' follows, Willard's hip hop beat underpinning a slowly-building keyboard pad in a track that builds, falls, builds again and finally establishes itself as a mid-paced uplifter. It's more about arrangement than riffs, though bassist Matt Wachter pulls out some cracking, driving sixteenth notes amidst the tune. Next up is 'Epic Holiday', which, were it not for the punkish rhythm section and the brutal sense of the heading into Tom's vocals about starting riots, could veer worryingly close to 'I Think We're Alone Now'. As Tom sings, though, life is just a game, the epic holiday of the title.

As with the previous two albums, there is a sense that this is indeed the soundtrack to a movie. The next song, 'Hallucinations', is different to what has come before on the album. Chuggy guitars are covered in squelchy laser sounds and the dreamy lyrics are skewiff and poetic. Worst song title on the album prize goes to 'The Moon-Atomic (...Fragments and Fictions)' which is another six-and-a-half minute composition with a crunched-up 'We Will Rock You' drumbeat moving things along niftily whilst the album's spacey narrative continues to unfold. Of great interest here is the lengthy coda: a minute of pure atmosphere complete with breathy, extended soft synths, ultra-processed vocals and heavily-echoed and delayed themes. It sounds like an astronaut floating off into space. Job done, then. It also forms the intro to 'Clever Love', Tom's vocal to the fore as the album and the story turns a little introspective for a moment. It takes nearly four minutes for a rock song to emerge from the set-up and is all the better for it. The blurring between outros, intros, bridging tracks and suchlike is more evidence that these songs are part of a greater whole – as we all are. 'Soul Survivor (...2012)' kicks in with a kind of Nintendo platform game-ish riff in a track that soon solidifies into one of the more conventionally pop, or, more accurately, stadium rock, moments of the record.

The penultimate track, 'Letters to God, Part II' is another brilliantly-conceived '80s-prog suite as the protagonist seeks out some home truths about life, death, truths, lies and the rest of it. *Love* comes to an end with 'Some Origins Of Fire', which ruminates on people needing love, but love being tricky, because people are actually also difficult to love; and that loneliness is essential to completion. It's not the strongest album-closer that there's ever been but on the whole *Love* is emotive stuff that reaches for the stars and whilst only occasionally getting there, the ride toward the horizon is at times one of intriguing beauty.

By now, most magazines were well used to hearing Tom's grandiose plans and schemes. Long-time supporters of everything that came out of the blink camp (and the members' solo projects) are *Absolute Punk*, whose review gave the LP 77%, noting that whilst the songs were arguably overlong and there was little here to entice new fans, it was a satisfying step up from *I-Empire*. The website picked out 'Young London' as a decent track and felt that whilst 'Shove' would make a good single, it also drew on AVA's previous 'Distraction'. Likewise, 'Epic Holiday' had more than a hint of the riff from 'Everything's Magic'. The production and proggy stadium rock feel were both praised, and the review concluded by advising DeLonge to stop trying to change the world – because he'd already done that in blink without trying. *Alternative Press* gave it 3 out of 5, not a bad score at all, in a review that praised stomping drums, shimmering guitars and lyrics that were anthemic. A physical version of the album would subsequently be made available on CD.

The message, though, was clear: AVA were here to stay, and they could and would co-exist with blink-182. That was something, of course, that DeLonge had been insistent on for quite a while. What 2009 and 2010 proved more than anything was that the trio's musicality spanned a range of approaches, genres and personnel that would never be able to be held inside one band. Simply put, there was a blink-182 mode, and there was a musician mode, and the two were clearly not the same thing, at least not always. Sometimes a break can do people the world of good.

Back in blinkland, album sessions continued through the spring of 2010, with the trio absolutely delighting fans in Europe with the news that they would be touring there in August and playing oodles of major music festivals – including those at Reading and Leeds. Hundreds of thousands of fans across the continent and the UK readied themselves for a slew of breast references, daft banter – and some of the catchiest punky pop songs that had ever been written. The hiatus was well and truly over, as if anyone really needed confirmation.

⋆

From first dates to family reunions, the ongoing story of blink-182 has been a complex one of triumph, tragedy, happiness and hard times. It's encompassed skating and farting, tears and disappointment, exciting new opportunities and dark nights of the soul. The guys have started families but experienced harsh mortality. There have been men overboard and friendships lost seemingly forever, only to be found again. Whether joking around, trying to change the world, losing direction or seeing through tragedy what is truly important in life, it has been, and continues to be, one hell of a timeless tale.

It's a story of a band, sure, but equally a study in friendship, brotherhood and, ultimately, love.

All The Big Things, you might say.

Footnotes & Index Of Articles Referenced

1 Interview from www.cacophony.com, 1996
2 Interview with www.cacophony.com, 1996
3 Interview with John Robb, 2000
4 Ibid
5 Interview with Thrasher, 1996
6 Interview with Hard Jargon, 1994
7 Lewis Carroll was the alter ego of Charles Dodgson, an eminent mathematician. Legend has it that Queen Victoria, much enamoured of the Alice books, requested a copy of his next tome. Dodgson, not a man without humour, duly obliged with *An Elementary Treatise On Determinants*. He denied this had ever happened.
8 Interview with www.cacophony.com, 1996
9 Dermot Lambert: "Other producers on the album were Gil Norton (we were all Pixies fans), Steve Hillage and David Pine."
10 Dermot continues: "In April 1994, while we were playing a student gig in Oxford with Oasis and My Life Story, Brian Message from Parlophone, who was working closely with us through this time, and who has since gone on to manage Radiohead, joked that we should consider calling our act McDermot's Blink. That's how *not* seriously we saw the whole thing. Our label didn't seem to mind too much either."
11 Other claims blink-182 have made in various interviews are that the 182 was Mark's ideal weight (presumably pounds, not stone); the number of Mark's grandfather's WWII boat; a numerological one with the 18 signifying the eighteenth letter of the alphabet (R) and the second (B) which stands for Rancho Bernardo, Scott and Mark's stamping ground. It's probably worth picking one you like and sticking with it.
12 To further add to the confusion, a Danish band called Blink also existed but they changed their name to BL!NK.
13 Interview with www.launch.com. 2000.
14 Apparently this is a 1985 movie featuring Kim Cattrall, which is more than enough reason to steer clear. She is from Widnes, not Liverpool, by the way.
15 There are many silly instances of tension in various interviews over the years but Lambert is keen to hold out an olive branch: "Come on Tom, let's have that dual release of 'All The Small Things', blink-182 featuring Blink... that'd be fun. Thank God for Bono. I'm serious." The campaign starts here.
16 I looked this one up too, apparently it means something along the lines of 'extreme, over the top pleasure to the point of being unbearable'. A bit like listening to Lenny Kravitz.
17 Interview with Heckler Magazine, 1997
18 Interview with iZine, 1998
19 Interview with Anonymous Magazine (Aus), 1998
20 Interview with Slamm Magazine, 1999
21 Interview with Thrasher Magazine, 1996
22 Interview with John Robb, 2000
23 Interview with Circus Magazine, 1997
24 Interview with Heckler Magazine, 1997
25 Kerrang! Review, 1997
26 Interview with Shane Brown, 1998
27 Interview with iZine, 1998
28 Interview with Kerrang!, 2001
29 From Transcript Of Interview with John Robb, 2000
30 Interview with Warped Magazine, 1994
31 Interview with Thrasher Magazine, 1996
32 Unfortunately not named after Elvis Presley's original drummer, DJ Fontana, although that would be cool.
33 Plus the possibly-apocryphal Eric Tronic
34 Interview with MTV, 2000
35 Interview with Drumstuff.com, 2001
36 Allmusic.com review, 1997

37 Absolute Punk review, 1997
38 The track Raynor refers to is the very emotive 'Turn The Page', released in 1973 on the *Back In '72* LP. Yes, I said LP, etc. It's worth listening to it. Metallica's version was released on the 1998 *Garage, Inc* album and subsequently stayed at Number 1 in the *Billboard* Hot Mainstream Rock Tracks for eleven weeks.
39 Interview With Rolling Stone, 2000
40 From Transcript Of Interview with Bobby Gorman
41 Interview With MTV, 2000
42 Check out: http://www.kungfurecords.com for their excellent roster
43 Pat Secor nows runs the successful 11345/Hi Fidelity merchandise operaton: www.11345.com
+44 *Buddha* LP sleeve notes, Kung Fu Records, 1998
45 There is a nine-song demo from these sessions that has subsequently appeared which shows also a couple of tracks which didn't make the final album – an instrumental titled 'Life's So Boring' and 'Man Overboard'. Tracklisting: Aliens Exist/Anthem/What's My Age Again?/Dumpweed/The Party Song/Dysentery Gary/Man Overboard//Wendy Clear
46 Interview With Liner Notes, 1999
47 Interview With MTV, 1999
48 Interview with adkg.com, 1999
49 Interview With Entertainment Weekly, Feb 25, 2000
50 Interview with Launch.com, 1998
51 Popular history holds that there is a version of 'Aliens Exist', likewise 'Mutt', in demo form with Scott Raynor on drums as recorded in the early days of 1998. Raynor himself recalls it differently: "We recorded 'Mutt' and 'I Won't Be Home For Christmas' [with Mark Trombino]. The tracks on the record were re-recorded and feature Travis on drums."
52 The lyrics also allude to Nirvana's 'Come As You Are'.
53 There's a hidden phrase in the artwork underneath where the CD sits, on the inner spine that reads, 'Viking Wizard Eyes, Wizard Full of Lies' in white text. This has caused some debate as to whether it was a lyric fragment or even a mooted album title. It was used by Mark as a screen log-in for Yahoo! chat for a while. Other possible album titles were apparently *Turn Your Head And Cough* and *Electric Boogaloo*. But as ever with blink-182 those should probably be taken with a fistful of salt.
54 Originally her hat had a red cross on it but that was removed on request by the Red Cross organisation. Initial copies also came without the voluntary-but-expected 'Parental Advisory: Explicit Content' sticker.
55 Rolling Stone Magazine album review, June 1999
56 Kerrang! album review, June 1999
57 Interview with adkg.com, 1999
58 Interview with nyrock.com, 2001
59 NME single review, 2000
60 NME album review, September 30 1999
61 Interview With Entertainment Weekly, March 30 2000
62 NME Live Review, October 15' 2000
63 Interview with John Robb, 2000
64 Interview With MTV, 2000
65 Kerrang! Live Review, September 25, 1999
66 Rolling Stone Live Review, November 17, 1999
67 See endnote 1 in *Kasabian: Sound, Movement & Empire, Shooman. J (Independent Music Press, 2008) ISBN:1-906191-00-X*
68 Interview with Kerrang!, January 2005
69 Interview with MTV, 2000. hur hur. 69.
70 Q Review, April 2, 2000
71Press Statement, March 2000
72 http://www.adamsletter.com/ is where you can find the whole shizzle.
73 A full explanation from John Cosper: "I wrote *Adam's Letter* after having written and produced a play in the wake of the Columbine massacre called *The Waiting Room*, which spoke specifically towards school shootings and the root causes for student-on-student violence. The one recurring theme that kept coming up as I researched Columbine and others was the need for students to love one another. Every student in every school has issues and problems, and the biggest factor in how they cope with them is whether they have a support system or not – be that friends, family, etc.

Thus, the central message of *The Waiting Room* was to stop pointing fingers and learn to look out for one another. With *Adam's Letter*, I hoped to expand on this theme and develop it further. A wide range of characters were created, each with their own problems, and set in a typical American high school. Their world and their secrets are then ripped exposed by a loner who kills himself and posts his suicide note on the internet. This action forces everyone to bare their true selves and leads some – though not all – to open themselves up and love their fellow students in a new way. The final scene of the play has an optional ending with a Christian message that can be cut for productions in public schools.

One of the original ideas that led to this play was the concept of posting a real website with the deceased character's suicide note. The site would serve as a home page for the play and include the full text, but it would also act as a portal for students who did need to reach out and know someone cared. I compiled a list of websites and phone numbers on a wide range of needs and issues – from suicide to teen pregnancy to drug abuse – and posted that list as well.

I was somewhat inspired by *The Blair Witch Project* and how they marketed the film as a documentary. I thought the suicide note on the home page might help the play get a little more attention, particularly from students.

The site has drawn a tremendous amount of attention, but not by my design. As I said before, the naming of the lead character, Adam, was a total coincidence, and I have no idea how my character and my fake suicide note became connected to the blink-182 song, 'Adam's Song.' I first became aware of this connection about two years ago when the visitor stats for adamsletter.com went through the roof, often drawing 500 hits a day or more. I started Googling "Adam's Letter" and "Adam Krieger," and I soon discovered that my play had become part of an internet urban legend.

At no time have I ever tried to further the case that the song and the play are linked. When people ask if the note is real, or if the note inspired the song or vice versa, I tell them no. *Adam's Letter* is fiction. Adam Krieger never existed. And no, I never heard 'Adam's Song' until long after the play was finished. But I am thankful that ministry has been done thanks to an urban legend."

74 Interview with nyrock.com, 2001
75 Interview reported by Denver Post, 2000
76 Interview with Rolling Stone, 2000
77 Interview With MTV, 2000
78 Melody Maker Album Review, 2000
79 Spin Magazine Album Review, 2000
80 Interview with Paul Brannigan.
81 Interview with MH18, 2002
82 Interview with MH18, 2002
83 Interview with Guitar Center, 2001
84 Interview with mtv.com, 2001
85 Rolling Stone Album Review, June 2001
86 Kerrang! Album Review, June 2001.
87 The FTC also cited Crazy Town and Rage Against The Machine, among others.
88 Interview with mtv.com, 2001
89 From Transcript Of Interview with Ben Myers, 2001
90 Ibid.
91 Interview with Teenpeople.com, 2002
92 Ibid.
93 From Transcript Of Interview with Bobby Gorman
94 Allmusic.com Album Review, 2002
95 NME Album Review, May 25, 2002
96 Q Album Review, June 2002
97 Blender Album Review, 2002
98 Interview with Guitar Center, 2002
99 From Transcript Of Interview With Bobby Gorman, 2003
100 There may have been other factors at work as time went by, however, with DeLonge saying in various 2002 interviews that Box Car Racer would indeed continue as a going concern to blink-182. For example, in response to a question from a Teenpeople.com web radio fan, he seemed definite about it: "We do plan on doing another record, but we need to focus on this [next blink album] right now. It just came out. Sometime within the next year, hopefully, we'll get back in the studio and do it again."

101 Interview With San Antonio Express, 2002
102 Interview With Alternative Press, 2002
103 Spin Magazine Live Review, 2002
104 San Francisco Chronicle Live Review, 2002
105 Orange County Register Live Review, 2002
106 Rockzone.com Live Review, 2002
107 Interview With Kerrang!, 2002
108 Interview With Rockdirt.com, 2002
109 Interview With Tastes Like Chicken, 2003
110 Rolling Stone Album Review, 2002
111 Allmusic.com Album Review, 2002
112 USA Today Album Review, 2002
113 Interview with LA Stories, March 2002
114 Interview with Aversion.com, 2002
115 The company was Garnier
116 Interview With blogcritics.org, 2005
117 From Transcript Of Interview With Bart Niedzialkowski, 2003
118 From Transcript Of Interview With Bobby Gorman, 2003
119 From Transcript Of Interview With Bart Niedzialkowski, 2003
120 Interview with Punkinterviews.com, 2002
121 NME single review, 2002
122 Punknews.org Live Review, 2002
123 Interview with MTV, 2002
124 Statement To The Press, 2003
125 Interview with Staticmultimedia, 2003
126 Interview with Rhythm Magazine, April 2003
127 Therip.com Live Review, Apr 2003
128 Kevchino Live Review, Apr 2003
129 Interview with Punk-it.net, May 2003
130 Foster was a member of the early '70s band Skylark but is possibly best known for his production work on a massive amount of artists including Kenny G, Olivia Newton-John, Whitney Houston and many others. Dave Carlock's 'punk' credentials – or lack of them – are amusingly illustrated by an incident on the Transplants' 2003 tour with Foo Fighters. "The Foos saw us mostly in soundchecks and in one when I was getting my stuff together I was running through 'Roundabout' by Yes, playing Rick Wakeman licks on the organ and stuff and suddenly out of nowhere from backstage running full speed was Taylor Hawkins. He says, 'That's YES! Man" and he leaps up behind his drums to play 'Yours Is No Disgrace' which I didn't actually know at that point but I went back to the bus and learned it in case it happened again. He came to us in Dallas in this gigantic rodeo place, it sat about three thousand and we had this mess hall, having lunch and Taylor came up to where we were having lunch and says, 'This guy knows way too much about Yes to be in a punk band' to which Tim Armstrong looked up and said, 'Yes he does.'"
131 Interview With Rolling Stone Magazine, 2000
132 Interview With Blender Magazine, 2004
133 Interview With Rolling Stone Magazine, 2004
134 From Transcript Of Interview With Bobby Gorman, 2003
135 Ibid.
136 Ibid.
137 Rolling Stone Album Review, 2003
138 Kerrang! Album Review, 2003
139 Blender Album Review, 2003
140 Ign.com Album Review, 2003
141 Entertainment Weekly Album Review, 2003
142 Spin Magazine Album Review, 2004
143 The Onion Album Review, 2004
144 Mojo Album Review, 2004
145 Q Album Review, 2003
146 Another draw for potential purchasers was the existence of one Willy Wonka-style, 'golden ticket'. Whoever got the LP with the golden ticket would be treated to a private blink-182 concert for

themselves and fifty friends.
147 From Transcript Of Interview With Bobby Gorman, 2003
148 Plus the Nirvana 'smiley face' is pretty much a direct quote of the rave scene's famous avatar. As the show presented by the much-missed Tony Wilson was named: So It Goes.
149 From Transcript Of Interview With Bart Niedzialkowski, 2003
150 Interview With MTV, 2003
151From Transcript Of Interview With Bart Niedzialkowski, 2003
152From Transcript Of Interview With Bobby Gorman, 2003
153 Interview With TheCelebrityCafe.com, 2003
154 From Transcript Of Interview With Bobby Gorman, 2003
155 Ibid.
156 And of course, blink-182 being the group they are, they also concurrently lent 'I Won't Be Home For Christmas' to *A Santa Cause*, a compilation LP for AIDS charities
157 Music OMH Album Review, 2004
158 A propos of nothing in particular, The Kinison hail from the brilliantly-named Oblong, Illinois.
159 Concertlivewire.com Live Review, 2004
160 Live Daily Live Review, 2004
161"My favourite track is 'Dementia'," Scott Raynor revealed. "You can hear three of the songs here: http://www.purevolume.com/thespazms . We only recorded four tracks – we had a whole set but we had to edit since we only had one day of tracking."
162 Interview With Blender Magazine, 2005
163 Interview With Rolling Stone Magazine, 2004
164 Speaking at Teen Choice Awards, August 2004
165 Interview With *Billboard* Magazine, 2006
166 Interview With Blender Magazine, 2006
167 Interview With Channelv, 2006
168 Travis and Shanna had tied the knot on October 30 in an unconventional ceremony based on the movie *A Nightmare Before Christmas*.
169 From Transcript Of Interview With Bobby Gorman, 2003
170 From Transcript Of Interview With Bart Niedzialkowski, 2003
171 As posted on www.6767.com on February 19, 2005
172 Press Statement, February 22, 2005
173 Interview With K-ROQ Radio, February 23, 2005
174 From Transcript Of Interview With Bart Niedzialkowski, 2003
175 Ibid.
176 Rolling Stone Album Review, 2005
177 Blender Album Review, August 2005
178 All Music Guide Album Review, 2005
179 The Onion Album Review, 2005
180 NME Album Review, July 2005
181 Spin Album Review, August 2005
(blink-)182 Kerrang! Album Review, June 2005
183 The ever-engaging Mr. Carlock continued down quite a left-field road at this point in our interview, pondering something that's nobody else would ever dream of having on the tip of their tongue: "Are the Transplants the Yes of punk? That's the big question…!"
184 From Transcript Of Interview With Trevor Baker, 2006
185 Interview With MTV, 2005
186 For some time in the early '00s Travis also managed to keep up a roster of teaching drums to several pupils although increased commitments made it correspondingly more difficult to do so. It's to his credit that his prices were at least the same as other teachers and in some cases even cheaper!
187 From Transcript Of Interview With Trevor Baker, 2006.
188 Another statement referring to blink's hiatus was reported widely in the summer of 2005
189 It's abbreviated to AVA rather than A&A as a graphics-based tribute to his daughter Ava Elizabeth. It's not a V either, it's an upside-down letter A.
190 Interview With Top Of The Pops/BBC, 2005
191 Interview With Rolling Stone, 2005
192 Interview With MTV, 2005
193 From Transcript Of Interview With Jason Tate, 2006

194 Interview With Ultimate Guitar, 2006
195 From Transcript Of Interview With Tom Bryant, 2006
196 Interview With Channelv, 2006
197 Unbelievably, distressing rumours also circulated in the gnarlier reaches of the net that Heller had passed away. This was obviously untrue and Mark was moved to say so on the band's MySpace page.
198 Interview With Ugo, 2006
199 Alternative Press Album Review, May 2006
200 Kerrang! Album Review, May 2006
201 Entertainment Weekly Album Review, May 2006
202 Spin Magazine Album Review, July 2006
203 Uncut Album Review, July 2006
204 Rolling Stone Album Review, May 2006
205 Boston Phoenix Live Review, July 2006
206 Birmingham Mail Live Review, June 2006
207 From Transcript Of Interview With Jason Tate, 2006
208 From Transcript Of Interview With Trevor Baker, 2006
209 Interview With Blogger, 2006
210 Interview With Island Jenn, 2006
211 'Make You Smile' was originally called something rather different, a track so poppy that Carol Heller, tongue massively in cheek, posited that they ought to name it 'Puppy Killing Machine'.
212 Interview With Ign, 2006
213 Interview With Live Daily, 2006
214 NME Album Review, 2006
215 Rolling Stone Album Review, 2006
216 Entertainment Weekly Album Review, 2006
217 Blender Album Review, 2006
218 Q Album Review, 2006
219 From Transcript Of Interview With Jason Tate, 2006
220 The tour support opportunity had come in late for The Tommys, so much so that Stevie and Fran of that band didn't yet have passports – in the rush to get themselves the required documents they missed the European leg's first date.
221 Interview With WWE, 2007
222 Interview With Baller Status, 2005
223 Interview With XXL Magazine, 2007
224 Live Review On Himynameismark.com, 2007
225 Widely reported, but sourced here from NME, 2007
226 Press Statement, 2007
227 From Transcript Of Interview With Stevie Chick, 2007.
228 Ibid.
229 From Transcript Of Interview With Brad Streeter, 2008
230 Ibid.
231 Ibid.
232 The other tracks were acoustic run-throughs of 'Everything's Magic', 'The Gift', 'Good Day', 'Do It for Me Now' and 'The Adventure'
233 Soundfires Single Review, 2007
234 From Transcript Of Interview With Shane Richardson, 2007
235 Rolling Stone Album Review, 2007
236 IGN Album Review, 2007
237 Blender Album Review, 2007
238 *Billboard* Album Review, 2007
239 The Onion Album Review, 2007
240 NME Album Review, 2007
241 Kerrang Album Review, 2007
242 From Transcript Of Interview With Brad Streeter, 2008
243 Ibid.
244 From Transcript Of Interview With Shane Richardson, 2007
245 From Transcript Of Interview With Brad Streeter, 2008
246 Ibid.

247 Interview With Metromix, 2008
248 As Posted On HimynameisMark.com, August 2008
249 Interview With XFM, February 2009
250 Quote Reported Widely, Sourced From MTV
251 Press Statement, September 2008
252 Modcam Transmission, October 2008
253 Interview With US Weekly, October 2008
254 Interview With TMZ, 2008
255 Grammy Awards Ceremony, 2009
256 Interview With Alternative Press, 2009
257 There had actually been a rumour flying around that during Travis' recuperation blink would reform with an 'old friend' in tow. It was another bit of internet silliness speculating that Scott Raynor would return to the drum seat. "I am going to school full-time for the next couple of years, then; who knows?," Scott told the author (Raynor is now studying art and literature at university). "Same with the blink guys. I wouldn't say it's likely that we will ever play together again, but I also wouldn't say it's impossible."
258 Interview With LA Times, 2009
259 Interview With The Aquarian, August 2009
260 Interview With Real Detroit Weekly, August 2009
261 Information sourced from People.com
http://www.people.com/people/article/0,,20308920,00.html and widely reported elsewhere
262 Onstage, Saturday August 29, 2009 and rebroadcast on Youtube and other sites from many fans' phones.
263 Press statement reported widely, 2009

Acknowledgements

Massive thanks to the interviewees for sharing their thoughts for this project: Sam Boukas; Dave Carlock; Donnell Cameron; John Cosper; Adam Deibert; Jack Endino; Joe Escalante; Jeff Forrest; Josh Franceschi; Brian Gardner; Steve Kravac; Dermot Lambert; Denny Jegard; Duane F. Okun; Scott Raynor, Patrick Secor; Stevie Shepperson; AK Skurgis; Drew Stuzan.

Thanks to Mischa Pearlman for his help with the discography and additional research. For kindly making their transcripts and expertise available for research and the project massive thanks to Trevor Baker; Tom Bryant; Scott Colothan; Stevie Chick; Bobby Gorman; Emma Johnston; Ben Myers; Bart Niedzialkowski; Brad Streeter; Shane Richardson; John Robb; Jason Tate.

Useful magazines in researching this book included *Alternative Press, Billboard, Blender, Bodacious Spills, Guitar Center, Kerrang!, Mojo, Music Week, NME, Q, Rock Sound, Rolling Stone, Slamm, Spin, The Fly, Warped* and countless other zines and mags across USA, UK, Australia and others. Websites useful in the research process included *Absolutepunk.net, Archive.Org, BBC.co.uk, Drownedinsound.com, google.com, Himynameismark. metacritic.com, MTV.com, MySpace.com, Theonion.com, Thepunksite.com, Punkplanet.com, Punkdisasters.com,* and hundreds of others as detailed where appropriate.

Thanks to Mart and Dave, my IMP compadres. Muchas gracias amigos.

Diolchiadau enfawr a cariad i fy nheulu i gyd: Nanny Drake; Matthew, Annie, Harry, Molly, Lily, Louis; Daniel, Louisa, Megan, Owen, Martin Faulkner, Stephen Faulkner, Cathy Balcomb, a Steven 'Robidoux' Faulkner. Loads of love and thanks to mam and dad for everything, ever.

Suzy, fyddwn i'n dy garu di at diwedd yr byd. Mae'r dyfodol yn disglair dros ben.

Vielen danke Robert Whiteley für das acht jaren im der Dorritschloss.

Fyddwn i byth anghofio'r brenhinau dan ni wedi colli dros y blynyddoedd.

To Vaffan Coulo, on hiatus: we did a good thing.

This book was written and recorded by Joe Shooman at Dorrit Sounds Studio 3 and Vista Visual-sonix, Room 2 and mixed at Whitewood Studios, L8. Mastering by IMP.

Practice Education in Paramedic Science

Theories and Application

By

Karen Gubbins MSc, PGCert, BSc, FHEA, Registered Paramedic

Sharon Hardwick MEd, PGCert, BSc, FHEA, Registered Paramedic

Disclaimer

Class Professional Publishing have made every effort to ensure that the information, tables, drawings and diagrams contained in this book are accurate at the time of publication. The book cannot always contain all the information necessary for determining appropriate care and cannot address all individual situations; therefore, individuals using the book must ensure they have the appropriate knowledge and skills to enable suitable interpretation. Class Professional Publishing does not guarantee, and accepts no legal liability of whatever nature arising from or connected to, the accuracy, reliability, currency or completeness of the content of the text. Users must always be aware that such innovations or alterations after the date of publication may not be incorporated in the content. Please note, however, that Class Professional Publishing assumes no responsibility whatsoever for the content of external resources in the text or accompanying online materials.

The information presented in this book is accurate and current to the best of the authors' knowledge.

The authors and publisher, however, make no guarantee as to, and assume no responsibility for, the correctness, sufficiency or completeness of such information or recommendation.

Printing history
This edition first published 2019

The authors and publisher welcome feedback from the users of this book. Please contact the publisher:

Class Professional Publishing,
The Exchange, Express Park, Bristol Road, Bridgwater TA6 4RR
Telephone: 01278 427 826
Email: post@class.co.uk
www.classprofessional.co.uk

Class Professional Publishing is an imprint of Class Publishing Ltd

A CIP catalogue record for this book is available from the British Library

Paperback ISBN: 9781859596692
eBook ISBN: 9781859596708

Cover design by Hybert Design Limited, UK
Designed and typeset by S4Carlisle Publishing Services
Printed in the UK by Short Run Press Limited, Exeter

Table of Contents

About the Authors

Karen Gubbins started a career in healthcare at the Birmingham Dental Hospital in 1992. She moved to the West Midlands Ambulance Service NHS Trust in 1996, qualifying as a paramedic in 1998. She worked at a number of stations within the West Midlands Ambulance Service NHS Trust, gaining a promotion to Clinical Supervisor then to Training Officer. She worked in training and education for the Trust for a number of years before moving to the University of Worcester as Senior Lecturer in 2007. She now works for Birmingham City University as Senior Lecturer in Paramedic Science. She remains a practising and registered paramedic. She has studied and gained a BSc (Hons), a PG Cert in Learning and Teaching and an MSc.

Sharon Hardwick joined West Midlands Ambulance Service NHS Trust in 1995 and in 1998 she qualified as a paramedic. In 2001 she moved to Hereford and Worcester Ambulance Service NHS Trust in the capacity of Clinical Supervisor. She quickly progressed on to work as a Training Officer and subsequently gained the position of Training Manager for the Trust. After helping to design the Foundation Degree in Pre-Hospital, Unscheduled and Emergency Care for the University of Worcester, in 2007 she successfully gained employment at the University as a Senior Lecturer. She was also instrumental in the development of the BSc Paramedic Science, which commenced in 2017. She remains a registered and practising paramedic. She has studied and gained a BSc (Hons), a PG Cert in Learning and Teaching, and an MEd. She now works for Birmingham City University as Senior Lecturer in Paramedic Science.

List of Abbreviations

ECA	Emergency Care Assistant
HEA	Higher Education Academy
NMC	Nursing and Midwifery Council
NQP	Newly Qualified Paramedic
PAD	Practice Assessment Document
PEd	Practice Educator
PTSD	Post-Traumatic Stress Disorder
RCN	Royal College of Nursing
SpLDs	Specific Learning Difficulties
SQA	Scottish Qualifications Authority

Introduction

It is a requirement for student paramedics to be allocated Practice Educators (PEds) whilst they gain experience within the practice environment (College of Paramedics, 2015). The role of the PEds could be considered equal to that of the placement facilitator or the mentor.

The title of PEd is utilised in this book as it is a term used by the College of Paramedics and a number of ambulance services. The terms 'mentor' and 'coach' tend to be utilised interchangeably throughout published works, but here we will define and discuss them as separate concepts. It is recognised that the role of the PEd incorporates mentoring, coaching and leadership, as well as a number of other concepts that are discussed in this text.

Regardless of the title 'PEd', 'mentor' or 'coach', these members of staff have a great responsibility to their learners and the profession. They are the people who will guide the learner, often maintaining a great deal of contact throughout the learner's education.

The College of Paramedics (2015) requires PEds to be:

- appropriately registered;
- educated as a PEd.

Appropriate registration would suggest that the PEd should be registered in the profession that they are supervising. For example, if the learner is being supervised within a hospital placement, their PEd could be a nurse registered with the Nursing and Midwifery Council (NMC). However, during ambulance service placements, paramedics registered with the Health and Care Professions Council would be the logical choice of PEd.

Many universities that offer an accredited paramedic programme will also offer post-qualification or postgraduate education for PEds. This book intends to assist this educational process and provide background and supportive information for those undergoing their education, as well as those who are currently working as PEds.

Scope of the Text

This text will cover many aspects of practice-based education and thus it will not focus purely upon mentoring as may be expected. In fact, mentoring (see Chapter 6) is just one small part of the PEd's role. It is not expected that a PEd reads this text from cover to cover in order of chapter; it is anticipated that you, the PEd, will read the relevant chapters and refer back to the text as required.

Within this text, PEds, mentors and placement facilitators will be referred to as PEds in order to ensure consistency.

This text contains many interactive sections for you to learn from, including reflections and case studies to consider. Full engagement with these sections will allow you to gain the most from the text and develop your skills more effectively.

Part I

Background and Basics

Chapter 1

What is a Practice Educator?

Learning objectives

1. Rationale for the role of PEd
2. Scope of the PEd role
3. Formal versus informal support
4. Teaching in practice

This chapter will outline the rationale and evolution of the PEd as well as showing the suggested boundaries of PEd practice. Teaching theory will be briefly discussed to assist the PEd in their role.

Paramedic education has moved almost exclusively from traditional 'in-house' education to higher education. Since this move, there are greater demands being placed on practice educators, mentors, paramedics and indeed anyone who supports paramedic learners whilst in education and practice. The College of Paramedics (2015) states:

> [Placements] must be undertaken with appropriately trained and registered paramedic educators (PEds) so that every patient encounter becomes an opportunity for learning to prepare the contemporary learner paramedic for ongoing development within evidence-based autonomous practice.

The Health and Care Professions Council (2017) states in SET 5.5:

> We also expect you [the education provider] to make sure that the qualifications and experience of staff are appropriate to the specific aspects of practice-based learning they are involved in, and that they are able to effectively support learning and assessment.

Thus, it is vital for PEds to have sufficient education and indeed resources to support their role.

The College of Paramedics (2015) requires that the PEd:

> [E]nsures that they also help to educate and guide learners through their practice placement experiences.

The College of Paramedics (2015) further states:

> The role of the paramedic educator is extremely important and comes with significant responsibility. The actions and examples set by the paramedic educator during clinical placements have lasting consequences, which include positive and negative influences.

Learners identified a number of key areas that they expected from a PEd: communication, support, organisation and qualities such as appropriate use of humour and being accepted by their PEd (Lane, 2014).

Clearly, the PEd role is a very significant one and, whilst it provides support to learners, is one that also requires support from others to ensure its effectiveness.

Reflection

What does support of learners *actually* mean? Explain in your own words.

There a number of words associated with support:

- Provision
- Backing
- Facilitation
- Establishment

How do these words relate to the role of the practice educator?

Formal versus Informal Support

As previously stated, the Health and Care Professions Council (2017) and the College of Paramedics (2015 and 2017a) have guidelines as to who should be a PEd, and provide formal support in the practice environment. However, it is argued that there is a valuable place for informal guidance, mentorship and practice-based education. Mohtady et al. (2016) argue that informal and formal support are complementary and equally important within healthcare.

Informal support can theoretically be provided by any individual in contact with the learner. For example, in the practice environment, ambulance technicians and emergency care assistants (ECAs) can be a valuable source of learning. It is important to remember that the learning opportunities provided in an informal manner should be provided by the most appropriate people in the same way that formal support is provided. For example, it may be unreasonable to expect an ECA to provide support for a learner in an advanced assessment technique. However, they are likely to be very adept in supporting the learner in communication skills or basic airway manoeuvres.

How Experienced Should a PEd Be as a Clinician?

There has been anecdotal discussion about how much experience a clinician should have prior to becoming a PEd, but there is no definitive answer to this debate. The College of Paramedics (2017b) suggests that PEds will usually be paramedics selected from the Health and Care Professions Council register, who are at least 12 months post-qualification. However, this is not a requirement and may not always be put into practice. Lane (2014) states that learners:

> ... seemed to be looking for experienced PEds who were knowledgeable about their Higher Education (HE) programmes and had a genuine desire to mentor them.

Yet, this statement still does not address the amount of time that should elapse between qualification and PEd status. Likewise, Health Education England (undated) states that the:

> Provider must ensure that learners have an appropriate level of supervision at all times by an experienced and competent educator, who can advise or attend as needed.

In the absence of a well thought-out and researched timeframe, it could be argued that there should not be a set amount of time post-registration as individuals develop and gain experience at different rates. In addition, background, previous employment roles and other personal experiences may well play a large part in a person's ability to be an effective PEd. It is therefore suggested that rather than a set amount of time, a robust selection process may be more effective in assessing suitability for the role of PEd. The details of the selection process would be best determined nationally and therefore this is outside the scope of this text, although certain areas are recommended by Nasser-Abu Alhija and Fresko (2014) (see Figure 1.1).

Figure 1.1 Examples of personal qualities of a PEd
(adapted from Nasser-Abu Alhija and Fresko (2014))

How Many PEds are Too Many?

Again, this is an ongoing and controversial issue with no real resolution. Some learners express the desire for one PEd only, whereas other learners prefer multiple PEds (Lane, 2014). Certainly, having one PEd should provide consistency for the learner, which could be disrupted by multiple PEds. Conversely, multiple PEds are likely to give a more diverse experience and knowledge base for the learner to further their development. In other words, the learner can select the most appropriate part of each PEd's practice and integrate this into their own practice. This point is argued by Kostrubiak et al. (2017), who state that learners benefit from multiple mentors, as each will have different abilities and strengths, all of which may not be present in a single person. However, it is also recognised that too many PEds could be unhelpful for the learner, as they may feel like they are starting afresh every time they attend a placement (Lane, 2014). It is recommended that a balance is sought between too many and too few PEds. It is likely this will be an individual requirement for each learner. Thus, discussions should be had with the learner to ensure they are receiving the most appropriate range of PEds for their needs.

Is a PEd a Teacher?

It could be argued that education and teaching are the same concept; however, the definitions demonstrate a subtle difference, in that education is the *facilitation of learning*, whereas teaching is the *imparting of knowledge*. Teaching thus suggests a directive approach that is potentially in opposition to education, which supports a person to learn. The imparting of knowledge is within a PEd's role; however, this should take place in an environment (both physical and emotional) which allows the learner to learn and develop. Indeed, many PEds perceive teaching as part of their role (Lane, 2014), as well as education.

Should a PEd Have a Teaching Qualification?

Whilst having a teaching qualification is required within a formal teaching environment, it is not required within the informal and supportive setting, such as those experienced by paramedic learners on placement. However, it is helpful for both the PEd and the learner for the PEd to have some basic understanding of learning and education processes. These are covered within Chapter 5.

A PEd may of course be inspired to continue their education to gain a teaching qualification, and indeed their PEd experience and knowledge is likely to be invaluable for this. This could be incorporated into the College of Paramedics' (2017a) aspiration that all PEds are working towards a level 6 qualification. In real terms, it *could* be an advantage for both learner and PEd if the PEd has a teaching qualification. This topic is potentially a contentious one, and it is not the intention to show that PEds with teaching qualifications are better than ones without. All PEds (with and without teaching qualifications) are valuable people who are best placed to support the learners in practice. Figure 1.2 shows just a few of the pros and cons to the PEd being a teacher.

This text will not make the recommendation that the PEds *should* have a teaching qualification. At this time, it is recommended that each PEd should consider the pros and cons for their own practice environment and choose their own path.

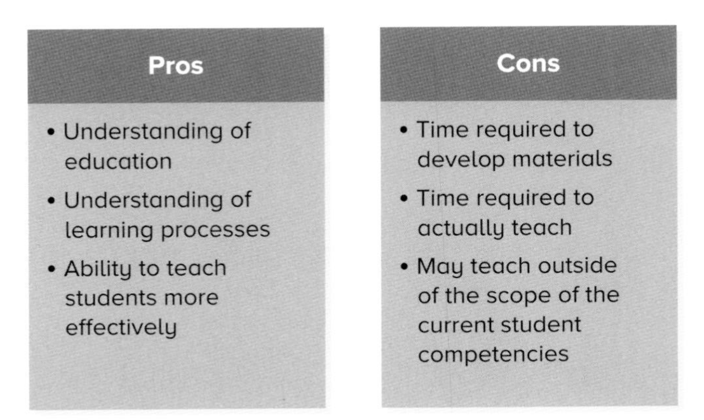

Figure 1.2 The pros and cons of a PEd being a teacher

Education and Teaching Theory in Brief

Education theory is an enormous subject and therefore will not be covered in great detail in this text.

There are two common terms used in education:

> **Pedagogy** – this is commonly more of a children's education-based concept, whereby the teacher/PEd teaches the learner.
>
> **Andragogy** – this is generally an adult education-based concept, where the teacher/PEd facilitates learning.

The above is a general guide as to the historical context of the theories; however, both pedagogy and andragogy can be utilised with both adults and children depending upon the subject matter and the ability of the adult/child learner.

Bloom's Taxonomy

Bloom's (1979) taxonomy recognises six levels of cognitive ability which build on each other in order to develop understanding of topics (see Figure 1.3).

It is helpful for the PEd to have a brief understanding of each of these areas and how they relate to the learner's educational process as recommended by Fry et al. (2009).

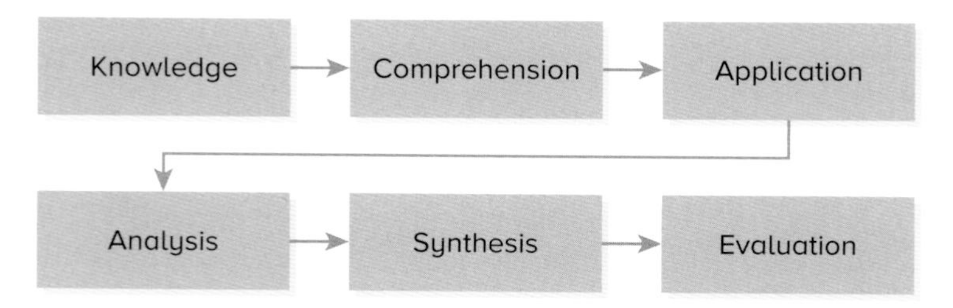

Figure 1.3 Bloom's six levels of cognitive ability
(adapted from Fry et al. (2009))

Knowledge – is about what we expect the learner to know. This skill requires the learner to be able to:

- Reproduce information
- Give details
- Describe a process
- Identify equipment.

In practice – knowledge could include selecting the appropriate equipment to undertake a blood pressure or blood sugar test. It could also comprise information such as the anatomy of the respiratory system.

Comprehension – requires a little more understanding from the learner. They should be able to, for example:

- Explain a process
- Summarise a concept
- Interpret meaning
- Select equipment.

In practice – comprehension could be demonstrated by the learner explaining to their PEd how to interpret a 12-lead ECG or inferring meaning behind differing pulse rates.

Application – expects a learner to be able to use the information they possess. For example:

- Problem solve
- Practise a procedure
- Demonstrate a skill
- Classify information.

In practice – the learner could show their PEd how they cannulate a patient or how they would immobilise a dislocated limb.

Analysis – requires the learner to relate constituting parts of a concept and show their interrelationship. For example:

- Differentiate between concepts and information
- Debate concepts and thoughts
- Appraise information
- Investigate concepts and theories.

In practice – this is likely to be more of a discussion-based skill, whereby the learner and PEd debate, for example, extrication techniques or equipment for moving a patient.

Synthesis – the learner will work with theories and concepts to create new ways of working. For example:

- Design a new process
- Construct a theory
- Propose a new standard
- Formulate a new assessment.

In practice – this is more likely to be a theoretical process that is undertaken outside of clinical practice. The learner could conceivably propose a new piece of equipment or medicine. It is likely that this is outside the scope of the PEd.

Evaluation – whilst this possibly sounds like one of the more simple constructs, it is more complex than the previous elements. For example:

- Defending a new theory
- Making judgements based on theory.

In practice – this is again a theoretical concept, whereby the learner will be questioned significantly upon their new proposals. It is likely that this will be outside the scope of the PEd.

Generally, the concepts discussed by Bloom (1979) can be related directly to higher education levels as suggested by the Quality Assurance Agency for Higher Education (2015) whereby learners at level 4 (year 1 at university) are expected to have knowledge and some comprehension. Level 5 learners (year 2) develop comprehension and application, and level 6 learners (year 3 BSc Hons level) progress into application and analysis. Synthesis and evaluation are often considered postgraduate skills (levels 7 and 8), although there may be times when undergraduates are expected to synthesise areas of knowledge.

Expectations may overlap these levels depending upon the information and skill required. For example, learners at level 4 may be expected to select appropriate equipment, or explain blood pressure variations, which may be considered a level 5 skill.

Ozuah (2005) asserts that adults learn most effectively using an andragogical approach and makes certain assumptions (seen in Figure 1.4) that the learner wants to learn.

The role of the PEd incorporates creating an environment of learning; therefore, the PEd may need to encourage the learner to experience each of the elements in Figure 1.4.

It could be argued that the majority of the support undertaken by the PEd will be skills-based, where the learner may need to be shown how

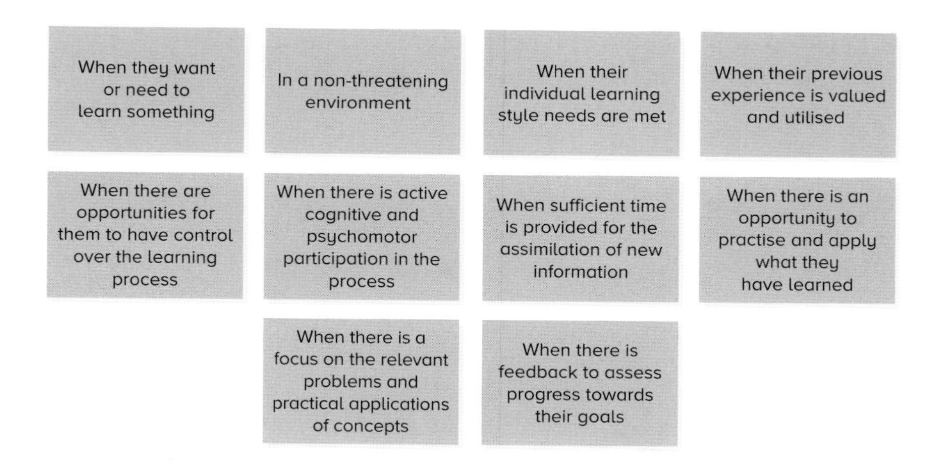

Figure 1.4 Assumptions regarding learning
(Ozuah, 2005)

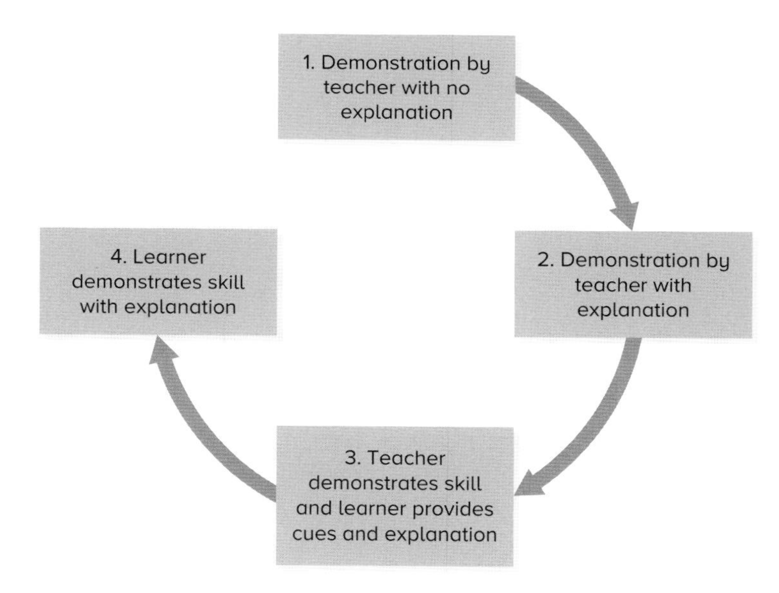

Figure 1.5 Peyton's four-stage approach
(adapted from Peyton (1998))

to undertake a specific procedure. Peyton (1998) advocates a four-stage approach (Figure 1.5) for this kind of teaching, which may be very helpful for the PEd and the learner.

Utilisation of Peyton (1998) is similar to the anecdotally often used 'tell – show – do' approach to skills, although it incorporates a little more explanation, which learners can find helpful.

Whilst the PEd's role may initially be thought of as being centred on ambulance skills (skills like cannulation, verbal and non-verbal communication or clinical decision making), the learner is likely to approach their PEd for assistance with other learning areas. Therefore, it is helpful for the PEd to be able to support the learner with these topics, for example, anatomy, physiology or research. Thus, the PEd may need to draw upon other areas of education to support the learner. The PEd could follow a discussion-based approach to these areas, for example, whereby the PEd draws out the information from the learner by asking supportive questions, which is an example of coaching skills, which are discussed in Chapter 7. As previously stated, it is not required for the PEd to be a teacher *per se*; however, the use of skills developed within this text will assist the PEd in supporting the learner in all areas. Education theory goes hand in hand with learning theory, which is discussed in Chapter 5 and should be reviewed alongside this chapter.

Do I Need to be a Teacher?

Although PEds are primarily considered facilitators and educators rather than teachers, the roles may overlap at times. For example, a learner may require the PEd to show them how to undertake a specific skill.

The majority of current or future PEds are likely to have taken a new member of staff 'under their wing' and to have supported them unofficially through the transition from being new staff to being experienced staff. This informal role is part teacher, educator, mentor, coach and leader. All of these skills are covered within this text.

Case Studies

You have a first-year learner who lacks the ability to undertake blood pressures correctly. How can you use Ozuah's (2005) point that learners learn best 'When they want or need to learn something' to encourage the student to learn the skill?

Which of Fry et al.'s (2009) areas do you think undertaking a blood pressure fits into and why?

Reflection

How do you believe the roles of a teacher and educator differ?

Give examples from your own experiences.

Chapter 2

Reflection

Learning objectives

1. What is reflection?
2. What to reflect upon
3. Models of reflection and their use
4. Legislation and ethics of reflection

This chapter has been placed near the beginning of this book as we will be asking you to reflect upon areas of your PEd practice during the remaining chapters.

Reflection is many things to many people, and we would not advocate that the message in this text is all-encompassing. Reflection is something that we all do automatically and often; we do it without realising. How often have you considered something you have said or done and thought 'that was good' or, conversely, 'that didn't go according to plan'? These thoughts are reflective. However, these thoughts need to be expanded and developed. Reflection is not always an easy process, as you may feel that you should not be pointing out where you did things wrong or did not do as well as you would have liked. Yet, without reflecting on the negatives, it is difficult to correct them. Thus, reflection is the process of looking at what you have done or are doing in detail (Schön, 1987). Schön (1987) also advocates reflecting upon events that are still happening, so that you can influence the result (referred to as *reflection in action*). For paramedics, in general the 'event' has a tendency to be a case that you have attended (referred to as *reflection on action*); however, you can reflect upon anything that happens at any time. *Reflection in action* is as vital as *reflection on action*. As such, reflecting upon actions whilst you are in the midst of a case and adapting your practices based upon your reflections is useful and something that invariably is done without conscious thought. For example, you may be wishing to move a patient, however, after completing an assessment, you change your mind as to the most appropriate way of moving them. This would likely be down to reflecting upon the choices available, your previous experiences and the patient's condition. It is recommended that as a PEd, you not only reflect upon clinical topics, but also your role and actions as a PEd.

Reflection on action, i.e. reflecting upon a case *after* the event, is vital for learners to develop. Commonly, after a case, PEds and learners complete a debrief, which often incorporates elements of refection. These discussions can be very useful, especially as the case is usually very fresh in the memory. The disadvantage can be that resources may not be available immediately for checking information. For example, if there is a debate regarding the aetiology of a specific medical condition, the PEd and the learner may not be able to access texts to resolve the debate. In this instance, it is useful for the PEd and the learner to agree a plan of action to complete the reflection.

Both forms of reflection suggested by Schön (1987) are useful tools for both the PEd and the learner, and therefore both should be practised as appropriate in the given situation.

The Goals of Reflection

1. Think about links between what actions you took and what you felt, i.e. did your actions influence your feelings or did your feelings influence your action?
2. Are there any questions that you need to be answered about the event?
3. What action(s) was successful in the event and why? Here you need to consider what other people have written about the subject – this may lead to a better understanding of what you did OR show you that there are alternative ways of doing something.
4. What action(s) was unsuccessful in the event and why? You would use the same principles here as in the section above. The idea of this section is to look at alternatives to what you did so that in future you may be more successful.
5. What changes (in your practice if you have reflected on a case) would you now make based on what you have learnt? There may be no changes; conversely, you may drastically change your actions based on your reflection.

How Do I Choose What to Reflect on?

Theoretically, you can reflect on any event in your life. However, Jasper (2006) suggests a number of reasons for reflection:

1. If an event will not 'go away' (i.e. it is something you keep thinking about).
2. If the event is preventing you from moving on in a relationship with another person (this could be a personal or professional relationship).
3. An event has shown a skill or knowledge deficit (something you didn't know).
4. You have witnessed something you would consider poor professional practice.
5. An event you cannot easily share with other people (this can be for many reasons, for example, you may be self-conscious about sharing the incident).
6. An event that breaks your ethical or moral codes.
7. An event that was particularly successful.
8. An event that involved a new experience.

Rolfe et al. (2001) advocate the use of a 'critical incident', a term which is often misunderstood. The 'critical incident' or event does not have to be one of monumental proportions, just one that allows you to analyse its occurrences.

The Role of the PEd in the Learner's Reflections

The PEd is best placed to encourage *reflection in action*, as they are present during practice and can highlight areas for consideration and reflection. However, the PEd needs to consider the appropriateness of the reflective process; for example, where a patient requires a great deal of intervention, it may not to be appropriate to undertake reflection at this time.

The PEd is also in a position to assist the learner with the actual reflective process; however, in order to achieve this, the PEd needs to understand the processes and be able to effectively apply reflective frameworks. In order to assist the learner, the PEd could ask reflective questions, pose different scenarios and supply or suggest published material for the learner, amongst other supportive methods. If the learner has provided a written reflection, the PEd could review it and make suggestions for improvement or guidance for published literature.

Reflective Journal

A reflective journal can be a diary or simply a small book with blank pages. If you plan on using a diary, it would be helpful to have the kind where each day has a page or half-page. This will give you plenty of space to write your thoughts. However, a small book (with lined or unlined pages) is just as appropriate. If you choose to use a book rather than a diary, it may be helpful for you to write the date on each entry. This may help to jog your memory further if you choose to write the case as a full reflection. Of course, verbal reflection is also a valid and useful tool.

It is important to note at this point that confidentiality is vital within a learning journal and indeed within any communication, be it written or verbal. Specific detail like case numbers, patient names and addresses, and location of incidents add nothing to a reflection, and could potentially breach confidentiality laws and guidelines. Therefore, it is imperative that no patient-recognisable data is recorded.

What Do I Write in My Journal?

You have a number of choices here, but the simple answer is whatever will jog your memory if you choose to reflect fully on the incident.

Here is an example of a journal entry:

> Date: 21 October 2018
>
> Female 80 yrs fallen in living room 5 hrs ago, no heating on, patient is possibly hypothermic. She has not eaten for a few hours.
>
> Full assessment done by learner Elle – she needs to work on medical history order.
>
> What was good – Elle was supported and encouraged when she forgot questions in the medical history.
>
> What was not so good – my communication with the patient was lacking at times because I was directing Elle.
>
> Comments: need to remember the patient.

Reflective Models

If you are not experienced in reflection, it can be helpful to use a reflective model to support the process, as without this, some people find that they merely tell the story of the case, which is only a small part of reflection. Using reflective models has a number of benefits:

1. Help us to learn from our experience because they are practitioner focused. As part of this process they help us to develop a greater sense of personal–professional biography and history.
2. Engage us in the process of knowledge creation by helping us to move from tacit knowing to more conscious and explicit knowing.
3. Help us to overcome professional inertia by asking us to look at what we do, our taken-for-granted clinical worlds and that which is atypical, 'critical' and professionally significant.
4. Tend to add more meaning and ascribe new and relevant meaning to our clinical practice through reflexive conversations with clinical situations. In this sense they enhance meaningful dialogue.
5. Have some significance for future personal and sometimes collective future action.
6. Celebrate the role of human agency.

(Ghaye and Lillyman, 2006)

Gibbs' Reflective Cycle

Gibbs' reflective cycle (1988) is, as the name suggests, a cycle. Therefore, you could theoretically start at any point and finish at any point. However, it seems logical to start at the description and end at the action plan (see Figure 2.1).

The purpose of each section is as follows:

Description – describe the event you are going to reflect on: you may write a very detailed account or prefer to keep it brief – the choice is yours.

Your feelings – write about how you felt at each stage of the event: before, during (including any changes) and afterwards, looking back on the event. Try and focus on emotions and avoid comments like 'I felt that what we did was right'. This does not convey an emotion; however,

'I was angry about what had happened' successfully conveys emotion. Consider why you might have felt the emotions you did.

Evaluation – in this section, you state what the positive points were and what were the negative points (if there were any) about the event you are reflecting on. For example: 'My communication with my learner was ineffective, but my communication with the patient was excellent.'

Analysis – this section should cover the same things as you mentioned in the evaluation; however, this time, you relate the subjects to published theories and processes. For example: 'When communicating with my patient, I tried to maintain eye contact. However, Hall (1990) points out that eye contact with an elder person in the American Indian culture can be considered rude, and potentially aggressive.'

Conclusion – here, you need to identify what else you could have done during the event. It is worth thinking particularly about areas you may have said were not as good as they could have been. If you have read around the positive and negative points, you will probably have some ideas that are new – you can put them in this section. For example: 'I could have asked about any cultural aspects that the patient would like me to have observed.' This section will probably be focused around any negative points you have raised. However, it is possible (and desirable for progress) to consider the positive points too, so you may find out something new about an aspect of the event that went well.

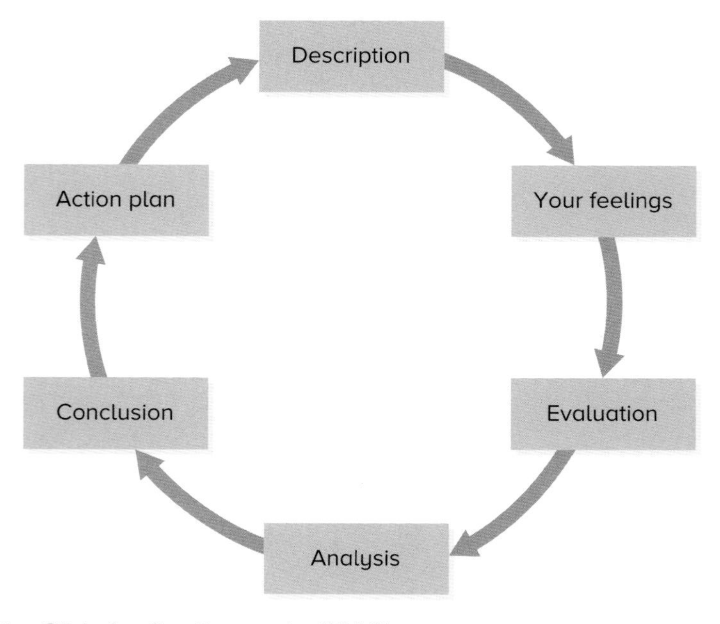

Figure 2.1 Gibbs' reflective cycle (1988)

Action plan – this comes from the conclusion; basically, you pick out the things you would like to try next time you encounter the same or a similar event. This section should really only contain things that you have mentioned in the conclusion. Again, this section can include solutions to aspects that you consider negative points, but do try to consider the points that went well too.

Once you have written the action plan, the idea now is that when you experience a similar event, you try out the things identified in your action plan. You can then reflect on how effective your adaptations were ... and so it goes on. The circle can theoretically go on forever – but clearly we are not suggesting you do this.

Gibbs' (1988) reflective cycle could easily be used to inform action research, where you find out what is wrong in a certain area of your PEd role or clinical practice, consider what can be changed (description, feelings and evaluation), how they can be changed (analysis, conclusion and action plan), implement the change(s) (do the actions, then back to the description) and evaluate the results (back to feelings and evaluation).

Example

Description – we attended an 87-year-old gentleman who has fallen. He had no injuries, Alan (who is at the end of his first year) was unsure of how to move the patient from the floor to his chair. I advised the use of the Mangar Elk.

Feelings – I felt happy with the situation; however, when it came to options for moving the patient, I did not allow Alan time to consider the options and discuss them logically. I now feel disappointed with myself for this.

Evaluation – the use of the Mangar Elk was effective and efficient. However, I did not allow Alan the opportunity to use problem-solving techniques in this situation, which was poor.

Analysis – Lewin et al. (1939) recommend the use of democratic leadership where appropriate. In this case, it could be argued that it was appropriate as the patient was uninjured and not distressed. Therefore, I could have employed this leadership style rather than the autocratic approach I used.

Conclusion – I could have used Lewin et al.'s (1939) democratic or laissez-faire approach. However, the laissez-faire approach could have put Alan in a difficult position, as he may not have been able to provide an appropriate solution to the situation. Thus, the democratic approach would be more appropriate.

Action plan – next time I am in this situation, I will allow Alan some time to think and offer questions to elicit thinking and structured problem solving. I will ensure we discuss the pros and cons for each option for moving the patient and come to a solution together.

References

Lewin, K., Lippitt, R., White, R., (1939) Patterns of aggressive behaviour in experimentally created social climates. *Journal of Social Psychology, Political, Racial and Differential Psychology*, 10(2): pp 271–299.

Johns' Model of Structured Reflection

Some people find Johns' model (1994) more structured and thought-provoking, as it asks more questions than Gibbs' (1988) cycle does. You do not have to answer all of the questions posed, but you may gain a more complete reflection if you do. However, Johns' structured reflection has questions specifically aimed at clinical events, for example: question 2 – *What were the consequences of my actions for the patient/family?* In order to reflect purely on a PEd event, you could ignore or adapt this question:

1. Description of the experience
   - Phenomenon – describe the here-and-now experience.
   - Causal – what essential factors contributed to this experience?
   - Context – what are the significant background factors to this experience?
   - Clarifying – what are the key processes for reflection in this experience?
2. Reflection
   - What was I trying to achieve?
   - Why did I intervene as I did?
   - What were the consequences of my actions for:
     Myself? The patient/family? The people I work with?
   - How did I feel about this experience when it was happening?

- How did the patient feel about it?
- How do I know how the patient felt about it?

3. Influencing factors
   - What internal factors influenced my decision making?
   - What external factors influenced my decision making?
   - What sources of knowledge did influence/should have influenced my decision making?
4. Could I have dealt with the situation better?
   - What other choices did I have?
   - What would be the consequences of these choices?
5. Learning
   - How do I now feel about this experience?
   - How have I made sense of this experience in light of past experiences and future practice?
   - How has this experience changed my ways of knowing (Carper, 1978):

     Empirics – scientific

     Ethics – moral knowledge

     Personal – self-awareness

     Aesthetics – the art of what we do, our own experiences.

Carper's (1978) 'ways of knowing' are incorporated into Johns' reflection (question 5c). Carper (1978) suggests there are four forms of knowledge:

Personal – knowledge stemming from your own understanding and empathy.

Ethical – knowledge that comes from your own moral and ethical codes.

Aesthetic – Carper considered nursing and healthcare to be an art form, but it also relates to an awareness of the current event and current actions and experiences.

Empirical – this relates to evidence that can be clearly shown, usually through research or science.

These concepts can be quite complex and may require considerable thought and discussion with others.

Example

Description of the experience

We attended an 87-year-old gentleman who has fallen. He had no injuries, Alan (who is at the end of his first year) was unsure of how to move the patient from the floor to his chair. I advised the use of the Mangar Elk. I am unhappy with the directive approach I took with this incident. I may have done this as a reflex action, as I did not really consider the needs of Alan prior to making the suggestion of the Mangar Elk.

Reflection

I was trying to ensure that the patient was moved safely, utilising the correct equipment. I was also trying to ensure that Alan was not put in an awkward position as initially he seemed unsure as to how to move the patient. This led to me being directive rather than discussing options, which meant Alan did not receive a problem-solving opportunity. At the time, I felt this was appropriate; however, now, I am disappointed and believe that Alan missed out on this opportunity.

Influencing factors

I made this decision as a reflex, I think. I am new to the PEd role and it was not in my conscious thought to provide a learning opportunity for Alan. I could have led a discussion with Alan suggesting equipment and asking for his opinions, pros and cons for each, using a democratic approach (Lewin et al., 1939).

Could I have dealt with the situation better?

Utilisation of Lewin et al.'s (1939) democratic approach would have been more appropriate here than his autocratic approach, which is the one I applied. This would have been better for Alan and would not have been detrimental to the patient or myself.

Learning

I believe that in future I will give more conscious thought to the learning needs and opportunities for learners. I am now more self-aware as well as more aware of the needs for Alan and my other learners. Thus, my practice will change as a result of this experience.

References

Lewin, K., Lippitt, R., White, R., (1939) Patterns of aggressive behaviour in experimentally created social climates. *Journal of Social Psychology, Political, Racial and Differential Psychology*, 10(2): 271–99.

Burton's 'What, So What, Now What' Model of Reflection

Burton (2000) bases her model on three questions: *what*?, *so what*? and *now what*? In order to achieve these, there are guided questions which include the following:

What...? (This includes a description)

1. Is the purpose of returning to this situation?
2. Happened?
3. Did I see/do?
4. Was my reaction to it?
5. Did other people do who were involved in this?

So what? (Analysis of the event)

1. How did I feel at the time of the event?
2. Were those feelings I had any different from those of other people who were involved at the time?
3. Are my feelings now, after the event, any different from what I experienced at the time?
4. Do I still feel troubled – if so, in what way?
5. What are the effects of what I did (or did not do)?
6. What positive aspects now emerge for me from the event that happened in practice?
7. What have I noticed about my behaviour in practice by taking a more measured look at it?
8. What observations does any person helping me to reflect on my practice make of the way I acted at the time?

Now what? (Proposed actions following the event)

1. What are the implications for me and others in clinical practice based on what I have described and analysed?
2. What difference would it have made if I chose to do nothing?
3. Where can I get more information to face a similar situation?
4. How could I modify my practice if a similar situation were to happen again?
5. What help do I need to help me 'action' the results of my reflections?

6. Which aspect should be tackled first?
7. How will I notice that I am any different in clinical practice?
8. What is the main learning that I take from reflecting on my practice in this way?

(Adapted from Driscoll, 2007)

Some people find Burton's (2000) framework the easiest to use.

Example

What?

We attended an 87-year-old gentleman who has fallen. He had no injuries, Alan (a learner at the end of his first year of study) was unsure of how to move the patient from the floor to his chair. I advised the use of the Mangar Elk. Alan accepted my recommendation without question and we moved the patient from the floor successfully and safely.

So what?

I am unhappy with the directive approach I took in this incident. I may have done this as a reflex action, as I did not really consider the needs of Alan prior to making the suggestion of the Mangar Elk. I could have used this opportunity as a learning experience for Alan and allowed him to problem solve (with support and discussion). Alan did not directly say he was disappointed with not being able to think through the options; however, he can see the value of these opportunities. I suspect I have done this type of thing on a number of occasions, which is not ideal for a PEd.

Now what?

In future I will try to ensure I have a supportive discussion with my learner in order to allow them to figure out the most appropriate equipment to use. Using Lewin et al.'s (1939) democratic leadership style will assist in this process. I will ask my learners to prompt me to adopt this approach if it seems I am not going to do so. My PEd practice is still developing and I need to keep evaluating my own practice to ensure that I am providing the most appropriate learning environment for my learners.

References

Lewin, K., Lippitt, R., White, R., (1939) Patterns of aggressive behaviour in experimentally created social climates. *Journal of Social Psychology, Political, Racial and Differential Psychology*, 10(2): 271–99.

There is no one recommended framework to use in different situations. It is very much a personal choice for PEd and the learner, and individuals may utilise different frameworks to reflect upon the same case. In order to discover which framework is best for you and for different situations, it is recommended that you try out all three and analyse the ease with which you use them and the results you gain from these.

Making Reflections Effective and Safe

There are a number of pitfalls in reflection that you would benefit from avoiding. Some of the common issues faced are discussed below; however, this is not an exhaustive list.

Description

Reflection is not about telling a story. In fact, when you reflect, you do not need to discuss the whole experience; you can select areas that are meaningful. When you become competent at reflection, you only need to reflect on the element that you learnt something from, whether this is a positive or negative learning experience (Ghaye and Lillyman, 2006). However, you can choose to reflect upon an entire case/experience if you find that useful.

When reflecting, the descriptive part of the reflection is ideally kept to a minimum and thus should be brief. It is used to purely to set the scene so that the reflection makes sense. The descriptive element of the reflection can be easier to control if you choose to reflect using a recognised reflective model (like the ones discussed in this chapter). If you choose not to use a model, be cautious this does not result in you purely telling a story, as this does not address the reasons why things occurred in the way that they did. It is the addressing of the 'why things happened like they did' question, and the comparison of your actions to published literature that makes the reflection analytical, and therefore provides you with an experience you are able to learn and develop from.

Legal and Ethical Issues

When writing your reflections, you must always remember the laws and codes of practice you are bound by, for example, the Data Protection Act (2018) and the Health and Care Professions Council Standards of Conduct, Performance and Ethics (2016). You will not benefit from identifying the patient or your workplace within your reflection, so it is imperative that you refrain from adding any information that contravenes these codes of practice or laws. If you deliberately or inadvertently disclose information that allows the patient, your colleagues or workplace to be identified, you are likely to be breaking one or more of the standards set by the Data Protection Act (2018) and the Health and Care Professions Council (2016).

> ***Remember**: Your reflection should not be traceable back to a particular learner, patient or event.*

Time

Having sufficient time to reflect effectively is always an issue for PEds and paramedic practitioners alike. Taylor (2010) highlights that reflection does take a degree of 'time, effort and continuing commitment'. It is worth persevering with reflection, as the benefits can improve your PEd (and paramedic) practice and can highlight any educational development needs as they arise (Taylor, 2010).

Catharsis

Many people will choose to reflect on an incident for carthartic reasons, i.e. it releases pent-up stresses or worries, relieving emotional pressure. Whilst this may be therapeutic and very beneficial to the individual, it is not recommended for a formal reflection. Often in these cases, the reflector will become 'caught up' in the case and often will not reflect; instead, they may vehemently explore their feelings and frustrations. In no way is it recommended to avoid reflecting upon these cases/incidents; however, the reflective process may not be followed effectively, so it may be best to put these reflections to one side as a purely cathartic exercise. As a PEd, you may be required to advise a learner on the appropriateness of a case/incident for their reflective portfolio. In this instance, it would be helpful for the PEd to explore if the reflective process will be a cathartic one. If the PEd believes the learner is in need of catharsis, they may choose to manage this using a method other than reflection.

Using References and Literature

When reflecting, you must refer to literature published on the subject upon which you are reflecting. For example, if you are reflecting upon a communication issue, it would make sense to refer to published communication texts and theories. It is not intended for you to prove that you are wrong; in fact, ideally it should prove your actions are correct. However, on occasion, you may discover that there are different ways of achieving or approaching a task/problem. For example, prior to reading this book, you may believe that you create the perfect learning environment for your learner. After reflecting, you may discover theories presented in this text that challenge your way of working and provide alternate solutions for you, creating a learning experience for you. The idea of most reflective cycles is that after the learning experience shown above, you try out the new theory/method and reflect upon its effectiveness.

Case Studies

Consider the last learner you worked with. Think about your communication with the learner. Write a brief reflection utilising each of the three models provided in this text. Use the same learner and incident for each reflection. This will allow you to compare the models directly.

Reflection

Consider the last learner shift that you undertook. Consider one aspect of your interactions.

Examples of aspects you could reflect upon: clinical support, communication, creation of learning environment for learner.

Use all three models within this chapter to complete a reflection on an area of your practice. Analyse which of the frameworks you find most effective.

Write a brief reflection using any of the three models in this text regarding the process you followed above.

Chapter 3

The Role of the Practice Educator

Learning objectives

1. Role of the PEd
2. Types of support for learners

This chapter will give an overview of the role of the PEd and will introduce some theories applicable to the practice environment.

The Health and Care Professions Council (2017) requires effective learner support within all learning environments. In addition, the Council states that practice placement settings should be 'safe and supportive', with 'appropriately qualified and experienced staff' who have 'relevant knowledge, skills and experience'. There are a number of supportive roles within the ambulance service and the NHS in general that the PEd and the learner may come into contact with.

Morton-Cooper and Palmer (2000) give an overview some of the common roles that can be assigned to a PEd (see Figure 3.1).

Along with the College of Paramedics (2015), the Health and Care Professions Council (2017) requires PEds to be appropriately registered and to have undertaken specific training for the role.

There are a number of fundamental roles that the PEd is required to undertake: confidante, supporter, leader and educator, to name but a few. The roles required will vary from learner to learner and even between PEds. The College of Paramedics (2017a) defines the role:

> A Practice Educator (PEd) is a multi-faceted role, these include being a Leader, Role Model, Coach, Teacher, Mentor, and Assessor, with a responsibility of ensuring the clinical supervision, leadership and

development of a learner (learner paramedic) in the practice-based education environment.

Assessor
A competent practitioner in their field, who is able to assess a learner performing specific skills
Clinical supervisor
A competent practitioner who is responsible for supporting, assessing and initiating reflection in others
Mentor
A person who provides an empowering environment to assist others in their development
Preceptor
A competent practitioner who provides support for others
Role model
A competent practitioner who demonstrates practices that are appropriate for someone else to learn from

Figure 3.1 Some common roles that can be assigned to a PEd (adapted from Morton-Cooper and Palmer (2000))

Morton-Cooper and Palmer (2000) suggest three main areas of work that can be applied to the PEd role. These areas can be subdivided into smaller sections, seen in Table 3.1, and will be discussed in detail below.

Table 3.1 Three areas of work in mentorship

Functional support	Personal support	Relational support
• Teaching • Coaching • Role model • Counsellor • Support • Advisor • Guide • Resource	• Personal development • Growth • Self-confidence • Creativity • Fulfilment of potential • Risk taking	• Interpersonal skills • Social relationships • Networking • Sharing • Trust

(adapted from Morton-Cooper and Palmer (2000))

Functional Support

Teaching – this may not be considered a traditional PEd skill. However, it is something that is generally done on an informal basis. If a learner experiences a completely new situation, the PEd may show them how to approach it. For example, a new learner is sent as part of a crew to a road traffic collision. The PEd may show the learner how to park the ambulance in the 'fend off' position. Whilst the majority of formal teaching will take place outside of the practice placement area, informal teaching will be very important for the learner.

Coaching – coaching is an important aspect of the PEd role and is covered in Chapter 7 of this book.

Role model – learner paramedics are aspiring to become excellent paramedic practitioners, so it is vital for them to have good practices and behaviours to emulate. In some aspects of practice, learners may not have the ability to recognise the difference between good and poor practices until late in their education. However, in other aspects, they may recognise good and poor practice quite early on. For example, a new learner may recognise that forcing an oropharyngeal airway into a patient's mouth whilst their gag reflex is intact is poor practice. However, they may not recognise that making a patient walk to the ambulance when they have cardiac chest pain is poor practice. It is therefore vital that the PEd is a good role model, demonstrating exemplary practice at all times. This will allow the learner to develop their own exemplary practice.

Counsellor – it is inevitable that some learners will require some form of counselling during their educational experience. This may be related directly to the programme or work placement, or completely unrelated to their course. Often, they turn to the people they know and trust for advice and support – this may well be the PEd. PEd training often does not encompass counselling, which is a comprehensive and complex skill; therefore, any support offered should be of an informal nature and should not take the place of formal counselling. The main skill for the PEd here is active listening. Coaching skills may also be applicable; however, it is important to recognise when true counselling is required and refer the learner to the appropriate resource. The main skill for the PEd here is understanding when they should refer the learner on for formal counselling. Seeking advice from the educational establishment to which the learner is attached is also very helpful.

Support – this may take the form of counselling; however, it may be less serious in nature than for those requiring counselling. Learners often require support if they have been unsuccessful in an assessment or procedure. They may require emotional support if they feel they are not performing well in the theoretical and practical aspects of the programme. As above, the issue may be related to the programme or completely unrelated. It is important for the PEd to recognise when a learner requires support, informal counselling and formal counselling. If a PEd is unsure, it is advisable to refer the learner on for formal counselling. Much support offered by PEds will be related to the learner's skills and performance; these are usually readily and effectively managed by PEds with little input from other agencies.

Advisor – learners will have questions at most stages of their education. For example, they may have been shown several different ways of undertaking a procedure and they may approach their PEd to clarify the 'correct' one. Therefore, the PEds should be open to answering questions and have the knowledge to answer them or show the learner how to obtain the answers they need. The PEd also needs to recognise when to refer the learner to another appropriate person, for example, university staff.

Guide – guidance can be considered to be similar to advice; however, advice is often sought by the learner, whereas guidance may not be. Thus, guidance may be unsolicited by the learner. An example of guidance may be feeding back to a learner about a behaviour that was inappropriate in a particular circumstance. Guidance by its nature tends to be a negative experience, pointing out to the learner that they have not done something well. Therefore, careful thought should be given to the manner in which this is done. Without guidance, learners may not develop appropriate behaviours, which subsequently may cause issues for them in later placements.

Resource – learners expect their PEds to have a greater knowledge base than they do. This may be unfounded, as some learners may be shown new techniques or procedures that the PEd has not been privy to. A good PEd/ambulance service–university relationship is important in order to ensure that PEds are kept up to date with current teaching. In order to maximise PEds as a resource, it is helpful to include PEds within university education. For example, PEds could assist with practical sessions in university. In addition, it is helpful for PEds to be up to date in terms of current research and publications; therefore, if a learner asks about a specific topic, the PEd will have the current knowledge and resources to pass on to the learner.

Personal Support

Personal development – every learner paramedic is undergoing development on a fundamental level, as they are learning a new way of behaving and interacting with other people. Some learners take to this change more readily than others. Sometimes this transition is easier due to the learner's past experiences. The PEd's role here is to guide these changes, praising good behaviour and moulding inappropriate behaviour.

Growth – this can be linked closely to personal development, but it also relates to the development of physical skills and intellectuality. Many learners 'mature' over the course of their learning, which is likely to be as a result of their experiences and interactions with patients and staff. PEds can influence this growth by being positive role models and providing a supportive environment for the learner.

Self-confidence – confidence often comes with experience. Benner (2001) discusses experience at great length and is a valuable resource here. Confidence will naturally develop as the learner learns and is successful. The PEd is able to enhance and assist in the development of confidence by the provision of a supportive and positive learning environment. Some learners may be overly confident and may therefore require help in reducing their over-confidence, which can be more challenging. The PEd may need to seek support from the educational institution in the case of over-confident learners. Self-confidence may go hand in hand with social relationships and interpersonal skills.

Creativity – in the paramedic environment, creativity may not appear to have any relevance. However, there may be circumstances where a problem is not straightforward and the paramedic needs to 'think laterally'; in other words, to be creative in their approach to problem solving.

> For example: a patient who has a dislocated shoulder may have their arm positioned out to the side pointing above their head – it will require some creative thinking to devise an appropriate method for supporting the patient's arm during their transport to hospital.

University education is intended to teach problem-solving skills and PEds can play a large part in a learner's creative experience in the practice environment. If the PEd is able to demonstrate how they have solved problems in the past and to discuss options, the learner will develop an understanding of how to solve problems themselves in the real world. Challenging the learner to think laterally without giving answers can also be helpful, as long as the challenge is appropriate and support is given as required.

Fulfilment of potential – learners often require the encouragement of their PEd to reach their full potential. Some learners do not realise what their potential is or how far they could go should they wish to. PEds are in a unique position to see the potential of their learner first-hand and are therefore best placed to guide the learner towards it.

Risk taking – this could be rephrased as 'appropriate risk taking'. Within the paramedic area of work, risks tend to be commonplace. For example, do you take a pregnant lady to hospital or deliver the baby at the scene? The role of the PEd is to help educate the learner to ensure they take educated and sensible risks rather than act on rash or ill thought-out ideas. Again, the PEd's experiences here are very valuable to the learner.

Relational Support

Interpersonal skills, relationships, networking, sharing and trust can all fit into the bracket of social skills. The PEd will assist their learner by setting a good example in all of these areas. These subjects tend to cross over into each other as well as into parts of the other two categories of functional and personal support. For example, interpersonal skills between the PEd and the learner are maintained by effective communication, advising, guiding and supporting, with the goal being development and growth for the learner (and sometimes for the PEd). If a PEd maintains inappropriate relationships with learners or staff, they are potentially a poor role model and may take inappropriate uneducated risks.

Using Morton-Cooper and Palmer's (2000) framework, it can be seen that functional support is the area that most paramedics and PEds would associate with being a PEd or mentor. However, on closer examination of past learners, most PEds or mentors would see that their protégés have also developed in many other areas as well.

Connor and Pokora (2012) suggest that both mentoring and coaching are helpful tools:

> Both coaching and mentoring are learning relationships which help people to take charge of their own development, to release their potential and to achieve results which they value.

Connor and Pokora (2012) go on to suggest that the role of a mentor is a supportive one, which challenges the learner into seeking answers themselves rather than merely giving information. Challenging the learner in this way is more associated with coaching than mentoring in Morton-Cooper and Palmer's (2000) framework. Like Connor and Pokora (2012), many authors consider mentoring and coaching to overlap, so the terms are often used interchangeably. In fact, there are many similarities between the definitions from Connor and Pokora's (2012) and Morton-Cooper and Palmer's (2000) work.

Both Morton-Cooper and Palmer's (2000) and Connor and Pokora's (2012) theories of the mentor role can be applied to the PEd. However, each learner will require the PEd to adopt a slightly different role in order to meet their individual needs. Paramedics and PEds are used to adapting to the requirements of others within their normal working environments and, as a result, they may adapt their style of mentoring without recognising that they are doing so.

Case Studies

Consider the most appropriate PEd roles for the following situations based upon the information in this chapter. There may be more than one answer for these scenarios:

1. First-year learner Adam has difficulty in taking a blood pressure reading. He says he cannot hear the changes in sounds through his stethoscope.
2. Second-year learner Rebecca has difficulty in communicating with older patients. She says she doesn't know what to say to them and feels awkward if they don't hear her correctly.
3. Third-year learner David cannot decide on a topic for his dissertation. He has two in mind: 1. Prevention of post-traumatic stress disorder (PTSD) in paramedics. 2. Assisted suicide: is it right or wrong?

   How will you as a PEd support David in his decision?

Reflection

Reflect upon a time where you have used relational support.

Reflect upon a time where you have used functional support.

Reflect upon a time where you have used personal support.

Reflect upon your role as an assessor with a first-year learner.

Chapter 4

Getting the Practice Educator/Learner Relationship Right

Learning objectives

1. Theories on PEd/learner relationships
2. Maslow's hierarchy of needs
3. Personal qualities and attributes of an effective PEd
4. How to avoid toxic relationships
5. Building an effective relationship

This chapter will consider what makes an effective relationship between the PEd and the learner, and it will present appropriate theories for use by the PEd in the practice environment.

The relationship between the learner and the PEd is one that usually lasts for at least two/three years, depending upon the length of the learner's course and subsequent post-registration employment. Thus, it is important for the PEd and the learner to have a good working relationship. Health Education England (undated) states that learners should be 'in an environment that delivers safe, effective, compassionate care that provides a positive experience for service users'. It is unlikely that this would be possible in a negative working relationship. Ideally, the PEd and the learner should choose each other to ensure they have a good rapport. However, in practice, this is not always practical and can lead to the PEd and the learner picking each other for the wrong reasons, e.g. they know each other.

Authority Gradients and the PEd/Learner Relationship

Authority gradients are generally accepted as being a perceived or actual power balance between differing members in a relationship. For example, the PEd may be perceived as being higher up the gradient when compared

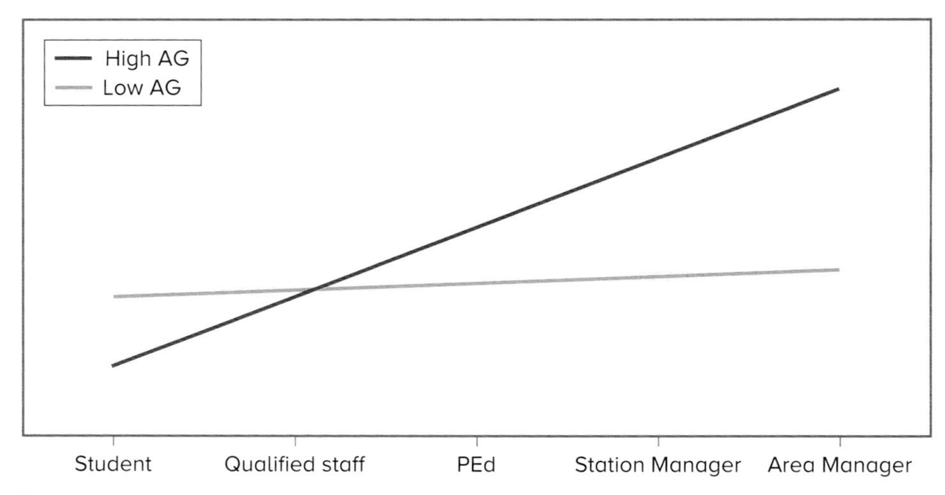

Figure 4.1 Difference in perception between a high- and low-authority gradient

to a student paramedic, but lower than, for example, an area manager. It is recognised that authority gradients can lead to errors and communication issues within the medical environment (Cosby and Croskerry, 2004), so the PEd should be aware of the phenomenon and how to mitigate its effects. Figure 4.1 shows how a learner may perceive themselves in terms of other staff within a typical ambulance service setting, in both a high and low authority gradient (AG) environment. Having a steep AG can limit communication and lead to people lower on the AG being unwilling or feeling unable to air their viewpoints. It is recognised that the AG should change based upon different situations. For example, in a serious clinical situation, the AG may become steeper with the PEd being more authoritarian; however, in general learning situations, it is beneficial to have a less steep AG to ensure the learner feels valued and that they can ask questions and make comments. Effective management of AG requires good communication and leadership skills (see Chapter 7) alongside other skills found in this chapter.

Morton-Cooper and Palmer's Three-Stage Relationship

Morton-Cooper and Palmer (2000) show a three-stage relationship between the mentor (PEd) and the learner (Figure 4.2).

The initiation stage is arguably the most important stage, as the bonds and ground rules of the relationship are laid down here. It is important for both the PEd and the learner to explore their needs and requirements. For

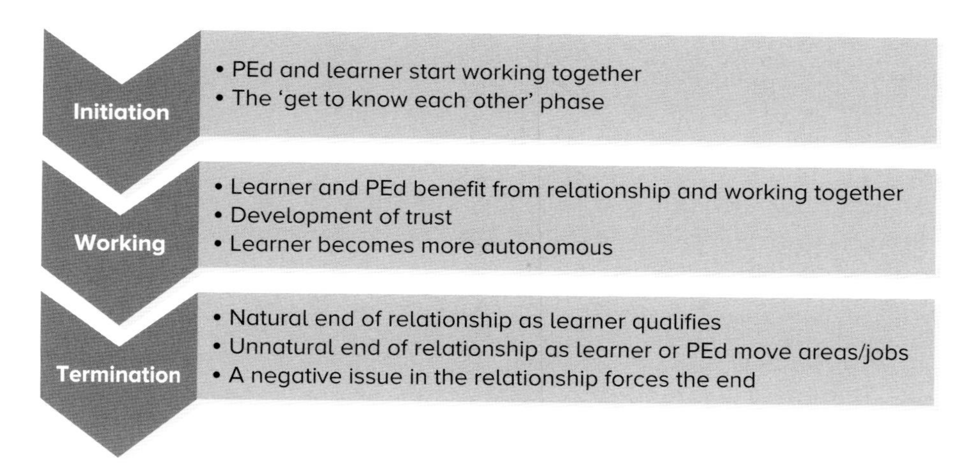

Figure 4.2 Three-stage relationship between PEd and the learner (adapted from Morton-Cooper and Palmer (2000))

example, if the learner requires the PEd to complete documentation, when and where this will be done is a matter for discussion. Should a PEd (or learner) display negative traits in this phase, it will be difficult to overcome them, so the section on toxic mentoring is important to bear in mind here. The initiation phase is also the one where an intervention or even dissolution of the relationship is required, should either party identify an issue. The length of this phase will vary significantly between PEds and learners, but may last from 1–2 shifts up to 5–10 shifts. The length may also be determined by how often the PEd and the learner work together. For example, if a learner is working with their PEd for one shift once a week for 12 hours, it is likely that phase one will be longer than for a learner working three 12-hour shifts in one week with their PEd.

The working phase is the most substantial phase in terms of time and action for both the PEd and the learner. The learner starts to develop as an autonomous practitioner with the support of the PEd. The benefit of this relationship and learning is a mutual one, whereby the PEd can learn from the learner as well as the learner from the PEd. This stage is vital for the learner to develop and become independent, and this stage will usually last until the learner qualifies.

The termination of the relationship is usually as a result of the learner finishing their placement and/or qualifying. This is obviously the most sought-after ending; however, this is not always the case. In some situations, the PEd and the learner do not form a positive relationship, resulting in it becoming unhealthy and destructive. This will necessitate the end of the relationship, for the benefit of both the learner and the PEd. In some circumstances, the

PEd may move into a new role or different working location and the learner may be unable or unwilling to move with the PEd. Regardless of the reason for termination, if the learner has not completed the placement, they will require a new PEd and will start the three phases again. The impact of this must not be under-estimated, especially if the learner had an excellent relationship with their previous PEd. In this instance, the new PEd will need to be especially mindful of the initiation phase, as the learner may be upset, angry or confused about the change.

Morton-Cooper and Palmer's (2000) three-stage relationship is similar to Kram's (1983) work; however, Kram shows four stages, where the last stage is 'restarting', where the PEd/learner relationship may endure, but in a different format. For example, if the learner qualifies and gains employment at the same location as their former PEd, they may find that their former PEd is now their work colleague. This can be challenging for both the PEd (who may still view the former learner as a learner) and the former learner (who may feel their former PEd is judging them). The 'restarting' phase could almost be thought of as a new initiation phase, where new boundaries and ground rules are set, and the PEd gets to know the newly qualified paramedic (NQP) as a practitioner (not learner) *and* the NQP gets to know the PEd as a practitioner (instead of as a PEd).

Personal Relationships

On occasions, conflicts of interest may arise, whereby a PEd and a learner engage in a personal relationship. It is incumbent upon the PEd and the learner to declare this relationship to the employing service and educational institution in order to ensure that a conflict of interest is avoided. Whilst at no point is it suggested that the PEd and/or the learner would behave inappropriately, it would be difficult to argue that the PEd could be unbiased when assessing the learner. Thus, a different PEd should be sought for the learner.

Maslow's Hierarchy of Needs

In addition to PEd actions having an impact upon the PEd learner relationship, Maslow's (1987) hierarchy of needs (Figure 4.3) could also have an impact. Maslow stated that in order to reach the top of the pyramid and achieve the best that a person can be, the previous layers of the pyramid need to be solid. Thus, if a learner does not have their physiological and safety needs met, they cannot progress up the pyramid to feel love and belonging. It is acknowledged that a learner may not have all of their needs met all of the time – for example, on shift the learner may feel cold and hungry, which would be a negative impact upon the physiological stage of the pyramid. However, these short-term deficits would not necessarily

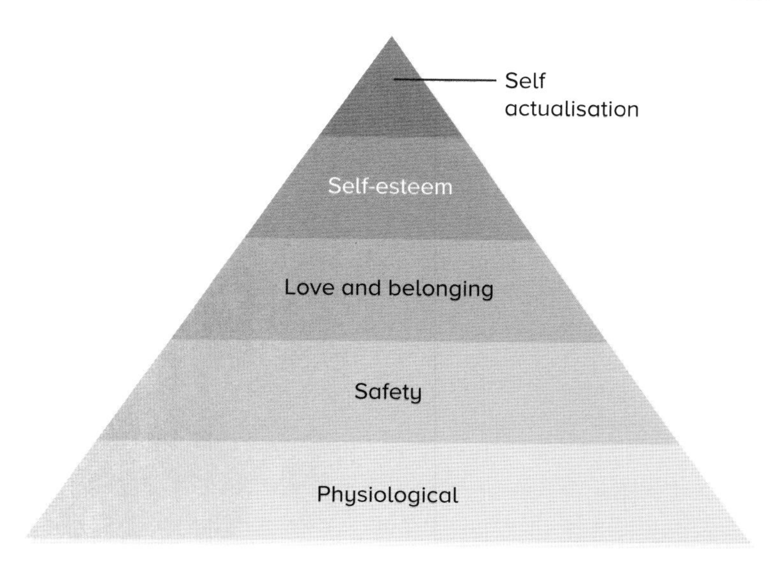

Figure 4.3 Maslow's hierarchy of needs (1987)

have a major impact in the long term. However, if a learner is living in a poor situation where they cannot heat their rooms or afford sufficient food, they will not be able to work and learn as efficiently as another learner without these issues.

Whilst a PEd is not intended to act as a social worker and manage these types of difficult situations for or with learners, it may well be that the PEd identifies these issues by the nature of the PEd/learner relationship. It is important for the PEd to know where to seek support for themselves and the learner in these situations. This is covered in more detail in Chapter 9. The PEd does have influence over some of the areas that Maslow highlights, for example, belonging and self-esteem.

Qualities and Attributes of PEds

In relation to Maslow's hierarchy of needs, the personal qualities and attributes of both the PEd and the learner can of course influence the PEd/learner relationship positively or negatively. The PEd can ensure they bring positive interactions by carefully considering and adapting (if necessary) their demeanour.

Personal qualities can be thought of as someone's standards (*Oxford Dictionary*, 2012a) and attributes as a characteristic or an inherent part of someone (*Oxford Dictionary*, 2012b). These two aspects of people overlap considerably, so should be considered in tandem. Table 4.1 shows *some* important qualities and attributes for PEds.

Table 4.1 Qualities and attributes of an excellent PEd

Approachable
Learners will have moments when they feel inadequate or upset. Being able to approach their PEd for advice or simply to have their concerns listened to is very valuable.
Honest
Learners benefit from being told the truth about their progress. It is pointless telling a learner they are doing well when in reality they are not. Likewise, it is unhelpful to fail to give feedback – avoiding the issue does not make it better.
Good communicator
This covers all kinds of communication – for example, active listening, use of appropriate language and vocal tonality, able to give concise verbal and written feedback.
Knowledgeable
Learners will have questions regarding their practice. As a PEd, it is beneficial to have the answers or to know where to get the answers to these questions.
Empathetic
This is the ability to appreciate the learner's position. Learners benefit from mentors who remember what it was like to be in training. These PEds tend to be more accepting of small errors and sympathetic when issues arise.
Good role model
Learners benefit from being shown good practice. They will emulate and learn from it. They will also emulate and learn from poor practice; however, they may not recognise that it is poor.
Able to motivate
Learners will become disheartened or demotivated at times. This could be as a result of poor performance, stress of the course, inability to achieve a set goal or tiredness, to name but a few examples. The ability to motivate learners at these times is valuable to both the PEd and the learner.

Table 4.1 Qualities and attributes of an excellent PEd *(continued)*

Enthusiastic
Enthusiasm assists with the PEd being a good role model, it also helps with knowledge acquisition and motivation.
Desire to help
PEds who opt to become PEds may be better than ones who are reluctant or who are persuaded to do so. The motivation for someone becoming a mentor should be considered in order to ensure they want to do it so as to help the learners become good paramedics.

Toxic Relationships

Darling (1986) considered the phenomenon of toxic relationships, which are the antithesis of effective relationships. She considered four main characteristics that are inappropriate in people who are in a supportive role (Table 4.2). It is important that PEds are aware of these areas so that they can be avoided. If PEds are recruited appropriately, it is likely that most toxic traits will be avoided instinctively. Support for the PEd is also crucial (see Chapter 9), to avoid PEds becoming disillusioned and taking their frustrations out on the learner, inadvertently causing a toxic relationship. Health Education England (undated) also states:

> Learners must not be subjected to, or subject others to, behaviour that undermines their professional confidence, performance or self-esteem.

Morton-Cooper and Palmer (2000) also discuss disruptive personalities, highlighting a number of points (see Table 4.3).

It can be seen that points raised by both Darling (1986) and Morton-Cooper and Palmer (2000) have similarities and crossovers.

It is recognised that to be a perfect PEd 100% of the time is unrealistic. As such, toxicity can occur as a one-off situation and, if it does, could arguably be due to the PEd having a bad day. Whilst ideally this should be avoided, a one-off occurrence is less likely to cause an issue for the learner than an ongoing toxic relationship. Whilst toxicity can have a devastating effect upon a learner's ability to learn as well as their confidence, it also has to be remembered that learners often feel awkward or unjustified in terms of raising issues surrounding toxic relationships. Learners do not want the

Table 4.2 Toxic traits

Avoiders
These PEds will avoid situations where meaningful relationships are required. They may avoid their learners by changing shifts or not being available to help the learner when they require assistance.
Blockers
These PEds will literally block the learner's development and learning; this can be achieved in a number of ways, for example, preventing the learner from practising skills.
Dumpers
These PEds will 'dump' the learner in at the deep end with little/no support. The learner then will not necessarily be able to achieve a good standard as they have not been supported in an appropriate manner.
Destroyers
These PEds may use destructive techniques, for example, humiliation of the learner, providing insufficient support and then telling the learner that they are no good.

(adapted from Darling (1986))

Table 4.3 Disruptive personality traits

Rigid mind
Where the PEd will not allow the learner to think creatively or with originality.
Ego mind
Where the PEd does not encourage objectivity and considers themselves to have the most important viewpoint.
Machiavellian mind
Where the PEd is manipulative, devious and deceitful.

(adapted from Morton-Cooper and Palmer (2000))

situation to get worse (similar to the schoolyard bullying situation) and thus will often not say anything to exacerbate the situation. Thus, the toxicity could go on unchecked for some time. Other PEds or other staff may in fact be in a position to be the first to see the signs of a toxic relationship. They may notice a strained relationship between the PEd and the learner or they may witness inappropriate behaviour from the PEd. Regardless of who identifies the issue, it is one that needs to be raised in a supportive manner for both the learner and the PEd. Support for PEds is covered later in Chapter 9.

Communication

Communication is something that people generally take for granted. However, it does require a level of skill and consideration. Effective communication is a vital two-way process between the PEd and the learner, and ineffective communication can lead to conflict, lack of learning and a toxic environment. Kilgallon and Thompson (2012) demonstrate that in order to avoid conflict, the PEd should recognise that there is an issue, use empathy and consider the other person's point of view, demonstrate their understanding of the other person's perspective, give their own viewpoint, be respectful and try to achieve a mutually agreeable solution.

Figure 4.4 provides an overview of how communication works. The sender is the person initiating the communication, i.e. the speaker, while the receiver is the person the communication is aimed at, i.e. the listener. It requires the sender to correctly code and send the message, which then requires the receiver to correctly decode the message. Breakdowns in communication tend to occur as a failure in one of these two points.

For example, it could be that the sender sends the message verbally, but with a significant facial expression; the receiver will not receive the facial expression as the sender has failed to notice that the receiver is facing away from them. Thus, it is vital for not only the verbal content of the message to be sent appropriately, but also the non-verbal part of the message needs to be sent appropriately.

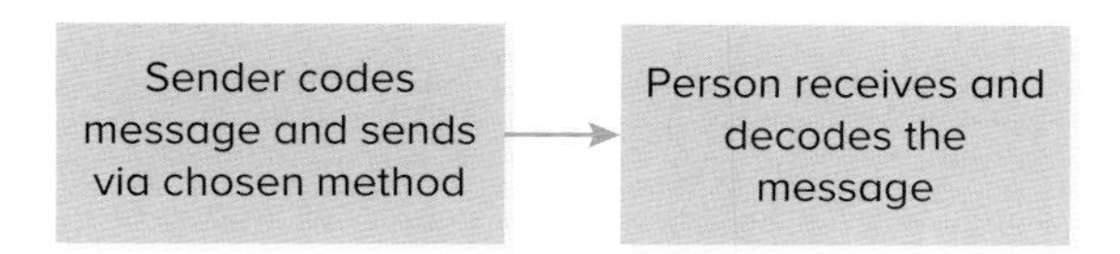

Figure 4.4 Communication process
(adapted from Gubbins and Nixon (2013))

Verbal and Paralinguistic Communication

It is widely recognised that verbal communication is only part of any communication, with non-verbal cues playing a bigger role than the spoken word. Paralinguistics literally means 'alongside linguistics' (Schuller et al., 2013); in general terms, it relates to the part of speech that does not involve the actual words spoken. However, paralinguistics is often not considered in as much detail, which can lead to misunderstandings and potentially conflict. Figure 4.5 shows the main elements of paralinguistics as discussed by Gubbins and Nixon (2013).

Pace – often people will speak more slowly if they know the person they are talking to is hard of hearing or does not fully understand the same language. However, a slower pace can also be used to make a point more profoundly. For example, long pauses between words can be used as punctuations or even threats. Consider the following phrase: 'Do you understand?' This is an innocuous phrase that can be used without fear of misunderstanding; however, now consider putting a pause between each word: 'Do ... you ... understand?' Suddenly, the same phrase feels more threatening and it *could* take the person on the receiving end of the phrase back to their childhood and instil negative emotions. Of course, the emotional response to communication is very individual and will vary based upon a person's life experiences.

Conversely, a fast pace of questions could bombard and overload someone. They are more likely to answer the last question they hear and ignore or forget the first set of questions. The PEd should be aware of the pace of their communication and adapt it appropriately for each situation.

Pitch of voice – pitch (or the note of voice) can again impact significantly on the message being received by the other person. Something said in an unusually high pitch can come across as being frustrated or anxious, whereas using a deeper voice than normal can feel menacing. The PEd should use pitch in a supportive manner to ensure that the learner is not made to feel useless or in the way.

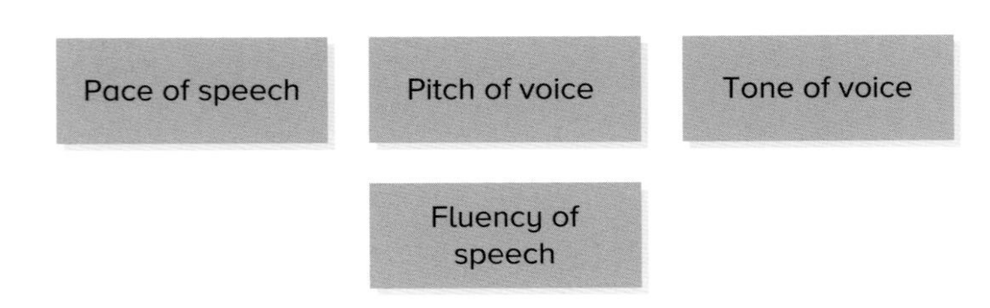

Figure 4.5 Paralinguistics
(adapted from Gubbins and Nixon (2013))

Tone of voice – this relates to the harshness or softness of the voice. Again, this can impact significantly upon the words being said. Using a harsh tone is likely to convey anger or frustration, whereas a softer tone is likely to evoke kinder emotions or feelings of empathy. It is possible that the PEd will be in situations with learners that involve some frustration; however, care should be taken not to allow this to come across in their verbal communications. In addition, a sense of urgency could come across as harshness in the vocal tone; if a PEd uses this tone (possibly accidentally), it could pressurise the learner, which could lead to a negative experience.

Fluency of speech – lack of fluency of speech can indicate a lack of belief in what is being said, an incomplete thought process or an inability to formulate a cogent argument/statement. It can show that the person talking is unfamiliar with the topic of conversation or is uncomfortable with the conversation. The PEd should try to portray confidence, which may be made difficult through lack of fluency. It is therefore important that the PEd has prepared their thoughts, prior to difficult conversations especially. Think about a time where you have seen a politician on television who has struggled to answer a question, giving lots of pauses and insertions of 'er...' in their reply. Consider how you felt about that individual – did you feel confident in their understanding of the situation? How did you feel about their ability to handle the situation?

Choice of Words

The actual words used are also vital in any communication alongside paralinguistics and body language. It is important to consider where it is appropriate to use jargon, colloquial terms and formal terms. Learners are likely to pick up terms used by the PEds, so if the PEd is consistently using jargon with patients, it is probable that the learner will adopt this practice. Sometimes it can be difficult to find exactly the right word for a given situation, in which case it may be better for the PEd to explain using a number of words/phrases or examples rather than taking the risk of using the wrong word and causing conflict or upset.

Body Language

As with verbal and paralinguistic language, body language can portray a whole range of emotions and opinions, and can give away someone's true feelings despite the verbal language being used. Boyes (2005) shows that much of our body language is not controlled by our conscious thought. However, this does not mean it cannot be adapted. The PEd should treat every interaction with their learner as an important one, so the PEd's body language should portray interest, alongside their verbal and paralinguistic language. Egan's (1990) SOLER acronym can be used to show how interest can be portrayed (see Figure 4.6).

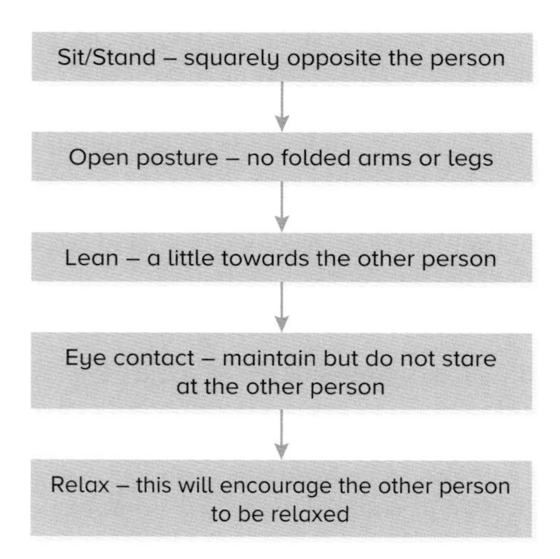

Figure 4.6 Egan's SOLER acronym
(adapted from Egan (1990))

Table 4.4 Aggressive versus assertive behaviours

Aggressive behaviours	Assertive behaviours
Standing with hands on hips	Face to face
Folded arms	Comfortable but direct eye contact
Direct and prolonged eye contact	Appropriate facial expressions
Using a loud voice unnecessarily	Clear voice – not harsh tone
Threatening or harsh tone of voice	Calm voice – not high or low-pitched
Threatening or provocative body language/gestures	

(adapted from Gubbins and Nixon (2013))

Mirroring can be a powerful tool in the escalation of a heightened situation. Mirroring involves the PEd adopting the same position as the learner; however, if the PEd can then gradually change their pose to a more relaxed and open position, it is likely that the learner will then mirror the PEd and become more relaxed in the process.

Where conflict is likely or unavoidable, it is important for the PEd to be assertive and that they avoid aggressive behaviours. Table 4.4 shows some aggressive behaviours that should be avoided and assertive behaviours that should be adopted by the PEd.

Another element of body language is the facial expression. Some expressions are cultural (for example, nodding the head back and forth to acknowledge something is not utilised across the globe) and therefore the PEd would be advised to have a little understanding and patience if they are supporting learners from different cultures.

Barriers to Effective Communication

Schiavo (2007) identified some barriers to communication that are especially common within healthcare, which can be seen in Figure 4.7.

Figure 4.7 Barriers to communication
(adapted from Schiavo (2007))

Some of the areas identified by Schiavo (2007) will not apply to the PEd's situation – for example, it is doubtful that they will have an elderly learner to support. However, some of the barriers will apply frequently, for example: learner stress, jargon and level of understanding. It is therefore important for the PEd to understand that these are barriers and adapt their communication accordingly to ensure that a positive learning environment is maintained for the learner.

Case Studies

1. Abdul has been a PEd for two years. He has a first-year learner, Kelly, who is particularly nervous when talking to patients.

   Identify the personal qualities that Abdul requires in order to help this learner.

   Identify your rationale for each of your selected qualities.

2. Lisa, a third-year BSc learner, has complained to you that her PEd is not communicating effectively with her. What questions would you need to ask Lisa in order to address this issue with her PEd?

3. Graham is a PEd with two first-year learners, Steve and Isobel. Isobel has approached you for help with Graham. She says that Graham has told her off in front of patients for not knowing the answers to his questions. You speak with Steve to see if he has the same experiences; reluctantly, Steve admits that this has happened to him too. Explain the Darling theory that fits with Graham's behaviour and consider how this could be addressed.

Reflection

Table 4.1 shows some qualities/characteristics of effective PEds; what other qualities/characteristics do you think PEds should have?

Why are these important? Please give some examples.

How do your attributes positively influence your colleagues?

How do your attributes positively influence your learners?

How could your attributes negatively influence your colleagues?

How could your attributes negatively influence your learners?

How can you adapt your attributes to ensure you have a positive impact upon colleagues?

How can you adapt your attributes to ensure you have a positive impact upon learners?

Consider if you have ever been guilty of toxic mentoring. If you have, explore the reasons for this and how you can avoid this situation in the future.

What can you do to help build an excellent working relationship with your learners?

Part II

Theories and Application

Chapter 5

Learning Theory and Learning Environments

Learning objectives

1. Understanding the importance of learning styles
2. Creating a positive learning environment

The relationship between the PEd and the learner is vital. The learner relies on this relationship during their paramedic education as the practice placement elements have just as much emphasis placed upon them as taught theory content. It is also important that the PEd helps create a positive learning environment where possible in order to help the learners transition into practice. This chapter will examine the importance of this relationship in terms of understanding the individual learner's learning style and how the PEd can help develop a positive learning environment to best support the learner as a result.

Learning Styles

When a PEd supervises a learner, it is important that they become aware of their learner's learning style. In addition, the PEd needs to be aware of their own learning style. It is not uncommon for the learner and the PEd to have different preferred learning styles, which may cause difficulties with the relationship if this fact is not recognised. If differing learning styles do occur, then the PEd needs to attempt to find a common ground or adapt their practice to suit the learner's learning style.

For the PEd, the starting point has to be the following question: 'What is a learning style?' Gopee (2015) describes a learning style as the way someone responds to the situation in which they find themselves, ultimately enabling them to gain knowledge or a new skill. The end goal of the learner's journey will be to gain knowledge and experience, but the journey they take to get there may be different from that of the PEd or a different learner that the PEd may be supporting.

A variety of learning styles have been identified over the years – for example, Kolb (1984), Honey and Mumford (2006) (see Figure 5.1) and visual, aural, read/write, kinaesthetic (VARK) (Flemming, 1992). Learning styles can be explored by completing self-test questionnaires. However, completing these questionnaires is not always practical in the clinical practice environment due to time and cost constraints (on occasions you have to pay for the licence to run these tests). Although it is difficult to find a solution to this, the PEd should take time to get to know their learner and examine how the learner learns best. When considering learning styles, it is possible that the learner may naturally utilise a combination of learning styles (Gopee, 2015), as every individual learns differently and these styles are not 'one size fits all'. In addition, the learner's learning style may change as they become more experienced and knowledgeable or when they encounter a different case or environment. It is up to the PEd to be able to facilitate these adaptations and enable the learner's development. To do this, it is recognised that the PEd needs to adapt to the learner's learning style where possible. This can be difficult for the PEd; however, it could be as simple as providing the learner with some time to reflect or to make a topic more visual if the learner's learning style indicates they would benefit from this.

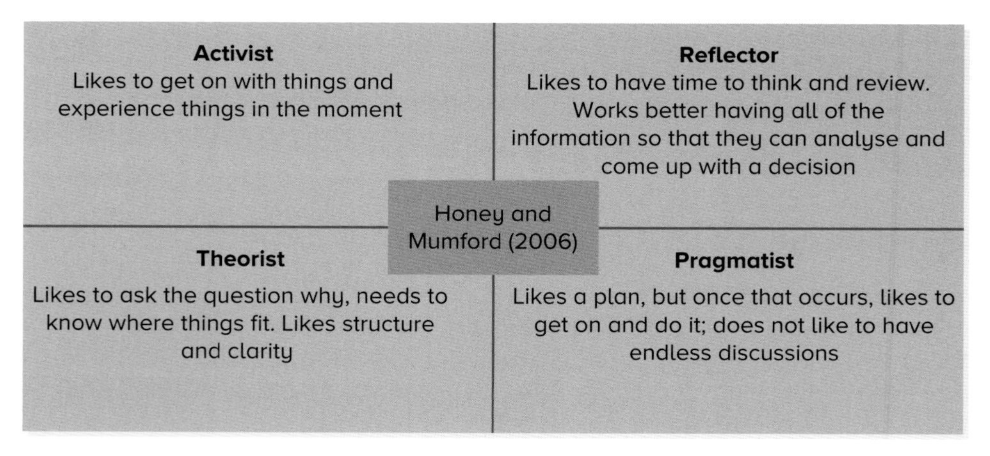

Figure 5.1 The four main learning styles
(based on Honey and Mumford (2006))

Each learning style comes with its own strengths and weaknesses as detailed in Table 5.1. It will be up to the PEd to help develop this learning style but also try to develop the positive elements of other learning styles relevant to the paramedic role. There can be occasions where the learner does not naturally fit into an ideal learning style for paramedic practice.

Table 5.1 Overcoming strengths and weaknesses

Style	Strength	Weakness	Role of the PEd
Activist	Enjoys being challenged and placed in new situations Enjoys and works well with others, enthusiastic	Does not enjoy working on own Does not enjoy theoretical lectures Can rush to take action without thinking	Important to show the relevance of learning the academic theory of the programme May need to control and closely supervise the learner's eagerness initially
Reflector	Methodical and thoughtful Rarely rushes to conclusions	Can hold back and be too cautious Can be slow at making decisions	Provide encouragement to learners when they are making decisions Help facilitate the learners to make decisions in a supportive environment
Theorist	Self-disciplined Asks probing questions Rationale, objective and logical in their thoughts	Does not tolerate disorder or ambiguity Restrictive in their lateral thinking	Encourage learners to think of alternative solutions Facilitate learners in gaining answers to their own questions to aid learning
Pragmatist	Practical in their thinking Task-focused	Can downplay the theory side of the programme Finds it difficult not to go with the first solution	Important to emphasise the need for theory within the role Encourage the learner's ability to engage with the task Promote reflection on alternative solutions and not going with the first solution every time

(modified from Poon et al. (2000))

It will then be the role of the PEd to help develop the learner and also develop the remaining styles, thus strengthening the learner's ability for the role.

Coffield et al. (2004) discuss that labelling someone with a learning style poses risks. They note that there is a strong possibility that the learner will be labelled in a particular way. Coffield et al (2004) argue that if learning styles are to be taken into account, they are used as a reflection tool so that learners can be aware of their own abilities, but are not limited by them. However, the users must be aware that there are a large number of recognised learning styles/models and they are not all of equal worth. Research carried out by Peterson et al. (2009) question the views raised by Coffield et al. and state that learning style awareness can be important when trying to fully understand an individual and their subsequent performance. Taking all of these views into account, it is important for the PEd to see the student as an individual, whilst recognising that students learn in different ways and that this way may be different from how they approach a situation or learn best.

Learning Environments

Think back to your first day in your current role or when you first started working as a clinician – how did you feel? Were you nervous? Can you remember why? Learners feel exactly the same when they are attending their clinical placements for the first time. Learners worry about how they will be greeted and welcomed into the placement, whether they will be able to settle in and whether they will be able to cope. The initial impression the learner gets of their placement will generally set the direction of the placement and the PEd/learner relationship. As a result, it is the role of the PEd to make this process as smooth as possible in order to ensure that the learner feels welcome and that the environment is supportive, where the learner can raise any concerns or ask any questions to aid their learning. Olander et al. (2018) discuss that when PEds spent less time welcoming their learners into placements, this impacted on the learner's experience and view of the practice placement. They go on to state that learners valued their placement more when the PEd was welcoming and took the time to get to know them.

One of the top priorities for the PEd is to put the learner at ease. This needs to start during the learner's first shift where possible and must continue throughout the length of their course. By doing this, the PEd will immediately foster a relationship where the student will feel comfortable approaching the PEd with any questions or concerns they may have. However, it is not just the responsibility of the PEd to create this environment. Fostering this culture must be part of the organisation's culture, which means senior managers and other staff, who are not directly responsible for the learner, also must play their part. The College of Paramedics (2017b) highlights the need for there to be a positive relationship between the PEd and the learner, but it also reiterates the need to keep the relationship professional and ensure that clear boundaries to the relationship are identified. This is especially important when the PEd is potentially faced with a struggling student as it may be necessary for difficult conversations to take place.

When allocated responsibility for a learner, the PEd needs to arrange an initial meeting between both parties; this should occur early in the learner's journey. Gopee (2015) states that during this time, it is important for the PEd to be ready to receive the learner so that they can be prepared, as well as prepare for the learner to be introduced to the other important members of the learner's journey. During this initial meeting, the PEd can also set ground rules for how the placement will operate. This may involve developing a learning contract and addressing any concerns the learner may have. It is also important for the PEd and the learner to minimise the common barriers faced when mentoring and assessing students.

During the placements, the learners will face a number of challenges due to the unpredictable nature of the paramedic role. The Health and Care Professions Council (2017) Standards of Education and Training state that the learner must experience a safe and supportive practice environment, and that the PEd must have the appropriate knowledge and experience in order to help facilitate this. It is the role of the PEd to discuss these challenges in order for the learner to develop. This can only be done by creating a learning environment where the learner is comfortable enough to ask questions and approach the PEd with any challenges they may be facing. A study by Pitkanen et al. (2018) showed that healthcare learners are more likely to recommend their practice environment if they received one-to-one support from their PEd and if the practice environment and general support they received were positive. They also evaluated the practice environment as a positive experience if they believed it was learner-focused and they were made to feel like they belonged there. These are important messages to hear as a PEd, as the learners' knowledge is more likely to develop in a positive setting than in a setting where they feel isolated or threatened.

In addition to ensuring that the learner is safe and supported, practice placement providers and PEds must ensure that the learning environment and culture they promote supports the learner to be open and honest with patients and service users when things go wrong – this is known as the Duty of Candour (Heath Education England, undated). Health Education England also stresses the importance of the PEd in developing the learner's tact, sensitivity and empathy when communicating to patients, service users and other professionals they will encounter during their placements.

Case Studies

1. You are due to be mentoring a first-year BSc learner for their very first shift. They have attended their ambulance service induction, but have no other experience of the ambulance service.

   How would you approach the initial meeting?

   What could you put in place to ensure that the learner feels welcome and starts to relax?

   Are there any initial ground rules you would wish to set?

   How would you approach gaining information about the learner's learning style?

   What barriers might you face?

2. You are working with a second-year learner and it is clear that your learning style differs from theirs.

   How will you approach this with them?

   What can you do to help minimise any difficulties this may cause?

   What barriers might you face?

3. Think of a time you have mentored a student where their preferred way of learning was different from yours.

   How did you overcome this?

   Did you discuss this with the student at the time?

   Did this difference impact on the student's learning and your ability to effectively mentor them?

   Were you able to alter the learning environment in any way to help overcome these challenges?

Reflection

Looking at Figure 5.1 and Table 5.1, think about your preferred learning style. Within your role, what are the challenges you face as a result of this learning? How can your strengths help you overcome these challenges?

As a PEd, what can you do to make the learner feel welcome when they attend their practice placement? Are there any barriers you might face when doing this and can these be overcome?

Chapter 6 Mentoring Theories and Application to the PEd

Learning objectives

1. Basic understanding of where mentoring originated
2. Benefits of mentoring to various groups
3. Theories of mentoring and their application to the PEd role

This chapter will provide an overview of the origin of mentoring in history and how mentoring theories can be applied to the PEd in practice. It will present and discuss two mentoring theories that are ideal for the role of the PEd. This chapter has been deliberately placed at this point in the book as it relates specifically to the development of mentoring and not the role of the PEd. As shown already, the PEd's role is multifaceted and mentorship is just one small part of it. Previously we have considered how the PEd role has developed; now we consider the development of mentorship.

The History of Practice Education and Mentoring

One of the fundamental principles of practice education is that of mentoring. The term 'mentoring' originates from ancient Greek mythology and there are a number of stories that could lay claim to the origins of the term:

The first is the story of Perseus. He was born to Zeus and Danaë (daughter of Acrisius, King of Argos). Acrisius had previously been warned that his grandson would kill him, so he sent Danaë and Perseus away (rather than killing Perseus). They were taken in and cared for by Dictys, whose brother Polydectes fell in love with Danaë. Polydectes held a banquet where guests were expected to bring lavish gifts (knowing that Perseus could not do this) as a plot to remove Perseus from Danaë's life. Polydectes demanded that Perseus bring him the head of Medusa, which was considered to be an impossible task.

In Perseus' pursuit of Medusa, Athene (who had turned Medusa's hair into snakes) assisted him by giving him a protective shield. She also advised Perseus to seek out the appropriate weaponry in order to kill Medusa. The shield Athene gave Perseus acted as a mirror and allowed him to see Medusa without being turned to stone. Thus, he used the shield mirror to see her and cut off her head using the weaponry suggested by Athene.

Athene was also influential in Hercules' quest to capture Cerberus by leading him out of the underworld.

But the story that is most commonly linked to mentoring is that of Odysseus (King of Ithaca), who went to war with the Trojans. He left his son (Telemachus) in the care of Mentor, who was an old and trusted friend of Odysseus. It is suggested that the goddess Athena took on the appearance of Mentor in order to guide Telemachus effectively. Athena (disguised as Mentor) guided and supported Telemachus to find out what had happened to his father Odysseus.

It can quite clearly be seen that regardless of the story, the nature of Athena/Athene was an assistive, nurturing and supportive one. Thus, the story of Mentor is one of assistance and support.

Later, in 1699, François Fénelon, a French author, used the term 'mentor' in his fictional retelling of the story of Telemachus (Roberts, 1999). Roberts (1999) believes that the modern term 'mentor' stems from Fénelon's (1699) work.

In 1978, Levinson et al. conducted research around male development and utilised the term 'mentor' to mean 'someone, often half a generation older, who could help accelerate the development of another in his age-related transitions' (Garvey, 2011). This linked an older, wiser person who gave advice to a younger, less experienced person. This could be considered to be the role of a mentor.

Regardless of the origin of the word, the ethos of the mentor is one of support, advice, nurturing and acting as a role model. All of these qualities are applicable to the PEd, as seen in Chapter 4.

The nursing profession had similar developmental processes to paramedic science and it has recognised the need for mentorship. The Nursing and Midwifery Council (2006) states:

> Learners on NMC approved pre-registration nursing education programmes, leading to registration on the nurses' part of the register, must be supported and assessed by mentors.

Furthermore, it says:

> From September 2007 a sign-off mentor, who has met additional criteria (paragraph 2.1.3), must make the final assessment of practice and confirm that the required proficiencies for entry to the register have been achieved (paragraph 3.2.6).

Since the success of this initiative, it has subsequently been applied to the paramedic practice placement area and PEds have taken on the role of mentor.

Benefits of Mentoring

There are many benefits to mentoring, for both the learner and the PEd, as detailed below (Figure 6.1).

In addition to the personal benefits given above, the practice placement provider will also gain benefits – for example, PEds should keep their knowledge up to date; therefore, they may work more effectively in their paramedic positon as well as their PEd role. PEds have the opportunity to shape learners in order to become effective members of staff for the service. Learners are able to learn the ways of working within a service, prior to

Learner's perspective

- Development in all areas of paramedic science
- Quality guidance
- Someone to approach
- Opportunity for new experiences
- Sounding board for questions/opinions
- Stability of practice – although working with a range of PEds gives a range of experiences
- Empowerment

PEd's perspective

- Able to shape new learners
- May learn from the learners
- Keep up to date
- Job satisfaction
- Personal development for future roles

Figure 6.1 Benefits of mentoring

applying for a job, so induction programmes may not need to be as long. The service gets to know the learner prior to their application for a job, giving them the opportunity for employment within an appropriate environment. As such, it makes sense for ambulance services to take an active interest in their PEds, learners and their progress.

Think about the benefits you have gained from being a PEd. If you are not yet a PEd, think about what you gained from helping someone in the work environment.

Mentoring Models

There are a number of different mentoring models that the PEd can draw upon; two of these are discussed below.

Pegg's Theory of Mentoring and Application to the PEd

Pegg (1999) discusses the push/pull theory of mentoring, whereby the mentor either pushes the learner, or pulls them, utilising the examples given in Figure 6.2.

Pulling involves the provision of a safe environment for the learner in order to enable them to consider their goals, actions and skills. The environment allows the learner to feel secure and therefore they will feel more comfortable in taking safe risks. These risks could be physical ones – for example, the learner may wish to try an ankle assessment. This will be risky for the learner if the skill is a newly acquired one, as the patient may object, experience pain or refuse to allow the learner to undertake the assessment.

Risks can also be mental or psychological – for example, a paramedic learner could be trying to understand the electron transport system (ETS)

Pull	Push
• Sanctuary for the mentee	• Stimulation
• Safe place for sharing	• Ideas
• Listening	• Challenges
• Asking questions	• Offers tools
• Drawing out of answers	• Wisdom
	• Rewards

Figure 6.2 Pegg's Push/Pull theory
(adapted from Pegg (1999))

and they may choose to tell their PEd what they understand. The learner may see this as a risk if the PEd has not created a safe environment for doing so, as they may believe that the PEd could ridicule their ideas and thoughts.

A thoughtful PEd will ensure that risk taking is undertaken appropriately and with support. For example, they may guide the learner during the assessment of the ankle or they may share their understanding of the ETS.

Pushing is a demanding process, where the PEd challenges the learner; this does not directly refer to a competition type of challenge, but more of a goal setting. For example, the PEd may challenge the learner to complete only a small section of the ankle assessment or they may provide a way to remember the ETS process (paramedics are well known for their use of acronyms).

Zachary's Theory of Mentoring and Application to the PEd

Zachary's (2011) four-phase mentoring model (see Figure 6.3) starts with the PEd preparing themselves for the relationship and task of mentoring the learner. This may include a reflection of their own abilities, skills, areas for development and understanding of the task of mentoring. This is the best time for PEds to remind themselves or reflect upon appropriate theories and their application, so that they can be fully prepared to assist the learner. The preparation phase is also an ideal opportunity for the PEd to consider their personal qualities and attributes (see Chapter 4) that make them a positive PEd, and it offers the opportunity for the PEd to address negative issues which could lead to a toxic relationship. In this phase, the PEd would also benefit from having a conversation with the learner so that the PEd can analyse the learner's position and ability prior to the negotiation phase.

Negotiation is described by Zachary (2011) as the point at which ground rules are developed. The PEd and the learner should meet and clarify their expectations (from both sides), their responsibilities, goals and other aspects related to the relationship which are deemed to be important. This phase can be thought of as a learning or mentoring contract, whereby both parties agree the rules of conduct and engagement. In some circumstances (but not all), a written contract may be appropriate to avoid any misunderstandings.

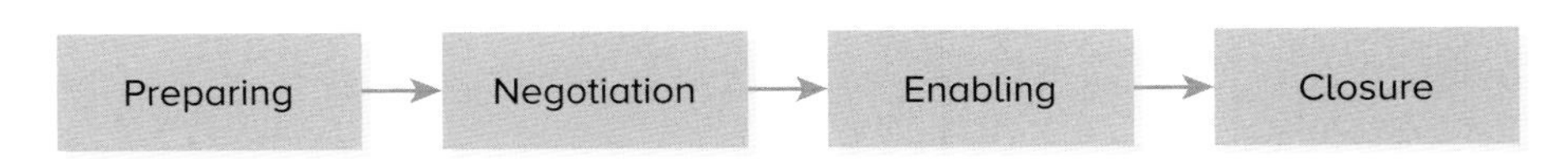

Figure 6.3 Zachary's (2011) four-phase mentoring model

The third phase of Zachary's (2011) model is enabling. This is the point at which the learner is encouraged to learn, flourish and achieve the goals set at the negotiation stage. The PEd should encourage the learner gently, through affirmation, constructive feedback and having an open and honest dialogue. This phase will often be the longest in terms of timescale as it may require the learner to attain many small goals in order to achieve the overall goal. The PEd will be gently guiding and supporting the learner throughout each small goal to ensure that learning (and competence) is achieved prior to moving on to the next goal. This phase may not progress smoothly and the PEd may have to revisit the first two phases of this model to establish unforeseen goals and/or circumstances in order to assist the learner to meet their overall goal effectively.

The final phase of Zachary's (2011) theory is closure. This is when the learner has met the goals and outcomes required. This phase is a reflective one for both the PEd and the learner. It is the time to reflect formally or informally upon the process and learning they have achieved. The PEd can utilise the time to consider their effectiveness and any changes they would make should these same experiences occur again. It is also the best time for the PEd and the learner to discuss the relationship and highlight areas of good practice. Depending upon where the learner is in their course, it may be possible or required for the PEd to start the process again with a new set of goals for the learner, in which case the first two sections could be considerably shorter in timescale and process.

Case Studies

1. You have a first-year learner, Ben, who has just been allocated to you. He is entering the ambulance service work placement for the very first time. Explore the use of Zachary's (2011) theory to show how you can support this learner with the first block of his placement. Consider the skills Ben would need to develop in this timeframe.
2. Grace, a second-year learner, approaches you for some advice. She has been told that she is going to fail her practice assessment. She is worried that her PEd doesn't like her and will fail her for that reason. Which part(s) of Pegg's (1999) theory would you be likely to use in this case?

Reflection

Think about the benefits you have gained from being a PEd. If you are not yet a PEd, think about what you gained from helping someone in the work environment.

How can you use Pegg's pull theory on sanctuary? Give two examples.

How often will you utilise Pegg's pull theory on listening? Why have you given that answer?

What rewards can you offer your learners (without them being considered inappropriate)?

When may it be appropriate to reward a learner?

How could you utilise Pegg's (1999) push/pull theory to support the final phase of Zachary's (2011) four-phase model?

Chapter 7

Coaching and Leadership Theories

Learning objectives

1. Role of coaching in supporting learners
2. Coaching frameworks
3. Leadership theories and the benefits for the PEd and the learner

This chapter will introduce you to coaching and leadership theories. It will highlight the importance of coaching and high-quality leadership when providing practice education support to learners. By using coaching and leadership techniques, the PEd will support the learner in taking control of their own learning to help develop autonomy during the learner's progression through their education.

The Role of Coaching and Coaching Frameworks

When the PEd supports their learners, the use of coaching techniques often occurs, sometimes without either party realising it. This chapter will formalise and discuss coaching theories and frameworks, which will help the PEd give control to the learner so that the learner does not rely on the PEd for all of the answers when it comes to their learning.

Coaching is seen not only as a conversation, but also as a way to facilitate enquiry and discussion (Starr, 2016). The PEd is there to encourage and promote learning, and Starr (2016) emphasises that it is better for the person to gain their own answers and insights, rather than have someone tell them what they have to do and why. It is recognised in coaching literature that it is better for the coach to be more interrogative in their questioning rather than providing all of the answers. As a result of the learner exploring their own questions and coming to their own conclusions, it is more likely that they will

Directive	Less directive
• We need to discuss the positives from that last case • I am thinking it was caused by a lack of communication • I know a book you could read to help – it is really good • I think you need to revisit that handover	• How do you think that last case went? • What do you think caused that? • What other options were there? • What do you think stopped you from providing a succinct handover?

Figure 7.1 Direct or indirect questioning techniques

take ownership of that decision and the knowledge gained. This also means that the learner will be able to draw upon this knowledge in future cases and it will be transferable in their career.

Starr (2016) discusses that coaching can be directive or less directive in nature (see Figure 7.1). A PEd needs to think about which style suits their situation. Ideally, a less directive style would be used, enabling the learner to come to their own decisions. A directive style can lead the learner to think that the PEd has more knowledge than they do; this may lead the learner not to volunteer answers to questions or promote discussion. A directive approach may also make the learner feel like they are being told to do something rather than being allowed to explore possibilities (Starr, 2016).

Benefits of Coaching

There is no one recognised way to coach and mentor (Garvey et al., 2011). A coaching culture has been used in business for a number of years and is seen as pivotal to enable staff development and growth. Whilst its use in healthcare is relatively new, it is increasing.

Garvey et al. (2011) recognise the importance of coaching for people in new roles and roles that require development. As the PEd, it is important to use coaching techniques as part of the support given to the learner as they start and develop on their learner paramedic journey. In order to truly benefit from coaching, both the PEd and the learner need to actively listen to the conversations taking place and reflect on them. This reflection will help change or cement practice as a result.

Coaching Frameworks

When coaching, there are a number of frameworks which can be used to help the PEd guide their learner.

The GROW Model

The GROW model (Whitmore, 2009) (see Figure 7.2) is a set of headings that are to be used to help sequence the questions asked.

Whitmore (2009) states the importance of visiting all four stages when discussing a new topic or issue. Once the task or case is in progress and is just being revisited, the learner and the PEd can enter and leave the framework at any stage.

At any point, the learner or PEd should feel comfortable in asking questions and/or revisiting previous stages. It is important to remember that working through this framework should help promote awareness (Whitmore, 2009), especially for learners, as this will also encourage ownership of the goal and help the learner come to a decision on how to achieve it.

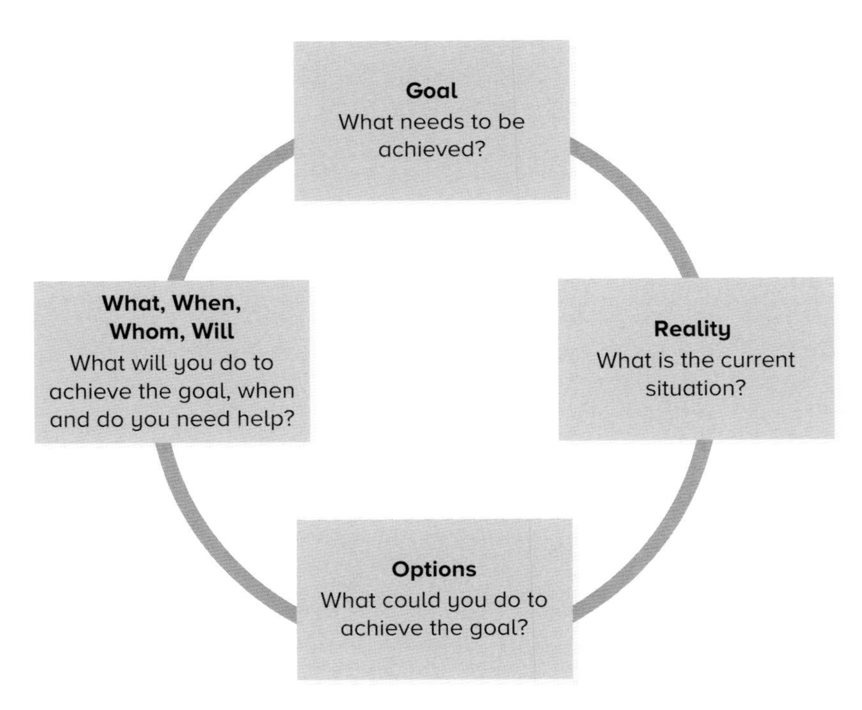

Figure 7.2 The GROW model
(adapted from Whitmore (2009))

An example of the GROW model and the questions that the PEd may wish to ask is given below:

GOAL – what does the learner want to achieve? The goal must be achievable and realistic in the given timeframe, and all parties must be able to decide if the goal has been achieved once the deadline has been reached. To help with clear goal setting, the PEd may wish to follow the SMART acronym, which helps achieve all of the above (this acronym is explained in more depth in Chapter 9).

> Example: 'The learner wishes to successfully complete the second year of their clinical practice for their Paramedic Science BSc.'

Questions the PEd must ask:

- Is this a realistic goal?
- Does this fit within the overall objective for the learner?
- How will you measure the attainment of this goal?

CURRENT REALITY – here the learner and the PEd need to understand the learner's starting point.

> Example: 'The learner has successfully completed year 1 of the programme and is currently undertaking their first year 2 practice block.'

Questions the PEd must ask:

- Where is the learner in terms of their current development?
- Are they on track?

OPTIONS – what are the current options available to the learner to help them reach their goal? It is important to let the learner offer solutions at this point.

> Example: 'The learner is worried about lack of patient exposure and wishes to complete some of their practice hours within a more urban area than where they are usually based.'

Questions the PEd must ask:

- What are the positive and negatives of each solution given by the learner?
- Are there any obstacles in the way?

- What else could be done?
- Are the options given realistic? Think about service requirements.

WHAT, WHEN, WHOM, WILL – at this point, the learner should have an idea on how the goal can be achieved. This is an important section as this is when the learner will commit to specific actions to help achieve the goal.

> Example: 'The learner commits to travel extra distance to facilitate shifts in urban area. The learner will ensure that their practice assessment document (PAD) is kept up to date with regular feedback included from mentors out of area.'

Questions the PEd must ask:

- How can the learner be kept motivated to achieve their goal?
- When would it be necessary to review the goal with the learner?
- Does the plan need to be changed?
- Is the goal still achievable after the review? Does it need to be revised?

> As a PEd, think about a goal that you may have. Use the GROW model to help you come up with a plan for achieving that goal.

The Five Cs Model

Effective communication between the PEd and the learner is of paramount importance in order for the relationship to be successful. Inam (2014) discusses the five Cs in relation to successful conversations and providing high-quality feedback. These conversations can benefit both the coach and the person being coached. Figure 7.3 provides some guidance in terms of what constitutes a successful conversation. Inam (2014) states that it is not just about what is said when there is a conversation to be had, but it is also about how the information is being relayed – for example, the environment in which the conversation is being held, the body language used and the tone in which the information is being discussed.

Clarity
Be sure about what you want to communicate. What effect do you want to have on the learner?

Compassion
Think about what you are going to say and how you are going to say it. Remember the way something is said is more important than what is said.

Curiosity
Coaching is more about listening and asking useful questions rather than just talking. The coach needs to try and come from a place of curiosity rather than judgement.

Confirmation
Pay attention not only to what the learner is saying but also how they are behaving and how their body language is coming across. Confirm these points with them with the questions you ask.

Commitment
The PEd and the learner must have commitment to the results and the relationships they are building. By doing this, the PEd will strengthen the commitment to the process and promote trust from the learner.

Figure 7.3 The five Cs to a successful conversation
(Inam, 2014)

Leadership

Paramedics' knowledge and experience in leadership has developed over a number of years (Blaber and Harris, 2014). Although often linked to career progression, paramedics have also developed their leadership skills by undertaking the PEd role. Ultimately there is a link between high-quality leadership and the development of an individual (Blaber and Harris, 2014), which in this case would be the learner. Blaber and Harris (2014) also discuss the fact that an effective leader shares their knowledge with others, including learners. However, an excellent leader does this in a supportive manner and does not do it as a show of authority – this is similar to coaching, as discussed above.

The Health and Care Professions Council discusses the importance of clinical leadership in both its Standards of Conduct, Performance and Ethics (2016) and the Standards of Proficiency – Paramedics (2014); this includes recognising the importance of mentorship and how this fits within the profession.

Over the years, there have been numerous authors discussing theories and styles of leadership, including Lewin et al. (1939) and more recently

Adair (2005). Each author has described what they believe makes an effective leader and what can be done to develop leadership skills. These theories can be used by the PEd when mentoring their learners. The work of Lewin et al. (1939) and Adair (2005) will be briefly discussed in this chapter.

Lewin's Leadership Theory

Lewin et al.'s (1939) research identified that there are three different styles of leadership: autocratic, laissez-faire and democratic. The autocratic leader makes all decisions on their own and does not take any other person's opinions into account. This style of leadership could result in a poor learning experience. If the PEd made all of the decisions all of the time, how will the learner learn? There may be occasions when the PEd needs to adopt an autocratic style – for example, in time-critical situations – but this should not be a style they use all of the time. If this style is needed, it is important that the PEd reflects with the learner after the event, so that learning can be achieved.

Lewin et al. (1939) identifies laissez-faire as a leadership style which is at the other end of the leadership spectrum. The laissez-faire leader leaves people to make their own decisions and does not get involved. For the PEd, this may be a style chosen when their learner is coming towards the end of their programme and is developing their autonomous practice. However, as Lewin et al. (1939) identify, the leader (PEd) still has overall accountability for the decision made, so this style of leadership should not be used without recognition of this fact.

The final leadership style introduced by Lewin et al. (1939) is the democratic style. This is seen by Lewin et al. (1939) as the preferred style, as everyone is involved in the decision-making process, even if the leader makes the final decision. Therefore, using this style, the PEd would ensure that their learner has full involvement in the case, that their opinions would be sought and that a decision is then made. This style would also help the learner to reflect on the case and how they can develop their practice in future.

Adair's Leadership Theory

John Adair is a British academic and is a leading authority on leadership and leadership development. Adair states that in leadership, there are three elements to always consider: the individual (PEd or learner), the task (case/patient) and the team (PEd and learner(s)) (Thomas and Adair, 2007). He investigates the needs of each of these elements and how it impacts on the overall leader, which in this case is the PEd (unless the learner is taking the lead).

Task (case being dealt with/patient to be treated)

- The task has to be completed regardless of people's needs.
- Can add pressure to all involved depending on the type of case/the patient's needs.

Team (PEd and learner(s))

- Every team has needs.
- A team has to be cohesive and 'stick together'.

Individual (either learner or PEd)

- Needs recognition for the role they are undertaking.
- Needs to feel that what they are doing is worthwhile.
- The need to give to the task as well as to learn from others.

Adapted from Thomas and Adair (2007)

So, with all of the above in mind, the leader (which is the PEd) has a pivotal role to play in the following ways:

- The PEd will help the learner achieve the task.
- The PEd will build good team dynamics and create a good working environment.
- The PEd will respond to the learner's needs and will meet them where possible.

Thomas and Adair (2007) recognise that all three elements will overlap and that one element can ultimately affect another (Figure 7.4). For example, if the team fails, the task may fail and the individual may lose their sense of personal satisfaction (Thomas and Adair, 2007). For an optimum result, all three elements need to be addressed, which involves meeting the needs of both the individual and the team, and successfully addressing the task.

Regardless of the theories, it is clear that the PEd plays a pivotal role in leading the learner, the team and the case. The type of leadership style used needs consideration, especially given the learner's stage of study.

A PEd will have access to and be influenced by a number of publications. In terms of leadership, the Clinical Leadership Competency Framework

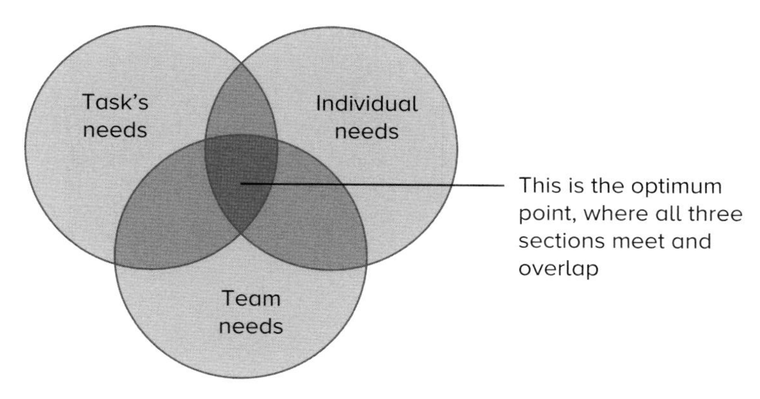

Figure 7.4 Leadership Theory
(Thomas and Adair, 2007)

(CLCF, 2011) is a document compiled for all healthcare workers by the NHS Leadership Academy. All professional bodies and healthcare professions were consulted during its production, including paramedics and the Health and Care Professions Council. The CLCF examines the behaviours required to contribute to effective leadership. These behaviours are demonstrating personal qualities, working with others, managing services, improving services and setting direction (NHS Leadership Academy, 2011). It is advisable that PEds read this document and examine how elements impact on their role or can influence their development as a PEd and when supporting learners.

Case Studies

You are the first ambulance on scene at a four-car road traffic collision with a first-year student. What types of leadership styles would be suitable given the situation in terms of the PEd and student relationship? Why have you chosen these styles for this situation?

You are acting in the capacity of a first line manager at your base ambulance station. A member of the Patient Transport Service approaches you asking for help in becoming a paramedic. How could you use the various coaching techniques to help you structure this conversation?

A student for whom you are not a PEd approaches you with concerns they have about their assigned PEd. How are you going to manage this situation? What would you say to the student and who else would you approach for advice?

Reflection

Reflect on the three different styles of leadership. How and when would you choose to use these styles? What leadership style would suit each student year group and why?

Think about a situation where you have faced a certain leadership style. Was it appropriate for the situation? Would a different style have been more effective and why?

Think about how coaching can be beneficial when dealing with students on an educational programme. Is there a time where you feel coaching is not appropriate? If so, why?

Chapter 8

Assessment of Learners

Learning objectives

1. Understanding of different types of assessment areas
2. Understanding of different assessment methods
3. Importance of assessment planning
4. Importance of assessment feedback
5. Moderation

This chapter will discuss how the PEd can effectively assess learners in the practice environment. It will equip the PEd with some tools for assessing learners and demonstrate where they can be used.

An inevitable part of the PEd role is to assess learners in the placement environment. Educational institutions rely on PEds to assess the learner in real situations and ensure that they practise safely and to appropriate standards. Assessments can be formal or informal, depending upon the situation and level of the learner. Informal assessments may take place when a learner undertakes a new skill, where the PEd ensures that the correct procedure is followed and gives feedback to the learner. Formal assessment will often take place as a visual assessment of the learner completing a task, supported by a practice assessment document (PAD) supplied by the education institution (see Figure 8.1).

Assessment of practice can be thought of as comparing the learner's actions to a given set of rules or a recognised process. Thus, it is imperative that the PEd understands the techniques taught at the educational institution at which the learner is learning. In addition to pure assessment, a learner often requires a grade/mark (see Figure 8.1) to be given and feedback to be provided so they can improve their practice.

Demonstrate safe and effective communication
The learner should: • Demonstrate effective communication via a number of different means, including face to face, over the phone and via vehicle radio. • Must use all forms of communication appropriately and responsibly, including devices, social media and networking websites. • Practise in accordance with current legislation and national, regional and local guidelines, protocols and policies. • Adapt communication style used to suit the setting/service user. • Use the correct abbreviations, medical terminology and slang when communicating. • Ensure that changes to the situation or circumstances are reported to the appropriate personnel. • Be aware of their body language and non-verbal communication at all times. • Communicate effectively and co-operate with mentors and staff members in their practice placement area to benefit service users and carers. • Should ask for, listen to, think about and respond proactively to feedback they are given. • At all times act in accordance with the expectations issued to them by the Health and Care Professions Council, their university and practice partner. All communication should be professional and appropriate.
The learner should demonstrate developing knowledge and understanding of: • Current legislation and national, regional and local guidelines, protocols and policies. • Correct radio procedure when transmitting messages. • The recognised abbreviations in relation to communication. • Alert procedures.

Figure 8.1 An example skill from a PAD

Learning outcome: Achieve level 4–5 in year 1			**Competency assessment observed through:** (Mentor to tick where appropriate)					
			Observation *Discussion* *Simulation*					
Learner completes			**Mentor completes**					
Date	Case	Learner comments to include references to legislation and national, regional and local guidelines, protocols and policies *(following discussion with mentor)*	**Level**					Mentor Signature
			1	2	3	4	5	

Mentor comments/reason for level achieved: *(optional to complete)*

Figure 8.1 An example skill from a PAD *(continued)*

Types of Assessment

There are two overarching types of assessment that the PEd is likely to be involved with: informal and formal assessments.

Informal Assessment

Generally, informal assessment (also known as formative assessment) is considered a practice attempt or a developmental assessment to prepare learners for the formal assessment process, i.e. a practice run. The learner should be given either the same task as the formal assessment or a series of tasks that build into the formal assessment. Appropriate feedback is essential in order for the learner to be able to develop between the informal and formal assessments.

Formal Assessment

Formal assessment (also referred to as summative assessment) is usually thought of as an end point assessment, which may or may not be the case. These assessments should not really be grouped at the end of a year or course; ideally, they should be spread throughout a given block of time to ensure that the learner can develop effectively. Whilst many formal assessments may be the learner's final assessment, it is still advisable that constructive feedback be given as the learner can still develop beyond the assessment process.

Regardless of the type of assessment, the process should encourage learning as well as assessing the understanding of the learner.

PEds will be asked to assess learners formally or informally (or both) in a number of areas of the learner's work. Some examples are shown below:

- Communication – with patients, members of the public and other ambulance service staff as well as staff of other organisations.
- Scene management – this will cross boundaries with communication, as the learner is likely to require good communication skills in order to manage scenes (especially complicated or difficult ones). However, possessing good communication skills will not automatically mean that the learner can manage complex situations. The learner may be required to liaise with a number of different groups of people in order to manage a scene.
- Patient management and treatment – again, some of this will be incorporated into communication; however, the physical assessment and management of a patient is a vital part of a paramedic's skill set. This area of work may well incorporate problem solving and decision making, as the paramedic is an autonomous practitioner, so the learner is also required to develop these skills.
- Resilience – currently there are a number of pieces of work being undertaken concerning resilience in healthcare staff, including ambulance service staff. The PEd is in a prime position to be able to influence and support the learner in terms of resilience, as well as to assess if the learner is robust and capable of withstanding the pressures of the role.

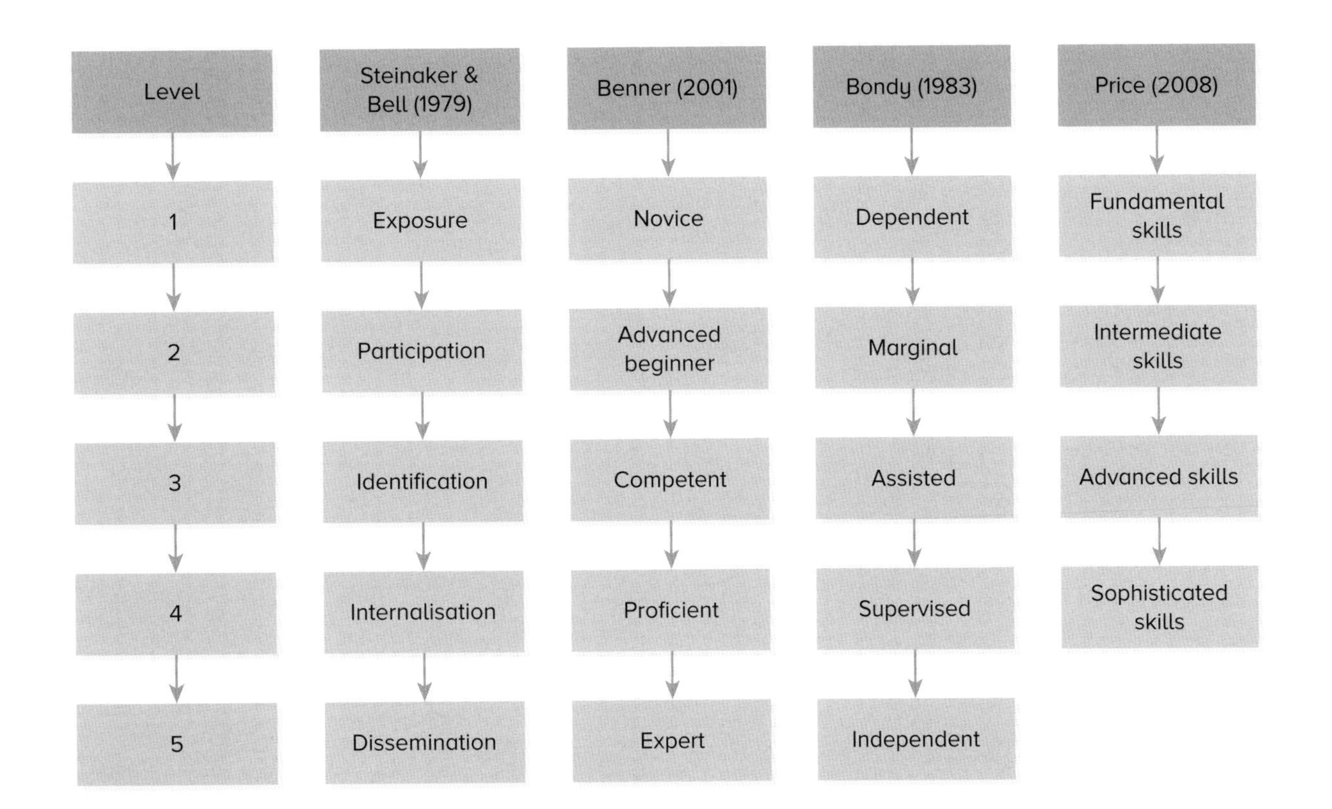

Figure 8.2 Gopee's framework for assessment
(adapted from Gopee (2010))

These areas of work fall into three overarching categories as described by Bloom (1956):

Cognitive – thinking and mental processing.

Psychomotor – physical acts and skills.

Affective – emotional aspects and skills.

Gopee (2010) draws upon the work of four renowned authors to show a framework for assessment at differing levels of practice (see Figure 8.2).

Figure 8.2 can be used to give the PEd an indication of the level a learner should be at whilst assessing them in practical skills; however, as with Bloom's (1979) taxonomy, consideration should be given to the actual skill being performed. For example, a level 3 learner may be considered competent according to Benner (2001), but in real terms, the expectation may be one of proficiency, which is level 4 according to Benner (2001). Attempting to assess the learner against the incorrect level could lead to the learner becoming disheartened or labelled as incompetent. Both of these outcomes are likely to lead to a negative relationship between the learner and the PEd. Thus, as with Bloom's (1979) taxonomy, adjustments may be required to ensure that the appropriate level is used when assessing a learner.

It is also important for the PEd to consider the role of the assessment – for example, is the assessment intended to be an informal assessment of current level of skills or it is a formal sign-off assessment to show competency? The following section will assist the PEd in deciding the most appropriate type of assessment in a given situation.

Methods of Assessment

Whilst assessments often take the form of a direct visual observation, a learner may not have the opportunity to demonstrate a skill in the practice environment at the appropriate time. Thus, the PEd must consider how else to assess the learner. Some institutions may put the onus on the learner to decide how best to demonstrate their competence; however, it is also helpful for the PEd to have some ideas to support the learner. Figure 8.3 shows some examples of how learners could be assessed either formally or informally. The PEd should give consideration to the areas discussed by Bloom (1956) when considering assessment strategies.

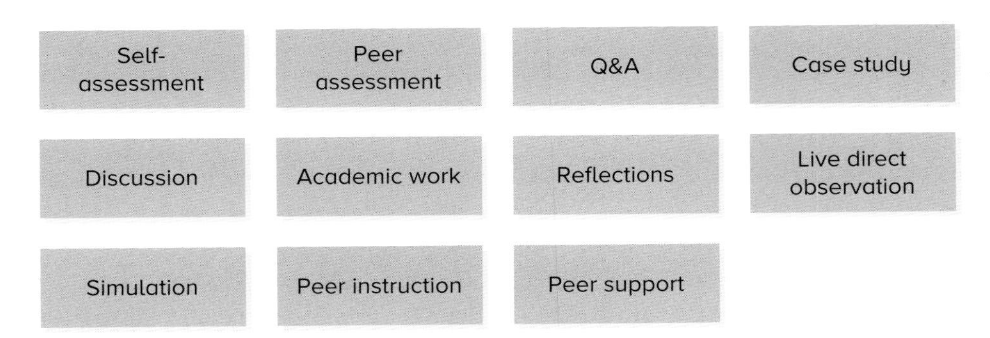

Figure 8.3 Examples of assessment methods

Question-and-answer sessions, case studies, discussions, academic work and reflections are useful for less practical skills, for example, understanding of the Mental Capacity Act, stages of labour or the pathophysiology of asthma. Self-assessment or peer assessment can be particularly useful for informal assessments.

Live direct observation (i.e. on a real patient), simulation, peer instruction and peer support are more useful for practical skills, for example, obtaining blood pressures, undertaking chest compressions or cannulation. The background knowledge behind a skill is as important as the skill itself; therefore, particular attention should be paid to the underpinning knowledge a learner has, as this may also influence the type of assessment allocated for the skill. In some cases, it may be beneficial to utilise more than one method of assessment – for example, cannulation can be assessed by direct observation. However, the underpinning knowledge (vein selection, cannula sizes, etc.) may be assessed by Q&A.

Planning Formal Assessments

The planning of formal assessments is an important part of the PEd role. The educational institution may give some guidance on when formal assessments should take place; however, there is usually latitude in terms of timescales. It is important that the PEd plans any formal assessment in advance to ensure that they get the best from the learner. The most important aspects of assessment planning are shown in Figure 8.4.

Time
• When is the right time for the assessment?
Nature
• What type of assessment is best for this learner and the skill?
Learner
• Does the learner know what is expected? • Has the learner had the opportunity to practise the skill? • Is the learner ready for the assessment?

Figure 8.4 Important aspects of assessment planning

Where a learner has a number of assessments that cannot be undertaken in the live practice environment, it may be worth creating an assessment plan with the learner:

> It is good practice to draw up an assessment plan that aligns the Unit Outcomes with the learning process and the acquisition of knowledge and skills, and indicates how and when the unit will be assessed. In a course or programme of learning consisting of a number of units, it is likely that a range of assessment methods will be used.
>
> Scottish Qualifications Authority (SQA) (2017)

Moderation

Moderation involves checking that the assessment process is undertaken fairly and that any grades or awards are applied in line with appropriate marking criteria. For example, in practice, this would mean that all PEds assess blood pressure taking against the same criteria. Moderation is considered a normal practice in higher education; however, it tends not to be undertaken so readily in the practice environment. Discussions between PEds and educational institutions regarding assessments and expectations are especially recommended for newly appointed PEds. Experienced PEds can also support new PEds by direct observation of the new PEd assessing the learner (Smith, McAskill and Jack, 2009); this would be considered peer observation. It is also recommended that educational institutions provide PEds with sufficient information surrounding each area that they are likely to assess in practice in order to allow the PEd to fully understand the requirements at the assessment.

Feedback

Appropriate and timely feedback is vital to enable learning and development. The SQA (2017) advocates '*process-orientated praise*, in which feedback focuses on the effort and strategies that a learner has used' alongside traditional feedback on how well a task was performed.

Health Education England (undated) states that:

> Providers must ensure that work undertaken by learners provides learning opportunities and feedback on performance, and gives an appropriate breadth and depth of experience appropriate to individual learner needs.

The Higher Education Academy (HEA) (2014) highlights the importance of feedback:

> Feedback can...
>
> - Raise learners' consciousness of the strengths of their work
> - Boost learners' confidence and self-concept regarding personal strengths and abilities
> - Provide guidance on areas for further development of skills and enhancement of work
> - Enhance learners' own judgement, understanding of assessment criteria and ability to self-audit their work.

These features are all beneficial to the learner and their progression. The HEA (2014) also recommends considering the purpose of the feedback being given. If feedback is intended to give advice on how to improve, the PEd may wish to consider given written feedback so that the learner can take the notes and study them later. If there is an issue that requires immediate feedback being given to a learner, verbal feedback may be the best tool.

Gibbs and Simpson (2005) discuss the content of feedback, where they suggest it can either tell a learner that they are 'hopeless' or give information on how to improve, the latter obviously being more appropriate and supportive. They also go so far as to suggest that where feedback is given, but a grade is not, learners are more likely to read the feedback. Informal assessment lends itself to this type of feedback, as no grade (or pass/fail indication) is required.

It is important that informal assessment feedback is given frequently and in sufficient detail for the learner to understand how to progress (Gibbs and Simpson, 2005). It also needs to be given at the appropriate time, i.e. as close to the assessment time as possible, so that the learner can relate the feedback directly to their actions (Gibbs and Simpson, 2005).

The PEd may wish to utilise differing forms of feedback depending on the learning styles of the learner (see Chapter 5).

Race (2015) recommends:

> Students and teachers become responsible partners in learning and assessment.

Race also recommends:

> [S]tudents progressively take responsibility for assessment and feedback processes.

Thus, the PEd could gradually introduce some responsibility for the learner across their placement time. Race (2015) also recommends that there is a dialogue between the PEd and the learner regarding feedback content; therefore, the learner is required to engage with the feedback, but can also clarify points as required.

Giving Feedback without Causing Distress

As previously discussed, learners benefit from feedback as they can apply the comments to new situations and develop/hone their skills based upon the information given. However, it can be quite easy to cause unintentional distress or anxiety when giving feedback.

Careful consideration needs to be given to both the content and the manner in which feedback is given. Poor communication could irrevocably damage a PEd/learner relationship, so a working knowledge of communication is recommended (Chapter 4).

LeFroy et al. (2015) make some specific feedback recommendations which can be directly applied to the PEd:

- Feedback is a social interaction, not just information provision – communication is key.
- Reinforce areas that have been achieved well.
- Focus on how a task was done and how it should/might be done rather than what was done wrong.

- Use a reflective process rather than an instructive process.
- Learner motivation is key to their learning.
- Tailor feedback to the learner – do not assume a one-size-fits-all approach to feedback methods.
- Consider the emotional state of the learner and how much feedback may be too much.
- Promote regular feedback for everyone in the environment, as this can help to normalise the process, thus make it less intimidating for the learner.
- Consider if feedback should be given to the learner in front of other people.

The PEd/learner relationship can have an enormous impact upon both the learner and the PEd when it comes to assessments. If the PEd and the learner have a close relationship, it could be very hard for the PEd to be objective when assessing the learner, which could lead to the PEd passing a learner when in reality they should not pass. Thus, it is important for the PEd to consider all of the information given in this chapter.

A final note on feedback from LeFroy et al. (2015) is as follows:

> Helpful feedback is a supportive conversation that clarifies the trainee's awareness of their developing competencies, enhances their self-efficacy for making progress, challenges them to set objectives for improvement, and facilitates their development of strategies to enable that improvement to occur.

Case Studies

1. You are required to formatively assess Ellen, a first-year learner, in her patient assessment. How would you assess her? How would you give feedback to her?
2. Frank is coming to the end of his two-year course and he needs all of his second-year skills signed off. Plan how you would undertake this task. Consider how many shifts may be required. How much time away from shifts may be needed and what methods you could employ to assess skills that he cannot perform live.

Reflection

How easy do you find it to assess your learner's objectively, i.e. with no preconceived ideas about how good they will be?

Consider one of your colleagues at work that you also consider a friend. Could you fail them if you needed to? How hard would it be to fail them? Now consider how hard it would be to fail them if it meant them losing their job.

Consider how you could use each of the assessment methods shown in Figure 8.3.

Consider how you have given feedback to learners previously – has it been effective?

How will you change the content of feedback/the way in which feedback is given based upon the information in this chapter?

Chapter 9

Support for Learners, PEds and Action Planning

Learning objectives

1. Support required for the learner and the PEd
2. Role of action plans
3. Constructing a successful action plan
4. The failing learner
5. Role of the organisation/practice placement in supporting the PEd

This chapter will analyse the support that should be made available to PEds to enable them to successfully carry out their role. This will include the role of the educational establishment (where appropriate) and the employing organisation/service. It will also provide information relating to developing a successful action plan for a learner who may be struggling to complete their practice placement.

Support and Action Planning

Ultimately, the responsibility lies with the learner for their learning and the PEd is present to facilitate learning. The PEd can use skills such as coaching (see Chapter 7), but the learner must be fully committed in order for learning, and ultimately competence, to occur. The learner's Practice Assessment Document (PAD) is of paramount importance in achieving competence. The PAD is a set of competencies which must be achieved in order for the learner to successfully complete their practice placement. It is the learner's responsibility to ensure that the PAD is completed and signed by the designated PEd. It is widely accepted that paramedic learners may not get to experience every clinical opportunity or demonstrate every clinical skill. As a result, the learner needs to highlight alternative ways to demonstrate their learning in order to allow for these elements to be 'signed off' by the PEd. This can include using simulation or questioning as an alternative.

Regardless of whether the learner is likely to pass or fail, they require a high level of support from the PEd. During this support, the PEd should use the coaching and leadership theories discussed in Chapter 7. This does not mean providing the learner with all of the answers; rather, the PEd should look to point them towards the resources which will help the learner find the answers and evidence they require. If a learner has been identified as struggling, the PEd will have to provide more structured support and will also need to make this support more formal.

Support for Learners with Learning Difficulties

The Health and Care Professions Council is clear that all learners must meet its Standards of Proficiency to enable their application to the register; however, it also states that there is no one way to meet these standards and providing reasonable adjustments must be considered (Health and Care Professions Council, 2015). In a nutshell, the destination that the learner must reach cannot change, but the route taken to get there can be different depending on the learner. It is recognised that enabling reasonable adjustments in the classroom is easier than when the learner is attending their placements. It is important that these considerations take place and the Health and Care Professions Council (2015) advises that all parties should meet to discuss what support can be offered.

Specific Learning Difficulties (SpLDs)

The most common learning difficulty PEds will encounter with paramedic students is dyslexia. A PEd may also come across other learning difficulties such as dyspraxia and dyscalculia. It is illegal to discriminate against any learner based on these difficulties (Equality Act, 2010). Learners apply for and will receive an assessment through their education provider; this assessment then entitles them to access the support and reasonable adjustments offered to them. It is then important that the education and placement providers facilitate these adjustments when appropriate.

In order for the PEd to support the learner, the learner must disclose their learning difficulty to those supporting them in their practice placement. If a disclosure is not made, then reasonable adjustments cannot be put in place. To enable learners to feel comfortable in disclosing this information, the Royal College of Nursing (RCN) (2010) advises that practice placements promote a culture of support and positivity in which learners will feel comfortable disclosing their challenges without fear of punishment or negativity. If the learner chooses not to disclose their learning difficulty to the education provider, this is their right and it cannot be done on their behalf. However, it is important to inform them that without making a disclosure, they cannot receive any of the reasonable adjustments that are potentially available.

Dyslexia

Dyslexia is believed to affect approximately 10% of the population (British Dyslexia Association, undated). For people with dyslexia, it is common for them to mix up their words and letters, which impacts their writing skills and sentence construction (British Dyslexia Association, undated). The British Dyslexia Association goes on to state that learners with dyslexia can also have problems with their memory, organisational skills and information-processing speeds.

Although learners with dyslexia can face a number of challenges, they can also present strengths. It is up to the PEd to tailor their support to help highlight these strengths, which in turn should help the learner with their journey to reaching the required standards. A learner with dyslexia is more likely to be kinaesthetic and visual with their learning, instead of learning through listening and talking things through (Reid, 2016). As a result, when assessing competence, it is advisable to use role play or simulation rather than conducting a Q&A session. Learners with dyslexia are recognised to have strengths in terms of lateral thinking, as well as being able to see the bigger picture when others may struggle (Reid, 2016). Taking these recognised strengths into account, the PEd needs to encourage and support the learner's strengths and to help them overcome the challenges so that they will excel in the healthcare arena.

Dyspraxia

Dyspraxia is a learning difficulty which impacts on fine and gross motor co-ordination, thus causing problems when completing certain activities (British Dyslexia Association, undated). The learner's dyspraxia may impact on their ability to retain and repeat tasks being shown to them. This group of learners may also have difficulties dealing with their emotions. Dyspraxia is known to run in families and is more prevalent in males than females (NHS, 2017). Often learners with dyspraxia will have developed excellent coping strategies for overcoming their challenges, so the PEd may not even notice a problem. This group of learners is often very determined and hardworking, as well as being highly motivated to achieve their end goals (Dyspraxia Foundation, 2018). Learners will always be encouraged to disclose their difficulties, especially if it could have an impact on their work or placement experience. In order for the learner to feel comfortable doing this, the PEd needs to foster a positive learning environment so that the learner feels able to talk about both their challenges and personal strengths.

Dyscalculia

Dyscalculia is all about numbers and symbols, so the learner may have problems with maths and may have the inability to master basic numeracy skills (British Dyslexia Association, undated). Unlike dyspraxia, dyscalculia is just as common in females as it is in males (Dyslexia Association, 2018). It will not be uncommon for a PEd to have a learner with dyscalculia who also has one of the other main types of learning difficulties. As dyscalculia deals with maths and numbers in terms of processing and memorising mathematical information, the PEd may find it best to refer the learner to their education provider for more structural support and learning strategies. It is still important for the PEd to create a positive learning environment so that the learner feels comfortable disclosing information and also does not shy away from engaging with important tasks, which can be common for this group of learners.

As highlighted by Reid (2016), it is important to treat each learner as an individual and not to compare learners with each other. It must be recognised that progress will be different depending on the learner. This means that goal setting may be different and cannot be generalised across a student group. It is important for the PEd to remember that all of these challenges and developments form part of the learner journey to reach the destination of successful course completion.

The Failing Learner

The failing learner can raise a number of concerns for the PEd. It is important to ensure that a learner receives the required support to try to address the weaknesses they are experiencing and that they are fully informed throughout the process. The amount of support a failing learner requires can be a challenge for a PEd. Hunt et al.'s (2016) research states that healthcare professionals worry about being labelled a bad assessor when they need to fail a learner; this may mean that the learner can pass their placement when this is not appropriate. Within the research, it is highlighted that healthcare professionals are also worried about the time it will take to support the failing learner and how failing a learner will make them feel isolated as a PEd (Hunt et al., 2016). In these circumstances, it is important to ensure that the PEd has support from their employing organisation and the learner's university. A comprehensive action plan will help everyone see what is required for a positive outcome and whether the actions set are being achieved. A good action plan is regularly reviewed as it is important for all parties to see if there has been any progress; this can also have a positive impact on the learner's confidence.

To ensure that the failing learner is being supported, it is important that all feedback provided is constructive. Duffy (2013) highlights that learners want and will benefit from regular feedback on their progress, and not just the formal feedback meetings dictated by the education provider. She also highlights that it is important to provide the feedback immediately so that the learner can correct what they are doing wrong. This can prove challenging in the pre-hospital arena, but the PEd must try to provide this feedback as soon as possible whilst it is still fresh in both the PEd's and the learner's minds.

> Think of a time when you were supporting a failing learner. What feedback did you provide? How could this feedback be improved?

The PEd must feel supported when undertaking the task of failing a learner. This support must commence as soon as the PEd has identified a potential problem. This will enable the PEd to identify learners causing concern at an early stage (Skingley et al., 2007). Pre-empting this failure can result in a positive outcome for all concerned. The university and the PEd must work together to support each other and the learner (Skingley et al., 2007); this also triangulates all of the information, ensuring that everyone is fully informed throughout the process.

Whilst ensuring that the learner is supported, the PEd must ensure that all concerns are comprehensively documented. This is important should evidence be required at a later date as part of the learner's journey. In addition to an action plan, any meetings held must also be documented. This will include the initial meeting, the mid-point review and the end of practice placement meeting. Depending on the education provider's process, these meetings may occur throughout the year or in various practice placement blocks. The learner must also have access to the documentation in a timely manner so that they are fully aware of what they need to achieve and have the necessary time to do so. If, as a PEd, support is required completing the documentation liaison should take place with the education provider, who will be able to offer assistance and support during the process.

Action Planning

Should a learner be struggling or require extra support or focus, an action plan can be used. This should contain clear goals for the learner to achieve, guidance on how they can achieve these goals and the timescale in which these must be achieved. A well-written action plan will provide both the learner and the PEd with clear actions/goals that the learner must consistently demonstrate in order to achieve competence, and will also guide the PEd to help facilitate these achievements. However, it could also be argued that all learners would benefit from an action plan giving them clear guidance in terms of their development and achievement.

It is important that both the PEd and the learner agree with the developed action plan. This will result in both parties taking ownership of the plan and its success. An example of an action plan template can be seen in Figure 9.1. The action plan completed must be comprehensive and clearly identify any concerns, how these are to be overcome and a clear, achievable deadline date for doing so. Once documented, the student and the PEd must have a copy of the plan so that there are 'no secrets' to what is required to achieve the required standard.

It is also imperative that the PEd liaises with the education provider; this will be a university in most cases, so it too can offer support to both the PEd and the learner. Duffy's (2003) research highlights the fact that at times PEds found it difficult to fail learners for a number of reasons; this included not wanting to upset the learner or the fear of being seen as a bad PEd. This then resulted in the learners passing the clinical practice element of their healthcare programme when they were not ready to do so. Kilgallon and Thompson (2012) discuss the feelings of guilt a PEd has when needing to fail a learner. By using the action plan, the PEd has an objective document to measure the learner against. If a learner who is seen to be failing does not receive an action plan with enough time to complete it and address the points of concern, the learner will have the right to appeal any decision made (Gopee, 2015). Therefore, action plans will support both the learner and the PEd when it is necessary to potentially make the tough decisions in terms of the learner's progression.

Formulating an Action Plan

When supporting a potentially failing learner, it is important that the action plan clearly sets goals and actions for achievement. Kilgallon and Thompson (2012) argue that a learner may not be aware of the gaps in their knowledge and as a result they may do nothing to rectify it. Therefore, the development of an action plan can help fill these gaps as well as offer advice on what success would look like.

An action plan can only be of benefit if the actions set can be understood by and are clearly defined for all involved. One way of ensuring a clear action plan is to set SMART goals for the learners to achieve. The idea of SMART objectives was originally developed by Doran (1981).

So what does the SMART acronym mean and how can it help the PEd? A description of each of the SMART elements based on Doran's (1981) work is given below:

S = SPECIFIC

Be clear – know exactly what you want the learner to achieve.

The learner needs to know what is expected of them, otherwise how will they be able to meet any of the goals set for them?

M = MEASUREABLE

How will you know that the goal/action has been achieved?

What does success look like?

What does the learner need to do in order to achieve the goal?

Failure to set a measurable goal may result in confusion on both the part of the learner and the PEd.

A = ACHIEVABLE

The goal needs to be achievable by the learner within the timeframe given and with the available resources.

The PEd may need to break the overall goal down into more bite-size actions to make it seem more achievable.

R = REALISTIC

Can the learner achieve the goal in the timeframe given?

Is the goal realistic considering the learner's current level on their course?

It can be challenging, but it is important that the PEd understands the stage at which the learner is during each stage of their studies, so that unrealistic goals are avoided.

T = TIMESCALE

Time on the course is limited, so the PEd needs to take this into account when setting the goals.

The timescales need to be realistic and achievable for all parties.

It may be worth considering introducing review points, especially for goals with longer timescales.

Table 9.1 Action plan template

Concern	Action to be taken	Help to get there	Success measurement	Date to be completed

The Role of the University and the Placement Provider

In order to achieve a positive learner journey, it is important that the university and the placement provider fully support the process. The key to achieving a positive experience for all is communication. Communication needs to flow in a variety of ways (Figure 9.1).

If one of these communication streams breaks down, the learner experience will be impacted.

The Health and Care Professions Council (2017) is clear that learners, PEds and placement providers must be fully prepared for undertaking the practice element of the programme.

The university must ensure that the learner is fully briefed on the expectations of the practice placement and what they are expected to achieve. It must make the learner and the PEd aware of the documentation

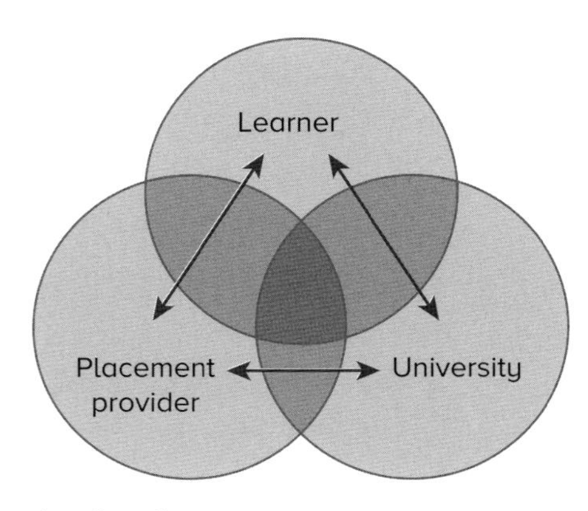

Figure 9.1 Communication flow

to be completed and what is expected in terms of achieving a pass grade. It must also ensure that it is responsive to any questions raised by the PEd in relation to the learner and the university processes. It is also the role of the university to support the PEd in any practice reviews or meetings held with their learners, especially if the learner is seen to be struggling.

The role of the placement provider is to ensure that the PEd is fully briefed. This includes making the PEd aware of the learners they will be supporting and making available the relevant university contact details. As an organisation, it also needs to support the PEd in their role so that they can deliver high-quality support. This includes providing the PEd with time to meet with their learners as well as providing opportunity for the PEd to update their knowledge where appropriate. Enabling this can be challenging for organisations due to operational pressures; however, it is of paramount importance when considering both the learner journey and the morale of the PEd.

When communicating, it is important to recognise the staff who will be contributing to the learner's journey in addition to the PEd; this may be grades such as Emergency Care Assistants (ECA), Emergency Technicians or administrative staff. These staff play an important role in the learner's experience and it is important to communicate with these groups too (Blaber, 2015).

Support for the PEd

When supporting learners, it is important for the PEd to have access to the education provider so that they can gain the required support; this is especially important if the PEd is supporting a struggling learner. A PEd should arrange to meet with their learner at various points in their programme to discuss their progress. There may also be times where the PEd requires a practice facilitator or lecturer to be present, especially if an action plan is being developed (Gopee, 2015). To access this support, the PEd should be provided with contact details for their local practice placement manager/facilitator. This individual will then either contact the university on their behalf or will provide the PEd with the relevant details, depending on the local policy. It is also best practice for each education provider to develop a raising concerns algorithm highlighting how both PEds and learners can contact the education provider should there be any concerns with the clinical placement. This is commonly found within the PAD. Ultimately, if the PEd has any questions or queries, they need to approach the university or the person responsible for student support within their organisation.

Case Studies

You have been assigned a second-year learner and they are struggling to take a comprehensive history from patients; they are halfway through their placement. They are constantly asking the same questions and they are unable to make any decisions based on the answers they are receiving. You have spoken to the learner and have informed them that they will need to be placed on an action plan:

- Think of the actions for this learner's action plan.
- What timeframes do you think would be reasonable for achievement?
- Are the actions you set SMART in their design?

A student approaches you stating that they are dyslexic and are worried how this will impact upon their placement:

- What questions do you need to ask the student as a result of their disclosure?
- Do you need to make any reasonable adjustments as a result of their disclosure? What may they be?
- Can you make changes to the students Practice Assessment Document to ensure that the student can meet the competencies?

Reflection

How effective are the communication strands within your area? What are the strengths in terms of the communications and where do you think communication could be improved? As a PEd, what impact could you have on improving the communication threads?

As a PEd, how do you deal with a struggling learner? What mechanisms of support do you put in place and who do you communicate these with?

What are the challenges faced when completing an action plan? Are there any ways in which these challenges can be overcome? At what point do you feel it relevant to notify the education provider of any concerns?

Have you ever compiled an action plan for a learner? Why did you do this? Did you find the process beneficial? How could you improve the process should you ever be required to produce an action plan in the future?

Part III

Perspectives

Chapter 10 The Learner and PEd Perspectives

This chapter explores the placement educational experiences from the perspective of the learner and the PEd. Direct quotations will be used to give the most powerful and genuine messages possible.

The Benefits of Mentoring

'Having realised my dream of becoming a paramedic, it was immediately obvious to me that my next goal was to become a mentor for others. Helping students to achieve their ambitions and follow the same path I have experienced is one of the most gratifying aspects of my job. Although challenging at times, the feeling of satisfaction that I gain from successfully mentoring future paramedics fills me with a sense of achievement and fulfilment of which I am confident no other role could replicate.'

'There are many pleasurable moments to discover when mentoring students. The students normally arrive as a blank canvas, keen to learn and eager to impress, but also apprehensive. They are in unfamiliar territory, new and often large environments, and in particular within the Ambulance Service this environment changes with every case they attend.'

'New students require hand holding, a friendly smile and to be reminded that we have all been that person with the academic knowledge and not a clue how to put it in place and that, yes, we do all remember that day and the mistakes we made along the way. However, when you see their faces light up, when their learning is able to be put into practice and suddenly things fit, that is such a joy to see. Moving through their placements and watching them grow.'

'Being a mentor has a positive impact on my role as a clinician. Working with a student leads me to reflect on cases much more and, with the student sharing current updated knowledge with me, enables me to provide best patient care. Working with students gives me great satisfaction and pride when I see their confidence and abilities grow and develop over time.'

'There is no feeling like when your blank canvas has fulfilled their dreams. To remember that nervous student that now bears no resemblance to their early days. To put your signature of competency in their books and to watch your fledgling soar is a feeling we should all experience.'

Challenges of the PEd Role

'It's often hard to have that conversation that maybe there are areas they need to work on. However, if you have shown them that they can trust you and that you are there to help, it is often just a hurdle. The hardest part of mentoring is to actually fail a student. You question yourself, 'Did I do everything I could?' There is no easy way to fail a student, it just takes a long time as a mentor to realise that sometimes this just has to be done and that it is the right thing to do.'

'It can be difficult to give students the time they need, often due to workplace constraints, whereby it is not possible to have as many shifts with your student as you would like or indeed need. Plus, given the growing number of students you can often find yourself mentoring several students on any given cohort.'

'As a mentor you have to have the professional confidence to allow the student space to develop their own way of patient care and assessment and be very creative on ways to help your student develop. A sound knowledge of learning styles and requirements helps to develop the student's learning plan.'

Mentoring Hours

'Generally, I believe the number of hours are sufficient for a student to gain the experience needed to qualify (except possibly if most [shifts] are in a rural area, seeing less than three patients per shift).'

'I find the Ambulance Service fails to provide enough time during shift for the mentor to give sufficient reflection and feedback to the student. So the student needs to be very proactive to ensure that work books [PADs] are kept up to date with signatures.'

Supernumerary Status

'I believe supernumerary hours work best, especially to begin with. Of course, university students are always supernumerary, but "in-service" students are not; I believe if these students were supernumerary, especially at the beginning of their training for at least a few months, this would be beneficial to them. The benefits I've seen for students being supernumerary are that they can stand back and observe the crew working, and begin to assist. I believe watching is important to start with, and in-service students are very much expected to begin attending patients immediately. This is very difficult for some and may have an adverse effect on their self-esteem if they get things wrong or do things that are different to what is expected. What I view as an ideal is for over the two years, the student to begin by observing, then gradually becoming more and more involved in patient care, then finally spending their final few months attending and getting used to being the lead clinician.'

Learners as Part of the Crew

'On the other hand, in-service students experience being part of a crew, which I believe is very beneficial, and would be beneficial to university students at the end of their training. Sadly, I understand this is not possible for many, as few university courses offer driver training as part of it.'

Number of PEds

'I believe that during the first few weeks, and possibly months, it is great to experience shifts with lots of different members of staff. This way they can gain an awareness of different approaches, meet several members of staff, and begin to form an idea of what approaches they would like to take when they begin to practise themselves. I believe there is a problem when a more experienced student works with different crews every week, or sometimes even every shift. Many students have discussed this with me, stating they feel they need to "prove themselves" every shift. I believe this is especially bad for their confidence. This can be a bad thing for the mentors as well. Working with a different student every shift means assessing a different person's skills every shift. Students will have their own strengths and weaknesses, and if a mentor does not know that student, it may take the whole shift to find what they need to improve on, and then they're working with a different student the next day. A student may be confident with a certain type of patient group, but not confident with another. If a student starts their day with a patient group they are unconfident with (e.g. a child), the mentor may believe they are not as proficient as they are with other patient groups and may not allow them to lead jobs for the rest of the shift, or will be more likely to "take over" quickly.'

Links with Education Establishments

'I find working at university enables me to forge a closer working relationship with lecturers, which can strengthen the student experience with a mentor due to continuation of support.'

'Communication with universities can be sporadic, often dealing with several universities at any one time and they all run their courses slightly differently. Communication with your employer can also be hit and miss as some don't fully understand the mentor role and see you as an employee rather than a mentor.'

A Final Note

'It is difficult for me to personally remember many more stressful experiences than that of entering the ambulance service as a student. Needless to say, the mentorship and guidance I received have shaped the way I carry out my duties to this day. I continuously strive to emulate the actions of my mentor who will remain my primary role model throughout my career and who ultimately gave me the courage and ambition to reach my goal of becoming a paramedic.'

Chapter 11 Reflections and Case Studies

Learning objectives

1. To draw together the knowledge gained in this text
2. To highlight any additional learning required by the PEd

This chapter will focus on you as a potential or practising PEd. These case studies and reflections have been written to promote reflection on your own experiences and to apply theories contained in this (and other) texts. They are designed to make you reflect upon your learning and consider the practical application of practice placement education.

Case Studies

For each case study below, ask yourself:

a. How do I best support this learner to ensure appropriate learning and development?

b. What theory/theories from this text are appropriate to utilise in each situation and why?

c. Where would I seek extra help from should I need it?

1. Marcus is a second-year BSc paramedic learner attending university full time and is on placement with you for blocks of six weeks at a time. He identifies to you that he is struggling with maintaining his clinical abilities when he is in university blocks.
2. Anna is a first-year DipHE learner who is on placement with you for two weeks. She has had basic skills education at university; however, she is very nervous about her shifts with you. She has commented that she really knows nothing and has no idea what to do.

3. You attend a road traffic collison (RTC) with your Ambulance Technician colleague Chris and third-year learner Asha. You discover one patient who is complaining of neck pain only and his vital signs are stable.
4. Craig, your first-year learner, is having difficulties revising for his anatomy exam in four weeks. He states that he cannot remember anything, even though he spends four to five hours at a time reading his textbooks.
5. Neil has declared to you that he has dyslexia, but he has not informed the university he is studying with of this fact. He is struggling with the university portion of his course.
6. Ranjit has confided in you that she has overheard one of her fellow learners discussing with a friend that he took money from a patient's house.
7. You notice that your learner Brian (who is 20 years older than you) does not accept criticism from you. However, he does accept criticism from your colleague Harry, who is a similar age to him.
8. You have a new first-year learner Leanne for her first shift. You attend a patient, Mabel, who has fallen with no injuries. Leanne is keen to assist with getting Mabel up from the floor.
9. Keith is a first-year learner; he has been self-employed for 20 years as plumber. He has a great deal of misplaced confidence, which means he does not listen to your advice. His patient questioning is very abrupt and borders on rudeness.
10. Chao is just 18 years old and is studying away from home for the first time. He is incredibly homesick and has come to you for some advice.
11. Sean is a third-year learner who is due to be formally assessed on his airway management skills. Consider how you can facilitate the assessment and the format of any feedback given.
12. First-year learner Lianne has asked you to check her method of taking a blood sugar reading. Consider how best to facilitate this and how you would give her feedback.

Reflections

Consider and reflect upon these statements and questions from your own perspective:

1. What is your learning style?
2. How does your learning style influence your continuing professional development (CPD)?
3. What is your experience of being mentored?
4. How do your experiences of mentorship affect your practice as a PEd?
5. How does your personal life affect your practice as a PEd and a clinician?
6. How do you intend to apply the most relevant topics?
7. Would you be comfortable dealing with each of the cases in the section above? If so, why? If not, why not?
8. Reflect upon the last learner assessment that you undertook (formal or informal). Consider the points raised in Chapter 8 with regard to assessment methods, planning and feedback.
9. What aspect of this text do you find most relevant and why?

Conclusion

So you have read the book from cover to cover and have undertaken all of the case studies and reflections. You now expect to be the perfect PEd! Sadly, no one is ever perfect; however, this text will give you the tools to develop and hone your PEd skills.

It is likely that you will have learnt a great deal from this text, and whilst we hope you have read it all, we do not intend for it to be read and then put away forever. We would like to encourage you to revisit this text on a number of occasions in the future – perhaps when you have challenging learners or a new situation. Maybe you will revisit the text if someone has asked for your help and you wish to reflect upon your actions. Your CPD activities will naturally ask you to consider and reflect upon your actions at regular intervals, and whilst you may reflect upon your clinical skills, you may also wish to reflect upon your personal and PEd skills. Remember the theories used are there to help you with the practical application of supporting and assessing your students.

We hope this text will follow you throughout your career and will prove to be an invaluable tool.

Thank you for taking the time to read to the end.

References

Adair, J. (2005) *How to Grow Leaders: 7 Key Principles of Effective Leadership Development*. London: Kogan Page.

Benner, P. (2001) *From Novice to Expert*. Upper Saddle River, NJ: Prentice Hall.

Blaber, A. (2015) *The Learner Paramedic Survival Guide: Your Journey from Learner to Paramedic.* Maidenhead: Open University Press.

Blaber, A. and Harris, G. (2014) *Clinical Leadership for Paramedics*. Maidenhead: Open University Press.

Bloom, B. (ed.). (1956) *Taxonomy of Educational Objectives, Handbook I: The Cognitive Domain.* New York: David McKay.

Bloom, B. (1979) *Taxonomy of Educational Objectives, Handbook I: The Cognitive Domain*. New York: David McKay.

Bondy, K. (1983) Criterion-referenced definitions for rating scales in clinical evaluation. *Journal of Nursing Education*, 22(9): 376–82.

Boyes, C. (2005) *Need to Know Body Language: The Secret Language of Gestures and Postures Revealed*. London: Collins.

British Dyslexia Association (undated) What are specific learning difficulties? Available at: https://www.bdadyslexia.org.uk/educator/what-are-specific-learning-difficulties.

Burton, A. (2000) Reflection: nursing's practice and education panacea? *Journal of Advanced Nursing*, 31(5): 1009–17.

Carper, B. (1978) Fundamental patterns of knowing in nursing. *Advances in Nursing Science*, 1: 13–23.

Coffield, F., Moseley, D., Hall, E. and Ecclestone, K. (2004) *Should We Be Using Learning Styles? What Research Has to Say to Practice*. London: Learning and Skills Research Centre.

College of Paramedics (2015) *Paramedic Curriculum Guidance and Competence Framework*. Derby: College of Paramedics.

College of Paramedics (2017a) *Paramedic Curriculum Guidance*, 4th edn. Derby: College of Paramedics.

College of Paramedics (2017b) *Practice Educator Guidance Handbook.* Derby: College of Paramedics.

Connor, M. and Pokora, J. (2012) *Coaching and Mentoring at Work*, 2nd edn. Maidenhead: McGraw Hill/Open University Press.

Cosby, K. and Croskerry, P. (2004) Profiles in patient safety: authority gradients in medical error. *Academic Emergency Medicine*, 11(12): 1341–45.

Darling, L. (1986) What to do about toxic mentors. *Nurse Education*, 11(2): 29–30.

Data Protection Act (2018) Available at: http://www.legislation.gov.uk/ukpga/2018/12/contents.

Doran, G. (1981) There's a S.M.A.R.T way to write management goals and objectives. *Management Review*, 70(1): 35–6.

Driscoll, J. (2007) Supported Reflective Learning: The Essence of Clinical Supervision? In J. Driscoll (2nd edn) *Practising Clinical Supervision: A Reflective Account for Health Care Professionals*. Philadelphia: Elsevier: 27–52.

Duffy, K (2003) Failing students: a qualitative study of factors that influence the decisions regarding assessment of students' competence in practice. Glasgow: Caledonian Nursing and Midwifery Research Centre, School of Nursing, Midwifery and Community Health, Glasgow Caledonian University.

Duffy, K. (2013) Providing constructive feedback to learners during mentoring. *Nursing Standard*, 27(31): 50–56.

Dyslexia Association (2018) What is dyscalculia? Available at: http://dyslexia.uk.net/specific-learning-difficulties/dyscalculia.

Dyspraxia Foundation (2018) Dyspraxia in the workplace. Available at: http://dyspraxiafoundation.org.uk/dyspraxia-adults/workplace-employees.

Egan, G. (1990). *The Skilled Helper: A Systematic Approach to Effective Helping*. Pacific Grove: Brooks Cole publishers.

Equality Act (2010) Available at: http://www.legislation.gov.uk/uksi?title=Equality%20 Act%202010.

Flemming, N. (1992) Not another inventory, rather a catalyst for reflection. *To improve the academy*, 11: 137.

Fry, H., Ketteridge, S. and Marshall, S. (2009) *A Handbook for Teaching and Learning in Higher Education: Enhancing Academic Practice.* Abingdon: Routledge.

Garvey, R. (2011) *A Very Short, Fairly Interesting and Reasonably Cheap Book about Coaching and Mentoring*. London: SAGE.

Garvey, R., Stokes, P. and Megginson, D. (2011) *Coaching and Mentoring, Theory and Practice*. London: SAGE.

Ghaye, T. and Lillyman, S. (2006) *Learning Journals & Critical Incidents: Reflective Practice for Health Care Professionals*, 2nd edn. Dinton: Quay Books.

Gibbs, G. (1988) *Learning by Doing: A Guide to Teaching and Learning Methods.* Oxford: Further Education Unit, Oxford Polytechnic.

Gibbs, G. and Simpson, C. (2005) Conditions under which assessment supports learners' learning: learning and teaching in higher education. *Learning and Teaching in Higher Education*, 1: 3–31.

Gopee, N. (2010) *Practice Teaching in Healthcare*. London: SAGE.

Gopee, N. (2015) *Mentoring and Supervision in Healthcare*. London: SAGE.

Gubbins, K. and Nixon, V. (2013) Consultation and Communication Skills. In V. Nixon (ed.), *Professional Practice in Paramedic, Emergency and Urgent Care.* Chichester: Wiley-Blackwell: 22–49.

Hall, E.T. (1990) *Understanding Cultural Differences, Germans, French and Americans*, Yarmouth: Intercultural Press.

Health and Care Professions Council (2014) Standards of proficiency – paramedics. HCPC: London.

Health and Care Professions Council (2015) *Health, Disability and Becoming a Health and Care Professional.* London: Health and Care Professions Council.

Health and Care Professions Council (2016) *Standards of conduct, performance and ethics*. London: Health and Care Professions Council.

Health and Care Professions Council (2017) *Standards of Education and Training*. London: Health and Care Professions Council.

Health Education England (undated) *HEE Quality Framework 2017–2018*. Available at: https://hee.nhs.uk/our-work/quality.

Higher Education Academy (2014) *HEA Feedback Toolkit*. York: Higher Education Academy.

Honey, P. and Mumford, A. (2006) *Learning Styles Questionnaire: 80-Item Version*. Maidenhead: Peter Honey Publications.

Hunt, L., McGee, P., Gutteridge, R. and Hughes, M. (2016) Failing securely: the processes and support which underpin English nurse mentors' assessment decisions regarding under-performing learners. *Nurse Education Today*, 39: 76–86.

Inam, H. (2014) Transformational leadership: coaching and leadership development. Available at: http://www.transformleaders.tv/five-cs-of-great-coaching-conversations.

Jasper, M. (2006) *Reflection, Decision-Making and Professional Development*. London: Wiley-Blackwell.

Johns, C. (1994) Nuances of reflection. *Journal of Clinical Nursing*, 3: 71–5.

Kilgallon, K. and Thompson, J. (2012) *Mentoring in Nursing and Healthcare: A Practical Approach*. Chichester: Wiley-Blackwell.

Kolb, D. (1984) Experiential learning: experience as the source of learning and development. New jersey: Prentice-Hall.

Kostrubiak, D., Kwon, M., Lee, J., Flug, J., Hoffman, J., Moshiri, M., Patlas, M. and Katz, D. (2017) Mentorship in radiology. *Current Problems in Diagnostic Radiology*, 46: 385–90.

Kram, K. (1983) Phases of the mentoring relationship. *Academy of Management Journal*, 26: 608–25.

Lane, M. (2014) Learner perceptions in relation to Paramedic Educator (PEd) roles. *Journal of Paramedic Practice*, 6(4): 194–9.

LeFroy, J., Watling, C. and Teunissen P. (2015) Guidelines: the do's, don'ts and don't knows of feedback for clinical education. *Perspectives on Medical Education*, 4(6): 284–99.

Lewin, K., Lippitt, R. and White, R. (1939) Patterns of aggressive behaviour in experimentally created social climates. *Journal of Social Psychology, Political, Racial and Differential Psychology*, 10(2): 271–99.

Maslow, A. (1987) *Motivation and Personality*, 3rd edn. London: Harper & Row.

McLeod, S. (2007). Maslow's hierarchy of needs. Available at: http://www.simplypsychology.org/maslow.html.

Mohtady, H., Könings, K. and van Merriënboer, J. (2016) What makes informal mentorship in the medical realm effective? *Mentoring & Tutoring: Partnership in Learning*, 24(4): 306–17.

Morton-Cooper, A. and Palmer, A. (2000) *Mentoring Preceptorship and Clinical Supervision*, 2nd edn. Oxford: Blackwell Science.

Nasser-Abu Alhija, F. and Fresko, B. (2014) An exploration of the relationship between mentor recruitment, the implementation of mentoring and mentor attitudes. *Mentoring & Tutoring: Partnership in Learning*, 22(2): 162–80.

NHS (2017) Dyspraxia (developmental co-ordination disorder) in adults. Available at: http://nhs.uk/conditions/developmental-coordination-disorder-dyspraxia-in-adults.

NHS Leadership Academy (2011) *The Clinical Leadership Competency Framework*. Coventry: NHS Institute for Innovation and Improvement.

NMC (2006) *Standards to Support Learning and Assessment in Practice*. London: NMC.

Olander, E., Rayment, J., Bryar, R. and Brook, J. (2018) Midwifery learners in health visitor placements: the importance of student-mentor relationships. *Midwifery*, 62: 49–51.

Oxford Dictionary (2012a) Quality. Available at: http://oxforddictionaries.com/definition/english/quality?q=Qualities+#quality__3.

Oxford Dictionary (2012b) Attribute. Available at: http://oxforddictionaries.com/definition/english/attribute?q=attributes.

Ozuah, P. (2005) First, there was pedagogy and then came andragogy. *Einstein Journal of Biology and Medicine*, 21(2): 1–5.

Pegg, M. (1999) *The Art of Mentoring*. Oxford: Management Books 2000 Ltd.

Peterson, E., Rayner, G. and Armstrong, S. (2009) Researching the psychology of cognitive style and learning style: is there really a future? *Learning and Individual Differences*, 19(4): 518–23.

Peyton, J. (1998) *Teaching and Learning in Medical Practice.* Hertfordshire: Manticore Europe Limited.

Pitkanen, S., Kaariainen, M., Oikarainen, A., Tuomikoski, A., Elo, S., Ruotsalainen, H., Saarikoski, M., Karsamanoja, T. and Mikkonen, K. (2018) Healthcare learners' evaluation of the clinical learning environment and supervision: a cross-sectional study, *Nurse Education Today*, 62: 143–9.

Poon, J., Stevens, C. and Gannon, M. (2000) Effects of training method and learning style on cross-cultural training outcomes. *Research and Practice in Human Resource Management*, 8(2): 73–97.

Price, B. (2008) Enhancing skills to develop practice. *Nursing Standard*, 22(25): 49–55.

Quality Assurance Agency for Higher Education (2015) *The UK Quality Code for Higher Education: Overview and Expectations*. Gloucester: Quality Assurance Agency.

Race, P. (2015) *The Lecturers Toolkit: A Practical Guide to Assessment, Learning and Teaching*. Oxon: Routledge.

Reid, G. (2016) *Dyslexia: A Practitioner's Handbook*, 6th edn. Chichester: Wiley-Blackwell.

Roberts, A. (1999) The origins of the term mentor. *History of Education Society Bulletin*, 64: 313–29.

Rolfe, G., Freshwater, D. and Jasper, M. (2001) *Critical Reflective Practice in Nursing and the Helping Professions.* Basingstoke: Palgrave Macmillan.

Royal College of Nursing (2010) *Dyslexia, Dyspraxia and Dyscalculia – Toolkit*. London: Royal College of Nursing.

Schiavo, R. (2007) *Health Communication: From Theory to Practice.* San Francisco: Jossey-Bass.

Schon, D. (1983) *The Reflective Practitioner: How Professionals Think in Action*. London: Temple Smith.

Schön, D. (1987) *Educating the Reflective Practitioner*. San Francisco: Jossey-Bass.

Schuller, B., Steidl, S., Batliner, A., Burkhardt, F., Deviller, L., Müller, C. and Narayanan, S. (2013) Paralinguistics in speech and language: state-of-the-art and the challenge. *Computer Speech and Language*, 27: 4–39.

Scottish Qualifications Authority (2017) *Guide to Assessment.* Dalkeith: Scottish Qualifications Authority.

Skingley, A., Arnott, J., Greaves, J. and Nabb, J. (2007) Supporting practice teachers to identify failing learners. *British Journal of Community Nursing*, 12(1): 28–32.

Smith, A., McAskill, H. and Jack, K. (2009) *Developing Advanced Skills in Practice Teaching.* Basingstoke: Palgrave Macmillan.

Starr, J. (2016) *The Coaching Manual*. Harlow: Pearson.

Steinaker, N. and Bell, M. (1979) *The Experiential Learning: A New Approach to Teaching and Learning*. New York: Academic Press.

Taylor, B. (2010) *Reflective Practice for Healthcare Professionals*. Maidenhead: Open University Press.

Thomas, N. and Adair, J. (2007) *Best of John Adair on Leadership and Management.* London: Thorogood Publishers.

Whitmore, J. (2009) *Coaching for Performance*, 4th edn. London: Perseus Publishing.

Zachary, L. (2011) The Mentor's Guide: Facilitating Effective Learning Relationships. Available at: https://www.wiley.com/legacy/landing_page/images/Zachary_Mentors_Guide_Transition_Guide.pdf.

Index

References to illustrations are in **bold**.